AWAKENED BY YOU

AWAKENED BY YOU

K L STOCKTON

authorHOUSE®

AuthorHouse™ *UK Ltd.*
1663 Liberty Drive
Bloomington, IN 47403 USA
www.authorhouse.co.uk
Phone: 0800.197.4150

© *2014 K L Stockton. All rights reserved.*

No part of this book may be reproduced, stored in a retrieval system, or transmitted by any means without the written permission of the author.

Published by AuthorHouse 07/28/2014

ISBN: 978-1-4969-8610-8 (sc)
ISBN: 978-1-4969-8611-5 (hc)
ISBN: 978-1-4969-8609-2 (e)

Any people depicted in stock imagery provided by Thinkstock are models, and such images are being used for illustrative purposes only. Certain stock imagery © Thinkstock.

This book is printed on acid-free paper.

Because of the dynamic nature of the Internet, any web addresses or links contained in this book may have changed since publication and may no longer be valid. The views expressed in this work are solely those of the author and do not necessarily reflect the views of the publisher, and the publisher hereby disclaims any responsibility for them.

For Ian
My husband, my best friend, my soul mate.
Thank you for your love, patience, support and belief.

Acknowledgments

I would like to give a huge shout out and thanks to the following ladies and goddesses for your time and honest feedback.
Lorraine Milench, Donna Turner, Claire Ball,
Ella Worthington, Linda Wightman.

Chapter One

CLAYTON

Christ I hate small talk, look business is concluded, now piss off. Oh how I wish to I could verbalise that thought. Instead I smile pleasantly at the four men surrounding me as they laugh like fucking hyenas at some inane joke their boss just made. Sighing inwardly I look around the foyer of my building.

My building, Blake Tower, wow! I always get a surge of pleasure and accomplishment when I think of that. I remember the day when my father, Marcus Blake, brought me here twelve years ago like it was yesterday. He told me I inspired him to buy it. Five years ago I took full ownership due to his passing. Hell, I still miss him. I find myself rubbing my chest over the ache that's suddenly come on at the thought of him. None of my party notice my actions thank Christ. I can do without false pretences after my health.

The foyer is a hive of activity with workers and visitors, being six foot four gives me the advantage of having a clear view of the entire space. Natural stone marble for the flooring and pillars, the circular dark mahogany wood reception desk being the centre piece, the odd tree planted in large natural stone pots adding splashes of color and broke up the simplicity but kept the lines clean. As is my habit I run a critical eye over the staff at the desk and the security guards, I take pride in what I see, smart business appearance with a genuine smile of welcome and farewell. My attention is diverted as I notice people coming in quickly shaking coats and umbrellas, shifting my gaze I look out of the glass frontage to see torrential rain coming down in sheets like a waterfall.

"Hell of a down pour" one of the group whose name escapes me says leaning around his colleague to see what I am looking at, as the words left his mouth a loud rumble of thunder could be heard, a few startled shrieks permeate around the foyer causing more people to stop and look outside at the sudden storm.

A quick flash of movement in my peripheral vision catches my attention. One of the security guards had stepped forward to open the side door for a woman. I frown wondering why he would do such a thing when the revolving doors are working perfectly. I can't see the woman's face because she has her hood up, however the security guard looks dazed, besotted wonder has come across his features as she talks to him. He points her in the direction of the reception desk. As she moves in that direction his eyes follow her every move.

Fascinated I study the woman in more detail, well what I could see of her. She's wearing a form fitting coat that reaches her calves and it shows off her ample chest, boy she has some rack on her. Her black boots are a style I've never seen before, the heels are high with a silver coating, running up the side of her leg I catch glimpses of multiple buckles that flash as she walks, my eyes travel up her slim body and I notice she's carrying a very large flat case, it's an art portfolio idiot, my brain so kindly informs me, hence the reason for coming in through the side door. She moves away from the reception desk and I spy the visitors pass in her hand, she's moving towards me and my group. Damn I still can't see her face, for some obscure reason it suddenly becomes very important to look at her face, to know her. She walks right passed me heading for the elevator, she doesn't even look nor do a double take in my direction which is typical of women's behaviour around me, not to be egotistical but I am good looking. Hell all of my family are handsome, it's in the genes. Usually I find women's reaction to me a pain in the fucking ass and I ignore it and them, but now….

With her back to me I stare and start to will her to take down her hood and turn around, I make it a mantra almost. She shifts slightly and looks behind her, she must sense me watching her, but I still can't see her face. God damn it, this is frustrating me.

The elevator pings it's arrival, miraculously nobody else moves into the car with her, she leans over to her left and presses the floor button she needs then turns and faces outward, letting go of her portfolio she raises her hands to her hood, relief sweeps through me, finally I will see her face, only the elevator doors begin to close.

I choke back on crying out "no." Checking myself I quickly look at my visitors, good no-one has noticed I've been pre-occupied these last few minutes. As I turn back towards the closing doors a man ran up and stuck his hand out to stop them closing, thank you for small mercies. As the doors re-opened to reveal my mystery woman her hands are at her hood. As she lifts the hood off her head she is looking down at the floor, look up damn it, her hair is blonde, no wait that's not right, it is silvery blonde almost white, under the lights it shines like the moon. Abruptly she lifts her head and looks directly at me.

Holy fucking hell, she is beautiful. Big eyes I can't determine the color but I swear they shimmered, high cheek bones, delicate fair skin, full lips. I feel the full impact of her stare, the floor feels as if it's tilting, all surrounding sounds are muted by the loud thundering of my heart, I'm struggling to breathe. It's as if she's stripped me naked right to my very soul. My body is reacting to her even my cock twitches and hardens, she is calling to me. The doors close breaking whatever spell she has cast on me. I exhale loudly, I feel dizzy, disorientated. No woman has ever affected me like that before. In this precise moment I know two things for sure: I have to know who she is and then claim her as mine.

With those things in mind I bring the small talk to an end and see my visitors out of the building, heading straight to the reception desk and the visitors signing in book.

"Mr Blake, how may I be of help" the young receptionist asks breathlessly, smiling widely and fluttering her eye lashes. I bite my tongue to hold back the "I'm not interested love" retort that is on the verge of coming out of me.

"Give me a minute" I scan the register. Damn, there are five signatures within a few minutes of each other "There was a woman who's just signed in, dark coat hood up, which one is her sign in?" I say tapping the book.

She takes the book and taps away on the keyboard looking at the computer screen "Skye Darcy visiting David Smith of Phoenix PR on the twenty third floor sir" she says smiling back at me.

Yes, thank god for super-efficient staff. I smile warmly at the receptionist, not fair of me I know, but you've got to keep them sweet "Thank you Lucy, you've been brilliant, keep up the good work"

Poor thing I can practically see her glowing from the praise. Hell, I didn't care that I further cemented her crush on me but if it meant I got her working for me for another six months it was worth it. One of the many important lessons I learnt from my father, know all of your employee names, even the cleaning crew and if you can their spouse and children's names too. Give recognition for a job well done no matter how small, frivolous and irrelevant it may seem and regardless of their position it shows you notice and recognise that individual plays an important role. The workforce in return pays you back with loyalty.

Heading back to the elevator I mentally shake myself and give myself a talking to "Right back to business, focus on the meeting coming up later this afternoon" only I know I'm kidding myself because the first thing I will do back at my desk is to do a search on my mysterious woman Skye Darcy. I stop short, I was thinking of her as mine already, really! "Ah fuck, I'm in trouble" I mutter to myself, with a resigned sigh I step into the elevator.

SKYE

"The meeting was a complete utter waste of my fucking time" I growl into the phone to Macy my PA and friend as I stood in the corridor waiting for the elevator.

"Whoa, it must have been if it's got you swearing like that and you don't swear" she says with a slight quiver of a laugh.

"Put it this way" I snap "it's two hours of my life I am never getting back, the guy is a total moron, an egotistical nit wit. He even had the audacity to say he was doing me a favor, me!" my voice is rising and I don't care I'm on a roll, venting my anger at Macy, who I knew didn't deserve it "The bloody prat is delusional, he introduced himself to a colleague of his as my new agent" I pause for breath.

"You did correct him didn't you?"

I could detect Macy's pique making me feel justified in my anger. I start to pace the length of the corridor trying to work off some of the irritation I'd been feeling throughout the meeting.

"Of course I did and you know what he said?" I didn't wait for an answer "he said oh, it's a minor detail, once we've thrashed out T&C's it's a moot point"

"Bastard" Macy spat, that makes me feel even better at being angry.

"My sentiments exactly, get hold of Simon, let him know I am on the warpath because I want to know who in the hell talked him into sending me on this, this.." I struggle to find the right words my brain isn't working quickly enough to articulate because I'm feeling so angry "waste of time, energy, pathetic excuse for a meeting" I know I'm exasperated because I'm wildly gesturing with my free arm, hey look at me the human windmill "I tell you I'm going to cut his balls off and serve them to him on a platter" I growl.

I sigh heavily as I turn to pace back. I notice a man midway down leaning against the wall, opposite the elevator, watching me. I didn't pay any attention to him as I stride past. I stab at the down button for the elevator, I realize I've been so wrapped up and bitching to Macy I hadn't done it earlier. Macy was saying she wouldn't be able to get hold of Simon for another hour due to various meetings then asked if I was heading back. I really should but I want to get rid of this aggression I'm carrying, it isn't right to go back and lay into people because of some jumped up arsehole, I need to work out then I have an even better idea.

"No, I'm going to work out, do me a favor and ring Phillipee, see if he's free, tell him I'll go to wherever he is. I can get to him within the hour" the elevator pings "the lift, sorry elevator has arrived, call me in five minutes I should be back on the ground floor" as we say goodbye I retrieve my portfolio from against the wall and step into the elevator. I'm back in America its elevator not lift I remind myself.

The man, who'd been leaning against the wall, straightens and enters the elevator and I get my first good look at him or rather I pay attention to him. Holy hell and Hades on a cracker the guy is an Adonis. Believe me as an artist I've drawn many a fine specimen of the male species, but this guy is something else. He's tall with really broad shoulders and he's well over six feet tall had to be at least six three or four, even with my killer heels on I only came up to his shoulder. Dark brown wavy shoulder length hair and the most amazing dark blue eyes that dance with amusement I have ever seen, they are surrounded by long thick dark lashes the kind most females will kill to have along with that luscious hair. My fingers twitch just at the thought of running my fingers through it. He has a strong straight nose, good cheek bones and a strong jaw line. He is very and I mean very easy on the eye, good looking not pretty boy but bad boy rugged. Oh my lord, his mouth, full sculpted lips a slight smile playing on them, his tongue darts out and licks along his lower lip. I suddenly feel very warm, heat flooding my body along with a giddy feeling in my stomach and muscles between my legs I had long forgotten about clench.

What the… I haven't had sex for… jeez; it can't be that long surely. My last proper relationship ended nearly six years ago, I have been out on dates none lasting past the third and definitely no sex. Ever since being brutally attacked at eighteen as a result I went off sex and I had never been sexually adventurous or promiscuous before it happened, so these feelings this complete stranger is invoking confuses the hell out of me and it's rather unsettling.

The elevator stops to let on more people. Craftily I move to a position which will allow me to study him inconspicuously, I notice the reactions the women getting into the car have toward him. All openly gape suddenly collecting themselves then smiling in what they obviously think is their most alluring come hither and get me look. Huh, well what do you know he's ignoring each and every one of them; it dawns on me belatedly he's looking directly at me, humph so much for my position of inconspicuous ogling. A few of the women give me a quizzical look when they realize it's me who has the focus of his attention. I put my head down and close my eyes, pinching the bridge of my nose I give myself a stern talking to. He's a man, a good looking, no he's gorgeous and sex on legs my inner goddess shouts, breathe. Two deep calming breaths, I lift my head and open my eyes looking straight ahead and watch the lights count down the floor levels. I can feel his gaze upon me the whole time. I suddenly remember the feeling of being watched I had when I arrived in the building and to getting in the elevator, was that him? I wonder, the one I briefly glimpsed just before the doors closed.

I'm used to male scrutiny and often told I'm beautiful but I never pay it any mind, I just thought they were being polite. I know I didn't give off any vibes to encourage such attention in fact I went out of my way to dissuade it at every opportunity. So why was he so fervent in his attention, maybe I've got something on my face and he's too polite or trying to work up the courage to say something, scrap the courage, he looks like the kind of guy who didn't need it. My money is on if he wants something, he takes it with confidence. Just to make sure and with the former thought in mind I turn to pick up my portfolio and take a furtive look in the mirror that surrounds the walls of the elevator. Nope nothing on my face, sneaking a quick look at his reflection his gaze catches mine, a lazy smile spreads across his face and he winks. Holy cow, he just winked at me! I blush like a silly smitten teenager and my body floods with heat... again! Oh, get a grip of yourself I scald which is mentally followed up by a slap to the back of my head from my inner goddess. I busy myself by rummaging for my phone in my bag—I cannot believe how flustered I've become—and getting ready for when the doors open as the elevator approached the ground floor.

As soon as the doors open I step out, my phone rings startling me. I didn't recognise the number and normally I wouldn't answer however on this occasion I did because I've a sneaking suspicion the Adonis is going to talk to me. "Chicken" my inner goddess says disdainfully. "Bite me" I say back mentally pulling my tongue out, childish I know but that's in retaliation for the head slap, and I sure as hell wasn't about to make polite small talk with a complete stranger no matter how sexy and good looking with the mood I'm in.

I answer the phone with a cautious hello and I am greeted by a smooth luscious French accent "Bonjour ma belle deesse, comment vas-tu" Phillipee, just the man I need, my face splits with a wide grin at the sound of my old friend's voice.

CLAYTON

Can this woman become even more adorable? I ask myself as I step out of the elevator behind her and listen to her conversation as she converses fluently in French.

She stops by one of the pillars, I move around the other side so I can watch and listen—lucky for me I am also fluent in French—hoping to learn something new about her.

True, I'd spent an hour on line searching for information on her. I found her website she's an artist and British. I don't know much about art but the work on display was breath taking. She is seriously talented and she specialises in the Fantasy and Sci Fi genre and from the look of things her work is in high demand, following links I discovered she also owns an art auction house in London England and along with other artists work she sells her own paintings through it. By all accounts she is one shrewd cookie, feisty too going by the way she was talking earlier in the corridor.

I focus on her voice just as I did in the corridor, it's husky and low, the kind of voice that would be in high demand if she worked on an adult chat line. Hell, I would spend a fortune just to listen to her talk. I quickly shut down that fantasy of listening to her talk dirty however just hearing to her English dulcet tones is sending a stream of shivers down my spine. She laughs, a deep throaty chuckle, my body reacts. Fucking hell how can a laugh make me hard? I can't believe the effect she is having on me and I haven't even spoken to her.

I move so I can get a better look at her, my attention snaps back to what she is saying when I hear her mention Premier Fitness and Health Centre, that's my gym. By the sound of it she's arranging to meet someone called Phillipee there, a thrill surges through me as I realize who she's talking to. It's my personal trainer and she's going for a work out. My mind starts to race through what I have to do for the rest of the day just to see if I can get to the gym earlier so I can see her again. Shit! I'm turning into such a sap over a woman I don't even know, but you want to know her my mind whispers back.

Her attention snaps to the entrance and I follow her gaze to a tall man with short cropped crew cut blonde hair walking towards her. He is well built in a sharp suit, boyfriend I wonder, a surge of jealousy sweeps through me taking me by surprise. I fight the urge to block his path and beat my chest, mark my territory and property. Shit where the fuck did that come from, get a grip of yourself. The man stops in front of her, without a word to him and continuing her phone conversation she hands him the portfolio and visitors pass then points to the reception desk, he nods to which she gives him the thumbs up sign. Lackey, I decide and let out a breath in a fast gust. As he came back to her she ends the conversation and asks if he knew where the gym is he nods yes, she gives him instructions of where to take her and when, she was going to be at the gym for four thirty, so I am right he is a lackey. I watch them as they exited the building his hand although not touching her is at the small of her back, just seeing that makes me want to rip his arms off and beat him to a pulp with the bloody stumps.

Jeez, Blake, get a grip of yourself! I admonish for what feels like the thousandth time in, I look at my watch, Christ has it only been two hours from when I first laid eyes on her.

Shaking my head in disbelief at how I am behaving I get back in the elevator. Oh if only my mother and brothers could see me now, the very thought is like someone pouring ice cold water over me, they would be merciless in tormenting me. As for my mother she would have the wedding booked and chosen names for the children in a blink of an eye. Just that thought alone should have been enough to put my focus back on work only it didn't. Damn it.

As I walk towards my office my phone rings, the call display shows it's my mother. Christ the woman is psychic "Hey Mom, I was just thinking about you" I answer to which she giggles with her girlie laugh.

"All good I hope"

"Absolutely" I lie "what can I do for you?"

"Liar" she retorts, see psychic what did I tell you "I need an escort for tonight and I want you to take me if you are free"

My mother the typical beautiful socialite at sixty two is not short of admirers, god knows me and my brothers had to fend off our fare-share of fortune hunters that seem to crawl out of the wood work. The fact she is asking me to escort her somewhere means it is to an event that will probably have a fair few of these shall we say questionable characters in attendance. I sigh. I couldn't say no to her "Okay, when, where, dress code".

Turns out it's an art gallery opening and it meant I could still make it to the gym. Maybe Skye would be at the opening, the sudden thought has me hopeful that the prospect of a potentially dull evening could turn out to be quite enjoyable.

SKYE

I flop down on to the sofa with a moan and as my head hits the cushion I close my eyes. I'm so going to pay for my work out with Phillipee in the morning. Oh my bruises are going to have bruises. I never learn, the guy is a black belt fourth Dan or whatever, three times world champion in mixed martial arts but he is an excellent punch bag to work off frustrations, aggression and general pissed off-ness.

I've known Phillipee for almost five years, first meeting him in France whilst I was there working on a commission. I turned up at the gym looking for someone to teach me self-defence, since my attack I had been trying out various martial art classes but none of it seemed to stick, until Phillipee introduced me to his fighting and defence style and for whatever reason it clicked with me and I love it. Phillipee moved to America not long after I finished the commission and whenever I can I fly to whichever state he is working in for a lesson, this is one of my few extravagancies but I don't care if it means I can defend myself effectively and cause as much harm in a few a moves as possible, so be it.

I was thrilled when I found out Paul, my bodyguard, knew the same style and now I practice regularly with him although he goes easy on me, even threatening to sack him doesn't work on getting him to hit harder. Paul is ex-military and a good southern boy, whose mother brought him up right and his manners are impeccable, after nearly four years of working for me he still calls me Miss Darcy, and he often says you don't hit a woman unless she is firing at you with a machine gun, I've offered to fire a rocket launcher at him to which he just laughs and shakes his head. Phillipee on the other hand has no hesitation in hitting back hard.

Whenever I am in the States I try to get in as many sessions as I can with Phillipee having said that it has been nearly two years since I have been in New York, lucky for me Phillipee moved here six months ago, I know when I or Macy ring he'll do whatever he can to accommodate as he likes to work out with me as well.

"Mon Cheri I will rearrange my whole diary for you just so I can fight someone so short and fierce."

I let out a snort as I remember what he said to me when I thanked him for getting me in at such short notice. I didn't take offense because I know the clients he can fight properly with are all male and as tall if not bigger than him and he's just over six foot.

My phone buzzes and rings with Macy's ring tone, keeping my eyes closed I fumble the phone out of my purse.

"Yeah" it comes out as a croak, I clear my throat and I try again.

"Don't you go falling asleep on me lady" Macy says in her school ma'am voice "I'll be round in half an hour with Shelley, so get yourself in the shower, now"

"What, why?" is all I can splutter with dread starting to creep in the pit of my stomach, I've been looking forward to having a night in doing nothing.

"Mr Smythe rang this afternoon, well whilst you were at the gym. He's invited you to the grand opening of his new gallery" I could tell by her tone she wasn't taking any prisoners, well me specifically "he'll be coming to pick you up at eight. Now before you go all 'how could you' on me you are only in New York for two weeks and not back until September you'll be away for three months and you need to establish contacts for when you open the new auction house"

"I know and you are right" I say as I heave myself off the sofa and head for the bathroom.

"I am" Macy says with uncertainty. I smile to myself as I know I've just taken the wind out of her sails she obviously expected a fight about accepting the invite, before I can say anything else she reaffirms "I am" again smugly.

My smile broadens as I picture her face going from a scowl to a self-satisfied aren't I clever, pleased as punch grin. Macy is a god send of a find, she had been a PA for a CEO of a large corporation when I met her five years ago. I was working on site doing a commission and we hit it off straight away, her boss treated her like shit and I told her so, six months later she quit fed up of his sexual advances. I offered her a job and we haven't looked back since. She organises me with military precision and doesn't take any crap off anyone, she protects me from a lot of day to day noise so I can concentrate on doing my job. I switch on the shower.

"Okay, I'll see you in half an hour, let yourself in" I hang up.

I look longingly and forlornly at my bath tub. Oh to have a nice long soak. I sigh inwardly and strip out of my work out clothes and step into the shower. I have spared no expense in my bathroom it's all white marble with gold and bronze veins threading through the tiles, the shower could easily fit four people and it has six power heads. The hot water pounds my body, massaging away the aches I'm beginning to feel.

I reach for the shampoo at the same time reminding myself to make an appointment to get my hair cut. My hair is long, naturally curly and a silvery blonde, who was I kidding it is practically white. It had been a dark blonde before the attack; afterwards sections of my hair turned white. Doctors said the cause was shock from what I had been through, and as a result my hair lost its pigmentation, it was rare but it happens, since then over the years these patches appeared to have spread now the majority of my hair is white with blonde highlights, most people would describe it as platinum blonde. Some women paid a fortune to have my hair color. I am tempted to dye it, color yet to be determined although I was leaning toward a deep fire red or a nice bright pink. The only thing putting me off actually going ahead is the thought of the up keep and having my roots done once a month, too much hassle considering I rarely visit the hair dressers but it definitely needs cutting, it is getting too long, dry my hair was at my hips, wet it was past my bum.

As I step out of the shower I hear Macy and Shelley shout hello. "I'll be ten minutes" I shout back giving me time to sort out my hair and clean my teeth, make up can wait.

Entering my living room wrapped in my favourite big comfy bathrobe, last year's Christmas present from Simon, Shelley is laying out three cocktail dresses across the sofa.

Shelley Mason fellow Brit and best friend, we met at Art College in London and instantly hit it off becoming best friends fast, after a few weeks we decided to share an apartment along with Simon, then about a year later I got an offer to study in New York. Shelley and Simon jumped at the chance to come with me. Shelley has established herself as a successful fashion designer. Three years ago I backed her financially to set up her own studio and now she is fending for herself as she puts it. I keep on at her to put on a show for fashion week all I get back is maybe next year.

Bringing myself back to the present and looking at the three fabulous dresses I ask "So what's the dress code for tonight?"

"Smart casual" Macy's voice drifts from the kitchen. I could hear cupboards opening and closing then the pop of a cork.

"So what's wrong with wearing jeans?" I ask just to be awkward as she comes in carrying wine glasses and a bottle of rose.

"Oh Skye, you never change and please don't" Shelley laughs and hugging me in a way of hello. I hug her back, god I love my friend, she is my sister in body and soul.

Macy pours out the wine and hands a glass to me "Cheers" I say and take a big gulp, Macy held a glass out to Shelley who looks at it uncertainly.

"Err, no thanks, I better not"

"It's not like you to refuse wine, what's the matter, you pregnant or something" Macy says laughing. A stricken look crosses Shelley's face then she blushes crimson.

"Oh my god" I gasp "you are, aren't you?"

Shelley blushes even more and looks down at the floor, taking a deep breath she looks back up with pure unadulterated joy on her face, tears shining in her eyes and nods. Macy and I shriek at the same time making her jump and wince at the noise, we descend on her firing questions.

"How long have you known?"

"When is it due?"

"Do you know what you are having?"

"OMG what was Phil's reaction?"

Laughing and disentangling herself from our group hugging she says "Phil is over the moon." They have been together forever, she met him not long after we moved to New York "due date is yet to be confirmed I have my appointment on Friday as in tomorrow, although I reckon I'm about six weeks, we found out yesterday, well I did a test yesterday because the last couple of days I've been feeling really rough and being sick."

"So was it planned?" Macy says wiggling her eyebrows.

"Macy, only you can make having a baby sound smutty" I admonish mockingly turning to Shelley I say "so was it?" and wiggle my eyebrows.

"Yes and before you ask it was a lot of fun" Shelley replies with a twinkle in her eyes.

"Oh I bet it was" Macy hip bumps her "that man of yours is mighty fine" she drags out the word fine finishing with an appreciative hum on the end "this causes for a proper toast, let me get you a soda first" Macy says disappearing back into the kitchen.

"Are you okay with this?" Shelley asks tentatively, gesturing her hands around her abdomen.

"Of course I am why wouldn't I be? All I want is for you and Phil is to be happy" I hug her gently. I know she is being cautious around me because I can't have children due to what the attacker did to me and her being sensitive to my feelings made my love for her grow stronger, a thought suddenly strikes me "I'm going to be an aunty" I pull back smiling wickedly "when it's older I can feed it full of sugar, teach it loads of stuff that'll drive you bat shit crazy and hand it back to you when its hyper as hell, what's not to love about that?" making sure to school my facial expression to one of innocence Shelley burst out laughing.

"Somehow I don't doubt any of that for a minute" she pauses takes my hands and squeezes "When 'it' is born would you be Godmother?"

Tears suddenly spring to my eyes and a lump the size of a golf ball in my throat makes it hard for me to speak "I would be honored" comes out in a hoarse whisper.

"Okay time for a toast" Macy says and we break apart to pick up our glasses.

I raise my glass and face my friend "To Shelley and Phil may you have a fabulous pregnancy, bloom with health, love and joy, to you Shelley my best friend, sister and mother of my god child" we salute her and clink glasses and take a drink.

"Not to be a party pooper but you madam" Macy gives me a meaningful look "have to get ready for tonight".

An hour later I was ready. With the help of my friends my hair has been dried and put up in a messy pile on top of my head, I remembered to ask Macy to arrange a haircut appointment, which led to the three of us agreeing to have a spa day on Saturday and since we are all attending a charity benefit that night it seemed the perfect excuse to go and get pampered.

The dress is beautiful as all of Shelley's creations are. I decided to go for the LBD number. The dress fits like a glove, Shelley refuses to put me in anything but fitted garments. "Show off your voluptuous figure" she says. My retort is always "That's just a polite way to say I've got big tits". Her come back is 'Women pay a fortune to have breasts your size."

The dress is silk with a layer of lace over the top and off the shoulder, it's fitted to my hips then the skirt flares out ending just above my knee. Although I'm not big on clothes I am on shoes so I have the perfect pair of killer heels to wear. I keep my makeup minimal, mascara, smoky grey eyeliner to enhance my eyes and nude lip gloss. My lips could be described as full or bee stung again I'm told women pay good money for lips like mine, so I'm conscious not to draw too much attention to them. With my slim figure, hair, tits and lips I am a walking talking Barbie doll. I've even had it said to my face by women who for some reason feel it necessary to put me down and I know it's definitely said behind my back. It used to get me down but with the help of Shelley and Simon I've learnt to accept myself inside and out and the jealous bitches can go fuck themselves.

When we first met the three of us were screwed up in some way and carrying baggage, over the years we have helped each other get over the problems and self-esteem issues. Even to this day we keep the pact we made eight years ago. Once a month we get together no matter where we are in the world, we spend a couple of hours listening and talking with each other about anything that is causing concern, thank heavens for Skype and face time. It doesn't mean we don't talk about our issues or concern at any other time we do, this allocated time means we can give it proper focus with those we trust and who are non-judgemental. In a way I find this time a soul cleansing, character building, affirmation of the positives in my life.

"You look stunning" Shelley says standing behind me and looking at my reflection in the mirror and pulling me out of my thoughts "Mr Smythe is here, ready?" she gives my shoulders a squeeze as I nod "come on then"

Mr Stephen Smythe—I guess him to be in his late fifties to early sixties—is the epitome of the distinguished gentleman, who enjoys the kind of lifestyle his wealth provides and it shows on his waist line. He is a flamboyant character and extremely camp. I'd got to know him through the multitude of Simon's gay friends quite a few years ago. He is very familiar with my work and never misses an opportunity to badger me about selling through his galleries. I'd politely turned him down now he's opened up in New York and come September when I'm going to be here on a more permanent basis I could envisage it becoming more and more difficult to decline, hmm mental note to self to talk to Macy about putting together a plan of action to head that one off.

"My darling Miss Darcy what a vision you are" Mr Smythe croons in his effeminate voice bringing his dainty hands up to his face, for a large man he has surprisingly small hands.

"Thank you Mr Smythe and I must say you look quite dashing yourself" I say smiling warmly, for all his faults I couldn't help but like him. Simon has told me on numerous occasions he could be a really vicious and bitchy queen.

"Shall we" he says gesturing grandly with a sweeping arm toward the door. I wave bye to the girls and tell them to lock up as I head out the door.

CLAYTON

I sigh and look around the cavernous room that is the art gallery, there are only a few pieces I would actually label and call art. My three year old twin nephews could produce better pieces than the crap that's on display here.

The place is reasonably full. I scan the faces again, Skye isn't here. We arrived half an hour ago and already I'm bored shitless out of my skull and sick to death of being pawed and mauled over by the women who know me. Thank god I hadn't fucked any of them and I have no intention of doing so. My mother however is in her element, surrounded by pretentious art luvvies. I pull myself up short, Skye is an artist and potentially I'm in a room full of her friends and acquaintances. Fuck! I need to make more of an effort if I want to get to know her.

What are you thinking, my brain shouts, you're talking as if you're going to be wining and dining her, being boyfriend material, you don't have time for that shit. My internal voice is practically screaming now. You made a right prat of yourself this afternoon rushing to the gym just to get another look at her. Instead you glimpse the back of her climbing in to an SUV then to cap it off you question Phillipee about her, who no doubt now thinks you're some crazy axe wielding stalker. Dude for all you know the guy could have called her and said "Hey not to cause you any concern or scare the shit out of you but watch out for a good looking, tall, dark haired and insanely rich guy, by the way the operative word is insane, he's got a thing for you and he's stalking you".

"Clayton darling are you alright?" my mother asks snapping me out of my mental tirade, concern marring her beautiful features "you seem distracted and out of sorts are you coming down with something?"

"No I'm fine Mom. Just thinking about tomorrow and work, nothing to worry about" I give her my brightest and most charming smile leaning in to give her a kiss on her forehead "sorry if I am spoiling your evening"

"Nonsense, I'm the one who should be apologising, dragging you to an event like this and I know you hate them" she murmurs quietly so those surrounding us wouldn't hear.

"How come you" I stop mid question as a surge of activity and excited voices near the entrance catches my and everyone else's attention.

"Oh how wonderful, Mr Smythe has finally arrived" one of the luvvies gushes "I do hope he is okay I believe a car tyre blew out on the way here, that's why he is so late. I must go and find out" he scuttles off.

I look back to the entrance to see a rather large man immaculately dressed come in through the door and steps to the side and turns to face the person behind him raising the crook of his arm out for them to take.

The vision walking in steals my breath. My heart stops. My sole focus is on her, everyone else in the room disappears. Skye, she's here my brain gibbers. I gulp air suddenly remembering I need to breathe. My heart restarts going so fast it gives me palpitations. I must've swayed on my feet as my mother grabs my arm.

"Clayton! Do you need to sit down? Are you sure you are not feeling ill. Let's go home." my mother sounds panicked.

"No, no I'm okay" I reassure her, I'm even better now Skye is here I add mentally.

I surreptitiously track her movement through the room as Mr Smythe leads her around introducing various people. Obviously the room isn't full of her friends and acquaintances as I first thought. I listen to my mother's running commentary about Mr Smythe and those she knew who he was talking to she did this right up to the point of him standing in front of us.

"My dear Mrs Blake how wonderful to see you, I am so glad you could make it" Mr Smythe has the art of air kissing down to a pat "may I introduce this beautiful and exquisite creature and my guest of honor Skye Darcy".

Skye flushes and looks embarrassed by the way Mr Smythe introduced her, she shakes mother's hand, both murmur pleased to meet you.

Mother without looking reaches behind her grabs my arm and pulls me forward "This is my son Clayton Blake"

Since I'm looking at Skye I see her reaction as soon as she looks at me and I know she recognises me from the minute flare of her eyes widening, followed by a slight frown. I shake Smythe's hand first as I reach for Skye's hand, my spine tingles and surprise, surprise my cock jumps to attention just at the thought of touching her "Calm down boy" I mentally tell my dick. Clasping her hand it feels warm small and fragile, her grip is strong and confident. The skin to skin contact sends a jolt of electricity shooting straight up my arm and down to my cock surprising the shit out of me. I see Skye's eyes widen as well, did she feel the same thing?

"Have we met before?" she asks in her sexy, husky voice "you seem vaguely familiar and I can't place where"

God I could listen to her for eternity, her voice did strange things to my body, a slow pleasant torture.

"No, we haven't met, although we have seen each other" I say. That got my mother's attention and before she could say anything I add "it was earlier today"

I see realization flit across those beautiful pale green eyes as she remembered and murmurs "The elevator" a soft flush blooms in her cheeks, obviously remembering me winking at her. I did that in a moment of, oh I don't know, playfulness, rogue-ness, flirting, take your pick.

I clear my throat. "Yes the elevator" I look at my mother and see her calculated scheming expression that usually means trouble for me with her match making efforts, on this occasion I wouldn't mind her meddling. "Miss Darcy was at my building visiting one of the businesses there, we happened to be on the same floor waiting for the elevator to the ground floor."

Mother's eyes sparkle, shit I could kick myself. I know I've given myself away by overdoing the explanation, volunteered too much information. Normally I would've said no we haven't met and left it at that but being the infatuated, lust driven sap I am, I want Skye to remember me, so I have just stuck a big red flashing sign arrowed straight at her for my mother to see I'm interested. Also my mother would draw the conclusion I had actively tracked Skye's whereabouts in the building down and lay in wait for her. Yep I'm definitely in stalker territory.

"Come my dear there are a few other people I wish to introduce you to" Smythe says taking Skye's arm and leads her away.

"Well she is absolutely stunning and I can see why you tracked her down" see I told you my mother would know "did you know she was going to be here tonight?"

My eyebrows raise at my mother in disbelief "Seriously" I say a tad sarcastically "it was you who wanted me to escort you here tonight otherwise I would be at home most probably working"

"Or thinking about a stunning creature called Skye Darcy" mother teases "tell me what does she do and don't try to play the innocence, I know you and you would have already done a search on her"

I laugh out loud, causing a few people to look our way, with a thrill I notice Skye looking over.

"Yes Mom you do know me, too well" I say affectionately "she is an artist, I looked at her web site this afternoon. She works in the Fantasy and Sci-Fi genre by all accounts she is an extremely talented and a shrewd business woman, she is also extremely rich and highly successful. As you heard she is British and came to America to study art when she was nineteen and she travels extensively with her work that's all I know" I neglect to add I have someone on the case digging up more information on her. I look down at my mother she has an expression I can't determine "what?"

Reaching up she cups my cheek, pure love shining from her eyes "Oh my poor boy you've got her bad you just don't know it yet"

"Don't be daft" I scoff, dread starts to grip me. I'm a love them and leave them kind of guy, I'm well known for it "what makes you say that?" I add with growing alarm.

"You haven't been able to take your eyes off her from the moment she set foot in the gallery" it was all said softly and as a statement. A large boulder feels as if it has suddenly taken up residence in my gut.

Luckily one of my mother's friends came over to spirit her away leaving me to my thoughts. No matter how much I try to deny my mother's words my eyes are constantly drawn to Skye.

Half an hour later I spy Skye on her own walking around looking at the paintings, she stops in front of a large canvass that is speckled with splodges of paint, a few squiggles and straight lines running through it, what utter crap.

Taking a deep breath I walk up behind her saying "The brush strokes show a determined mind and the aesthetically pleasing colors show an insight into the artist's character, don't you think?"

Skye startles and jumps at the sound of my voice stepping back into me. I place my hands on her waist to steady her. Fuck she feels good. I bite down on a groan threatening to escape my throat. It takes all I have to keep my hands from roaming all over her body. I'm not quite successful as my fingers flex and knead her tiny waist and the tops of her hips. Instead of moving out of my grip she leans slightly to one side and looks up at me then quickly glances around to see who is near then looks back up at me with a mischievous grin and glint in her eye.

"Bullshit, you just think it's a load of splodges, squiggles and straight lines and any three year old can do better" she says in her sexy throaty voice with barely contained mirth.

"Busted" I say around a surprise bark of laughter that escapes me.

Skye moves to turn and face me I let my hands drop, to stop myself reaching out to hold her again I put my hands in my jeans pockets.

"I do have three year old twin nephews to which you have just echoed my sentiments exactly that I had over an hour ago."

"So what kind of art do you prefer Mr Blake?" is that a hint of a challenge I detect.

"Please call me Clayton, Mr Blake is so formal plus it makes me feel old" I place a hand over my heart and give a slight bow.

"Clayton" she whispers, her husky voice washes over me sending my cock agonisingly harder. Her luscious lips curl in a slight smile, fantasies of those full luscious lips wrapped around my cock immediately spring to mind. As I bring my head up I look into her eyes and my breath catches. They are the most exquisite color I've ever seen. At first glance you would be mistaken to say they are pale green, however her eyes are more yellow and have a dark blue ring surrounding the outside of the iris.

"Your eyes" I breathe out in wonder, she frowns then raises an eyebrow at me.

"My eyes, well that's a first to be told they are a work of art"

"What" I say in confusion, to my horror I realize I've spoken out loud. I can feel the blood rush to my face "sorry, err, what I meant to say, err, was" fuck I'm flustered. Me! Clayton Blake, billionaire, master of industry who puts the fear of god in everyone who works for him and does business with is reduced to a quivering wreak by the goddess who stands before him.

"What's up? Cat gotcha tongue Clayton" she's teasing me and that mischievous grin is back her eyes sparkling with amusement. Did she know the effect she is having on me? Christ, I want to kiss her fucking senseless. Bringing my brain back on line I try to remember what the question was. Art, yes that was it; what art did I like? I open my mouth to answer when from behind me a loud effeminate voice squeals.

"Skye, oh my god honey there you are"

My instincts would normally be to scowl and tell the person to fuck off, however in this instance I welcome in the interruption. I move so I can see who is coming towards us. The man is average height and very slim, his hair is his crowning glory as it's artfully styled and holds that much product it didn't move. His suit is expensive and he carries it well plus he is blatantly gay given by the way he holds himself and walks. He descends on Skye giving her a huge hug.

"Okay Simon, let go I can't breathe" Skye mumbles as she pat's his back indicating she wants him to ease up.

Letting her go he says in a rush "I am so sorry about this afternoon, when Macy rang me I got on to it straight away. I must confess I have no recollection of a David Smith, I do know Phoenix PR but not him, anyway

I have put calls out so I should have answers for you tomorrow" he pauses for breath then notices me "helloooo gorgeous" he says blatantly dragging his eyes up and down my body, imagining me naked no doubt.

"Behave" Skye admonishes and slaps his arm "Simon this is Clayton Blake, Clayton this is one of my best friends and PR guru Simon Hanson"

Simon's eyes widen "The Clayton Blake as in billionaire business mogul, thirty years young free and single Clayton Blake"

"The one and only" I grin extending my hand.

He takes it and with his other hand he fans himself saying to Skye "Well shag me sideways I've found my sugar daddy for tonight, what are you doing?"

Skye looks at me nervously obviously trying to gage my reaction to her friend's outrageous behaviour. I laugh heartily mainly to show her I'm not offended and I find myself genuinely liking this guy.

"Unfortunately this sugar daddy is spoken for tonight so you'll have to find another one"

Right on cue mother appears at my elbow. I introduce her to Simon who charms her immediately by saying he could see where I got my good looks from.

"Are you ready to leave?" I ask her.

"Yes if you don't mind" I nod "we are going to be at the Bolton House Charity fund raiser on Saturday, will we have the pleasure of seeing you there?" mother directs the question to Skye however it is Simon who answers.

"Yes we have a table. I can't wait I just love the glitz and glamour all in the name of a good cause"

"Fabulous" mother practically squeals "I look forward to seeing you both there" she says air kissing with Simon, then surprising both me and Skye hugs her goodbye. I nod and shake Simon's hand then take Skye's hand raising the back to my lips and kiss her soft skin. I hold my breath as I don't trust what affect her scent will have on my body and brain. If just being in the same proximity has me hard and her voice sends my muscles into a quivering mess I know I will be lost completely if I take in her scent.

"Till Saturday" I murmur holding her gaze as I step back. I see her skin flush pink across her cheekbones, down her throat and over her wonderful ample bosom. The sight gives me a satisfying thrill I do have an effect on her.

SKYE

A loud groan escapes me as I slide deeper into the hot scented water, finally getting the soak in the bath I longed for hours earlier. I feel all of my aching muscles slowly relax. Mentally I run a checklist of what I have to do tomorrow. Hair cut at eleven, good old Macy had called a friend of hers after I left for the gallery and booked an appointment. Meeting at four, now that is going to be interesting as it is in one of those high end gentlemen's pole dancing clubs if everything went as planned then it will be a commission I would start when I came back in September. I've had quite a few conversations with the owner over the last few months so tomorrow is to view what space the painting will take up, then I can give him a rough indication of price. Then seven thirty meeting with Simon, Shelley, Phil and whoever else turns up at Gino's restaurant for a get together. At least I can get a good few hours of drawing done in the morning. I don't sleep much probably due to all the travelling I do and crossing various time zones constantly has screwed up my internal clock.

With a contented sigh I slip down further into the hot water and my thoughts turn to the evening and Clayton Blake. God my body tightens just at the thought of him, normally I am cautious and wary of new men I meet but for some reason he brought out the tease in me. A smile breaks out across my face as I remember how flustered he became when he mentioned my eyes. Huh! He didn't answer my question on the kind of art he preferred, mental note to self, ask him that when I see him on Saturday. A thrill jolts through me and butterflies take up residence in my stomach at the thought.

Bloody hell, I'm going to be a quivering wreck by Saturday if this keeps up, however I am proud of myself for being cool and calm around him especially when Smythe introduced me to his mother. I give myself a mental pat on the back at my cleverness for saying he seemed familiar but I couldn't recall where I knew him from. Of course I recognised him the minute I clapped eyes on him when I entered the gallery. I'm just thankful I didn't fall off my shoes at the surprise I had at seeing him there. For some reason it struck me that the gallery and the art it contained wasn't for him, a chuckle escapes me as he admitted as much when I'd called his bluff.

My thoughts drift to when I stepped back into him when he startled me. It was like hitting a brick wall, a deliciously hot brick wall. Just imagining what his chest and abs would be like had me squeezing my thighs together. I can still feel the heat of his big hands on my waist, his strong grip and flexing fingers; jeez I wanted him to run his hands all over my body. His touch sent riotous tingling sensations all over my body and I thought my heart was going to burst out of my chest; it beat so fast it made me light headed. My tits ache and nipples harden in agreement and boy oh boy he had smelt so good, a lovely musky, mildly spicy all male scent remembering that made my blood heat. Bloody hell I'm turned on, no-one has ever had an effect on me like he did.

Would I have sex with him? My body gives a resounding yes. Hell yes! Shouts my inner goddess but mentally was I ready? Park the brain and thinking my inner goddess snaps. Fair enough let's see how things progress, he might not even want me. Oh he wants you alright sweet thing, you did see the look he gave you when he kissed your hand. The guy wants to eat you alive and fuck you senseless. The heat in my whole body ramps up a thousand degrees as my imagination runs riot. Come on girl admit it Clayton Blake is sex on legs, he oozes it. Not only that, my inner goddess chides he's a billionaire!

I shoot up out of the water "Christ I'd forgotten about that" my words echo around the bathroom making me jump, laughing at myself I settle back in the water. Clayton being rich doesn't bother me, I'm extremely wealthy myself, not as rich as him of course but I'm a multi-millionaire in my own right. What's different is he wouldn't be interested in me for my money, that's one of the reasons why I'm wary of meeting new men it's determining and filtering out the fortune hunters. On the way home I asked Simon how come he'd known so much about Clayton.

"Darling, I'm in PR it is my job to know who the movers and shakers are, besides you've spent so little time in America over the last few years, plus it's almost two years since you were last in New York I knew you wouldn't have a clue who he is"

"And you knew who he was before you came over" I said a tad indignant recalling his spiel of Clayton being a billionaire, free and single.

"Of course, he definitely has a thing for you honey" he bumped my shoulder giving me a knowing wink.

I climb out of the bath, dry off and put on my bathrobe, I'm still wide awake. I head into the kitchen and make myself a drink of milky hot chocolate, in the living room I switch on the music centre and set the iPod on random. Rock music blares out. I turn the volume down then decide I want to listen to Evanescence, with Amy Lee's voice filling the room I walk over to my drawing desk, as I sit down Paul enters' the room.

"Hey, everything okay?"

"Yes ma'am, if you don't need anything I'll turn in"

"I'm good thanks, goodnight" as he turns to go I suddenly remember Sunday "Paul" I call him back, silently he comes back into the room and waits patiently for me to speak, it always amazes me how quiet he can move for a man his size, six one and built like a barn. "Sunday, do you still have Jack?" Paul nods warily "it's his birthday isn't it?" again a nod "what do you have planned?"

"I don't have anything definite planned, thought I would see what he wanted to do" Paul answers, he seems embarrassed he hasn't got his six year old, soon to be seven, son's day planned out meticulously, which is his usual style.

"Well I was thinking, how about we have a birthday lunch or tea for him here. I'll organise it all you have to do is turn up after whatever it is you decide to do and if he wants to bring some friends too that's fine" I couldn't fathom if I'd over stepped the mark as Paul's face was completely blank "anyway have a think about it, the offer's there, just let me know sometime tomorrow morning, that way it'll give me time to get groceries and make a cake."

Paul stood there motionless for a few minutes, to distract myself I take a drink to break eye contact.

"You'd do that for Jack?" Paul says quietly, keeping my head down pretending to be busy with what's on my desk I nod, it also meant I didn't see or hear Paul as he approached me. I nearly claw the ceiling as he touches my shoulder and says "Thank you" softly.

"Jeez, you scared the crap out of me" I say swatting him "I swear to god I am going to make it compulsory for you to wear a bell"

"Sorry ma'am" he chuckles not in the slightest "and thank you again, that's great. I think a birthday tea would be much appreciated"

"Sure you don't want it to be lunch" I ask double checking.

"Tea will be fine, besides you'll be out late Saturday or should I say early hours Sunday" he reminds me.

"Oh yeah" I screw my face up remembering the charity event "good point, tea it is. Okay so let me know what time tomorrow" he opens his mouth to say something I raise my hand to stop him and add "once you have spoken to Jack and find out what he would like to do then that will give you an idea what time you will be back here, plus find out how many of his friends will be coming."

Conceding to my points Paul nodded and yes ma'am me again, saying goodnight he left to go to his quarters.

Paul has worked for me for nearly four years and he lives in. Travelling everywhere with me and Macy, he has seen me at my worst, which doesn't happen often and thankfully he hasn't run in the opposite direction screaming. Like Macy he is another god send of a find. I've had other bodyguards before him but for whatever reason it didn't work out, usually the amount of travelling I did was the reason cited for them leaving. Actually I think it was more to do with the amount of time I spent out of the country when I was working on commissions in some cases it could be months in one country, so being away from family became an issue for many.

Macy didn't have family, well she did, she just didn't want anything to do with them and I'd never pried, I figured she would tell me whenever she was ready or wanted to and so far to date she didn't.

Paul Boyd came recommended by my last bodyguard. They had been in the military together serving in Iraq and Afghanistan. I clearly remember the day I interviewed him, as it's the only time I have seen him nervous. He'd been out of the military about nine months and working as a bouncer for a club of 'questionable activity' that's all he would give me when I asked why he was looking to leave. I admired he remained true to his integrity rather than get pulled in to the questionable activity. At the time of the interview he had no contact with his son due to his ex-wife using the boy as a weapon to get her demands met during a nasty divorce battle. As part of the terms for his employment I got him to agree to allow my lawyers to resolve the divorce issues, all at my expense, that way I know his mind is on the job at all times, not that I class myself as high risk but due to my work I have quite a fan base which means I have my share of nut jobs and stalkers hence the bodyguard. He couldn't argue with my logic so reluctantly he agreed. In return I have an extremely loyal bodyguard. Whenever I am in the States I make sure he has time with his son, the ex-wife can't refuse because if she does all the benefits she receives, again courtesy of me, disappear. When I'm travelling Paul face times or Skype's his son at least once a day. I've met his son a few times and he's a lovely polite kid and a softer image of his father. Paul has a rugged handsomeness about him but the horrors of war have left their mark and his features have a harshness that screams don't mess with me.

Making a mental note to buy Jack a birthday present I glance over at the wall clock, one o'clock. Oh well time to get some sleep. Switching everything off I take my cup into the kitchen rinse it out and put it in the machine. In my bedroom I switch my iPod to some calming meditation music and settle in to wait for sleep to claim me. My last thought and image is of Clayton Blake and how his eyes seared mine with promises of sin and decadence and how his lips felt as he kissed the back of my hand.

Chapter Two

SKYE

In the mirror I watch Simon pass behind me as I put on my mascara. I can tell something is on his mind and he has news or information I wouldn't like, he has a 'tell' when he's agitated, the clenching and unclenching of his hands, but he's putting on a front of calm. I refocus on my reflection and finish putting on my makeup. After a few more minutes I can't stand it anymore.

"Okay, spill" I say in my best don't mess with me tone as I can muster because I'm not really sure if I want to hear what he has to say, ignorance is bliss and all that.

"Oh honey" he says with a sigh setting alarm bells ringing and dread settling in the pit of my stomach "I don't know how to tell you without it sounding scary as shit" he's distraught.

I know I have a wide eyed look on my face because he winces at my reaction to what he's just said and he knew he'd already started to scare me. I stand and went to him, giving him a hug.

"We've been besties for eight years you know you can tell me anything, just come out with it and we'll go from there. I'm a big girl and I'm wearing my big girl pants, I can handle it" that got him to relax a little.

"Right, okay, give me a minute to collect my thoughts. I'll fix us a drink" he says walking out of my bedroom.

As I got dressed in my trade mark jeans and t-shirt, I thought back to when we first met at Art College in London. It was about a week after I started there and I'd already befriended Shelley. We were in the cafeteria for lunch and saw Simon stood alone with a tray of food looking lost and forlorn in the crowd of chatting groups surrounding him. I took pity on him and invited him to join us, for the rest of the hour the three of us didn't stop talking and laughing. Not long after that day we got an apartment together. Shelley and I guessed Simon was gay before he did, actually that's wrong, Simon knew he was gay he just hadn't accepted it himself. I think it was mainly down to his Catholic upbringing and having a controlling father and an indifferent mother it kind of messed with the guy's head. Not long after when we moved to New York he came out and has never looked back since and he found his calling in PR. He is an absolute star at what he does and he's established himself with a strong client base, including me.

Giving myself one final look in the mirror and fluffing out my hair, the stylist had done a fairly reasonable job the poor thing nearly had a heart attack when he saw how long it was. Now my hair is waist length and all natural cork screw curls, I blow myself a kiss and head out to find Simon.

He's in the living room pacing. On the table is a bottle of Southern Comfort, my favourite tipple, along with a glass that has a generous measure in it.

"Surely it can't be that bad if you are giving me the hard stuff" Simon jerks around at the sound of my voice, blimey he is jumpy. I sit down and take the drink in one hit. The smooth liquor burning its way down my throat to my stomach "okay hit me with it"

He sits next to me and takes my hands and looks me in the eye, sighing and dropping his gaze to our joined hands he says "Oh honey, I've screwed up big time" he sighs heavily again. I didn't react just gave him space to find the words he needs to continue "the meeting you had yesterday with David Smith" he pauses and looks at me worry lines creasing his brow.

"Yes how can I forget that prat, he took two hours of my life I will never get back" I say pleased with myself as I remain calm, yesterday I was willing and ready to commit murder I was so angry "did Macy tell you he has this idea he is signing me and he's already introducing himself as my new PR agent?" I add although it came out more forceful than I intended.

"Yeah, she did. The fucker is delusional" I nod my agreement "anyway" Simon takes a deep breath before he continues "about six months ago I was out with friends, you were in France" he shakes his head "that's by the by. It was one of those nights with lots of wine and boasting, my dad's bigger than your dad kind of boasting only it was about clients. I happened to mention you, as you know you are my number one"

"And most profitable" I chide with a smile.

"Yes that as well" he smiles back although it's strained "well at the time I was mega busy and I was saying I didn't think I could handle you when you came back to the States" I kept my face blank "David pipes up he would jump at the opportunity to represent you and would I arrange a meeting, well the alcohol was taking effect and" he pauses taking a deep breath saying the next bit in a rush "'I accessed your diary and put in the meeting sending him a diary request" he looks at me with such remorse it takes all I've got not to laugh, considering I should be mad as hell at him because nobody but Macy puts things in my diary "I'm such a dick and I'm so sorry. I want to continue being your PR agent and I swear to god I'll never do anything like that again" he looks at me with pleading eyes he breaks my heart and I know I can't be mad at him even though I've every right to be.

"Oh Simon, yes you are a dick" I say laughing "and I will let you keep your balls" relief sweeps through in him making his shoulders sag "seriously though I thought you were going to tell me you'd killed someone or lost a shit load of money" he gives a shaky laugh "so have you set this David straight?" I raise an eyebrow to prompt him; he looks back at me rather sheepish.

"Well, that's the thing David works for his uncle who is a big fish in the PR business and" he winces saying the next bit "if I tell him 'Oh sorry I was drunk that night and I screwed up and Skye Darcy is remaining my client' he can make things very difficult for me, so I was wondering..." he let the sentence hang and dutifully I pick up the thread.

"So you want me to be the bad guy" I say resigned, he nods giving me puppy dog eyes "you owe me, big time for this" and I punch his shoulder to make my point.

"Ouch" he yelps "am I forgiven" he says hopefully rubbing his shoulder.

"Don't know" then after a beat "just don't do it again because if you do I will definitely be serving you your balls on a platter"

"You're the best" he grins widely and gives me a big hard hug, I grumble at him under my breath and feel my ribs crack "so how are you going to handle it"

"Leave it with me. I'll have a brain storm with Macy for a plan of action" I look at my watch "come on time to go to Gino's, Paul" I yell, his yes ma'am response is immediate making me jump. I look at him and point "bells, now compulsory"

Simon looks at us puzzled and mouths bells to Paul with raised eyebrows. Paul put his head down and shakes it sighing as he opens the door. I laugh, poor man although it does give me an idea for his Christmas present.

Gino's is a lovely family run Italian restaurant. It was started by the current owner's great grandfather who immigrated to the States after the Second World War. Simon often jokes it's a front for the mob but none of us has the nerve to ask. The restaurant is done out in a homely traditional Italian setting, simple wooden tables covered in red and white gingham table cloths, decorated with scenic pictures of the Italian countryside.

When we first moved to New York we'd stumbled across this restaurant during one of our many adventures in getting to know the neighbourhood and since then we frequent it as often as possible, normally at least once a week usually on a Friday, especially when I'm around.

On route we picked up Macy so the three of us walk into the welcoming warmth and hospitality of Gino himself—it's a family tradition to call the first born son Gino— and when he sees me he greets me like a father would at the return of his much loved prodigal son, in my case daughter. Well it has been nearly two years since I'd last set foot in the place. Gino always speaks in Italian to me and he didn't care if no-one could follow the conversation as he knew I'd translate.

"Mia cara e stato trappo lungo, oh come ho perso te" he says giving me a bear hug making my spine crack, releasing me he bellows "Maria, Maria come see who is here"

The whole restaurant went deadly quiet and looks at us. Oh how I wish the floor would open and swallow me up. Maria is Gino's wife, she's a few inches shorter than me and round, her greying dark hair scrapped back into a bun, as she walks from the back of the restaurant she holds her arms open with a huge smile on her beautiful motherly face. I went to her and greeted her just as warmly. I feel myself filling up at the response they've given me. Maria starts to fuss saying how beautiful I am and I'm too thin. I laugh and say that's why I've come because I missed her fabulous cooking so much, which is true. I head back to the others as Gino is showing them to our table. Shelley and Phil are already there along with two friends of Simon's, plus Pete and his catty bitch girlfriend from hell Caroline. Shit that's the evening ruined.

Simon leant down and whispers "Sorry honey I didn't know they were coming. In fact I have no idea how they found out since we haven't been here in forever. Come on sit in between Harry and Mark they'll keep the bitch in check."

"You have just redeemed yourself, all is forgiven" I whisper back. Plastering a smile on my face I make my way round and greet my friends.

CLAYTON

Why, oh why do I put up with my mothers' match making attempts I ask myself for the millionth time as I look at my date across the table? She is dressed and made up to the nines, obviously expecting to be taken to some obscenely expensive restaurant she can later boast to her friends about via Facebook or Twitter or both.

Instead I've brought her to Gino's, my favourite Italian restaurant. I love the family atmosphere and the genuine welcome they give you. It's a far cry from the obnoxious or simpering welcome at some of the posh restaurants I've frequented. I can tell by her face she isn't impressed, well fuck her – hmm may be later. Suddenly thoughts of Skye come unbidden to mind, this has been happening on and off all day when I least expect it. I keep having fantasy after fantasy of getting her beneath me, each one being more graphic. My cock twitches at the direction of my thoughts and I shift in my seat trying to make room in my pants. Clearing my throat I look up from the menu I'm holding "So what are you going to have Pippa?" I ask politely.

As I ask my question the door opens and a group of people walk in, I'm momentarily distracted as I watch Gino welcome them, the guy seems vaguely familiar. I look back at Pippa and as she is about to answer Gino starts bellowing for his wife. Frowning I look at the group again and nearly fall off my chair as Skye steps into view and walks towards Maria with the most beautiful smile I have ever seen taking my breath away. Skye and Maria embrace, when they pull apart I can see genuine affection shining in both faces. I only know the odd word and a couple of phrases in Italian so I couldn't follow what Maria is saying. However Skye floors me even more when she laughs her deep throaty sexy laugh and answers Maria in fluent flawless Italian.

I can't take my eyes off her and watch as she moves across the restaurant back to her friends. Her hair is down, a mass of cork screw curls cascading down her back to her waist. Fuck I'd love to wrap my hands in it. She's wearing jeans, hipsters and I'm mesmerised as I watch her hips sway and her tight ass flex as she walks. She takes off her jacket to reveal a plain black V neck fitted t-shirt. I noticed yesterday she has big tits and I'd put money on the fact they are real and they suit her, she carries herself and them well. I stifle a groan as images of her naked and I'm sucking and fondling them come to mind, my cock throbs. Her waist is tiny and my hands tingle as I remember how she felt under them yesterday. Appreciating her figure that is more athletic than hour glass in build has me rock hard, no woman has ever gotten to me like she did. I continue to watch Skye as she greets each person at her table with a hug except one couple who she acknowledges with a strained smile, wonder what that's all about. Skye sits down between two men, smiling and laughing at whatever it is they've said. I have to fight an overwhelming urge to go over and join her table. I could feel my body preparing itself to stand, suddenly Skye looks up and straight at me and my heart does a funny flip flop. A slow shy smile breaks out across her beautiful lips, raising her hand she waves tentatively at me. Her action causes the rest of her party to turn around and stare. I wave back with enthusiasm and stupid grin on my face.

"So you actually know her then" snaps my date, what's her name again, oh yeah Pippa, fucking stupid name.

"Yeah I do" thankfully the waitress arrives to take our order and I bury my head in the menu so I don't have to look at her.

The meal is a complete fucking disaster. The food is outstanding as it always is and I eat heartily it's the company that's crap. I quickly discover my date has very little to say if it isn't about shopping, fashion and shoes or some reality TV show I've never even heard of she couldn't converse. She has done nothing of interest with her life and didn't work. She's a typical trust fund socialite looking for a rich man, so the majority of the time we are silent. Thanks Mom!

The only good thing is I can watch Skye from where I sit. I have a clear unobstructed view of her. Skye's group seem to be having a riot of a time. I recognise the guy she came in with as Simon from last night, they're loud but not boisterous enough to annoy the other dinners. I notice Gino and Maria sitting down and joining them whenever they could. At one point the whole group broke out in cheers and got up to hug and congratulate one couple, bottles of champagne were brought to the table, from what I could hear the toast indicated a baby and engagement for the couple.

As I ordered coffee I see Skye get up, panic surges through me I feel myself breaking out in a cold sweat I don't want her to leave yet. An older woman got up as well and they move towards my table, why is she coming to me, she's not idiot my brain snaps, she has to pass you to go to the bathroom. I feel myself flush at my own egotism. As she approaches I catch her eyes and hold them. I know I have my idiot goofy smile on my face, I can't help it. I stand and greet her.

"Skye how lovely to see you again so soon" my voice is low and seductive, pure proof to what this vision of beauty is doing to me.

"Clayton, a pleasant surprise" she replies in her low and sexy as fuck voice "how was your meal?"

"Wonderful it always is when I come here" I want her to know I'm a regular. The woman behind her shifts and clears her throat. Skye takes the hint and introduces her. I feel obliged to introduce my date which is the last thing I want to do.

"Well enjoy the rest of your evening, nice to meet you" Skye smiles at Pippa who does a piss poor job of being civil back. To me she says "and I guess I'll be seeing you tomorrow night"

"I look forward to it" and before I could stop myself I pick up her hand and kiss the back of it. I see the high flush of her cheeks and it makes me feel like a giddy teenager. Screw it tomorrow night I am going to make my move on her. I step aside to allow her and her friend to pass. As I sit down I catch the spiteful almost hateful look on Pippa's face and I realize she isn't a patch on Skye. I can see Pippa is dying to say something, I don't volunteer any further information and we remain silent for a few minutes.

"So who is the walking talking Barbie doll" Pippa finally spits out, her face screwed up with disdain "and what's this about tomorrow night?"

Pippa has seriously pissed me off so what came out of my mouth next, let's just say hell will freeze over before I apologise to my mother for tearing a strip off one of her friend's daughters.

"Skye" I enunciate barely reigning in my anger "is an extremely talented artist and successful self-made business woman who is widely travelled and speaks at least two languages fluently to my knowledge and I suggest you could learn quite a bit from her and apply it to your life to make you a more interesting human being because I think the brainless and plastic Barbie label is better suited to you" the look of shock on her face makes me feel justified "tomorrow night is the Bolton House Charity fund raiser I am attending and so is Skye" I neglect to say separately, by now anger has replaced Pippa's shock.

"I will not stay here and be insulted" hisses Pippa as she stands and throws her napkin on to the table then stalks out of the restaurant.

"Good riddance" I mutter under my breath. I pull out my phone and send a text to my mother explaining what has happened, the least I can do is forewarn her about the potential fallout heading her way.

SKYE

I can feel Macy's curiosity and eyes burning a hole in the back of my head as I focus on washing my hands, with a sigh I give in and tell her "I met him last night at the gallery opening. He was there with his mother who happened to mention they would be attending the charity benefit tomorrow. She wanted to know if I would be going. Simon told her we have a table"

There is no way in hell I'm telling her or my best friends about the elevator incident which happened earlier that day as they'll have a field day in teasing me. I turn around and pull out a couple of paper hand towels from the holder behind her.

"What, I didn't say anything" Macy says trying to look innocent.

"You don't have to it's written all over your face. You know curiosity will kill you one of these days" I say with mock stern chastisement making her laugh.

"I must say he is easy on the eye, very, very easy" she emphasises "I wouldn't kick him out of bed in a hurry" she winks saucily.

"Macy, I'm shocked" I laugh as I throw the towels in the bin "however, touch him and I'll rip your arms off".

"Ho ho ho" Macy chuckles with amusement "Skye Darcy, are you implying the deliciously delectable Clayton Blake is the first man in god knows how long to have caught your attention and you plan to do something about it?"

"Maybe" I say mischievously over my shoulder as I open the door of the restroom to head back into the restaurant.

As I walk through the door I see Clayton's date stomping out the front door, he on the other hand is still seated and scowling at his phone as he texts rapidly his fingers flying over the keys on his phone. As we pull level to his table and only god knows what possesses me to say it I ask "What did you say that was so bad to make her walk out?"

Clayton's head snaps up his scowl disappearing instantly to be replaced with a look I can only describe as chagrin. He looks back down at his phone and shifts in his seat, clears his throat and when he looks back up his face is set with determination, a crease forms between his eyebrows. His luscious sculpted lips press into a thin line then he lets out a heavy exhale.

"She insulted you"

I think my jaw hit the table. How can a complete stranger insult you when they don't know you? Oh wait a minute… yep… I do know this one.

"Barbie! By any chance" I ask.

The look of shock and surprise on his face is classic and it makes me chuckle, I'm right in my assumption.

"So what did you say in defence of our beautiful and brilliant Skye?" Macy says appraisingly.

Clayton's eyes flick to Macy then back at me, holding my gaze he says "Exactly that, she is beautiful and brilliant, plus she's a highly accomplished businesswoman and the Barbie insult was better suited to her than Skye"

This time my jaw hits the floor and I know my cheeks have gone purple with embarrassment because of the sudden heat flooding my body and face. I have absolutely no clue how to feel and think about what he's just said. It's bloody obvious he's done his homework on me. Macy on the other hand lets out a whoop of laughter and claps her hands.

"For such gallant and chivalrous actions towards our sensational Skye please come join our party and let us reward you with copious amounts of alcohol" Macy says taking my arm and moving me back towards our table gesturing to Clayton to follow.

My legs move woodenly, one foot in front of the other that's all I'm aware of along with Clayton's presence behind me as we walk back to our table. I'm in stunned shock. Simon being Simon—he never misses a trick—has been closely watching me and Macy with Clayton, he had already got an additional chair, made Harry and Mark move next to each other meaning Clayton will be sitting next to me by the time we got back to the table.

Clayton gallantly pulls out my chair and holds the back and moves it forward as I sit. I glance at Shelley who's grinning so widely her face is in danger of splitting in half. It's also apparent Simon has told everyone who Clayton is and of our meeting him last night.

I introduce him to everyone pointing out the couples. Harry and Mark both sigh and gaze at Clayton with open mouthed awe. Clayton handles their besotted attention well, it doesn't faze him one bit.

Now call me a bitch but I take great delight in watching Caroline's reaction. I just wish I could've filmed it or took pictures of her green with envy sour face for prosperity. This is a woman who unbeknownst to anyone but herself tries to make my life a misery whenever I'm in proximity of her and she always takes every opportunity to belittle me in front of everyone, a feat she rarely achieves thanks to my friends thwarting her attempts and slapping her down with their own bitchy comebacks. My friends only tolerate her because of Pete.

Pete had been my first proper boyfriend when I was seventeen and we dated for all of three months and I also happened to lose my virginity to him. He had been my cousin Alfie's best friend but I'd sort of known him since I was sixteen. I try never to have regrets but if I was ever given the chance to go back and change something in my life that would make the list.

Pete moved to New York about six years ago and we bumped into each other in the street, literally. I hadn't seen Pete since we finished going out together and because he told me I was the only person he knew—he'd been in New York for three weeks—and I felt sorry for him I extended an invitation to join us at Gino's, he jumped at the chance and has been coming here ever since. God knows why because I don't even class us as friends, I even struggle to call us associates or acquaintances. Pete's been seeing Caroline for about five years, she seemed okay at first but I think since she found out Pete and I had once been an item her animosity towards me just seems to increase each time she sees me. I'm just glad I don't have to see her too often.

I also happen to know she's not faithful to Pete and as far as I'm aware he and the rest of my friends don't know this. I haven't even told Shelley and Simon. I don't know why because we share everything, we have very few secrets. Admittedly there are things I haven't told them about my past and I'm sure it's the same for them but keeping the fact Caroline has been unfaithful to Pete three times that I know of something inside me was saying to keep quiet, so I am… for now.

"Skye" Clayton's deep raspy voice brings me back to the present.

"Hmm, sorry what did you say" I'm suddenly aware he or someone has asked me a question.

"Desert, what would you like?" he says with a smile playing on his sinful lips. You covered in chocolate, I nearly blurt out. I mentally slap myself and feel my cheeks warm. Clayton leans in close and whispers in my ear "whatever it is you just thought of, you can have later. For now choose from the menu" he taps the menu that has somehow miraculously appeared in front of me.

The combination of his body heat, scent, seductive voice and the proximity of his mouth next to my ear nearly causes me to combust. I look at the menu my cheeks on fire, deep breathes I tell myself trying to calm my racing heart. I clench my hands into fists to stop the tell-tale sign of trembling. Out of the corner of my eye I can see Simon and Shelley frantically whispering and looking at me then Clayton. Oh god help me what are they plotting.

"I'll have hot chocolate fudge cake with ice cream" I say to the waiter handing the menu to him. I'm thankful it's in a hard leather folder which means no-one will see my shaking hands although my fingers are cramping with gripping it so tightly.

"Excellent choice" Clayton murmurs "Chocolate and ice cream, the fun you can have with those"

Oh sweet baby Jesus, the man and his voice ooze sinful toe curling sex and for the first time in forever I feel myself getting wet.

"So Clayton" Simon says leaning across the table "what multimillion dollar deal are you working on at the moment"

For the remainder of the meal Clayton regales us with funny stories that have happened in his private and business life. He is witty, charismatic and eloquent putting everyone at ease. It doesn't escape my notice how he gets each of my friends to talk about themselves and tell him how they met me interestingly he didn't ask Pete or Caroline. At midnight Paul came in to the restaurant to take me home prompting me to call it a night. Settling the bill became a battle of wills with Gino and Maria, they insisted no payment was necessary. To avoid insulting them and their hospitality I pull four one hundred dollar bills out from my wallet and put them on the table telling Gino to split it between the staff, everyone else follows suit, except Caroline, who scowls at Pete when he put his money down. I know he wouldn't have been as generous as the rest of us, his act of putting money on the table is more about saving face and not looking tight fisted.

Outside we say our goodbyes and finalise arrangements for tomorrow's pampering session. Simon and Macy were getting a lift home from Shelley and Phil, I've no idea where Pete and Caroline have gone and I don't care. Paul pulls up to the curb in the SUV and remains in the car, engine running. I know even though it appears he's ignoring me and Clayton he is paying one hundred percent of his attention on us and our surroundings.

"Can I give you a lift home or where ever" I ask in the friendliest nonchalant manner I can muster.

"Thank you but no, my own chariot awaits" he nods in the direction of a Bentley parked across the street and a suited man, bodyguard I guess, stood by the rear passenger door "I look forward to enjoying yours and your friends company tomorrow evening, if tonight is anything to go by it's going to be highly entertaining" he leans forward an kisses my forehead then picks up my hand and kisses the back, his eyes never leaving mine and by god they promise all sorts of enjoyable and decadent things that makes my heart pick up speed, hell I'm practically panting and my body is tingling all over. Clayton opens the rear passenger door and helps me in to the car.

"Home" I say to Paul as I watch Clayton with his tight butt flexing and lithe long legs stroll cross the street and get into his own car "oh be still my racing heart" I murmur.

Chapter Three

SKYE

"I love being pampered" says Shelley as we—Macy, me and Simon—each sit in a reclining chair with a face pack on and a towel wrapped around our heads whilst a team of beauticians sit around us doing manicures and pedicures. A collective hum is all the answer she gets.

"So tell me Skye" Simon says "What are you wearing tonight to ensnare Clayton the sex god even more" Shelley and Macy snigger.

"No idea, what am I wearing Shelley" I throw back.

"Your birthday suit" she says round a laugh.

"Jeans and t-shirt it is then" I say smugly.

"Oh no, you're not!" three voices chorus together loudly, each of them know given half the chance that's exactly what I would turn up in.

I lift my head and address the beauticians "See what I have to put up with" I say trying to sound indignant and going for their sympathy instead they all grin back at me, not one look of sympathy.

We've been bantering and teasing, generally entertaining the staff for the last two hours. So far I have been waxed, plucked, buffed and now I'm being polished. Conversation ceased as the beauticians set about the task of removing the face mask and giving us each a facial. Shelley and Macy are having their makeup for tonight done. I prefer to do my own, no disrespect to the makeup artists but I always feel like a painted doll when they've finished with me. Instead I'm getting my hair done so I'm taken into the salon along with Simon when our facials are finished. Earlier I had a discussion with the stylist about what to do with my hair so as soon as I sit down he sets to work.

"Skye, honey" Simon leans across and takes my hand and I meet his gaze in the mirror, I frown because he looks deadly serious.

"What's the matter?" the concern I feel is evident in my voice.

He shakes his head "Nothing for you to worry about, I just" he pauses "I just wanted to ask, all joking aside but do you like Clayton, I mean really like him?"

I take a deep breath, okay moment of truth "Yeah I do" it came out quietly and it feels right saying it. I get a warm fuzzy feeling every time I think about him.

"Oh honey, protect your heart. I care and worry about you, you know that right" Simon squeezes my hand again, he always has my best interest at heart and is very protective of and towards me, Simon is a brother to me "I did some research on him. I can see he's in to you in a big way and tonight I think he is going to make his move. He has a reputation as a womaniser. You know, love them and leave them."

"I appreciate what you're saying and you're not the only one who has done their homework" I spent the morning researching Clayton online but my actions were more in response to his declaration to me when his date called me Barbie "I've also drawn that conclusion myself after seeing all those photo's on the internet" I pause collecting my thoughts, there had been hundreds of photos of him with different women, very few showed the same woman twice. I am under no illusions, he is man with a past "I do like him, what will be will be" I shrug "the way I look at it I have another nine days here then I'm out of the country and not back here for three months, so I'm going to let myself have some fun and you know that's long overdue. You never know maybe he'll fall for me hard and then spend all his time being miserable and pine for me and get blue balls whilst waiting for me to come back"

Simon burst out laughing "That's my girl" he splutters, his delight at my response is infectious and starts me giggling.

I catch the stylists gaze in the mirror who is smiling at us laughing, he winks saying "And may his hands be forever covered in blisters" making us laugh even harder.

CLAYTON

My jaw is beginning to ache as I grit my teeth listening to my mother berating me down the phone for my treatment of Pippa last night. She has been going on for nearly five minutes. Apart from saying hello I haven't said another word nor made a sound. I'm biding my time and waiting for her to run out of steam, if it doesn't happen soon I'm going to hang up and damn the consequences. I let myself into my apartment and throw my keys down on the table along with my gym bag and head to the kitchen to get a drink. I put my phone down on the counter top switching it on to speaker, my mothers' voice echoes around the room as her tirade continues. Grabbing a bottle of water I crack it open and drain half of it. Suddenly my mother stops speaking.

"She insulted Skye" I say through gritted teeth into the silence "and every word I said to Pippa she deserved it"

More silence and I let it drag out I can visualise my mother standing stock still, her mouth slightly open as she deciphers meaning from what I've said. I knew when she'd drawn her conclusion because of her sharp intake of breath.

"Oh, that just won't do" her voice soft with wonder. I wasn't about to enlighten her, as much as I love her she can deal with the fallout from her meddling in my love life "well, I'll see you tonight then dear" she hangs up.

I pick up my phone and quickly glance through my emails, nothing urgent requiring my attention so I head for the bedroom and strip off my workout sweats and walk naked into the bathroom. I decide to have a soak in the bath, Phillipee had really worked me over and my muscles are feeling it. I turn the faucets on then went to the sink and fill it with water so I can shave whilst I wait for the bath to fill.

I groan as I ease myself into the steaming hot water, my skin and muscles twitch as they get used to the heat. Holding my breath I submerge myself fully and stay there until my lungs scream for air. I have absolutely no idea why I do this, I've done it for as long as I can remember but I feel refreshed, rejuvenated and relaxed by the time I let myself up for air. Resurfacing I reach for the shampoo and body wash. As I wash my thoughts turn to Skye marvelling at how much I found out about her last night. How she is quick witted, sassy, extremely knowledgeable yet somehow she didn't make anyone feel awkward or dumb, she is very observant although that shouldn't be a surprise due to her being an artist, duh! What surprised me most is how good a listener she is. I mean she really listened and paid attention that was evident by the questions she asked, in some cases they were quite intrusive and personal in nature yet I had no qualms in answering her nor did anyone else for that matter.

My cock springs to attention when my thoughts stray to tonight and I speculate what she will be wearing. I start to imagine her in the sexy slinky black dress she wore on Thursday night at the gallery. I imagine her slowly taking it off revealing her luscious body; my cock jerks and aches, demanding attention. Taking hold of my erection I start slow long strokes, my hips thrusting upwards of their own volition. My fantasy shifts to Skye dropping to her knees and taking me in her mouth and those full luscious lips circling my cock. Groaning I imagine what it'll feel like as she teases me with her tongue and sucks me hard, taking me deep into her mouth. I can feel my climax building, fisting and gripping myself tighter I pump harder this time imaging her beneath me and how she'll feel clamped around me. I yell her name as my orgasm rips through me. Fuck, I haven't come that hard in a long time. What the fuck am I going to be like when I do get to be buried balls deep inside her?

Breathing heavily I reach for the cloth to wipe myself down. Once my heart rate is back to normal and my legs don't feel like jelly I climb out of the bath. Looking down at my cock it's still hard and begging for more attention. Cold shower time, at this rate I'm going to end up with blisters on my hands.

In my study going through my emails—I decided to do some work since I've a couple of spare hours before I have to get ready for tonight—sorting and prioritising things to address Monday I come across one from an old friend and college buddy Chuck. We keep in touch sporadically and get together when we can. I haven't seen him for nearly eighteen months. He'd been in New York on a business trip and looked me up, now he's living in England with his wife who is something in TV. He has a business proposition for me which looks fairly promising. I email him back expressing an interest and ask him to send more information. His response back is immediate then my phone rings. Before I can say hello Chuck's baritone voice booms down the line.

"Hey Clayton good buddy, how the devil are you?"

"I'm good my man, how's the family?"

"Excellent, Nessa is pregnant" his joy radiates through his words.

"Congratulations dude, so is it number two or three now?"

"This will be the second" he says proudly "anyway to business as I know you are a busy man. I've just sent you the proposal. If you want to attend there's going to be a presentation to all interested parties in about six weeks here in England, thought I'd give you the heads up so you've got plenty of notice to plan your diary as I know your schedule is chaotic"

"You've got that right" I grimace "do you have the exact dates for the meeting?"

"I'll have them finalised in the next day or so. I should know before end of play Monday" he pauses "either way I'll email you as soon as everything is confirmed"

"Sounds good my man, I'll have a look over the proposal now and I'll give you my answer Monday before lunch, just in case I want to consult with some of my people"

We chat for few more minutes and swap gossip about various business acquaintances and mutual friends then say our goodbyes.

I set the alarm on my phone so I won't lose track of time and end up being late for tonight. I'm already on my mothers' shit list and I sure as hell wasn't going to give her any more ammunition to make my life difficult.

SKYE

On my way home from the spa I went with Shelley to her studio to collect my dress for tonight. She wouldn't let me look at it there saying I could only do that when I got home. I feel sick to my stomach, I trust

Shelley implicitly I just don't like the idea of having no choice in the matter of what I'm to wear.

Standing in my bedroom I hang the dress bag up, I decide not to look at the dress until I have to put it on, that way I won't give myself time to have a panic attack. I look at the clock I've an hour and a half before I have to get ready. I go to the kitchen and make a sandwich to take the edge off the hunger pangs, carrying it over to my drawing desk I sit and start to sketch out some ideas that came to me whilst at the spa. I've no idea how long I'd been drawing when my phone rings with Simon's ring tone.

"Hey" I say around the last bite of sandwich as I continue drawing.

"Put down that pencil or paint brush. You have approximately twenty five minutes to get your slap on and in your dress. I'm on my way to yours now" then he promptly hung up.

Shit, with a quick rush of panic I jump up and run to the bathroom to clean my teeth and put my face on.

Now I'm standing in front of the mirror staring wide-eyed at my reflection. Oh my sweet fucking lord, I sigh as I take in the overall effect. The dress is fantastic as I knew it would be but if I stand at a certain angle my top half looks naked. The dress has no back, or so it would appear. It's actually made up of flesh colored silk and mesh. The front is a complex pattern of black lace and flesh silk and mesh across the chest, waist and sleeves. From the hips the floor length skirt flows and it's made up of black lace and silk. Scattered throughout the whole dress including the back are sequins and diamantes. My hair is a series of complicated twists on my head and threaded through it are diamantes and Swarovski crystals so when I move I twinkle as the light catches all the shiny things on me.

"Let's go knock 'em dead" I say aloud to my reflection with confidence I don't really feel. I pick up my clutch purse and check I have everything I need and head out to the living room. Simon wolf whistles when he sees me and indicates he wants a twirl, which I oblige.

"Oh honey, Mr Clayton Blake ain't gonna stand a chance" he drawls "he will have no idea what has hit him tonight when he gets a load of you. Shit, he'll be fighting off every man in the room just to get near you. Hell if I was straight I'd be making a move on you"

I laugh at Simon's compliment and link arms with him as we head out the door with Paul following.

CLAYTON

"So which one is she?" my brother Joshua asks as he hands me as glass of champagne.

"Who" I say distractedly, Skye hasn't arrived yet and I'm avidly watching the entrance.

"Who he says" Joshua scoffs "the beautiful creature that has captivated the elusive Clayton Blake, or so mother would have us believe"

"Leave him alone Joshua" chides his wife Elizabeth "besides if she was here, Clayton wouldn't be stood with us, would you?" I look at her and she smiles and winks at me, making me smile.

"Got that right" I say grinning "you should listen to your wife she has the brains" Joshua laughs good-naturedly.

"Holy hell, will you get a load of what has just walked in" Andrew my other brother says in appreciative awe as he hands Elizabeth her drink whilst looking at the entrance. It's not like Andrew to comment on women like that, but it might be because his long term girlfriend isn't here tonight.

I turn quickly to look back at the entrance, Skye. I suck in a sharp deep breath, my god could the woman get anymore stunningly beautiful.

"That gentlemen, is Skye Darcy. The beautiful creature who's captivated the elusive Clayton Blake" I relish the dumb struck faces of my brothers "if you will excuse me I need to go fight off hordes of lust hungry males"

I walk across the ballroom with purpose my sole focus is on Skye. If anyone greeted me I didn't hear, hell a bomb could go off and I wouldn't know. I am captivated by the vision of Skye. As if sensing my approach Skye turns to face me. I see her eyes widen and her lips part as if breathing has suddenly become difficult, or she could be turned on by you my mind whispers and the wicked thought makes me smile. My body thrums up a notch, my cock already hard throbs. As I get nearer a slow shy smile appears in welcome on her face, when I reach her keeping eye contact I take her hand and kiss the back with a long lingering kiss and I see the flush spread across her cheeks and her breath hitches.

"Hi" I say softly still looking deeply and getting lost in her yellow green eyes.

"Hi" she replies breathlessly in a hoarse whisper.

"You look absolutely stunning" I step back and indicate I want her to twirl, with a shy smile she obliges. Fuuuccckkk me! The dress has no back. Oh, wait it does as I realize her back twinkles as there are diamantes and sequins stitched into flesh colored mesh.

"You like?" says Simon with a knowing tone in his voice.

"Very much" I reply without taking my eyes off Skye.

"It's one of Shelley's creations, glad you like it" says Skye running her hands down the front of the dress.

"Skye darling" my mother calls out and I inwardly wince "so lovely to see you again" she elbows me out of the way and embraces Skye in a hug.

"Mrs Blake, so good to see you again" Skye replies her voice soft and husky, holy fuck was I going to survive the night the thought crosses my mind as my whole body tightens.

"Call me Stephanie, please. Mrs Blake is so formal. Let me introduce you to Clayton's brothers as I doubt he will do it" Skye looks at me and I roll my eyes, she tries and fails miserably to hide her grin which makes my heart fit to burst.

Skye introduces her party all of whom I'd met last night and we fall into easy conversation. Various people come over to say hello and dutifully they were introduced to the rest of the group. After half an hour I was about to ask Skye to dance when we are interrupted by a loud Russian. Skye spins around with a broad smile and shouts "Mr C" the rest of the sentence I have no idea what she's saying as she speaks to him in Russian, fluently. So that's three languages now. She obviously knows him very well as he hugs her and looks at her with avuncular affection. Skye turns back and faces the group.

"May I introduce Mr Boris Cheremisinova" she says to everyone then proceeds to introduce each of the party.

Joshua leans in to me and whispers "Not only is she stunningly beautiful but she is extremely well connected, that my dear brother is the Russian billionaire owner of Nova Industries you are meeting on Tuesday"

My head snaps around and I look at my brother's solemn face so I know he isn't kidding which also put paid to the "you shitting me" comment I'm about to make. Joshua is a lawyer and he acts as mine, his practice has a team purely dedicated to me and my business so he would have already been doing his homework on Mr Cheremisinova in readiness to brief me on Monday.

"And this is Clayton Blake" I turn around at Skye's husky voice.

"A pleasure to meet you Mr Cheremisinova" I smile as we shake hands.

"Ah, Blake Enterprise Holdings, we meet Tuesday" Mr Cheremisinova says delightedly.

"Yes, we do" I smile broadly "and I am very much looking forward to it"

"Me too, me too" he agrees "however tonight no business except Skye I have something to ask of you" Mr Cheremisinova turns his attention back to her "I know you come to me a week Tuesday, however I fly back to Russia a week on Sunday would you and your party like to come on my plane two days early" he asks her.

"Oh" Skye looks momentarily startled then quickly collects her herself "hang on and let me check"

Skye calls Macy over to her then I watch as she scans the room looking for someone, failing to locate the person she lifts her hand in a come here signal and Paul seems to materialize out of nowhere. Damn the guy is good at being invisible.

"Mr C has invited us to fly out with him a week on Sunday. If we leave two days early will it mess up any plans?"

Both of them pull out phones and appear to be consulting diaries, in unison they say "No" with Macy adding "There's a couple of appointments I can move forward into this coming week if you are okay with that"

Skye nods and instructs Macy to do it. Turning back to Mr Cheremisinova she says "We're good to go. If you get Hanna to send details of times to Macy we'll see you at the airport"

I listen to this whole transaction with growing dread. Skye is going to Russia. I have to find out for how long. I lean down and whisper "Dance with me"

SKYE

I know I must have a look of surprise on my face, had I heard right?

"Please dance with me" Clayton says again in his low raspy smooth as melted chocolate voice. A shiver runs down my spine and all I can do is nod.

We excuse ourselves from the group and head for the dance floor. All my friends are grinning at me like idiots and I roll my eyes at them. I didn't dare look at his family.

I'm amazed at how physically unlike Clayton is to his brothers. He definitely takes after his mother in hair and eye coloring as both his brothers are blonde and have paler blue eyes. Clayton is also a good three inches taller and broader in the shoulders plus he appears to be more muscular, yet when they all stand together there is no mistaking the family resemblance.

As we step on to the dance floor Clayton pulls me in close to him and sets off in a waltz. He dances well and I can feel his muscles flex as he moves. Oh he feels good, my hands and fingers itch to roam over his body. His scent surrounds me, intoxicating me as I breathe him in. He looks damn mighty fine in his tux and I can see nearly every woman in the place sneaking glances at him, some openly ogling lustfully and hoping to catch his eye but he seems to be oblivious to it all.

"How do you know Mr Cheremisinova?" his low raspy voice sends tingling sensations up and down my spine, good god will I ever get used to it.

"He's commissioned quite a few paintings from me over the last eight years. He had a daughter, Alexi. I was at college with her in London, we weren't friends, just knew each other through friends of friends. I suppose you could say we were acquaintances. She got in to drugs in a big way and the inevitable happened she OD and I happened to find her and saved her life" I pause remembering the harrowing day of finding Alexi in the toilets at college "anyway Mr C wanted to pay me which is his way, he uses money as a way of thanks. I wouldn't take it, didn't seem right somehow. A few weeks later he turns up on my door step demanding I do a painting for him. Alexi had told him I was an artist and he found out I did commissions, so he found the perfect way to pay me for saving Alexi's life" I shrug "I took the commission and the money he paid me made it possible for me, Simon and Shelley to come to New York and study"

I watch his face closely as I say all of this and I see a variety of emotions cross it, some I couldn't fathom others look like respect and admiration. I'm also acutely aware I've given him more information than I intended. I put it down to nerves for making me blab. A thought suddenly occurs to me, he is meeting with Mr C on Tuesday "If you're after any of his business secrets you have the wrong person, corporate espionage is not in my repertoire" mischievously I grin.

Clayton laughs "Busted again" he says and continues to chuckle, it's a lovely sound "but speaking Russian, Italian and French fluently are" he adds smiling.

"So is Spanish and Chinese" I smile impishly back, his eyes widen in shock.

"Wow, you are full of surprises" he says with genuine awe. I feel myself gleam with pride "how come you learnt so many languages?"

"Well Russian, Italian and French is because I have a lot of clients in those countries and over the years I've spent a fair amount of time there with work, so I learnt the languages out of necessity. I learnt Spanish and Chinese when I came to study here. There were two students who spoke little English so I agreed to teach them if they taught me their language in return. I just seem to have a natural aptitude for languages. If I am ever in a country for a reasonable amount of time I make the effort to learn the language"

"Fair point, you shame me" he says in all seriousness "I do business all over the world and I only speak French" he seems vexed at himself.

He shakes it off and his hand strokes my back sending tingles of electrical current zigzagging all over my body "how long will you be in Russia for?"

"Six weeks, however I'm not back here in New York until September so it means I will be away for twelve weeks" I cautiously add and watch his reaction, he jolts in surprise.

"Oh twelve weeks" he seems disappointed "where will you be the rest of the time"

I sense he's genuinely interested but his disappointment puzzles me "At the moment it is two weeks in France then on to Italy then LA however that could change" I pause debating whether to give more of an explanation when he doesn't say anything I add "sometimes a client can change location or I get the work completed sooner than expected" he nods his understanding.

"Had" Clayton says with a frown "you said Mr C had a daughter Alexi, past tense, what happened?"

"Alexi died about" I pause to work out when it happened "got to be three and a half years ago, she never did get clean of drugs. The sad thing is she had a daughter and she'll never know her mother. Aleksandrina is five now, lovely little thing and has Mr C wrapped around her little finger, she rules his household" I laugh remembering the last time I'd seen Aleksandrina all blonde curls and big blue eyes smiling sweetly at her grandfather and asking for a pony.

The band stopped playing and the Master of Ceremony announces dinner is ready to be served and for everyone to take their seat. Although we've stopped dancing Clayton doesn't let go of me, raising his hand to my face he trails his fingertips down my cheek "So beautiful, amazingly talented, highly intelligent, you have beguiled and bewitched me" he says softly looking deeply into my eyes.

Holy crap, my heart stops along with my brain, you could push me over with a feather "Come" he commands softly and leads me off the dance floor. I just about manage to put one foot in front of the other. I'm in a complete daze as he takes me back to my table and friends. It isn't until I sit down and I watch his retreating back that my brain kicks back into gear. Holy bloody hell is he serious!

"Skye, honey, are you okay? You look as if you have seen a ghost" Simon says looking concerned and squeezes my hand. All I can do is nod.

CLAYTON

Fuck, I'm in serious, serious trouble. I mentally kick myself as I head to my table. What in the hell possessed you to say that, you've probably scared the crap out of her I berate myself. Don't be surprised if she runs screaming to the hills. If she did I know I will chase after her. I'm going to fight to keep her. Keep her, I didn't even have her how can I claim her as mine, by next week she'll be on a plane to Russia. The very thought makes me sick to the stomach.

"Clayton darling" my mother calls pulling me from yet another of my mental tirades. I take my seat beside her "I must say darling, the two of you make a stunningly spectacular looking couple"

Here we go and right on cue my brothers start.

"Mom's booked the wedding" says Andrew grinning widely.

"Yeah, it's at her estate for three weeks today" Joshua adds chuckling.

"Damn, it's a shame Skye can't make it, she will be out of the country for twelve weeks come a week tomorrow" my comment is met with stunned silence. Bingo, just the result I'm after.

Mother recovers first "Twelve weeks, why?" she splutters.

I raise an eyebrow at her in a silent 'seriously' instead I say "She is a successful businesswoman mother, a highly accomplished, talented artist in great demand and she travels the world because of her work, as I've already told you before" I hope I don't sound condescending.

No-one has anything to say to that, the conversation turns to other topics as the first course is served.

"So what did you get out of her regarding Mr Cheremisinova" Joshua says wiggling his eyebrows.

Laughing I tell him verbatim what Skye said about being the wrong person for corporate espionage. After that the conversation shifts and all teasing ceases. I glance over at Skye she looks thoughtful probably trying to decide if I'm genuine in my declaration or if it's part of some elaborate ploy to seduce her. I have to convince her of my sincerity, as if sensing my gaze upon her she looks up, her large eyes beseeching me to give clarification of my intentions. I smile, I put all of my thoughts and feelings I have for her into it, admiration, respect, awe, love. Holy fuck! I'm falling for her fast and hard. Her returning smile although tentative makes my heart swell.

The meal seems to take hours. I desperately want to be with Skye. I watch her interact with the others at her table, at first she is subdued—no points for guessing why Einstein my conscious chides—but as time progresses she becomes animated and laughs easily.

As soon as the meal is over people start to table hop. I stand but before I can get away I'm cornered by a group of men all fawning and saying they have a business opportunity we had to get together and discuss, yeah right blah, blah, blah, I catch Skye's eye and mouth help. A wide grin spreads over her face I know if I was closer I will see mischief dancing in her eyes. She stood and walks towards me with sensuous grace. A thrill shoots through me a mix of desire and surprise as I didn't expected her to come to my rescue. The men surrounding me all have their back to her.

"Excuse me gentlemen" Skye's husky voice renders them all speechless and they part like the Red Sea. Skye steps into the space leans forward and grasps my hand "I simply must steal Mr Blake away from all this boring business talk and have my wicked way with him" she says looking each of them in the eye giving them a look of innocence with a mischievous smile. Looking back at me she gives a saucy wink and says "come on" tugging my hand, all the men look at me in astonishment. I shrug my shoulders and follow her with a goofy grin on my face, leaving the men behind with stunned confused looks.

After several steps I stop and pull Skye to a stop as she turns I step forward closing the gap between us, my hands grasp her waist pulling her to me, leaning down I whisper "Skye Darcy you are incorrigible"

Then I kiss her.

SKYE

Holy cow he's going to kiss me, the thought flits across my mind seconds before his beautifully sculpted lips meet mine. His lips are surprisingly soft and firm Clayton pulls away before anything else registers. "Sorry about that" his voice is low and seductive "I couldn't help myself"

"S' okay" is all I can mutter through my shock.

"Gentlemen's excuse me" Simon says from behind me "I'm claiming Skye for a dance" Simon grabs my arm and propels me towards the dance floor. I don't know whether to kick his shins or kiss him in thanks.

Simon takes me in his arms and starts to waltz. I catch glimpses of Clayton as he walks towards my table and sits down engaging my friends in conversation.

"You okay?' Simon asks softly, I nod "I just wanted for you to have a breathing space. You didn't seem yourself during the meal, well since you came back from dancing with him"

I sigh heavily "You were right about protecting my heart" I tell Simon what Clayton said to me about beguiling and bewitching him "I don't know if it's part of some elaborate plan to seduce me or if he's being genuine" I look over at my friends and Clayton "my instincts are telling me it's the latter"

"Oh honey" Simon groans in sympathy "what can I do to help?"

I know he is referring to my lack of experience in relationships, I shrug "Just be you and tell me if I'm making an idiot of myself"

"Always, honey, always"

For the rest of the dance Simon bitches about the lack of seriously good looking gay men at the function then he sets about picking on the straight men and coming up with ways to have his wicked way with them making me laugh and lightening my mood from my earlier deliberations.

When we get back to our table Macy is regaling a story to everyone about her previous employer and one of his hilariously funny attempts at getting her into bed, I sit down in the chair Clayton pulls out next to him. I've heard the story before and I still find it funny so I start giggling before she gets to the end.

"Pay back's a bitch" Shelley says wiping tears from her eyes.

"That's right sista" Macy agrees and they high five.

"And that's why you don't piss off a woman" Phil says laughing "okay time to be serious for a minute. Skye when are you back in September?"

"All being well the fifth, but if you're asking when will I be back in the States then it'll be August thirteenth, why?"

"So where will you be when you arrive back" Shelley asks rather than answer me.

"LA or Vegas could be both. Why?"

Shelley and Phil put their heads together, whispering, having reached an agreement they turn back to face me. "We're getting married on September twentieth and I want you to be my Maid of Honor" Shelley says beaming at me.

"Yay" I shout and clap my hands, jumping up grinning I give Shelley a huge hug "I'm thrilled to be your Maid of Honor"

Conversation around the table turns to the nuptials and good natured banter about the Bachelor and Hen parties which Shelley and Phil adamantly refuse to have.

Over the following couple of hours we have fun dancing and talking with those who come to our table. Clayton's family join our party and I sit back watching them interact with my friends, I also find it highly amusing at the number of women coming over and fawning all over Clayton. One in particular reminds me of an octopus, no sooner Clayton peels one hand or arm off she puts the other on him immediately. From the snippets of their conversation I overhear I guess her to be a former girlfriend or conquest, she's whining she misses him and why didn't he return her calls. I find myself wondering how many of the other women he's been with. I switch off then to stop that train of thought—protect your heart I tell myself—and distance myself from him. As silly as it is I move seats to talk to other people only to find Clayton follow me. I don't know whether to be annoyed or flattered.

"I'm going to the bathroom" I lean over and whisper in Shelley's ear so I wouldn't interrupt what Andrew is saying to her, Shelley acknowledges with a nod. I feel Clayton's gaze follow me the whole time as I walk out of the ballroom, my skin prickles at the nape of my neck and along my arms just as it did when I first arrived, it amazes me how a tuned to his presence I've become in such as short space of time.

Having relieved and refreshed myself I marvel at how much fun I'm having and I finally admit to myself I'm flattered and thoroughly enjoying Clayton's company and attention. With a spring in my step and a smile on my face I exit the bathroom. I immediately feel the all too familiar tingle in my body as my senses let me know Clayton is near. I look up and sure enough Clayton is stalking towards me. I slow to a stop and watch him.

His gait is sensual and predatory just as it was when he approached me when I first arrived causing the same reactions in my body, my mouth is dry, my heart beats faster and my skin flushes with the warmth pooling in my stomach. Clayton's long muscular legs eat up the distance between us with ease. His shoulder length dark wavy brown hair flowing around his face, my fingers flex at the thought of grabbing hold and pulling it, his face has an expression I can only describe as carnal and it has me rooted to the spot.

Oh hell, I suddenly understand what the romance novels I read meant by a virile male. Clayton is the embodiment of that description and he is heading straight for me. I try to take a steadying breath but my breathing has accelerated so much I'm panting. Christ he hasn't even touched me yet and I'm a quivering wreck. I lick my lips trying to get moisture in my dry mouth. A low growl emanates from Clayton. The very sound ripples through me I'm wet instantly. Oh my sweet lord. I put my head down and close my eyes trying to restore my equilibrium, I give up when I feel his large warm hands on my waist and in the blink of an eye Clayton has me in his arms holding me tight to his hard body and kissing me senseless, his lips soft and gentle yet demanding.

Somehow he moves us, I have no idea how but my back is to the wall. I respond to his kisses, I open my mouth to take more from him. His tongue darts in licking, stroking and tasting. Following his lead I do the same. Boy, the man can kiss. I feel my body responding. My nipples harden and ache to be touched; my skin is tingling all over. I want to rip his clothes off, my hands move up and down his back feeling solid muscles flex and move. I pull trying to get him even closer to me.

Clayton grasps my wrists and lifts my arms above my head securing them with one hand. His other hand running up and down the side of my body, from the side of my breast down to my hip and back, sending shivers of desire coursing through me, he shifts and uses his hips to pin me in place against the wall. I can feel his arousal pressing against my lower belly. A groan escapes me in response to the myriad of sensations he's creating in me.

"I can't move!" my brain suddenly screams. The fog of lust evaporates instantly and I'm catapulted back to the derelict office building. I'm restrained, the panic I feel at not being able to get away from my attacker surges through me. My body begins to shake in remembrance of the beatings and repeated rape. Clayton is kissing my neck and jaw line murmuring words I can't hear. All I hear are the vile and depraved words of my tormentor. My stomach churns and revolts, my gorge rising. Cold sweat breaks out across the whole of my body and I'm trembling, made worse as I swallow to stop throwing up.

"P-p-p-please l-l-let me go" I stutter in a frightened whisper.

"What baby" Clayton murmurs continuing to kiss along my jaw.

"Please, release me, let me go" I sob out louder, it comes out almost as a scream. My vision is blurry, I hadn't realized I was crying and I can feel hysteria taking over. Clayton let go of my hands and steps back instantly. My legs give way and I collapse to the floor on my hands and knees, my body dry heaving and I try to gulp in air, I'm shaking violently.

"What's wrong, what's the matter" he asks alarm in his voice, through my blurred vision I see his hands reaching for me again.

In a movement too fast for me to register Clayton is knocked to the side and pinned against the wall by Paul.

"Skye, Skye, what's happened" someone cries out terrified and kneels besides me wrapping their arms around me hugging me "What did you do to her" the person screeches at Clayton. I get my breathing under control and look up into Shelley's horrified stricken face.

"I-I-I'm o-o-okay" I stutter "h-h-he's n-n-not at f-f-fault" I manage to get out.

No-one is listening to me. Shelley continues to glare at Clayton, who looks grey and sick with torment. It registers Paul still has Clayton pinned by the throat. Clayton is taller than Paul by a couple of inches but that doesn't matter Paul is more muscular and a trained killer.

I take a deep breath and in as calm a voice I can muster I say "Paul, he's not a fault, stand down"

Giving him the command I know he will obey although he doesn't do it immediately. Paul looks at me, for the first time ever I see real emotion in Paul's face and I'm touched. He genuinely thought Clayton had hurt me and I know that if he had Paul would make him pay. I swipe the tears away from my face, my hands are still shaking in fact my whole body is.

"I'm okay it's not his fault" I repeat.

Without a word Paul steps away from Clayton and he reaches for me helping me up.

"Let's get you home" Shelley says soothingly, I nod. I turn to look at Clayton he looks confused and devastated, it breaks my heart to see him like that.

"I'm so sorry, I can't... I can't" I couldn't finish "I'm so, so, sorry"

Just then Simon appears, one look at the state of me and being support by Shelley and Paul he rushes at Clayton yelling "What did you do to her you bastard?"

I didn't hear Clayton's response because Paul having decided I'm not moving quickly enough for his liking picks me up into his arms and carries me out to the car. Paul loads me in like I'm a small child and Shelley climbs in the other side. I try to tell her to go back to Phil.

"Don't be silly, you are my priority. Phil is going to follow us back to your place with Simon" she says matter of fact and is not taking no for an answer. I take hold of her hand and squeeze it silently showing my appreciation. I'm thankful because I really don't want to be on my own, plus I want to tell them what happened so they wouldn't blame Clayton, poor guy. I feel saddened because after tonight I'm certain he wouldn't want anything to do with me.

Shelley, Phil, Simon, Macy and Paul all sit in my living room watching me pace as I try to find the right words to explain what happened.

"Look Clayton is not at fault" I can see they don't believe me. I sigh heavily "I had a panic attack, a stupid panic attack. He kissed me, things were..." I pause and my cheeks flame "anyway he got me in a position where I couldn't move, I was enjoying myself, I wanted it" I blush even more. I'm sure my face is now purple, the color of beetroot at least "only my brain decided to drag up memories of my attack and I guess it freaked me" I look pleadingly at my friends to understand.

"Oh honey I believe you" says Simon standing and gives me a hug.

"Really?" I ask for reassurance.

"Really" he smiles down at me "besides I haven't seen you blush so hard since, well never come to think of it" he squeezes me to him again.

"I feel such an idiot" I grumble "well, I guess I can chalk it all up to experience and I seriously doubt Clayton Blake will want anything further to do with me. He'll probably run as fast as he can in the opposite direction the next time he lays eyes on me"

"Oh don't write him off just yet" Simon laughs "he seems to me the kind of guy who doesn't give up without a fight"

Chapter Four

CLAYTON

Pouring myself another coffee I yawn, the jaw cracking ears popping kind of yawn. I haven't slept much. I couldn't. Every time I close my eyes images of Skye crying, shaking, struggling to breathe, the pain and fear in her face torments me. What in the fucking hell had happened to her in the past for her to react so strongly. The question circled my mind until it made me dizzy. I recall my brief conversation with Simon afterward.

He yelled at me "What did you do to her you bastard?" I could still clearly see the anger and fear in his face. Anger at me, fear for his friend.

"Nothing, I just kissed her" I said confused by what just happened and I watched helplessly as Paul picked Skye up and carried her away from me.

"Bullshit, you did something you bastard, what did you do" he radiated anger. If he had been Paul I genuinely would've feared for my life. That is the only reason why I didn't attempt to throw Paul off me when he'd pinned me to the wall by my throat "you did something to her whilst you kissed her" Simon accused.

Suddenly Simon stopped pacing turning to me his eyes widened as something occurred to him, in an almost whisper he asked "Did you restrain her?" I looked at him wondering what he meant, he picked up on that because he said again louder "did you restrain her, make it so she couldn't move"

"No I had her..." I stopped abruptly as I realized I put her hands above her head and pinned her with my hips. A move I'd done countless times to countless women and they all responded the same way, except Skye. Skye was different.

"Fuck" I felt sick. I told Simon what I had done.

"Shit" he hissed then he set off at a run to catch the others. I went after him calling to him to wait thankfully he stopped.

"What I did it means something, please tell me" I begged "tell me how to make this right"

"It's not my story to tell. Skye is the one you should be asking" he said looking at me apologetically.

I pulled a business card out of my pocket and wrote my personal phone number on it then handed it to Simon "Please call me and let me know how she is. Call me at any time" I reiterated.

He took the card and true to the silent promise he made he rang me at two in the morning. All he would say is Skye was fine and that my actions triggered a panic attack, he still wouldn't divulge information on the cause he ended the call by saying "She likes Calla Lilies and Blue Moon Roses, oh and she'll be in all afternoon"

"You dumb bastard" I mentally chastise myself, belatedly realizing Simon has given me an opening to approach Skye and chances were good she would see me if I turn up on her doorstep. Why else would he tell me she would be in all afternoon and what her favourite flowers are. Christ if I had a brain I would be dangerous.

I look at the clock it's eleven, excellent plenty of time to get ready. I went into my study and fired up my laptop. I find a florist who could do rush deliveries on a Sunday and had Calla Lilies in stock. I buy every single one they have. I arrange for the flowers to be delivered to me as I want to see Skye's face when I hand them over. With a renewed sense of purpose I head to my bedroom to get ready.

Fuck I'm nervous. Breathe deep breaths I keep telling myself as I get out of the car and look up at Skye's apartment building. It's one of the old brick style buildings, quite possibly it had been an old warehouse converted into apartments it looks well maintained. As I walk up the steps a young woman comes out and holds the door open, her smile is the kind I usually get and ignore. I nod my thanks and step in to the foyer, which is spacious, light and airy. The floor is made up of small black and white mosaic tiles and along one wall is an empty concierge desk. I head for the elevator. Simon hadn't told me where Skye lived I'd gotten the information from the report my security man had done, so I knew Skye was on the top floor. On the ride up my nerves get worse and my mind races with different scenarios and things to say. Hell man, get a grip of yourself what is the worst she can do? Throw the flowers back in your face and say she doesn't want to see you ever again. I seriously hope that didn't happen.

Taking a deep breath I knock on her door. I can hear the fast muffled beat of music then someone shout about getting the door, footsteps, must have a wooden floor the thought flits through my brain for some bizarre reason. The door opens and I'm hit by the blast of loud rock music and the smell of baking. Shelley stands before me, I smile tentatively not sure of the welcome I'm about to receive.

"Hi Clayton come on in" she smiles warmly and steps back not in the least surprised to see me. Well she's forgiven me for last night I think, that gives me hope. "You have a visitor" she yells trying to be heard over the music, turning to me she says loudly "this way, Skye's in the kitchen"

Shelley leads me down a short corridor which opens into a huge room. One half is living room with a large cream sofa and two lazy boys facing a huge fireplace and a large flat screen TV. A low overstuffed book case runs along the length of the wall under the windows and an artist desk sits in front of the largest picture window. The other side of the room is sparse in comparison. It holds four large easels each holding a huge canvass with a painting in varying degrees of completion and a large cabinet which I assume held art materials. I want to stop and study the paintings but Shelley continues through the room. She heads for the wide open doorway taking us into the kitchen which is a large square room and has a real homely feel to it. Skye is in the centre of the room with her back to us and she's bending over the centre island counter top.

"You've got a visitor" Shelley says loudly. Skye doesn't respond sighing Shelley picks something up off the counter and clicked a button, the music cut off.

"Hey, I'm listening to that" Skye shouts indignantly stopping what she's doing and turning around to glare at Shelley. Her eyes widen and she goes stock still like a statue when she sees me.

"As you can see you have a visitor" Shelley says smugly pointing at me over her shoulder "I'll be in the living room to set up if you need me" Shelley smiles and winks at me as she leaves the kitchen.

Huh, what's that all about? I puzzle as I turn my attention back to Skye, she appears to have collected herself.

"Hi" she says softly almost shyly.

I move forward cautiously, I don't want to frighten or startle her and hold out the bouquet of black and white calla lilies. "Hi, I just wanted to make sure you were okay after last night and to apologise for my actions and the distress I caused you"

Skye makes her way round the counter wiping her hands on a cloth hanging from the waist band of her jeans. She has flour flecked down her clothes and on her face, along with a smear of chocolate icing on her cheek. I'm sorely tempted to lean in and lick it off. I look past her to see the huge chocolate cake she's decorating.

"It's a birthday cake for Jack, that's Paul's son" she says following my gaze "in about two hours I'll have a house full of his friends for his birthday tea" she takes the flowers out of my hands and buries her nose in them and takes a deep breath "who told you these are one of my favourite flowers"

"I couldn't get Blue Moon Roses" I watch her as she closes her eyes and breathes in the lilies scent again, the look of peace a complete contrast to the fear and pain of last night.

"Simon" she chuckles "thank you they are beautiful" she pauses chewing her bottom lip and looks up at me "and it's me who should be apologising for freaking out like that, you deserve an explanation for my behaviour"

"No, no there's no need" I say although I did want to know, desperately so I add "well, only if you feel up to it"

Skye nods "I do, only I haven't got time now or for the rest of the day for that matter" she frowns "can you meet me for lunch tomorrow?"

"Sure, twelve suit you?" I should check my diary but damn I want to hear what she has to say and it seems important to her so I will move heaven and hell to accommodate "if you don't mind coming to my office, I'll get lunch in"

"That's great, can I get you a drink"

Skye moves to the sink and put the flowers in it. She bent down and opens a cupboard, oh damn me to hell and back, viewing her ass in the air like that has images flicking through my mind of taking her from behind. I'm hard instantly; quickly I adjust myself and clear my throat.

"No thanks I better get going and leave you to it"

Skye straightens holding a vase, disappointment flitters across her face.

"Oh okay" she put the vase down on the counter "I'll see you out"

I follow her out of the kitchen admiring the view of her ass as it hypnotises me with the swing of her hips. In the living room Shelley is setting a long dining table I didn't noticed earlier, she smiles as her gaze flicks from Skye to me.

"Leave the paintings I'll move them a little later" Skye says to Shelley, taking the opportunity I walk over for a closer look "that reminds me you never did answer my question on Thursday night" Skye says coming up behind me.

Knowing full well what she is referring to I look down at her with as much innocence and ignorance on my face as I can muster "What question was that?"

"Don't give me that" she shoulder bumps me. I pretend to stagger making her giggle the sound makes my heart flutter "what style of art do you like?"

I look back at her work, even though they are incomplete they are remarkable and I know they will be magnificent when they are finished. I decide to answer her honestly.

"I've never really had a preference before, don't get me wrong when I say I can take it or leave it" I shrug "but I know what I like" turning to her I hold her gaze as I say "I like this very much"

Her eyes widen and she flushes so I knew she picked up on the intended double entendre, so as not to embarrass her further I turn back to the paintings "Who are they for?"

"No-one, I get ideas coming to me all the time. Some of them I develop into finished pieces. These will go to auction" she says gesturing at the canvasses "I sell about ten to fifteen paintings a year that way" she pauses and has a look on her face which I'm beginning to recognise as one that told me she debated internally as to whether to divulge more information. I remain quiet and wait. My patience is rewarded when she adds "I own an auction house in London normally I sell these kind of paintings through that, but I'm opening a branch here in New York so I'll more than likely sell these in the first auction"

My interest is piqued the New York auction house is news and this kind of intelligence didn't appear in the search reports I got.

"When are you opening and in which part of town?" I ask with genuine interest.

"The when has yet to be finalised, the where might be decided this week. I'm viewing different locations all this week. I looked at a few in the past week but none were suitable" she wrinkled her nose "so fingers crossed"

"What will happen if you don't find what you need this week?"

"Nothing" she shrugs "all it will simply mean is I continue to look when I'm back in September"

"Do you have someone to look for you whilst you're away?"

"Why, you volunteering for the job" she teases giving me her adorable cheeky grin causing me to laugh.

"No, but I could get someone on the case for you all you need to do is describe what you need"

I can tell my offer surprises her and the look of gratitude makes me feel ten feet tall and I want to beat my chest.

"Thank you" she says softly "but it's not necessary. I already have someone on the case"

I deflate, idiot, I mentally slap myself of course she has someone she's an extremely successful businesswoman. A polite cough coming from behind us startles me. I forgot all about Shelley.

"Sorry to interrupt but Paul's just rung they'll be here in half an hour, the boys are hungry"

"Shit" Skye curses "okay grab a painting I'll put them in my bedroom out of harm's way and sticky fingers. The easels can stay as they are we'll push them further back against the wall"

I help move the easels and paintings, I would've liked to get a closer look at her bedroom but I didn't think my lingering would be appreciated.

Skye saw me to the door, I turn to say goodbye as I face her she lifts up onto her tip toes taking hold of the lapels of my leather jacket and tugs me down to her, she kisses me softly on the lips, my body thrums but before I can respond she breaks contact and whispers "Thank you for the flowers and I'll see you tomorrow"

I raise my hands to cup her face moving slowly giving her the opportunity to stop me. I lower my lips to hers again kissing her in return, moving back I say "You're welcome and I'll be counting the hours"

That is no joke I really will be counting the hours. What the fucking hell is this woman doing to me?

Chapter Five

SKYE

I ride the elevator up to the top floor to Clayton's office, jittery with nerves. All morning I've been distracted about this meeting. I haven't even been able to get into my painting which is unusual as nothing stops me once I pick up my brushes or pencils.

I deliberated on how much information to give Clayton, where did I start. If I missed things out would he pick up on it and think I was intentionally being misleading. Ah hell this was going to be more difficult than I imagined.

Treat it as if it's one of the sessions with Shelley and Simon, the thought suddenly pops into my head, before I can dismiss it the elevator stops and the doors ping open to reveal Clayton.

My heart judders to a stop, he is jaw dropping stunning and he looks mouth wateringly fabulous in his dark blue three piece tailored suit, his shirt and tie are a pale blue. Somehow he manages to pull off the bad boy image even when he's suited and booted, butterflies flit around my stomach making me feel giddy.

"Hi" he smiles shyly as he holds out his hand for me to take.

Oh I've died and gone to heaven I inwardly sigh as I look into his dark blue eyes and put my hand in his. As I step out of the elevator his large warm hand gently squeezes mine and his thumb brushes back and forth over the back of my hand sending a multitude of sensations racing around my body. He pulls me forward and bends to lightly kiss me. I breathe in his masculine scent and my nerves evaporate, he instantly calms me. I decide there and then I will tell him everything, well everything that will explain my freak out.

Clayton keeps hold of my hand as he leads me through the open plan office. People openly gawp at us. I guess this is a first for the work force to see the boss behave this way.

Clayton's own office is at the far end of the floor. I notice other smaller offices around the periphery some are occupied, others not. I take these to be meeting rooms. Desks are grouped together in clusters throughout the floor, the atmosphere appears relaxed and friendly although when people see Clayton they immediately straighten and suddenly appear to be extra busy.

As Clayton opens the door to his office he turns to his secretary, a sharp dressed woman I guessed to be in her late forties "No interruptions until I tell you otherwise" he didn't wait for an answer, this is a man who expects to be obeyed. With his warm hand at the small of my back he guides me into the office.

His office is typical of all the CEO offices I've been in. Large picture windows with a fantastic view of the city sky line, large desk with all the latest technology gadgets and gizmos, large comfy leather sofas and the pre-requisite multiple TV wall showing news feeds and stock market information from around the world.

I turn to face Clayton at the sound of the lock clicking in to place "Please take a seat" Clayton gestures to the sofa as he moves to the glass wall that faces the office floor and closes the blinds, he is ensuring we have complete privacy "what would you like to drink?" Clayton walks back to his desk and opens a cupboard at the side to reveal a mini fridge.

"Water please"

He takes out two bottles and I follow him to the sofa, on the coffee table is a platter of sandwiches and various nibbles. I take my jacket off and sit down.

"I hope I haven't disrupted your day too much" I take the offered bottle of water "I know it was short notice" I grimace, it didn't occur to me until after he left yesterday he probably would have to rearrange his day just to accommodate me.

Clayton waves a dismissive hand "Don't worry about it, this is important to you and I won't deny I am intrigued" he indicates towards the food "please help yourself"

I pick up a plate and select a few sandwiches and grapes, my appetite is non-existent I couldn't even eat breakfast because my stomach is in such turmoil. Taking a deep breath and before my courage fails me I ask the question that will determine my starting point.

"Before I start tell me have you done a search on me?" I look directly into his eyes. Clayton immediately stills and looks wary he also seems to struggle with how to answer, I take pity on him "it's okay if you have, hell I would be surprised if you said you hadn't. A man of your standing has to be careful"

He visibly relaxes "Yes I have" he says still cautious obviously wondering where I'm going with this.

"So correct me if I'm wrong, but I'm guessing your guy couldn't find any information about family or anything about my life before I attended art school in London"

I know from his reaction I'd hit the nail on the head because he looks at me in total astonishment. Taking another deep breath and a drink of water to collect my thoughts and buying time as I know my starting point will be like dropping the proverbial bomb. I brace myself and watch Clayton closely.

"That's because Skye Darcy isn't my birth name"

Clayton jerks in surprise he quickly schools his face in a blank expression. I feel panic starting to rise, my heart thudding painfully in my chest, breathe I tell myself. The worst thing he can do is ask you to leave. I wait a few seconds, Clayton nods as a means to acknowledge what I'd said and then indicated for me to continue.

"I was born Skynard Lillian Belling. Both my parents are dead and I changed my name legally when I was eighteen, after I had been disowned by my grandfather"

"Jesus" Clayton whispers, horror etched in his face "sorry please continue"

"Anyway, although changing my name has a correlation to what I've just said and to what happened to me, I hope you understand some of the information surrounding the event I don't wish to go into"

I look at him willing him to understand. His eyes soften, picking up my hand and rubbing his thumb across my knuckles his smile so tender it has my heart thudding in my chest.

"Only tell me what you are comfortable with. I feel privileged that you are sharing something so personal and you trust me with it" his eyes radiate warmth and sincerity. Butterflies flitter in my stomach and I know I'm in danger of falling hard for this guy, this Adonis. Protect your heart, Simon's words echo around my head, oh heaven help me "if at any time it gets too difficult just say and we'll stop, you don't have to do this now, today"

"I do" I say quickly, before my courage fails completely I plough on "I hadn't long turned eighteen, this was before I changed my name and started art school, I was attacked. I'm not going to give you the gory details but suffice to say I was restrained in such a way that I couldn't move and I was severely beaten and repeatedly raped"

Clayton is utterly still his eyes never left my face before I could continue he states "So when I held your wrists it brought everything back?"

I can see the horror dawn in his eyes as he realizes exactly what he triggered, a lump in my throat stops me from speaking all I can do is nod.

"Fuck" he barks viciously and squeezes my hand painfully making me flinch. Clayton stood abruptly and in jerky movements starts to pace, his hands fisting and pulling at his hair, he curses a few more times. I open my mouth to continue I want to explain it isn't his fault. I didn't want him angry at me or himself, before I can get anything out he stands in front of me and drops to his knees, startling me, taking my hands I look at his anguished face "I am so, so, very sorry, please tell me what to do to make amends" the remorse ripples off him, shattering my heart into a thousand pieces.

"Oh Clayton" I lift one hand to his face and stroke his cheek "you already have" I put my fingers to his lips to cut off his words "let me explain"

He kisses my fingers and sits back down only this time he picks me up and sits me on his lap and wraps his arms around me. Getting over my shock I gather my composure.

"I have only ever had three sexual partners" I feel him tense beneath me "two consensual the other not. The consensual ones were either side of the attack I was twenty when I had my last proper relationship and it lasted six months. I've been on dates but I've always shied away from getting too close or intimate. That is until I met you" I look up at Clayton and hold his gaze his dark blue eyes widen in surprise then soften "you've awakened something inside of me. You invoke emotions and feelings I've never experienced. Hell I've been having fantasies I've only ever read about" a shaky laugh escapes me and I can see Clayton wants to know what I've been imagining.

Suddenly feeling bold I shift position and straddle his lap. Thank god I'm wearing jeans. I can tell I've shocked the hell out of him but he doesn't move or tell me to get off. Instead he places his large hands on either side of my hips. I can feel the heat of his hands penetrating through my jeans. I resist the urge to squirm, as if reading my mind his eyes darken becoming heated with desire.

"When you kissed me Saturday night I liked it, I enjoyed the feel of you against me. I wanted you" Christ my voice sounds huskier than usual. I clear my throat "I guess on some unconscious level I haven't gotten over the attack" I cup his face searching his eyes to see if what I'm saying makes any sense "things happened a little too quickly and I panicked, my brain and body over reacting, so you see it's me that has the issues and baggage to boot. I am so sorry for all the anxiety I've caused you and the hassle I've put you through with my friends and Paul"

I can't read his expression waiting with baited breath I remain quiet giving him time to process all the information I've given him. I admire how he's taken it all. It shows the strength of his character, he is infallible. Clayton starts to rub his hands up and down the side of my hips. Christ I want those hands rubbing somewhere else.

"It's okay" he says softly, his action is reassuring me that it is "your friends are very protective of you and Paul was doing his job. You are very lucky to have them"

He's still distracted so I remain quiet giving him time to think. Suddenly he stops moving his hands and his focus snaps back to me, he opens his mouth then closes it again. He does this a few times. I start to move off his knee but his grip tightens on my hips effectively keeping me in place.

"Can I ask you some questions?" I look at him warily "if you don't want to answer just say, I won't be offended" he says softly. I nod "your name, what made you chose Skye Darcy?" well I didn't expect that, it must show on my face because he shrugs "I'm just curious"

"Curiosity killed the cat you know" I tease and he smiles "well I always liked Skynard, however growing up I was referred to by my middle name Lillian. So in honor of my first name I chose Skye, the spelling of which is after the Isle of Skye in Scotland. Darcy I chose because at the time I was a huge fan of Jane Austen"

Clayton bursts out laughing. I love the sound, a deep rich rumble emitting from his chest.

"One more question" he says asking for permission, I nod "you said your last proper relationship was when you were twenty" he pauses for clarification.

I nod, where in the hell is he going with this. I feel uneasy and I'm not sure if I'm going to answer this one but I'm a big girl and mentally I pull up my big girl pants "Go on" I prompt.

He seems to be choosing his words carefully "So am I right in thinking that the last time you had sex was then and you've not been with anyone since?"

I think the fact my cheeks go absolutely purple is all the answer he needs.

"Holy shit" he exclaims shocked "you are the most beautiful woman I have ever seen. I thought guys would be battering down your door" I shift uncomfortably "sorry I didn't mean to make you feel awkward" he says contritely.

"That's why I employ Paul" I sigh "as I said I've been on dates but I just" I pause struggling to find the right words "none of them felt right. Coupled with the fact my work is in such high demand I just don't have the time for a relationship and the guys I had dates with just didn't do anything for me. I had no inclination to jump into bed with them so they could scratch their itch"

Clayton roars laughing, his head thrown back into the cushions I can't help but smile "Oh Skye you have such a way with words, you are a breath of fresh air"

He looks at me intensely his eyes travel up and down my body and licks his lips. The muscles between my legs clench, heat starts to radiate upwards in my body. The look he gives me is unmasked unadulterated carnal lust.

"So those other guys did nothing for you" his voice dripping pure sex "yet you liked me kissing you, tell me Skye what is it exactly have I awakened within you?" his voice drops into a raspy whisper "do you feel it now"

Oh boy do I. Very slowly he lifts his hands from my hips to cup my face, his palms resting on my neck his fingers at the back of my head and tangling in my hair, his thumbs gently brushing my cheeks.

"I don't know and yes" I answer both questions my own voice a husky whisper.

Gently he pulls me towards him, I go willingly, my heart already beating rapidly feels as if it's trying to jump its way to the back of my throat. He places his lips over mine moving them slowly teasing a response from me. I melt against him. My arms find their way around his neck and my hands in his soft silky hair. Moving his arms he wraps them around me, one hand at the back of my head the other going to my lower back pulling me closer, shifting me forward in his lap so our hips meet. I feel his arousal as my hips grind against his, I gasp at the sudden sensation and his tongue darts into my mouth doing the sensuous stroking and licking he did on Saturday night. I catch his tongue and suck his responding groan vibrates through me, he tastes divine.

Clayton deepens the kiss his lips become more demanding and I want to give it to him, whatever 'it' is. His hands run up and down my back. I shift again whimpering as he lifts his hips pushing his erection against my clit. Pleasure shoots through me. The whole sensation is new to me and I want more, instinctively I rock my hips back and forth. Clayton let out a hiss. I stop immediately, I've hurt him.

"Oh baby don't stop" he groans between kisses, his hands return to my hips, thrusting his up as he pulls mine down the friction causes me to moan at the pleasure this causes "that's it baby enjoy the feel of me" he whispers trailing kisses and nips along my jaw and down my neck.

My breathing is becoming ragged as I continue to rock my hips enjoying the friction his hard cock gives against the ridged seam of my jeans that presses against my clit. A pleasant strange feeling pools in my lower belly and between my legs. I can feel muscles deep inside me clenching and releasing in rhythm to my rocking hips against Claytons erection. I'm panting heavily as if I'm running fast. My tits are heavy and ache I want to feel Clayton's hands on them. I arch my back, sensing what I want Clayton runs one hand up from my hip over my waist to my breast cupping it he brushes his thumb over my nipple, even through my t-shirt and bra I can feel his thumb work my nipple, causing a delightful tingling sensation to run straight between my legs.

"Oh yes" I groan and grind my hips harder against Clayton's cock.

"You like that baby" he says as he continues to rain kisses and nips along the column of my throat and play with my nipple, teasing and pulling at it, all I can do is whimper in answer.

As he continues his ministrations to my breasts, my hips move faster. Clayton moves his so our bodies work in a sensuous synchronization. All my nerve endings tingle making my skin hyper sensitive, my heart pounds faster. I can feel something building inside me wanting to be released. All I know is Clayton working my body with his hands, hips and lips. I'm a mass of sensations.

"Come for me baby, give me that" he coaxes.

The feelings and sensations in my body build to a crescendo, a thrust of his hips and a tweak of my nipple causes me to climax with such ferocity it rips through my body causing me to cry out. Clayton covers my mouth with his to muffle the sounds I make and holds me close as my body convulses and shudders with the aftershocks of my orgasm.

After a few minutes my breathing returns to normal and as my awareness returns I find I'm lying limp, boneless, against Clayton, my head buried in the crook of his neck and his hands rubbing up and down my back calming and soothing me, bringing me back down from the incredible high. I lift my head to look at him. His eyes hold such warmth it makes my throat constrict. He doesn't say anything I inch upward and kiss him when I pull back he smiles tenderly.

"So I'm guessing that was your first orgasm"

"Wow, is that what it was" I say trying to play the angelic virgin and failing miserably only for it to come out teasingly "and I have my clothes on. I'm impressed"

He chuckles "Vixen" he calls me as his arms tighten around me.

"I thought I was a siren" I joke back.

"Come on get something to eat" Clayton says sitting us both up. I move off his lap and sit beside him on the sofa.

We eat in silence for a few minutes. I don't feel as if I need to talk and I watch Clayton trying to gage if he is regretting what has just happened but he just smiles and winks at me. God I'm hungry, I never knew an orgasm could make you work up such an appetite.

"When can I see you again?" Clayton's question startles me out of my thoughts.

I have a busy week ahead. I dig out my phone and access my diary. Clayton gets his phone out too. We throw out the times we are available for each day. Two evenings I'm attending an event of some sort. Clayton makes a note of them and says he will see me there because I have escorts already, on the evenings I don't have an engagement Clayton did and he asks me to attend them with him, I readily agree. I tell him about Friday night being a farewell meal at Gino's with my friends before heading off to Russia and he is welcome to come. So it ends up I will see him every day sometimes for lunch as well as the evening which secretly thrills the hell out of me. When I look at the time I'm surprised to find two hours have passed so quickly.

"I better go and let you get back to work" I say standing and getting my things together. Clayton pulls me to him and kisses me so gently and sweetly I melt into him.

"Thank you for lunch"

"Isn't it supposed to be me who says that" I say with mock wonder, he grins.

"Minx" he growls into my ear sending a shiver through me "come on before I decide to keep you here chained to my desk"

"Why Mr Blake are you trying to tell me you're into BDSM?" I mock in my best southern belle accent.

"Want to stay and find out?" he counters wiggling his eyebrows and making me laugh.

Clayton walks me back to the elevator holding my hand all the way and once again people openly gawp at us. I'm tempted to say something but decide against it as he appears to be oblivious to his employee's reaction or maybe he isn't and just chooses to ignore it.

As I wait for the elevator Clayton asks for my phone and holds his hand out a gesture that shows he expects me to comply. I raise an eyebrow at him he doesn't flinch just returns the look with raising his own eyebrows. I give in and hand over my phone. He smirks as he busies himself inputting his contact numbers, when he's finished he presses a key and his own phone starts to ring.

"You now have all my contact details" he says handing my phone back "and I've got your number" he looks mighty pleased with himself. I don't have the heart to tell him my phone the majority of the time is diverted to Macy.

The elevator arrives and once it divests the occupants I get in. Turning to face Clayton I hit the ground floor button and smile sweetly "See you later"

He leans in, hands on either side of the doors preventing them from closing, and kisses me.

"You betcha"

Oh be still my beating heart I thought as the doors closed.

Chapter Six

SKYE

"Come on Misses, spill, I want all the details" Simon drags the word all out to emphasise his point about not leaving any detail out "you've seen Mr Moneybags every day this week, twice in some cases. So spill, I'm gossip deprived"

Simon lounges on my bed as I go through my wardrobe selecting clothes I'll be taking away with me. Before I can answer there's a knock on the door and Paul walks in.

"What are you still doing here" I say in a way of greeting. I'd given Paul the afternoon and all of Saturday off to spend with his son before we leave for Russia.

"Just making sure you don't need me for anything else or for tonight ma'am"

"Nope, go. I don't want to see you again until Sunday morning at seven" I say in my best mock school teacher voice and wag my finger at him then in a softer tone "go and enjoy quality time with your son, you deserve it"

"Yes ma'am, see you Sunday" Paul says giving me one of his rare smiles then left.

I head back into my closet and grab an armful of clothes off the rack and dump them on the bed. I start sorting through them with Simon who gives a yeah or nay to my choices.

"Come on give, spill, gossip now!" he says a tad impatient making me chuckle.

"There's not much to tell. We've had fun and enjoyed each other's company"

This is true, we've talked a lot finding out about each other, likes and dislikes across a wide range of topics. I found out what he did business wise which is a multitude of things, in some markets he dominates and others he dabbles as he put it. He has two main cores of business one is buying land and developing it the other providing private equity finance. Clayton has amassed a huge personal fortune. I know he's a billionaire but I haven't asked how many billions he has either way his fortune makes my personal wealth look like pin money.

We've also made out like a couple of randy teenagers although we haven't had sex or as Clayton joked we haven't made it past second base. I got the feeling Clayton is giving me space and time, letting me lead on how fast and far I wanted things to progress. This is something I really appreciate. I'm also one hundred percent certain this approach is a totally new experience for Clayton.

During the week I'd asked a couple of times if he was okay with the no sex which he assured me he was and we joked about him having blue balls and blisters on his hands. Thankfully I amuse him with my sense of humour but the last thing I wanted was for him to think I was a prick tease to use Simon's terminology of someone who gave off all the signals and negated at the last minute on the insinuated promises.

I told Simon all of this "I'll admit I really like him but I am not kidding myself about any rosy future with him and I am certainly not going to attempt a long distance relationship whilst I'm away, it just won't work and I can do without the worry and hassle wondering if he's being faithful" I finish being frank and honest.

"Whoa, honey you really have thought this through, haven't you" Simon says in awe.

"Protecting my heart" I repeat his words back "it's the only way I know how"

Simon climbs off the bed and hugs me "I'm really proud of you. I admire you and your strength" he kisses the top of my head "I love you and if he ever hurts you I'll have his balls"

I laugh "I love you too and you can't have his balls until I've had them"

"Oooh does that mean you're going to give it up" he says sassily.

"That my dear friend you will just have to wait and see" I say tartly "right help me sort out what to wear tonight"

Clasping his face in mock horror Simon squeaks "What no jeans and t-shirt" then pretends to swoon.

"Prat" I mutter under my breath but loud enough for him to hear "for that I am going to wear jeans and t-shirt"

"Oh no, no, no you don't" he says shaking a finger above his head as he disappears into my closest.

Clayton has offered to pick me up actually he told me he was picking me up after I mentioned I was giving Paul time off to spend with his son before we left the country. I have noticed Clayton can be quite demanding, oh who was I trying to kid, he is demanding. He is CEO of his own company and answers to no one. Like all powerful men I've met he is the dominant Alpha male. Secretly I've had fun all week telling him no, basically standing my ground or bossing him around just because I could and it was glaringly obvious he rarely got told no or had someone stand up to him. It amused me to watch his reactions. How he checked himself, either he shook his head and took a deep breath or he would run his hand through his gorgeous mane of dark brown wavy hair. It also earned me being called Vixen or Minx followed by a chaste kiss.

As I got ready for the night out I pondered on the fact we needed to have a conversation at some point over the next thirty five hours about what will happen when I come back in September. I know deep down that if he is free and single I hoped we could pick up where we left things if and it's a big if he feels the same way. The coward in me decides to leave it up to Clayton to raise the subject and I'll tell him truthfully, if he's free and still interested we could hook up, get together, date or whatever the current phrase is nowadays. Jeez… I'm so out of touch with this relationship malarkey.

I will let him know I have no expectations of him likewise he would have none of me. Suddenly I feel a whole lot better as if a great weight has lifted as I come to this decision.

"Duh! You like the guy" my inner goddess chides "you're anxious he will think you're the clinging girlfriend type, like one of those barnacles that has to be pried off if you bring up the subject"

I give myself one final look in the mirror. I'm wearing a pale pink capped sleeved blouse that is fitted so it emphasises my boobs and small waist, a purple flared skirt rests on my hips and finishes mid-thigh and a pair of purple platform killer stiletto heels. I've left my hair down, wild and curly since I've spent most of the week with it being done up in some kind of elaborate style. Mascara and lip gloss is the only make up I have on, again since I've spent every night of the week wearing a face full of slap I really want to be as au natural as possible tonight, in other words me.

"Let's see how many Barbie comments we get tonight" I say to my reflection then blow myself a kiss. I pick up my purse and head for the living room as I enter the external buzzer sounds, a thrill shoots through me and butterflies hit my stomach I grab my jacket and hit the intercom.

"I'm on my way" I wait for Clayton's reply. Paul would be proud, he's drummed it into me safety first.

"It could be any crack pot out there" he said each time he berated me. Out of all the bodyguards I've had he is the only one who tells me off for not following protocol.

"Okay baby" Clayton's deep sexy voice comes over the intercom.

Smiling like a silly idiot and feeling like a giddy teenager going on her first date I left the apartment. Clayton is waiting for me in the foyer as I step out of the elevator. He looks magnificent in black jeans that hug in all the right places and a dark blue v necked t-shirt that matches his eyes and shows off the expanse of his chest down to his flat stomach and muscular arms. As he moves towards me I can see his abs flex, oh my, my mouth waters at the sight of him.

"You look absolutely ravishing" he growls as he bends and kisses me "I see I am going to have to fight off every man and his dog again tonight"

I laugh "Does that mean I get to scratch every woman's eyes out again"

This has become a standing joke between us. He first said it on Monday night as I accompanied him to a function. I pointed out every woman in the place was lusting after him; he laughed and said he only had eyes for me. I retorted good so whilst he fought the men I would scratch out the women's eyes.

On entering the restaurant Gino greets me with his usual hug and Italian conversation. He is beside himself with joy that Clayton is with me. He shows us to our table; so many people have turned up the party takes over half of the restaurant. I'm so glad my table has Phil, Shelley, Simon and Macy already seated. As Clayton and I take our seats Pete and Caroline rush over and take the remaining two chairs.

"Shit" I curse to myself under my breath.

Clayton heard me and raises an eyebrow a silent query asking for an explanation. I lean over getting so close to him that my breasts brush against his arm. I put my hand on his knee and whisper in his ear "Remember when I told you I had two consensual sexual relationships?"

Clayton tenses and I feel the muscles in his thigh turn to banded steel. His eyes narrow as he glares at Pete, keeping his voice low but full of menace he murmurs "You're going to tell me he was one of them"

He turns to look at me, oh boy he has the whole dark and dangerous bad boy thing going on making my whole body thrum with excitement.

"Yes, he was" I whisper "Pete was my first proper boyfriend" I look into Clayton eyes trying to fathom the expression in them, then it hits me, he's jealous. Holy cow he is jealous of someone I'd been with nearly ten years ago. Confidence and mischief surge through me "don't worry you have given me something he never could" as I lean further in to him I move my hand further up his thigh and squeeze "an orgasm and he couldn't even do that with me naked"

"Be careful baby" Clayton growls his voice full of warning.

"Or what" I challenge and bite my lower lip.

"Or I will be throwing you on this table and giving you what for with everyone watching"

Before I can react Clayton pulls my hand to his crotch, I can feel how aroused he is. My fingers automatically flex feeling his hard length as he thrusts pushing himself further into my hand, I cup and squeeze him harder. Clayton claims my mouth kissing me senseless in a hard lip bruising kiss and I'm lost to him.

Something hits me on the side of my head making me break the kiss and brings me back to my surroundings. Luckily Clayton has angled his body so no one can see I've been fondling him under the table. I turn in the direction of the missile just in time to see a bread roll heading for me. I duck to a chorus of "Get a room" and "Save the porn show for later"

Laughing heartily Clayton pulls me protectively into his arms "Sorry guys couldn't help myself" he says as he dusts bread crumbs out of my hair "from now on I'll behave myself"

I pout which causes more laughter and Simon shouting "Down girl"

I feel as if I'm on cloud nine and I know I'm grinning like a goofy idiot but I don't care.

"It's so good to see you with someone and enjoying yourself" Caroline the Catty Bitch from Hell says "such a shame you're leaving the country"

And there is the sting or rather claws to put a dampener on my fun. The whole table went deathly quiet and scowls at Caroline; she looks back feigning innocence as if there's nothing wrong with what she has said. Fortunately the waiter arrives with menus and to take everyone's drink order.

Clayton leans in to me and in a low voice so no one else can hear "Tell me what it is with her?" distain mars his words.

I subtly shake my head "Later" I murmur back "however let's play a game" I smile, wickedness rushing through me and with a renewed determination that I wasn't going to let Caroline spoil my evening "let's count how many times Catty Bitch from Hell tries to put me down"

Clayton raises an eyebrow and mouths "Catty Bitch from Hell" I giggle.

"My nickname for her and you've already had a glimpse of the put down's she throws at me although that was quite tame even for her"

As it turns out she only manages another two and I think that's because of the faux pas she committed so early on everyone was ready for her, so the slap downs she received back were hard even vicious in Simon's case. Surprisingly even Pete at one point told her to shut up as she was becoming an embarrassment, that's a first. I've never heard him say something like that to Caroline before and from my friend's reaction, neither have they. Apart from the Catty Bitch from Hell the evening is a success and a good time is had by all.

In the car on the way home Clayton pulls me onto his lap, something he'd been doing all week it's as if he's holding onto me until the last available minute.

"Tell me all about Catty Bitch from Hell" he says with amusement "I must say it's a very befitting nickname"

Sighing and not at all surprised he's brought it up I tell him what she's like and the various things she's said to me over the years. "I have really no idea why she is like that. I mean apart from the fact Pete and I used to be an item, if you can call it that and it was nearly ten years ago back in England" I pause thinking "I think they had been seeing each other about six months when Caroline found that out. I don't know or care who told her, I do know it wasn't Pete. I felt sorry for the poor guy the grief she gave him about not telling her. Since then she's got more malevolent towards me each time she sees me, which I might add is not very often thank god, you know last Friday was the first time I'd seen and spoken to her and Pete in two years" I sigh as I resign myself to the fact that no doubt I will be seeing more of her when I come back in September "Simon says it's because she thinks I will take Pete off her and he's convinced Pete still carries a torch for me, which I think is absolutely ludicrous but that's his theory anyway" I scoff.

"She's jealous and I have no doubt that he does" Clayton says quietly. I must have a puzzled look on my face "Oh Skye, you really don't see it do you" he chides.

I shake my head completely at a loss. See what? Caroline is very pretty, her and Pete make a good looking couple and I think he loves her. I certainly wasn't attracted to Pete in any way and I certainly don't encourage or flirt with him.

Clayton hugs me closer to him, his mouth close to my ear, his warm breath tickles my skin sending delicious excited feelings rushing through my blood "You are a stunningly beautiful, hugely successful and incredibly rich, highly accomplished confident woman, who is comfortable in her own skin and body" my mouth falls open in astonishment at his litany of praise "you are a free spirit yet you are completely grounded. You are everything she wishes to be"

I don't know what to say to that, he has taken me by complete surprise. He's totally floored me. My brain is numb in fact it's packed its suitcase and gone on vacation. I pull away and twist to look at Clayton better. I think more than anything it's to make sure he isn't teasing me. What I see enthrals me. When we first met he told me I beguiled and bewitched him, I see that now. I really have, he is speaking from his heart. He is telling me what he thinks of me. My inner goddess fans herself "Oh my" we chorus together.

Cupping my face Clayton kisses me so softly and with such reverence the top of my head nearly blows off. I want him, badly. Pulling away I look him in the eye "Spend the night with me" I whisper.

His eyes widen, his mouth opens and he takes a sharp inhale of breath "Are you sure that's what you want?"

"Yes. I want you" I've never been so sure of anything in my life as I am of this. I lean forward and kiss him to show him just how much I want him. He chuckles darkly.

"Careful baby, otherwise we'll be putting on a show for Bruce"

His driver, shit. The raging desire I feel dampens as I remember we aren't alone. Both me and my inner goddess pout making Clayton chuckle even more.

"Oh baby the things I'm going to do to you" his voice is deliciously dark and low.

With those few words he has me wet instantly as images flash through my mind of what we are about to do and of the unspoken things he's promised, then apprehension hits me.

"What's wrong, changed your mind?" he cajoles sensing my shift in mood.

"No, no it's just" god this is embarrassing and I feel myself flush, I clear my throat "it's just that it's been a long time for me" I put my head down because I can't look at him as I feel so ashamed of what I'm about to say "you will be gentle with me won't you" my voice sounds small, unsure, strained even as I ask the question.

"Skye, look at me" he commands softly, I lift my head and he cups my face "I know this is a big step for you and at any time you can tell me to stop and I will, at any time" he reiterates.

Clayton is ingenuous when he says it and I know he will be true to his word no matter how much it left him frustrated. I nod to show I understand; gratitude has closed my throat.

"You know you could use a safe word"

Shock brings my voice back "As in BDSM safe words" I say causing him to chuckle.

"Those romance novels didn't happen to be erotica by any chance" he teases, I grin sheepishly and nod "okay how about we use red for stop and by that I mean we stop completely it's too much and yellow for carry on but slow down as I'm pushing your limits"

Even though he said all of this matter of fact he still manages to make it sound sexy as hell.

"Red and yellow I can go with that" I say confidently and I feel it.

"Your place or mine" Clayton asks and kisses my cheek lightly.

"Mine" I say without hesitation, if things don't work out I won't have to worry about getting home or doing the walk of shame for that matter. Plus I suddenly remember Shelley and Simon are coming round mid-morning to help me pack. At least they won't see me in the same clothes and this way I would avoid their scrutiny and questions.

"You okay?" Clayton asks bringing me out of my revive "we're here"

I'm so wrapped up in my thoughts I hadn't realized the car has stopped. I look up at Clayton to see solicitude in his expression.

"God I feel as if I'm about to lose my virginity" Clayton burst out laughing. Huh guess I said that out loud. I scramble off his knee as the door opens when Clayton climbs out I grab his hand "come on" and pull him towards the steps of the building.

CLAYTON

I give Bruce the signal to go as I let Skye pull me along toward the building. I can't believe she has asked me to stay the night. I've respected her boundaries all week, letting her show me how far to go. The heavy petting sessions took me back to my high school days. I'd come in my pants a couple of times something I haven't done since I was seventeen and I didn't care. I thoroughly enjoyed every minute of my time with Skye and now I get to make out and go all the way.

"Take your time, don't rush her or you will scare her" my conscious admonishes. My heart aches as I recall how she asked me to be gentle with her. If I ever meet the bastard who had hurt her I will rip him apart and then I will kill him.

We get into the elevator and Skye looks up at me, I can see the mixed emotions she is struggling with. God she steals my breath she is so beautiful. I pull her into my arms and kiss her gently and very slowly doing my best to calm her and put to rest any anxiety. I will never tire of the feeling of holding her in my arms and kissing her.

I've been hard from the moment I saw her earlier this evening, that doesn't bother me because I've been walking around all week either semi or full on erect. Now it's different, now my cock is throbbing painfully anticipating what is about to happen. I'm determined to savor every minute and part of her.

This past week has been a whole new experience for me, comprehension hits me. I'm so used to women throwing themselves at me I never bother getting to know them. I mean truly get to know them.

I've always categorized women into two groups; those that just want sex with me so they can boast to their friends and those that jump in the sack with me in the hope of getting to know me and taking things further, only I wasn't interested by then. Skye doesn't fit in to either of these groups.

She is in a class all of her own. Over the week we've gotten to know each other, she is genuinely interested in me and my business and not my money, hell she has plenty of her own. Not only that but she's challenged my thinking and business practices, she's even given me suggestions and ideas that I've implemented and I'm already seeing a return on investment and cost savings for Christ sake.

She didn't initiate sex. The heavy petting had been a natural progression from the heated kissing and god bless her she even asked me if I was okay with it not going any further, for the first time in my life I was. I really, really didn't want to fuck up what we have between us. Ultimately she has no expectations, hell she is about to leave the country. I jolt breaking the kiss; I realize the physical jolt is from the elevator stopping but the emotional jolt! I puzzle over this as we walk through her apartment. What did that mean? I push the thought aside as we enter her bedroom.

A huge bed dominates the room. I notice boxes and open suitcases around the rest of the space and heaps of clothes neatly piled in the cases or around the floor all evidence of the pending departure.

"Sorry about the mess" her voice quivers making me realize just how nervous she is and I notice she's trembling.

"We don't have to do this" I say putting my arms around her and rubbing her back in an attempt to soothe her, if my cock could speak it will be shouting shut the fuck up, yes we do.

Looking at me with wide eyes she whispers "I want to" raising on to her tip toes she kisses me.

Christ I love the taste of her and I want more a lot more but I want her to feel in control. I break the kiss and step back. Confusion flits across her face.

"Undress me" I keep the command soft. Skye will have the control, I will direct her actions. She reaches for my jeans "top first"

Skye lets out slow exhale and with trembling hands catches the hem of my t-shirt and lifts it. I bend so she can pull it over my head. A gasp escapes her as she takes her first look at my torso as I stand up to my full height. I look after myself and work out every day so I'm all clearly defined muscle. Her hands reach out to touch me then at the last minute she curls her fingers as if changing her mind or to stop herself. I want her hands on me. I crave her touch, to feel them run over my skin.

"Touch me" my voice rasps betraying my desire and need.

Her look of rapt awe heats my blood. Tentatively she runs her fingers feather light over my abs and up to my chest, circling my nipples, tracing my pectorals and back down stomach and waist. My whole body trembles and twitches at her soft caress. I have to force myself to keep still and bite back on the groans of pure pleasure I feel from her touch. Her hands continue to explore, she moves behind me and runs her hands over my back and down my spine, her touch becoming firmer, bolder as she gains confidence.

Skye steps back in front of me her fingers tips never leaving my skin, looking me in the eyes her hands travel from my wrists up my arms to my shoulders, across my chest and down trailing the muscles of my six pack. Her fingers slip underneath the waistband of my jeans sliding them around my hips. My heart is racing. I open my mouth to breathe trying to get more air into my lungs.

Skye drops to her knees. My cock pulses and throbs painfully. Oh fuck. I nearly come just at the sight of her in that position. Breaking eye contact Skye reaches for my left foot and takes off my shoe and sock, her fingers trailing along the sole and side of my foot sending spasms through all my muscles up my leg. I shift my weight as she repeats the process with my right foot.

Placing her hands on my knees slowly she moves them upwards, over my thighs. I hold my breath. Christ, she is torturing me. Slow sweet torture. Looking at her up turned face I reach out and run my hand over her head and round to cup her cheek, she turns her head and nuzzles my palm placing a kiss at its centre then circles her tongue over it. I let out a groan I wasn't going to hold back any more, I want her to know what effect she is having on me.

Her fingers trace the outline of my cock causing me to jerk and thrust my hips forward. I hiss a breath as she continues to tease and stroke me through my jeans. Licking her lips she reaches for the button and pops it open, taking hold of the zipper she pulls it down slowly brushing her fingers against my cock. My head drops back and I take deep breaths trying to keep control as I feel her grab the waist band of my jeans and boxers. When nothing happens I look back down, smiling she pulls and in one swift movement my aching cock is released. I chuckle the little Minx wanted me to watch her. I lift each leg at the silent command she gives with a slight pressure of her hands on my calf so she can remove the clothing.

I bend down and reach for her, to pull her to her feet. Skye shakes her head "I want to explore more" her husky voice resonating bone deep in me. I release her and stand breathing deeply preparing myself and mustering all of my control for what is to come.

Her hands and fingers start at my ankles and work slowly upwards, setting my skin on fire, making me moan with anticipation. I steel myself as her hands sweep over my thighs, my skin mists with sweat as the sweet torture continues. My cock is twitching, demanding and begging for her attention and touch. I watch as Skye tentatively reaches for my cock, I hold my breath which leaves me in a rush as she trails her fingers lightly along my shaft. I close my eyes and my head rolls back as she grips and strokes me, my hips thrusting forward slightly of their own volition.

"Fuck" I hiss as I feel her tongue slide over the head of my cock. I bring my head forward and look down my body meeting her gaze. The sight is so fucking hot. I can see Skye is enjoying herself torturing me as a mischievous grin plays across her lips. Her tongue darts out and swirls around my cock head "Oh sweet fucking Jesus" I groan.

An agonised cry of pleasure escapes me when she takes me in her hot, moist mouth. My hips thrust forward of their own volition again as she takes me deeper, sucking as she pulls back. Shit! I nearly come.

"Baby your mouth feels so fucking good" I pant.

It was a million times better than any fantasy I conjured or experienced before. Skye sets a rhythm working me with her tongue, mouth and hands. I bury my hands in her hair, my hips moving with her. My climax is building quickly perspiration covers me, my breathing becoming ragged as my heart pounds faster.

"Baby if you don't want me coming in your mouth, stop, I'm not going to last"

In response to my warning Skye sucks harder working my shaft with one hand and cupping my balls massaging them with the other. Instinct kicks in and I take over fucking her mouth.

"I'm coming for you baby" seconds later my orgasm hits hard "fuck, Skye" I shout my release as my body tenses then shudders and pulses as I keep pumping my seed into her mouth. Skye continues to work me sucking and swallowing every drop I have to give. I struggle to get my breathing under control I'm panting as if I've run a hundred metres in eight seconds. Skye is still licking my cock like it's a Popsicle, keeping me hard.

"Baby you can have more later" my voice comes out gruff "now it's my turn"

SKYE

I lick my lips savoring his tangy, slightly salty taste as I rise to my feet with Clayton's help. I feel giddy with anticipation wondering what he's going to do to me.

Clayton moves to the bed and I admire his muscular hard body. God he is a work of art. My fingers flex itching to explore again. Clayton pulls the covers back then sits down on the edge of the bed.

"Strip for me baby" his raspy command is soft so I know I can refuse if I want to, but I want to please him. I decide to put on a show.

During the week I'd spent some time at The Gentlemen's Club it's an up market pole dancing strip club. In order to get ideas for the commission I'd spent time with the girls, watching them work. I picked up quite a few tips and tricks so I sure as hell was going to put theory into practice.

I move to stand in front of Clayton then stop, music, I want music. Purposefully swinging my hips as I walk over to the dresser, the swing is made more pronounce since I'm still wearing my killer heels. I scroll through my iPod until I find the song I want, Muse's cover version of Feeling Good. I put it on repeat. The heavy guitar riffs and drum beats will be good to peel my clothes off to. The lyrics also hold significant meaning for me especially the chorus.

I switch the music centre on and start to walk back towards Clayton, as the guitar riffs blast out I move in time to the music and run my hands over my body and into my hair. Clayton's heated gaze follows my every move, he licks his lips and his magnificent erect cock twitches, he hasn't even softened after his orgasm. I had him, he is mine. Time to get naked, my inner goddess agrees.

I undo the buttons of my shirt slowly, watching Clayton's reaction. All the while I move my body, undulating with the music. I let the shirt drop to the floor. I run my hands across my stomach, up and over my breasts, up my neck and into my hair and back down to my skirt. Undoing the button and zipper it floats to pool at my feet revealing my pink lace boy short panties that match the pink lace bra.

I step back out of the skirt putting some distance between Clayton and me. I can see he is struggling to stay put. Clayton is gripping the edge of the bed, his hands flexing on the sheet. The strain shows in his arms as the veins and muscles stand out prominently and he's rocked forward a few times only to pull back. His expression is exhilarating, pure dark carnal lust for me. I feel light headed knowing that I'm responsible. I'm doing this to him. It makes me feel powerful, beautiful and sensual.

I undo my bra then turn my back to Clayton and look over my shoulder at him, I take off my bra and hold it out to the side letting go.

Turning slightly keeping my eyes on him I bend at the waist, thrusting my butt out and hooking my thumbs into the waistband of my panties. Clayton visibly swallows and takes a deep breath. He's on the edge of his control. Slowly I pull my panties down. A long low growl emanates from Clayton sending a thrilling surge of desire through me and making my core muscles clench. I shimmy my panties down my thighs in time to the music. I step out of them and turn to face Clayton, his eyes rake me from head to toe and back again. Keeping my heels on I walk toward him slowly and stop just out of reach.

Clayton slides off the bed and onto his knees, looking up at me I can see the barely contained desire he has for me. "You are truly a vision of beauty, a goddess. Let me worship you"

I can't speak his words take my breath away all I can do is nod.

Grasping my ankle he lifts my foot and removes my shoe and kisses the top of my foot. Then he repeats the gesture with the other. Clayton stands gracefully towering over me, bending slightly he scoops me into his arms and carries me to the bed, gently laying me down. I scoot over to the centre.

Clayton crawls onto the bed and climbs over me with the sleek sensuous grace of a panther. Supporting his weight on his arms he dips his head and kisses me. A gentle lingering kiss I try to deepen but he pulls away.

"Be patient my goddess" he rasps "I am going to worship every inch of your delicious heavenly body"

He proceeds to work his way down my body with kisses, licks and nips with excruciating slowness. He follows my jaw line then down the column of my throat. I thrust my head back to give him better access. His hands trail lightly over my skin leaving goose bumps and a burning tingling in their wake. Slowly moving along my arms, shoulders and between my breasts I groan in frustration when he doesn't touch them. Sweeping over my stomach and out over to my waist and hip then back again. I'm mindless with the sensations he's creating in me.

I cry out in pleasure when his tongue circles my nipple then his mouth closes around it and sucks, sending muscle clenching feelings straight to my core. My hips thrust upwards I want friction and attention given to my clit. I start to thrash and mewl. I'm going out of my mind.

"Shhh baby, I've got you" Clayton's voice calms me, my breathing is loud and ragged to my ears "your tits are fantastic" he praises cupping and pumping them with his warm large hands "made just for me"

He alternates working each nipple with a lick then a nip which sends sharp sensations of pain followed by a suckle giving me immense pleasure. I can feel my climax building steadily.

Clayton shifts and starts to work his way downwards kissing my stomach, making light traces with his tongue swirling and dipping into my navel then moving lower. He pauses and I lift my head to see why.

He's looking at my scar that runs from hip to hip just above my pelvic bone. Shit. Now is so not the time to get into the how and why. Clayton runs his fingers lightly over it. The scar isn't ugly in fact it is hardly noticeable, the surgeon had done a good job it is just very long. Clayton dips his head places kisses along it with such tenderness I have to fight the surge of emotion he invokes but I fail to stop the tears that escape and run into my hair.

"Open your legs for me baby" again a soft command, my muscles clench. I knew I wasn't going to last long if he went down on me. Clayton positioned himself lying prone between my legs, his broad shoulders making me spread them wider "Oh baby you are so beautiful down here and so ready for me" he blew lightly over my clit making me whimper. I nearly buck off the bed as his tongue traces over my slit "shhh easy" he croons "I've got you, let me take care of you"

His fingers circle my clit, desire and pleasure radiate through my body from the knot of nerve endings. He replaces his fingers with his mouth.

"Oh yes" I groan a loud, grinding my hips against his mouth.

"Like that baby" he chuckles "want me to do that again?"

"Yes, please" I spread my legs further to give him better access "please" I beg shamelessly.

Clayton obliges. His tongue circles my folds and his teeth graze and gently nip. His mouth suckles my clit, his tongue trusts into my entrance. I'm going out of my mind the sensations are so intense. He inserts his finger into me slowly then withdraws only to push back in with two fingers my hips move naturally to his rhythm.

"Baby you are so close I can feel it, your cunt is so greedy" he moves his fingers faster "come for me baby, let me hear you" his mouth closes down on my clit sucking harder as his fingers fuck me.

I'm helpless, groaning loudly, his words bouncing around my head send me over the edge. "Clayton" is the last coherent thought I have then I'm lost in a wash of pleasurable feelings and sensations, my body convulsing.

I'm vaguely aware of Clayton rising up over me, continuing to massage my clit he positions himself with his cock in his hand he puts the head at my entrance and pushes forward slowly. Clayton is big and I desperately want to feel him inside me. I thrust my hips up to meet him and he slides in further, the pleasure of penetration making us both groan.

"Baby you are so fucking tight. Tell me if I hurt you" Clayton gasps out.

"More please" is all I can say. I want all of him.

Clayton flexes his hips and pushes further in, my muscles clench around his cock, welcoming him.

"Fuck you feel so good" he moans as he pulls back and thrusts in slowly, moving my hips upwards so I can take more of him deeper I groan at the fullness and the stretch of him being inside me, it feels so good. I want more. I lift my legs and wrap them around his hips my feet resting on his buttocks taking him all the way to the root.

"You okay baby" he whispers in my ear his breath coming out in heavy gusts as he tries to regain his control.

"Yes, fuck me" I groan out with impatience.

"With pleasure baby" he chuckles at my demand.

He starts to move slowly at first giving me chance to get used to him and his size. I feel every delicious inch of him. I relish the feel of my muscles as they contract and clench around his cock. My hands explore his back, feeling his muscles flex and relax sinuously with each of his thrusts.

Clayton bends his head and suckles my nipples overwhelming me with sensations and my second climax is building fast. Clayton rolls his hips and thrusts deep, pulls back and repeats the move going faster, picking up pace. My body responds to his, my hips rising to meet every thrust so he hits a spot that sends pleasure thrumming through my body.

"I'm going to come" Clayton pants "Come with me, baby"

He thrusts hard twice and sends me spiralling "Oh god Clayton" I cry out as I rush head long hard into the pleasure abyss. Clayton follows me, we hold on to each other as wave after wave shudders through us.

We stay wrapped around each other until awareness comes back and our breathing becomes normal. Clayton lifts his head and looks at me moving my hair away from my face and kisses me gently. I know he is checking to see if he had hurt me.

"I'm okay" I say softly almost shyly. He smiles and kisses me again as he pulls out. I want him back inside me again. I don't like the emptiness I feel.

Clayton gets up and goes into the bathroom. I hear running water then he comes back with a cloth in his hand.

"Let me clean you up. I seem to have made rather a mess of you" he stops short and curses, running his free hand through his hair.

"What" I ask startled, the look on his face has fear pooling in my gut. I sit up and reach over for the remote on the bedside cabinet and switch the music off "what is it?"

"Protection" he snaps out and running his free hand through his hair again, a clear sign of his agitation "Christ I am such a fucking idiot. I should have used protection. I am so sorry, I was so wrapped up in the moment" he says apologetically looking me in the eyes.

"It's okay" before I can say anything else he cuts me off.

"No, it's not. It is irresponsible of me, please forgive me" he pleads.

"Are you clean?"

"What" confusion crosses his face, ah he's thinking of pregnancy not STD's it dawns on me.

"Yes or no are you clean" I ask again, Clayton nods still looking confused.

"Then there is nothing to worry about, you're clean and I am as well" I pause taking a deep breath "and I can't get pregnant"

I watch as Clayton sways on his feet probably from relief sweeping through him. He doesn't say anything, he doesn't need to as I see his eyes flicker down to my scar instead he simply nods and proceeds to take care of cleaning me and himself. He throws the cloth into the wash basket and climbs into bed pulling me into his arms and wrapping the covers around us.

We lay like this for a few minutes his arms flexing and holding me tighter, pressing kisses to the top of my head. I decide to volunteer information.

"I had a partial hysterectomy, that's what the scar is from, the operation" his arms tighten around me "because of the damage caused from the attack"

Clayton's whole body stiffens and he curses loudly. I remain still wondering what he will do. Gradually he relaxes but his arms remain tight around me if it's possible he pulls me closer to him. We fall asleep like this.

I wake up needing the bathroom. I can't move a flash of panic surges through me, my heart thunders painfully in my chest. I hear soft steady breathing close to me, spiking my panic further. I slowly turn my head in the direction of the noise. Clayton. My body goes limp with relief and I blow out a breath I didn't realize I was holding.

Clayton's face looks peaceful and heartbreakingly beautiful. He is wrapped around me, it's as if he's determined to hold on to me, protect me. Smiling I ease myself out of his grip disentangling our limbs without disturbing him. As I head for the bathroom I look at the clock it's four in the morning.

Whilst I relieve myself I check my body, it has been six years or there about since I last had sex so I was expecting to be sore and I am, surprisingly it isn't uncomfortable. My body definitely knows it has had sex and I thoroughly enjoyed every minute of it. An involuntary shudder goes through me as if my body is telling me it remembers too and I become aroused.

I recalled all of Clayton's words, his instruction and encouragement, praise and worship. Goddess, he called me his goddess. He certainly made me feel like one.

I realize with sudden clarity that he has in fact awakened my inner goddess. Now she and I are raring to go and we are hungry, starving in fact. We have six years to make up for. Poor Clayton he's not going to know what's hit him. I smile wickedly to myself as ideas and fantasy after fantasy spring to mind.

I start playing scenarios through my mind of the different ways of how to wake him up. I am most definitely going to put more of the theory I'd learnt from the strippers into practice. I look at my grinning reflection in the mirror as I wash my hands. My skin is flushed, eyes bright, lips kiss swollen. I look wanton, hell I feel it all because of the Adonis that is lying asleep in my bed.

Back in the bedroom I switch the music centre on, turn the volume down and put it on random play.

"You okay baby?" Clayton's drowsy gravelly voice comes out of the dimness.

"Yes" I whisper as I turn to face the bed.

"Good come back to bed, it feels lonely without you"

He throws the covers back and from the light of the moon shining through the windows my eyes take in his masculine physique and rake his body up and down. The defined muscles of his chest, abs, arms and thighs, his large cock lay flaccid across his thigh. He is mouth-watering and sexy as sin. I watch his cock twitch and get bigger as I approach. I look up at Clayton's face; his look is greedy as he takes in my naked body. Desire courses through me, he wants me as much as I want him. I climb onto the bed and he starts to reach for me I shake my head.

"I want to explore again, turnover"

A slow sexy smile spreads across his face and without a word he complies. I straddle him placing my hands at the base of his spine. I run them upwards to his shoulders applying pressure; his responding groan is long and low as I massage his shoulders and back. I run my tongue up along his spine and kiss and nip my way back down. He hisses and his hips grind into the bed. Shifting I move his legs apart and sit between them. I knead his buttocks and he thrusts again at my touch. I kiss and bite each cheek not too hard but not soft either. Leaning down I run my tongue along the crack of his butt.

"Holy fuck" he yells and jerks up, his butt cheeks clenching "Christ baby you are going to be the death of me" he pants.

Smiling and feeling empowered I work my way down each leg to his feet.

"Turn over" I command again without a word Clayton complies, his cock stands thick and proud pointing and reaching just past his navel.

Moving his legs wider I crawl up the bed towards him, keeping eye contact I lick my lips deliberately displaying my intention. His body responds. His hips surge upwards in anticipation of my mouth.

Clayton's eyes are half closed and his breathing heavy. I grasp his cock and stroke gently. Clayton throws his arms out to the sides and grasps the sheet throwing his head back into the pillows groaning. He is completely at my mercy.

"I'm going to make you beg" I say squeezing and pulling harder on his cock, his hips jerk upwards "you are going to beg me to let you come"

"Oh fuck" he groans as he gives himself to me.

Seaman pools at the tip of his cock, I lick it off then take him in my mouth as far as I can. I relax my throat so I can take him to the root and suck hard as I withdraw.

"Fucking hell" Clayton groans out and pants loudly.

I run my tongue up and down his shaft and cup his sack with my other hand and gently massage. When I know Clayton is back in control I take him in my mouth again, this time I grip the base of his cock and start stroking him as I concentrate on the head of his cock with my mouth and tongue. With my other hand I massage and scrape my nails over his sack.

"Yes, baby" Clayton hisses "that feels so fucking good"

As I massage his sack I extend my middle finger and stroke the perineum a few times then extend further and touch his anus, circling it with the pad of my finger then drew it back towards his sack, all the while working my mouth, tongue and hand along the shaft of his cock.

"Jesus, fucking hell" Clayton curses "baby you're killing me" he cries out.

Hearing him like this spikes my arousal even more. I work him harder causing him to curse more loudly. His chest and abs are glistening with perspiration in the moonlight. I feel his sack draw up and the veins in his cock pulse he is on the brink of coming so I slow down taking him away from the edge. Then I set about building him up again, I do this twice more when he starts to beg me to let him come.

I move to straddle him, holding his cock I positioned him at my entrance then take him inside me to the root in one swift move. Clayton yells and curses his shoulders jack knifing up off the bed. I push him back down and leave my hands on his glistening pectorals in fact his whole body is covered in perspiration and rivets of sweat run between the ridges of muscle. I can feel his heart hammering as his chest heaves gasping in air.

I relish the feeling of fullness and of him being deep inside me. When Clayton has his breathing under control. I start to move my hips, circling and undulating riding him all in time to the heavy beat of the music that's playing.

"Baby I'm going to come if you don't slowdown"

Clayton puts his hands on my hips gripping them trying to slow my movements but the pressure feels incredible and I keep going chasing my own release as I watch Clayton fall apart underneath me calling my name. I continue to move prolonging his orgasm. Seeing him unravel like this triggers my own release. I collapse on his chest as my body shakes in pleasure. Clayton's arms come around me holding me close to him.

When the last of the shudders leave my body I raise my head. Clayton has his eyes closed and is still struggling to get his breath under control. I can feel his heart is still pounding. I move forward and kiss him gently. Without opening his eyes he cups my face and deepens the kiss. When he releases me he keeps my face close and slowly opens his eyes, my breath catches at what I see; warmth, wonder, awe and something else I can't fathom.

"That was the best orgasm of my life" exultation sweeps through me "tell me, where in the hell did you learn that" he exclaims "I mean you've been celibate for six years, surely it wasn't from those erotic novels"

I laugh as I climb off him "You really want to know" he nods as I lie down beside him and he pulls me into his arms "I was simply putting theory in to practice and no it wasn't from a novel" I lean back to look at him "remember the gentlemen's strip club commission" he nods "well some of the girls agreed to be models for the paintings and I was there during the week taking reference pictures and I needed certain facial expressions so they started to share, let's say, very intimate details on various sex acts, basically turning each other on so they could get the look I needed" I shrug "that was about four different theories put into practice"

"And lucky ole me got to be your guinea pig" he chuckles "feel free to practice on me anytime" he kisses me so tenderly my body thrums with contentment "how are you feeling, are you sore?" his concern for me showing in his voice, it makes my heart swell.

"I'm good, a bit tender" I say shyly "nothing unbearable" I smile wickedly "put it this way I know I've had a good workout" I reach between our bodies and grasp his cock "hope I haven't worn you out because I would like to do that again"

He thrust his hips effectively stroking his cock into my hand and I can feel him getting hard again.

"You are insatiable" he rolls me onto my back and parts my legs with his and he nestles between them, rocking his hips the friction making him harder and massaging my clit at the same time "what is it I have started or should I say what is it I have awakened?" he says as he rolls his hips and slips inside me.

My back arches and I moan "My inner goddess and we're starving"

"Oh my goddess, you are mine to feed" he growls possessively and I'm lost to him as he makes slow sweet love to me.

Chapter Seven

CLAYTON

I watch Skye as she sleeps. She's lying on her stomach, face toward me. Her wild curly white blonde hair spilling around her giving the effect of a massive halo as it shimmers in the morning sunlight. Her arms are under the pillow and the bed sheets pool at her hips. I carefully move her long hair off her back so I can admire the curve of her spine and tiny waist. She is exquisite, how could anyone want to hurt her.

I thought back to the scar, I shudder as I remember her whispered words as to what had caused it. Skye shocked the hell out of me when she told me she couldn't get pregnant but I didn't think for one minute it was because she had a partial hysterectomy. I feel sick as my mind conjures up images of Skye badly beaten and bloody, she was so young to have suffered at the hands of some fucking sick bastard. Did she know who had attacked her and where was he now? I hope to god I meet the bastard one day because I will cause him pain like he's never experienced for the damage he has done to my beautiful goddess.

Then there is Caroline the Catty Bitch from Hell. Christ I feel violent towards the bitch. I've never felt the need to hurt or harm a woman. I despise those that did, but Caroline is a nasty piece of work. I should know I come across her type often enough thanks to my mother.

I marvel at how Skye handled Caroline and I salute Skye's friends in their loyalty and protectiveness to her. Last night was highly entertaining listening to the slap downs Skye and her friends dished back, it's obvious they are all well versed in Caroline's attempts to belittle Skye. I must admit Simon's were the best and I couldn't help but laugh when Skye whispered to me Simon had his Bitchy Queen head on. I made a mental note to ask Skye why she still has them in her circle of friends if she didn't feel anything for Pete but pity.

Skye stirs, she's waking up. I get out of bed and head for the bathroom to run a bath; she's going to be sore so a soak in a nice hot bath will help. Not only that but I know if I stayed in bed I will be on her the second her eyes open and that wouldn't be fair to her.

As I switch the faucets on my thoughts turn to the sex. Christ, it has been the best experience of my life. No woman has ever got me groaning and shouting as she did, normally I'm quiet, not a sound escaping me, not even a grunt when I came and I'm usually in complete control which I totally lost with Skye, not that I'm complaining.

I want to spend as much time with her today and this evening as I can. I want as much of her as I can possibly get in the little time we have left, would she feel the same? The thought sobers me and jolts me from the lust filled fantasies that started to invade my brain.

"Morning" Skye's husky sleep filled voice brings a halt to all coherent thought.

I turn to see her standing in the door way gloriously naked, my cock responds instantly. A lazy smile spreads across Skye's face as she sees my reaction to her and I walk toward her grinning back.

"Good morning baby" I bend and kiss her long and slow. I pull back and cup her face "I thought a nice long soak in the bath would be in order, help with the soreness"

"Thank you"

I can hear the gratitude in her voice, which pleases me having made the right choice and mentally I high five myself for thinking of her and not my dick.

"Do you have any bath salts?"

Skye shakes her head and walks into the shower coming back with body wash, shampoo and conditioner setting them on the side of the bath along with a wash cloth. She moves to the sink and cleans her teeth, when she's finished she offers the brush to me. I take it and clean mine the whole act seems natural and pleasantly domesticated. I like this and I want more of it with her.

I start as the thought stuns me, where the fuck did that come from? I finish and put the toothbrush back in the holder, turning I realize Skye has left the room. I test the bath water, the temperatures just right. Switching off the taps I shout "Bath is ready"

A muffled "Okay" comes back. I climb in. Skye re-emerges with towels in her arms and puts them onto the towel rail. I hold out my hand to help her into the bath. She lets out a loud ah sound as she settles into the water. I sit behind her and gently urge her to lean back against my chest. I soak the wash cloth and begin to trail water over her arms and chest. Skye let out a contented sigh. We stay in the companionable silence both enjoying the relaxing moment. It dawns on me this is the first bath I've taken with a woman.

"What are your plans for today?"

"Shelley and Simon will be coming over around ten-ish to help me pack" Skye let out a derisive snort "actually Shelley and Simon will be arguing about what clothes I should take would be more accurate. Mr C's person will be here about three to pick up my cases. Then it's a quiet night in with the pair of them along with Phil and may be Macy for wine and pizza with a debate over which film to watch"

"Would you mind if I hung out with you as well?"

Skye gasps and jumps in surprise at my request. "No, not at all, I'd like that" she sighs "but please don't feel obliged to stay"

"What do you mean?" I'm concerned at the obliged word she's used.

Skye sits up and turns to face me, water sloshing over the sides at her movements "It's just, well this week" she stops and looks down at her hands resting in her lap gathering her thoughts "In less than twenty four hours I'm leaving and not coming back to New York for three months. I've really enjoyed my time with you" she looks me in the eye and continues softly "last night was the best of my life. I just don't want you to feel you have to stick around"

It dawns on me she's giving me an out, one I'm not prepared to take. "Skye, I really like you. Really, really like you" I emphasise, her eyes widen at my declaration "and I want to spend as much time with you as you'll let me until you leave tomorrow. Will you let me?" she looks absolutely stunned "will you?" my voice comes out as a whisper and a hint of desperation. Fuck I know I will get on my knees and beg to have the time with her if I had to.

"Yes" Skye whispers, she didn't move and because I so badly want her in my arms I lean forward take her hands and pull her to me so she's lying on my chest, wrapping my arms around her I kiss her forehead and her damp hair.

"Thank you" I whisper then after a beat "listen, I'm not going to push you to keep in touch whilst you're away it would be unfair. But when you are back" I shrug, before I can continue Skye says

"And if you are free and single maybe we could pick up" she lifts her head probably to see my reaction.

Pure joy fills me. My cheeks ache at the size of the smile on my face. Skye is on the same wavelength. No strings, no pressure, no expectations "Yes, I would like that"

"Me too"

I pull her further up my body and kiss her senseless.

SKYE

We spend so long in the bath my hands have turned prune like but I enjoy every minute. Clayton has washed my hair and body with such gentleness and reverence it makes me feel special like a goddess all over again.

I still can't believe he'd asked to spend all of today and the evening with me. I nearly fainted when he said he liked me. "Correction" my inner goddess gloats "really, really like is what he said get it right" and to cap it all off we're on the same page about getting together when I come back in September. I'm in seventh heaven.

Clayton dries me with the same gentleness as he did washing me, then he carries and lays me on the bed going down on me until I beg for release. "Pay back for last night" he says with an evil grin.

We just finish eating breakfast when the buzzer sounds "That'll be Shelley and Simon" I say as I get up to answer and let them in. Clayton picks up the plates and cups taking them to the sink and starts to rinse them.

"I'm going to nip home and get changed, do you need anything bringing back?"

"No, only if there is something you want particularly to eat or drink otherwise today is about take out junk food" I say grabbing the dishes and load them into the machine. Crikey, look how easy it is for us to fall into such a domesticated routine.

Loud banging on the front door brought me out of my thoughts and I go to let the rabble in leaving Clayton to finish.

"Morning" Simon choruses in a sing song voice "how are you honey" he says he hugging me making my "I'm good" reply muffled.

Shelley walks in behind him looking pale. I hug her "What's the matter you look terrible"

"Morning sickness" she grimaces.

In the living room Simon has lain down on the sofa "Oh what a night" he mock groans "we went to Harry's afterwards and I didn't get in till four this morning"

Suddenly he shoots upright his face has shock plastered all over it.

"Good morning Simon, Shelley" Clayton says coming out of the kitchen "I'll see you in about an hour" he says to me giving me a quick kiss.

"Okay" I smile like the cat that's got the cream and I can feel my cheeks burn "Oh, take this with you" I pull a key out of my pocket "just in case world war three has broken out and we don't hear the door" I nod in the direction of Shelley and Simon as I hand the key over.

Smiling Clayton takes the key and kisses me again, a longer lingering one this time then left. I turn to face Shelley and Simon's totally shell shocked faces and burst out laughing.

Shelley recovers first "Did he and you?" she says wiggling her eyebrows.

"Huh, huh" I'm smiling so widely my jaw aches.

Simon miraculously overcoming his hangover points at the seat next to him and demands "Sit, details now"

Shelley shoving me in my back adds "And we've only got an hour before he's back"

"Oh no" I counter "bedroom, pack, details" I walk towards the bedroom with them hot on my heels firing questions at me.

As we sort and pack my clothes I answer their questions honestly and tell them what Clayton and I have agreed for when I come back.

"Holy cow" Shelley exclaims "he's willing to wait until you get back"

"No, if we are both free and single and we are both of the same inclination we'll pick up" I reiterate.

"And you're not going to keep in touch whilst you are away" Simon says almost disbelievingly.

"No we're not. It wouldn't be fair on either of us" I say patiently.

"Hello" Clayton's voice calls out from the living room. I get up and go out to meet him.

"Hey" I say as he greets me with a soft slow kiss "hmm, miss me" I tease as he breaks the kiss. He gives me a smile that makes my heart skip a beat.

"I brought lunch" he says bending down and picking up a couple of grocery bags. I also notice an overnight bag, wow he is serious about spending the night. Gleefully I hug myself.

"Excellent, stick it in the kitchen we've nearly finished so we'll eat in a bit" I say heading back to my bedroom.

An hour later my cases are packed and the food Clayton brought is spread out on the coffee table, as we eat conversation turns to last night at Gino's. Simon is full of gossip and making us laugh at the stories he'd been told by various friends and acquaintances.

"Oooh, yes and the best bit" he pauses for dramatic effect "Pete and Catty Bitch from Hell got into a huge row after you three; four if you include Phil, had left"

"About what" I ask, not that I really care.

"You" Simon says smugly pointing at me.

"Me!" I splutter "what in god's name could they be arguing about me for"

"Well according to George, Pete had a real go at Catty Bitch for being just that and how she embarrassed him in front of Mr Moneybags here" Clayton laughs at Simon's nickname for him "it turns out Pete had done some research since last week and was hoping to make an impression obviously with the aspiration to either get a job with your company" he points at Clayton "or he was hoping to tap you for some insider information of some sort"

"So the argument wasn't about me it was about Clayton" I say feeling relieved.

"Oh it was about you alright" Simon went on "Pete finally grew a pair and wanted to know why she has it in for you and tries to make your life a misery. George said she couldn't give a feasible answer"

I'm speechless, I don't know what to make of all this.

"What I don't get is why do you have someone so toxic and you don't like around you?" Clayton says directing the question at me.

"I don't" I say simply "I have nothing to do with either of them. Like I told you last night it's been two years since I last saw both of them. The only time I see them is at Gino's and on the very rare occasion at a function. Being perfectly honest I have no idea how they find out when I'll be at Gino's"

"I know the answer to that" Shelly says excitedly "apparently they go there every Friday in the hope of running into one of us"

We all look at each other and collapse into hysterical laughter. Clayton looks at us bemused "What's so funny?"

"Well considering the lovely Skye here" Simon says wiping his eyes "hasn't set foot in the place for two years and we" he indicates to himself and Shelley "probably have only been in about four times in those two years. Pete and Catty Bitch have been spending a hell of a lot of time and money unnecessarily and Catty Bitch hates spending money unless it's someone else's"

"How did you find that out Shelly?" I ask purely out of curiosity.

"Gino told me" she grins "Phil and I went in about six months ago on a Wednesday night. He commented my friends would be disappointed to learn they had got the wrong night. I asked him what he meant and which friends that's when he told me" we set us off laughing again "no wonder Pete was so pissed off" Shelley says wiping her eyes and gulping for breath "knowing it's going to be twelve weeks before you're back so he can get another crack at you Clayton"

Clayton raises his eyebrows and has a kind of a not bloody likely, over my dead body expression on his face which set us off again.

"I don't know why Pete's still with Caroline considering she's not faithful to him" Doh! I didn't mean to say that out loud. I mentally slap myself as my brain finally catches up with my mouth.

"Details, spill now" Simon barks at me.

I feign innocence "What the great gossip that is Simon Hanson doesn't know Catty Bitch is an unfaithful girlfriend. Oooh I know something you don't know" I sing teasingly.

"Details now Darcy, spill" Simon says in all don't mess with me sternness. I pull my tongue out at him for spoiling my fun causing Clayton and Shelley to chuckle.

"As far as I know there have been three occasions" I say pompously.

"Three!" Shelley and Simon chorus in disbelief.

"That I know of" I confirm.

"So there could be more" Shelley says incredulously.

"Could be" I say speculatively shrugging one of my shoulders.

"So how do you know of these three occasions and the Queen of Gossip here doesn't?" Clayton asks pointing at Simon.

I smile. One, because Simon practically preens at his new nickname and two, Clayton is as curious as my friends are.

"The three I know of is because they all happened to be my dates" I state matter of fact. Shelley and Simon gape at my openness in front of Clayton "each of them told me. Caroline came on to them and they didn't pass up the opportunity. Then during pillow talk she told them she didn't want to break up my relationship with them but was up for being the other woman. The guys that told me were convinced she was a bunny boiler. I thanked them for their honesty and told them she was" when everyone stopped laughing I continue "I also know she propositioned two others" everyone's eyebrows rose in further surprise "Harry told me about them because on both occasions he overheard her"

"So considering your dates" Simon finger quoted dates "you at most went out with the same guy no more than three times, she must have hit on them pretty much on your first outing with them"

"Yep" I say round a mouthful of food "that's how Harry came to know. On each occasion we'd been in Gino's and he overheard her hitting on them and in his words practically from the minute they sat down, so he eavesdropped. On the second occasion he heard her he decided to tell me but I already knew about two of the guys she'd slept with by then" I look at my friends shocked faces "I didn't say anything because it just didn't seem right" a derisive snort escapes me "actually it's probably got more to do with I didn't want to admit those guys had jumped straight into bed with a skank because I wouldn't. Anyway I didn't tell Harry either" I direct that at Simon because I know he will pull Harry up about it at some point.

"Is there any possibility Catty Bitch knows or even suspects that you know about her indiscretions?" asks Clayton.

I shrug "I've no idea. The only way is if she saw or spoke to those guys again and they told her they had told me"

"Are you thinking Catty Bitch is being malicious to Skye to provoke her into an argument hoping Skye reveals what she knows as a way to find out for definite what Skye knows" Shelley asks Clayton.

"It's a possibility" says Clayton nodding. I give him points for understanding what Shelley has just said.

"Well I don't care. She is the one with the problem. I've better things to do and think about so let's change the subject" I say with finality.

Instead the buzzer went startling all of us. I get up to answer. It's Mr C's men for my cases, they're early. Turns out they'd arranged it with Macy and she'd messaged me only I haven't looked at my phone all day. With Clayton's help I get Paul's cases from his quarters but I really think he just wants to have a nosey around and he confirms my suspicion when I offer to give him a tour and he jumps at it.

I have the whole of the top floor actually I own the building although it isn't common knowledge as it's under a company name for tax purposes.

The building is in a nice neighbourhood and not far from Central Park. It doesn't have the coveted park view but real estate in this area is in big demand. When I bought the building over four years ago it had been derelict for a long time and needed a lot of TLC. So I took it on as a restoration project with the intention to sell only I fell in love with it and whenever I come home I renew the love affair and I always feel a sense of achievement when I look at the building.

"Wow this is very impressive, so what's your landlord like?"

"Erm" I grimace "I own the building, so I guess you could say the landlord is witty, incredibly funny, highly intelligent, fantastic, kind and generous"

Clayton looks at me open mouthed. I reach up and push his chin up so his mouth shuts with an audible snap "Sorry, I just wasn't expecting you to say that. You took me by complete surprise. Although I should be used to it by now, you've been doing it all week"

"Got to keep you on your toes" I wink cheekily at him.

"Oh you've been doing that all right" Clayton chuckles.

Back in the living room Simon and Shelley are bickering about which film to watch.

"What time is Phil coming over?" I ask Shelley as I scan through my phone messages.

"About four but it's more likely to be closer to five as he's gone to help his Dad at the yard, why?"

"Macy's going to order the pizza's so she wants to know what time and which pizza does everyone want" I continue to read her message "also what preference on wine or other drinks to get"

Whilst I take everyone's order and text Macy back Clayton out of genuine interest asks Shelley "So what does Phil's Dad do?"

Clayton already knows Phil is an accountant and he did my books. It delights me he's taking such an interest in their lives, could it be he just wants to impress me by being cordial towards them. Oh hell what does it matter? In fifteen hours I'll be on a plane on my way to Russia.

Shelley came to the end of her explanation of the kind of waste management Phil's Dad handles as I get a final text back from Macy.

"Okay that's the pizzas ordered. Macy will be here about five with the wine and beer. So what film are we watching?"

Simon holds up Pirates of the Caribbean and Lord of the Rings.

"Pirates" Shelley and I say together "we can all ogle Johnny" I say then look at Clayton "you can too if you want"

He laughs and reaches for me pulling and tucking me into his side. I snuggle in as Simon puts on the film. About quarter of the way into the film soft snores come from Shelley's end of the sofa, looking over at Simon sat in the lazy boy he has his eyes closed. I debate whether or not if he's asleep. As if reading my mind Clayton murmurs "He fell asleep about ten minutes into the film"

"I'm getting a drink do you want one?" I say getting up.

Clayton's hand travels down my back and lingers on my butt sending a sudden surge of desire through me.

"Yes please" Clayton's eye darken, oh my! What is he thinking?

On my way to the kitchen I make a detour and grab blankets and put one over Shelley and another over Simon then went into the kitchen and put the kettle on to make tea. I bend down to rummage around in the cupboard for the box of tea bags. I shoot up when I feel a hand on my butt.

"Sorry didn't mean to make you jump but I couldn't resist, you bent over is just too tempting" Clayton says with a wicked smile and not looking in the least bit sorry.

"Humph" I make in response and turn to bend back down to resume my search, within seconds Clayton's hand is on my butt again.

"Christ your ass is gorgeous" he says rubbing his hand in big circular movements then up and down. Oh sweet Jesus I'm getting wet. I realize I've stopped looking for, what was it again? Sod it! who cares! I'm lost to the sensations and his hand. I moan in pleasure.

"Like that baby?" Clayton's raspy voice is rough with his own desire.

"Yes" I manage to groan as I feel his hand move to the waist band of my yoga pants, pulling them down to bare my butt. I rise and alter my position. Resting my arms on the counter top I thrust my backside out, moving my feet to hip width to give him better access.

"Oh you naughty girl" Clayton purrs and slaps me lightly. Although it isn't a hard slap I'm surprised by how much it excites me. Clayton continues to rub in slow circular and up and down motions over each butt cheek going down to the juncture of my thighs and back to my lower back.

I wriggle and push back in to his hand. Clayton's chuckle is low and sensuous resonating in my core at the sin it promises.

"You want me to take you from behind, here in the kitchen while your friends sleep in the living room" he lightly slaps me again when I don't answer "yes or no naughty girl"

"Yes please"

Hell I want him badly and I'm past caring. Wow! Does this make me an exhibitionist? Clayton steps behind me grabbing my hips and pulling me back on to his. I can feel his hard length through the rough material of his jeans against my butt.

"Are you sure baby, because I will. It's going to be hard and fast" I groan at the images his words create in my mind "you will need to be quiet baby unless you want an audience. Tell me what you want"

"You, I want you now, please" I whisper my voice betraying my need.

Clayton steps away from me and pulls my pants down lifting one leg out of the trouser so he can widen my stance unhindered. His hand cups my sex and I bite down on a loud groan.

"You are so wet and ready for me" he says in wonder as he slips a finger inside me, moving in and out.

"Take me now" I beg "I want your cock in me, I want to feel you"

"How can I refuse when you speak so eloquently" he chuckles.

The sound of his zipper coming down sends a fresh wave of need racing through me, anticipation making me wetter. I feel his cock brush against me as he pushes his pants down. I look over my shoulder and watch as he takes his cock in his hand and strokes himself, shifting my gaze to his face I can see his need is as evident as mine.

"Ready baby"

I nod, guiding his cock to my entrance he pushes slowly in. I moan as quietly as I can.

"Shhh, quiet remember" Clayton whispers "tell me to stop if it makes you too sore or hurts"

I nod it's all I can do. Clayton thrusts forward sliding deeper, pulls back out slowly, placing his hands on my hips he pulls my hips back on to him as his thrusts forward.

"Oh yes" I scream in my head, the delicious fullness and stretch. Clayton stays still giving me time to adjust. I clench my muscles around his cock loving the feeling of him deep inside me. A quiet groan escapes Clayton so I squeeze my muscles harder, he hisses in a sharp breath.

"Hold on baby"

On hearing the soft command I brace my hands on the edge of the counter and lock my arms as Clayton withdraws then slams into me. Holy fuck he's deep and it feels amazing. Clayton starts to move setting a fast rhythm, each time he enters me he pulls my hips back to meet each thrust. How in the hell I keep quiet I'll never know. I want to scream and shout as pleasure shoots around my body, I want everyone to know how amazing it feels. Clayton reaches round and cups my sex, massaging my clit. I'm helpless. I throw back my head, a low groan escaping me as my climax builds.

Clayton continues massaging and thrusting as he whispers to me "I can feel how greedy your beautiful tight cunt is for me" my muscles clench down harder on his cock "oh yes baby do it again"

I do and my orgasm starts to ripple through me. Clayton pounds into me hard three more times causing me to reach a shattering silent climax as he finds his own release. He collapses against me, wrapping his arms around me, both of us gulping in air trying to get our breathing under control.

Moving my hair over my shoulder Clayton kisses the back of my neck and pulls out of me "Stay there baby"

I watch as he grabs some tissues and gently cleans' me then helps me back in my pants. I love that he is so considerate seeing to me first before himself. As soon as my clothes are back in place I help him, taking great delight as I slowly put his cock back in his boxers and very nice Calvin Klein's they are. Then slowly refasten his jeans letting my fingers brush against his hard again cock as I pull the zipper up, I let my fingers linger and trace the outline. With a deep throaty laugh Clayton removes my hand and putting my arm behind my back bends me backwards, holding the back of my head with his other hand he kisses me soundly. My free hand sinks into his thick wavy hair.

"If your friends weren't here, right now I would have you naked and fucking the hell out of you again" Clayton says against my lips.

"Well we've christened my bed and now the kitchen, how about I kick them out and we can christen the sofa" I chuckle.

"Minx" he says bringing us upright and starts kissing me again. God I could spend hours kissing him. I wrap my arms around his neck as Clayton's hands grasp my butt lifting me off the floor. I wrap my legs around his hips and we groan in unison as our tongues intertwine tasting, licking and teasing.

"Perleeze get a room guys" Simon drawls.

"My house, there's the door" I retort against Clayton's lips.

"Yeah right sweet cheeks" Simon says heading for the fridge and getting a can of soda.

The buzzer went making me forget my come back retort. Clayton releases his hold on me letting me slide down his hard body "Oooh I like that ride I want to do it again" my inner goddess purrs. I answer the intercom and let Phil in. Thirty seconds later Macy buzzes.

Phil and Macy didn't show any surprise at seeing Clayton which led me to suspect the jungle drums are in full working order so I didn't feel the need to explain away his presence.

By seven we're all lounging around after eating too much pizza. Clayton picks me up and sits me on his lap much to the amusement of my friends although none of them say anything. It's a lovely relaxing evening watching a film no-one really pays any attention to, drinking wine and beer with good natured banter and teasing. At ten with the exception of Clayton everyone has left. Simon and Shelley making me promise a million times I would text them as soon as I land in Moscow.

"Do you want an early night, since you've got to be up early?" I can hear the consideration in Clayton's voice and I feel it in his touch as he gently rubs my leg.

"Well since I can catch up on sleep during a nine or ten hour flight I thought we could christen the sofa" I smile coquettishly.

I didn't see Clayton move, the next thing I know I'm flat on my back being pressed into the sofa cushions by Clayton's weight and being kissed senseless.

I shiver as the early morning breeze swirls around me. Clayton steps closer and put his arms around me to warm me up. Oh I'm going to miss this. I snuggle in to him. Paul pulls up in the SUV neither of us make a move.

"Time to go" Clayton says softly.

"Yeah" I look up at him memorising his face, dark blue eyes, arched eyebrows, straight nose, sensuous lips, chiselled jaw. His arms tighten around me as he bends and kisses me goodbye, long, slow and toe curling. Memories of last night come flooding back, not only did we christen the sofa but the reclining lazy boy chair, living room floor, kitchen counter and the shower twice and of course the bed. I'm surprised I can walk.

"Excuse me Miss Darcy" Paul says apologetically "we need to get going"

I break the kiss "Okay thanks Paul" he climbs back into the car.

Clayton doesn't let me go which makes me smile "What?" he says bemused.

"You need to let go of me" I say softly.

"What, oh yes" his arms tighten instead of relaxing. I chuckle and kiss him, breaking it before I get lost in him again.

"Goodbye Clayton" I whisper and move, sighing he releases me and leans to open the car door.

"Safe travels" he says helping me in then he runs his fingers down my cheek "include me in the group text to let me know you've arrived, please" I nod. He kisses me once more "look after her for me Paul"

That surprises the hell out of me. If Paul is offended he doesn't show it "Yes sir" he replies respectfully.

Clayton's gaze never leaves mine "Bye" I whisper, he kisses me again then steps back and closes the door.

Half way to the airport I realize he didn't say goodbye.

Chapter Eight

CLAYTON

What in the hell possessed me to make this trip to London, I wonder for the millionth time. I could've done all of this via video conference. Oh for fucks sake stop grouching I tell myself, if it wasn't so good a business deal I wouldn't be still here.

I attended Chuck's presentation two days ago with a group of other businessmen or I should say potential investors. Chuck is hoping to put together a consortium for this venture. I'm meeting with him this afternoon to give him my final decision, which will be good news for him depending on a few things so I'm going to make him work to get his hands on my money.

"Mr Blake may I get you a drink" the leggy bleached blonde PA asks licking her Botox plump lips, as I sit down at the boardroom table I undo my jacket her eyes raking my body giving away her lustful thoughts. Christ I'm so sick of that, before Skye I would have hit on her and had meaningless sex, not now.

"No thank you" my reply sounds curt even to my ears.

"Mr Johnson will be with you shortly" giving me one more lustful lingering look, she left when I give a nod to acknowledge what she's said.

Over the last five weeks I've thrown myself in to work, a snort escapes me what an existence. My whole routine has been work, exercise—a lot, eat, a little sleep and more work all in that order. My mother had done her damnedest to fix me up on dates with various women she knew or their daughters. After the forth horrendous so called date I had enough and completely lost it with my mother and her meddling. I shouted, cursed and shouted louder at her, she cried. Feeling an utter shit I apologised and mother went back to trying to fix me up. I stopped taking her calls and refused to see her. Joshua and Andrew ended up being mediators, now at best our relationship could be described as strained.

The frustrating thing is I couldn't explain to my mother that the women she is fixing me up with are all empty headed, self-centred bimbo's and their interests in life went no further than shopping for the latest fashion and getting the latest beauty treatment because mother would see nothing wrong with all of that. I want intellectual conversation, to be able to discuss business ideas and problems, debate the ethics and morals of what is happening in the world. Coming to London has been a means of escape.

I sit up straighter in the chair as the thought whispers through my mind. Why would I want to escape? Because you want to be faithful to Skye my unconscious whispers again. Crap. Memories of her swamp me, the conversations, her laugh, smell, taste, feel of her in my arms. My body starts to respond to the memories, my chest hurt, tightening, I rub at it. This is a regular occurrence whenever I think of her.

I haven't had sex since she left and this is the longest period in my life I've ever gone without it. I had plenty of offers and I took some of them up but when it came to doing the deed I couldn't go through with it. Even kissing another woman felt wrong, hence the reason for losing it with my mother. I didn't want to pollute myself or what Skye and I could have when she returned. I want to be able to stand in front of her and honestly say there has been no one since her, she is the only one for me.

I don't know why but I have a strong feeling she wouldn't be with anyone else, stop kidding yourself of course you fucking know, she'd been celibate for six years and the chances of her jumping into bed with the next guy who came along are nil, or so you hope, my mind snidely whispers. My stomach roils at the thought, please don't let that happen, I send the silent prayer up to whoever's listening.

It's killing me not being in touch with her. I miss her humour, her insight and the way she views the world. She kept her promise and sent me a text letting me know she'd arrived in Moscow. I accidently on purpose bumped in to Simon a few times and unashamedly asked after Skye. It was a relief to hear she is well and according to the information from Macy doing nothing but work all hours on the commission. I also got up dates from Mr C as we're still negotiating and collaborating on a business venture together. Mr C really does view Skye as being part of his family so I'm reassured she's in good hands.

I thought back to the Sunday morning of her departure, how I couldn't let go of her, you didn't want to my unconscious mind points out. Yeah, okay I admit I didn't want to let her go. Hell I couldn't even say the word goodbye or a variation of it. It just seemed too permanent, too final. I was afraid if I said it I'd never see her again. That scared me. I've never suffered or experienced grief from the ending of a relationship before but I sure as fuck know it now and five weeks on it isn't getting any easier. The real kicker is the fact we hadn't officially been an item and I'm a complete mess, could I last another seven weeks?

"Hey buddy, sorry to keep you waiting" Chuck entering the office snaps me out of my ruminating. I stand up and shake his hand mumbling what I have no idea "hope you don't mind' he waves his phone "but I'm waiting for an important call" he laughs heartily "hell who am I kidding.

It's not work related but it's a birthday surprise for Nessa. You're still coming tonight?"

Nessa's thirtieth birthday dinner party at his house "Of course I wouldn't miss if for the world" I give him a big warm smile that I don't feel.

"Excellent, if I can pull this surprise off it'll be Christmas for me every day for the next six months" he pauses "better make it twelve months, what with the baby an' all" he laughs at his own joke "anyway to business" he claps and rubs his hands together.

For the next couple of hours we thrash out the finer details and things are drawing to a conclusion when his phone rings, apologising he picks it up.

"Please give me some good news" he says in a way of greeting, he hummed and ahh'd for a few minutes as he listens to the other person "We're sitting down at seven….. yep….. huh, huh….. shall I send a car…. sure…. okay" a long pause "fantastic" he shouts his face splitting into a big grin as he punches the air. No prizes for guessing he's pulled off the surprise "tell her I can't wait to see her again and I know Nessa is going to freak." He hangs up looking very pleased with himself and smiling broadly "Man, tonight is going to be awesome" he says rubbing his hands together in excited agitation.

"Christmas every day for the next twelve months by any chance" I say stating the obvious and smiling broadly.

"Dude, I've pulled off the near impossible and got an old friend of Nessa's to come tonight. She is flying in especially for her party"

His excitement is infectious, I nearly ask him what is so special about this friend but resist because undoubtedly the match making instinct will kick in and I sure as fuck can do without that, instead I bring us back to business.

The screeching laugh grates on my nerves and I do my best not to wince as it assaults my eardrums. I've only been here fifteen minutes and I'm already regretting my decision to come to this dinner party. The women are circling like fucking vultures around me fortunately Chuck comes to the rescue in the nick of time.

"Clayton, come with me. Let me show you around the place and get you a drink" he says grabbing my elbow "excuse us ladies" Chuck gives them a dazzling smile under his breath he mutters "sorry about that had to take an emergency call. Nessa's friend is going to be half an hour late. Okay what would you like to drink"

Chuck steers me out of the living room into a spacious hallway where we meet Nessa coming from the direction of the kitchen.

"Clayton, it's so good of you to come" she says greeting me warmly. I hug her gently mindful of the baby bump.

"You look absolutely stunning, happy birthday" I kiss her cheek. I like Chuck's wife she's down to earth and a genuinely lovely person and she makes my friend incredibly happy.

Nessa laughs putting her hand on her belly and rubs "I always wondered what it was that I liked about you and now I know. I feel like the backend of a bus yet you make me feel like a super model" turning to her husband "the chef is ready to serve dinner, lets round everyone up"

The dining room is a good size and decorated tastefully with a crystal chandelier being the main focal point of the room. The dining table has twelve place settings except one is empty between Nessa and me. Nessa doesn't question the empty seat however it didn't stop one woman stage whispering very loudly how rude it is to be late. Her partner hushes her to be quiet. Chuck has no qualms stating loudly the missing guest has been delayed and is on route.

I notice during the first course Chuck has his phone on the table; he's checking it frequently and sending messages. This earns him a few frowns but he pays no attention to them nor does he apologise. That's what I like about Chuck he doesn't care what people think. If he's doing something he considers important and if you didn't like it you can go fuck yourself and he'll tell you to as well. The servers start to clear the first course plates away when the doorbell rings.

"Nessa my love" Chuck beams at her "will you answer the door please"

Before she can respond the loud whispering woman shot to her feet "I'll get it Chuck. Nessa needs to rest" she says this rather condescendingly.

"Sit down Samantha" Chuck enunciates each word almost threateningly and it stops Samantha in her tracks "Nessa will answer the door"

Nessa rose to her feet with a questioning look on her face to her husband. Chuck smiles back warmly and nods a go on signal.

Everyone is quiet listening to Nessa's retreating footsteps down the hall, the clicking of the locks being released and the door opening. A piercing scream rents the air. It has everyone to their feet in an instant some heading for the door with panicked looks. I look at Chuck as he walks past grinning widely and gesturing everyone back. Sitting back down I realize the surprise birthday present and guest has finally arrived.

A sexy throaty laugh drifts to my ears. My body stirs and my cock hardens at the sound. Nooo my mind calls out in exaggerated disbelief, it can't be. Only one person affects me like that and she's in Moscow. What are the chances of meeting two people who can have the same effect on me? A billion to one! A trillion!

Chuck comes back in the room looking smug and mightily pleased with himself "Ladies and gentlemen our final guest has just arrived. Please take your seats the ladies will be in shortly"

Five minutes later Nessa came in with… Skye!

My heart and world stop. Nessa is beaming from ear to ear, her mascara smudged from tears. Skye has her arm wrapped around Nessa and her attention is on her friend so she hasn't noticed me yet. It gives me the chance to compose myself. Skye is even more stunningly beautiful than I remember. My memories haven't done her justice.

"Everyone" Nessa calls out her voice wavering with emotion "I would like to introduce a very special friend of mine Skye Darcy"

Skye turns her attention to the room and sees me. I watch as surprise sweeps through her body and she collects herself quickly as Nessa introduces each person as she guides Skye to her seat next to me. I stand as Nessa says "And this is"

"Mr Blake" Skye finishes in her husky voice giving me a blinding smile that fries my brain.

"Miss Darcy" I say smiling like a goofy idiot, taking her hand and kissing the back of it. I fight every urge to throw her on the table and fuck her senseless. I feel the electricity surging and thrumming between us. I take in a deep breath drawing her scent into my lungs. My cock already hard goes agonisingly harder. Fucking hell I've missed feeling like this "so very good to see you again" my voice purrs.

"You know each other?" Chuck and Nessa say in shocked, surprised unison.

"Yes, you could say our paths crossed a few times in May when I was in New York" Skye chuckles taking her seat.

During the main course I watch and listen to Skye as she fills Nessa in on her recent stay in Moscow, how Chuck contacted her three weeks ago and she worked around the clock to finish the work early in order to be here. It turned out to be really eleventh hour stuff. Chuck's phone call this afternoon was from Macy informing him Skye had literally finished the painting and was getting onto a plane. Skye pulled out all the stops just for her friend and to make her birthday extra special. My admiration for Skye went off the scale.

"What is it you actually do?" asks loud whisper woman. I don't like the tone of voice she uses. I feel my hackles rise she reminds me too much of Catty Bitch from Hell.

"I'm an artist" Skye replies politely.

"Will I know your work?" says the condescending bitch. I decide to rename loud whisper to Catty Bitch Two.

"Unless you are into the Fantasy and Sci Fi genre then it's unlikely" Skye seems completely unfazed.

"No I'm not. I suppose you make some sort of living out of it" Catty Bitch Two says haughtily.

I seriously want to slap her, my hands clench into fists as I imagine doing it.

"You could say that" says Skye calmly and reaches out covering my hand with hers and giving a gentle squeeze silently telling me she can handle it.

"So out of interest how much do you make a year?" Catty Bitch Two causes a few people to tut at her faux pas. Catty Bitch Two doesn't take a blind bit of notice.

"Last year I made seventy five" Skye pauses and Catty Bitch jumps in.

"Seventy five thousand that's not bad going I suppose" Catty Bitch gives a fake laugh as she reaches for her wine and takes a drink.

"No seventy five million pounds not dollars" Skye says slowly and coolly enunciating each word so there is no way of mistaking what she has said.

Catty Bitch Two chokes on her wine, spraying it everywhere. Game, set and match. Skye winks at me setting me and everyone else off laughing. Oh how I've missed this woman. After that and for the rest of the meal Catty Bitch Two remains quiet and rather subdued.

"So tell me what did you get for your birthday" Skye asks Nessa. When Nessa finished giving a rundown of presents Skye whistles. "Good haul girl. So my present you'll get tomorrow. Chuck" Skye calls down the table when he looks at her she asks "are we all set?" he grins and nods. Turning back to Nessa she continues "okay tomorrow I will be picking you up at nine thirty and you're going to play being my assistant for a couple of hours. I have a very famous client flying in for a consultation briefing. We are meeting him at the airport" Skye grins wickedly.

"Who is it" Nessa asks her eyes sparkling "please, please tell me. Pregnant woman" pointing at her stomach to emphasise her point "suspense is not good for my blood pressure"

"Ha, ha, ha, good try" Skye teases "alright I'll give you a clue. Remember years ago we all got drunk and created the free pass shag list"

That gets everyone's attention and all conversations stop. Chuck laughs at Nessa's expression, a mix of shock and embarrassment. "Can you remember who you put down?" he asks. Nessa nods slowly and Chuck's grin gets wider.

"Anyway" Skye continues bringing Nessa's attention back to her "more importantly do you remember who you put down as number one" Nessa's eyes widen "yep it's him. Only you can't shag him. I promised Chuck I would make sure you behaved yourself" Skye deadpans.

Nessa is in utter shock her mouth gaping open. Chuck roars laughing at her stunned expression.

"Oh come on, who is it?" one of the women wails, a few others murmur they want to know as well. I must admit I'm more interested in finding out about this free pass shag list. Did Skye have one? A surge of jealousy sweeps through me at the possibility she could have a list of men she wanted to shag.

Nessa is too shell shocked to answer. Neither Skye nor Chuck succumbs to pressure to divulge the identity of the mystery famous person.

"After the meeting we are going to the Ivy for lunch and after that to the spa for pampering in readiness for the ultra-posh charity function we are going to. Shelley has created your evening gown and it's your birthday present from her and Simon by the way. Chuck has arranged Ella's care for the whole day and night. How's that sound?" finishes Skye.

My heart swells at the thought Skye has put into making a memorable day for her friend. I even have a lump in my throat as Nessa with fresh tears in her eyes gets up and hugs her friend whispering thank you.

Fuck! I love this woman. I know instantly in this moment I always have loved Skye. I've fallen fast and hard, hook, line and sinker. She makes me whole and complete. I hadn't realized until this moment that for the last five weeks I felt as if I've been missing part of myself. She is my soul mate. Shit my mother saw it that Thursday night at the gallery, her words coming back to me.

"You've got her bad you just don't know it yet"

I know now. Fuck did I…

SKYE

After the meal ended everyone gathers in the living room making small talk. Clayton is in deep conversation with Chuck but his eyes never leave me as I move around the room and it gives me quite a thrill. The attraction is still there and just as strong. I switch off from the inane conversation around me and enjoy the unobstructed view of Clayton.

Over the last five weeks I've thought about him often. Wondering what he was doing or who my snippy side would throw in whenever I got all rose tinted glasses about what could happen when I got back to New York.

Don't kid yourself girlie he's a womaniser. Love them and leave them. Remember protect your heart, all are reality check favourites. I imagine my snippy side to be like one of my old prep school teachers. Rail thin, harsh features, hair scrapped back into a severe tight bun, no boobs and mean.

When I saw Clayton in the dining room I nearly passed out in shock. If Nessa and I didn't have our arms wrapped around each other they would be still scrapping me up off the floor. How in the hell I got to my seat I'll never know but I'm thankful I was coherent at least and my brain hadn't completely fried or left to go on vacation.

As soon as Clayton was out of earshot I quizzed Nessa how she and Chuck knew him. It truly is a small world and a wonder we haven't crossed paths sooner. It got me thinking about how many times we must have come close to encountering each other and wondering would we still have had the same reaction to each other. God this is making my head hurt.

I stifle a yawn. It's been a long day, hell it's been a long three weeks. Since Chuck emailed me about Nessa's thirtieth birthday how could I not pull out all the stops to be here for my good friend?

Nessa had been our neighbour in the apartment building we rented when we first moved to New York. She took the three of us under her wing, really took care of us and became a big sister. As careers took off and we went our separate ways we kept in touch. We text or emailed most days and I always made sure I spoke with her once a month. I'd also been bridesmaid along with Shelley at their wedding.

I look over at Chuck and smile, he is the iconic image of the good all American boy. Blonde haired and brown eyes, sun kissed skin, straight white teeth. He's a big man although not as tall as Clayton and his physique is not as toned but the guy loves my friend in fact he worships the ground she walks on. They are soul mates and he willingly gave up everything to move half way around the world for her career.

My phone vibrates bringing me out of my reverie. I pull it out of my jacket pocket to see I have several missed calls from Macy and Simon. Hmmm something is up. I excuse myself and head into the conservatory. Paul has also texted saying he has checked us in at the hotel and he's on his way back. He would wait in the car until I was ready to leave.

I ring Macy first, she's still in Moscow tying up loose ends then she will be heading straight to Paris where Paul and I will meet up with her.

"Hi Macy you okay" I'm concerned because of the number of times she has rung.

"Yes I'm fine. I just need to go over some things with you before you call it a night and they can't wait until morning what with the time differences. So I've had Giles on" she says getting straight down to business that's one of the many things I like about her "they definitely want you for the Vegas Fantasy and Sci Fi convention. He's pushing for a meet and greet with the fans. I've got to go back with an answer ASAP so you up for it?"

"Sure why not! it's been a long time since I last did an appearance plus it'll keep Paul on his toes" I say laughing because I know he'll hate it.

"I'll let you tell him" Macy says chuckling with me "and I'll let you know what I negotiate for an appearance fee"

I don't do many appearances they are fun but also scary as hell at the same time. Some fans could get a little too enthusiastic.

"One last thing, I keep getting calls and emails from David Smith of Phoenix PR" I feel a prickly tingly sensation across my skin, I look up at my reflection in the conservatory glass and see Clayton standing behind me in the doorway watching and waiting. My knees go weak again "hello you still there?" Macy shouts bringing my attention back to her.

"Sorry Macy. What does he want?" for some reason the name rings a bell and I can't place it.

"He wants to know when you will be coming in to sign the papers"

"Papers" I frown "what papers" I'm at a loss.

"Something about him being your new PR agent. I didn't know you're getting rid of Simon"

I sense her curiosity and she's probably wondering why I haven't told her about it, which is very unlike me because I tell her everything to do with business and this is definitely business.

"I'm not" I say distracted as I try to remember. Suddenly the old brain kicks out the memory "Oh shit, I completely forgot to tell you" I exclaim.

"What you are getting rid of Simon" Macy squeaks in shock.

"No, no not at all" I laugh "Simon dropped a clanger. Whilst drunk he set up the meeting I had back in May with that stupid prat. Long story short I agreed to play bad cop and it completely slipped my mind"

"Hmmm and the distraction was called Clayton Blake" Macy laughs heartily, good job she can't see me blush.

"Anyway I agreed to save Simon's ass by playing hard ball and telling prat face I'm not looking for a new agent or I didn't think we were suited, something along those lines. I was intending to brainstorm with you a plan of attack before we left"

"No problem I'll deal with him. How ferocious can I go?"

"Nuclear if he's being a pompous git" I'm grinning because I know Macy can be a Rottweiler when let off the leash figuratively speaking "Simon's been trying to reach me and I'm guessing it's about this, will you call him and tell him first what you are going to say" I try to stifle a yawn on the last bit and fail miserably so it comes out garbled. Good job Macy is fluent in garbled.

"On that note I will say goodbye and goodnight. Enjoy London"

"Good night and safe journey to Paris"

As I end the call a pair of large warm hands circles my waist. I smile. Clayton. I turn to face him staying within his hands.

"Hi" we both murmur softly.

Clayton bends slowly and I meet him half way rising up onto my tip toes. Our lips meet. Heat instantly ignites and courses through my blood. My arms wrap around his neck and my fingers tangle in his silky soft wavy hair as his arms wrap around me pulling me close into his gloriously hard body. I melt and the kiss deepens. Our tongues caress and entwine reacquainting each other. Want and need explodes, the muscles between my legs clench hungrily, the feeling of his arousal against my lower belly making me even wetter. When the kiss finishes we are both breathing hard and Clayton hugs me tighter. God I've missed being in his arms.

"Christ I've missed you" his lovely gravelly voice rasps in my ear sending shivers down my spine.

"I know" I laugh and pull back to see his expression of surprised confusion "what, did you really think Simon and Mr C wouldn't tell me that you asked after me" I tease.

"Busted" chuckles Clayton.

Boy I've missed that lovely sound as well. I reach up and kiss him "I missed you too" I say against his lips. Clayton groans and deepens the kiss again. We are both panting heavily when the kiss breaks.

"Where are you staying" Clayton asks putting his forehead to mine.

"The Dorchester"

"Really, seriously" a wide smile spreads across his beautiful face.

"Ha! From the look on your face and correct me if I'm wrong but my guess is you're staying there as well" I say matching his smile.

"You would be right" he drawls seductively as he runs the back of his fingers gently down the side of my face.

"Want to get out of here" I purr.

"Why Miss Darcy are you planning on seducing me?" Clayton drawls using a southern accent.

"Hell yeah" I say enthusiastically "and I'm starving"

"So am I, want to split?" his rich voice promises untold decadence.

For an answer I grab his hand and pull him after me out of the conservatory and needless to say we make our excuses and leave.

Clayton's car and driver, Bruce, are outside and no sign of Paul. Climbing into Clayton's car I ring him, he's stuck in traffic. I tell him who

I'm with and to return to the hotel and I'd see him at eight in the morning. The instant I hang up Clayton pulls me onto his lap and kisses me senseless. His hands roaming my body it's almost as if he can't believe I'm real and he has to constantly check. I break the kiss just so I can breathe.

"Wow, you really have missed me" I tease.

Stroking my cheek Clayton sighs "Yes, I have" he answers honestly and simply "Tell me how was Moscow"

"Not much to tell. I painted, ate, slept and painted. In fact if it hadn't been for Macy I wouldn't have ate or slept" I chuckle "she is such a mother hen"

I remembered the times she'd stood over me and watched me eat and how at three in the morning pried the brush out of my hand and frog marched me to bed.

"When do you fly out to Paris?" Clayton asks squeezing me tighter to him.

"Sunday afternoon" I whisper "how long are you in London for and what brought you here. I know it wasn't Nessa's birthday"

"I'm here on business. Chuck is putting together a consortium for a venture" he shrugs "it looks promising so I came for the proposal presentation. I've preliminarily signed up. Everything should be finalised tomorrow so I will be heading home on Sunday" he pauses as if considering what he was going to say, he clears his throat "this function tomorrow night would you mind if I come too"

A thrill shoots through me "No not at all" I'm pleased he's asked "in fact I would be rather disappointed if you didn't"

By pure coincidence our hotel rooms are on the same floor, as I step out of the elevator Clayton tackles me, he would have done it sooner had the elevator been empty. Sweeping me into his arms I squeal in surprise.

"Shhh baby" Clayton admonishes in his sexy as hell voice "the last thing I want is Paul barrelling out of his room to protect you. I do value my life"

"Oops sorry" I try to look contrite and fail miserably so I kiss him instead which makes walking down the corridor very interesting.

We eventually make it to my room. Clayton kicks the door shut and literally throws me on the bed. He stands over me breathing hard, anticipation at what is to come has me squirming and wetter. Clayton backs away.

What the hell. Why is he moving away from me, we should be ripping each other's clothes off and the look on his face tells me he wants me, badly, his whole body is shaking with need. His hands clench and unclench. I rise up on to my elbows.

"What's wrong" I can hear anxiety and concern in my whispered question.

"I'm sorry baby. I want you so much, too much" his voice is a low growl and saturated with desire "if I come at you now in the state I'm in, I'm going to come at you hard and fast. I'm going to be buried in you balls deep before you take your next breath"

Holy shit he's scared of hurting and frightening me. Yet his words make me hotter and wetter. Sod this I want him balls deep and hard. In reply I kick off my shoes, lay back and undo the button and zip of my slacks "I can take it, hell yes"

True to his word Clayton moves fast. My slacks are off and my panties disintegrate as he rips them off me in one swift action. Before I can blink he is buried deep inside me. Both of us curse and groan as he enters me. Claiming my mouth he starts to move in and out, two slow strokes then he loses control and hammers me into the mattress. Animalistic and carnal he claims me body and soul. I'm lost to him, he owns me. I meet his thrusts wanting to take him even deeper, my muscles clenching tight around him. I'm delirious at the feel of him. I feel his cock thicken filling me even more. His primal need for me drives the swell of my rapidly building climax ever closer.

"Come with me baby. I can't hold on" Clayton growls out his command, two deep thrusts, Clayton throws back his head "Fuck, Skye" he bellows, his whole body stiffens. I feel his cock jerk and pulse as he releases inside me and it sends me over the edge. We hold each other as our orgasms roll through us hard in wave after wave.

As consciousness seeps in and the realization Clayton is still fully clothed and I'm naked from the waist down has the saying and meaning of "wham bam thank ma'am" bounce around my head and sets me off giggling.

Clayton lifts his head an amused puzzled smile on his face "Well that's a first, a woman having a fit of giggles on me after an orgasm"

"Wham bam thank you ma'am" is all I can get out before collapsing into fits of giggles again.

Clayton put his head down next to mine and joins in my laughter. After a few minutes the giggles subside and the kisses begin to get heated "I want to get you naked and explore" I say against Clayton's lips.

A deep rumble vibrates from his chest and he starts to move in jerky movements. He continues to kiss me and he's still inside me so his movements start to stimulate me making me gasp and groan. I realize he's taking his clothes off. Once his are off he removes the rest of mine then he starts to move in and out of me in slow languorous movements. I'm in heaven.

Kissing down my throat, the side of my neck and down to my breast Clayton catches my nipple with his teeth, gently tugging and teasing with his tongue, suckling. He's maddeningly slow, cognizance jolts through me. He's making up for the ferocity of earlier, he's making love to me showing me it isn't just about sex and I mean more to him. I'm not the only one who is falling hard and fast although I've already fallen.

I lose all sense of time as I absorb the feel of him deep inside me, his hard body, soft demanding lips and his wickedly talented tongue and fingers. I commit it all to memory. He is indolent yet diligent, the combination is mind blowing. I feel my climax build slowly and steadily.

"Faster, harder please" I beg but he continues to torture me with his slow steady pace, he wants this to last. He's setting the rules for the rest of the night. He whispers between kisses how he's missed me, my mind, my body, my taste and scent. He rolls his hips as he thrusts in to me; the spot he hits sends a surge of sensations racing through my body "again" I groan. He hits the spot again and again.

"Oh god Clayton" I cry out as my body tenses and releases my orgasm giving me a delightful sense of floating and soaring at the same time. Clayton continues his slow steady pace keeping my climax going and climbing ever higher.

He holds me close whispering in my ear "Keep coming for me baby, you feel so good" only then did he pick up the pace chasing his own release. When he climaxed he calls my name with adulation and reverence.

I fall asleep wrapped in his arms sated and boneless. I don't have the energy to go exploring.

Chapter Nine

CLAYTON

"Come on ladies, the car is here" Chuck shouts up the stairs.

I can see he's nervous or anxious about something. I give up trying to read his body language "You okay buddy?" I ask instead.

"Yeah" he says distractedly straightening an already straight bow tie then seems to check himself "it's just, well kind of" he pauses as his eyes flick to the stairs, anxious I decide "this is going to sound daft but the dress Nessa is wearing tonight Shelley had to make it without her knowing so there's been no fitting and I had to email all of Nessa's measurements" he barks out a laugh "I had to take them whilst she slept and that wasn't easy I'll tell you. Oh god I hope it fits"

Chuck went to the bar in the living room and pours himself a brandy, silently offering me one I decline.

"I hope that's the first and last until we get to the function" Nessa's voice came from behind me. I turn to see her standing in the doorway.

Nessa is positively glowing. Shelley is a truly talented fashion designer. The floor length gown emphasises her full pregnant body making her look sensuous and captivating. The russet color complementing her skin tone and up swept mahogany hair. I turn to look back at Chuck, the glass he raised to his lips stays suspended in mid-air, his eyes and mouth getting wider.

"Well what do you think" Nessa says giving a twirl.

Chuck put the glass down and walks over to his wife, the love shining out of his eyes makes my heart ache. He takes both her hands and kisses them.

"Wow. You look absolutely stunning my love" he says with reverence and awe, he kisses her forehead obviously not wanting to spoil her lipstick.

I turn away to give them some privacy then I see Skye. Oh my fucking god. She looks sensational. The off the shoulder floor length gown clings to her like a second skin, it is beyond classy. Shelley has out done all of her previous creations I'd seen Skye in. Her wild curly hair has been teased into a chignon exposing her slender neck. The blush pink of the satin material emphasises her English rose complexion. Skye has her ears pierced multiple times and I notice she is wearing small diamond studs where she normally wore silver hooped earrings; apart from the earrings she has no other jewellery. She didn't need any other adornments. Without prompting she twirls for me. She is perfection.

I went to her and copying Chuck I take her hands and kiss them. Otherwise I would throw her over my shoulder and head for the nearest bedroom. Fuck any room with a lockable door. I didn't say anything. I didn't need to. I can tell by the blush on her cheeks she could see what I want to do to her. I can feel the unmistakable thrum building between us.

"Right folks, shall we" Chuck says gesturing to the door.

After being at the venue for about an hour I decide I'm really going to enjoy tonight because Skye and I didn't know anyone which meant I have Skye all to myself. Chuck and Nessa are off networking. I was listening to Skye as she regaled the events of her meeting with the famous actor.

"Jason was brilliant with Nessa. I had warned him to behave and that she is pregnant but it didn't stop him being devilishly naughty" she laughs "his poor PR"

"Lillian" an elderly gentleman interrupts her, standing before us he looks intensely at Skye "it's good to see you"

Skye's demeanour changes instantly. Her face becomes blank and her eyes cold as stone, her whole body stiffens.

"I'm sorry you mistake me for someone else" her voice is cold, flat and emotionless, she turns to walk away.

Fuck what in the hell has just happened. It's as if someone has flipped a switch on her personality. I didn't say a word and start to follow her. The old man steps forward and grabs her arm.

"Lillian, please wait" his voice is a command even though the words are a request.

Why in god's name is he calling her Lillian. Skye spins round pure hatred and anger on her face the old man flinches even I take a step back.

"Lillian is dead" Skye spits through gritted teeth in a low angry voice "she no longer exists, she ceased to exist the day you turned your back on her. The day she needed you the most and you disowned her and kicked her out onto the street. Lillian died that day"

Fuck me this is her grandfather. The vehemence she spoke with scared the shit out of me. She is so cold with hatred I could see icicles form on the words she spoke and aggression rolls off her. I shiver.

Skye yanks her arm out of his grip. Paul suddenly materializes surprising me. I didn't even know he was here, damn the man is good.

"Keep this bastard away from me, break his fucking legs if you have to" Skye snarls the instruction to Paul.

Is it wrong to be turned on by the cold heartless bitch side of her? Before I could answer my own question the old guy blurts "I'm dying Lillian. I want to make amends"

Skye lets out a derisive laugh "And why the fuck should I care, but you know what. I'm glad, it couldn't happen to a nastier person, send me an invite to the funeral and I'll throw a fucking party on your grave as for making amends you're too fucking late. Eight years too fucking late. Rot in hell" Skye walks away with Paul shadowing her.

The old guy looks after her retreating back with pain, sadness and resignation on his face 'I deserved that' he says softly his voice full of sadness and regret then he left.

I find Skye at the bar downing a very large measure of liquor.

"Come dance with me" I bend and say low in her ear, taking her hand and gently tugging. She let me lead her to the dance floor and I wrap her in my arms.

Christ she is so tense her body is trembling. I try to relay through touch I'm here for her. Instinct is screaming at me to stay quiet to give her time and space to work out whatever is going through her head. At the end of the second dance Skye let out a long audible sigh and physically relaxes, sagging almost against me.

"Do you want to leave?" I keep my voice as soft as I can. I will give my left testicle to see her smile and be happy again. Skye shakes her head.

"It's Nessa's night. I don't want to spoil it for her"

Christ can this woman be any more perfect, she is putting her friend's feelings before her own needs.

"I'm sure Nessa would understand" I hedge.

"No" determination has her gathering her resolve "I'm not running away"

Shit I so want to ask her what she means by that but I bite my tongue now isn't the time nor the place to get into it.

"Shall we dance or would you like to get a drink"

"Drink" says Skye and smiles at me, but it's strained and doesn't reach her eyes.

I lead her off the dance floor where I pick up two flutes of champagne off a passing waiter as I hand her a glass dinner is announced.

All through the meal and for the rest of the evening Skye put on a good show. To the outsider she appears to be her usual funny, witty and polite self but I can see the pain and anguish in her eyes. Thankfully we get dropped off at the hotel first. I don't make a move on her in the elevator or down the corridor like I did last night it doesn't seem appropriate. I don't touch her either. My instincts are screaming at me to give her space. I desperately want to hold her, my arms ache from holding them tense as it takes all of my strength to keep myself from reaching out for her. Instead I stand as close as I can letting her feel my presence.

Skye opens her door and went into the room I didn't cross the threshold. I want to give her a choice, she will decide if she wants me to stay and I will respect her wishes. Halfway into the room she realizes I'm not with her and she turns to face me. The lost look on her face breaks my heart.

"Do you want me to stay?" I ask, please say yes my mind shouts. Her smile breaks my heart all over again it's full of so much sadness. I seriously want to break the old guy's fucking legs myself for whatever painful memories he has dragged up for her.

"Please. I don't want to be alone"

Although she isn't crying I can hear the unshed tears in her voice. Christ I feel so fucking helpless. I went to her enfolding her in my arms again trying to transmit the depth of my love through touch. We get undressed and climb into bed. I don't make a move on her I will leave it to Skye to initiate making love if it's what she wants. I simply gather her in my arms, holding her close, protecting her and giving her the most tender kiss I possibly can and being a gentleman I trap my cock between my legs to hide my arousal from her.

SKYE

I can't sleep. I listen to Clayton's breathing, slow and steady. I know it had been a while before sleep claimed him, for me it remains elusive. I'm restless. I need to do something. The mixed emotions I'm experiencing since seeing my grandfather are driving me mad. I need to make sense of them.

Draw, the command my brain throws out has me removing myself from Clayton's comforting arms and out of bed. On the desk I pick up my art sketch book and pencils. I sit on the sofa and turn the side light on, altering the angle mindful that it doesn't disturb Clayton. I start to draw. As usual when I draw or paint I lose all sense of time and with my self-imposed drawing therapy I start to work through the anger, angst and hatred until it all ebbs away.

At some point I start to think about Clayton. I put down my pencil and art book. I bring my knees up and wrap my arms around my legs. I realize I'm naked and starting to feel the cold but I can't make myself move. I stare into space reflecting how silently supportive Clayton has been all night. Holy crap what must he think of me. The snippy side of me tries to make me believe he thinks I'm a cold heartless bitch and will want nothing more to do with me. But his actions and the tenderness he has shown me, the silence to give me thinking time and space, the choice he gave me to decide if I wanted him to stay told me otherwise.

Oh that's right convince yourself he's a good guy and sensitive to your needs, get real he's hoping for one final shag before you both leave tomorrow.

No, he genuinely cares for me he hasn't made a move on me all night. He's being respectful of the emotional state I'm in. Letting me dictate what happens.

A blanket being wrapped around me startles me out of my mental debate, argument, whatever. Clayton crouches in front of me concern etched in his beautiful face and eyes.

"Hey baby you're shivering" moving slowly he sits beside me, he's naked. Hmmm lovely!

In what is fast becoming a familiar move he picks me up and sits me on his lap and just holds me, I love being held by this man, his arms, is my favourite place. I snuggle in.

"You must think me a cold heartless bitch" I find myself voicing snippy.

"On the contrary" his low raspy voice close to my ear sends shivers through me and my body starts to respond in its usual way "I find you to be selfless, kind and warm hearted, considerate, strong, do you want me to continue" a giggle escapes me and before I can say anything Clayton asks "what were you drawing, will you show me"

I nod. Clayton reaches over for my art book. I hadn't realized how many pictures I'd drawn. Variations of hands with a heart being crushed or ripped apart, empty chest cavities, faces in silent anguished screams. The last picture has a crumpled figure on the floor in the background, in the foreground is a female figure holding a smoking gun in one hand and a huge knife dripping with blood in the other. A psychiatrist would have a field day interrupting all of this.

Clayton chuckles "I agree" damn! I didn't realize I had spoken out loud "however I think it's self-explanatory" he says "the earlier pictures show the internal turmoil seeing your grandfather again and the emotions it triggered" he pauses looking for clarification he's right, I give a short nod "this last one my guess is you killing off your past to be the strong, self-sufficient, determined, stunningly beautiful woman I am fortunate to have in my life"

Shocked my mouth pops open. I gape at him like a stupid idiot. Clayton looks at me with such tenderness my heart stutters. He raises one hand and cups my face looking deep into my eyes.

"Skye Darcy I love you"

Holy fucking shit did I hear him right. He put his finger under my chin and my mouth shuts with an audible snap. He leans forward and kisses me before I can respond he pulls back and gently strokes his fingers down my cheek.

"I love you Skye and I really want us to work. I don't care about your past. All I care about is a future with you in it with me"

Speak. Say something my mind is screaming but I can't form a coherent thought let alone a sentence.

"I just want you to know how I feel about you" he cups my face again, his thumb brushing my cheek "I'm here for you no matter what"

My vision is blurry; his thumb continues to brush my cheeks. Tears, he's wiping away tears. I wasn't even aware I'm crying. A sob escapes me.

"Oh baby, tell me how I can make you feel better"

The flood gate opens and I cry hard, wracking sobs. All the while Clayton holds me, soothing me, rocking me. Not once saying "it'll be alright" nor berating me for being silly. He's letting me cry to get rid of years of pent up anger, injustice, frustration and letting the scared little girl go. This is something I have never done because I'd buried it deep, too deep.

Clayton magically produces tissues from god knows where and hands me fresh ones, taking away the sodden snotty wet ones without a single complaint.

I want to talk, to tell Clayton why I'm acting like this. Christ where do I start, the whole thing is a mine field. I took the fresh tissue Clayton handed me. I'd stopped crying but took it anyway. Clayton put his arms around me and hugs me, holding me tight to him.

"As a child growing up there was nothing I wanted more than this, to be held, hugged" I say, suddenly realising I have my starting point I continue "I don't remember my mother. She died when I was three. Actually she committed suicide"

I feel Clayton stiffen then relax. His arms continue to hold me close, his hands rubbing my arm and back in gentle soothing movements.

"Of course I didn't find that out until I was much older. Pills and booze apparently" I sigh "my father moved us to live with his parents. The estate is huge and the place is fabulous but I hated growing up there. The people, my relatives are all cold, hard and ruthless individuals. Showing any form of affection was frowned upon. It was seen as a weakness. All created by my grandfather. He controlled everyone's life with an iron fist" I let out a derisive laugh "the epitome of the draconian patriarch. My father died of a drugs overdose when I was ten. That's how I knew what to do with Alexi, Mr C's daughter when I found her it was because I had seen my own father overdose three times before he finally succeeded in taking his life. People always say it's a cry for help. I guess my father was screaming he wanted out of his miserable existence and didn't love me enough to stay. Well that's what I thought until I met Shelley and Simon"

In my mind I replayed their horrified reaction the first time I said it, now I repeat what Simon had said "I realize now he was a selfish bastard who was too weak to stand up for himself and chose to escape from his reality" I pause and look at Clayton.

His expression is one of hard cold anger. I know it isn't directed at me but at the strangers who inflicted the pain I had gone through. I try to smile but it doesn't quite work. He tenderly kisses my forehead and I snuggle back into him enjoying the feeling of being protected after a few minutes I continue.

"You know my grandfather disowning me and kicking me out was the best thing he ever did. Don't get me wrong I meant every word I said to him tonight but hindsight is a wonderful thing. If I had stayed right now I could be an alcoholic mess or a wasted junkie or both" I shudder "either way my life wouldn't be my own. I certainly wouldn't be doing what I do, so I am thankful the bastard gave me the opportunity to have a rich and fulfilling life. I don't mean rich in the monetary sense that's just an added bonus as far as I'm concerned. But I will never forgive him for the things he said to me as I lay in the hospital bed after the attack. When I needed love, help and support the most he turned his back on me and I died. When I got out of hospital I went back to the estate, in my room the servants had packed all my belongings up it was then I realized my grandfather meant every word he said that day and I died all over again. He gave me a month to get out. I found a place within two weeks, I moved as far away as I possibly could which was London. Those final weeks in the house were awful. Everyone acted as if I didn't exist. None of the family knew of the attack, grandfather had kept it from them. The only people who would talk to me were the servants and that was only when I forced them to acknowledge me. It was during that time I came up with my new name. It gave me a sense of hope, a fresh start. I was setting out on an adventure. I was fortunate I wasn't penniless I had my inheritance money from my father. One hundred thousand pounds, for someone who had not long turned eighteen it was a fortune to my grandfather it was a pittance. Before I got to London I formed a plan for my new life and the new me and the rest they say is history. You're right when you said seeing him tonight triggered all the old memories and when he said he wanted to make amends" a hollow laugh came out of me "does it make me a bad person to wish him dead already" I ask, uncertainty evident in my voice.

"No baby it doesn't"

"I almost went nuclear when he said that. If I hadn't walked away I would have killed him. Hell I had six different death moves play out in my head as I said those words to him" I snort "you know what stopped me" I didn't wait for an answer although I could feel the shake of his head "I thought he's an old man, got to be at least seventy five, let the miserable bastard suffer in his final days, comeuppance for making everyone else's life a misery. Karma"

I fall silent and mull over everything I've said and how I feel now. I realize I've finally let go of the ghosts from my past, well the majority of them. I'm a stronger person for it. I couldn't have achieved all that I have if I wasn't. I have a new family and people who love me unconditionally.

Hell, I'm sat on the lap of a gorgeous man with a body built for sin, who I might add is very naked and says he loves me. He wants me in his future and that is before I'd spilt my guts, does he feel the same way after my big baggage reveal?

I shift and look up at Clayton his face hard with tension. I lift my hand and stroke his face, his chin rough with stubble. I smooth the lines in his brow and run my fingers through his sleep mussed hair. As I do this I see the tension gradually leave him, softening his features. I lean forward and kiss him.

"Thank you" I whisper, he kisses me back.

"What for"

"For listening, for being here with me and not running screaming out of the door" I look into his deep blue eyes and whisper "for loving me"

"Always" then he claims my lips making my heart soar.

I want him. I want him to make the pain of the last few hours become a distant forgettable memory.

"Make love to me" I say against his lips "make me feel alive again"

Clayton stood in one smooth fluid movement with me in his arms and gently lays me on the bed. He makes love to me with deliberately slow tender caresses and when I climax I cry only this time with joy.

Sunday afternoon saw us part ways at the airport neither of us wanting to let the other go. My flight is called first with a final parting kiss I murmur "I love you"

Clayton told me countless times last night and during the morning he loved me but I hadn't felt ready to say it. He looks at me dumbstruck then a huge smile lights up his whole face making his eyes sparkle. He picks me up and swings me round laughing with joy putting me back on my feet he kisses me soundly.

"I love you, safe journey and ring me when you can" he looks over my shoulder "keep her safe for me"

I wonder for a second who he's talking to. Paul. I'm definitely going to get him a bell. Clayton turns me around to face Paul.

"Go on, go, before I kidnap you and take you back home with me"

Laughing I wave goodbye. Paul hands me my carryon bag and boarding pass. I went through the gate and turn for one final look at the man I love. Clayton blew me a kiss then waved me off. As I turn back I catch Paul smirking at me.

"What" I ask innocently or try to look it at least.

"Nothing ma'am" Paul's smirk gets bigger "it's just good to see you so happy" then his expression sobers "and just so you know if he hurts you I will break every bone in his body"

"I don't doubt that for a single minute Paul" I say laughing.

I'm still chuckling as I take my seat. Clayton the poor man truly doesn't know what he's taking on and god help him if he did hurt me. Simon wanted his balls and Paul every bone in his body. Shelley and Macy would take whatever was left.

Chapter Ten

CLAYTON

The sun blinds me as I step out onto the deck. I fumble my sunglasses out of my shorts pocket. Breathing deeply I take in the hot sea smelling air. I look out over the calm water towards land, seeing the faint outline of Corsica in the distance. A deep chuckle came from behind me and a meaty hand lands on my shoulder.

"She will come, she will come" Mr C says in his heavy Russian accented broken English "no worry, soon Skye will come"

In the two weeks since I last saw Skye in London we have spoken as often as possible each day through email, text and verbally including Skype. On her second day in Paris she emailed saying Mr C invited her plus a guest to join him on his yacht for a ten day trip around Italy and it's islands, would I like to join her as her guest. I have never cleared my diary so fast in my life.

Helena my secretary had even said "Who are you and what have you done with Mr Clayton Blake?"

I laughed heartily. I do that a lot now ever since Skye told me she loved me at the airport. I still get a thrill whenever I recall the moment and those words especially being said in her soft husky voice.

"Is that a polite way of telling me I was a miserable bastard before"

Helena's response was a raised eyebrow which made me laugh again "All I'll say is she must be one hell of a remarkable woman. You've never taken a holiday in the seven years I have worked for you"

That sobered me up. Helena was right I didn't take vacations. I travelled for business but I never took time out to relax or sight see but the thought of eight bliss filled days with Skye had me grinning again.

"My dear Helena you are absolutely correct she is an incredible woman"

Skye is joining the party two days late due to work commitments in Milan where she has been for the last week or so and she should be arriving on board today.

There are four other couples of mixed nationalities on the trip, two married couples one French the other English, a Russian and his Spanish girlfriend and two American women both married but minus the husbands and both have been coming onto me strong, one more than the other.

Maxine is a skinny fake tits peroxide blonde. She hits on me at every opportunity she gets. I even lock the door to my cabin whenever I'm in it.

On the first day I'd been on board less than two hours when she walked in without knocking, I was getting changed luckily I had just taken my shirt off. Licking her Botox lips she offered to help me with the rest of my clothes whilst she took off her bikini top. I shoved her out of my room fast, shut and locked the door on her startled face. She makes my skin crawl. Being thrown out of my room however didn't deter her, even last night she knocked at my door and tried the handle after I'd gone to bed so Skye's arrival couldn't come soon enough.

"Have you heard from her Boris?"

Mr C insisted I call him Boris only Skye can get away with calling him Mr C. Fortunately he'd laughed when I said it without thinking.

"I will find out" then he yells in Russian. A crew member appears instantly. Mr C continued to speak in Russian when he finished the crew member did a slight bow and disappeared "come Clayton join me in a drink"

We went up onto the top deck, most of the other couples are there and I groan inwardly when I see Maxine. She attempts to get me to rub sun cream on her at every chance she can, I refuse to oblige then she offers to return the favor, just the thought of her hands and bony fingers on me makes my skin itch. I make a point of sitting in the shade, Skye is the only one who is going to touch me and I sure as fuck wasn't going anywhere near Maxine.

The crewman reappears and speaks to Mr C who beams at me "Good news Clayton, she has just left the harbour and is on way. ETA is thirty minutes" he turns and points toward the main land "that is direction she will come"

"Thank you Boris" I can't help but smile at the joy I feel surging through me at the news.

"Someone else coming aboard" Maxine says sidling up beside me doing her best to rub her fake tits against my arm. I take a step away from her.

"My final guest" says Mr C.

I didn't say anything and neither does Mr C but I can tell she is itching to know why Mr C has made a point of telling me.

"Excuse me" I say and move away making a point of joining Jean-Paul and engaging him in conversation. It's the perfect opportunity to practice my French and keep one eye on my watch and the other on the horizon.

After twenty minutes I spot a dot moving fast towards us. Unable to contain myself I stand and watch the speed boat approach. I can't believe the level of suspense and anticipation that is building in me at the thought of seeing Skye again. The speed boat slows down as it gets nearer. I head down to the lower deck. Out of my peripheral vision I see Maxine get up and follow.

As I descended the stairs the speed boat engine cut out so as I get to the lower deck I'm just in time to see Skye being helped aboard.

She takes my breath away as always. Skye is tanned a lovely golden color making her white blonde hair which is braided standout even more. She's wearing a flowery sundress underneath I see cycling shorts as the skirt flares up in the breeze, good thinking on her part I muse. On her feet are Timberland boots, only Skye can pull off that look.

I rush to her. The crewmen see me coming and quickly get out of my way otherwise they'll end up being thrown into the sea in my haste to reach Skye.

Skye greets me with a huge smile and opens her arms. I bend as her arms wrap around my neck and I grab her ass and lift her up making her wrap her legs around my hips and I kiss her soundly. I'm greedy like a man who has been in the desert without water and is being offered his first drink. When the kiss breaks Skye chuckles her beautiful throaty laugh and it makes my heart soar.

"Wow. I take it you missed me"

Those of the crew close enough to hear her laugh heartily.

"Skye, my dear Skye so good you could come" Mr C says loudly, reluctantly I put her down.

Mr C wraps her in a huge welcoming hug. I move out of the way for the crew so they can bring aboard her bags and something large but light wrapped in plastic refuge bags to protect it. Mr C sees it and stops conversing in Russian with her.

"Is that" he says pointing and not finishing his question.

"It is" Skye smiles brightly.

"You finish it already" Skye nods "Can I see?"

"Of course but let's get it inside though before opening it"

"Yes, yes this way. Bring painting and be very careful" Mr C orders the crewman who is holding it. I see him visibly gulp.

In the state room Skye carefully peels off the wrapping to reveal an exquisite work of art.

"It's Mr C's granddaughter, she wanted to be a fairy and a mermaid with a pet unicorn" Skye explains "hopefully she'll like it"

Mr C turns and looks at Skye, he has tears in his eyes, speaking to her in Russian. Whatever he says makes her gasp then she hugs him. She speaks softly to him and he nods turning to me she takes my hand and pulls me out of the room. I look at her quizzically, she shakes her head but I know she will tell me in private.

"Let me show you our room"

The yacht truly is luxurious, no expense spared. It's a floating five star hotel so when I open the door to our room Skye let out a low whistle.

Her bags are already in the room and the maid is finishing unpacking. Skye went to the back pack that is on the bed, opened it, took out her art book and pencils, put them on the dresser and put the back pack in the closet.

"You know most women usually put make up, hair brushes and jewellery boxes on a dressing table" I tease.

"Good job I'm not most women" she retorts "so tell me about the platinum blonde with a face like a bulldog that swallowed a wasp"

I wince. Shit Skye noticed, I laugh at my own idiocy at forgetting how observant Skye is of course she would have noticed.

"That bad" Skye asks with a raised eyebrow. Skye thanked the maid as she left the room and closed the door.

"You have no idea" I pull Skye to me, wrapping my arms around her and burying my face in the crook of her neck. I take a deep breath pulling in her scent which is mingled with sun cream and sea salt "I have willed away the last two days and done my damnedest to keep out of her clutches" I tell Skye everything Maxine has done and said.

"Oh my poor baby" Skye mock croons trying her best not to laugh but failing miserably as usual, I pout at the lack of sympathy which sets her off even more, after a few seconds I join her.

"So what's up with Mr C" I say to change the subject.

Skye moves out of my grip and sits on the bed to untie her boots. I kneel and undo the other.

"The painting of Alexsandrina apparently she's the image of Alexi at the same age, he just never noticed it until now. Mr C has a tendency to remember Alexi as a wasted drug addict, no that's not right" she pauses and starts again "drugs robbed Alexi of her beauty and Mr C finds it difficult to forget that, so seeing the painting it was a bit of a shock for him"

A knock on the door interrupts Skye.

"Come in" we both call out. Paul opens the door and steps into the room.

"Ma'am, sir" he nods to me.

"All sorted" Skye asks him.

"Yes ma'am. I'll be heading back unless there's anything else"

"No, you and Macy have a fantastic time and I'll see you in eight days"

"We will ma'am. Enjoy yours too" he says then he's gone.

Curiosity gets the better of me "Where are Paul and Macy going" I take Skye's foot in my hands and start to massage it.

Skye let out a low moan "Oooh that feels good. They're going to tour main land Italy, visiting various vineyards and then spending a couple of days in Sicily, turns out Paul has family there"

"I thought Paul came from the south" I realize what I've said is stupid so I slap myself on the forehead making Skye giggle.

"Yes he is, born and bred. His grandparents came to the US during the fifties so it's their families he is visiting"

"Are Paul and Macy an item?" curiosity is getting the better of me again.

Skye shrugs "I guess so. I've never asked. I know they hook up and they care about each other but they don't advertise the fact they're officially a couple" she pauses "I suppose their situation is similar to ours"

That stops me dead "What do you mean?" I ask not really sure I want to know or hear her reasoning.

Skye looks me in the eye then leans forward cupping my face in her delicate hands. I kiss the palm of each hand causing her to smile tenderly.

"They are two people who get together whenever they can. They feel deeply for each other but have no official status that defines their relationship to the outside world"

Put like that I totally get what Skye means, however I want the world to know Skye is mine and I'm hers.

"How would you feel if we made it official to the outside world, you know let people know we are a couple" I ask tentatively.

"I would like that" Skye smiles shyly "what about you?"

"I want the whole world to know you are mine and I am yours" I whisper.

"Okay so we are officially a couple to the outside world" Skye's voice is soft and low "although I do have one reservation"

Alarm fills me "What" I almost shout.

"Your mother"

"Oh fuck" I groan. We both start laughing "I am seriously fucked, she's going to have a field day and that's not including the merciless piss taking I'm going to get from my brothers" I moan which sets Skye off laughing again "for Christ sake I am a thirty year old man who is scared to bring home his girlfriend"

"Well on the bright side it's four weeks until I'm back in New York so you don't have to tell her or your brothers straight away"

"Well that's one consolation I suppose"

"Poor baby" Skye croons running her hands through my hair and cups my face.

There's a knock at the door "Come in" I call out.

"Excuse me sir, ma'am" says the maid opening the door wide enough to pop her head in "Mr Cheremisinova has asked if you would join him on deck for a drink"

"We'll be there in five minutes' Skye says "let me get changed"

I stand and enthusiastically help her out of her clothes and after ten minutes I reluctantly help her get dressed again.

SKYE

Mr C's yacht is seriously over the top luxury, I love the thick carpets, they're the kind your feet sink into and I'm dying to take my sandals off and make scrunch toes in the pile. Soft cream kid leather seats and highly polished oak wood panelling throughout.

As I climb the stairs to get to the upper deck Clayton's hand skims up the inside of my leg and inner thigh. I bite down on a squeal. I stop with one foot on the next step his hand continues to rise and cup my sex. Holy hell he makes me instantly wet. I turn my head to look at him on the step below me his eyes sparkling with mischief. Oh what is he thinking?

His fingers move my panties to one side and he slips two inside me causing me to gasp and grip the hand rail. He moves in and out of me slowly. I'm so turned on my muscles clench and grip his fingers.

"Baby your cunt is greedy for me" he growls pulling his fingers out and puts them in his mouth "hmm the taste of Skye. Delicious"

"Mr Blake" I admonish my voice purring "you sir are incorrigible" I bend down and kiss him running my tongue over his lips and dipping inside his mouth. I can taste myself "hmm I do taste good don't I" I chuckle at his shocked expression. Two can play this game and I carry on up the stairs.

I've been on the yacht for less than an hour and already we can't keep our hands off each other, how in the hell are we going to survive the next eight days. I have visions of us shagging ourselves to death, it makes me smile.

"What on earth are you thinking Miss Darcy?" Clayton's seductive voice rasps in my ear.

"How we are in danger of shagging ourselves to death over the next eight days, just think of the fun we can have" I reach behind me and cup his crotch giving him a squeeze, he's instantly hard.

"Oh baby I am going to fuck you at every opportunity I get" he growls thrusting into my hand as I stroke him.

"There you are" Mr C calls out "what would you like to drink?" he asks as we approach.

"I'll have a bottle of beer please" it's too early to start on the wine for me.

I get introduced to the rest of the party. Clayton never leaves my side and he always has one hand touching me. He takes great delight in introducing me as his girlfriend. I hit it off with Jean-Paul and his wife Marcelle. They are thrilled to learn I speak fluent French and that I've been in Paris recently. Likewise Alex who I knew is a cousin of some sort to Mr C and his Spanish girlfriend Maria, Andrew and Martha both English are all welcoming.

It's the two American women—Maxine and Penny—I know I'm going to have problems with if I let them get to me with their snide remarks and attempts to lure Clayton away. I know their attempts will fall flat on their face so bring it on bitches, let the games begin.

Later back in the cabin we are getting ready for dinner, Mr C said it is informal so I'm stood looking through my dresses deciding which one to wear when I realize I'm actually choosing what to wear based on out doing those two bitches. I mentally slap myself and select a dress that hugs me and is comfortable. It's also the kind of dress you don't want to wear underwear as it shows off every lump and bump. Smiling to myself I know it will drive Clayton crazy even more when he discovers I'm not wearing panties. Lucky for me the dress has a built in bra. I quickly put the dress on so by the time Clayton came out of the bathroom I'm sitting at the dresser putting on my mascara.

In the mirror I watch him as he moves about the room getting dressed. Clayton's body is every artists dream, sculpted in every way and not an inch of body fat. God I want to sink my teeth in to him.

"Keep looking at me like that baby and we won't make dinner" he drawls and winks at me.

I shiver with need and anticipation. I blow him a kiss and carry on applying mascara.

We meet everyone on the upper deck for pre-dinner drinks. Whilst talking with Alex, Maria, Jean-Paul and Marcelle, Clayton runs his hand over my back and down to my butt. He continues this for about five minutes when he bends down and whispers in my ear.

"Are you wearing anything underneath this?"

"Of course" I smile and I wink at him "my birthday suit"

"Fuck me" he curses and groans.

I chuckle. I'm thrilled because now he will be thinking of ways to get inside me as soon as possible. He couldn't keep his hands off me and at every opportunity he grinds his arousal into my butt, letting me know exactly what I'm doing to him.

Dinner is being served on the lower deck as we walk down Maxine is instructing everyone to sit at their designated place. Clayton flatly refuses when he finds he is sandwiched between Maxine and Penny and promptly sits himself down next to me grumbling about it all being a set up. I put my hand on his knee and slowly run my hand up his thigh. He picks up my hand and kisses it then replaces it on his thigh.

Dinner is very enjoyable. Mr C is on the other side of me and I get him to tell me how he knows everyone on the trip. Alex is not only his cousin but also a business partner. Jean-Paul heads up the French business interests he has and Martha is Jean-Paul's equivalent in England. Interestingly Maxine and Penny are the trophy wives of two American friends. The husbands had cancelled at the last minute but still sent the wives thinking it would keep Mr C happy.

"Personally I would rather they weren't here" Mr C speaks to me in Russian "they are like two bitches in heat. I have a good mind to send for the husbands to keep them in line. I feel sorry for Clayton. Now you are here, he is a happy man" he pats my hand with my free hand I pick up my wine glass and drink "you will invite me to the wedding, yes"

I snort my wine. After I'm able to breathe again from nearly choking to death and Mr C can stop laughing at my reaction I manage to squeak.

"Mr C have you been talking to Clayton's mother by any chance" he set off laughing again. Clayton lifts an inquisitive eyebrow at me "match making and wedding bells he hears the same things as your mother"

Clayton rolls his eyes and seeing the piqued interest of those around us he delights in telling the story of how we first met and his mother within five minutes was already planning the big day.

"As you can imagine that scared the crap out of me and I ran in the opposite direction as fast as I could" I deadpan making everyone laugh.

After dinner I went up to the top deck with Maria as Alex and Clayton have disappeared with Mr C to talk business. I ask her if she wouldn't mind speaking in Spanish just so I can practice as it has been a long time since I conversed in the language and no one was around so we wouldn't be considered rude. Maria is more than happy to oblige.

I find we have a lot in common. We share the same taste in music, heavy rock. She has a keen interest in art and dabbles occasionally. She already knew I'm an artist and made a living from it, she surprises me by talking about all the work I've done for Mr C and she picks my brain about the business side of it.

"So is it something you want to get into, professionally I mean" I ask.

"I don't know. I don't need to work because of Alex" she told me earlier they have been together for over ten years and just never got round to getting married "but I need to do something to occupy me"

"Besides doing the full time charity thing" I hedge a guess and she nods.

My grandmother had filled her days doing constant charity work and events purely because grandfather didn't want her working. She never said it but I could tell it bored her shitless sometimes. There is only so much you could do on the do-gooder bandwagon, well in my opinion.

"I have a few artist friends who do it as a part time business. They produce four to six paintings a year and I sell them through my auction house. They get good prices and it saves them being committed to a gallery or hassle of trying to sell the paintings themselves also I do know a few of them pick up the odd commission. Have a think about it and if you want more information I'll give it to you"

Maria's eyes lit up with the potential opportunities. She continues to quiz me on my work and how often I travel even when Clayton and Alex came to us Maria carried on.

"There you both are" Maxine drawls stepping out from behind Clayton and Alex. I hear Maria curse under her breath. Huh, guess she's not a fan either.

Clayton has two bottles of beer in one hand and a blanket in the other with mischief written all over his face. Oh what is he planning!

"Hey baby, you okay" he asks bending and kisses me. He puts the bottles on the table, picks me up, sits in my seat and places me on his lap. He put the blanket down beside us "for later if it gets cold" then he wraps his arms around me and I snuggle in.

"Whatcha talkin about" Maxine asks as she drags a chair over to the table since neither Clayton nor Alex made any attempt at getting one for her.

Maria and I look at each other, willing the other to answer. Maria buckles first. "I'm getting valuable information and advice from Skye about how to make a living from being an artist"

Maxine's lip curls. Here it comes, the malicious bitchy comment. I brace myself in readiness but before she can get it out Alex steps in "That's great, tell me about it"

I settle back into Clayton's arms and lean against his chest as he rests his chin on the top of my head. Maria tells Alex everything we've discussed whilst I add the odd bit or clarify a particular point on the inner workings of selling at auction. During this time the others join us and pick up the thread of the conversation. Jean-Paul asks if I have any work with me to which Mr C delightfully shows off the painting he commissioned of and for his granddaughter.

"Something I keep meaning to ask" Clayton says "how come you travel so much to work?"

"Well it's usually because the commission is huge and it makes it difficult to ship. Well not difficult it's more awkward. There are so many restrictions, the time of exporting, papers, red tape, the list is endless and depends on the country. Plus you run the risk of the painting being damaged in transit no matter how well it is packed. Not to mention it all adds to the cost of the commission for the client. In Mr C's case the six weeks on site was finishing off a painting fifty foot in length by twenty foot in height" that causes a few whistles "for the client it works out cheaper, in the majority of instances, for me to travel and work on site"

Alex asks Mr C if he can see the painting when they got back which he agrees that prompts Jean-Paul and Martha to ask if they could see it the next time they were in Russia.

"How many commissions do you do roughly in a year" asks Jean-Paul.

"It varies" I shrug "for example the last two years I've travelled constantly simply because all the commissions have been large or it was simply easier to be on site and work" I did a mental calculation "rough ball park figure about twenty per year for private commissions, but I'm also approached by companies to produce art work for products, comics and films, which reminds me" I twist to look at Clayton "I'm heading straight to LA from here I don't need to go back to Paris" a slow smile of delight spreads across his face "and the last weekend of August I'm going to be at the Vegas Fantasy & Sci Fi convention. Simon, Shelley and Phil are coming out to join me, do you want to come?"

"Absolutely, just try and stop me" his smile getting wider "you going to be working the whole weekend"

"Just for a couple of hours on Saturday for a meet and greet with fans then an hour on Sunday for a Q&A. I'm on a panel with other guest artists. The rest of the time is do as you please"

"I would like to do as I please right now" Clayton whispers in my ear and rolls his hips making me shiver with lust "cold baby" he says loudly and picks up the blanket placing it across my legs and wrapping his arms back round me.

Conversation shifts to other topics. I notice Maxine is watching me and Clayton like a hawk and listens to everything we say but doesn't join in, creepy bunny boiler my mind shouts. The yacht's engine starts up startling a few of us and we begin to move.

"We are going to new location" Mr C announces in his broken English, he wouldn't tell us where we are going all he would say "it is surprise, you will know in morning"

"Come on baby let's call it a night" Clayton says standing and taking me with him.

We say goodnight and head to our cabin with the others who also decided to turn in as well. All the way Clayton is cursing under his breath.

"What's wrong" I mutter. He doesn't answer just shakes his head. As soon as we set foot in our room I turn to him "okay, spill. What's bugging you?"

"That fucking bunny boiler"

Blimey, he's seething. He paces the room like a caged panther. Whoa where did this come from, I've never seen him this angry. He vibrates violence. He is trying to contain himself. I think back trying to pinpoint what has set him off then I realize he's been quiet most of the night only participating in the conversation when he had been asked a direct question. Most telling is the fact he didn't touch me intimately as I expected him to when he put the blanket over us. I need to distract him.

I take off my shoes and put them in the closet "What did she do?" I ask knowing full well who bunny boiler is.

"All night she has stared at us, giving you daggers. She was lying in wait outside Mr C's office whilst we were in there discussing business" I switch off whilst he rants.

I let him vent and work it out of his system for a few minutes whilst I take off my mascara. Standing where he can see me regardless of where he paces and I start to slowly peel my dress off. When I expose my breasts he abruptly halts, his heated eyes follow the slow descent of my dress and I step out of it.

His eyes greedily rake up and down my naked body that alone gets me thrumming with need and heated desire courses through my blood. I reach up and take the clips out of my hair letting it fall around my shoulders and down my back. Clayton is breathing heavily through his mouth.

I walk towards to him. He reaches for me. I shake my head silently telling him no, he drops his arms and clenches his fists.

I undo the buttons on his shirt slowly, peeling it off him, running my hands slowly over his gloriously muscled front and back. Christ he is tense, hard as iron. I continue to stroke him lightly reacquainting myself with his chest, abs, waist, arms and back continuously moving my hands until I can feel him start to relax and enjoy my touch calming and soothing him.

Standing in front of him I undo his cargo shorts and let them fall to the floor. I'm not the only one to go commando tonight. Clayton steps out of the pants kicking them to the side. His cock stands hard and proud, it twitches and bobs demanding attention, so I oblige dropping to my knees I take him in my mouth.

I suck hard and cup his balls, teasing and stroking his sack as I work his shaft with my other hand. Clayton groans thrusting his hips forward, his hands rest on my head with his fingers sinking into my hair. He soon takes over and starts to fuck my mouth. I relax my throat taking him deeper. I hold on to his ass, letting my fingers kneed his tight flexing buttocks as I hollow my cheeks and suck his cock harder, tasting him. I feel the veins in his cock pulse as he gasps "I'm coming baby" warning me his climax is imminent. I suck even harder. He comes loudly, as he stills his cock twitches pumping his seed into my mouth, calling my name as his fingers clench and tighten in my hair, pulling to give a slight sting of pain on my scalp. I continue to work him with my mouth drawing every last drop out of him and making him shudder as I draw out his orgasm and bring him down.

I rise to my feet and kiss him. Clayton wraps himself around me, burying his head in the crook of my neck and breathing deeply.

"Now tell me again what was it that got you so worked up?" I say softly.

"I have absolutely no idea" Clayton tightens his arms and chuckles lifting his head he looks me in the eyes "oh baby excellent distraction and diversion tactic" he kisses me so passionately he literally takes my breath away "I love you Skye" he whispers stroking my face.

He picks me up in his arms and carries me to the bed, making slow sweet love to me.

Chapter Eleven

SKYE

After my first night on board and for the rest of the holiday Clayton doesn't let Maxine's antics get to him. In fact he is openly rude to her. I don't admonish him, she deserves it.

Whenever we are sunbathing either on the yacht or beach Clayton frequently tells me I need more sun cream, not one to spoil his fun I let him apply the cream. I love the feel of his hands on me and needless to say he cops a sneaky feel at every opportunity and I return the favor.

Maxine would ask him to apply her cream, he refused every time until she one day she says "Please, I'm sure Skye won't mind you having your hands on me"

"Skye might not mind, however it has nothing to do with how she feels about it but I do, I mind and I have no intention of putting my hands on you" Clayton snaps back. I muffle a snort of laughter and she never asked again.

After her third attempt at trying to manipulate the seating arrangements at lunch and dinner, Clayton thwarts each one politely telling her to fuck off, she gave up.

Each time we went ashore Maxine would try to separate us by arranging the girls going on shopping trips whilst the men go for a drink. Yeah right, in other words she would conveniently lose the girls and head off to find the men. I thwart these by saying I don't do shopping and I'm going to explore the countryside, mountain, art galleries, museums, whatever the local town offered as places of interest to visit.

It surprises me how many of the others decide to join me and Clayton on these expeditions. Maxine only came on the one of them. We were climbing a mountain—well it could be better described as a very big steep hill—at the top is a restaurant reputed to serve fantastic food all freshly made from produce from the surrounding land.

The path to it is rocky terrain. Maxine turned up in entirely inappropriate sandals whilst everyone else including Penny is wearing trainers or boots. About quarter of the way up Maxine starts complaining loudly, Mr C told her to turn back. Maxine asks Clayton if he would be a gentleman and accompany her back. Clayton told her he isn't a gentleman and carried on walking.

Even Penny refused to go back with her, telling her it was her own stupid fault for ignoring the advice given by the steward that morning. Maxine ended up being escorted back alone by one of the crewmen.

It doesn't escape my notice that Penny seems to be distancing herself from Maxine. More frequently Penny would hover or sit close by listening quietly and appeared to be genuinely interested in the business orientated conversations I was having with the other women and men. Subtly I included her into the conversations whenever she was near.

The restaurant lived up to its reputation, the view was fantastic and the food mouth wateringly fabulous. Shame Maxine missed out, not.

At breakfast on the morning of my fourth day on board Mr C informs Maxine and Penny their husbands are joining the party for the remainder of the holiday and will be arriving around lunchtime. Penny looks thrilled. Maxine well let's just say bulldog and wasp.

Later in the morning Mr C admits to me that he has summoned the husbands because he is fed up with Maxine's behaviour especially towards Clayton and he values our friendship and our budding relationship more than his so called friends.

"You make a beautiful couple, so much in love and I really do want an invite to your wedding" he chuckles at my expression and kisses my forehead.

As lunch is being served the husbands arrive. Maxine's husband Brett is exactly as I expected and imagined. Maxine truly is a trophy wife. I estimate her to be mid-thirties, hard to tell with all the Botox. I put Brett close to Mr C's age around the late fifties, early sixties. Brett is short, bald and fat; he is a heart attack waiting to happen. He also looks like a bull dog. Maxine has obviously married the money not the man. No wonder she made a play for Clayton in the way she did. Clayton is the exact opposite of her husband.

Penny's husband Mike is nothing like what I was expecting. He is younger, I guessed late forties and although his waist line is thickening he is still physically fit. Fairly good looking with a full head of blonde hair kept buzz cut short and tall around six foot.

Mike it turns out is also a huge fan of my work and is quite star struck when he's introduced to me, something Clayton finds highly amusing. Just wait till Vegas I think then you won't find it so funny. However during dinner that night Clayton gets a good idea at just how big my fan base is which stops his celebrity jibes.

"I really am dating a celebrity" Clayton says in wonder after Mike tells him about a convention he attended where I was appearing and how ten thousand fans turned up just to see me and all the ensuing chaos it caused.

"As soon as the news broke you are appearing at the Vegas convention I bought tickets" Mike admits sheepishly "I'm lucky to get them, the whole event sold out within thirty minutes of the press release going out"

Clayton's jaw hit the table. I know the event is a sell-out, what I didn't know is that it had been within thirty minutes of my attendance being announced.

It transpires Mike has been following my career for years, apparently some friends of his commissioned work from me when I first started out and that is how he got to know about me. He has copies of all the books and calendars I've published along with limited edition prints and on the rare occasions I did appearances he attended and after all these years he finally got to meet me.

Maxine, I think mainly trying to make up for her behaviour towards Clayton and to appease me says loudly to her husband "Darling we simply must commission Skye to do a painting for us"

"You'll be lucky" Mike says before Brett could open his mouth "Skye has a two year waiting list" I look at Mike and raise an eyebrow in a silent how in the hell do you know that. Blushing he clears his throat "I made enquiries. I'm on your waiting list, have been for the last nine months"

I laugh at his bashfulness, it's true I do have a waiting list and I make them wait twelve months before I make contact. Macy would call to see if they are still interested if it's yes I know they are serious about the commission and they will agree to my terms and conditions although I don't tell Mike. I decide that if I like Mike at the end of the holiday I will tell Macy to upgrade his tickets to VIP for the convention and if I still liked him after that I will bump him up the waiting list. His chances are good as I'm already warming to Penny.

Everyone retires to the stateroom after dinner as the weather has turned going colder due to a storm approaching. As usual Clayton has me sitting on his lap and no one bats an eye lid except Brett and Mike who are briefly surprised at Clayton's actions. I'm not quick enough to stand for Clayton's liking as I'm engrossed in conversation with Martha and Penny so I didn't see him approach. He scoops me up in his arms, sits in my seat and repositions me on his lap. Martha, bless her, doesn't miss a beat in what she is saying. Just goes to show how everyone has gotten so used to Clayton's open display of affection for me. Did I show my affection and feelings for him so openly? I shove that thought aside to examine later as I refocus on the conversation.

I find Martha fascinating, I rarely meet female CEO's and she triggers all kinds of images and ideas I want to put down on paper. Penny likewise proves to be an astute businesswoman. Penny runs her own online business, party items and fancy dress costumes. I can tell from Mike's reaction she's surprising the hell out of him with the way she converses with Martha and me. I get the impression he's starting to look at her in a different light. I will go as far to say he looks at her with admiration for her mind not her body. She might play the blonde bimbo but she is one shrewd cookie and I bet she's showing a side he's never seen before.

"Forgive me" Clayton murmurs in my ear. I turn to look at him, puzzled by what he's said. For the life of me I can't think of what I would need to forgive him for. He hasn't upset or offended me "I seriously underestimated you" he whispers. Again he's lost me. I must look really confused as I feel "I know you are seriously talented and highly successful as an artist I just didn't realize there is a whole industry surrounding you" he sighs "I am so, so sorry"

He looks so miserable he makes my heart ache. "Does this new found knowledge change how you feel about me" I ask quietly, fear creeping into the pit of my stomach and bones.

"Hell no" he says louder than he intended causing those around us to stop talking and look in our direction.

Relief floods through me. I cup his face, looking into his beautiful dark blue eyes I whisper "Good because I am still the same person I was when we first met in the gallery as I was an hour ago when you found out" I kiss him gently.

"God I love you" he says loudly, again. I blush as cheers and ahh's went up around the room and he kisses me hard.

"When can I expect my wedding invitation" Mr C calls across the room.

"Fuck off" both Clayton and I say at the same time then the three of us burst out laughing much to the stunned amusement of all the other guests.

"By the way" says Clayton "you're flying back to the States with me" I start to protest but he stops me by putting a finger on my lips so I mock mumble "I've already spoken to Macy and told her to cancel your flights. The three of you will fly with me to LA and before you say I should have consulted you first" he shrugs "I figured it was worth it to get the extra time together" he looks at me with uncertainty trying to gage my reaction.

"You're right you should have asked me first" I mock scold "and I'm glad you thought of it" I add softly giving him a chaste kiss.

"Excuse me Skye" I look up to see Maria "I've given it a lot of thought about what you said about selling through auction and I would like to give it a go"

"Fantastic" I beam at her "sit down, what else do you want to know?"

For the rest of the evening I answer Maria and anyone else's questions. Clayton simply listens and holds me in his arms.

By the time we get back to our cabin Clayton's mood is best described as cogitative, pensive almost. I leave him to his thoughts and go into the bathroom, as I get ready for bed I decide to tackle him. I have a feeling his mood is due to or connected to his apology. I've a sneaking suspicion that whatever information his security guy dug up on me it didn't reflected my so called celebrity status.

When I come out of the bathroom Clayton is already in bed. Purposely I get undressed slowly. I know Clayton likes to watch me strip so standing at the foot of the bed I put on a show. His eyes darken and I get a thrill as I see his cock harden through the sheet pooling at his hips.

I crawl onto the bed maintaining eye contact and climb up his body. I nuzzle his cock through the sheet causing his hips to jerk and thrust upward. Using my teeth I pull the sheet down to expose his huge thick cock. Hmm my mouth waters, I run my tongue from the base of his cock up his shaft to the head, circling my tongue around the tip and licking off the dew drop of cum. Clayton let out a low groan.

"Like that? Do you want me to do it again?" my voice comes out in a husky whisper.

"Yes please baby"

I run my tongue over him again only this time I take him in my mouth and suck the head of his cock teasing more pre cum. I moan at the taste of him the vibration causes Clayton to hiss in a breath. I open my mouth and throat and take his cock as deep as I can before my gag reflex kicks in. As I withdraw I let my teeth lightly graze over his cock as I suck hard.

"Holy fuck" Clayton shouts, his hips jerk upwards.

I repeat the action three more times when Clayton begs me to stop.

"Please baby, I don't want to come in your mouth, stop, please"

I don't stop straight away. I make him beg again before I comply and shift to straddle his hips. Taking his cock in my hand I position his head at my entrance and lower myself slowly down, loving the feeling of him filling and stretching me. I take him to the root. God I really love the sensation of him inside me, the fullness. I lift clenching my muscles so I can feel every inch of him then slowly lower again.

Clayton sits up suddenly causing me to gasp at the wonderful feelings racing around my body as he hits my g-spot. Clayton places one hand gripping my hip and the other at the back of my head fisting in my hair, effectively holding me in place as he claims my mouth with such passion and ferocity he makes my head spin.

Releasing my mouth he trails kisses down my throat pulling on my hair to move my head further back, the slight pain is lost in the pleasure his lips bring on my skin. Clayton leans me further back giving him easier access to my breasts as the hand on my hip moves upwards skimming my waist to cup my breast bringing it to his mouth.

His tongue circles my nipple making it harder, aching for more attention but he continues to tease the areola circling inward to the nipple. His mouth closes around my nipple and he sucks sending my core muscles into spasm, clenching and gripping his cock.

"Oh yes" I moan as he continues to suckle, my hips moving of their own volition enjoying the friction I start to gyrate. It isn't long before instinct takes over and Clayton surges his hips in rhythm to my movements.

A loud clap of thunder sounds outside and rain starts to fall. The sound of the rain hitting the sea and the rumble of thunder fills the room. The gentle rock of the yacht becomes a dip and roll making our movements more pronounced, intensifying the sensations of each thrust and grind of our hips. I can feel my climax building quickly.

"You feel so good" I groan and move faster creating the friction I want and need.

"Oh baby I can't hold on you're making me come" Clayton rasps "Ride me baby, ride me harder"

His words intensify my desire for him even more and spurring me on. He shudders, wrapping his arms around me and throws his head back, his face screws up and his jaw clenches the veins standing prominent in his forehead and throat. He's desperately holding off his orgasm waiting for me. I work my hips faster.

"Skye, fuck" he roars his release and thrusts up hard and deep into me igniting my own orgasm. My release hits in great waves, it feels like they're matching the waves rocking the yacht.

When awareness comes back to me I realize Clayton has his head in the crook of my neck and is holding me tightly against him, his warm gusting breath tickling my skin. I run my fingers through his damp hair and down his sweat slicked back. It dawns on me that Clayton has told me nearly every day that he loves me and I've only said it once to him, suddenly anxiety hits me. I'm not sure if my actions tell him how much he means to me, having grown up in an environment that frowned on any kind of affection being demonstrated has me worrying and questioning was I doing enough?

"Clayton" I tug his hair to make him lift his head so I can look at him. I run my fingers over his brow and down his cheek "I love you so much. I know I don't say it often and I'm not even sure if I show you how much you mean to me, will you tell me if it's not enough and that you need more. This whole thing is new to me and I don't ever want to lose it or you because I fail to tell or show you" I search his face for some clue as to what he is thinking and feeling. His eyes glisten and his throat works a few times "I love you Clayton" I whisper.

"Skye, baby" his raspy voice low and sexy as sin "you are my world. I will never let you go. Yes it's nice to be told and I love to hear you say I love you, but only say it when you want to and not when you think I want to hear it. You show me how much I mean to you in so many ways and I treasure those moments. But yes I will tell you if it will help put your mind at ease"

"Thank you" I kiss him tenderly, lovingly.

Clayton lies down taking me with him. We fall asleep wrapped around each other, the rock of the yacht lulling us with the rolling waves and the sound of the rain pounding the water and yacht.

Chapter Twelve

CLAYTON

Something woke me. Lying still I listen, nothing. I move my arm to reach out for Skye only my hand meets cold empty sheets then I hear a rustling sound, lifting my head I see Skye sitting at the dresser, she's drawing and gloriously naked.

This is a familiar sight, she doesn't sleep well or as she puts it her internal clock is screwed because of all the travelling she does across various time zones. Personally I think it's because her mind never switches off, she constantly draws the ideas that pop into her head. Skye is a workaholic although I seriously doubt she will see it that way.

Hell, I seriously had my eyes opened this evening. I'm an arrogant fucker. I thought I knew everything about her but Mike put paid to that. He followed her career for Christ's sake. The real shocker had been how many fans she has, the ten thousand turning up at the convention is a mere fraction of the world wide fan base populous and he had known she has a two year waiting list. Shit I knew she was in high demand I just didn't realize how much.

There is a whole industry built around her, at the age of twenty six she has amassed a personal fortune of over three hundred million dollars from scratch. I'm a fucking idiot for not working that one out.

Skye is the only wealthy woman I know who is self-made and she doesn't care about money, status or the trappings it all brought and she loves me, for me. Not my money, status or the privileged life I can give her. Cold realization sweeps through me as I become aware there is nothing I could buy her she couldn't buy herself. There is nothing I can do to impress her that I would normally do to impress any other woman.

I apologised for seriously underestimating her but I hadn't explained myself well enough going by the confusion I caused her. I felt as if my heart had been ripped out when she asked if my feelings for her had changed due to Mike's revelations. She did it again after we made love. It took courage to admit she didn't know if she was affectionate and attentive enough. It doesn't surprise me one bit considering the loveless and attention deprived up bringing she had.

The selfish bastard I am wants her all for me, I feel jealous a complete stranger knows more about her career than I do, that is what I tried to tell her. You fucking moron get out of bed and explain it to her.

I climb out of bed and stand behind her watching her work. Skye doesn't realize I'm there; she's lost in her imagination and the music she is listening to on her iPod. I move to the side so she will see me in her peripheral vision and kneel down. It works Skye turns to look at me her bewitching yellow green eyes have an unfocused glaze to them, she's in the zone, then she blinks and it's gone she's back in the present.

"Sorry did I disturb you" she asks taking the ear buds out and turns the music off.

"No baby and I should apologise for disturbing you but I do want to talk to you"

"Oh" she whispers and a myriad of emotions flash across her face.

Taking her hands I marvel at how small and delicate they are compared to my large square ones. Focus I admonish.

"I didn't explain myself properly when I asked you to forgive me last night" Skye opens her mouth to say something but I put my finger tips on her lips to stop her "please it's important to me that I explain. I need you to understand and it has nothing to do with nor does it change how I feel about you"

Skye kisses my fingers and takes hold of my hand putting it back in her lap. The love and trust shining from her eyes gives me the courage I need.

"I realized last night there is an area of your life I knew very little about. I'm an arrogant and selfish bastard. I thought all the information I had dug up on you and what you have told me was everything I needed to know. It took a complete stranger who knew more about your career to show me how wrong I was and listening to you talking business and holding court further proved how sagacious a businesswoman you are. Shit I haven't even given you credit or thanks for the ideas and suggestions you gave me in the first week of us being together. I implemented them straight away and I have seen immediate returns, considerable returns" Skye's eyes widen "there are many layers to you Skye Darcy and I now know I have only seen the tip of the iceberg, that is why I'm asking for your forgiveness and what I meant by seriously underestimating you" I sigh "can you forgive me and I promise never to make that mistake again with you"

I search her face trying to see what is going through her mind. Fuck I wish I had a mind reading superpower. Skye sighs. Shit is that good or bad. Reaching up with both hands she cups my face, holding me still. Christ I can lose myself too easily in her eyes.

"There is nothing to forgive Clayton" I hold my breath "our relationship is still very young and discovering each other's nuances and idiosyncrasy is part of the journey. Just because someone knows more about my career than you is irrelevant. I'm sure I have met and going to meet people who know more about your career than I do but it is all part of the learning process. Because we didn't reveal the information doesn't make us bad people or deceptive, we just haven't got round to talking about it. If Mike hadn't revealed my fan base last night you will see part of it for yourself in Vegas. As for my business acumen we'll have got to that eventually. You have never been condescending or odious towards me when we have talked about our business affairs believe me if you ever do I will slap you down, hard. As I see it we've had more important things to talk about" Skye shrugs "we've only known each other a few months and if you add up the number of actual days we've spent together it's less than a month. I don't know about you but I have never learnt so much about a person in such as short space of time. As for being selfish, well that's human nature. Everyone is selfish to some degree, we all want to have and keep something all for ourselves and I am just as guilty of it as well. You are the most considerate, affectionate and loving man I have had the good fortune to meet and I love the fact that each day I learn something new about you and I treasure that nugget no matter how big or small it is, and it doesn't matter if that nugget comes from the external persona Clayton Blake shows the outside world or from the private intimate Clayton I am the only person who gets to see him. I love you Clayton and those daily nuggets regardless of who or where they come from make me love you even more. Sometimes the love I feel for you hurts so much" Skye moves her hand over her heart "I never knew it could be like this and I love every minute and I don't want to get off the ride" Skye leans forward and kisses me so tenderly my heart aches. She pulls back and gently strokes my face, smiling shyly "you okay?"

I nod. I'm speechless this beautiful creature before me is so insightful it humbles me. Someone so inexperienced in relationships and demonstrating affection is teaching me, showing me the way to move forward. I know bone deep I will be the biggest idiot alive if I ever let her go.

"I love you Skye so much. I don't know what I have done to deserve you"

I pull her into my arms and hold her for a long while. Skye lets out a sigh of contentment or is that a yawn.

"Come on back to bed" I say softly, I stand pulling her with me.

As we lie wrapped in each other's arms a thought occurs to me "You will tell me if I ever get over bearing or if you feel suffocated by me"

"I promise" Skye chuckles "just so you know and not to put a dampener on the moment but if you ever hurt me, emotionally that is although they could mean physically as well either way Simon will have your balls and Paul will break every bone in your body"

I chuckle, although Simon's threat is figurative and I've already had a taste of Simon's tongue lashing I know I will survive a full blown lashing. Paul however is something else, his threat is deadly serious and it makes it all the more real because he has told Skye his intent.

"Yes ma'am message received loud and clear" I kiss the top of her head.

Skye falls asleep pretty quickly and as I listen to her soft breathing I run everything she'd said over in my mind. I'm such a fucking dolt and I mentally slap myself. She's right in her approach to our relationship. I need to take a leaf out of her book. I vow to myself to learn something new about her every day. A nugget she'd called it, good phraseology and I wasn't going to be an ass about the source the information came from. I want this woman in my life permanently and forever. She is my soul mate and I'm going to marry her. I feel giddy at the thought of introducing her as my wife. But will she accept?

Fuck the question leaves me cold and fear grips my heart. If I propose now it will be too soon for her that I know for sure. Baby steps don't push or rush her. I'll look for signs from her as to judge when the time is right. I fall asleep thinking of more and more elaborate ways in which to propose.

I wake to an empty bed, again. I'm going to have to shackle Skye to the bed I grumble to myself as I head for the bathroom. Yeah you bloody idiot if you do you can kiss her goodbye. She'll kick you to the curb so fast you won't see it coming, my voice of reason jeers. I kick myself for even thinking such a thought.

I get dressed and go in search for Skye. I find her in the gym. Her body glistens with sweat as she pounds the treadmill. I stay in the doorway watching her, admiring her lithe physique as it moves sensuously. Skye slows down to a brisk walk cooling down to a slow pace then she moves to the multi gym setting the machine to work her arms and inner thighs. Christ watching her work out is turning me on. Fuck it I want her. I step inside the room and lock the door behind me. As I walk over to her Skye smiles then her expression changes, her eyes widen as she reads my body language.

I stand in front of her and hold out my hand, releasing the machine she takes my hand and stands removing the ear buds. I can hear the driving heavy rock music she listens to as she switches off the iPod.

"Good morning baby" my voice purrs "I was disappointed to wake up alone, so I am going to strip you naked, sit you back down on the machine and lick and eat your pussy then I am going to fuck you" she gasps and her eyes widen, her gaze flicks to the door "don't worry we won't be disturbed. I locked it"

I pull her to me and kiss her hard. Skye responds with enthusiasm, she's game. I peel off her work out clothes and sit her back at the machine.

"Do some exercises for me" I command.

Skye complies squeezing her legs and arms together to work the weights controlling the outward movement so her wet glistening pussy is slowly exposed for me.

"Hold that position" I stand back and admired her, my cock is throbbing. I put my hand in my pants and lazily stroke myself "Christ you look so fucking gorgeous"

"Glad you like the view" Skye smiles wickedly and licks her lips.

"Do some more exercises" I command again. As she moves the machinery I continue stroking myself.

"Let me see you" whispers Skye.

I strip then fist my cock and stroke "Like what you see baby"

"Very much" taking her arms off the press she cups her tits and pulls on her nipples. Oh fuck she is tormenting me as much as I am her. I went to her, drop to my knees and put my head between her legs.

I swirl my tongue around her folds and clit, her hips surge up to me and she groans. I love hearing the noises she makes. I lick and nip working her up to a frenzied state. I place my hands under her ass and lift her so I can penetrate her with my tongue. Her work out has made her scent stronger, it is intoxicating at the best of times, now it's pure concentrated Skye and I can't get enough, she tastes divine. I put my mouth over her clit and suck hard making her cry out and her hips buck.

"Do you want me to make you come this way baby?"

"No" she pants "I want your cock deep inside me"

Kneeling up I look at her, she is at the right height for me to penetrate her in the position she's in but it means she won't be able to move.

"Baby I can fuck you in this position but you won't be able to move your legs plus you might want to hold on to the arm press, effectively making you immobile" I watch Skye carefully as I let my words sink in and I see comprehension dawn across her face "do you want me to fuck you like this?"

Skye's breathing speeds up. I can see the pulse in her throat indicating the hammering of her heart beat, she licks her lips "Yes I want you to fuck me like this" she whispers.

I stroke her cheek and kiss her "Remember the safe words if it gets too much" I say against her lips.

"Okay, red and yellow" she says softly, showing me she remembered them.

Skye's next move shocks the shit out of me. She raises her arms and places them back in position in the arm presses "Fuck me Clayton" her husky voice commands me.

"With pleasure my love"

I claim her mouth and slowly work my way downwards. I run my tongue over every inch of her body, savoring her taste, the saltiness of her sweet smelling sweat. Lapping the taste of her pussy, swirling my tongue over the folds and sucking hard on her clit making her writhe and moan loudly. Then I work my way back upwards. Licking and kissing her stomach back to her fabulous heavy breasts, suckling and nuzzling them.

"Please Clayton" she begs around her groans of pleasure.

"What do you want baby, tell me" I say against her nipple.

"You, your cock now" she gasps "inside me now"

Skye's need for me has my cock twitching painfully. Taking hold of my cock I stroke myself as I position the head at her entrance and thrust forward. Skye is so wet I slide in seamlessly. Her cunt is hot, tight and greedy for me as always.

"Oh baby you feel so good" I groan.

I love the sensation of her cunt muscles clenching around my cock, gripping me tightly, milking me. Pulling back slowly I feel her muscles pulse, sending tingling sensations shooting through my cock into my balls and straight up my spine. Fuck this is heaven.

Lust fogs my brain and instinct takes over and I begin to move. Thrusting in and out fast and hard, circling my hips to hit new spots inside her. I listen to the sounds Skye makes, when she cries out louder I know I've hit her g-spot. It spurs me on and I repeat the move over and over again, in and out, deep thrusts, gripping her hips and pulling her onto me to get deeper still. I can feel her climax building, the muscles gripping my cock harder and pulsing bringing my own climax on, my ball sack tightens and draws up. I thrust back and forth harder and faster, my breath coming in short bursts. Skye's orgasm starts I keep the momentum up chasing my release.

"Keep coming for me baby" I bark the command.

Her muscles grip me hard triggering my own orgasm on the second thrust I explode, shouting "Skye" as my release floods into her. My body seizes and all my muscles clench as pleasure surges through me. My heart pounds in my ears. When consciousness returns I find myself wrapped around Skye, holding her tightly. I lift my head from her shoulder.

"You okay baby"

"Hmm" is all the answer I get.

"That good" I chuckle.

"Hmm" Skye moves her arms; she winces and makes an oomph sound.

Shit did I hurt her? I massage her shoulders. "Talk to me baby are you hurting" I'm starting to feel sick to the stomach, worrying she'd used her safe word and I hadn't heard her.

"I'm fine. I just gripped the arm press too hard to stop myself from touching you" she blushes "I enjoyed that, really enjoyed it"

Holy fuck! Skye purposely restrained herself. Shit the things I could do to her now "Would you like to do that again?" I ask not being able to stop the question "be restrained"

"Maybe, I could be talked into it" Skye says coquettishly.

"I can be very persuasive you know" I chuckle.

We get dressed and after unlocking the door I hold it open and mock bow indicating for Skye to lead the way. Reaching the stairs to go down to the cabin we bump into Brett and Maxine who are coming up them heading for breakfast.

"Had a good workout?" Brett comments to Skye as he leers at her.

I want to rip his fucking eyes out of their sockets. With a broad smile and eyes twinkling Skye huskily replies "Yeah you could say that" and winks at him.

It wipes the leer off his face. That's my girl, pride floods through me. Skye really does have a knack for turning things in her favor she's not intimidated at all. Maxine gapes at Skye. I would go as far to say she is shocked at the way Skye has spoken to her husband, hmm interesting.

We shower, make love, shower again then get dressed and head for breakfast. We are the last to arrive. Mr C gives a rundown of the activities that have been planned for the day.

"What do you fancy doing" I ask.

"Shopping" Skye laughs at the surprise on my face "I want to get gifts for Shelley, Phil and Simon"

"Shopping it is then"

I'm going to pay special attention to the things she looks at and the comments she makes especially when it comes to jewellery. I've noticed the only jewellery she wears constantly is earrings. Skye has multiple piercings in each ear. She also wore rings and necklaces occasionally when she attended functions but she didn't seem to have any favourite pieces that she wore all the time. Her birthday isn't until the end of November and I want to get her something sooner.

The other thing I notice is how people follow Skye. They naturally gravitate towards her. During the whole trip each day everyone would state their chosen activity or someone, namely Maxine, tried to organise a group thing, the minute Skye stated her choice practically everyone, male and female, changed their mind and opted to join her. If this bothered Skye she never showed it or voiced it.

It occurs to me that I've never heard Skye complain whinge or grumble about anything. Well I've heard her grumble but that was done good naturedly and it was over nothing serious or prolonged. I feel pleased with myself I've learnt two new things about her and its only mid-morning.

Shopping with Skye is an educational experience. I've been on shopping sprees with my mother and various women I dated which consisted of being dragged in and out of well-known designer shops along the high street.

Skye ignores all of these; instead she went into the local boutiques, craft shops and headed for the back streets. I ask her why she ignores the high street stores.

"Why buy a gift from there when you can buy the same thing in any of their stores in any country. If I got a gift from any of those places I'd feel cheated and I also like to support the local businesses, put money in their pocket rather than the large corporate"

This opens up a whole new world of shops that the locals use. It is in these shops Skye finds her gifts. One of the stores we come across is kind of new age, selling crystals, incense and jewellery along with cheap tourist tat. Skye buys herself a couple of semi-precious stone dangly earrings and it turns out the owner made them.

We come across a lovely little restaurant to have a very late lunch. I don't think the owner knew what hit him when we all walk in. Our party consists of Mr C, Alex and Maria, Penny and Mike, Jean-Paul and Marcelle. Andrew and Martha elected to stay on the yacht. Low and behold we lost Maxine and Brett, actually as soon as we all got to the high street Maxine tried to dictate which shops we would visit starting with Gucci. Everyone bar Skye followed Maxine into the store, when they realized Skye wasn't in the shop they came out and found us. Maxine complained loudly like a petulant teenager she wanted to shop in Gucci.

"What's stopping you?" Skye replied.

Maxine looked perplexed "Nothing"

"Have fun" was all Skye said and continued walking up the street.

Maxine looked flabbergasted as everyone else turned and followed Skye, in a huff Maxine stomped back to Gucci with Brett trailing behind her and we haven't seen them since.

I also discover how handy it is to have a girlfriend who speaks the native language fluently. Within five minutes of being in the restaurant Skye has the owner and the waiters wrapped around her little finger. The food and wine is excellent. Mr C insisted on picking up the bill. Skye left a generous tip, everyone else follows suit.

Another thing I discover about Skye is she really doesn't care what people think of her actions, she is a free spirit and she treats others in the same respect. I broached the subject with her after the Maxine mini shopping run-in.

"Has it ever bothered you that someone wants to do something different to you and expects you to comply with their wishes?"

Skye looked at me as if I'd grown two heads "No, why should it" she says simply.

"None whatsoever, I just wondered if it bothered you"

"The way I look at it is life is too short to pander to someone else's whims if you've got something better to do" she shrugs "if others come with you that's their choice. I don't force my will on anyone and I won't bow to anyone's will if I don't want to. I have a choice. If that person doesn't like my choice that's their problem, not mine. If someone labels me as difficult or awkward all it simply means is that I won't comply and do what they want me to do"

"Wow you have really given that a lot of thought" I say amazed.

Skye stops walking and looks up at me lifting her sunglasses so I can see the sincerity in her eyes, taking my hands she sighs heavily.

"I spent the best part of eighteen years growing up being dictated to. No choice, being told what to do and when. Then I was set free, I vowed never to live like that again. If that makes me selfish or difficult in some people's eyes so be it. I really don't care" Skye pauses and looks away, getting the contemplating expression on her face, returning to meet my eyes and in a soft low voice "you should know that if someone applies pressure, you know keeps on at me hoping to wear me down, to give in" I nod to show my understanding "I will walk away. In the past I have cut all ties with those that have not taken no for an answer, business and personal"

My suspicions are confirmed I have to tread carefully and take my time with her if I'm going to propose. The message is received loud and clear. She loves me but she also values her free will and she won't sacrifice that for anyone, even if it meant walking away from someone she loves. Skye would get over it she is a survivor. I bend down and kiss her tenderly.

"I love you Skye. If at any time you feel that I am not giving you a choice or infringing your free will, kick me and tell me I am being an ass" I told her this last night, no harm in saying it again.

"You got yourself a deal" she chuckles, standing on tip toe she pulls me to her and kisses me "thank you for understanding" she murmurs against my lips.

After we left the restaurant by general consensus we head back to the high street. Skye is content to wander and go where ever anyone else wanted to go and guess what like sheep they follow her. I seize the opportunity and steer Skye towards a jewellers. I was wondering how to get her opinion on certain pieces without looking suspicious when Penny did just that, I could have kissed her in gratitude. Skye doesn't like the big rocks she called them ostentatious. I should've known Skye didn't flaunt her wealth, she did point to rings of an unusual design. Duh! Of course she would, she's a Fantasy and Sci Fi artist therefore she would appreciate something that is unique and not mass produced. Penny also asked if she wore rings, again I could have kissed her.

"I do but I take them off when I paint and I forget to put them back on" Skye replies with a roll of her eyes.

When I get back to New York I'm going to commission a piece of jewellery for her and decide to enlist the help of Simon and Shelley.

Chapter Thirteen

SKYE

"I can't believe how fast the last eight days have gone" I say to Clayton. We are on our way to the airport. He raises my hand and kisses the back of it "have you enjoyed it?" I ask tentatively. I don't know why I'm asking because I know he has, reassurance I suppose. We'd learnt a lot about each other, soul baring stuff, especially on my part.

Clayton smiles his eyes sparkling obviously remembering some of the things we'd gotten up to. Clayton held true to his promise of fucking me at every opportunity, just the thought has me squeezing my thighs together.

"I have loved every single second" he murmurs close to my ear "and I can't wait to have you on my plane, we have nine hours and I plan to fuck you the whole time" a thrill of excitement shudders through me "wet for me baby" his low seductive growl is turning me on even more.

"Hell yes" I say enthusiastically "I'm going to be joining the mile high club" Clayton chuckles sinfully.

"So tell me" Clayton changes from seducer to serious inquisitor. This I recognise is his way of understanding me as a person, getting me to voice my thoughts and opinions on different scenarios or other people's behaviour. I don't mind this because it gives me the opportunity to be honest and open about something that is important to him, likewise it gives me an insight into his thought process and invariably I turn his own questions on him. I know I've given him more than enough food for thought and he genuinely spent time thinking through what I've said and changed his perception on a number of things simply because as he said I made him look at them from a different angle or I brought other ideas, possibilities, options to the table "who out of the party are you going to keep in touch with, aside from Mr C of course?"

"Well Mike and Penny, we'll be seeing them next weekend in Vegas. I'm going to get Macy to upgrade their tickets to VIP passes and Mike will be commissioning a painting. Maria and Alex although probably Maria more because she wants to sell paintings through auction. I would like to keep in touch with Martha, maybe see her whenever I'm in England but I doubt it'll happen" I shrug "what about you?"

"Definitely Jean-Paul and Marcelle, he's given me some good insights into the French marketplace that I can use and he's invited us to stay with them. They have a chateau and vineyard, did you know?" I shake my head "like you Mike and Penny, they are a nice couple" he pauses and I leave him to his thoughts "you know Mike looks at Penny in a different light now because of you"

"What you mean she's no longer a blonde bimbo and eye candy on his arm, that she is actually an intelligent and shrewd business woman" I say jokingly although to my ears I sound sarcastic.

"Exactly" well that shut me up "Mike told me last night"

When he doesn't volunteer any further information I cave "Okay, spill, details now" I demand.

Clayton smiles impishly "Channelling Simon I see" I narrow my eyes at him threatening untold pain if he doesn't concede "okay, okay I give. Christ you can be scary when you want to be" he laughs.

"I know, now spill" I smile sweetly.

"Remember Mike and Brett's first night on board" I nod "you, Penny and Martha were discussing e-commerce and throwing ideas around, looking for gaps in an already saturated marketplace, standing out from competitors and a load of other related stuff, well it started then"

"Hmm, yeah I remember thinking he looked at her as if he had never seen her before. I admit that night I changed my opinion of her. So what else did Mike say?"

"You brought out a side of Penny that for years she kept hidden. Apparently you forced them to talk about their relationship and how he viewed her" bloody hell, I'm gobsmacked. Well push me over with a feather. Clayton chuckles at the look of shock on my face "you inspired her to reveal her true self. This was the first time she's been around like minded businesswomen and she craved intellectual conversation instead of ones revolving around shopping, fashion and cosmetic surgery"

"So that's why Penny distanced herself from Maxine" I say in wonder as understanding hits me.

"Yes and not only that Penny told Mike she's not going to continue pandering to the expectations of the wives of his so called friends and business associates. She is no longer hiding her light behind a bushel or whatever the saying is"

"What's Mike's reaction to this declaration of Penny's" inside I'm cringing. I really don't want to be held responsible for the breakdown of their relationship.

"He's delighted" Clayton barks out a laugh "he said it's like going home with a new woman and he loves it"

I smile at that and I hope it makes them stronger as a couple. Well I guess I'll find out next weekend. The car drives us straight into the private area of the runway where Clayton's plane is waiting for us. An official met us at the steps and checked our passports and wished us a safe journey.

Inside Clayton greets the crew warmly and introduces me. Macy and Paul are already seated, I wave to them. Both look relaxed and tanned. Clayton finishes his conversation with the pilot and we head to our seats. The stewardess, Linda, takes our drinks order as we settle into our seats.

"You both look well, tell me all about your trip" I say looking at both of them.

For the next hour I listen as Macy and Paul talk about the places they visited and meeting Paul's family in Scilly. I laugh my socks off when Paul told stories of thwarting attempts as various female members of the family conspired to marry him off. They only stopped when he came clean about his and Macy's relationship. I can see they're apprehensive about my reaction to their revelation. I'm thrilled they have finally admitted it.

"I've known about you two for years. I know you have never publicised the fact not just to me but to anyone. I am happy for you. So when's the wedding"

Paul sprays his drink all over the table. Macy looks shocked. Clayton roars laughing.

"How did you know" Paul splutters. Ha! That's a first, I've made Paul flustered.

"Female intuition" I wink at him "besides Macy's kept her left hand underneath the table this whole time, so have you set a date yet and let me see the ring" I indicate to Macy to show me, she lifts her hand up from under the table "oh that is beautiful" I say taking hold of her hand.

It is an oblong cut two carat diamond with smaller oblong diamonds either side set in platinum and it blinds you as it sparkles, just what every girl wants, if you like sparkly things that is.

"We haven't set a date yet we wanted" Macy pauses as Linda wipes the table.

Clayton asks Linda to bring champagne. I realize Macy has stayed quiet a little too long then it dawns on me. "You wanted to see what my reaction would be" both nod with anxious expressions "ah guys come on you know me better than that"

"I know you treat us as friends and part of your family" Macy says "but we are your employees first" she grimaces as she says the last bit.

Macy has a very valid point I can't argue with. I do blur those lines. "You are right. I do see you as friends and part of my family; to me you are no different than Simon or Shelley and Phil for that matter. I pay each of them for the services they provide me" I pause as Linda hands out glasses of champagne, I raise my glass to toast them "to you both I wish you much happiness in your new life together and neither of you can leave your life of servitude to me. I won't let you. How's that?" we all laugh "seriously though, I am genuinely thrilled for both of you, congratulations"

We clink glasses and drink. We start discussing their wedding plans and diaries, well my diary after half an hour it looks like they are going for a spring wedding.

"I'm paying for the whole thing" I hold up my hand to stop their protests "it will be my wedding gift to you both" both nod their acquiescence.

Clayton stands and holds out his hand to me which I take and rise to my feet "Congratulations to you both" Clayton says smiling "now if you will excuse us I am going to spirit Skye away for some alone time"

Paul and Macy grin at me and I blush, oh it is so obvious what we are going to be doing. Smiling I wave as Clayton leads me to the back of the plane to the bedroom.

Chapter Fourteen

SKYE

"Skye, honey it is so good to see you" Simon squeals as I step aboard Clayton's plane. He jumps out of his seat and rushes me.

"Humph" the air leaves my lungs as he collides with me and wraps me in a huge hug.

"I've missed you" he squeezes me tighter.

"Missed you too" it comes out wheezy due to the lack of air in my lungs. He releases me and Shelley takes his place, we hug hard our gesture demonstrating what we feel rather than saying the words.

"Oh my god" Simon squeals dancing on the spot and clapping his hands "Macy, Paul congratulations"

Simon is seriously hyper and in full on queen mode. Shelley joins Simon and they hug Macy then ooh'd and ahh'd over the ring. A pair of large warm hands land on my shoulders and spin me around, Clayton, his smouldering look ignites my blood. He bends and kisses me. My arms wrap around his neck as his wrap around my waist, he lifts me off my feet, deepening the kiss as he stands straight. Our tongues dip and dance reacquainting and tasting each other. We are both breathing hard when the kiss finishes.

"Hi" I say panting softly.

"Hi. I've missed you" Clayton whispers.

"I love you" I whisper back. Clayton's eyes sparkle and a heart stopping smile spreads across his face.

"Put her down Clayton" Simon calls "don't worry love I'll tell him for you" looking over my shoulder I see a blushing Linda stood next to Simon "come on Mr Money Bags put her down, they want to take off. You can do all the smooching you want when we get to Vegas"

Clayton laughs, putting me down he apologises to Linda. The crew make preparations for take-off once we are all seated.

"Okay peeps" Macy calls for everyone's attention "I need to go through a few things regarding the weekend" she hands out passes "these you will need to wear at all times when you are in the convention areas. It is an access all areas VIP pass. If you are attending with Skye you will need to follow protocol for security and safety reasons, Paul"

Paul nods his thanks and starts giving his briefing, everyone pays attention. "Whenever Skye is in public she will have security detail. On the casino floor up to six guards will shadow her at all times. In the convention areas this will be as many as ten. It all depends on how enthusiastic the fans are. Should the fans get over zealous security will close in two in front and at the back, one either side. Expect to get moved out of the way, their priority is Skye and her safety. If you get caught up do exactly what they tell you and when, do not argue as they will move fast" he pauses making sure everyone understood "security will be situated on Skye's floor and outside the suite. They have your names and your passes will also be your form of ID, don't miss place them" Paul enunciated the last four words "when Skye does the appearances I advise you make your way down to the VIP area twenty minutes before Skye's due time" Paul looks at Clayton "that includes you too sir" Clayton nods his acquiesce, I told him earlier in the week Paul might give him specific instructions and he would need to comply "once the appearance is over Skye will be escorted directly to the pre-arranged rendezvous. Any questions"

No one had any.

"Here is a copy of Skye's schedule for the weekend" Macy says handing out a sheet of paper to everyone "tonight there is a dinner being hosted in Skye's honor by the hotel owners and organisers of the conference, everyone is invited. You will notice the plan is color coded. Green means anyone can attend. Yellow means if you want to attend you can if you haven't already done so you need to let me know, at least two hours beforehand. Red is a no go for anyone" Macy looks at Clayton.

"That includes me" Clayton says beating her to it. Macy smiles apologetically and nods. I squeeze his hand in a silent thank you for being so understanding.

"Any questions" Macy finishes looking around the group.

"Does this mean you are working the whole weekend?" asks Shelley.

I shake my head but it's Macy who answers "No the green is free time. Yellow indicates when Skye is doing appearances and red means"

"She is having sex with Clayton" Simon pipes up gleefully causing everyone to laugh.

"No that's the green" Clayton deadpans "and no we're not inviting anyone to join it's just the majority color on the plan" Clayton winks at me, heat floods through me and I feel my cheeks burn which makes my friends laugh harder.

"Okay one final thing" Macy says when the laughter subsides "the hotel has arranged for limo's to meet us at the airport. Paul will go with Skye and Clayton in one, the rest of us in the other. On arrival at the hotel we will be met by their welcoming committee and escorted to our rooms"

"What no check in" Phil says in astonishment.

"No check in" Macy clarifies "it's already been taken care of" turning to me she says "Penny and Mike have had their booking upgraded, they don't know this by the way, they'll find out when they check in and they are registered as your guests. I will meet them later this afternoon to give them the passes and your schedule also I'll invite them to dinner tonight" I nod my agreement to her plans "everyone clear" nods all round "that's it unless there are any other questions"

There aren't any. Macy and Paul have covered everything between them.

Clayton leans over and murmurs "You really do have two gems there. I am surprised they've never been poached"

"Oh they have. Well attempts have been made I should say" Clayton raises his eyebrows in surprise "turned the interested parties down flat, must get two or more offers a year, each that is"

"They have told you this" Clayton's amazement sounds in his voice.

"Yes, well not at first. I found out from the people trying to poach them. When I asked them about it they admitted it. Both of them are bloody good at what they do" I state as a matter of fact.

"Wow, you are obviously one hell of a boss and friend to inspire such loyalty" he says with awe. I shrug.

"We talked about it. They were upset I found out. I was upset that I'd been told by someone else who I might add was trying to stir up trouble and hoping I would sack them so the three of us made a deal. Whenever they get approached they tell me, then I will take out the competition" Clayton looks startled then chuckles at my poor joke "seriously though I talk through the offer with them. I let them know I don't want to lose them but if they felt strongly enough and didn't want to pass up the opportunity I won't stop them. So far no offer has tempted them away"

"You are an amazing woman Skye Darcy" Clayton kisses the back of my hand, his love for me shining in his eyes.

"Skye tell us about Italy and where is my present" demands Simon.

"Honestly you are worse than a child" I admonish getting up to retrieve my hand luggage to get the gifts. For the rest of the flight I tell stories about Maxine's attempts at seducing Clayton much to his chagrin and my friend's amusement.

Clayton whistles low and long as we enter our suite. It is huge with views of Vegas seen all around the living room. The furniture, fixtures and fittings scream money and top of the range expensive. At one end of the room there is a bar and a pool table at the opposite end a baby grand piano, in the middle a huge white kid leather sofa and an equally massive flat screen TV.

"They really are pushing the boat out for you" he says in awe.

"Well she is the star attraction" Macy says coming in behind me and closing the door "plus Skye is the reason this hotel and the all the surrounding hotels are booked to capacity"

Clayton's jaw drops my celebrity status finally hitting home. I chuckle then stop short when Macy's words resonate in my brain "Really" comes out as a startled squeak.

"And that's why I didn't tell you sooner because I knew you would freak"

"Ha, so the ploy was get me here knowing full well I wouldn't refuse or walk away"

"Bingo, got it in one" Macy winks "do you need anything before I go and unpack"

"No I'm fine"

There's a knock on the door and Macy opens it. Shelley walks in with Phil carrying a number of dress bags.

"I'll see you at six downstairs. Paul will be here in about twenty minutes to introduce the security detail. See you later" Macy calls out to the others as she leaves.

Shelley shows me the Vegas evening dresses she has brought for me to wear and that is the start of the next hour and a stream of people coming and going. From the hotel owners Marco and Vinny, the convention organiser Giles all making sure I'm happy with the suite to the bell boy bringing our luggage and other senior people from the hotel and convention popping in to discuss various details. Paul introduced the security detail I will have the most contact with, all of them are carbon copies of him; somehow I don't think these guys work for Marco and Vinny.

All the while Clayton sits at the bar and watches the whole circus. I worry that he will feel left out and at first I find myself looking over frequently to make sure he is alright, each time he simply smiles and winks at me, after the tenth time and his demeanour hasn't changed I focus on what was going on around me. When the last person left Clayton came to me, wrapping me in his arms, I sag against him.

"At last I have you all to myself" he murmurs into my hair "come on let's have a nice long soak in the bath"

He leads me to the bathroom, a huge oval bath is already full of hot jasmine and lavender scented water. Clayton undresses me, as skin is exposed he kisses me, once I'm naked I return the favor.

"I need to take you baby" Clayton groans "I need to be inside you"

As soon as he steps out of his jeans and boxers he picks me up and sits me on the counter. The cold marble against my butt makes me gasp.

"Cold" Clayton smiles wickedly as he rests his hands on my knees "don't worry I'll soon warm you up"

Grasping the back of my knees in his warm hands he lifts and moves my legs apart. Clayton positions himself between my legs and thrusts forward. We both groan as he enters me.

It's only been five days since we've last seen each other and I missed him and the feel of him inside me something terrible. Clayton starts to move slowly dragging out the sensations for both of us.

"I've missed you and this" Clayton says hoarsely then he takes my mouth and proceeds to fuck me and my mouth.

My body is so greedy for him my climax hits surprisingly quickly and the sounds I make echo around the room. Clayton moves faster chasing his own release and prolonging my orgasm. My legs are wrapped around his waist urging and pushing him deeper into me using the back of my heels against his taught flexing buttocks. I feel his cock thicken, stretching me further, delicious friction rekindling my orgasm.

"That's it baby come for me again" Clayton gruffly commands.

I dig my nails into his back as my second orgasm hits, the pain of my nails dragging across his back causes Clayton to curse loudly and I feel every inch of his release.

Clayton lifts me off the counter and helps me into the tub. As he settles in the water he lets out a hiss "What's the matter?" I ask looking at his screwed up face concerned.

"I'm fine baby, just my back it's a bit tender from where you marked me"

"Oops sorry" I feel awful "I didn't mean to hurt you. I couldn't help myself" I blush, why am I blushing?

Seeing my discomfort Clayton chuckles and turns me around so my back is to his chest and sink us both further into the water "It's okay baby. I like that you have marked me as yours"

Marked him as mine, I run the words through my mind over and over. I feel delirious with joy. I hug myself, he likes the fact I've marked him as my own. How would I feel if he marked me as his? Mixed emotions flit through me, fear and anxiety when I think what the mark could be, worst case scenario I would have a scar. I shudder. Automatically Clayton's arms wrap around me in response, he wouldn't hurt me. I know that with all of my heart. I'm precious to him.

How would I feel if it was a hickey? Humph, I wouldn't be impressed.

What about a ring? An engagement ring my mind whispers. Every muscle in my body tenses. What are you worried about he's not going to ask you I scoff at myself.

Yes but he has said you are his future and he doesn't want to lose you because of his behaviour, he's also said he's never going to let you go. Stalker, my mind screams. I mentally slap it down.

But what if he did ask me, it's too soon we haven't known each other long enough.

Do you want to spend the rest of your life with him? Hell that's the sixty four thousand dollar question, I don't know.

Okay if he was to walk out of your life right now what would you do? I would survive, purely by throwing myself into my work. I would eventually get over him. But would I? I love him so much. No I don't think I would get over him, he calls to my very soul.

Shit, he's my soul mate. I feel complete when I am with him. I sense him before he gets near me. My body and soul recognise his, it always has.

If I didn't have him in my life I would go back to how it was before, empty and lonely. Sure I have friends who love me but until now I had no-one to share my life with, my inner most thoughts and feelings. I told Clayton things I have never mentioned to anyone. The thought of losing all that makes me feel sick.

Yes I do want to spend the rest of my life with him and I know deep down in my heart of hearts I will fight tooth and nail to keep him.

"What are you thinking" his lovely voice rasps close to my ear.

Instead of answering him I turn to face him. God he is so beautiful. I run my fingers over his eyebrow and down his cheek then over his lips. He kisses my fingers making me smile. He is such a strong, vibrant and sometime ferrous, red blooded male who is also tender, gentle, considerate and above all loving. I lean in and kiss him trying to relay all my love for him through the touch of our lips. I pull back his dark blue eyes showing a mix of love and bewilderment.

"I love you Clayton" I whisper and kiss him again before turning back to enjoy being held in his arms.

"Are you going to tell me what you were thinking in the bath" Clayton asks as he zips up the back of my dress, his fingers trail across my bare shoulders as I turn to face him.

I can feel the curiosity rolling off him. It's killing him. I smile I'm not ready to tell him yet. I shake my head and reach up to caress his cheek.

"Let's just say I had an epiphany" lifting up onto my tip toes Clayton bends to meet me. I kiss him tenderly.

"So it was a good epiphany" he murmurs against my lips.

"The best" I pause "I'm just not ready to tell yet" Clayton looks at me puzzled and worry mars his handsome face "I love you so much" I kiss him again like I did in the bath.

Clayton growls deep in his chest. Holy crap on a cracker the sound spikes my desire for him off the scale.

"Finish getting ready baby otherwise I'm going to be tying you to the bed for the weekend"

Just the thought makes me wet. I was debating to launch myself at him when Simon's voice drifts from the living room.

"Damn" I mutter causing Clayton to laugh as he went into the living room. I turn to the dresser to put my make up on.

"Wow baby girl you are looking mighty fine" Simon drawls as I walk into the living room.

The dress is strapless and as usual fits like a glove, it came to mid-thigh. Rich purple in color with sequins covering the chest area that peter down my rib cage. I'm wearing my purple killer heels; I love the fact Shelley matches the dresses to my shoes. My hair is down all wild and curly. Clayton and Simon are stood at the bar and I do the obligatory twirl when Clayton silently signals with a twirl of his finger.

Simon wolf whistles as Clayton stalks towards me. His gait is predatory and the look he gives me is hot and lustful. I shiver in delight at the effect I'm having on him. Clayton looks divine in black jeans, white dress shirt open at the neck and a black suit jacket. His dark wavy brown hair shines as the light hits it. God I want to sink my hands in to it.

He stops in front of me and takes my hands kissing the backs "Absolutely stunning"

"Okay love bugs" Simon calls to us "time to go"

Clayton offers me his arm. Paul is waiting for us in the corridor with two of the security detail.

"Is everything okay?" I ask because I could've sworn the detail isn't starting until tomorrow morning.

"Word has got out and spread you are here and quite a lot of fans are hanging around downstairs" says Paul.

"Ah crap" I mutter "the circus starts early. Okay guys let the game begin" I smile brightly doing my best to cover how pissed off I feel.

We get about a quarter of the way across the casino when an excited shout goes out like a war cry "There she is, Skye" and my name being continuously called out. Within a blink of an eye the security team appears out of nowhere to usher us to the restaurant.

As I walk I smile and wave to the fans as calls of "See you tomorrow" are shouted. Thankfully no-one makes an attempt to ask for a picture or autograph, although pictures are being taken I just didn't have to pose, so we got to the restaurant without incident.

"OMG" Simon exclaims "that was surreal, is it going to be like this all weekend"

"It will be worse tomorrow" says Paul.

"Oh honey you have my sympathies" Simon says with such sincerity it makes me laugh, he has absolutely no idea how bad it will get.

"Now you know why I don't do many appearances, just bear all of this in mind" I gesture to the security team "the next time you plan or try to talk me into public appearances. This weekend is cutting ten years off Paul's life span" I pat Paul on the shoulder, he grunts a response but his eyes continuously scan our surroundings as are the other security guards.

Safely delivered to the restaurant the security detail including Paul melt into the background and we are met by our hosts who make a fuss about the fans but I'm not fooled because I know they are secretly pleased at the fans invasion, more money in their coffers.

Mike and Penny greet us full of thanks for the VIP tickets and gush over the room they've been upgraded to. I introduce them to my friends. Penny has dyed her hair brunette, back to her original color she informs me; the difference is astounding.

"It's like you're a new woman" I say fingering a lock of her hair admiring the chestnut color.

Penny gives me a wink and whispers "You're not the only to have said that" and she nods in Mike's direction where he's stood talking to Clayton.

"All good with you two" I ask anxiously as I remember what Clayton told me when we'd left Italy and his conversation with Mike.

"Fantastic" Penny smiles broadly "and it's all thanks to you"

"Me" I act surprised and shocked.

"Yes you, when you talked business with Maria and Martha I realized I had been an idiot for years by hiding my business acumen, mainly out of fear. Fear of being ridiculed. You don't conform and you challenge the status quo, you inspired me to show the world what I am capable of and" she pauses and looks lovingly at Mike, I can practically see her hugging herself "Mike loves it, the new me"

"I am so pleased for you" I say with genuine affection and hugging her "for both of you"

Dinner is a relaxing and pleasant affair. My friends make Mike and Penny welcome and they seem to genuinely like them. Simon as usual is his outrageous self and is the source of comedic entertainment. Vinny asks if he ever did stand up, I'm sure if Simon had said yes Vinny would've signed him up there and then.

Discussion turns to moving onto a club, leaning into Clayton I whisper "I'm not going to go, tomorrow is going to be crazy so I want an early-ish night but you go and enjoy the rest of the evening"

"Not a chance" he growls then in a low voice so only I can hear "you are my enjoyment. I go where you go" his thumb draws lazy circles on my back giving me goose bumps.

"So who's up for going to a club" Simon calls out.

Shelley and Phil decline along with me and Clayton. I stand and say goodnight, arrangements are made for meeting at breakfast and somehow everyone is meeting in my suite. Guess that's because I have the biggest room. As we come out of the restaurant I see the large crowd of fans that's gathered and security are keeping them at bay.

"Security is certainly earning their pay tonight" Clayton murmurs as he puts his arm around my waist.

Paul signals to start moving, as like earlier the fans keep their distance respecting this is private time for me, tomorrow it will be all bets are off and a free for all, tomorrow, I was theirs.

Back in our suite Clayton indicates for me to sit on the sofa while he went to the bar to fix my favourite drink, Southern Comfort.

I kick off my shoes and flop down on the sofa putting my feet on the coffee table. Clayton hands me the drink as he sits down next to me. He reaches for my legs and puts them across his thighs and starts to massage my feet and ankles with his magical fingers.

"Oh that feels good" I sigh as the light pressure works its way through to other parts of my body.

Clayton is quiet, too quiet. I watch him as he massages the soles of my feet, he looks contemplative. I leave him to his thoughts, since arriving in Vegas he has seen an area of my life very few people get to see. If this evening has unnerved him god knows what tomorrow will do to him, there is nothing I can say now that will appease him. I will just have to deal with whatever issues he has tomorrow.

Clayton takes a breath as if he is going to say something but changes his mind. He does this a couple more times. Crap, here it comes. I'm going to have to deal with it now. He's working up the nerve to say it.

"Spit it out" I say softly "whatever it is that's bugging you"

He looks at me sideways and softly snorts shaking his head. I raise an eyebrow in a silent try me challenge.

"I'm sorry baby" ah, this doesn't bode well "but I've got to ask"

"Go on" I sound as cautious as I feel.

"Your epiphany" well I wasn't expecting that and I know my mouth gapes to show my surprise, in a rush he continues "I know you said you weren't ready to tell and I vowed to myself to give you all the time you needed, but I'm not a patient man" he sighs putting his head back against the sofa and runs his hands through his hair, when he looks back at me the despair in his eyes and face breaks my heart. I'm killing him "I need to know" he whispers "please"

Holy shit, fuck, fuck, fuck my mind shouts as I look at the drink in my hand. You're a big girl, step up and stop being a coward I scold myself. I down my drink for Dutch courage. When the burn eases from my throat I look up into his tormented eyes.

"Do you believe in soul mates" I ask hesitantly, actually I'm bracing myself for his laughter and ridicule. It doesn't come and I can't decipher the expression on his face, I've never seen it before.

"Yes, your epiphany was about us being soul mates" his voice is barely a whisper.

I can't speak; my voice has left the building, so I nod. A huge smile and sheer joy lights up Clayton's whole face.

"Finally" he shouts and laughs.

"Finally... what... when" I splutter, now my brain has packed its bags and left, I can't get a coherent sentence out.

"What am I on about?" Clayton says for me. I nod since speech is also eluding me, again "baby we are soul mates"

"Wait, hold on, back up a minute" my brain and voice are back in the game "are you saying you already had an epiphany" Clayton nods grinning manically, shocked I sit up "when" I say in a high pitched squeak.

Clayton pulls me onto his lap. I twist so can I straddle him I want to see his face properly. I have to hitch the dress up so I can do it, Clayton's gaze darkens and he licks his lips as he watches me. Oooh yes please, I want his mouth on me. I slap the thought away, for now this is more important. I tilt his head back so his eyes meet mine.

"Focus" I snap the word at him.

"Yes ma'am" he drawls, his hands cup my ass and slide me further down his thighs so our hips meet. I feel his arousal and he surges his hips into me the friction causes my pulse to kick up twenty notches.

"Behave, this is important, stop distracting me" I admonish and playfully slap his chest, although my voice purrs giving me away. Clayton's lascivious smile tells me he knows exactly what he is doing to me "when was your epiphany?" I demand.

"London, to be exact whilst you were talking to Nessa, possibly about ten minutes after you arrived" well shag me sideways as Simon would say, all those weeks ago and to top it off he went on to shock me even more "being brutally honest, I knew you were meant for me the minute I laid eyes on you. I also knew I was in trouble that night at the gallery and you sealed my fate on the Saturday night at the charity gala"

Holy shit, he has known all along and he's been waiting for me to play catch up. He strokes the back of his fingers down my cheek.

"I thought I had everything I wanted in my life but you came along and turned it on its head. I realized how empty and meaningless an existence I'd been living, you filled the huge gaping hole in my life. I had previously avoided facing this truth because I didn't want to admit to myself I was lacking something. You complete me Skye. I am nothing without you" he sighs "you call to my very soul. That day you walked into my building, seeing you walk through the foyer even though I couldn't see your face, you had your hood up" he explains, I must have looked puzzled "I had this overwhelming urge to make myself known to you. I was willing you to take your hood down so I could see your face the second you did I was lost to you" he barks a laugh "I even tracked your whereabouts down and lay in wait for you just so I could see you again"

"Stalker" I tease.

"Oh that's not the half of it. I heard you on the phone to Phillipee"

"You followed me to the gym" I give a wide eyed shocked look whilst being secretly thrilled to learn I had such an effect on him so early on.

"Not quiet. I had a session booked with him although I did try to get there earlier to see you but I only caught the back of you climbing into an SUV. Needless to say I gave Phillipee the third degree about you. I'm surprised he didn't call to tell you to be on your guard and before you jump to any conclusions Thursday and Friday nights were pleasant coincidences and if you recall I was at both venues before you" he cajoles.

"I'll give you that" I grin "wow I had no idea. Why didn't you say something earlier?"

Clayton shrugs "I didn't want to scare you off and when you told me about your past and how inexperienced you are regarding relationships I knew you had to go on your own journey of discovery. Remember you said so yourself in Italy how learning each other's nuances and idiosyncrasies was part of the journey, I already knew if I came at you all guns blazing like I wanted to I would scare the crap out of you and you would have run to the hills screaming. Then I really would have become a stalker because I would have tracked you down"

The enormity of what he is saying hits me. If I have considered spending the rest of my life with him that means he has too, his words come back to me "you are my future," "I don't want to lose you." Bloody hell he has also thought about marriage, suddenly my stomach roils. I feel queasy.

"Yes I do want you to be my wife and for us to spend eternity together" the man is bloody psychic, he is seriously hot-wired to my brain, how else could he know what I'm thinking. Clayton rubs my arms, I realize I'm shaking "but only when you are ready and when you want to" he emphasises the word "you" each time letting me know I'm the one that has the control in this situation. It's my decision, my choice.

"Thought you weren't a patient man" I say through chattering teeth, was I in shock?

"So long as you are in my life and that one day you will do me the honor of becoming Mrs Blake I will wait for you. You own me Skye mind, body and soul"

A thought pops into my head and before I can put my brain in gear I blurt it out "Children, I can't have them. You still want me even though I can't give you a family of your own" I search his face for any clue this will change his mind but I can't find one.

"It's you I love and you I want. Having you in my life is all I want. I can't bear the thought of you not being in it" the pure unconditional love he is displaying makes me so happy I want to weep. Clayton reaches up and runs his thumb across my cheek, it feels wet, well what do you know I am weeping "if you decide at some point you want children" he shrugs "we can adopt or borrow nieces and nephews that way we can hand them back" he smiles impishly.

Could I fall any more in love with this amazing man than I already am? My heart aches with joy and happiness. Leaning forward I kiss him. I made my decision.

"I love you Clayton and I would be honored to become Mrs Blake someday"

Clayton's mouth pops open and he trembles then he physically shakes himself, shaking me in the process. Wonder, surprise, joy and love light up his face "Is that a yes, as in yes now" he's excited. I nod not quite trusting my voice. Clayton stands suddenly and unceremoniously drops me on the sofa "stay there" he commands as he leaps over the back of the sofa and sprints into the bedroom.

I've just righted myself and straightened my dress when Clayton reappears in front of me and kneels on one knee in his hand is a ring box. Holy shit he's had the ring this whole time. Clayton looks sheepish.

"This ring wasn't intended to be an engagement ring. I was waiting for the right time to give it to you as a gift this weekend" he pauses and opens the box turning it around saying "Skye Darcy I love you with all of my heart and soul will you marry me?"

I gasp the ring is exquisite and unique it takes my breath away. He has obviously had it specially made. I look back up at him, my vision blurry and nod, answer him numb nuts my brain shouts.

"Yes" I croak out.

Taking the ring out of the box and lifting my left hand Clayton slides the ring onto my ring finger. It fits perfectly. I hold my hand up in wonder and admire the ring. The centre diamond is a large tear drop shape, the platinum setting and band appears to be a swirl of Celtic knotting which is covered in tiny diamonds. The ring is big but not tacky ostentatious big.

"You like it" Clayton asks uncertainly.

"I love it" I look at him "and you"

I put my arms around him and kiss the hell out of him. Clayton pushes me back onto the sofa and lies on top of me.

"So" he says against my lips "are we rushing down to the Little White Wedding Chapel or are we going to wait, my vote is for the Little White Wedding Chapel, now"

His enthusiasm makes me laugh, I think hysteria sets in because I get a fit of the giggles then I think about him telling his mother which makes me even worse.

"What's so funny" Clayton is bemused at my reaction.

"I don't think your mother would be too pleased you telling her on Monday back in New York, by the way Mom I'm married" I set off laughing again at the look on his face, he curses "not only that but word will get out tomorrow and the press will have a field day now that one of New York's most eligible bachelors is off the market and just happens to be in Vegas"

Clayton's tanned face turns white then a shade of green "Fuck that my mother is going to have a field day" he chokes out "she will be unbearable, I can't win either way"

"Oh my poor baby" I mock in a commiserating tone, although I do genuinely feel sorry for him and I tighten my arms around him "tell you what, how about we put off making the announcement. Put the ring back in the box and wait a month. I'll have been back in New York for a few weeks and you can tell your family in your own time"

He considers it for all of a second "Fuck no. I love my ring on your finger. It is not coming off now, you are mine and I want the world to know" he says possessively "fuck it, I will step up to the challenge that is my mother and call her tomorrow morning before we head for the convention"

"Would you mind if we held off setting a date" I ask apprehensively.

"Whatever you want if it makes you happy" he kisses me tenderly "you just tell me where I am to be and when and I'll be there. Also I will forbid my mother from asking and talking to you about it"

Just like that he's given me full control, no asking for an explanation or trying to second guess me.

"Thank you" I whisper.

"Come on, let's go to bed" Clayton starts to lift himself off me and I pout. Clayton raises an enquiring eyebrow.

"I thought we could make out on the sofa for a while" I say trailing a finger down his chest.

"Oh Skye you naughty girl" he growls, chuckling darkly he lowers himself back down.

Chapter Fifteen

CLAYTON

I stretch then reach for Skye only to find the bed empty. Opening my eyes I look to the dresser to see if she is drawing, nope. Jumping out of bed I head to the bathroom, empty, although the last of the steam filling the room wafts like a slow moving fog tells me she hasn't long showered. I head for the living room, opening the door I stop short as I hear voices.

"Crap there goes our morning of making love and christening new surfaces" I mutter as I pull on sweat pants making sure my erect cock is trapped by the waist band "sorry buddy you're going to have to wait" I grab a t-shirt and head into the living room.

Skye in yoga pants and vest t-shirt is sat cross legged on the floor with her back to me. A man is standing over her. What the fuck, I just manage to stop myself from shouting out. As I move closer I notice her hair is wet and she has a towel wrapped around her shoulders, the man sections her hair and pulls a comb through it lifting the section of hair straight up. I hear a snipping sound. Idiot she's having her hair cut.

Skye's hair is that long in order for the stylist to be able to cut it she has to sit on the floor and it doesn't seem to bother her. By the sound of the conversation Skye is quizzing the guy about living and working in Vegas.

"I bet you've seen some sights then over the years, so go on what's been the funniest thing that's ever happened to you?" before he can answer she sees me, her eyes light up and she gives me a heart stopping brain frying smile "good morning, this is David" she points up at the hair stylist.

I nod to him. His jaw drops and his eyes lustfully rake my body up and down then he blushes, definitely gay.

"Excuse me" I say to him and I drop to my knees, lean in and give Skye a long lingering kiss "morning baby I missed you" Skye chuckles as I stand and put on my t-shirt "what time is breakfast and everyone coming?"

"They'll be here in about half an hour"

I do a quick calculation of time difference "Right I'm going to call my mother, get it over and done with" I say as I head back to the bedroom.

"Good luck" Skye calls after me "go on David what's the funniest thing to happen to you?"

I leave the door open. I can't make out what David is telling her, I just get the rise and fall of the tonality of his voice, he sounds quite animated. Skye let out an "Oh my god" squeal then roars laughing, I love that sound and love watching her laugh, I have to hold myself still because right now I want to be out there with her and see the happiness and joy emitting from her beautiful yellow green eyes.

Skye has made me the happiest man alive by saying yes last night, she is finally mine and the world is about to find out. I hadn't pushed her for an explanation as to why she wanted to hold off setting a date, it just didn't seem important to get into it. Whatever her reasons I knew each and every single one of them would be valid. Hell she's probably thought of things I haven't like living arrangements when we got back to New York. Shit we've a lot to discuss and sort out as a number of things start to flit through my mind. Stop, there's plenty of time to have those conversations and Skye is right we do need to hold off on setting the date.

Right now it's time to make the call. I find my phone in my jacket pocket. I glance at the missed calls and messages, without thinking I start to go through them.

"Stop procrastinating, you fucking idiot and call your mother" I mentally harangue myself after a few minutes. Before I could think of anything else to do I pull up her number and press call. My stomach starts to knot. Jesus I'm nervous, my hands are getting clammy. I haven't been this nervous since I was a kid and I had to own up to some misdemeanour I'd committed.

"Hello Clayton darling, what a lovely surprise" my mother's voice is soft but cautious. She's probably bracing herself for a tirade of abuse from me for meddling. My mouth has gone dry. Christ I've been a right shit to her "Clayton, hello" hearing the concern and worry in her voice snaps me out of my deliberations.

"Yes" I clear my throat "Mom, hi how are you" I make a conscious effort to keep my voice light. I think I succeed.

"I am well and you" she's still cautious.

"I'm good, in fact I'm better than that I'm fantastic" I knew she would pick up on the happiness that is evident in my voice, taking a deep breath I plough on "the reason for my call is to let you know I'm engaged and it's most likely to hit the news later today"

"Engaged" I barely hear my mother's shocked whisper. I let the silence hang "do, do I know her?" she seems almost too afraid to ask.

"Yes. It's Skye" this time I hear the loud gasp of surprised shock "you were right Mom" I say softly "she's my soul mate and she's agreed to be my wife" I hold my breath waiting for her reaction. I hear a sniff, then another one "Mom are you okay"

"Oh Clayton, I am so happy for you" she wails "can I tell your brothers and the rest of the family? Date! When is the wedding? Oh we have so much to plan" and she's off.

"Mom, Mom" I have to shout to stop her wittering.

"Sorry darling. I am so excited" she makes a funny squealing sound.

"We haven't set a date yet and we're not going to" before I can finish she cuts me off.

"What!" she exclaims "don't be silly of course you need to set a date. Don't worry I'll organise everything"

"No you will not" I enunciate each word, I'm proud of the fact I keep aggression out of my voice "we will set the date when we are good and ready. Also I do not" again I enunciate "want you harassing Skye about setting a date or anything to do with the wedding. Do you understand?"

"Yes" she says meekly in a small whisper. She got the message, if she wants to piss me off this is the way to go.

"I would be grateful if you told Joshua and Andrew for me and do it sooner rather than later, it's up to you if you choose to tell the rest of the family" I couldn't care less about the rest of them however I don't want my brothers finding out on the evening news "tell Joshua and Andrew I will speak to them on Monday when I'm back"

"Back, where are you?" she says startled.

Fuck, I forgot to tell her "I'm in Vegas with Skye" a sharp intake of breath from mother makes me chuckle because I know full well what she will be thinking "relax Mom I'm not married, nor am I getting married this weekend, besides Skye didn't fancy the idea of the Little White Wedding Chapel. Skye is star guest at the Vegas Fantasy and Sci Fi convention and I'm here as part of her entourage"

"Oh, oh I see"

From her tone I know she doesn't quite believe me and she'll be straight on the internet the second this call ends to check it out. I hear more voices and laughter coming from the living room.

"Look Mom I've got to go, I'll see you on Monday"

"You'll bring Skye with you. I would so like to see her" says mother quickly.

"No, Skye will be in LA, she'll be back in New York the following week, maybe we can arrange something for then"

"Okay. I love you Clayton and I am really happy for you both, send her my love"

"I will and I love you too Mom, see you Monday" I hang up, relief flooding me. I hadn't realized now tense I was.

Skye is still sat on the floor with David doing the finishing touches to her hair. Simon is half lying on the sofa looking a bit worse for wear along with Mike and Penny who were trying not to laugh at him.

"Good night at the club Simon" I say chuckling.

I get a grunt for a reply. Macy, Shelley and Phil come in all calling morning then laugh when they get a load of Simon and good humoured ribbing starts. I went over to Skye as David helps her up.

"Thank you David, it feels tonnes better. What do you think?" she asks turning to me.

"You look fabulous" I say leaning down to kiss her.

"How'd it go?" she mumbles against my lips as I continue kissing her. I kiss her a little longer before I answer.

"She's thrilled and sends her love. I'll tell you more later on, are we going to announce it now?"

Skye's eyes sparkle as she nods. Paul enters holding the door open for room service and the trollies delivering breakfast.

"Paul can you stay a moment please" Skye calls out to him as he went to go back into the corridor.

Once room service has left I call for everyone's attention "Before you all dive in for breakfast we have an announcement to make"

I look down at Skye, these are her friends and this is her moment, grinning she lifts her left hand flashing the ring.

Shelley and Penny are the first to make the connection and scream, both rushing to hug Skye and me.

"Fucking hell" shouts Simon as he leaps off the sofa "lemme see, lemme see" he elbows the girls out of the way "holy shit" he exclaims "so this is the reason you wanted to know her ring size?" shocked blood shot eyes look at me.

"And pick our brains about what Skye would and wouldn't like at the jewellers" Shelley adds.

Smiling Skye looks at me and raises an eyebrow.

"Busted" I shrug happily "I wanted a unique and exquisite ring for my beautiful fiancé" I bend and kiss her.

"Okay get a room before I hurl" Simon mocks throwing up.

"You're in it so close your eyes" I retort.

Skye moves out of my arms raising a finger she mouths "one minute" and went over to Paul by the door. I watch as they speak quietly, of all the times I have seen Paul he rarely shows emotion. This is the first time I've seen him show affection, he embraces Skye in a brief hug. Macy joins them. Seeing the three of them together in this intimate moment I realize even though Macy and Paul are Skye's employees to a certain extent they play the role of older brother and sister in the family Skye has created and everyone in this room plus Mr C and Nessa will probably be the only people she'll have at the ceremony. Sure Skye can fill it with acquaintances but somehow I doubt she will.

I make a mental note to tell mother the ceremony will be immediate family only, that's going to be fun because she'll want to invite every man and his dog.

David the stylist joins Skye at the door. He has cleaned and packed up so quietly I'd forgotten he was here. Paul hands something to Skye, money I realize as she pulls bills off the roll and gives them to David handing the rest back to Paul. I walk over.

Paul and David have gone by the time I reach her and I catch the tail end of what Macy is saying.

"He seems like a nice guy and he's done a fantastic job on your hair" Macy reaches out and touches Skye's hair "how did you find him?"

"I didn't. I got fed up of fighting with my hair this morning in the shower so I rung reception and asked if there was a salon on site. The lady I spoke to said they could send someone to the room, within fifteen minutes David turned up. He's done a great job, best cut I've had in years. I can see I'm going to have to come here every time I want a haircut" she let out a bark of laughter.

Somehow I didn't think Skye was joking.

"Come and get something to eat" I say guiding her to the breakfast trollies.

We grab a plate of food each and join the others sat on the sofa. Skye chose to sit on the floor putting her plate on the coffee table, I join her. Conversation stops for a few minutes and the sounds of eating fills the room with the odd comment on how tasty the food is.

"What's everyone doing between now and the meet and greet?" Phil asks.

Calls of shopping, going back to bed from Simon, exploring, gambling went around the room.

"What time does the convention start?" I ask no-one in particular.

"Eleven" Macy says "Meet and greet is at two"

"Go and have a walk round with Mike and Penny" Skye encourages me "get an experience of the atmosphere"

"What about you?"

"I'm staying here. I've been advised to, apparently fans are already descending and it's mayhem down there"

"Excuse me Ms Darcy" Paul calls from the door. I look up to see the guy from the convention standing next to him. Skye stands and walks over. I follow.

"Good morning Giles want some breakfast?" Skye points to the breakfast trollies with the croissant she's holding. Giles shakes his head "so what brings you this early?"

"Just to see how you are and if you need anything and I've come to ask a small favor"

I see a cringe flash across Giles' face before he schools his expression, did Skye catch it I wonder.

"That sound ominous" Skye says round a mouthful of croissant.

Giles clears his throat "Its bedlam downstairs"

"So I hear" Skye cut in.

"Thing is" he pauses and shifts uneasily. Skye just looks at him. Her eyes seem to see right through him. His throat works "thing is" he shifts again.

I look at Skye. Her face is completely expressionless her eyes have become more yellow and hard. Giles couldn't look at her and his nerve is failing rapidly. I hear him curse under his breath. If Skye heard him she doesn't give any indication that she has. Giles sighs heavily "Listen I hate to ask this but" he stalls again.

"You see an opportunity to make more money because god knows how many more hundreds if not thousands of people have turned up to see me. Correct me if I'm wrong" Skye says without any inflection. Fuck, the guy is shitting himself "well?" Skye says softly and raises an eyebrow.

"Yes you're right" Giles replies resigned. Skye had instantly seen right through his purported small favor request.

"So tell me all about the money making ideas that have gone through your head Giles" Skye's voice is soft but I detect the underlining menace.

Holy shit this guy is going to get his balls served up on a silver platter if he says something she doesn't like and boy he knew it too. Giles runs his hand across the back of his neck as he contemplates his answer and clears his throat a few times.

"Marco and Vinny have given us more room. Stall holders are being spread out across all the rooms effectively getting more space. I wondered if you would open the convention and do an extended meet and greet today and do another tomorrow"

"Extended" Skye looks at Giles with a blank expression, she is giving nothing away "how extended?"

"Four hours today and the same tomorrow"

Giles cringes when he says it and I don't blame him. Skye looks at him with cold dispassionate calculation. Christ she is scary and hot as fuck. I'm seriously getting turned on.

"Triple my appearance fee plus ten thousand for opening" Skye holds his eyes as she says it.

Giles looks as if he's going to try to negotiate but one look at those cold hard yellow eyes and he bottles it "Agreed" he says almost reluctantly and holds his hand out for Skye to shake, which she does.

"Get the new paper work to Macy within the hour and we're good to go" Skye instructs, she's taking no prisoners.

"Excellent. I'll be back in half an hour" Giles says as he opens the door.

I pull Skye into my arms "You are one scary businesswoman" I say in a low voice and kiss her.

"The great Clayton Blake, billionaire extraordinaire and business mogul sacred of lil' ole me" Skye chuckles and shakes her head in disbelief.

"Terrified" I mock shudder "and you are hot as fuck in business mode" I growl in her ear.

"I thought you found me hot as fuck full stop" she purrs and runs her hand down over my semi hard cock making me rock hard instantly. I hiss in a breath at the surge of lust the sensation creates.

"Oh baby I am going to fuck you senseless when this lot go" I kiss her running my tongue along the seam of her full lips, she parts them and I deepen the kiss, dipping my tongue into her mouth, tasting her.

A burst of laughter brings me back to my surroundings and I break the kiss, damn I get lost in her so easily.

"Are you going to be okay hanging with the others whilst I work?"

"What would you do if I said I wasn't going to be okay?"

"Nothing, tough you're a big boy in more ways than one" Skye cups me again and squeezes gently "I'm sure you can find something to do"

"Careful baby" I growl. I'm close to taking her here and now on the living room floor, even with an audience.

"What did Giles want?" Macy asks coming over to us.

Skye twists round in my arms to face Macy and put her hands behind her back and continues to fondle me. Fucking hell it takes all I've got not to bend her over and nail her hard.

"He wanted to see if I would do extra hours due to the amount of people that are turning up and I've agreed. He'll be back shortly with the new paper work. Four hours today and tomorrow for meet and greet, plus I'm opening the convention. He's agreed to my terms. Triple my appearance fee plus ten grand for opening"

"Seriously" Macy says astonished.

"Yep seriously" Skye says, I nod to back up Skye. I have to concentrate on what is being said rather than Skye's fingers lazily stroking the outline of my cock.

"I'm missing something here, what is it?" I ask.

"It means I'm getting one hundred thousand dollars for this weekend instead of thirty thousand" Skye says matter of fact.

I whistle "Wow and it took less than five minutes for you to get an extra seventy thou" I'm impressed and in awe of her "come and work for me"

Skye laughs "I got the extra because I already knew what was going on downstairs. They need me more than I need them. I could have pushed for a percentage of the ticket sales but that just gets messy. As it is at the moment Giles will be calling me all the names under the sun but by the end of tomorrow I will be the best thing since sliced bread"

"I'll let Paul know of the changes" Macy says heading for the door.

"I need to get ready if I'm opening the convention at eleven" Skye says moving out of my arms, catching my hand and tugging me with her to the bedroom not that I need telling or any encouragement.

"Fuck me" I exclaim aloud. I'm stood in the VIP area at the balcony looking down onto the entrance of the convention area where Skye will be opening the show. All I can see is a seething mass of bodies. There's not one inch of visible floor space.

"Scary isn't" Mike chuckles next to me "plus if it wasn't for this" he holds up his all access VIP pass "I would be one of those heads down there"

"All these people just to see Skye" I'm in total shock. I thought I had a handle on her celebrity status.

"Even scarier, this is only a fraction of her fan base" Simon adds, he's looking slightly better than he had done an hour ago.

The crowd let up a cheer and I look back down to see Giles had taken to the stage. Suddenly the place explodes with noise, the cacophony of cheers and whistles is deafening. Skye has stepped onto the stage. In the lights her white blonde hair a cascade of spiral curls shimmers around her, truly making her appear as an apparition.

She is dressed in black skin tight pants, knee length boots, the ones with the silver heels and buckles running up the side, these are the ones she'd worn the first time I saw her. I'm so going to fuck her wearing those later. Her black vest t-shirt is covered in rhinestone skulls and roses and to finish off the look she's wearing a motorcycle jacket. Very rock chick, very fuckable and very mine.

I swell with pride, she has caused this mayhem. It takes a few minutes before the noise subsides enough for Giles to speak into the microphone, when he mentions Skye's name and hands her the microphone the place erupts again. I find the adoration overwhelming Christ only knows what affect it's having on Skye.

I look around the stage and see Paul plus three other security guards positioned strategically around the outside, continuously scanning the crowd. Thank fuck the guys are all built and look ex-military like Paul. God help any overzealous fan who decides to storm the stage.

"Good morning ladies, gentlemen, boys' and girls'" Skye's sultry voice echoes around the room "it is an honor to be here and it gives me great pleasure to welcome you to the Las Vegas Fantasy and Sci Fi convention, I look forward to meeting as many of you as possible over the next two days. The show is now open, have fun and enjoy your day, thank you"

The cheering and whistles erupts again. Skye is immediately surrounded by security as she steps off the stage.

Mike leans towards me and says in a low voice so only I can hear "If you think you had your eyes opened in Italy by me that is nothing compared to what you will see today and tomorrow" shit I've nothing to say to that so I just nod. I told him earlier how he opened my eyes to areas of Skye's career I hadn't taken into consideration "in half an hour we'll take a walk around and I'll point out all the things Skye has had a hand in"

I'm astounded there are very few products on sale Skye didn't have a hand in.

"Not only is Skye ingenious but she is also very resourceful and extremely calculating, see these" Mike points to a collection of figurines which are characters from a computer game "she had the hindsight to copyright her artwork and designs; she also chose to take a percentage of royalties rather than get paid a flat fee. So every figure, poster and game sold Skye gets a cut, this is the number one selling game and has been for the last six years. She does this with every company who engages her. The companies don't care they will meet her terms and conditions, she has the Midas touch. Every company which has employed her services for revitalising a failing product or new launch has seen a profit immediately and return on investment double the following year"

"How in the hell do you know all of this?" I know my amazement came out in my voice. Mike looks rather smug if it wasn't for the fact I liked the guy I would've smacked the fucker.

"The company I work for years ago employed her services. It was before my time. When I first joined a few years ago as CFO I looked into all the company's financials and contracts. Skye's being one of them. Being new and wanting to make an impact namely cost savings etcetera"

"You tried to terminate the contract" I cut in laughing.

"I did" he says laughing with me "until the CEO and lawyers pointed out I was about to cost the company approximately fifty million dollars" I whistled "you see Skye has this clause based on current royalties being paid and times that by a lifetime which is twenty five years that is the amount we had to pay" I'm laughing hard now "and of course this fucking idiot here not only picked the CEO's favourite artist but most profitable product line to cut costs on" Mike is shaking his head at himself "good job the CEO is my Dad otherwise I would have been out on my ear"

I'm laughing so hard I have to hold onto Mike to stay upright, people are giving me funny looks but I don't care. It is funny as fuck "So you've never met Skye before, until Italy" I manage to ask between splutters of laughter.

"That's right she does so few appearances and last time I only caught a glimpse of her" he snorts "if I had known right at the beginning Skye was on the holiday I would have cut my business trip. Poor Penny I gave her some grief about not getting in touch with me to tell me Skye was on board. Penny bless her didn't realize she was The Skye Darcy" Mike mimicked Penny actions and all "then I finally get to meet the artist in the flesh and I get all-star struck and tongue tied like an adolescent teenager making a right prick of myself"

I should have felt uncomfortable with this man telling me about his obsession with my fiancée, wow the thrill that word gives me, but I didn't he admired her talent and business intellect that is evident. I think he has her on a pedestal and wants to keep her there.

"Clayton, Mike" a female voice calls out.

We had walked around the halls and we were heading back to the VIP section when I turn to see Macy fighting her way through the crowd.

"Glad I found you. The meet and greet has been brought forward it's going to start in fifteen minutes. I suggest you head over now before it's announced to avoid getting caught up in the scrum"

"How come they've brought it forward?" I ask puzzled as we follow her in the direction of the meet and greet room.

"See that queue" Macy points to a line of people in front of us "it starts over there" she points in the direction at the far end of the corridor where we are heading "and it's snakes all the way into the casino with more people joining it by the second"

Realization hits "That's the queue for the meet and greet" I say flabbergasted.

"Bingo. Come on hurry up"

We got to the head of the queue and flash our passes to the security guards. The meet and greet room is huge and Skye has it all to herself. Throughout the room are roped aisles so the queue will snake around the room at the top end is a table standing on a raised platform where Skye stood talking to Giles and a few other people. Behind the desk are big display boards, getting nearer I see it's a montage of her work. A PA system hisses and makes a high pitch ear splitting squeal making everyone physically flinch. Then a disembodied voice announces the meet and greet is starting early due to the large crowd already gathering. We hear the muffled cheer of the gathered crowd.

"Okay people take your places" Giles calls out to the room in general.

Skye turns to sit at the table, sees me, smiles and walks to me. I open my arms and she steps into them, we kiss tenderly.

"Hmm thank you I needed that" she says breaking the kiss "got to get back to work"

For the next few hours I watch Skye interact with her fans. She is ebullient. Her smile never once slipping as she signs whatever is put in front of her and poses for photos. She speaks to everyone and gracefully accepts the gifts given to her. The only time I was scared for her was when the doors opened and the crowd surged forward and ran at her. Thank fuck for the roped aisles as it was the only thing that slowed them down.

Skye however seems to take it in her stride, welcoming the first fans with a dazzling smile. I look at my watch it's now three and she's still going strong. Skye hadn't taken a break although she is given a constant supply of drinks. I went to find Macy to express my concern.

Another eye opener is behind the scenes it's a hive of activity. I find Macy barking orders at a group of servers. I wait until she's finished.

"Hey Macy" I call her over "look I'm concerned Skye has been going for well over three hours and she hasn't had anything to eat"

Macy expression softens and she smiles "Skye is fine, believe me we would know about it if she wasn't" there's no condescension or patronising tone when she says it however her tone brokers no argument "see the drinks on the table" I nod "the blue bottle is a protein drink" as she says this Skye picks it up and drank as she puts it back down she shakes it from side to side "and that is the signal for another one"

Macy snaps her fingers in quick succession over her head, one of the servers ran over and she pointed to the table. Within seconds a fresh bottle is placed and the old one removed.

"You really do look after her" this comes out softly and reflects the wonder at what I have witnessed "forgive me I meant no disrespect"

"None taken" Macy says still watching Skye "and that's the signal for a nature break. Excuse me but we need to manage the crowd"

Macy steps onto the raised platform, picking up the microphone and announcing Skye is taking a short recess and would be back in less than ten minutes. Surprisingly there are only a few groans.

I snatch another kiss and assure Skye I'm perfectly fine hanging around which is true because it gives me the opportunity to talk with other people to gain insights into Skye's working life.

Marco and Vinny are beside themselves with joy at the revenue they are pulling in because of Skye's presence. Everyone adores her and literally fall over themselves to fulfil any request on the rare occasion she makes one.

News of our engagement has filtered out and I've had an exceptionally high number of men congratulate me and call me a lucky bastard to which I smugly replied "Yeah I am"

By four thirty Skye autographed the last thing a fan gave her to sign. I didn't realize they shut the door an hour earlier and told the remaining crowd to come back tomorrow. I made my way to Skye as she stood and stretched. I open my arms; ignoring everyone around her she comes over to me and sags into me.

"Tell me what you need" I murmur.

"Bath, massage and fuck in that order" she mumbles against my chest. I'm hard instantly.

"Coming right up" I chuckle. I love how she speaks her mind and gets straight to the point.

"Excuse me Miss Darcy"

I reluctantly let her go as she pulls away and turned. It's one of the servers, a young guy, who had been the one to change her drink bottles. He's nervous and is blushing profusely in his hands he held a pen and one of Skye's books.

"Yes Bradley" she says with a tinge of weariness then she sees what he's holding, without a word she takes them from him. Poor guy is shaking. Skye gives him her brain frying blinding smile and the lad's jaw unhinges. As Skye writes in his book she says "thanks for all your hard work today, I appreciate it" then she kissed him on his cheek and put the pen and book back in his open hands. Bradley is too stupefied to do anything.

"That was very unfair of you" I say as we walk away.

Skye grins wickedly "I know"

"She has no shame" I mocked horror which set Skye off giggling, Christ I love that sound.

The debriefing lasted all of ten minutes and arrangements are made with everyone to meet for dinner at eight. Security tail us to the elevator luckily the bulk of the crowd has dispersed and security keep those that linger from approaching. We get in the elevator a man and young boy are the only other occupants. They didn't pay any attention to us as the boy I guessed to be around eight is crying and the man, I figured to be his father, is crouched down trying to console the boy. As Paul hits the floor button and the doors close the man is murmuring.

"Never mind son, we'll try again tomorrow, we'll get there early okay"

The boys head is hung low and gives such a pitiful nod it even tugs at my heart strings.

"Hey little fella, what's all the tears for?" Skye's husky voice coaxes.

What happens next is comical. The little boy lifts his head and his tear filled eyes go wide and his jaw drops open. The father as he rises from his crouch starts to say "He wanted to see" when he got a load of Skye he gets the same expression on his face as his son.

"See what?" Skye prompts looking at both of them. The little boy grabs his father's trouser leg and tugs.

I chuckle it's her they wanted to see "Skye, baby. I think these two fine upstanding men have spent the best part of today queuing to see you and got turned away. Is that right?"

Both nod still open mouthed. Skye's megawatt smile is frying their brain. She crouches down to the boys' height "What did you bring for me to sign" he still couldn't speak instead he lifts up his back pack. Skye takes it from him and opens it "wow, all this?"

Dad found his voice "I did tell him to select one thing but kids being kids he insisted on bringing as much of his collection as he could possibly carry"

Skye snorted a laugh, sitting on the elevator floor she pulls a sharpie pen out of her pocket, the young lad sits down next to her "What's your name?" the lad looks at Skye with such adoration if he was older I would have been fighting him off.

"Danny, his name is Danny" his father supplies and the boy nods.

Skye is great with the kid, she keeps talking and asking him questions until he got over his star struck shyness. His Dad pulls out a camera and asks if he can take pictures, Skye nods.

"This is so cool" Danny squeals in excitement "no-one is going to believe me at school"

"I think they will your Dad has got enough photos to fill an album" Skye jokes "plus you've got enough to sell and make a nice profit to buy more for your collection" she winks.

"No it's going towards his college fund" his Dad jokes back.

I help Skye to her feet as Danny zips up his back pack his face flushed and glowing with joy.

"Thank you so much" Danny says then he launches himself at her. Skye just manages to catch him in time as he gives her a huge hug and a sloppy wet kiss on her cheek.

The elevator dings and the doors open "My pleasure" Skye says as she sets him on his feet and waves bye as the doors close.

I take hold of Skye in my arms "You were brilliant with him you will make a fantastic Mom" Skye stiffens immediately. Shit why the fuck did I say that. I feel awful, sick even "I'm sorry I didn't"

"It's okay" Skye says softly cutting me off "I will take it as the compliment it was intended to be"

"Christ I feel such a fucking shit"

Skye lifts her head and looks at me with beautiful yellow green solemn eyes "It is not the first time it has been said to me and it sure as hell won't be the last" she reaches up and tenderly trails her fingers down my cheek "sooner or later your family are going to say it or ask when we will be starting a family or even worse why am I not pregnant yet" that makes me suck in a sharp breath. Shit I hadn't considered any of this.

"I am used to it, so don't worry about offending me. You just surprised me that's all" she plants a soft kiss on my chin "you are the one that's going to have to learn how to deal with it and not treat me with kid gloves, okay" the smile she gives me is so sweet it makes my heart ache.

"Okay and I am sorry for how I reacted" I bend and kiss her as the elevator pings and the doors open.

Paul steps out, holding the door open whilst he checks the corridor. The guy is seriously good at being a shadow I forgot he is with us, again.

"Bath's ready" I speak softly in Skye's ear as I crouch next to her, she'd dozed off on the sofa "come on baby" I pick her up and carry her to the bedroom as she's groggy. I sit her on the edge of the bed and she flops back "do you want a nap first" I ask taking off her boots and socks.

"No" she says round a yawn "I'm just crashing from the after effects of the adrenalin rush. I'll be fine in a bit"

I pull her arms to get her to sit up and take off her jacket, t-shirt and bra then lower her back down so I can peel off her pants. Being the perfect gentleman I don't make any sexual moves on her. I want to, my cock is throbbing painfully and I'm aching to be inside her but her energy levels are low and besides I'm giving her what she wants a bath, a massage then a fuck in that order.

Within five seconds I've stripped and carrying Skye into the bathroom. I lower her into the bath and climb in behind her. I wash her slowly deliberately enjoying the feel of her wet skin under my hands, she went to return the favor but I stop her.

Instead I put on a show for her, spurred on by the heated look in her eyes as they follow my hands as I run them over my body. Skye licks and bites her lower lip as my hands travel lower and I take hold of my cock and begin stroking myself. She wants me.

"Like what you see baby" my voice a hoarse rasp, Skye's eyes light up in response.

"Show me how much you want me. Come for me" Skye whispers.

Seeing her lust and desire for me has me thickening and my balls drawing up. Fuck this is erotic as hell, watching her watching me. I start to pump my cock faster my hips thrusting upwards. Just as I'm reaching my climax Skye leans forward and takes the head of my cock in her hot moist mouth, that and the swirl of her tongue has me releasing instantly.

"Fuck yes baby" I cry out as Skye continues sucking the head of my cock and I pump and stroke out my orgasm. Skye swallows every drop.

"Mmmm delicious" Skye purrs as she licks her lips when there is no more to be had.

After drying her and wrapping her up in warm towels I carry her back to the bed and lay her gently in the middle placing the bottle of body lotion beside her. I turn on the music centre and go through the music list on her iPod. Skye likes rock music but she also has meditation music in the play list. Selecting the Native American Indian flutes she sometimes played at night to go to sleep to I put it on repeat. The soft relaxing music fills the room. Skye has her eyes closed and a contented smile on her face. I climb on the bed.

"I'm going to remove the towels" I keep my voice low so as not to startle her. It's like unwrapping a present "turn over for me baby"

Without a word she complies. Fuck I want to take her now and giving her this massage is seriously going to test my control. I reach for the lotion and squirt some on my hands the sweet buttery fragrance fills my nostrils. I straddle her and put my hands at the small of her back with my thumbs either side of her spine, applying pressure I run my hands upwards pressing my fingers and thumbs into the knot of muscle at her shoulders.

Skye lets out a long low moan "Oh boy that feels so good" is muffled.

I work her whole body, paying attention and repeating moves that get the deepest groan and when she lifts and pushes herself into my hands.

"Turn over time to do your front"

I move to her feet and sit back to give her room to turn over. Skye spreads her legs and her pussy glistens, seeing how wet she is I can't help myself I lean forward and run my tongue up her slit and swirl my tongue around her folds and close my mouth on her clit and suck. Skye cries out and her hips surge upwards.

"Mmmm delicious" I murmur.

I pick up the lotion and start to massage her arms. Skye keeps her eyes closed the whole time. I massage her breasts with my mouth toying with her nipples until her breathing is ragged. I expected her to stop me, but she doesn't. Skye obviously enjoys the slow sensuous torture. My mind starts to conjure up other things I want to cover her with and have fun licking off.

I massage her legs and as I get to her upper thighs she spreads her legs further. I lean in and lick her again, she whimpers, she's close to coming. Placing my hand on her stomach I clamp my mouth onto her clit and suck hard. Skye came immediately, crying out my name. As her hips buck I press my hand down lightly to keep her in place. I slide my tongue inside her entrance catching and drinking her juices as her body shudders from the orgasm rolling through her.

Before her climax subsides I mount her, the still contracting muscles grip my cock, welcoming and drawing me deeper. Fuck I love the sensation of being inside her, she is so tight. I pull back and thrust forward sliding balls deep, her warmth surrounding me.

"Baby you feel so fucking good" my words come out on a long low moan.

Skye wraps her legs and arms around me, the heels of her feet pushing into my butt urging me to go deeper. Her fingers flex and knead the muscles on my back. Her hips meet each of my thrusts. Christ I love to see and feel her writhing and undulating beneath me. I claim her lips kissing her hard and deep. Her tongue dips into my mouth and I suck on it causing her to groan. I start to thrust harder and faster, my climax building as I can feel Skye's building too.

"Oh yes, harder" Skye pants out.

A film of perspiration breaks out across my skin and my heart pounds as I move faster and drive harder into Skye. Reaching down with one hand I grip Skye's butt and lift her hips up and thrust deeper.

"God yes again" Skye calls out, who was I to deny what she wanted. I gladly pound into her.

"Squeeze me baby"

Her muscles clamp down hard on me and it triggers her orgasm, her nails dig into my back bringing a pleasurable pain. Slipping my arms around Skye pulling her closer so I can feel her shudder and spasm as her orgasm rolls through her I bury my head in her neck and chase my own release absorbing the feel of her all around me.

Chapter Sixteen

CLAYTON

A light knocking sound disturbs me, lifting my head off the pillow I look at the clock it's six thirty. The knocking came again. Skye is fast asleep. I ease out of bed without disturbing her. I pull my sweat pants on and head for the door, opening it a crack to see Paul stood there.

"Sorry to disturb you sir but I need to speak with you and Miss Darcy"

"Skye is sleeping can you just tell me" I speak in a low voice.

"I could, but with all due respect sir, Miss Darcy is my main concern and I would prefer to speak with her" and Skye is his employer and he is answerable to her not me is the underlying message.

"Is everything okay" Skye's sleep filled husky voice comes from within the room.

I step back opening the door and gesture for Paul to enter. I switch the side light on. Skye looking adorably rumpled is sat up in bed with the covers pulled around her.

"Pardon the intrusion Miss Darcy but your engagement has hit the news and your whereabouts has been publicized also" Paul says getting straight to the point "the TV crews and reporters along with the paparazzi have descended on the hotel"

"So I am to be confined to the room I take it" Skye says with a resigned sigh.

"We" I point out indicating to both of us "we are" Skye smiles apologetically. It didn't annoy me she assumed she would be in this on her own.

"Purely for safety reasons" Paul nods "Marco and Vinny have contacted the police just to confirm you are both on the premises in case anything gets out of hand"

"Can you get Simon, I think it best if we" Skye emphasises we smiling at me "issue a statement"

"He's already in the living room ma'am"

"Let me guess you drew the short straw to break the news and wake me up" Skye chuckles.

"Yes ma'am" Paul says smiling "also if you decided to hit someone they knew I could take it"

"Okay, give me five minutes and I'll be out. Who else is in the living room?"

"Everyone including Marco, Vinny and Giles" Paul says then left.

"Welcome to the circus" Skye sighs sardonically and got out of bed.

I hold my arms open and she approaches me in a slow seductive walk. Confident and comfortable in her nakedness, god I love her, I would give her the world if I could.

Sliding her arms around my waist she places her lips on my chest over my heart and kisses tenderly. Looking up at me with her chin resting on the spot where her lips have just been she murmurs "If you want to head back to New York I understand"

My heart aches with love for her. Skye wants to protect me from this circus as she calls it. Taking her face in my hands I kiss her "I wouldn't leave you to fend off this pack of wolves on your own. I'm staying. I love you. Wherever you go, I go. Now get dressed before I have my wicked way with you" the last bit came out as a growl.

Instead of moving away Skye reaches up and kisses me so tenderly my heart shatters with the love she is demonstrating through the kiss. Another thing I've learnt about Skye is that she didn't verbalise her feelings often but she told me through kisses and touch how much she loves me.

"Thank you" she whispers.

SKYE

I step in to the living room to be met by a wall of noise with all the different conversations going on, all discussing the same thing no doubt.

Clayton is stood with Simon watching the TV and surprise, surprise both our pictures take pride of place in the centre of the screen. I can't hear what the news reporter is saying nor can I read the strapline running along the bottom of the screen from where I'm stood. No-one has seen me yet.

A sense of dread shoots through me. Oh what have I done? You are a big girl, you can deal with this and you are not alone. After giving myself the pep talk I mentally pull up my big girl pants and head for Clayton and Simon. As I approach I catch the tail end of what Simon is saying.

"I really don't want to step on anyone's toes. PR in my opinion is a fickle business, I am more than happy to temporarily represent you under Skye's umbrella but I strongly advise you get your PR people on to it. Who are your PR people by the way, maybe I could collaborate with them to issue a joint press release or statement"

Clayton turns to face Simon "I don't have PR people, never needed it until now. So consider yourself hired Mr Hanson" Clayton says heartily patting Simon's shoulder with such force it almost makes his knees buckle. Clayton smiles at the stunned look on Simon's face. Simon is rarely speechless. It's a sight to behold.

"What's up Simon, cat gotcha tongue" I tease.

"Hi honey" he says smiling and giving me a hug "I guess you are not the only one to be making an obscene amount of money this weekend"

"That's his way of letting you know he's expensive" I say to Clayton, he chuckles shaking his head "right gentlemen fill me in. What's going on?" I call out to Paul, Marco, Vinny and Giles.

For the next half an hour I'm briefed along with Clayton about the chaos the press and paparazzi are causing. It's decided Simon will deliver a statement to the news crews in the hope they would leave. The paparazzi we could do nothing about. Giles is worried I'll bail he doesn't say it outright but the insinuations are there and his body language screams it. He nearly cries when I say I have every intention to fulfil my commitments tomorrow the only request I have is to use the staff access routes to get from the suite to the convention rooms citing it'll cause less disruption and headaches all round for security. Paul smiles and winks showing me he approves so I know I've scored brownie points with him. Yay for me my inner cheerleader shouts doing back flips and ra ra'd with her pompoms.

My stomach growls loudly and I realize I haven't eaten anything since breakfast.

"Hungry baby" Clayton's voice rasps in my ear.

Hell yeah, you in bed with your cock in my mouth and the accompanying image flitting through my mind and has me smiling.

"For food" he growls.

"I know a fun way to get protein, want me to show you" I purr and lick my lips. Clayton's eyes darken. Ha, I got him good all I need to do now is reel him in.

"Food" he mouths.

"Damn" I pout. Clayton laughs as I get up and walk to the bar and pick up the menu "I'm ordering food does anyone want anything since I'm, sorry we" I correct myself and indicate to Clayton and me "are grounded and won't be going out for dinner later"

"Please allow us to bring dinner to you all here it is the least we can do" Marco says getting to his feet, Vinny follows.

"Thank you, we appreciate it" says Clayton.

Marco and Vinny leave with everyone's food order and a promise it will be with us within the hour. I went behind the bar to get some nuts and potato chips I need something to eat now. Sod it! I'm going to have a drink I decide as I spy the mini fridge. I open the door and bend down to have a look at what drinks it stocks. Mineral water, cans of soda, white wine, a variety of bottled of beer, I reach for the beer. A hand strokes my butt, startled I shoot up. Whoa the room spins and two arms come round me to hold me steady.

"Sorry baby I didn't mean to startle you" Clayton drawls in my ear.

"S'okay can't beat a good head rush. Want one" I hold out the bottle of beer.

Clayton takes it and I bend down to get another one. No sooner had I bent over Clayton's hand is back on my butt, rubbing me. I stay bent over longer than I need to.

"You know if you stay in this position much longer I'm going to take advantage" Oooh yes please, I wiggle my butt. Clayton spanks me "naughty girl" he growls.

I'm instantly wet. Holy cow I like that and I want more as I stand a wicked idea comes to me. I turn to face Clayton his bright eyes are promising all sorts of sin. The bar is quite high, chest level on me, and no-one is paying us any attention. I take hold of Clayton's wrist, pull the waistband of my sweat pants out and guide his hand to my sex, he cups me. Leaning into him as his fingers circle my clit I purr "I want to be really, really naughty"

A rumble emits from Clayton's chest as he slips a finger inside me. Oh heaven. I adjust my stance and move my hips, grinding myself into his hand. Clayton slips two fingers in.

"You are so fucking wet, what naughty thoughts are you having" Clayton's voice is thick and raspier than usual.

"I liked you spanking me just then" another idea is forming in my head. I bite my lower lip to stifle the groan that is threatening to escape.

"And you want more" he finishes. Clayton thrusts his fingers in and out of me faster making my muscles clench, my breathing hitches "there's something else isn't there?"

How in the hell did he pick that up. I'd been thinking about the pool table. He smacks me with his free hand and thrusts his fingers in deeper at the same time. I bite back a cry of pleasure but it still comes out as a strange strangled note.

"Shhh baby you will draw attention to us, now tell me"

Bloody hell this is so erotic. Clayton finger fucking and spanking me, getting me to tell him about a fantasy whilst my friends are twenty feet away, another spank and deep thrust of his finger has pleasure hurtling around my body. I'm close to coming. I drop my head onto Clayton's chest, my fingers dig into his muscular arms.

"Tell me" Clayton growls, another spank, oh sweet lord.

"Play a game" I manage to pant out "later, pool table"

It's all I can say because the images I have going through my head sets off my orgasm. Clayton shifts so his body blocks me from anyone looking over. His free arm holding me to him all the while he finger fucks me. He kisses me to muffle mewls of pleasure I make. I let go and enjoy the roller coaster ride of my orgasm and not caring if anyone sees me.

"You are one lascivious, wanton and extremely naughty girl" Clayton's voice shamelessly lustful whispers darkly in my ear as I come back to my surroundings.

"Yes and I wonder who's made me that way" I retort "at least I'm your lascivious, wanton naughty girl. I can't help myself" I say as innocently as I can, actually I'm astounded at myself but damn! I enjoyed it. My inner goddess is shamelessly jumping around shouting let's do it again… I wouldn't say no to round two.

"Damn right you are" Clayton says removing his hand from my pants and puts his fingers in his mouth, he licks and sucks his fingers clean making sounds of appreciation. I lick my lips as I think about going down on him and wondering if we could get away with it.

"No baby we won't" Clayton says reading my mind. How does he do that! I grin impishly and reach for him willing him to give it a try. He catches my wrists and shakes his head "you can have me all you want later, after everyone has gone and when we play pool" I am so going to have my wicked way with him then. I pick up the beer bottle, open it and rather suggestively take a drink "oh dear what have I done" Clayton tries to be all serious but fails miserably.

"Oh my god" Penny suddenly squeals excitedly drawing everyone's attention "Simon's on TV quick, quick turn it up"

The whole room went quiet as we listen to the newscaster explain they are going live to Las Vegas. Simon looks cool, calm and collected in front of the mass of microphones. I know this is the biggest gig of Simon's career and it will really put him on the PR map. Although he held the statement in his hand not once did he look at it, he had memorised it. My heart swells with pride. Behind him I can see Marco, Vinny and Giles all smiling. When Simon finished he fielded the reporter's questions. We'd previously agreed the amount of personal information to be given should certain questions be asked, the rest of the answers would be no comment.

The remainder of the press conference is about why I'm in Vegas giving Giles, Marco and Vinny publicity for the convention and the hotel. Simon did a sterling job. I know I would have crumbled at the first hurdle.

"You know I think we should celebrate, have a party" I say to Clayton.

"Good idea, champagne" he says moving to pick up the phone to ring down to room service.

"Yes and more bottles of beer" turning to the rest of the room I announce "party time"

Simon arrived back fifteen minutes later to cheers and shouts of well done, you were fantastic and with perfect timing the extra booze arrived as well. I hug him.

"You were absolutely brilliant, thank you"

Everyone gathers around firing questions at him about what was it like and was he nervous.

"I was terrified. Don't get me wrong I mean I'm used to dealing with the media but that" he pauses for dramatic effect "to coin the phrase being thrown to the wolves I totally get it now. It is absolutely mental down there. Skye I think you are doing the right thing tomorrow and using the staff access areas. I found out from Marco some of the press donned staff uniforms and have tried to get up here"

"Fucking hell and crap on a cracker" I bark out, it's all my brain can come up with in response to that news. My stomach drops to the floor.

At the look of shock on my face Simon quickly adds "Don't worry they didn't get very far, apparently Vinny has assigned specific staff to you and the security team know who they are so the second the reporters tried to get off the elevator at this floor security closed in and turfed them out"

"Thank fuck for that" Clayton says with relief handing me and Simon a glass of champagne "listen Simon I really do want to employ your services on a more permanent basis, when we get back to New York come to my office and we can draw up a contract. You really impressed me by the way you have handled everything since the news broke. Well done" Clayton pats Simon's shoulder then moves away to talk to Mike and Penny.

"Well wonders never cease" I laugh "that is the second time in less than two hours I have seen you speechless"

"He's serious isn't he" Simon says in wonder.

"Yep and he's genuine with his compliment and I have to say I agree with him one hundred percent"

"You really love him don't you, I mean really, really love him" Simon says softly, his eyes searching my face.

"He's my soul mate" I whisper looking at Clayton, suddenly I feel incredibly emotional "we complete each other. I never realized how empty and lonely my life was until I met him and it was the same for him" I look up into Simon's face searching to see if he understands what I'm saying "I can't imagine my life and world without him in it" The beaming smile Simon gives me tells me he knows exactly what I'm on about "Simon when we do eventually set a date for the wedding, will you give me away?"

And that's three occasions Simon has now been rendered speechless. Grabbing me in a rib cracking hug he tearfully accepts.

Shelley comes over as we break apart, seeing Simon wipe away tears her smile fades to be replaced with concern. Her frown mars her lovely face "What on earth is the matter?" Shelley says reaching out and rubs Simon's back, giving me a quizzical look.

Simon can't answer he just waves his hands in front of his face in an attempt to stem the tears from running down his cheeks.

"I've just asked him to give me away and I would like you to be my Maid of Honor, will you?"

"Hell yeah" she shouts with a huge grin on her face then she hugs me "will it be presumptuous of me if I said you want me to make your dress?"

"I wouldn't trust anyone else, besides it wouldn't surprise me if you've already got it designed, hell knowing you, you've probably already made it" I joke. Shelley's cheeks turn beetroot and she looks down at the floor so I know I've guessed right. I start laughing at my own surprise "you have haven't you?"

Shelley nods "Please don't be mad at me" she looks at me imploringly "but when you started seeing Clayton in New York I could see how much he loved you and you were falling for him so I" she pauses and shrugs looking guilty "I got carried away, my imagination ran riot, plus I was making your bridesmaid dress"

"It's okay" I stop Shelley blabbing and take hold of her hands, squeezing gently to give reassurance "without even seeing it I know it will be stunning. I trust you and thank you. It is one thing less I have to think or worry about. Come on group hug and share the love"

We all laugh because it's our motto. When we first became friends and we realized we each had shitty baggage because of our pasts we came up with it and whenever we have one of our sharing sessions we finish with a group hug and shared the love.

A knock on the door has us breaking apart. Paul came in and held the door open as room service brought in dinner.

By eleven o' clock everyone has gone. Clayton locks the door and draws the curtains over the windows. Ho, ho, ho he's making sure we don't get disturbed; anticipation has my heart rate speeding up.

"Fancy a game of pool" he says picking up the cue his voice velvet and inviting.

Hell yeah! I'm up off the sofa in a flash "I'll be back in a minute, you set up" I say as I head for the bedroom. Okay I run. Time to get dressed for the occasion, I feel giddy with excitement. I'm about to fulfil a fantasy.

As I walk out of the bedroom I know by what I'm wearing Clayton, from the second he sees me, understood the kind of game I want to play. I have on my shortest skirt, a fitted blouse—with the buttons across my boobs fastened the rest left open so as I walk it shows flashes of my stomach—and my knee length high heeled Goth boots, the heels are chrome and buckles run up the side. Call it sixth sense but during the day I got the distinct impression Clayton has his own fantasy about fucking me whilst I'm wearing them, time to test my hunch.

Clayton watches my every move. I went to the bar and pour myself a very large Southern Comfort with lots of ice.

"Do you want a drink?" I ask casually.

Oh my sweet lord the look Clayton gives me is lecherous. He is going to devour me until I scream. I'm soaking already. Clayton slowly shakes his head and raises a bottle of beer, salutes me and takes a long pull. Game on.

I saunter over to the pool table deliberately swaying my hips. Again Clayton tracks my movements.

"I'll break" I say picking up a pool cue from the rack.

I can't play pool, I'm hopeless in fact but I'm sure as hell going to have fun trying tonight.

As nonchalantly as I can I lean over the table and line up my shot. Clayton moves around the table. I can feel his eyes running over my body. My skin tingles with the burn of his gaze. I make sure my stance is a provocative as possible.

I hit the white ball, the crack as it hit all the other balls and the resulting scatter resonates around the room. I pocket two colored balls, beginner's luck my snippy side quickly threw at me and stops me from gloating. I line up the next shot and miss.

As Clayton lines up his shot I move to stand opposite him. I bend low so he gets an eye full of cleavage. Clayton stills watching. I slowly undo the buttons and remove my shirt revealing the white lacy bra I'm wearing. His eyes smoulder. I stretch my arms out along the edge of the table.

"Whatcha waiting for take your shot" I purr. Smiling Clayton refocuses takes his shot and misses "too bad"

I get ready to take my shot. Clayton straightens put his cue to one side and slowly peels off his t-shirt, he runs his hands over his chest and down his washboard stomach. Yum, I lick my lips.

"Like what you see baby?" he teases then he mimic's my pose of stretching his arms wide along the edge of the table "take your shot"

I do and miss. We grin at each other and circle the table. Clayton bends to take his shot. I slowly peel my mini skirt off deliberately thrusting out my butt as I lower it over my hips revealing my white lacy thong.

Clayton licks his lips and takes a deep breath. He refocuses taking his shot and pockets a stripe. As he lines up his next shot I put my leg up on the table and start to unzip my boot.

"No baby, keep the boots on" Clayton's voice is thick and velvet smooth.

"Like them do you?" I tease as I refasten the boot.

"Yes" he whispers.

Bingo! I was right. Gleefully and smiling knowingly I put my leg down and reach behind my back and undo my bra. Keeping myself covered I raise an eyebrow in a silent "take your shot" command. Just as Clayton pulls the cue back and starts the forward strike motion I drop my arms and bra. He misses the shot in fact he misses the white ball completely.

"Oh dear, two shots for me I think"

I parade around the table in as a languid manner as I can, taking my time to select the best shot. Ha! As if I know what that looks like.

Clayton's eyes never leave me and he stands stock still, he's gripping his pool cue so tight the muscles and veins in his arms stand out in relief.

I position myself next to him and bend over, provocatively thrusting my butt out, to take my shot. Clayton stays as still as a statue. Damn. I'm willing him to touch me. I take my shot and pocket a colored ball. Huh, go figure. I move to the other side of Clayton to line up my next shot. Just as I'm about to strike Clayton's hand strokes and caresses my butt, I miss. He pats me lightly.

"Too bad baby"

I watch Clayton's muscles flex as he moves around the table sizing up his next shot, he takes his time letting me enjoy the view. As he lowers into position I move, Clayton stills and watches me. Standing beside him I angle myself so I can run my hand over his chest, across his abs and cup him between his legs. I feel his thick rock hard cock twitch through the material of his sweat pants. Leaning over I whisper in his ear "Take your shot baby" I squeeze slightly, a groan rumbles through him. I keep rubbing him very slowly as he tries to take his shot and fails miserably "oh dear" I mock.

I line up my next shot. Clayton slowly removes his sweat pants, he isn't wearing any boxers. His cock long and thick bobs and twitches begging for attention. A drop of cum glistens on the end, my mouth waters and I swallow audibly. Clayton strokes himself. Bloody hell he looks fucking hot doing that.

"Take your shot baby" he rasps.

Needless to say I miss.

Clayton gets in position to take his shot. I approach him, he doesn't move a muscle. I kneel down and take hold of his cock and run my tongue over the head licking off the cum. Clayton hisses in a breath. I don't take him in my mouth I just run my tongue over the sensitive tip.

"Take our shot baby" I say between licks. It takes a few minutes before he can do it and he misses. I wonder why "missed again" I feign concern.

The look Clayton gives me has my sex clenching. Oh what is he going to do as pay back I wonder as I strut my stuff walking around the table. I stop and contemplate my next move stroking my hand suggestively up and down the pool cue, as do I notice Clayton has managed to get his breathing under control, not for long I think smugly. I pick up my drink and take a swig taking an ice cube into my mouth. I suck on it and spit in back into the glass. It gives me an idea of what to do to Clayton on his next shot. With a smile on my lips I bend to take my shot.

"Stay as you are baby" Clayton's soft command has me holding still.

I have to breathe through my mouth as he approaches me. Anticipation has my heart racing flat out. Clayton places his hand on my butt and rubs moving in slow circular movements.

"Are you fond of these panties baby?" his hands grab the string waist.

"Yes" I whisper, they are part of a set.

"Shame" he says as he pulls and rips them off me. Holy hell this is fucking hot. Clayton runs his hand between my legs, cupping my sex he inserts a finger, the slow penetration makes me moan "you are so wet" Clayton rasps in my ear moving his finger in and out maddeningly slow "take your shot baby" he says with a hint of challenge.

Blindly I take a shot and pot a ball, what the… "Oh dear" Clayton mocks "that was one of mine" he chuckles as he moves away from me.

I pick up my drink and take a swig, taking an ice cube in my mouth. I smile at Clayton as innocently as I can as I put my glass down. Don't want to give the game away.

I move behind Clayton as he bends to take his shot. I place my hands on his tight ass. He stills. With one hand I rub his ass, with the other I take out the ice cube and run it along the crack of his ass.

"Fucking hell, shit" Clayton shouts loudly and jumps upright.

"Cold baby" I feign innocence when Clayton glares at me over his shoulder. I pop the ice cube on my tongue and suck.

Without a word Clayton resumes his position. With my right hand I reach between his legs and grasp his cock, with my left hand on his left buttock I push outward, separating his cheeks. I stroke his cock as I place my now cold tongue on his scrotum, running my tongue up over the perineum and up to his anus. I circle with my tongue then press against the sphincter not penetrating just applying pressure. I feel the veins in his cock pulse as he cries out in pleasure. I stroke and repeat the path my tongue had made.

"Take your shot baby" I challenge continuing to stroke and lick him, swirling my tongue and biting his ass with little nips.

Clayton is breathing hard and his body is trembling as he fights to keep control as I torture him with pleasure. He takes his shot—god the man has got control and then some over his body— and pots a ball. I'm impressed. I release him and stand moving quickly out of his reach because I'm sure he's about to launch himself at me.

Holy mother if his gaze alone ravages my naked body, god knows what he will do once he is unleashed. I don't want the game to end so I leave him alone for his next two shots. Instead I walk; okay I strut around the table stopping to take a drink every now and then.

On his third shot I drop to my knees and take him in my mouth. I swirl my tongue around his cock, taking him as deep as I can, sucking hard as I pull back. I hear the clatter of the cue as it hits to the floor. I open my eyes and can just make out Clayton's arms as they brace against the edge of the table, his head thrown back. He's close to coming so I stop and move out of the way.

"Take your shot baby" I purr.

Sweat trickles down Clayton's back. I run my fingers along his spine and he shudders, cursing under his breath he bends to pick up his cue. He lines up his shot and misses, on purpose I bet.

"Your turn" he says looking at me with hooded eyes.

I haven't quite bent over to take my shot when Clayton is on me. His hands snake under me and cup my breasts. I can feel his cock hard as steel pushing against my butt. Clayton adjusts himself so his cock goes between my legs.

I shift my stance so his cock is against my slit and I move my hips to gain friction at the same time Clayton rolls my nipples between his fingers sending sweet delicious spams straight to my core. I move my hips to such an angle so the head of his cock finds my entrance. I push back causing him to slide inside. We both groan. Clayton doesn't move.

"Take your shot baby" he says heavily between sharp in takes of breath.

I revel in the fullness his cock creates at my entrance. I want him deeper but he has one hand on my hip holding me still.

Somehow I pot one of my balls, I take the shot with so much gusto the white ball rebounds back to a place which means I don't have to change position.

"Lucky you" Clayton says darkly in my ear.

I feel his body flex and he inches deeper into me.

"Oh yes" I moan and my muscles clench around him trying to take him deeper.

"Take your shot" Clayton says and he thrusts deep.

I can't focus on the table all I'm aware of is his hands as they run over my stomach. One hand moves up to cup my breast and plays with my nipple whilst the other heads south his fingers circling my clit. The sensation's he's creating in me has my brain taking a vacation. My breathing sounds ragged in my ears. Suddenly Clayton stops and pulls out of me, the emptiness is excruciating, stepping away he trails his fingers down my spine then he spanks me. The sting of pain makes me moan as it mixes with the pleasure coursing through me.

When I'm capable of coherent thought and my brain has come back from its vacation I take my shot and pot another of my balls. What the hell…

Clayton drinks his beer as I assess my next shot, well I pretend to, secretly I ogle his magnificent naked body. As I get into position Clayton comes to me, I hold still. He gets down on his knees and turns so he's sat on the floor. He shuffles and moves my leg so it means I'm straddling him. His mouth latches onto my clit. I gasp as fizzy lukewarm liquid hits my clit, beer. My knees nearly buckle as Clayton sucks and laps at me. I hold onto the edge of the pool table for dear life.

"Oh god" I moan loudly as Clayton inserts his fingers into me and starts a slow in and out thrust with them.

"Take your shot baby" he says between licks to my clit.

Shot, what's he talking about my brain asks as the lust fog sets in again, I flex my hand because I'm gripping something so tight it hurts my fingers. It helps me focus, pool cue, shot, okay I can do this. I hit the white ball not caring where it goes or what it hits.

Clayton stops what he's doing and gets up standing in front of me, his chin and chest glisten with a mix of sweat, beer and me. I lean forward and lick up his chest to his neck. I reach up and grasp his hair pulling his head down so I can lick the rest of his neck and chin, humming my appreciation at the taste of him. When I get to his mouth I kiss him hard, his tongue invades my mouth, the taste of me, beer and Clayton is intoxicating and I demand more.

Clayton picks me up and sits me on the pool table. I inch backwards as he crawls up. Balls scatter in all directions as I lie down and Clayton mounts me.

His cock slides in smoothly, taking him to the hilt in one swift thrust of his hips. Heaven I'm in glorious heaven. My eyes roll to the back of my head and my back arches. I lift my hips to meet his thrusts groaning loudly.

Clayton's breath is hot against the side of my neck, his body slick with sweat glides against mine. His hard muscles flexing and relaxing with each thrust, I run my hands over his back and down to his ass pushing him into me harder. He starts to move faster "Oh yes" he's chasing his release and taking me with him. My sex clenches around him and I feel his cock pulse. My orgasm hits and rips through me.

"Oh god Clayton" I cry as my nerves scatter and body shatters.

Clayton wraps his arms around me, holding on as he rides out his orgasm saying my name over and over like a prayer.

I'm brought back to awareness by Clayton kissing me. Feather light kisses across my forehead, cheeks, jaw and neck. I open my eyes to see Clayton looking at me with a myriad of emotions on his face love, awe, admiration and fascination.

"I love you" he whispers then he kisses the hell out of me.

Clayton helps me down off the pool table "I must say that is the best game of pool I have ever played"

"Me too" I say grinning.

"I've got to ask, yes curiosity" he cuts me off as I'm about to make a snarky comment "where in the fuck did you get the idea?"

"Imagination" I pause thinking, then add "and following my instinct. Plus it's amazing what you pick up from books" I wink at him "so you like my boots" I lift one of my legs to show him.

"Oh fuck yes" he growls picking me up and carries me to the bedroom.

Chapter Seventeen

SKYE

"Deep breath" I tell myself for the umpteenth time, my nerves are kicking in. I pace the suite waiting for Paul to give me the okay to head downstairs.

Clayton had left twenty minutes ago with everyone else. I had to kick him out. He went reluctantly and only because I pointed out he would be on his own in the suite until mid-afternoon as he wouldn't be able to get into the VIP areas once I arrived due to the new security measures.

The press and paparazzi are still out in force; yesterday's press conference has done little to thin out the hordes of journalists and photographers. According to the news reports rumours are abound we plan to get married today. Well they will be sadly disappointed.

Clayton has been lovingly attentive all morning. He'd woken me with kisses all over my body and brought me to orgasm three times before he sought his own release. My gaze lands on the pool table and I feel my body stir as I recall what we'd done to each other. Hmm would Clayton be game trying out the piano tonight. A smile spreads across my face as ideas form. Clayton changed his plans to stay another night when he found out yesterday I am travelling back to LA Monday morning. Shelley, Phil and Simon are heading back later this afternoon on Clayton's plane which is then coming straight back for us. I tried to have a dig at Clayton about his carbon footprint, he shrugged it off.

"Sue me, but if it means I get to spend extra time with you it's worth it"

I couldn't argue with that.

Giles turned up whilst we ate breakfast to let me know of another change. Due to the volume of people turning up the afternoon Q&A has now been brought forward to this morning and the meet and greet will start immediately after. Another long day, I thoroughly enjoyed yesterday and I'm looking forward to today with apprehension. I'm more worried about what the fans reaction will be to all the press around. I hoped they didn't blame me for spoiling their convention experience. I voiced these thoughts during dinner last night and everyone said I'm being over sensitive. I snort a derisive laugh, that's just a polite way of saying I'm being silly. It doesn't stop me worrying though.

I think that's part of the reason why Clayton was making such a fuss of me this morning, trying to distract me. I look out of the window taking in the Vegas landscape it makes me realize I've never done the tourist thing or spent time gambling whenever I came to Vegas. I've never experienced the thrill of winning or the disappointment of losing. When all this madness has settled down I am so coming back here to do all of those things, I nod to myself in agreement.

"Skye we're ready for you" Paul says softly from behind me.

I yelp and jump about a mile in the air; he scared the crap out of me. I hadn't heard him. I turn to glare at him. Paul is trying desperately not to laugh.

"You are so going to get bells mister" I threaten whilst clutching my chest and rattling heart.

"In my defence I called you three times" he holds up his hands in surrender "are you okay?" he asks softly, his usually hard features softening with concern.

"Nervous" I admitted "how bad is it?"

Paul knew better than to try and placate me or fob me off with everything will be fine crap.

"Mental doesn't even start to describe it, the good thing with the route you will be taking you won't get to see any of it" Paul put his hands on my shoulders and gently squeezes "I won't let anything happen to you I promise"

I nod, I know Paul will do everything in his power to protect me and I trust him implicitly. I run my sweaty palms down the front of my jeans and straighten my AC/DC rhinestone logo t-shirt, it has a worn battered look to it then picked up my lightweight soft kid leather jacket. I'm wearing killer heels, I might not be able to run fast in them but I sure as hell can use them as a weapon if I need to. I left my hair down and mascara and lip stick is the only make up I have on. I'm as ready as I'll ever be.

Stepping into the corridor I'm immediately surrounded by five other security guards. I look at Paul "Seriously it's that mental?"

"Don't worry. I won't let anything happen to you"

It isn't until we get in the service elevator I realize Paul didn't answer my question. I decide to let it go. I really, really don't want to know.

I find it fascinating how different the staff only areas are to the luxury and opulence of the guest areas. Whitewashed walls, linoleum flooring and visible pipes it is all clinically clean. I'm taken through one of the kitchens and I'm amazed at the sheer scale of it and it's a mass of activity. As we walk through shouts of congratulations, cheers and clapping went up. I smile, wave and shout thank you back to the staff.

I get to the Q&A VIP area without incident. Clayton is the first person to greet me the second I set foot through the door, to say he pounces on me would be an understatement.

"You okay baby?" he asks anxiety is rolling off him and his relief is palpable. He holds me at arm's length scrutinising and checking for signs of what I have no idea, injury maybe. He brings me in to him for another hug. I lean back to look at his anxious face.

"I am absolutely fine. The only people I saw were kitchen staff. Who by the way are all cheerful and shouted congratulations to me as we passed through, Paul and the guys did a sterling job" I say trying to reassure him, then it occurs to me something must have happened on his way down because he's rattled "how about you?" I ask softly.

"There was a near riot when the press saw me walking through the casino" he sighs and runs a hand through his hair "good job Marco and security were with us. Marco managed to get us into the staff only entrance which is security coded. I tell you it was fucking scary. We seriously need to discuss upping security when we are back in New York" his tone brokers no argument.

I rub his arms, in a way I suppose I'm subliminally calming him "Sure lets discuss it tonight along with some other things, it'll be easier with everyone gone" Clayton nods his agreement and kisses me tenderly "I love you" I whisper.

Clayton's smile lights up his whole face it's as if I've given him the best gift in the world. Actually I suppose it is considering how wealthy he is. It's something he can't buy. Hmm that gives me an idea for his birthday which is coming up at the end of October.

I catch up with each of my friends making sure they are okay. Mike and Penny are absolutely thrilled with the way the weekend is turning out.

"You know being this side of things has really opened my eyes" says Mike "I always knew you were a star now I know you are a mega super star of the Fantasy and Sci Fi art world and you have honored me and Penny by giving us this unique experience into your life and sharing it with us. This weekend has been the best of my life"

"And mine" Penny echoes "we have loved every single minute of it. Your friends have been so welcoming and considerate towards us. I feel as if we've known them forever"

"I am so pleased you're both having such a good time" I smile at their enthusiasm.

"Miss Darcy excuse me" I turn to see Paul making his way towards me "time to head down to the auditorium"

I shout my goodbye and see you in a few minutes as I follow Paul out. I dawns on me then Paul has started to call me Skye—and he has since Italy—when we are in private and using formal address in public. I wonder if Macy has anything to do with it, I make a mental note to ask her.

The trip to the auditorium is another change, due to the large volume of ticket sales. The Q&A is being done with three other artists although we all work in the same genre our styles couldn't be more different including the medium we chose to work in. I know the other artists and we all got on well so I'm thankful there will be no animosity towards me.

"Hey Skye, long time no see" Todd drawls sarcastically as he greets me with a hug.

I had met up with him for lunch earlier in week in LA. Todd is a good fifteen years older than me and cultivates the half-starved waif artisan look complete with goatee. It fooled no-one who is in the know because Todd is a multi-millionaire. A lot of his work is to do with the film industry. I'd been fortunate enough to meet him not long after moving to New York right place, right time kind of thing. Every now and then he'll get in touch and offer me work on a film project, if my work load and diary allows I will take it on.

"Congratulations on your engagement. Will I get to meet the lucky bastard?"

I laugh and blush "Of course, he'll be here in a few minutes"

"Skye good to see you" Jules and Ben the other two artists say together and hug me.

"Trust you to cause absolute bedlam again" Jules says emphasising the last word.

He's laughing obviously remembering the last appearance we did together a few years ago where we were both guest artists and speakers.

"Hey you know me bedlam is my middle name" I joke "but guys on a serious note I'm sorry for any inconvenience all this has caused you"

"Are you kidding me" Jules barks out a laugh "after your last appearance I got so much work I had enough to keep me going for over eighteen months this time I'm banking on you setting me up for life"

"Freeloader" I deadpan and roll my eyes making them all laugh, I happen to look over at the door to see my entourage arrive. I wave to Clayton to come over "you are about to meet the lucky bastard" I say to Todd.

They all turn and watch Clayton approach.

"Oh my I've died and gone to heaven" Ben says in a hushed voice.

"I bet Skye does several times a day" Todd says giving me a saucy wink and I blush to the roots of my hair.

"Love that color on you" Jules chuckles.

Clayton looks at me bemused and raises an eyebrow. I shake my head I'm so not going to tell him the tone of this conversation. Instead I duly introduce him to the three artists.

I stand back and watch Clayton work his charismatic magic. I swear within thirty seconds he has them eating out of his hand. It hasn't escaped my notice this weekend that Clayton always asks certain questions of the people who know me. How did they meet me? How long had they known me? What work had we done or collaborated on together? He very cleverly threw these questions in at random intervals and that took the creepiness out of it. If he asked the questions altogether I would definitely be running for the hills screaming at the top of my lungs.

Clayton has told me he didn't have friends in the same context as I did. He has his family for all the personal stuff as he put it. He immerses himself in work and he has plenty of associates but no-one knew him soul deep and I'm the only person with that privileged insight.

"Show time folks" Giles calls out rubbing his hands together as he walks towards us. Giles has a rather manic look on his face probably a combination of the stress from all the press and fans along with ticket sales surpassing his wildest dreams "everyone ready" he says looking at each of us.

We all nod, my stomach flip flops. I really hope people will not fixate on my engagement.

"By the way, we've had the audience write down the question they want to ask then we will draw them out of a drum so they will be random" Giles clears his throat then looks at me almost embarrassed.

"Please tell me you've filtered them and got rid of the personal ones" I say in alarm.

Giles relaxes and nods, "thank you" I mouth, we're both on the same page.

"If everyone is in agreement the order I'll introduce you all on to stage will be Ben, Jules, Todd then Skye"

I look at the guys and they readily agree. I could take it as an insult no-one wants me to go first but I know, and so did they, I will get the biggest welcome reception and no-one really wants to follow that. Can't say I blame them, I wouldn't either if it was one of them in my situation.

Giles heads out and we all follow him. Clayton and my friends make their way to their seats in the audience. Standing in the wings I get a sudden bout of nerves, my heart pounds and my palms become sweaty. Breathe, deep breaths, in through the nose out through the mouth, I chant to myself.

I can hear Giles on the stage welcoming the crowd and explaining what is going to happen then he starts introducing each of us giving a brief bio then calling a name. Ben and Jules get polite applause. Todd's is louder and with cheers. When Giles calls my name it sounds as if a jet is coming in to land. Yesterday I thought the reception at the show opening was mind blowing, today holy fucking hell today, now I know what it's like to be a rock star at a sell-out stadium gig. Taking a deep breath I step out.

"Oh my god honey you were absolutely sensational" Simon squeals as he enters my suite and runs to me giving me a hug "I swear every person in that room fell more in love with you. You owned it baby girl. Mr Money Bags has his work cut out" Simon sing-songs in a loud stage whisper.
"I heard that" Clayton calls from the bar.
"You were meant to" Simon retorts unabashed.
The Q&A had gone on for three hours due to every seat being filled and the sheer amount of questions, the majority were for me but I threw the questions out to Todd, Jules and Ben to answer as well or I blatantly said one of the others was better qualified to answer as it was their field of expertise. The guys each thanked me separately after the Q&A for being selfless and involving them more than I needed to. I joked they owed me big time and I would come knocking on their door when I was broke and destitute. That was when each of them got serious on me and vowed to be there for me should I ever need help of any sort. I was touched by their sentiments and being a girl I filled up but I managed to hold back the tears.
I had an absolute ball during the time on stage. We bantered, mocked and joked with each other. A couple of times the guys got a dig in about the press frenzy. We had the audience in stitches. When the audience realized Clayton was in the auditorium they chanted until he finally came on stage to huge cheers. Clayton came to me and kissed the back of my hand and returned to his seat. Some lucky sods will be making a fortune now for pictures and video footage of that moment.
I did a couple hours of meet and greet with the fans and now I'm relaxing and enjoying a very, very late lunch with everyone before saying our goodbyes. I told Macy to speak to Mike about getting dates so we could get together to discuss his commission, the pair of them have really won me over and I could see a budding friendship forming between Clayton and Mike.

I sigh in contentment. Everyone has gone home, I'm all packed and it's early evening, I'm lying on the sofa after a hot soak in the bath wrapped in my bathrobe and watching TV with Clayton curled around me. We are still hot news and video footage of Clayton coming on stage and kissing the back of my hand at the Q&A is the main story.

"You know they must seriously be struggling for something news worthy if we are one of the main stories" I say failing to hide my contempt.

"And on that note, now would be a good time to discuss security" Clayton murmurs in my ear.

"Yes what are you going to be doing" I say twisting round to face him.

"Me!"

Ha! That startled and shocked him going by the high pitch of his voice "Yes, you Mr Blake" I poke him in the chest and raise an eyebrow at the surprised expression on his face he obviously thought he would be discussing getting extra security for me "my security is already in place for LA and when I'm back in New York. Paul doesn't wait to be told. So what are you putting in place for you or should I get Paul to sort it?"

Clayton gapes at me then throws back his head and roars laughing.

"What's so funny?" he's puzzling me I can't see the joke or the funny side of having to organise more security because to me it's an absolute ball ache.

"Me. Here I am worrying about you and your safety when you have an ex-marine working for you, who has done a sterling job this weekend keeping us both safe" he sighs "Christ I feel such a fucking idiot"

"Yes you are a prat but it still doesn't tell me what you are putting in place"

"I'm sorry" he plants a kiss at the end of my nose when he realizes how serious I am "I already have security detail in place. Bruce like Paul is ex-marine and he too will see to it without being told"

"What about your family?" it suddenly occurs to me the press would hound them. I don't have that problem.

"They will contact Bruce if things get too bad. They have security anyway but it will be increased if they felt they needed it" Clayton pauses his dark blue eyes searching my face "you mentioned about other things to discuss" he says this very softly almost warily.

Ah hell. Me and my big mouth, I'm mentally biting off my tongue. Thinking back to this morning at the time when I said that it seemed like a good idea to get some things out in the open for future discussions we will need to have. Looking into his beautiful eyes I can see his love for me, the coward in me is hiding behind the sofa. Big girl pants time, taking a deep breath I pull them up.

"Expectations" I say in a low voice. I see the perplexity this one word causes him "I think we need to discuss each other's expectations for when I am back in New York. For example: living arrangements. I mean do you expect to move in with me or vice versa straightaway or do we get a new place at some point in the future?"

"What would you like to do?" his voice still a soft rasp.

Smooth move, get me to spill first "I don't know. I know we enjoy each other's company but we've been in a bubble of bliss. It's a going to be different because the outside world is going to intrude, plus I've never seen where you live" Christ the last bit comes out lame.

"All valid points, what other concerns do you have?"

"Attending functions, the big one though" I sigh, deep breath "pre-nup" I search his face for a reaction all I see is love. Anxiety is eating at me and my stomach is in knots.

"Again all valid points and my love, you are six steps ahead of me. As I see it the most pressing is living arrangements plus it's the only one I have really thought about" he smiles at me so sweetly I feel my anxiety ebb away 'how about we don't make any decision for at least a month, I do however expect to spend each night with you either in your bed or mine. As for functions and other social events let's play it by ear and I am certain at some point there will be one where it is important to one of us to attend so the expectation will be for the other to go as eye candy. How does that sound?" his eyes twinkle with amusement. I smile and nod he makes it sound so simple and he is willing to give us time "I can live with that and we promise each other to let the other know if something isn't working" he finishes.

"I can live with that too" I kiss him "I just want you to know that when the time comes I am ready to discuss pre-nup. I know my lawyers are going to insist on one so I can sure as hell imagine yours are going to as well" I stroke his cheek tenderly hoping to take the ugly sting out of the harsh reality our union presents.

"You are an amazing woman Skye Darcy. I would give you the world if I could, instead I will give you everything that is mine" holy shit, I gasp "I told you on Friday my life is meaningless without you in it. I was an empty shell until you came along. There is nothing I can give you that you can't buy or get for yourself. All I have is me and I want to share everything I have with you"

I'm speechless he's telling me he doesn't want a pre-nup. I've no idea what to think or how to feel about it. My brain has definitely gone on vacation, a long one.

"I can see I've surprised you and you were fully expecting to sign a pre-nup and you are right our lawyers are going to want us to protect our personal wealth and business interests. But I realize now the only thing I want to keep and protect in my life is you"

My heart swells and surges with the love I feel for this man, this Adonis before me "I love you so, so very much" I whisper fighting back the tears that blur my vision.

A devastatingly beautiful and shy smile spreads across his lips, lighting up his whole face making him impossibly more stunningly handsome.

Clayton trails his fingers down my cheek "I have something I want to tell you" his smile fades to be replaced with a frown. My anxiety comes back full force, I sense I'm not going to like what I'm about to hear "you know of my reputation as a womaniser and my past of casual sex" I nod.

I'm starting to feel sick, has he cheated on me already since we have been together as an official couple? Clayton's arms tighten around me pulling me back to him. Unconsciously I'm pulling away from him and my body is preparing and getting ready to run.

"The first two weeks when you left New York I went on four dates" I drew in a deep breath, it's before we were officially a couple but his admission still stings "my mother set them up and badgered me until I gave in, but that's no excuse. Before you came along I would have fucked them and left them, never giving them a second thought"

"You didn't sleep with them" I cut in, I feel sick; my stomach roils with anxiety and relief.

"No, I didn't" he whispers "the offers were there but I didn't want to, couldn't. You were constantly in the forefront of my mind. I was comparing them to you. I was grieving for the loss of you in my life and I wanted to fill the huge hole you had left. Anyway after the fourth disastrous date I realized more than anything I wanted in the world was for us to work and I didn't want to taint what we could have when you came back in September" he sighs heavily "I lost it big time with my mother when she started meddling again. It got so bad I wouldn't speak to or see her" he let out a derisive laugh "my brothers had to act as mediators. I even went to London to escape her at that point our relationship was best described as strained. Christ I was such a shit to her"

"'But you are okay now?" the last thing I want is to be the cause of a family feud.

"Yeah" he snorts "look the reason I'm telling you all this is because I want you to hear it from me what I did even though we weren't official but I felt I cheated the memory of you and there is bound to be gossip concerning me and those women"

"Thank you for your honesty, I appreciate it" I place a kiss over his heart, a thought occurs to me that has me grinning like a Cheshire cat "so when we saw each other in London you hadn't had sex for five weeks?"

"Yes ma'am" Clayton's grin matches mine "and I was suffering from a severe case of blue balls and blisters on my right hand"

I laugh with joy and relief, Clayton had kept himself pure for me, he truly wants me and loves me with every cell and bone in his body, heart and soul and he always has. I am his world and he is mine.

I kiss him in the way I do to show him through touch and sensation what he means to me. What starts out as slow and tender, the dipping and tasting of our tongues ignites into hungry need. I have no idea who did what but in no time at all we are naked and I'm beneath Clayton. He is inside me moving in and out with languorously deep deliberate thrusts. I feel every glorious thick inch of him as I meet his thrusts and clench my muscles to hold onto him as he withdrew. We came hard together, holding on tight and calling each other's name.

Chapter Eighteen

CLAYTON

The traffic crawls forward agonisingly slow, horns blare as taxi drivers cut each other up. Bicycle couriers on death wishes weave in and out of the slow moving almost stationary cars.

I love the city but it's empty without Skye. Christ I fucking miss her. It has been just over forty eight hours since I'd left her in LA and I have another seventy two before I can hold her in my arms again. I've seen her via video call this morning but it isn't the same, I want her in the flesh.

The weekend in Vegas has been the best of my life. I grin like a stupid fucker when people congratulate me. I don't care if they think I'm a sap. I know my staff have seen a new side to me and it totally threw them. Helena my secretary jokes she likes the new Clayton Blake. I need to give her a pay rise she has gone above and beyond the call of duty in fending off the press this week and without complaint plus the media interest shows no sign of letting up.

The success of the convention and the pulling power of Skye really captured the media's imagination. The press are billing us as New York's most powerful and glamorous couple when they realized how wealthy Skye is in her own right and self-made like me. The phrase 'powerhouse' is being used to describe us.

The newscasters never got tired of showing the clip from the Q&A when I went on stage, fuck it had been one of the most, if not 'the' most nerve wracking experiences of my life. Skye was welcomed on stage like a rock star. The noise had been incredible, deafening but incredible and she had taken it all in her stride, looking cool calm and collected. Skye also endured herself more to her fans because she made sure her fellow artists had an equal share of the attention and limelight, she didn't have to but she chose to.

The press got hold of this plus other stories from fans who met her, the most prominent being Danny and his father. I saw the interview Danny gave, the pictures his father had taken flashed on screen to back up Danny's story of Skye sitting on the elevator floor to sign all of his memorabilia. I smile as I remember the journalist trying to suggest Skye did it under duress because he'd been so upset. Danny soon put paid to that and on live TV as well. Lesson learnt by the journalist don't try to disrespect an eight year olds heroine.

Simon has proven to be worth his weight in gold as well. I met with him Monday afternoon, he impressed the pants off me in Vegas and he blew me away within the first fifteen minutes of the meeting, so much so I got all my executives in because a lot of what he covered they needed to hear it as well. Before he left he had a signed contract. The only thing I changed was his fee, I increased it. He will have earned every penny of it by the time I married Skye.

A white blonde curly haired woman getting out of an SUV further up the road catches my attention. Is it, I lean forward trying to get a better look; no it can't be Skye is in LA. Fuck I'm missing Skye so much I'm hallucinating images of her.

I focus on the woman, she has her back to me; she's greeting a man as another woman joins her. Christ that woman looks just like Macy. My heart is beating so rapidly it feels as if it's in my mouth. The white blonde turns and looks directly at me as we pass, Skye.

What... when... how... my mind splutters. I'm in shock.

Why hadn't Skye acknowledged she had seen me?

Fuck that why didn't she tell me this morning she was coming back early?

I'm getting angry, why the fucking hell hadn't she rung me to tell me she is back the minute she landed?

Spurned into action I take out my phone from my jacket pocket, no missed calls or email from her. I feel like punching something. I've missed the opportunity to get out of the car to confront her. How dare she not fucking tell me and why the fuck is she keeping it from me? Who is that fucker she is meeting?

It's obvious she doesn't miss me as much as I miss her and where the fuck is her security my mind shouts as I didn't even see Paul.

My mood is getting blacker. I could have told Bruce to turn around instead I ring her, it went straight to voicemail. Shit. I hang up too angry to leave a message.

By the time I get back to the office I'm in the foulest mood I have ever been in for a very long time. Picking up on my bad mood my employees immediately run in the opposite direction and I literally bite the head off of anyone who is foolish enough to approach me or not get out of my way fast enough. Helena the professional that she is says nothing but follows me into my office puts my messages on the desk telling me the top one is urgent, when she leaves I slam the door after her. I really, really want to hit something.

SKYE

Helena meets me at the elevator. I rang her as I got to the office to see if Clayton is free. I want to surprise him. I went back to LA and worked around the clock to finish the commission in record time so I could come home early. I missed Clayton. Helena told me I have all access to Clayton whenever I wanted if he is in the office. I'm surprised to see her waiting for me as I step out of the elevator, after greeting each other the reason becomes apparent.

"I have to warn you Mr Blake is in a foul mood. I have not seen him in a mood like this since he has met you" Helena blushes "sorry that was unprofessional and inappropriate of me" she says quickly.

"Don't worry about it, any idea what could have set him off?" I say trying for easy going manner in order to put her at ease, it works.

Helena sighs exasperated "None whatsoever and I've been racking my brain. This morning he was his usual happy pleasant self. He went out for a business meeting and returned half an hour ago in the foulest mood I've not seen in months"

"Where was Clayton's meeting?" Suspicion grips me. It's possible I'm the cause of his bad mood.

"It was across town" is all Helena supplies.

It's enough. I am the cause. I made a stop en-route to meet with Billy my property agent. He called Macy just as we left the airport to find out when I would be available to view a building he had just seen. Paul said we passed the building in question on our way to Clayton's office. I decided a quick stop to see if the building was worth making an appointment to view. Billy said he'd wait for me.

When I'd stepped out of the car the hairs on the back of my neck prickled. I knew I was being watched. I started to tingle it was the kind of tingle I get when Clayton is near. I turned and looked around me, I couldn't see him. A Bentley with blacked out windows went past, at the time I speculated Clayton could be in the car, now I know he was and he had seen me. Right this minute he is stewing I didn't tell him I was coming back early. God damn it, his current mood pissed on my chips as Shelley would say. Well you will just have to get creative and improvise I tell myself.

Just like last time all those weeks ago, all staff gape openly at me only this time some have that star struck look as I walk the length of the office with Helena.

"Mr Blake has a meeting in forty five minutes" Helena says subtly letting me know how long I've got. I like this woman.

"Let me see if I can work my magic on his mood" I wink and open the door.

Clayton is stood with his back to me. He's looking out the window, hands on his hips. My mouth waters as I admire his narrow hips and tight ass encased in navy blue trousers. His broad shoulders emphasised by the dark blue silk vest worn over a crisp white shirt.

"It's not fucking good enough" Clayton suddenly barks making me jump. I nearly bolt out of the door. I can feel the aggression rolling off him "no. I am not fucking signing anything. The whole thing is a fucking sham. Shit my three year old nephews can do better"

He's on the phone my mind breathes a sigh of relief. As I close and lock the door quietly I glance at the glass wall, good the blinds are closed. I move further into the room. Clayton spins round stopping dead when he sees me. Surprise flits across his face but I can also see anger there.

I undo my jacket as I walk slowly towards him, his eyes follow my movements. Underneath I have on a short sleeveless shirt waister style black dress; I also have on mine and his favourite boots. I put my jacket over the back of a chair and continue walking towards him.

"I don't care. Tell them to go back to the drawing board. I am not putting my name or money to that piece of shit"

Clayton stands like a statue as I reach him. I put my hands on his chest, I can feel his heart pounding, and look into his eyes. I can see he is fighting a myriad of emotions. I reach for his tie and tug. Clayton resists for all of two seconds. I lift to my tip toes as I bring him to meet me. I kiss his lips tenderly, as I start to pull away Clayton's arms snake around me and he deepens the kiss. I can hear the other person in his ear piece. I break the kiss.

"Continue your call" I whisper.

My hands move down to his waist band and I undo the button. Clayton grasps my wrists his look is full of dark warning. As if that is going to stop me, my inner goddess is free and we are hungry.

"Fulfilling a fantasy" I whisper and smile lasciviously.

Clayton's mouth pops open and his eyes widen in surprise. I drop to my knees and he lets go of my wrists. Keeping eye contact I lick my lips as I pull his zipper down.

"Yes, I'm still here something else got my attention for a minute. Say that again"

Taking the waist band of both his trousers and boxers I tug them down together, far enough to release his gloriously erect cock. I run my fingers over his shaft following the veins.

"You are just telling me the same fucking thing in a different way. I'm not buying it'" he still sounds angry "still not good enough, the whole thing fucking stinks" I take him in my mouth and suck hard.

"Fuck" Clayton barks out "no I just split water over my desk"

Nicely covered I grin and mentally give him a gold star for thinking so quickly. I run my tongue over the head of his cock and push the tip into the slit. Clayton hisses. I look up at him. His face is set hard in concentration. Still keeping eye contact I open my mouth and take as much of him as I can. I lightly drag my teeth over his cock as I withdrew. Clayton's eyes roll, his head falls back. The veins in his neck bulge over his collar, I've got him.

I start to work him, stroking with one hand and cupping his balls in the other I massage and lightly scrape my nails over his sack.

"Get them to do a presentation" he is breathing hard now and trying not to let whoever it is on the other end hear, I pick up the momentum "no… tomorrow. Helena will give you a time"

Clayton's hips begin to move to my rhythm. A salty tang hits my tongue, he's close. I suck harder.

"Shit, call me back later" Clayton rips the ear piece out and flings it in the direction of his desk.

Clayton places both hands on my head, burying his fingers into my hair. The slight sting on my scalp as he pulls my hair I find a huge turn on, I'm unravelling him. He takes over and fucks my mouth. I grip his hips my fingers flex against his tight ass as he pumps.

"Harder" Clayton hisses the command "that's it baby. I'm coming. Oh fuck yes"

His release fills my mouth. I swallow quickly so I can take more of him. I suck and lick until I have every last drop, then I suck and lick him clean reluctantly putting his cock back inside his boxers when I've finished. Clayton helps me to my feet and kisses me.

"Feeling better now? I hear you were in a foul mood" I grin mischievously.

Clayton buries his head in the crook of my neck "Why didn't you tell me you were coming back early?" it came out muffled. Clayton breathed in deeply and the expelling hot breath sends goose bumps all over my skin.

"I wanted to surprise you, besides I wasn't certain when we spoke early this morning" I shrug "I didn't want to get your hopes up only to disappoint you later if things hadn't panned out. So tell me" I lift his head off my shoulder and cup his face so I can see him. Clayton stays bent so we are eye-level "this bad mood, actually let me guess. You saw me in the street. You were in the Bentley with the blacked out windows and ever since you have been tormenting yourself as to why I didn't call"

Clayton looks adorably sheepish "Busted" he seems to consider what I've said because his eyes widen and he flushes "actually I just realized, I was convinced you had seen me and you chose to ignore me. I forgot the windows were blacked out"

"Oh my god! Clayton you numpty" I laugh.

"Numpty" he says smiling "that's a new one. Is that a new way of calling me an idiot by any chance?"

I nod and beam at him, then kiss him "I've missed you" I say against his lips and kiss him again.

"So what you just did that was a fantasy fulfilled" his eyes darken with lust.

"Oh yes, did you like it?" I purr.

"Very much, feel free to come by any time you have the urge to play out a fantasy or two"

"Hmm, I better get my thinking cap on, although" I reach down and rub his cock through his boxers, his trousers are still open "I do have one thing I would like to leave you with" Clayton hasn't softened completely and he becomes instantly hard as I touch him, his hips surging as I continue to fondle him.

"Tell me baby" his voice rasps in a groan.

"A memory" I whisper.

He looks at me puzzled "A memory" he repeats.

Nodding I slip my hand into his boxers and grasp his cock and start stroking him.

"Yes of you fucking me on your desk"

Clayton didn't need telling twice or any further encouragement. Picking me up and he carries me over to his huge wooden desk. Putting me down on my feet he lifts the skirt of my dress to my waist and slips his hand down the front of my panties, massaging my clit. I moan when he slides his fingers inside me.

"Oh baby, just as I like you wet and ready for me as always" removing his hand he pulls down my panties "and you're wearing my favourite boots as well"

From his kneeling position Clayton runs his tongue over my slit and circles my clit "I love the taste of your pussy" he murmurs "sit up on the desk" I do as he instructs.

"Spread your legs for me" I did. I undo the top buttons of my dress to expose my breasts and look up at Clayton through my lashes "you look so fuckable" a growl rumbles deep within his chest.

In one swift move Clayton pulls down his boxers and is buried deep inside me before I take my next breath. Oh heaven. I lean backwards and rest on my elbows and lift my legs around his hips, tilting my hips to take him deeper with each thrust.

"Oh yes" I moan as pleasure courses through me as I feel him slide in and out. I'm addicted to this, to him.

"I'm going to move fast and hard, you'll need to be quiet baby" Clayton says bending over me and kissing me hard, bruising my lips. He's letting me know he's about to lose control. Anticipation for the imminent pounding makes me even wetter. Standing he positions himself and adjusts his stance, gripping my hips he lifts me as he withdraws then pulls me onto him as he thrusts forward hard.

I bite down on a cry of intense pleasure. I take every inch of his thick long cock as he sets a punishing pace. He possesses me, claiming ownership of my pleasure and I love every minute of it. The fact he is fucking me in his office and we are fully clothed drives me toward my climax.

"I can feel you baby, come for me, now" Clayton rasps the command slamming into me setting off my orgasm. I hold onto Clayton for dear life as he thrusts faster chasing his own release making my orgasm roll into anther more intense one, with one final thrust Clayton groans out my name. I can feel his cock twitching and pulsing as his release fills me.

Clayton collapses on me, his head resting on my breasts. He rains kisses over them whispering how much he's missed and loves me and that one day he is going to fuck my glorious tits.

"Come on let me clean you up" Clayton lifts me off the desk and carries me to the bathroom; the door is cleverly hidden next to a large cabinet that holds decanters and various glasses.

"What are your plans for tonight" Clayton asks as he tenderly wipes a cloth between my legs.

"Apart from shagging you senseless and eating, nothing" I say it matter of fact making Clayton chuckle "why what have you got planned?"

Clayton threw the cloth into a basket and straightens my dress before answering.

"Family dinner, will you come with me?" the hope in his face makes my heart ache "I can't get out of it. I should have gone on Monday to see my mother but I cancelled and promised faithfully I would go tonight. It will be the first time I will have seen any of them since our engagement. So will you come, please?"

The puppy dog eyes did it, how can I say no. "I would love to go with you" he gives me the sweetest of smiles "are you going to tell your family I'm coming?"

The smile turns impish as he shakes his head "I'll pick you up at six and thank you"

We finish straightening ourselves up and I realize I didn't have my panties and went back out into the office to look for them around his desk.

"What are you looking for?" Clayton stands in the door way of the bathroom watching me.

"My panties, do you remember what you did with them?" I say searching the floor.

"Yes" I look up at him. Grinning he put his hand in his trouser pocket and slowly pulls out my blue lacy boy short panties. I walk toward him and hold out my hand for them. Clayton slowly shakes his head.

"You are not getting them back, these" he holds them higher "are mine to keep as a memento" Clayton holds my panties to his nose and inhales deeply "my favourite perfume" he sighs.

Holy hell that is erotic to watch.

"You only want them so you can masturbate as your memory re-enacts this afternoon you pervert" I mock scold.

The phone on Clayton's desk buzzes and Helena's voice fills the room "Your three o'clock meeting is waiting for you Mr Blake"

"My cue to leave" I say going to the chair to pick up my jacket, putting it on as I went to the door and unlocked it. Clayton got his jacket "I'll see you at six"

"Wait I'll walk with you to the elevator" I open my mouth to say he has a meeting and it isn't necessary when he cut me off "they can wait. Shall we?"

Clayton held out his arm and I take it. He pulls me to him and kisses me long and slow making my toes curl.

"Come on before I decide to chain you to my desk" his voice is husky and lustful.

"Wow, de ja vu" Clayton raises an eyebrow at me "you threatened that last time I was here or should I say promised" I tease coquettishly.

"So I did" Clayton wiggles his eyebrows making me laugh as I open the door.

Helena stood as we come out of the office. She looks at Clayton's smiling face then at me. I wink at her and wiggle my fingers in Clayton's direction. Helena put her head down quickly but I can see her silent laugh as her shoulders shake.

"I'll be five minutes Helena please let them know in the boardroom"

"Yes Mr Blake. Goodbye Miss Darcy" she smiles at me knowingly.

The walk to the elevator has the staff doing the usual gawp. One young lady smiles and says congratulations to us as she passes. Poor thing blushes beetroot as both Clayton and I acknowledge her and say thank you.

"So what's the dress code for tonight" I ask as we reach the elevator.

"Wear whatever you'll be comfortable in. Dinner will be at mother's house with my brothers and their partners"

"Smart casual then, great that narrows it down, not" I say sarcastically.

The elevator pings notifying me of its arrival and the doors open.

"I will be wearing black jeans with a shirt and blazer if that helps" Clayton says in an effeminate voice making me chuckle.

I give him a quick kiss and step into the elevator "See you at six" I say and blow him a kiss as the doors begin closing. Clayton pretends to catch it and places his hand over his heart.

CLAYTON

I arrive at Skye's building to find security on the door and in the foyer.

"Good evening Mr Blake, please go right up" the guard indicates to the elevator.

I'm impressed. I didn't see any paparazzi around but that doesn't mean they weren't lurking. It won't take long before they realize Skye is back in New York. Who was I fucking kidding they probably already knew! Skye must have come straight from the airport to my office and I have no idea what she has done since leaving me a few hours ago.

My thoughts turn to the blow job she'd given me whilst I'd been on the phone. Fulfilling a fantasy, I chuckle as I recall my shock when she'd said it. I really want to find out more about her fantasies, fucking her on my desk fulfilled one of mine and set off ideas for some others. Skye might be inexperienced but by Christ she is adventurous.

We'd set up safe words and not once has she used them. Maybe it's time to have a conversation about what she's willing to try.

The elevator pings and I step out onto Skye's floor, time to get my mind out of the bedroom. I raise my hand to knock on the door when it suddenly opens. Macy shrieks then bursts out laughing as she clutches at her chest.

"Jeez you scared the crap out of me Clayton. Come on in, Skye's in the bedroom" Macy steps back as I pass her Macy heads out "enjoy your evening" eyeing the holdall in my hand she adds "and I'll see you in the morning" as she closes the door.

I head for Skye's bedroom. The door is open and Skye is stood in her bra and panties looking at the various clothes on the bed frowning.

"You have to pick the clothes up and put them on, frowning at them doesn't work"

Skye looks up and gives me the most beautiful welcoming smile. I go to her and kiss her slowly savoring the taste of her.

"Hi" she whispers when the kiss finishes.

"Hi" I nod to the bed "what's up can't decide what to wear?"

"Yeah, my idea of smart casual doesn't fit with the general populace idea of smart casual" she sighs.

"Would it help if I said my mother will be wearing either slacks or a skirt and blouse, Joshua's wife the same and Andrew's partner always wears slacks. I've never seen her in a skirt. Would it also help if I said wear a skirt as it will make it easier for me to feel you up under the dinner table" I say the last bit in a low seductive voice with my mouth close to her ear.

Skye trembles and I'm getting harder just at the thought. I'm already hard from seeing her in her lacy underwear. Skye looks at me with sparkling eyes, oh she's game. Skye bends and picks up the clothes off the bed taking them back into her closet.

I put my bag on the bed and open it taking out my suit, shirt and toiletry bag. I take the toiletry bag into the bathroom and empty the contents. When I get back in the bedroom my suit and shirt have gone. Skye came out of the closet.

"I've hung up your suit" she says pointing behind her.

Skye is wearing a dark pink dress with red roses printed all over it, the skirt of the dress flares out at her hips and finishes two inches above the knee. The dress is sleeveless with buttons running down the front and it shows just the right amount of cleavage. On her feet are red killer heels, as she calls them. I am so going to fuck her wearing them later, my cock throbs in agreement. Skye gives me a twirl.

"Smart casual enough?" she asks, I nod my approval "okay I'm ready to meet my prospective in-laws"

Shit I'm a schmuck. Skye is nervous this is a big deal for her. I've been so wrapped up in not wanting to go on my own and having to endure my brothers ribbing and mother's Spanish inquisition I'd not given a thought to Skye and her feelings. I went to her and wrap my arms around her.

"I'm a selfish bastard" I kiss the top of her head "I'm sorry I didn't even consider the affect tonight will have on you"

Skye looks up at me and smiles sweetly, almost shyly "I'm going to have to do this at some point so sooner rather than later and at least this way it'll get your mother off your back about bringing me to dinner, plus it will probably shut your brothers up as well"

I laugh "Considering you have met my brothers once and my mother twice you are spot on. Man, you are perceptive" I kiss her again "come on we best get going it's going to take us about an hour to get there"

"Are we going in your car or mine" Skye asks.

"Bruce is waiting outside"

"Do I need to bring Paul?" that stumps me before I can answer Skye states "I'm bringing Paul just in case"

"Good call" I say as we head out into the living room.

In the car Skye asks about my day. Whilst I tell her about a deal I have my suspicions about it dawns on me to ask her to attend the meeting tomorrow because the proposal being brought to the table is by two Russians. Skye speaks fluent Russian. I put the suggestion to her.

"So you just want me to sit in and suss out if they're dodgy?" she asks clarifying what I'd said. I nod "sure why not. I've got nothing to do tomorrow"

As we get closer to mother's house I start getting nervous. True to my word to Skye this afternoon I haven't told them she is coming mainly because mother will have invited other members of the family who would have turned up just to ogle at her. Skye doesn't deserve that. We pull up in the drive; taking hold of Skye's hand I kiss the back. "Ready?"

Skye takes a deep breath and lets it out slowly through her mouth and nods "As I'll ever be"

Joshua opened the front door "Hey baby bro" he greets me smiling "so the elusive Clayton Blake has finally…"

I step aside to reveal Skye and his words dry up in his throat, stunned to silence, perfect.

"Skye you remember Joshua"

Her smile is dazzling further stupefying my brother, if this is the effect she is going to have on him and Andrew I'm going to enjoy tonight after all.

"Clayton darling so glad you could…" and that is my mother rendered speechless when she sees Skye.

I pull Skye over the threshold and close the door.

"Good to see you Mom" I bend and kiss her cheek "I've brought an extra guest, found her wandering outside and thought I'd bring her in and give her a good meal" I wink at Skye.

"Oh Clayton" mother admonishes and slaps my arm "Skye it is wonderful to see you and welcome to the family" she embraces Skye "Joshua stop catching flies and go get the champagne out of the cellar. We have reason to celebrate. Come into the living room my dear" mother links arms with Skye "and I'll introduce you to the others"

Others, my heart sinks. Fuck I should have realized she would have invited more relatives regardless of Skye being with me or not. Tonight is like hitting the jackpot for my mother. As we walk in to the living room the soft conversations going on immediately stop.

"Everyone" my mother calls out beaming "I would like to introduce you to the newest member of our family. Skye" Mother proceeds to take Skye around the room, I follow. "Of course you have met Elizabeth and Andrew" both hug and welcome her, congratulating both of us "this is Mandy, Andrew's girlfriend"

I've never really taken to Mandy, it's something I couldn't put my finger on but seeing the look she gives Skye makes me want to slap her. It's nasty. Mandy obviously thinks she is far superior. Fuck! Mandy looks just like Pippa when she called Skye a Barbie doll. I'm going to tear a strip off Mandy if she attempts to be condescending.

The other people in the room are my grandparents, both sets. All of them make a fuss of Skye and in turn she charms the pants off them.

Dinner is interesting. I don't get to feel Skye up under the table. Mother thwarts that by insisting Skye and I sit either side of her.

"Skye darling I am only going to say this once because I have been given strict instructions not to harass you about the wedding" mother glares at me to make her point, I look back nonchalantly "but whenever you both set a date I am here at your disposal. You know to help pick a venue, caterers, flowers, table plans, choosing your dress anything at all"

"Thank you Mrs Blake that is very kind of you to offer" Skye says softly and smiles at me. I can see the gratitude in her eyes. I told her in Vegas I would forbid my mother from discussing the wedding with her. I hadn't told her I'd actually done it.

"Stephanie, please call me Stephanie"

"I remember going to get my dress" Elizabeth says leaning across Joshua to speak to Skye "I was overwhelmed by the choice on offer. I spent whole days just trying on dresses. You've got such a fabulous figure you'll be spoilt for choice"

"Actually" Skye shifts in her seat and flushes her eyes flit to me "the dress is already sorted"

I smile at her, understanding her uneasiness. Skye is the one stonewalling a date being set but she has her dress already.

"Shelley" I say.

Skye nods sheepishly "Designed, made and ready to go"

"When did you find out?" I laugh.

"Vegas, after Simon came back from doing the press thing. I asked him to give me away and Shelley to be Maid of Honor that's when she told me. Apparently she got carried away whilst she was making her dress and my bridesmaid dress"

Seeing the stunned faces around the table made me chuckle, this is fun.

"You all remember Shelley don't you? You met her at the Bolton House charity gala back in May. The fashion designer, she's the one that designed and made the dress Skye was wearing that night" I prompt their memory "she gets married in a few weeks. Joshua you spent most of the night talking with her partner Phil"

"Oh my god, I remember" Elizabeth breathes in awe "she's designed and made your dress" Skye nods "I bet it's stunning. Is it?"

"I don't know, I haven't seen it yet"

Everyone looks at Skye puzzled or in disbelief.

"Skye only got back from LA late this afternoon and it's been almost twelve weeks since she was last in New York" I point out and got nods of understanding as realization dawns.

"So what were you doing in Vegas?" Mandy asks as if she didn't know.

I roll my eyes. Skye saw and gets a mischievous glint in her eyes. A thrill shoots through me. Skye is going to wipe the floor with Mandy. I sit back to enjoy the show.

"Getting paid an obscene amount of money for about nine hours work"

Mandy's jaw drops, she wasn't expecting that answer.

"I heard the convention was a sell out with thousands turning up without tickets" Joshua says "and the organiser had to get additional space pronto"

"It happened on the first day and they asked Skye to extend the meet and greet. Then on the second day the Q&A was moved to the auditorium in the hotel because of the amount of people that turned up and it ran for three hours. All because of Skye" I say gloating with pride. I raise my glass to salute her causing her to blush even more.

"If you don't mind me asking but I'm curious. How much did you get paid?" Joshua asks.

"Ha! Curiosity a family trait'" Skye says smiling at me, then turns to Joshua "one hundred and fifty thousand dollars for roughly nine hours work"

Mandy chokes on her drink, everyone else stunned silence. I wink at Skye.

"Hundred and fifty thou, I thought you renegotiated from thirty thou to a hundred thou on the Saturday morning when Giles asked you to do the extra"

Skye plays along "I did, but I renegotiated again on Sunday when he wanted the Q&A to run an extra two hours, not only did I get an extra fifty thou for me but the other three artists as well"

"That's my girl not just a pretty face but a ruthless businesswoman who takes no prisoners" I beam at her.

Mother recovers her composure "I saw the interview with the young boy who met you in the elevator, did it really happen as he said?"

The conversation shifts to discuss how accurate the reports were that came out of Vegas. No-one asked any intrusive questions again. Well not until Mandy decided to have another go at Skye.

Standing in the living room after dinner with Joshua, Elizabeth, Andrew and Mandy the conversation is mainly around Skye's travels and her client base when Mandy pipes up "So tell us Skye what exactly attracts you to Clayton?"

Where the fuck is she going with this, Skye squeezes my hand. I realize I'm scowling at Mandy.

Skye smiles brightly "Oooh good question. Let me see. His business mind, his wit and sense of humour, his devilishly handsome good looks and rock hard body and of course his"

"Bank balance" Mandy cuts in sardonically with a snide smile.

"Nah, his cock" Skye deadpans.

Andrew sprays his drink everywhere. Me, Joshua and Elizabeth all burst out laughing at the look on Mandy's face. I high five Skye and kiss her soundly.

"God I love you woman" my jaw aches I'm smiling so hard.

After two attempts at trying to put Skye down in front of everyone I thought Mandy would give up but no she has to go for round three. I'm at the bar fixing a fresh drink for Skye when I hear Mandy ask her "So when is it due then?"

I freeze. Fucking hell, shit Skye warned me this would happen. I just didn't think it would come so soon. I speed up what I'm doing so I can get back to Skye and slap Mandy down.

"When is what due?" Skye feigns ignorance.

"The baby, when does it arrive?" Mandy speaks to Skye as if she's a simpleton making my blood boil.

I start back towards Skye anxiety is eating at me.

"I have absolutely no idea what you are talking about" Skye says as I give her the fresh drink turning to me she says "have you ordered something and forgotten to tell me" Skye winks to let me know she is okay and relief floods through me.

"Erm" I drag out pretending to think "nope. Why?"

"Oh no reason, Mandy seems to think we've ordered a baby and is asking when it's going to arrive"

Clever, Skye is twisting Mandy's words, this is fun. Mandy opens her mouth probably to correct her meaning in what she originally said. I beat her to it.

"Well if we do get a baby sent to us by mistake and if you don't like it you can always send it back" Joshua and Elizabeth snigger "do you even like children?"

"Oh yes" Skye says in all innocence "but I could never eat a full one"

Joshua and Elizabeth are howling with laughter and holding on to each other. Andrew is scowling at Mandy, I high five with Skye again. Mandy stalks off.

"What is her problem bro?" Joshua asks Andrew "that is the third time she's had a dig at Skye"

Andrew blushes. I feel sorry for him he doesn't do well with confrontation.

"I'm sorry if she has offended you, she isn't normally like this" Andrew says to Skye.

"None taken Andrew" Skye says graciously.

"I don't know about you lot but I thought that was funny as fuck" I grin "I've not had this much fun at a family gathering in… well never"

"I must say Skye you are wicked" Elizabeth says wiping tears from her eyes "I nearly wet myself I was laughing so hard"

"I know it was funny but I don't understand what has gotten into her" Joshua says aiming it at Andrew.

Rather than provide an answer Andrew excuses himself. He obviously doesn't want to get into a debate about Mandy's bizarre behaviour.

"Well my guess, she's got it into her head I'm some sort of gold digger" we all look blank at Skye. She sighs and holds up a finger "one, the reference to Vegas, land of the impromptu wedding. Possibly to Mandy me inviting Clayton to the convention was a ploy to get him to the alter" I snort I wanted to do that Skye didn't "two, his bank balance dig when she asked what attracts me to Clayton and three the only logical explanation to getting engaged after such a short time of knowing each other is that I'm pregnant and what better way to get access to his bank balance and get him down the aisle" Skye frowns and chews her bottom lip as she holds up three fingers "actually four Mandy has the hot's for Clayton and she wanted to show me up for a blonde bimbo Barbie who is just after Clayton's money"

"I want to say all of that is ridiculous but I'm having a hard time to put up a counter argument" Joshua says, I can tell Skye has impressed the hell out of him "you're definitely not pregnant?" Joshua has his lawyer head on now, I can tell by the tone of his voice.

"I am not pregnant" Skye confirms.

I sigh, Skye looks up at me. I am going to have to tell the family. "Excuse us a minute" I pull Skye to one side before I can say anything she trails her fingers down my cheek. I catch her hand and kiss her palm.

"It is up to you if you want to tell them. I don't mind, although" she pauses and glances over at Joshua and Elizabeth who are both watching us with open curiosity "I would suggest you leave it until the end of the evening and tell them altogether otherwise it will put a dampener on the rest of the night"

Skye is right. Me, I would have blurted it out right now and then Skye would have to put up with intrusive questions and pitying looks. I take her in my arms bending close to her ear I murmur "You are the most amazing woman I have ever met. I love you" her arms tighten around my waist "would you be okay if I told them on my own?"

Tilting her head up Skye's beautiful yellow green eyes radiate so much love it takes my breath away. "No not at all. I'll wait in the car for you" she whispers.

An hour later I'm stood in the kitchen with my brothers, mother and Elizabeth. I have no idea where Mandy is, she's kept out of the way since stalking off earlier. Skye waited in the car. We came up with a ruse to leave and I'd come back into the house on the pretence I've forgotten something. I manage to get everyone I wanted, well almost, together.

"Look I need to tell you all something" I look each of them in the eye, their demeanour changes instantly when they realize I'm serious "Skye knows I am telling you this. I wouldn't be telling you at all if someone hadn't forced my hand and thought it was clever to ask Skye if she is pregnant" Andrew shifts uneasily and mother looks confused "I want to make one thing very clear. Skye is not pregnant" I enunciate "in fact Skye can't have children"

In the shocked silence I hear a gasp from behind me. I turn to see a white faced Mandy, the rest of the family are likewise pale.

"I'm sorry I didn't mean to" Mandy starts to blab, I cut her off.

"Save it, I am not interested" I snap I'm getting angry at the sight of her, she has seriously pissed me off "in fact I am not the one you should be apologising to"

Mandy starts to say something else I hold up my hand to stop her.

"You've had it in for Skye all night. If you think for one fucking minute that Skye is trying to trap me or only after my bank balance and you've said what you did out of some misplaced loyalty to me, you can fuck right off. He is your concern" I point at Andrew "not me" the volume of my voice rises as I've been speaking so I'm nearly shouting at the end.

"How do you know she isn't after your bank balance or she can't have children" Mandy retorts lifting her chin in defiance. I hear Andrew groan obviously wishing Mandy to shut the fuck up.

"Not that it is any of your fucking business but I will tell you anyway" I say through gritted teeth, I'm losing it and I'm prepared to rip her to shreds if I have to.

"Skye has a personal fortune of three hundred million dollars, she is self-made. For reasons I am not going to go into Skye had a hysterectomy when she was eighteen. I know this because I have seen the scar and for the fact we have been fucking like rabbits for the last three months and we don't use protection that's a big fucking clue" I know I've gone TMI but I want blood. Mandy's to be precise.

"So get this into your fucking head. I am the one who pursued Skye. I am the one that asked her to marry me. I am the one that wanted to get married in Vegas at the weekend. Am I fucking clear enough for you" I practically roar.

I see the whole family cringe and shrink back from me. Mandy has gone from white to green. I try to reign in my temper, deep breath.

"Skye is used to the idea of not being able to have kids. She doesn't want or need your pity. What I don't want is any unnecessary pressure from people asking when we will be starting a family or why isn't Skye pregnant yet? We would have told you together may be in a few weeks but motor mouth here put the kibosh on that" I point at Mandy "I love Skye for the amazingly beautiful soul she is and she loves me for me. I am the happiest man alive she has consented to be my wife. If there ever comes a time when Skye decides she wants kids then we will adopt, that will be her decision" I sigh "don't worry about Skye if you are around her and someone asks when is it due, you all saw first-hand how she handles it" mother looks even more puzzled "one of these will tell you later Mom" I indicate to Elizabeth and my brothers "the press are probably going to be speculating about pregnancy and doing the baby bump watch. Let them do that and not you"

It suddenly occurs to me Skye's predicament is known only to a handful of people and those people would never sell out on her.

"Oh and FYI if it ever gets out in the press that Skye can't have kids I will personally fucking skin you all alive because it isn't common knowledge" this came out as menacingly as I meant it.

I look at each of them in turn lingering the longest on Mandy, she couldn't look me in the eye. She knew she'd fucked up big time and judging from the look mother is giving her it will be a long time before she'll be forgiven and by Christ, Mom can hold a grudge. I look at my watch, it's getting late.

"I'm leaving, thank you for a lovely evening and making Skye welcome" I didn't look at Mandy when I say that "I'm just sorry it ended this way. I'll speak to you tomorrow Mom" I kiss her cheek "Joshua I'll see you tomorrow afternoon" I kiss Elizabeth, clap Andrew on the shoulder and walk out ignoring Mandy, petty I know, so fucking what I don't care.

I climb in the car to find Skye has fallen asleep and has someone's jacket draped over her. I move her so I can cradle her in my arms. I notice Paul is minus his jacket.

"Thank you Paul" I let the gratitude I feel show in my voice.

He nods "It's been a long couple of days for her sir"

I immediately get the insinuation of his words that Skye worked around the clock so she could come home early to be with me.

Skye has completely crashed. She doesn't even stir when I carry her up to the apartment, strip her clothes off and put her in bed. I fall asleep holding her in my arms.

Chapter Nineteen

CLAYTON

I come awake to the sound of Skye's laughter. Her side of the bed is empty. I'm about to get out of bed to find her when Skye comes in carrying a tray and speaking rapid Spanish. She puts the tray down on the bed and smiles as she carries on her conversation picking up her phone off the tray. As she climbs on the bed she asks "Do you have any plans tonight?"

"No" I mumble around a piece of toast.

A few minutes later she finishes her conversation.

"That was Maria, her and Alex are coming to New York for a few days, they will be here by lunch time so we are going to meet them for dinner tonight. Where would you like to eat? Oh almost forgot" Skye leans over and kisses me "good morning"

"Good morning" I grin at her "and I don't mind anywhere is fine by me"

"I quite fancy Gino's it'll be a nice reminder of the Italian holiday" Skye says getting a faraway look in her eyes.

Half an hour later I'm standing in Skye's kitchen drinking coffee and ready for work. I watch Skye as she potters around her kitchen she's wearing her slops as she puts it. A baggy over-sized t-shirt and sweat pants, even her hair is tied back in a sloppy pony tail and she still manages to look sexy as hell. I feel myself getting hard.

"Hello earth to Clayton" Skye waves her hand in front of my face.

"Sorry baby" I smile apologetically.

"You were really spaced out there" Skye's husky voice is full of concern "you okay? Not worrying about last night?"

I told Skye everything I said to my family whilst I got ready for work, she just nodded when I said she was right about Mandy's motivations.

"No, I was just thinking you look sexy as hell in your slops" I put my hand on my crotch and adjust myself.

"That's because you've not had sex since yesterday afternoon" she laughs reaching out and cupping me between the legs "hmm can't have you going to work and taking out your frustration on your unsuspecting employees now can I"

Skye undid my trousers and drops to her knees. I grip the kitchen top counter as she takes me in her mouth. I groan as the warm moistness envelopes my cock. Her tongue swirls around the head and licks up the shaft. Taking my cock back in her mouth she takes me deep to the back of her throat and sucks hard as she pulls back. Pleasure races along my cock and up my spine.

"Oh fuck yes do that again baby"

My eyes roll and my head falls backwards as I absorb the sensations of her tongue, mouth and teeth as they lightly scrape my shaft. Skye starts to work my shaft with one hand and massages my balls with the other as she continues to lick and suck me.

"That feels so fucking good"

My hips start to move to her rhythm. I bury my hands and fingers into her hair. I'm not going to last much longer as I give myself over to the pleasure sensations she is creating in my body. Instinct takes over my hips move faster as I fuck her mouth and chase my release. I feel Skye's hands grip my hips and her fingers dig and flex on my ass. I thrust deeper into Skye's mouth. My breathing is ragged as my heart pounds. I open my eyes and look down at Skye and seeing her full lips wrapped around my cock tips me over the edge.

"I'm coming" I manage to gasp out before my orgasm rips through me "fuck, Skye" I shout, my spine and hips locked and my fingers clench in her hair.

I feel Skye's mouth work me as my cock pulses and twitches pumping everything I have to give and Skye greedily takes it all, every last drop.

I feel sated and alive. Skye tucks me in and refastens my trousers. I help her to her feet and kiss her long and hard, tasting myself and her.

"Feeling better now?"

I chuckle. Skye asked me exactly the same thing after the blow job yesterday afternoon "Fantastic, like I could conquer the world"

"Good. Now what time do you want me for this meeting?"

"Meeting is at three but how about coming in for one and have lunch with me?"

"Sure sounds good. Any preference on how you want me to dress?" she rolls her eyes at my lascivious smile "I mean do you want me as a sexy business executive or naughty secretary?"

"Definitely naughty secretary"

Fuck me! My cock agrees by jumping to attention as Skye walks into my office, she is seriously working the naughty secretary look. White fitted blouse showing just the right amount of cleavage. Black fitted pencil skirt the hem line finishing just above the knee. Sheer black stockings with the line running up the back of her legs and high black heels, my imagination is running riot speculating what lingerie she has on underneath. It takes everything I have not to shove her skirt up around her waist and fuck her against the wall. Later, you can do that later.

Joshua turns up whilst we are eating lunch effectively thwarting my role play fantasies. If Skye is disappointed she doesn't show it.

Joshua wanted to talk about the upcoming meeting he has his reservations as well, hence the reason for him turning up early. I explain Skye is going to sit in and hopefully she will be able to pick up on something which would either confirm our suspicions or show they are unfounded. When Skye visited the bathroom Joshua turns to me.

"Bro you are one lucky son of a bitch" I raise an eyebrow it isn't like him to comment on my girlfriends "not only is she stunningly beautiful with a smoking hot body but she is intelligent and an extremely astute businesswoman"

"I know so keep your fucking hands off" I snap. It also occurs to me Joshua has been doing his homework on Skye to make the comments he has.

"Only window shopping baby bro" Joshua chuckles at my reaction and holding his hands up in surrender "listen have you spoken to Andrew or Mandy this morning?" I shake my head "neither of them has been in touch?" again I shake my head.

Skye comes back into the room with her phone to her ear and walks over to my desk, picking up a pen she bends down to write on a pad. The whole pose just begs for her ass to be spanked then fucked from behind hard. I'm so going to do that the first chance I get. Skye is going to be staying at my place tonight maybe I can get her to bring the outfit with her.

The phone on my desk buzzes "Mr Blake your three o'clock appointment has arrived and they are setting up in the boardroom" Helena announces.

"Have they been in touch with you?" I ask as I stand.

"Andrew has, he says Mandy is really sorry and wants to apologise"

"Like I said last night it's not me she needs to apologise to"

Joshua drops the subject as Skye walks over to us.

In less than five minutes of the meeting starting Skye wrote on the pad in front of me, fake accents not Russian. Fifteen minutes later Skye is frowning at the hand out material the fake Russians have circulated. She picks up her phone and starts messaging someone, she does this discreetly under the table. This went on for five minutes. I'm fascinated as I watch her. A few minutes later her phone buzzes she answers and slips out of the room.

When she came back in a few minutes later from the look on her face I know something is up, something serious. Leaning into me she whispers "I need to speak with you, call a halt to this meeting but keep them in here" she inclines her head towards the two fake Russians.

"Gentlemen" I call out and stood "I need to attend to an urgent business matter. Please continue and I will be back in a few minutes, my executives will brief me of anything important I need to know" I indicate to the three sat round the table.

I look at Joshua and incline my head toward the door. We follow Skye out and into the nearest meeting room. As soon as we enter Skye starts talking fast.

"The whole thing is a scam they are not Russian. The reason I know this is because they have mispronounced name places, also this belongs to Mr C" she opens the hand out and points to the site the proposal centres around, her phone buzzes "this is him now"

Skye answers in Russian—her face transforms with a warm smile—converses for a minute then alters to English. "You are on speaker phone Mr C. I have Clayton and Joshua Blake with me. I've explained the land being pitched for sale is yours. I'll let them explain the business proposition"

I give a brief outline of what is being proposed.

"You have the men there in your office now" Mr C asks.

"Yes they are" I confirm.

"Good. I have been aware of this scam for some time but have been unable to locate the culprits. Can you keep them there? I have Alex on his way to you now"

"I'll ask Helena to get security up here" Skye says and left the office.

"I am indebted to you Clayton. I owe you" Mr C says with gratitude.

"It's not me you should be saying that to, this is all Skye's doing. I just asked her to sit in on the meeting because she knows Russia and speaks the language. I thought she could tell me how authentic the details are. She knew within the first few minutes these guys were fake"

Skye comes back in with Helena behind her. "Security is on the way up and Helena has notified the front desk to send Alex up immediately"

"Excellent. Helena, tell security to stand outside the boardroom doors. Boris, I'm going back into the meeting, I'll speak to you later" I hand Skye her phone back and kiss her "Mr C has something to say to you"

As Joshua and I leave the room Skye is conversing in Russian and I see Helena's eyes widen in surprise. Pride surges through me at how talented Skye is.

"Helena when Mr Alex Cheremisinova arrives please show him in straight away"

To stall for time I make the two fake Russians go over the bits I had missed. Skye enters the office fifteen minutes later with Alex. They are conversing loudly in Russian, immediately picking up this is a ploy of some sort I quickly shift my attention back to the fake Russians. Their reaction is hilarious; I bite the inside of my cheek to stop myself from laughing. The pair of them have the whole bug eyed gold fish look going on, momentarily stunned at the new arrivals then they look at each other uneasily, I visibly see them gulp.

Alex addresses the two fakes and it's obvious he expects them to answer him, when they look at each other blankly Alex repeats what he has said more slowly. Panic flashes across their faces as they realize they've been rumbled. Skye in her sultry voice translates.

"Mr Cheremisinova" the two fakes turn green at the mention of Alex's name "would like to know who has given you permission to sell this land"

One of the guys starts to babble Skye holds up a hand to stop him. "Do yourself a favor and drop the fake accent"

The guy physically sags. The three executives all sit open mouthed. It dawns on me Daniel is the one to bring this deal to the table in the first place, is he in on this scam? I'll have his balls if he is, by Christ he'll wish he'd never been born by the time I finish with him.

"You two come with me, you have answers to give" Alex says in broken English.

"We're not going anywhere with you and you can't make us" one of the fakes says rather cockily.

"Very well" Alex replies as he opens the door and four gorillas walk in. They definitely aren't my security people, guess Alex has brought his own "please escort these gentlemen to my car, do not worry I will bring your equipment"

For a few seconds it looks as if the two fakes are going to make an attempt to get away, possibly run and jump out of the window. Falling thirty floors is certainly more appealing than going god knows where with those gorillas. Not surprisingly the two fakes go rather meekly. The sadistic bastard in me is disappointed; I was looking forward to some high drama as a finale to this charade.

Skye helps Alex pack up the laptop and hand out material the whole while Alex talks in Russian. Skye nods and occasionally says something back. It appears he is briefing her. When they finish Alex comes to me and holds out his hand which I shake.

"Boris wishes me to extend his gratitude in this matter and he still holds to what he said earlier. He also wishes me to say congratulations and looks forward to receiving his wedding invitation" Alex grins making me laugh as it's obvious we're both remembering Mr C on the yacht in Italy and his not so subtle hints.

"Thank you and I'll see you and Maria later"

Alex turns back to Skye and speaks to her in Russian again, they converse for a few minutes she has the most dazzling brain frying smile on her face it makes me wonder what he's saying. He kisses both her cheeks and took his leave.

Skye sits down next to me. Trying not to and failing miserably my three executives all openly gawp at Skye. I'm tempted to pick her hand up and kiss it but I know it will embarrass her so I refrain.

"Gentlemen, may I introduce you to Skye Darcy. If you have been following the news recently you will know she is my fiancé, what isn't common knowledge is that Skye is fluent in five languages and as you've just heard Russian is one of them. As you also all bore witness to she is extremely well connected"

I let my words sink in. I'm quite proud of myself for remaining calm up until this point. Now I'm going to let rip.

"So one of you fuck heads better tell me how come it took Skye less than thirty minutes to work out this deal was a fucking scam when you have all been involved with it for the last three weeks" my voice is threatening violence.

A wall of silence, I let it drag out. Skye and Joshua sit still as statues. The three executives squirm. Daniel clears his throat.

"I'm sorry sir. I take full responsibility. I didn't do the proper checks. When they mentioned the Cheremisinova name I assumed they were representatives and as we have done business with them recently I thought" he sighs and shrugs "no I assumed the deal was genuine"

"So you got fucking lazy. I told you yesterday and last week something wasn't right and still you did fuck all about it" I shout.

Daniel's shoulders slump "Yes sir"

At least he didn't say it won't happen again otherwise I will fire his ass here and now.

"You're a fucking idiot. If it wasn't for the fact you are bloody good at what you do you would be clearing your desk right now! Christ, Daniel if this deal had gone ahead you will have lost us fifteen million dollars and not only that but destroyed all forms of relationship I have with Mr Boris Cheremisinova, who is a close personal friend of Skye's"

I let the severity of the implications of what I said sink in. Daniel looks as if he's about to be sick.

"As it is and fortuitous for you Mr Cheremisinova feels indebted to me for catching the fraudsters. However, you and I both know this is all Skye's doing and for that reason it is because of her you still have a job" relief flashes across Daniel's face.

"Thank you sir, it won't ha..." I glare at him cutting his words off.

"Do not finish that fucking sentence" I growl through clenched teeth enunciating each word "otherwise I will kick you to the curb, am I clear?" he nods "that goes for all of you" I glare at each of them in turn "from this point on anyone and I mean anyone found cutting corners I will serve you your fucking balls on a platter"

My threat is met with a collective "Yes sir"

"Right go back to work and redeem your selves" I point at the door dismissing them.

To say there is a stampede for the door would be an understatement. Joshua whistles through his teeth and loosens his tie. "There is never a dull moment with you baby bro"

"That's why you enjoy being my lawyer" I retort. I turn to Skye and pick up her hand and kiss the back "I'm intrigued, tell me how you knew the land belonged to Mr C"

Skye's smile dazzles me. I swear to god my brain short circuits each time she turns it on me.

"When I was there in June Mr C had a hell of a time sorting out a problem. It's very rare for him to show anger, scared the crap out of all his staff I'll tell you. Anyway I got him to talk through the problem, turned out it was the second time it had happened. Someone was selling" she uses quotation marks with her fingers "a substantial plot of land that had planning permission for development. This land was his as I'm sure you've guessed. The sale had what looked like authentic paperwork along with forged signatures of Mr C's, both parties claimed the men where representatives of Mr C. By the time he got details of the con artists whereabouts they would be long gone. Mr C showed me everything the con artist used so when I saw the hand out it was familiar and took me a while to remember why. When I left the office it was to put a call in to Mr C. I checked with Hanna his PA the location of the land so I knew it was a scam. I told her to get Mr C to ring me as the con artists were here attempting to sell his land to you"

"So when you and Alex came in" I left the sentence unfinished. Skye grins impishly she knew what I was getting at.

"That was my idea. I wanted to scare the crap out of them. Alex agreed to go along with it" both Joshua and I laugh at Skye's smug look "although Alex's goons did that too"

"Dare I ask what's going to happen to them?" asks Joshua.

"They'll probably get smacked about a bit, knee capped and have their toes and fingers hammered to extract information from them" Skye shrugs.

"Holy shit" Joshua audibly swallows.

"Nah, just messing with you" Skye's smile is positively wicked I burst out laughing at Joshua's expression of disbelief "Alex is delivering them to the FBI apparently these con artists are wanted internationally. Mr C is on his way so expect a visit at some point in the next twenty four hours"

Joshua's phone rings and he digs it out of his pocket, he frowns at the screen then answers it. I kiss the back of Skye's hand again.

"I can't tell you how much I am indebted to you. Thank you for everything you did" I decide I want to buy her something to show my gratitude.

"Glad I could be of help. I quite enjoyed myself if I'm honest, sure beats the hell out of watching afternoon TV"

"He's sat right next to me" I turn back to Joshua and raise an eyebrow "Andrew" he mouths "yes I told him and his reply is the same as last night"

I know instantly what he is going on about. It is unfair of Andrew to put Joshua in this awkward position so I take the phone from Joshua.

"Andrew what is it you want?" I speak in as civil a tone as I can because frankly I want to shout at him for being so fucking childish and using Joshua as a go between just because he hates confrontation. I want to yell at him to grow a pair of balls for once.

"Mandy is really sorry for last night and she wants to apologise" he says quickly.

"To whom"

Silence, that's stumped him. "Err to you and Skye" Andrew says hesitantly.

"How and when"

"I'm not sure what you mean" again he's hesitant.

"How is she going to do it and when" he's stumped again because he remains quiet, so I add "or is she hoping with you ringing on her behalf and saying she wants to apologise to both of us will be sufficient?"

"I'll find out and ring you back" he says quickly.

"You do that, better yet get her to do her own fucking dirty work if she wants to earn any credibility back with me" I hang up and hand the phone back to Joshua "don't let yourself get stuck in the middle not over that bitch. Has she apologised to you and Elizabeth?"

Joshua shakes his head "Andrew said the same to me. I think you're right in what you said to him. Mandy tried to apologise to Mom after you left. Mom wouldn't hear it until we explained what Mandy had said even told her Skye's come backs. Mom went ballistic and tore a strip off her and then some. I've never seen Mom so angry" Joshua physically shudders at the memory.

"I don't want a rift in your family over something like this. Mandy made a bad error of judgement. It's not as if I haven't had to deal with the Barbie misconception before. Hell it's practically an everyday occurrence for me" Skye holds up her arm and pinches the skin "look, elephant skin on top of rhinoceros skin. Can't get any more thick skinned than that. I'm sure she felt a complete and utter shit when she heard I can't have kids and she'll feel like that every time she sees me. It wouldn't surprise me if she didn't show her face at family gatherings for a while"

"You shouldn't have to put up with that kind of prejudice from family members" Joshua says quietly "you are an amazingly strong woman Skye, it is inexcusable for someone even though not officially a family member but has been part of the family for so long they are treated as such to attack the character of the newest member they know nothing about. It is also unacceptable"

I couldn't have put it better myself.

"Fair enough, but just so you both know and you can tell the rest of your family I bear her no ill will, yes her behaviour was unacceptable and I'm not condoning her prejudice toward me but I am not going to bear a grudge and hold it against her. I have got better things to do with my time and energy"

"Baby bro you seriously need to get this woman down the aisle and fast" Joshua says slapping me on the shoulder.

Joshua has a look of awe and adulation on his face, the fucker has fallen under Skye's spell. Skye laughs and shakes her head. Her phone rang.

"Excuse me" she says as she answers.

"I need to get going" Joshua says getting to his feet and walks to the door, I rose as well and follow him "speak to you tomorrow"

We embrace and he waves bye to Skye and left. Turning my attention back to Skye I listen to her side of the conversation.

"Blimey that's quick I thought it would be a few weeks before I got to view it… really… okay… you mean now" she looks at her wrist as if to look at a watch and realizes she isn't wearing one "what time is it… no…

I'm finished here now… yeah… okay… tell Paul to meet me in the foyer in ten minutes… bye"

Skye stood and walks towards me "Business calls I have a viewing in half an hour on a property which is going to auction tomorrow"

I open the door and we head back to my office so she can get her things.

"What time will you be finished, sorry let me rephrase, what time will you get to mine?" I ask as I help her into her jacket.

"Probably about six, gives me time to nip home change and grab my bag"

"Do me a favor" my voice comes out low and deep.

Skye's eyes widen then sparkle "What?" she says breathlessly.

I pull her to me cup her ass and lift her against me so she can feel my arousal "Keep the outfit on I want to play naughty secretary when you arrive"

Skye's breathing hitches with her lips close to mine she murmurs "Thought you'd never get there" then she kisses me long and hard.

Not long after Skye left I call it a day and went to the jewellers. I want to get a gift for her as a way of showing my gratitude and thanks for what she did today. I shudder to think what could've happened if she had not been there.

"Welcome Mr Blake good to see you again" Gerrard the shop owner says as I walk in. His shop is one of those old antiquated establishments, not only did they do one off commissions but sold traditional as well as modern pieces. I'm one of his best customers. "How may I be of help?"

"Hello Gerrard, I'm after" I stop I have no idea what to get her "I've no idea! I want something exceptionally special that can be worn on a daily basis. Does that make sense?"

Gerrard beams "Yes sir. May I be so bold and ask is this for the same lady you had the ring made?"

I match his smile "Yes it is"

"Congratulations on your engagement sir. Did she like the ring?" a look of horror flashes across Gerrard's face "I am sorry it was presumptuous of me to think you've given it to her"

Gerrard's team pulled out all the stops to get the ring made on such short notice. I came to the shop with Shelley and Simon Monday lunchtime and picked the finished ring up first thing on the Friday morning we flew out to LA and Vegas.

"Skye loves it. In fact it's her engagement ring. I didn't intend it to be as you know it was made to be a gift" my jaw aches I'm smiling so much I can't help it. Gerrard's practically glowing with happiness.

"Does she have pierced ears?"

"That's an understatement" I bark out a laugh. Skye has her ear lobes and the tops of her ears pierced multiple times.

"Being an artist I take it she wouldn't care for the majority of what is on display here" he indicates around the cabinets. Huh, he has a point "don't worry sir I am not offended. However, come with me and let me show you some pieces, since your last visit and the ring you commissioned it inspired one of my jewellers and for a while he has been working on a…. let's say unique range"

Gerrard leads me through the back of the shop and into a workshop where he has a small team working industriously at various polishing machines and work benches.

"Matthew" Gerrard calls out. A young man wearing goggles switches off the machine he is using and turns around "this is the one who made your ring. Matthew this is Mr Blake"

The young man's eyes widen, he takes off his goggles and wipes his hands before shaking my extended hand.

"Pleased to meet you Matthew and thank you, you did a fantastic job on the ring"

He nods and blushes at my praise. Poor guy is shy. God help him if he ever gets to meet Skye.

"Matthew would you please get all the pieces you have been working on" Gerrard instructs, he blushes even more and rushes off.

Whilst we wait for Matthew to come back Gerrard talks about the workshop and answers my questions about the various processes. Matthew places a wooden box on the long bench like table that is in the centre of the room. He lays out a black velvet cloth and starts to layout various pieces, separating out finished and unfinished earrings, necklaces, bracelets and rings, all of them exquisite. One of the finished rings catches my eye and I pick it up for a closer look. Out of the corner of my eye I see Gerrard nod to Matthew giving him a prompt to tell me about it.

"It's… err… it's…" he clears his throat and tries again "its moonstone and diamonds set in platinum. The ring can be adjusted to fit the finger by squeezing it. It's designed to be wrapped around the finger and extend above and below the knuckles" Matthew points to the knuckle on his hand and to the knuckle on the finger to demonstrate his meaning.

Skye would love it. There are also two pairs of earrings similar in style to the ones she bought in Italy and another pair fashioned like an upside down Calla Lily with an amethyst protruding from the petals, on closer inspection the lily part is encrusted with diamonds.

"I'll take the ring and these three pairs of earrings. I would also like to commission you to make our wedding rings" Matthew's face is a picture, shock doesn't even cover it "the ring you made is now Skye's engagement ring so the wedding band needs to be designed around it" from the look of him I think Matthew is about to keel over in a dead faint I look at Gerrard concerned.

"It would be an honor sir" Gerrard says "you'll have to forgive Matthew he is a huge fan of Miss Darcy and her work. Up until now he had no idea the ring he made was for her"

I burst out laughing and it explains Matthew's stunned, startled look. God help him if he ever gets to meet Skye in the flesh, my callous side takes over before I can stop it.

"Well I'm guessing you are going to need the ring in order to design the wedding band. Maybe I can talk the lady herself in to coming to see you, how about Saturday?"

I look at Matthew when I say this however it's Gerrard who answers "That would be most excellent sir"

Back in the shop I peruse the store whilst I wait for Gerrard to box up my items. I look at the watches and remember Skye back in the boardroom looking at her wrist for the time. I buy her a Rolex as well, nothing too flashy, just something she can wear every day.

SKYE

"This building is fantastic" Simon's voice echoes around the cavernous room.

I bumped into Simon as I left Clayton's office. Simon was leaving the building next door after a meeting and promptly invited himself along to view the property with me as he had nothing better to do. Of course he also wanted to know why I'm dressed like someone's secretary. On the way over to the viewing I filled him in on my afternoon's escapades, which earns me a rare dumfounded look.

"Skye Darcy you will never go to heaven" Simon giggles after I'd finished regaling what I'd said to Joshua.

"I'm having way too much fun so I don't want to go" I retort "besides you don't get chocolate up there so I'm definitely not going"

The vast open space will be ideal for holding auctions in, with plenty of room and wall space to display artwork. I head towards the back of the room to the stairs so I can look at the rooms on the upper floor which will become offices. Billy and Simon follow me, picking my way through remnants of office furniture I make mental notes of work that will need to be done and visualising an open plan modern office with meeting areas and enclosed offices for privacy. The property is located in a prime location, easy access and it ticks all the boxes on what I needed.

"Are they open to offers?" I ask Billy.

"I'll find out"

He walks away to make his call. I like that about Billy he didn't try and fob me off with half assed guesses and then try and get an answer but then again he'd worked with me long enough to know better.

"Hey honey what are you doing tonight?" Simon asks pulling me out of my thoughts.

"Going to Gino's for dinner with Alex and Maria" suddenly realising he has no idea who I'm talking about, coupled with his blank look I explain who they are "why don't you join us, actually" I pull out my phone "I'll ask Shelley and Phil to come as well. Do you have someone you would like to bring?" Simon blushes "ho, ho, ho Mr Hanson, details, spill, now" I demand.

"Remember the guy who cut your hair in Vegas" he says quite excitedly.

"David" I say to show I do, it dawns on me "you two hooked up didn't you?"

Simon grins sheepishly and nods. "Anyway he's in town visiting family until Sunday then he's heading back to Vegas" Simon does a kind of little jig and claps his hands.

"Good for you. It'll be nice to see him again" I smile at Simon.

I ring Shelley and invite her and Phil then I ring Gino's to change the booking. Billy has been waiting patiently for me to finish.

"Sorry Billy just organising my social life" I apologise, for some reason I feel guilty my calls weren't business related.

He waves away my feeble apology "I have good news" must be with the way he is smiling "they are willing to listen to what you might want to offer"

"Do you have any idea what they are hoping to get at auction?"

Billy puffs out his cheeks. I know him well enough to know he's thinking "I tried to find out but couldn't get a definite figure. Suggestions range from ten to fifteen million and before you ask I think they might struggle to get the top end"

I nod appreciating his opinion. Billy did his homework he has ways of finding out all sorts of information even the downright obscure but it all helped when putting an offer in or negotiating a price.

"Put an offer in, go in at whatever price you think is best and go up to fifteen million if you have to. If they turn it down we'll go to the auction tomorrow. Ring me when you get an answer"

I look at my watch for the time, damn it, I keep forgetting I've lost it, I miss my watch. I'd misplaced it somewhere between Vegas, LA and here. I dig out my phone and check the time. Jeez where has the time gone! I need to get a move on if I'm to get to Clayton's for six. A thrill shoots through me and anticipation makes me giddy. I'm so looking forward to playing naughty secretary.

I remember Clayton's heated stare as I leant over his desk to write a message. I did it deliberately to see what reaction I would get and boy I wasn't disappointed. I know if Joshua hadn't been there Clayton would've been all over me like a rash.

I left Billy to his phone calls and to lock up. I dropped Simon off at his place then headed home to pack an overnight bag. On the way to Clayton's I broach a subject with Paul which has been niggling me.

"Paul" he glances at me in the rear view mirror "I'm going to talk with Clayton over the weekend about our current arrangement, you know taking it in turns staying at each other's apartment. I'm conscious this is going to be a real ball ache for you and Bruce"

"There's no need ma'am" he says cutting me off, I raise an eyebrow "Bruce and I have already talked it through and agreed tactics" well push me over with a feather. Paul chuckles at my surprise "thank you for your consideration Skye it means a lot" I can hear his appreciation in his voice.

"So put my mind at ease, explain how it's going to work" I'm curious.

"Bruce has similar living quarters to mine so when you stay over at Mr Blake's I will stay with Bruce in his spare room. Likewise Bruce stays in my quarters when Mr Blake is with you"

Huh, so simple.

"Macy doesn't mind this?"

I suggested to Macy she move in with Paul when they'd got engaged, she is moving in this weekend.

"Macy is more than fine with the arrangement. She understands it is my job plus she got to know Bruce in Vegas"

"Bruce was in Vegas!" I'm shocked "I never saw him. Mind you I never got to see much of Vegas come to think of it" I grumble.

Paul chuckles "He helped out with getting the security detail organized and shadowed the first line of guards whenever you ventured out. Just shows how good he is at his job if you didn't see him"

"So when did you arrange all of this?"

"Vegas. As soon as you announced your engagement"

Huh, go figure. He's two steps ahead of me.

Suddenly the car went dark, a flare of panic surges through me. I mentally slap myself. We've entered the underground parking garage you numpty. Paul helps me out the car and hands my overnight bag to me then points to where the elevator is and gives me the code for the penthouse.

On the ride up I adjust my skirt and undo the two top buttons on my shirt to reveal more of my cleavage. I have butterflies in my stomach and my heart is already pounding. The elevator slows to a stop smoothly and the doors open. My heart stops.

Clayton stands with his arms braced on either side of the doors, a dark smouldering look rakes me from head to toe and back again.

Oh my! He is going to eat me alive. I squeeze my thighs together as desire pools in my lower belly. Clayton holds out his hand and I take it.

He has me in his arms and is kissing me senseless before I even blink. Not that I'm complaining. Clayton can kiss and given half the chance I would spend all day kissing him.

His lips are soft yet firm, his tongue lazily licks inside my mouth. I love the taste of him. He makes my toes curl. The kiss only ends because we need to breathe.

Without a word he picks up my bag and leads me inside. My phone rings. I take it out with the intention of switching it off then see its Billy so I answer.

"Good news Skye" Billy says before I can say hello.

"Go on then" I'm smiling and surreptitiously crossing my fingers.

"I went in with an offer of eight million and they accepted" I can hear his gleefulness in his voice. I squeal and do a little jig. Clayton looks at me with a mix of bemusement, indulgence and as if I've lost my marbles "I hope you don't mind but I said it would be a cash sale and we would sign the papers tomorrow. I think that's what swung it"

"No it's absolutely fine, email me times and where you need me to be and well done. Enjoy your evening" I hang up "yay I just bought a building" I jump up and down on the spot clapping my hands.

Clayton laughs at my silliness "Well done baby. Come on tell me all about it whilst I give you a tour"

Clayton leads me into a huge room which is obviously the living room. It's a mix of rustic and modern, in most cases I would have said putting the two styles together shouldn't work, but it did. Huge picture windows give fantastic views of the city skyline and Central Park.

Wooden flooring, big soft leather sofas, huge TV and a pool table. I smile as memories of Vegas flash through my mind. Clayton with a salacious smile winks at me. Oh yes he's on the same wavelength. Looking around the room I notice he doesn't have any art on the walls.

At the far end of the room is an open staircase which he leads me towards. Instead of going up the stairs Clayton went along the side of them and into the kitchen. All stainless steel and black, very masculine and cold, it's the opposite of mine. I take an instant dislike to the kitchen.

Through the kitchen and an archway is the dining room it has a beautiful long black glass table with high backed leather chairs, I count twelve seats. Through the dining room and another archway brings us back into the living room. I realize what I'd thought was an alcove is in fact an archway to the dining room.

By the time the tour of the ground floor is finished I've told Clayton everything about the building and my plans for turning it into the auction house.

"That's fantastic and you've got a bargain. I know the properties in that area are highly sort after" Clayton says as he leads the way up stairs.

At the top is a corridor as we go along Clayton opens each door. One is a well-equipped home gym, another is his home office and two guest bedrooms the door at the very end is his bedroom, the master suite.

A huge wooden framed bed dominates the room. The size of the bed shouldn't have been a surprise considering he is six foot four. My bed is big but I know it isn't long enough for him. Last night I'd joked about chopping his feet off to make him fit more comfortably.

Clayton places my bag on the bed then he walks towards a cabinet as he went he points to a door to the left of the bed "Bathroom is through there and the closet is there" he points to the opposite side.

He picks something up off the cabinet and turns to face me although he's looking at the floor his brow wrinkles in a frown. In his hands is a carrier bag and he playing nervously with the top of it, I notice it's from a jewellers and Clayton seems to be struggling with what to say. I wasn't going to help him. I sit on the bed and wait.

Actually I admire the view because Clayton quite frankly looks hot as hell. He's wearing a tight white t-shirt which shows off his sculpted chest and arms, washboard stomach and slim waist. The black combat trousers hug his ass and thighs, I can see the bulge of his cock and he has a semi. I grin salaciously as I know I own his pleasure and I'm the cause of his aroused state.

I lean back with my hands out to the sides to support me and cross my legs. The more I look at Clayton the more I fantasize about peeling him out of his clothes.

Clayton sighs "Skye what you did today" he stops and still doesn't look up "fuck" he curses quietly under his breath and runs a hand through his dark wavy hair "Skye" he looks up and his eyes darken becoming heated, predatory even. He stalks towards me, oh yes! It takes everything I have to hold still. Clayton drops to his knees before me and holds out the bag.

"I wanted to give you something that would show my gratitude and appreciation for what you did today for me and my company"

I take the bag and sit up looking inside there are lots of boxes. "Bloody hell, Christmas has come early!" I say in startled surprise.

Clayton shrugs a shoulder and looks adorably sheepish. "What can I say, I got carried away" Clayton rises and sits next to me, taking the bag off me he pulls out a couple of boxes "here open these first"

Inside are long dangly earrings, a more expensive version of the one's I bought in Italy. "They're gorgeous and just my style" I smile at him.

"I wanted to buy things you would wear every day" Clayton says softly as he hands me the next box.

"Oh these are beautiful" I breathe heavily.

The earrings are exquisite, diamond encrusted long drop earrings in the shape of a Calla Lily with an amethyst protruding from the bottom. I run my finger over the earrings I am definitely wearing these tonight.

With an indulgent smile Clayton silently hands me the next box. He's enjoying giving me these gifts as I am at receiving them. Inside is a ring, my jaw drops. I look at Clayton speechless. I put the ring on the middle finger of my right hand, it fits perfectly. The ring design is to wrap around the finger in a spiral between the two knuckles and it's studded in diamonds and moonstones.

"You like it?" asks Clayton, I hear the uncertainty in his voice.

Nodding "I love it" I whisper as I admire the ring on my hand.

"The jeweller who made it and the earrings also made that" he indicates to my engagement ring "I've also asked him to make our wedding bands" he takes a deep breath and I know he's about to say something he thinks I will have a negative reaction to "I would like us to go see him on Saturday"

My gut tells me he's already made the appointment and I'll put money on the fact he scared the crap out of the jeweller, unintentionally of course, poor guy. I'm not angry, in fact I'm pleased. Hell, I already have my dress.

"What time is the appointment?" Clayton barks out a laugh "I know you Mr Blake. I think it's a great idea"

"Last one" he hands me a box which is bigger than the rest. I gasp inside is a Rolex "I noticed a couple of times this afternoon you looked at your wrist for the time"

My smile got bigger he doesn't miss a thing when it comes to me. "Thank you. I've misplaced my watch somewhere between Vegas, LA and coming home. I do miss it. This is gorgeous, all of it is. Thank you"

I have no intention of saying you shouldn't have or it wasn't necessary. Clayton has bought me things he knew I will wear and I'm touched by his thoughtfulness and consideration.

I kiss him to show him how much I love his gifts, passion soon ignites. Clayton pushes me into the mattress his hands are everywhere. He starts to undo my shirt.

"I know I said I wanted to play but right now I want you naked and to be buried balls deep inside you" he growls and my whole body tingles and thrums in response.

I grab the hem of his t-shirt and pull it off him. The next few seconds are a frantic pawing and grappling to get clothes off of each other. My libido is in overdrive and Clayton's appetence for me pushes me to new heights that are hedonistic.

"Are you ready for me baby because I can't wait another minute"

"Yes"

I push back further onto the bed, laying back down I open my legs. I can feel my juices flowing ready to welcome Clayton's magnificent cock.

"Baby you are so fucking beautiful" Clayton growls hoarsely as he crawls up my body.

Clayton lowers himself down on me. I can feel the head of his cock parting my lips then slide inside me. I thrust my hips up to take him deeper. Clayton dips his head and catches my nipple and sucks, the pull sends sensations racing to my core muscles. I feel them as they clench and grip his cock. We both groan our pleasure.

Clayton pulls back and thrusts forward plunging deeper, he holds still as he kisses up my neck along my jaw and claims my mouth. I start to move against him, taking control grinding my hips and clenching my muscles around his cock.

"Oh yes baby" Clayton moans against my lips "fuck me baby, fuck me good"

Not needing any further encouragement I work us both into such a frenzy Clayton starts to move fast, pounding into me hard, nailing me into the mattress. Pleasure sensations hurtle around my body, I feel as if my climax is running full pelt to dive off the precipice.

"Come with me" Clayton growls through gritted teeth. I dive off. My orgasm erupts like a volcano and flows through me like the lava rushing down the mountain side. I hold onto Clayton feeling his body shake and his muscles spasm as his orgasm claims him.

Clayton's bathroom is as big as mine. A walk in shower big enough to hold six people, a large bath tub actually his is a mini pool compared to mine. The whole room is done in natural stone tiles with white marble wash basins and counter top.

I finish putting my mascara on and look at my reflection and admire my new lily amethyst earrings as the light dances off the diamonds. I decide to keep my hair up to show off my gift. Clayton came in he still has the towel wrapped around his hips. I'm in my bra and panties.

"Don't be mad but I lied when I said the watch was the last gift" he says abashed. I turn to face him and hold out my hand "greedy" he laughs.

"No, expectant, give it up" I snap my fingers "I hope you realize you have made a rod for your own back" I add tartly making him laugh more.

"Honest to a fault and what a stunningly beautiful monster I have created" he mock sighs putting one hand over his heart whilst with the other places a jewellery box in my hand.

I open it to find six pairs of small hooped diamond studded earrings.

"I just had to make your other holes sparkle" we both chuckle at his poor joke.

"They're lovely, thank you" I kiss him and turn to face the mirror.

I take out the plain silver hoops I have in and start putting in the new ones. The hoops hug my ears. I'm thrilled they are exactly what I would have bought myself. I turn back to Clayton.

"What do you think?" I've never asked him before what he thought to the amount of ear piercings I have and suddenly I feel apprehensive. I kick myself; get a grip if he didn't like them he wouldn't have bought enough diamond hoops.

"Dazzling just like you" he bends and kisses me.

My arms snake around his neck and I deepen the kiss. I can feel his cock hardening. My body responds and I press myself closer to him.

"Behave" Clayton growls.

"Do I have to?" I'm trying for peevish instead it comes out sounding tantalisingly seductive.

"Are you going to explain to Alex and Maria why we are late?" that has me pulling away making him chuckle "I'll have to remember that one for the future"

"Actually it was the thought of telling Shelley, Phil, Simon and David as well" Clayton looks at me puzzled then I remember I haven't told him "I invited them and they are meeting us at Gino's. David is the guy who cut my hair in Vegas. Apparently Simon hooked up with him and he's in town visiting family"

"Excellent, it'll be a good evening. Gino will be beside himself, does he know we're all coming?"

"I think so. I rang the restaurant to alter the booking"

I turn back to the mirror, picking up my eye liner I lean over to apply it. Clayton slaps my butt making me yelp but at the same time a surge of desire settles in my belly. Clayton winks at me saucily as he turns and walks out dropping the towel flashing his tight ass. I am so going to sink my teeth in that later.

We are the last to arrive at the restaurant having picked up Alex and Maria from their hotel en-route. On the way to the restaurant I tell them about my other friends joining us which they are fine about. Alex notices and comments on my earrings, expressing how much he likes them. I proudly show off my ring and watch telling him they are all gifts from Clayton, who adds it's his way of showing his appreciation and gratitude for what I'd done this afternoon.

"Although I will forever be in her debt" he finishes kissing the back of my hand.

"As will Boris and I" says Alex "he will be landing tomorrow mid-morning. If you are both free tomorrow night he would like to take you to dinner"

"That would be lovely. I've no plans do you Clayton" Clayton shakes his head.

"Good Boris will be pleased. I will let him know"

I tell Maria about the building I've bought for the auction house and ask how she is getting on with her painting. She admits she's made little progress and vows to make more of an effort when she gets home now she has the incentive and deadline to work to. I also tell her about Penny and how much she has changed appearance wise since Italy. By the time we get to the restaurant it feels like we haven't been apart for three weeks.

Gino greets us with his usual enthusiasm and warmth. He welcomes Alex and Maria as if they are lifelong friends. I introduce my friends and within ten minutes everyone is getting on like a house on fire. Gino brings over two bottles of champagne and toasts Clayton and me on our engagement.

"Hey honey how do you feel about having an engagement party?" Simon calls across the table.

Oh hell no! That is so not going to happen "I would sooner stick pins in my eyes!"

"See I told you" Simon says turning to Shelley, who shrugs nonchalantly.

"It was just a suggestion"

Clayton put his hand on my knee and squeezes. I look at him but he continues his conversation with Alex. His hand travels up my leg. I'm wearing leggings so he has nothing to push out of the way. I try to focus on the menu. My heart starts to pound as he reaches the apex of my thigh. I feel his fingers splay out as his hand moves to my inner thigh. Automatically my body shifts position and my legs part allowing his hand better access and more freedom to move. His little finger skims my sex. A deluge of excitement has me wet instantly. I resist the urge to squeeze my legs together.

Periodically throughout the meal Clayton runs his hand along my thigh but not every time did he go high enough to titillate my sex. The bastard has me highly strung with anticipation, halfway through the main meal comprehension dawns. He's fulfilling a fantasy. He wanted to do this last night at the family dinner only Stephanie thwarted his plan.

"You okay baby" Clayton's husky voice rasps low as his hand does its circuit on my leg, inner thigh and brushes my sex. A shiver runs through me.

I lean over making sure my breast rubs against his arm and I cup his crotch feeling how hard he is. I kiss him to cover the hiss he makes as I squeeze and fondle him.

"I am now" I purr pulling back and pick up my glass of wine. I take a drink and engage David in conversation.

Chapter Twenty

SKYE

"What are your plans for today?"

Clayton is shaving and I sit on the side of the bath tub watching him. We have showered and I'm wrapped in Clayton's bathrobe, he has a towel wrapped around his hips, obviously I'm ogling the fabulous view.

"I'm meeting Billy at ten thirty to finalise the buying of the building. I'm meeting Shelley and Maria for lunch and then they are taking me shopping" I shudder at the thought I hate clothes shopping, shoes no problem, clothes ugh "oh, and I've got my bridesmaid dress fitting afterwards. What time are we meeting with Mr C? Alex and Maria will be there tonight as well in case you didn't know"

"Yes Alex mentioned it last night and he's going to let me know a time later this afternoon. But I think it's safe to say seven thirty to eight"

Clayton finishes shaving and dries his face. He turns to me taking my hands and pulls me to my feet then wraps his arms around me and softly kisses me. I breathe in deeply, absorbing his clean, fresh musky masculine scent and soap. When he pulls away he tenderly strokes his fingers down my cheek.

"I know we agreed to wait a month before we made a decision to discuss moving in together, but can we do it this weekend please" he says softly.

He does the puppy dog eye thing on me again. Damn, but I can't help agree with him. I've been thinking it will be easier for everyone concerned plus I want to.

"Yes, Saturday morning at mine"

"Wow! That was easy" Clayton says surprised.

"What! You expected a hissy fit from me?"

I mock scowl and punch him, not hard but he still says "ouch" and rubs his arm feigning a hurt expression.

"I just thought you would put up a strong argument for sticking to the original agreement"

"No you're right we do need to discuss it. I spoke with Paul yesterday because I was concerned of the ball ache the toing and froing will cause him and Bruce, needless to say they have already sorted it out between them. But it also concerns Macy, she's moving into Paul's quarters this weekend"

Stupefaction is the only expression I can see on Clayton's face.

"Us moving in together affects and involves others so we need to consider their living arrangements not just our own" I run my fingertips down his cheek to take the sting out of my admonishment.

Clayton sighs heavily and puts his forehead against mine "Christ I am a selfish bastard" he whispers "here I am thinking of my own blissful gratification and you sucker punch me out of it. Thank you for the reality check"

"Not a problem anytime you want the rose tinted glasses removing I'm your girl. Now you need to get ready for work" I kiss him then push him back gently.

"Yes ma'am" he chuckles and went into the bedroom.

I clean my teeth and put on my mascara. Clayton is dressed and on his phone when I enter the bedroom.

"Let me log in, give me five minutes and ring me back" Clayton hangs up "I'm going to be in my office. I shouldn't be long" he kisses the top of my head and left me to get dressed.

I begin putting my clothes from yesterday into the bag. I never did get to play naughty secretary I pout to myself. What am I, stupid? I mentally slap my forehead. I can play now. Clayton is working in his office. Quickly I put the underwear and outfit on and head for his office giddy with anticipation. I really hope Clayton wants to play.

Clayton is talking and tapping away on his keyboard when I walk in. He glances up and back at his screen then his head snaps back to me so fast he almost gives himself whiplash and he stops talking. His eyes darken with lust as his gaze rakes me from head to toe and follows my every move. I walk to his side of the desk and perch on the end. I cross my legs and pick up a pad of paper and pen poised as if ready to take notes. My heart is pounding and I'm half expecting him to hiss at me to get out.

"Sorry Tom I got distracted for a minute, say that again"

Clayton pushes back his chair and appraises me, he rubs his index finger across his lower lip, contemplating. I take it as a sign he wants to play. He looks hot in his shirt sleeves, tie and vest. Unabashed I rake my eyes over him from head to toe, my eyes lingering on his crotch and the noticeable bulge. I lick my lips thinking of all the times I've sucked him off.

Clayton obviously thinking the same thing opens his trousers and releases his cock. Fisting his cock he strokes himself. Holy hell, watching him as he pleasures himself whilst on a call makes me even wetter. I'm itching to take him in my mouth but I want Clayton to call the shots in this game after all I am his secretary to do with as he pleases.

"Hold on a moment Tom" Clayton presses a button on his ear piece "Miss Darcy I have a job for you, come here" I hop off the desk and stand in front of him "kneel" he commands, excitement thrums through me as I get into position "suck my cock but don't make me come" I open my mouth and lean forward "what do you say?"

"Yes sir" my voice is low, throaty and sultry.

Clayton's eyes widen briefly, hmm he liked that. Wonder what reaction I will get if I call him Master. Save that thought for another day.

I run my tongue up the length of his shaft and take him in my mouth as far as I can and suck hard as I pull back. Clayton groans as his hips surge upwards.

"Don't make me come" he repeats the command "Tom, talk me through what the next stage entails"

As Clayton conducts his conversation I lick and suck his cock alternating between soft and hard sucks. I feel the veins in his cock pulse and taste cum, he's close. He has one hand on my head stroking and caressing my cheek and hair.

I can resist anything except temptation, the Oscar Wilde quote floats around my head as I wonder what Clayton will do if I defy his command. Sod it, I give in to temptation. I suck hard twice and on the third he came. A grunt is the only sound he makes. I continue to lick and suck every last drop out of him.

I put his cock back in his boxers and fasten his trousers. I sit back on the desk waiting for him to finish his call. Clayton's eyes never leave me and his face is impassive. I have to hand it to him his control impresses the hell out of me. I look back at him as nonchalantly as I can although I'm quaking inside.

A few minutes pass, when the call ends Clayton removes his ear piece slowly.

"Miss Darcy I had such high hopes for you in your role as my secretary" his voice is rich and smooth dripping with decadence "however I am disappointed you don't take instruction well" he stands and steps close to me, running a finger down my cheek "I think disciplining you will teach you a lesson. What do you say?"

My mouth goes dry. I try to swallow it didn't work. I'm excited as hell. "Depends on the discipline sir" I say hoarsely.

His eyes sparkle and a salacious grin spreads across his face. "Spanking"

Oh my sweet lord, that one word ignites my desire, in fact I feel as if I'm about to combust.

"You like that don't you Miss Darcy, don't deny it I can see it in your beautiful eyes. I think six of the best should do it" he steps back "get off the desk" I did "turn around and bend over"

Holy hell, those commands have my juices flowing. I bend over the desk and feel his hand on my butt immediately rubbing backwards and forwards, up and down. His hand left me, the slap lands and I yelp more from the unexpectedness of it rather than the pain.

"Count" he barks out the command.

"One"

Clayton went back to rubbing. Slap.

"Two" I breathe heavily. Slap.

"Three" I moan, god this is such a turn on.

"Tut, tut Miss Darcy you are enjoying this too much"

Clayton moves behind me, both hands on my hips he pushes himself against my butt. I can feel how much this turns him on as well. His hands fist in my skirt and pull up revealing my stockings, garter belt and black lace thong.

"Oh fuck me" he groans the curse and runs his hand over my butt.

My muscles tighten sending delicious pleasure sensations racing around my body. Clayton slips his fingers into the waist band of my thong and slowly pulls it down to my thighs. Bloody hell this is so erotic. Clayton's hand moves in between my legs. I adjust my stance to give him better access; his fingers run along my slit, parting my lips and folds, circling and teasing my clit with light pressure. I moan at the pleasure the sensations create.

"Oh dear Miss Darcy you really are enjoying this far, far too much" Clayton's voice betrays his own lust as he places a kiss on each butt cheek.

His wet fingers trail up to my back passage and circle the rim then applies a slight pressure on the sphincter. I fight the instinct to pull away.

"Tell me Miss Darcy have you ever been fucked here" he pushes his finger into my ass. I gasp and groan at the brief painful alien intrusion "answer me Miss Darcy"

He slaps my butt, my muscles clench down on his finger. He rubs my butt as he slowly moves his finger in and out of my ass. I'm overwhelmed with sensation; the pain is now replaced by intense pleasure.

"No. Four" I gasp trying to get my breathing under control.

"Good girl" he continues to move his finger in and out "one day I am going to fuck you right here. Would you like that Miss Darcy?"

He pushes his finger in further and slaps me at the same time. I cry out as the pain and pleasure is all consuming.

"Answer me Miss Darcy" his voice stern yet seductive.

"Yes. Five" I heave in breaths trying to stem my panting.

Clayton continues to move his finger alternating from short shallow fast thrusts to slower deeper penetration. I moan as I feel my climax building from the pleasure Clayton is drawing out of me. I never knew it could feel like this.

"Your ass is just as delightfully tight as your cunt which I am going to fuck now"

He slaps my butt then rubs as he removes his finger from my ass. I hear the zipper of his trousers go down then his hands grip my hips. Clayton's foot taps mine in a silent command to widen my stance. As I move I feel his cock slide along my slit, coating it with my juices as he teases me. Clayton guides his cock to my entrance and pushes in slowly. I feel every ridge of his thick cock. When he is fully inside me both hands return to my hips and grasp tightly.

"Hold on Miss Darcy I'm going to fuck you hard and fast"

He slides out slowly then pulls my hips back onto him as he rams forward. In and out over and over each time impaling me, his balls slap against my clit stimulating me further. I'm moaning and groaning loudly.

"Your cunt is so fucking tight Miss Darcy and it belongs to me"

Clayton slaps my butt as he slams in to me.

"Oh yes" I cry out as the unbelievable sensations of pleasure crash around my body, my muscles clench hard around his cock.

Clayton slaps me again as he penetrates me and my orgasm rips through me. I cry out in surprise at the intensity of it. Clayton continues to pound into me chasing his own release. Another orgasm hits me before the first one subsides, my arms give out and I collapse face down on the desk.

"Skye, fuck, Oh Skye" Clayton roars out.

I feel his cock twitching and pulsing inside me as he holds still and pumps his release into me. He collapses against me his head resting between my shoulder blades. If I hadn't been resting on the table we would be in a heap on the floor, the table is the only thing keeping me on my feet because my legs have turned to jelly. Clayton wraps his arms around me and our heavy breaths are in sync.

Clayton straightens my clothes then sorts himself out. Taking me in his arms he hugs me.

"I enjoyed that" he says against my hair.

Leaning back I look into his dark blue eyes, so much love it makes my heart ache.

"I did too" I whisper "I love you"

"I love you too Miss Darcy" then he kisses me in a way it should be illegal, not that I'm complaining.

CLAYTON

Shit, it's only three o'clock. I can't concentrate it will be another three hours before I see Skye. I'm like a junkie going through withdrawal. My mind keeps going back to this morning and the scene we played in my home office. I've been permanently hard all day. Everything that had taken place turned me on. How Skye had given herself to me, the trust and when she called me sir, fuck I'd nearly ejaculated when she said that.

I push away from my desk and pace around the office. I've never been this restless in my life. Calm and focused that's me especially when I'm working. I run a hand through my hair.

There's a knock on the door and it opens Helena walks in, a brief flash of surprise crosses her face when she finds me the other end of the office pacing.

"Sorry to disturb you Mr Blake but your mother is on the line"

"Thank you" I walk back to my desk and pick up my phone and see two missed calls from her. I've been so wrapped up in thinking about Skye I didn't hear it, I also hadn't heard my desk phone I realize for Helena to come in and tell me I had a call. I pick up the desk phone.

"Hi Mom everything okay?"

"Hello darling, yes of course I'm fine" she says matter of fact, alarm bells ring, something is up when she uses that tone "have you spoken to Andrew?"

Here we go, inwardly I brace myself "Not since yesterday afternoon. Why?"

"So he was telling the truth" she sighs heavily "he wants me to get everyone together tomorrow night so Mandy can apologise to us all. Will you and Skye come over about seven?"

"What do you mean he was telling the truth?" it comes out harsher than I intend.

"When he said he had spoken to you I didn't really believe him because he shies away from any type of skirmish or argument. I'm just surprised he rang you. So will you come?"

"He didn't ring me" for some reason her assumption annoys me "he rang Joshua who happened to be here. I took the phone off Joshua to speak to him obviously what I said to him has sunk in. I'll have to come back to you. I need to check Skye hasn't organised anything else"

"So Skye will come" mother says hopefully.

"Yes, she has already told me and Joshua she bears no ill will towards Mandy. It's the rest of us that has the problem with her" I pick up my phone and send a text message to Skye about Saturday night "Skye is used to the kind of prejudice Mandy showed and she handles it brilliantly. Skye says it's not the first time and it sure as hell won't be the last but as Joshua said it's unacceptable when it comes from someone who is practically family" my phone chimes with Skye's reply.

"I was so ashamed and embarrassed when Elizabeth told me what Mandy had said to Skye then I got angry. So help me god I wanted to hurt Mandy badly. I thought Skye wouldn't want anything to do with us ever again, most of all I was worried she would break up with you. You have waited so long to find happiness. It's lovely to see you so much in love" her voice is soft with wonder.

"Skye is an amazingly strong woman, she's just responded to my message. She says she'd love to come so you can take it we'll be there"

We chat for a few more minutes before hanging up. I'm still restless. Fuck it, call it a day and go to the gym. I shut down my computer and grab my jacket.

"Helena" I yell she appears at the door within seconds "I'm calling it a day, you go home too and have a good weekend"

"Yes sir, have a good weekend too" Helena says quickly getting over her shock.

"Okay spill mister" Skye says as she hands me the night cap and sits beside me on the sofa. We've just gotten in from diner with Mr C "you've been in a funny mood all night, not that anyone else noticed but I have. So what's bugging you?" Skye's voice brokers no argument.

Skye shifts her position, curling her legs underneath her and turning to look at me and takes a sip of her drink. I look at mine and swirl the brandy around the glass. She's right I've been out of sorts all day. I just can't get the scene out of my head and how turned on we both had been.

I need to know how far she would like to take this. The realization punches me in the gut. Fuck how do I start this kind of conversation? I didn't want to frighten her off. I look at Skye, her beautiful face expectant, she wanted an answer. Crap, here goes. I take a large gulp of the brandy. It burns the back of my throat, heat pools and radiates outward as it hits my stomach.

"The scene we played this morning you said you enjoyed it and I know it turned you on" I pause to watch her reaction. Skye nods and her yellow green eyes sparkle as she remembers what we did "would you do that again? And a variation of it?" again she nods, no hesitation "what part of the scene did you really like and don't say all of it be specific"

Her eyes widen and her cheeks flush. "I liked the spanking and everything you did to me. I liked the commands you gave and I liked sucking you off whilst you were on the phone call" her voice is huskily soft with no trace of embarrassment "I enjoyed the thrill and anticipation the whole role play gave me, I especially enjoyed the intense orgasms" her cheeks flush again as she smiles shyly.

"What would you be willing to try?"

A slight frown crease appears between her eyebrows as she works through my meaning, she makes an audible gasp as she got there a few seconds later.

"You want to tie me up" she whispers.

I can't fathom how she feels because there is no accusatory tone, no fear in her eyes and she's holding herself perfectly still.

"I would never do that without your consent" I watch her reaction closely, again nothing "I was thinking more along the lines of the spanking, using a paddle and or a flogger"

This time her eyes widen but still no fear.

"You really are in to BDSM" a whispered statement.

Be honest with her, don't fuck this up, she has always been open and honest about her past give her the same respect.

"Not really" I clear my throat "when I was in my late teens and early twenties there was this college buddy who got into the scene. Being a curious, horny and randy young man I tagged along. I went through the training. I was I suppose what you might call a dabbler. Building my business empire was more of a priority"

I take another large gulp of my drink. I've never told anyone about those few years and my college buddy would never talk because he fully embraced the lifestyle even to this day.

"Skye I want to make love to you and fuck you in so many ways, take you to the heights of pleasure you don't even know exist"

"So as a Dominant you want me to be your Submissive" a whispered statement not said as a question my mind warns.

"Fuck no" I say this forcefully so she would know I'm not expecting that "baby you are not a submissive, even sexually you take charge and I love it when you do, but this morning you were submissive and I loved it just as much" I pause giving her time to process what I've said "what I'm getting at is there are toys and equipment which we can use to heighten the sexual experience and test our limits"

"So the things you want to do to me I can do them to you?"

I nod. Skye doesn't say anything else. After a few minutes I can't stand the silence any longer.

"Talk to me, tell me your thoughts" I whisper a plea "please, tell me if I've over stepped the mark and scared the crap out of you"

"I don't know how I feel about it. Yes it sounds sexy and erotic as hell yet equally scary" she sighs "I guess I just need time to think it through. Will you give me that?" Her eyes plead with me to be patient, to understand.

"Of course, all I ask is you consider it and if you decide no then its fine with me. All I need to know is what and how far you are willing to go. The last thing I want to do is something that sends you running and screaming for the hills"

Skye snorts a laugh "If I did you would only follow me"

"True I would, but I wouldn't drag you back kicking and screaming. I would stay and follow you around like an adorable lost puppy" I give her a doleful look, Skye laughs. I smile as it seems to lighten the mood in the room. Standing up I hold out my hand "come on it's getting late and we both need our beauty sleep"

SKYE

I let out a long sigh, sleep is eluding me. I look at the clock it's three in the morning. Clayton's words from earlier are constantly circling around my head. I still can't truthfully say how I feel about his proposal to use BDSM toys and props. Yes I'm turned on at the thought of some but scared shitless at others.

When we came to bed Clayton made love to me slow and steadily, he brought me to orgasm three times before he sort his own release, that made me wonder what it would be like when or if we played as he wanted.

I got out of bed carefully so as not to disturb Clayton and quietly got a vest t-shirt and shorts from the dresser. I put them on and headed for the living room.

I pick up my bandanna and iPod from my drawing desk, I'm going to draw and paint out my thoughts. I find this a therapeutic exercise as it helps me understand my feelings about a situation or decision I have to make.

I move my easels out of the way and tape the largest sheets of paper I have up onto the wall. I tie back my hair and put the bandanna on as the last thing I want is paint in my hair which sadly for me isn't unusual, hence the bandanna. I went to the cabinet that holds my art materials. Sitting the iPod on top of the speaker docking station I switch it on setting it at random then opening the cabinet I take out acrylics, pastels, chalks and charcoal setting them on the floor in front of the papered wall.

I start with the first image in my head, being bound and blind folded holds the most fear for me. No shit Einstein my mind mocks.

Time to switch the brain off and get into the zone, I never know when this happens. For a few years I tried various things to try and pin point when my conscious brain left on vacation and my unconscious side took over, I never did find out. Now I don't bother. I immerse myself in the music and my imagination and begin to draw.

CLAYTON

A beautiful haunting female operatic voice sings to me, lulling me back to deep sleep. Something has disturbed me. The singing tempts me back to slumber. As I drift back off I turn to pull Skye into my arms, the heavy beat of rock music accompanying the haunting voice has me wide awake instantly and sitting bolt upright. Skye is up and drawing, I knew this before I open my eyes. I look at the clock, five am. Getting out of bed I grab my bathrobe and go to find her in the living room.

As I enter I automatically look at her drawing desk, she isn't there. The music volume is low had she been on her own it would be blaring out. Movement in my peripheral vision has me turning in that direction.

Skye stood in front of the wall at the far end of the room. She's moved the easels which normally stand there with canvasses on out of the way. I move towards her, getting closer I see a montage of images.

Fuck me. I stop dead.

They scream BDSM and they are of me and her in various poses and positions. Some bound, some shackled, alternating dominant and submissive roles for each of us.

Skye told me in London that if she has something on her mind she often drew what is in her head to help her understand what she is feeling and it aides her decision making.

I guess I'd given her a lot to think about.

Shit, I'm the cause. I've pushed her too far, it was too soon.

I'm forcing her to face her demons. I've never outright asked her about what happened to her when she was attacked, of course I've wondered and drawn conclusions from the volunteered brief snippets she has given and I trust she'll tell me the rest one day when she is ready, I know she had been restrained and beaten. Shit, I'm such a fucking selfish idiot why didn't I use my brain instead of my dick, I'm asking her to voluntarily to be spanked and flogged being restrained heightens the sexual experience, she will be reliving a past experience which is a nightmare for her. That's why the bondage features so heavily, she will be surrendering control regardless of how much she trusts me.

Despair and the weight of what I'm putting Skye through brings' me to my knees.

I watch helplessly as Skye continues to paint, she is lost in her world. I can't see her face, part of me doesn't want to.

Fucking coward man up! Take her in your arms and tell her to forget everything you've said.

Think of her and her needs for a change you conceited narcissistic bastard.

I didn't move, couldn't or was it more wouldn't. Either way I'm staying put as I helplessly watch her work.

The artwork even in its rough form is fantastic and detailed. I notice in a few images of me I'm wearing tight black leather trousers, my torso and arms naked. All muscle definition and veins coursing my arms are done from memory. I continue to watch her. I decide to stay as I am on my knees until she finishes then I will beg for her forgiveness.

SKYE

I straighten and step back from the wall. Yawning I stretch and feel rather than hear my spine pop. Man I'm tired. I have no idea how long I've been at this but it's been worth it. I'm at peace. Looking at all the images in front of me I know I will give it a go but I have questions for Clayton. I trust him and I know he will never hurt me, it would kill him if he ever did even if it was unintentional.

The images of being restrained told me what I already knew; this will be the biggest hurdle to overcome. I don't know if I ever will get past it, but I want to try. I've come too far. If I got over this will I be completely free of my past?

Clayton is the one to show me the way.

I put the palette and brush down on the floor next to the other art materials. I'll clean them up later, right now I want to crawl into bed and get a few hours' sleep, picking up the rag cloth I wipe my hands and turn…. Holy cow! Clayton is in his bathrobe on his knees with the most unusual expression on his face.

"I am so, so very sorry, please forgive me"

The remorse in his voice and the sadness that is emanating from him has me rushing to him and dropping to my knees, anxiety and concern eating at me.

"What's the matter?" I search his face. His eyes shine with tears. Holy mother what has he done to get in this distraught state "talk to me please you're starting to freak me out" I say earnestly.

Clayton reaches out and tenderly touches my cheek "I never meant to put you through this, force you to face your demons. I pushed you too far and too soon. You look exhausted all because I was, no I am, arrogant enough to think you want to please me and because you enjoyed the scene you would want to do more of it"

Oh Clayton. He's been torturing himself, blaming and most probably cursing as well whilst he watched me work.

I lean forward and kiss him mainly to reassure him I'm okay. I pull back just enough to look him in the eyes. I pour sincerity into my voice and hopefully he sees it in my eyes as well.

"I asked you to give me time. Time for me to work through how I feel about it and that's exactly what I have done" I nod to the wall "I am at peace. I have made my decision" I let my words sink in.

His eyes widen "You have?" he couldn't believe it that is very evident.

"What does the picture or I should say images say to you?" I move so he can see the wall better.

"Bondage is an issue" he whispers.

"Yes you're right. Now look past that, what else do you see?"

I stay still and quiet as Clayton studies to interpret the images. After five minutes he inhales sharply turning to look at me his eyes shine with love and awe.

"You want to give it a go"

I nod my acquiesce "As I've said to you before I don't know if I will ever get over being restrained, but I am willing to try. I trust you to find a way. I want to be free of my past in that respect. I want to enjoy the heights of pleasure you have promised to take me to. The pressure is on you now mister" I prod his chest "to deliver"

"Skye Darcy I love you so much" he whispers and kisses me.

"I love you Clayton Blake" I say against his lips and kiss him back.

There is nothing sexual in the kiss just tenderness and love.

"Now I need sleep" I say as I pull away.

I stood then help Clayton to stand up; his legs have gone numb because he's knelt for so long. I crawl into bed and Clayton's arms and promptly fall into a dreamless sleep.

Chapter Twenty One

CLAYTON

I wake Skye up with breakfast in bed at two in the afternoon. She looks mussed and well rested and fuckable.

"Good morning beautiful" I kiss her awake. Skye mumbles or rather grumbles something incoherently "if we didn't have to go the jewellers I would leave you to sleep"

"What time is it" she snaps grumpily around a yawn and stretch.

Skye really doesn't like being woken up, although she is adorably grouchy. I can't help but smile at her.

"Two o'clock"

She bolts upright wide awake "Damn! I promised to give Macy and Paul a hand" she snaps out.

"Don't worry. Bruce has helped and they are all done, now breakfast eat"

"Bossy" she mutters scowling at me, it makes me laugh.

I watch her as she munches on the toast and sips the juice.

"You're staring, have I sprouted another head? No wait, have I got a pimple?" Skye mocks horror.

"I was going to say I'm enjoying the view, but damn that pimple is having a party all on its own"

"Ha ha you're funny, not" Skye says trying hard not to grin.

I continue to watch Skye as she finishes off the toast and juice, gauging her mood aside from the grumpiness of being woken up I want to make sure she is still at peace with what we had discussed last night and the early hours of this morning.

Skye has set me the challenge of finding a way which would help get her over the fear of being restrained. I had lain awake for hours thinking about it. I'm determined not to fuck this up. I thought back to the training I had gone through and an idea hit me, show and tell.

I rang my old college buddy whilst I made Skye her breakfast and gave a brief explanation for my request. Thankfully discretion and confidentiality are paramount in his lifestyle so he didn't push me for any further information. Another bonus is he's going away on business first thing in the morning and would leave a key for me at the front desk with the concierge.

Now it's time to put my idea to Skye. I take a deep breath "Listen, I've been giving it some thought"

"So that's what the whirring noise is, it's your brain!" Skye cuts in grinning impishly.

I roll my eyes at her "As I was saying" I say pompously "further to our conversation earlier this morning" Skye drops her mischievous act becoming serious and attentive "I have an idea. The college buddy I mentioned he has a play room and he is willing to let us use it and everything in it" Skye's eyes widen "I thought, if you are willing, we could go over there tomorrow, he won't be there by the way" I add quickly as I see panic flash across her face "I can show you the different types of restraints, talk you through the functionality and the positions they would put you in, if you wanted you can try them out, get a feel for them" I shrug hoping she picks up my underlying meaning as I didn't want to blatantly say face your fear or worst nightmare "Also the various toys which can be used to heighten the sexual experience I can show you those as well. This is the only way, I think, that will be an open, honest and safe environment for you. What do you think?"

I hold my breath as I wait for her response. My heart feels as if it's in my mouth it's pounding so hard. Skye's face is expressionless.

"You will do that for me" she whispers.

Cautiously I nod. Shit what is she thinking? At this moment I really, really want to climb inside her head to find out.

"Thank you I would like that" I sag with relief. Skye leans over and kisses me.

"Mmmm, Skye and toast, delicious" I murmur against her lips, my cock twitches "and as much as I want to fuck you senseless we haven't got time so Miss Darcy get your butt out of bed, shower and dressed in half an hour please"

Skye crawls across the bed muttering under her breath. I slap her butt it's too tempting not to. Skye yelps then wiggles her butt at me daring me to do it again. I like this game so I lift my arm higher that makes Skye move faster off the bed and run giggling into the bathroom.

The bell jingles as I open the door to the jewellers and hold it open so Skye can enter first. As I follow Gerrard comes from behind the counter to welcome us. The shop is quite busy and most of the patrons gawp at us, I ignore them and focus on Gerrard.

"Mr Blake welcome back" I match his smile and shake his extended hand.

"Gerrard good to see you again, this is Skye"

"Miss Darcy it is such a pleasure to finally meet you" Skye gives him her brain frying megawatt smile as she shakes his hand. Gerrard is momentarily stupefied "come, I shall take you through to Matthew"

"By the way Skye I should warn you, Matthew is a fan" I say chuckling, the malicious bastard in me is looking forward to seeing his reaction at meeting her.

"Yes he is. Poor lad was in a state of shock for hours when he found out the ring he had made was for you. I'll be surprised if you get a word out of him for which I will apologise now just in case" says Gerrard trying not to chuckle, he obviously has images in his head of how the meeting is going to pan out.

"Don't worry I'm used to it" Skye says smiling.

As we enter the workshop all activity ceases. Matthew, sitting at the table in the centre of the room rises shakily to his feet, is white as a sheet. Poor lad looks as if he is about to pass out. I watch Skye as Gerrard introduces her. Skye gives him her megawatt smile, it makes my brain short out fuck knows what she is doing to his.

"It's a pleasure to meet you Matthew. I absolutely love everything you have made and I look forward to working with you" Skye's low husky voice resonates around the room it is so quiet "I would also like to see the other pieces you designed, Clayton told me you have made a range"

Matthew blushes purple and nods. He tries to speak but a squeak comes out instead. Skye takes a step closer to him and puts a hand on his arm.

"I'm only human and I promise not to bite" she makes Matthew laugh and he visibly relaxes "that's it and don't forget to breathe" Skye chuckles.

"It's an honor to meet you Miss Darcy" Matthew finally says.

"Skye, please call me Skye" she says kindly as she pulls out a stool and sits down. I follow suit.

"I will leave you in Matthew's capable hands. Can I get you both a drink?" Gerrard asks as he makes his way to the door.

"No thanks" we both chorus.

Matthew is nervously playing with an art pad he has in front of him "Err, what would you like to see first, the wedding band designs or the jewellery pieces?" he stumbles through the sentence.

"Let's see the designs first" Skye says then turns to me "you okay with that?" I nod.

I watch Skye work her magic on Matthew just as she did with the young boy Danny in the elevator in Vegas, she asks him questions in such a way she gets him talking and within five minutes he is a completely different young man.

Matthew becomes animated as he describes his ideas going through his pad and Skye listens attentively; she asks questions I never would have thought to. Before I know it they have agreed the design to her ring. Matthew has designed my ring to be the masculine version of Skye's.

"If Skye is happy with it then so am I" is all I say when they both look at me for my input.

Skye laughs "But you've got to wear it" she counters.

"If you like it, I'll love it. I trust your judgement" I raise her hand to my lips and kiss it.

"Soppy git" Skye snorts much to Matthew's bewilderment "okay so that's the bands sorted; let me see these other pieces"

Matthew takes my ring finger measurement then went off to get the other pieces.

"Happy?" Skye asks me.

"Ecstatic" I lean forward and kiss her "you?"

"Very" Skye smiles so sweetly it makes my heart swell.

A throat being cleared has us pulling apart. Matthew has returned with his box of jewellery.

"Sorry" Skye apologises.

Matthew lays out the pieces on the black velvet cloth just like last time separating the finished from the unfinished

"Wow, these are awesome" Skye says picking up the bracelets and necklaces she looks at them closely "these are the best interpretation of my art work that I have ever seen"

Matthew went purple either at the praise Skye has just given him or from the fact Skye has recognised the designs as hers.

"You are seriously talented Matthew"

"You're not mad that I used your art work" Matthew whispers I detect worry in his voice.

"Hell no" Skye exclaims "I'm flattered you've used it to inspire you to design and make these"

Skye continues to examine the finished and unfinished pieces closely and getting what I recognise as her thoughtful ideas look on her face. Matthew watches her with uncertainty and worry etches his face, he glances at me and I smile trying to reassure him Skye isn't angry.

After a few minutes Skye hasn't said anything else and I'm starting to feel sorry for Matthew "What are you thinking baby?" she snaps out of her thoughts.

"Huh, what" Skye looks at me then Matthew "sorry, I was just thinking. Matthew I often get asked by people to design or make the pieces that appear in my paintings but I've never really been inspired or had the inclination to do anything about it, until now. Would you like to collaborate with me in putting a range together?"

Matthew's legs give out and he collapses onto the stool, his face is blank. I laugh silently to myself, gleeful that I'm not the only guy Skye could floor with words. Skye looks puzzled by Matthew's reaction.

"Skye baby" she looks at me "you have just shocked the shit out of the poor lad. You have just offered him a chance of a lifetime and it means he is going to be working with his heroine if he chooses to take you up on it. Give him a few minutes"

Skye's eyes widen as she comprehends the truth of my words, she opens her mouth to say something then decides against it and nods. A few minutes pass before Matthew manages to speak or squeak rather.

"Seriously you want me to work with you?" Skye nods "I, I, I would be honored" Matthew takes a few shaky deep breaths "wow, oh wow!" he exclaims putting his hands on the top of his head as if to hold on to it before it blew off.

"Excellent, how about I come in next week and we can go through the legal aspects. Let's say Tuesday, that'll give you a chance to speak to whoever here if permission is needed plus we can discuss marketing platforms" Skye is in full business mode.

"Sure, sure Tuesday is good for me" Matthew says still stunned. I'm sure he is still pinching himself to check he isn't dreaming.

"I would also like you to make me two more pairs of these" Skye lifts her hair to show the amethyst lily earrings "I'd like one pair to be ruby and the other moonstone"

"Make another pair with diamonds" I add Skye looks at me open mouthed I raise an eyebrow daring her to say differently instead she smiles her megawatt smile and my brain fries.

Before we left the shop Skye told Gerrard about the collaboration she wanted to do with Matthew. Gerrard has the same reaction as Matthew. I thought the old guy was going to keel over.

"Miss Darcy you bestow a great honor on us and Matthew knows of this?"

"Yes and I apologise if I over stepped the mark by speaking with him first. Please don't be angry with him, it's all entirely my fault. I'll be coming in on Tuesday to discuss the partnership so I'll have my business advisor and legal counsel with me so I recommend having yours present too. The sooner we can get the legal side finalised the quicker Matthew and I can set to work"

"I shall make sure everything is ready for Tuesday"

The shop door opens and Paul walks in coming straight to us "Excuse me Miss Darcy, sir. We have a situation outside" turning to Gerrard he says "may we use the back exit to leave the premises" to me he says "Bruce has the car waiting in the alley by the doors"

Gerrard quickly got over his surprise and starts to lead the way out.

"What is it?" asks Skye, she is cool, calm and collect. I can feel the adrenalin pumping through me ready for action, fight or flight.

"Paparazzi" is all Paul says. Shit.

We get into the car easily enough. Bruce angled the car in such a way the open door blocked the view from anyone looking into the alley and it was one step from the building doorway into the vehicle.

"Well I suppose we've been lucky it lasted this long considering you've been back since Wednesday"

Skye nods her agreement as she pulls her phone out of her pocket and hit a button "Hey Simon... yes I'm fine... Listen, Clayton and I have just been in the jewellers and we've had to leave through the back exit... bingo... uh huh... yep... Gerrard speak to him. Also I'm collaborating with Matthew the jewellery designer on a range to go to market I'll need you on Tuesday for the meeting, let me know what time you can do.... no... I trust you just run with it... okay... speak to you later" Skye hung up.

"Simon is going to put out a press release about why we were there it'll go out within the hour" Skye says as she scrolls through her contacts "damn" she mutters under her breath as she hit another button.

"Hey Macy, how's it going" Skye chuckles "yeah sorry about letting you down this morning" Skye's eyes snap to me "he did, did he" she raises an eyebrow at me "well he's got to put those muscles to some use, can't all just be for decoration" a deep throaty laugh. What the hell is Macy telling her? I only helped with a couple of boxes "we're heading back now but I need Lar's number I have a meeting on Tuesday and I require his services. I just want to give him as much notice as possible... are you sure?... okay... well just find out what time he's free. I'm waiting for Simon to come back with his availability... cheers... do you need anything picking up from the store... see you in a bit" Skye hung up.

"You really are a powerhouse" I say in awe "I'm fascinated that you have accomplished so much in so few words in such a short space of time"

Skye winks at me saucily "I have the right people around me and they know how I think" then she changes the subject "right we need to discuss moving in together when we get back" Skye pats my leg "but I want some information from you Bruce"

Bruce's eyes snap to mine in the rear view mirror. I shrug I'm at a complete loss as to why she would want information from him.

"Paul, obviously I know yours and Macy's requirements. Is there anything else that needs consideration?"

"No ma'am nothing has changed"

What the fuck is she going on about? My confusion must be showing on my face because Skye looks at me. "I've told you us moving in together affects other people so we need to put their requirements into the pot when we discuss our own, that will determine where we live"

I feel such a shit she has to point it out again, "As always my love you are right" I kiss the back of her hand then undid her seat belt and pull her onto my lap. I want to hold her in my arms. I refasten my seat belt around both of us. Skye is so used to me doing this she complies without complaint.

"Bruce, I am aware of the current arrangements you and Paul have made. What I would like to know is what your living accommodation requirements are?"

"I'm not sure I follow ma'am" Bruce says his uncertainty evident.

"Well on a more permanent basis you will want your own space and privacy. Do you have a partner or like Paul a child that may come to stay with you or family. So at least you would require two bedrooms or do you have a particular hobby which requires a certain amount of space"

A smile spreads across Bruce's face he is touched by her thoughtfulness and consideration for his needs. I see the look Bruce and Paul exchange and the imperceptible nod Bruce gives him. I would put money on the fact it is in acknowledgement to a previous conversation they've had about Skye and Bruce is seeing first hand her altruistic nature.

"Thank you for asking ma'am but I have no specific requirements and I have no family" Bruce says in his usual brisk gruff voice although there is an underlying softness I've never heard before. Bruce's eyes flit to mine. I give a brief nod to let him know all is well. Skye has him wrapped around her little finger.

I watch the fading sunlight dance across Skye's hair and face. When the light catches her at the right angle it appears she shimmers giving her an otherworldly aura, the diamonds in her ears flash and sparkle adding to the illusion.

We are sat at the breakfast bar in her kitchen compiling our living space requirements. Skye's kitchen has a warm homely feel to it not cold and clinical like mine. I don't like my kitchen, not that I use it much because I can't cook, but that's what you get when you leave it to someone else to decorate and they give you the ultimate bachelor pad costing a fucking fortune.

"You're not paying attention Mr Blake"

Skye looks at me with what I can only describe as a school teachers expression, a stern eyebrow raised in I'm not impressed kind of look. I give her my most dazzling smile and try for contrite.

"Sorry ma'am. You are absolutely right. I was greatly admiring the stunningly beautiful goddess before me"

I lean forward and kiss her. I stroke her luscious full lips with the tip of my tongue. Her lips part and I dip inside lazily exploring and tasting. Skye's arms snake around my neck and her fingers tangle in my hair. Neither of us deepens the kiss. I think we both know it will be dangerous as we'll be fucking in no time considering the passion we have for each other. So instead I enjoy the slow almost lethargic tenderness of the moment.

"You ready to focus now?" Skye says against my lips.

"Nope" I kiss her for a few more minutes. I have to pry myself away "Christ I could kiss you forever"

"Ditto" Skye chuckles.

"Sorry my love you were saying" I prompt her.

Skye is writing out the list of what we need for our living arrangements. We've already agreed neither of our current apartments ticked all the boxes.

"So you will need an office. I need studio come office space. At least three bedrooms one being master en-suite with the other two being guest rooms, kitchen, living room, dining room and security office. Staff quarters one to be two bedroomed, bathroom, living room and kitchen, the other a one bedroom with the same amenities, finally a room to use as a gym for everyone's use. Can you think of anything else to add?" Skye looks up from reading the list.

"Ideally we would need security on the front desk, coded access and sufficient secured underground parking, that'll keep Paul and Bruce happy" Skye adds the extra to the list "so who are we going to give this odious task to?"

"Odious!" Skye scolds, but the twinkle in her eyes gives her away "looking for our future home is odious is it?"

"So you're doing it then" I state matter of fact.

"Hell no, I was thinking of giving it to Billy" she laughs "unless you know of anyone"

I shake my head and Skye picks up her phone, scrolls her contacts and hits the call button.

"Hey Billy… no, no all is well, I have another job for you" Skye read out the list "Everything on there is minimum requirement… yes… yes… no… yes… sooner rather than later, end of the month"

I raise an eyebrow she has piqued my curiosity "timeframe" she mouths. A warm glow spreads through me; Skye wants us living together as soon as possible just like I do.

"Okay Billy enjoy the rest of your weekend" Skye hangs up "Billy is getting on with it straight away"

"Do these people not mind you ringing them on a weekend about work?" I ask intrigued.

"Don't know" Skye shrugs nonchalantly "they all work for themselves so I know they will be working in some sort of capacity besides it's a Saturday and it is still a working day plus I'm their best client so I don't feel guilty" Skye gives me an innocent smile.

I can't argue with her logic, mind you it would be hypocritical of me because I'm guilty of calling people outside of office hours on work related issues. I glance at the clock on the oven, shit we need to get going if we're going to make it to mothers for seven. I'm not looking forward to tonight.

"Come on baby we need to make tracks if we're to make it to mothers on time" as I stand I see Skye grimace, I wrap my arms around her "I'm not looking forward to it either and I make no apologies for anything I say tonight to anyone especially to that fucking bitch"

"Promise me one thing" Skye leans back to look at me, she runs her finger tips down my cheek, I love it when she does that it makes me feel treasured "please don't be the one to antagonise or start an argument"

"I'll be on my best behaviour, scout's honor" I say as solemnly as I can.

"Now why do I find it hard to believe you were in the scouts" snorts Skye.

"I was" I feign as much hurt feelings into those words as I can "I got kicked out mind you, but I was in the scouts" I grin wickedly as memories flit through my mind.

"Now that I can believe" Skye pats me on the chest as she gets off the stool.

"Baby wake up, we're here"

I coax Skye awake by rubbing the back of my fingers down her cheek. Skye dozed off halfway through the journey. Slowly she opens her eyes. I watch those gorgeous yellow green eyes go from unfocused sleepy to bright alertness. Skye sits up and stretches, one of her tits is dangerously close to my mouth. Fuck it, I open my mouth and bite the nipple then suckle her through the material of her t-shirt.

"Clayton!" Skye squeals and swats at me.

"Awake now" I grin salaciously.

In retaliation Skye squirms and grinds her butt against me. Christ that feels too good, my cock agrees.

"I am now" Skye retorts then putting her mouth next to my ear she murmurs "and wet"

Fucking hell! That makes me even harder. I really want to find out how wet she is but before I can do anything the door opens. I'm about to growl at Paul or Bruce to close the door when my mother's voice intrudes.

Skye climbs off my lap and out of the car. I follow to see my mother embracing Skye in a welcoming hug. My heart swells at the sight. My mother did and said a lot of things that drove me bat shit crazy but I could never fault her in her genuine affection for Skye, from the moment mother had met Skye she had taken an instant liking to her.

Inside everyone is gathered in the living room. Andrew is stood talking to Elizabeth and Joshua, Mandy is sitting on the sofa looking mournfully into a glass of wine.

Mandy looks up as we come in, she wouldn't meet my eyes and I can see she is crapping herself. Good, I feel vindictive the bitch deserves to feel crap.

Mandy waits until we've said hello to everyone and have a drink in our hands before standing and calling for attention. Either she is being polite or it takes her that long to work up the courage.

"Excuse me everyone" she has to say it twice as the first time her voice fails her, nervous, good.

"Skye, I am so very sorry for my behaviour towards you on Wednesday evening. It was uncalled for and you didn't deserve it. I had no right to say the things I did. It was mean and malicious of me. I sincerely hope in time you will see how out of character it was of me. To everyone else I am sorry for the embarrassment, anger and hurt I caused because of my actions towards Skye, it will never happen again"

Mandy is visibly shaking by the time she has finished. Skye moves toward Mandy.

"Thank you, apology accepted" Skye says loudly then she speaks to Mandy quietly.

Mandy sags and puts her head down, she nods a few times. Skye puts a hand on her arm and rubs when Mandy looks up her eyes are shining with tears and the smile she gives Skye is grateful. I know I will never forgive the fucking bitch but for Skye's sake I will attempt to be civil to her.

Skye came back to my side and I raise my eyebrow in a silent query. I want to know what she has said to the bitch "later" Skye mouths, yeah she's right now isn't the time or the place.

"Skye have you saved any other companies millions of dollars by catching international fraudsters lately" Joshua calls from across the room.

"Nah, only his and Mr C's" replies Skye nonchalantly.

Of course everyone wants to know what Joshua is going on about so I take great pleasure in telling the story. Emphasising the importance of Skye's part, Joshua helps by backing me up and waxing lyrical about how amazing she was. I want Mandy to feel even more of a shit, vindictive of me? Fuck yeah.

"Will you all have to give statements?" mother says in a horrified breathless voice.

"Probably but they haven't been in touch yet" says Skye.

"Actually I gave a detailed account yesterday" Joshua chipped in "and I know Mr C did as well, so you might not have to"

"Excuse me ma'am" the housekeeper interrupts by announcing dinner is ready to be served.

Mother wants Skye next to her and I wasn't going to be separated from Skye and I refuse to sit on the opposite side of her, childish, probably but I don't give a fuck.

Dinner is going well until mother decides to quiz Skye about her family. Dread, anxiety and tension shoot through me. I glare at her and she looks back puzzled. Skye places her hand over mine and squeezes it gently reassuring me she is okay; it makes me relax a little. It's a gesture that doesn't go unnoticed by mother.

"Both my parents are dead and I lived with my father's parents until I left at eighteen to go to college and study art" is all Skye says.

You couldn't accuse Skye of lying. Everything she said is the truth she just left out huge chunks of information. My mother thank god has the sense not to push for details. Mother would however try her damnedest to get it out of me at a later date. Good luck with that I am saying nothing.

"So is that when you came to America?" mother asks instead.

"No at first I studied in London, in order to help pay my way through college I started selling paintings and doing commissions. I was fortunate enough to pick up a commission which paid extremely well and it meant me, Simon and Shelley could come and study here in New York, so I was nineteen"

"And the rest they say is history" I say with a meaningful glance to mother to drop the personal questions only to have Joshua pipe up with…

"How did you get to know Mr Cheremisinova?"

It took all I had not to throw my fucking plate at him.

"I knew his daughter when I was at college in London. It was through her I got a commission from her father. He liked what I produced and since then he has commissioned numerous other pieces"

Again Skye told the truth leaving out huge chunks of information. I can tell Joshua has picked up on this and is about to go into lawyer mode when I catch his eye and subtly shake my head warning him not to push it, he got the message.

"I understand from the gossip columns you two were seen wedding ring shopping today" Elizabeth says with a fucking great big smirk knowing full well it will set mother off. Surprisingly mother didn't rise to the bait and doesn't say a word. Skye left me to field that one and I shock the lot of them by admitting it was true.

Back in the living room after dinner I'm stood at the bar watching Skye talk with mother, Elizabeth, Andrew and Mandy. Christ the woman never ceases to amaze me.

"Tell me baby bro what is she hiding?" Joshua says in a low voice.

"Skye is hiding nothing" I reply nonchalantly as I can and keep my focus on her.

"Okay so fill in the omissions"

I sigh he isn't going to let it go. "Skye saved Mr C's daughters life after she had over dosed. Skye found her in the toilets at college. Mr C did commission her as a way of thanks, that was the large commission enabling her to come and study here and before you ask Mr C's daughter died about three years later of drugs"

"Jesus, I'm sorry bro. No wonder you stopped me, but I've got to ask your reaction to when Mom asked about her family, what's that all about?"

"Fuck you're like a dog with a bone" I frown at him "Skye's mother died when she was three, suicide. Her father when she was ten again suicide. She was brought up in a loveless, attention deprived environment and through no fault of her own got kicked out and disowned by her grandfather when she had barely turned eighteen"

"Fucking hell" Joshua whispers horrified "bro I'm sorry. No wonder you want to keep it quiet" Joshua looks at Skye with awe "makes you wonder how she's turned out the way she has with all that baggage"

"She has two very good close friends and a small team of people who work for her that love and respect her, the lot of them together are her family and support network. I'm one lucky son of a bitch to be part of it"

Joshua pats my shoulder and moves off to talk with the others. I stay where I am and continue to watch Skye. I reflect on what I said to Joshua about her background growing up, it's so far removed from my own.

I grew up in a loving and supportive environment. I idolised my father, he was my hero and mentor. As a kid growing up I always asked him questions about his day at work as I got older my questions were more about getting to understand the business.

I remember his deep bass voice and bellow of a laugh. He invented a game to play with me making the learning about business fun. During school holidays he would take me into the office, letting me sit in on meetings as I got older he set me to work in the different departments he would tell his employees I was learning the ropes.

My brothers never showed any interest in his business but he was just as supportive in developing them for their chosen career paths. When I went to college I started my own acquisition and mergers business venture buying small failing businesses and turning them around. I was very successful at it, still am in fact. After graduating I went to work for my father starting in a junior role that had been my choice. At the same time I continued with my own business with my father's blessing. He recognised my aptitude and talent for making huge profits and mentored me. I was devastated when he died. I lost my father, mentor and best friend.

"Hey you okay?" Skye's low husky voice brought me out of my reverie.

I look down into her big yellow green concern filled eyes. I take her in my arms and hug her, holding her close, breathing in her mild floral scent. She is home for me, grounding me, calming me.

"I was just thinking about my Dad. God I still miss him. I wish you could have met him. He would have loved you on sight then he would have commandeered you and talked business all night"

"From what you and your Mom have told me he sounds like he was an incredible man" Skye says softly.

"He was my mentor, best friend, my inspiration. I idolised him" my voice is thick with the emotions I'm feeling.

"What's triggered all these thoughts?" Skye runs her fingers down my face, soothing me. I catch her hand and kiss her palm.

"You" she raises her eyebrows "Joshua wanted to know the omissions to the information you gave about your family and Mr C. I filled in a couple of blanks, just enough to shut him up anyway it got me thinking about how different our upbringings have been and remembering what you said about your father I compared mine" I shrug I didn't know how to finish without it reminding her of something she never had and then she floors me.

"I am so glad you had someone in your life who loved you so much and demonstrated it on so many levels and shaped you into the man you are today and I love the fact that I get all the benefits of it" lifting up onto her tip toes she kisses me "I love you Clayton"

I tighten my arms around her and kiss her back pouring all my love in to it. I don't fucking care I'm making a spectacle of myself in front of my family they'll get over it.

"Feeling better now" Skye murmurs when the kiss finished.

Chapter Twenty Two

SKYE

Ah crap. What in the hell possessed me to agree to try this? My stomach is in knots as I try and fail miserably not to think about what is coming up. I feel sick, a couple of times I had to swallow down bile. I couldn't eat breakfast so my stomach is empty, at this rate I'm going to end up with an ulcer and wouldn't that be the icing on the cake.

"You okay baby?" Clayton's voice is a soft murmur in my ear.

I'm sat on his lap, it's practically a given thing whenever we travel in the car actually whenever Clayton can get away with it he sits me on his lap just as he had done in Italy. It's a good job the windows are blacked out in all our vehicles otherwise we would constantly be pulled over by the police.

I nod although I know I'm not and I wasn't fooling him. Clayton is doing his best to soothe me by rubbing my arm and leg, it isn't working but I don't want him to stop.

"We don't have to do this we can turn around and go home. Do you want to go home?"

I shake my head. I'm not going to chance talking because I know I will throw up if I do. I've been quiet all morning, as we got ready and the nearer it got to the time for us to leave the quieter I became. I haven't said a word for nearly half an hour. I'm not going to back out and I just hope and pray I don't freak out on Clayton to such an extent it ruins our relationship.

This is your opportunity to get over your fear and turn something which is part of a horrifying nightmare experience into something sensual and erotic and shared with the man you love. I keep telling myself this over and over.

Clayton, bless him, gives me the space I need to work through my inner turmoil. I take hold of his hand and link our fingers; mine feels fragile small and cold against his big warm strong hand. He raises our linked hands kisses my fingers and then the back of my hand, his lips are just as warm and soft. I try to smile and I'm sure it looks more like a twisted grimace.

I look out of the window to try and distract myself it works for all of thirty seconds. I keep conjuring up images of what the play room will look like and scaring the crap out of myself. The current favourite is an all-black room filled with medieval torture instruments.

"We're here baby" I didn't notice the car has stopped. Paul and Bruce have got out. "Just say the word and we'll head home. I honestly don't mind"

I see the sincerity in Clayton's dark blue eyes and face.

"I'm okay" I whisper and move to get out of the car.

I look up at the building. It's a high rise apartment block all modern and glass. Clayton told me during breakfast the college buddy was still a friend of sorts and a business associate. I have absolutely no idea how I will react if I ever meet him. Probably die of embarrassment because he would know or at least have a bloody good idea what we had done in his play room.

"Come on"

Clayton holds out his hand and I take it, he leads the way inside. He heads for the concierge's desk to collect the key. The guy's apartment—I hadn't asked for his name and Clayton didn't volunteer it, best way to remain anonymous—is on the top floor. I have no idea how long it took to get up there and I couldn't tell you what his apartment looked like, it's all a blur. Now the moment of truth is on me as I stand in front of a solid wooden door.

My heart is racing, making me short of breath. You can do this, you can do this. The mantra has been going through my head since I got out of the car.

"Skye" Clayton turns me around to face him; he looks solemn "at any time you want to leave just say okay" I nod "ready?"

I close my eyes and take a deep breath letting it out slowly. I feel a soothing calmness come over me for the first time since waking up. I open my eyes and nod. Clayton searches my face for a few seconds then nods himself answering his own internal question.

Reaching around me he unlocks the door and pushes it open. He waits for me to move, when I don't because my feet feel as if they have been nailed to the floor he steps around me and enters. Lights come on. Clayton doesn't say anything he just waits patiently for me.

From where I'm stood I can see the room is a deep dark red with soft lighting. The fact it isn't black and I can't see any medieval torture looking equipment has me moving forward. Clayton leaves me alone whilst I look around the room, which is surprising large, and take in its contents.

To my right is a large four poster bed covered in what looks like black satin sheets and pillows. Immediately in front of me on the wall is a large wooden X which has shackles on each of the arms. I've read about these in the erotic novels I borrowed off Macy. Fascinated I walk over to it. I run my fingers over the highly polished surface then pick up one of the leather cuffs. I'm surprised at how soft the leather feels.

Next to the X hanging and running the length of the wall is a selection of canes and whips along with some other odd shaped looking things I have no idea what they are. I don't feel brave or curious enough to give them a closer inspection.

On the opposite side is a bench, I go over to it for a better look. It isn't a bench more of a table; it's padded and wide and long enough for someone to lie down on it. Next to the table is a high backed leather chair.

I look back at Clayton his face gives nothing away. He's standing in the centre of the room with his arms folded across his chest, his head is bowed slightly but his gaze is on me, following me. He looks menacing and sexy as hell then I notice something hanging from the ceiling behind him, chains. I go over for a better look, now I'm curious. I reach up and run my hands over the links feeling the cold of the metal, at the end is a leather cuff, I notice the other lengths of chain have the same cuff fitting.

The room itself isn't scary; I realize I've looked around the room with a detached curiosity. I'm not afraid, nervous or panicked by any of the things I see. They are inanimate objects. The fear is what my mind makes it to be. I have to be honest with myself, so I am. I admit to myself that I'm scared of my memories. It's what is inside my head I have to overcome. Well no time like the present to make a start. I take a deep breath and look at Clayton.

"I'm ready"

He smiles so sweetly and tenderly as he strokes his fingers down my cheek.

"You are so brave" I don't feel it "I've had an idea which might help you, would you like to hear it?" I nod. I'm willing to hear anything if it will help. "Remember back at the gym on the yacht" he pauses to let me think.

We had a very nice work out session on a multi gym, I held... Holy hell... I had purposely restrained myself using the arm and leg bars. I more than enjoyed the experience. Clayton carries on with his idea when he sees I got the gist of what he wanted me to remember.

"Rather than fastening you into the cuffs just hold on to the chains and if it gets too much you can let go. The alternative is when you feel ready I will fasten the cuffs and you safe word if it proves too much"

He really has thought about this, I also realize that having done this before with Clayton and thoroughly enjoyed the experience I could do it again because I trust him. I'm sure I could try being restrained.

"Yes I can do that" saying it out loud gives me the confidence and conviction to see it through "where do we start"

Clayton takes my hand and leads me over to the wall where the canes and whips hang. I now notice various riding crops and what I guess to be floggers thanks to the descriptions given in Macy's erotic romance novels.

"In a play room the rules of engagement are pre-arranged between the Dominant and the Submissive, they will have gone through an extensive list and discussed their limits, what they are willing to do and what is a no go" Clayton looks me in the eye "unless you decide to fully embrace the lifestyle then we will do that as it stands at present all I am proposing is using some of the toys in the bedroom and being completely open and honest I would love to tie you up sometime"

Sweet Jesus on a cracker. Even though Clayton said it all in a matter of fact tone, hearing him admitting he would love to tie me up and using the toys on me has desire thundering through me. I so want to get this party started.

"These are the things I would like to use" he picks up a riding crop, a flogger and a flat oblong thing. Holding it up "this is a paddle" he says handing it to me, it's lighter than I expected and flexible "as much as I enjoy using my hand spanking you this will give a different sensation. These two" he holds the riding crop and flogger up "are also used to work the whole body, to sensitise it. It is common to be restrained when these are used although you don't have to be"

I nod to show my understanding. He puts them back on the rack. Taking my hand he leads me to the wooden X.

"This, the bed and the hanging chains all have the same cuff attachment. Want to try?"

I hold my arm out without hesitation. I see a small smile on Clayton's lips as he takes a cuff and quickly fastens it around my wrist. He moves me to stand with my back against the wood.

"The cuff won't leave a mark, give it a tug"

I do. I'm surprised how comfortable it feels and I can still move my arm even though I couldn't lower it. I'm not completely immobile.

As if reading my mind Clayton says "If the Dominant wanted to he can make it so the Sub is completely immobile, however common practice is to train the Sub to hold still, should that be the Dom's wish" Clayton reaches up and undid the cuff "the bed and cross gives the options of having you bound spread eagled or just having arms or legs bound. If you are spread eagled once the Dom has finished using the toys in the majority of cases the ankles are released so he can either fuck you standing up" he nods to the cross "or on the bed putting your legs where he wishes whilst he fucks you"

I must have looked confused, so much information and too many images are flashing through my mind and by god I'm feeling horny.

"Would you like me to demonstrate?" what the hell this is show and tell after all, I nod "get on the bed and lie on your back"

I didn't need telling twice. Clayton climbs on the bed and reaches to the sides above my head.

"Lift your arms above your head"

I do as he instructs, taking one arm he moves it out to the side and places something in my hand, I twist to look at what he is doing, it's the restraint.

"Hold on to this"

I do. Clayton moves and does the same with my other arm as soon as I feel the restraint I grab hold of it.

"Good girl, now open your legs for me"

Clayton settles between my legs. Looking down at me he smiles, he doesn't say anything but I bet he is thinking about me naked. I can feel him getting harder, I so want to grind my hips against him but being a good girl I stay still.

"'Position one the missionary"

He flexes his hips and grinds into me, desire pools between my legs instantly and I bite the inside of my cheek to stop the moan threatening to escape.

"Position two"

Clayton rears up grabs my hips and lifts them up, my lower back lifts so only my shoulders remain on the bed he pulls my hips towards him as he thrusts forward, the much welcome friction makes me gasp.

"Position three"

He lowers me back to the bed takes hold of my ankles and raises my legs and puts them against his body, he thrusts his hips again.

"Position four"

He leans forward so my legs slide over his shoulders bringing my knees closer to my chest again he thrusts his hips. Sweet lord I'm breathing heavy I'm so turned on.

Moving back up onto his knees Clayton takes my right leg and places it back on the bed then he straddles that leg, holding and keeping my left leg in the air.

"Position five"

He thrusts his hips forward. I whimper as pleasure surges through me. Holy hell I so want to try all these positions naked, Clayton moves off me. I bite my tongue as I nearly shout at him to carry on.

"The good thing about all those positions is you can do them without being restrained" I smile as images flash through my mind "up for trying them at home baby?" Clayton's voice is seductively low and velvety smooth.

"Hell yeah!" I say with much more enthusiasm than I intended. Clayton's eyes sparkle and his knowing chuckle is deep and sinful.

"Come on there are some other things I want to show you"

He leads me to a chest height cabinet with lots of narrow drawers standing to the side of the door. I didn't notice it earlier. Clayton pulls open the top draw all I can see are vibrators. Clayton starts to close the draw then stops reaching in he pulls out a box and opens it and shows me the contents, two silver balls which are linked together.

"Do you know what these are?" he says taking them out of the box and placing them in my hand, I shake my head "they are love balls sometimes called eggs. They go inside you. You can wear them all day if you wanted to and you will be in a constant heightened state of arousal. Also if you wear them whilst being spanked I believe it makes the experience even more enjoyable"

The balls are weighty and my vagina muscles clench when Clayton mentions the heightened arousal state. Hmm might be worth a try. I think my face gives me away because Clayton gives me a knowing smile as he takes them off me and puts them away.

I spot another box and point "What are those?"

Clayton lifts the box and opens it showing me the contents. Inside are various sized conical shaped things.

"These are called butt plugs" he picks up the smallest one and hands it to me "these can heighten penetrative sex, imagine being filled both holes. Plugs are also used to train the anus so it makes it easier to be penetrated by a cock and yes, I do want to fuck your ass"

Again I find his frank openness and honesty as hot as hell, so much so I have to squeeze my thighs together only it doesn't give me the relief I want or need.

"These are anal beads" Clayton swaps the plug for a long thing which has small progressing to larger circular beads along its length "these are inserted into the back passage like so"

With one hand he makes a circle with his index finger and thumb forming and O shape, then picking up the smallest bead he threads it into the O, he continues until he's pushed in the last and largest bead leaving the thread hanging.

"At the point of climax pull these out" he takes hold of the thread and pulls, the beads pop out one after another "and it will intensify the orgasm"

I'm seriously turned on. I squeeze my thighs again desperately trying to get some relief even my boobs feel heavy and my nipples are tingling. Clayton smiles his knowing smile again as he puts the things away and closes the draw. Damn it, am I really that obvious?

"Ah, this is what I was looking for" Clayton says as he opens the next draw. He starts taking out number of items and puts them on the top of the cabinet.

"These are the things I would like to use to sensitize your skin" he pauses "how do you feel about being blindfolded?"

My stomach roils at the thought "If it means being tied up at the same time, no" I hear the harsh finality in my voice.

That is definitely too close for comfort, the very thought has me shutting my eyes cringing and my body shuddering. Clayton's arms come round me in a protective embrace.

"Forgive me" he murmurs his lips on the top of my head "it was insensitive of me, forget I ever mentioned it"

"I don't think I can handle both together, not straight away. I think I can do one at a time. At least I can open my eyes if I was bound and I could see what was happening if it was too much or I could remove the blindfold if my hands were free" I lift my head so I can look at Clayton "knowing I had some form of control gives me power over my memories and imagination"

All I see is love and wonder in Clayton's eyes, he bends and kisses me so tenderly it makes my heart soar, he gives me the courage to say the next bit.

"Carrying on the subject of no goes, as far as restraints go it is a huge no to rope and electrical cable, likewise to being made completely immobile"

Clayton's eyes widen and his whole body goes ridged as comprehension hits with the meaning behind all of what I've said. Clayton has never pushed me for information about my attack and at the moment I'm not ready to go there, hell even Simon and Shelley don't know all the details, I've given Clayton bits of information and now I've just let him know how my attacker restrained me and with what. I reach up and touch his face.

"I know you would never hurt me and I trust you implicitly. I just need to go slow in some areas so I can reign in my imagination and put past memories to rest"

"You are an incredibly strong and brave woman Skye Darcy. I love you so much" Clayton says with such reverence if it's at all possible I fall in love with him all over again "I think we've covered enough for today, let's go home"

No I want to play! My inner goddess cries and stamps her foot.

"Before we go I'd like to try something"

"Sure whatever you want baby"

Clayton releases me as I pull out of his arms. I went to the wall where the canes hang and pick up the flogger and riding crop. I take them back to Clayton and give them to him; he has a heated but puzzled look on his face. I move to the centre of the room where the hanging chains are, reaching up I grasp the links and look at Clayton smiling seductively.

"What are you waiting for?" my voice is low and sultry. I'm more turned on by all this than I realized.

Clayton is totally shocked it takes him a minute to recover. I'm expecting Clayton to ask if I was sure I wanted this but he doesn't. Instead he puts the flogger and riding crop on top of the cabinet then takes off his shoes, socks, t-shirt and jeans, leaving his boxers on. I want Clayton to undress me so remain in my position.

Clayton stalks towards me, his chest and ab muscles flexing as he prowls. His boxers barely contain the impressive bulge of his erection, his eyes darkening as he rakes my body from head to toe. I feel naked by the time he gets to me.

Taking the hem of my t-shirt Clayton pulls it up over my head but he leaves the shirt covering my eyes and claims my mouth, his warm hands travel over my back and waist. His lips trail kisses down my throat and chest, his teeth tease my nipples through the lace of my bra sending tingling sensations all through my body and pooling between my legs. His hands trail down my stomach to the waist band of my jeans I feel the tug as he undoes the buttons, slipping his hand inside my panties; his fingers circle my clit and slide inside me. Oh that feels soooo good. I moan out loud.

"Baby you want this bad, you are so creamy and wet" I hear the wonder and lust in Clayton's whispered voice; he's turned on by the fact I'm so turned on.

I can feel Clayton's breath close to my neck. My imagination supplies the image of what the look on his face would be like, scorching appetence for me. He moves his finger slowly circling the walls of my vagina then thrusting in and out of me, my hips buck to the rhythm of his movements. "Oh yes" I moan. Clayton's other hand strokes lazily over my back and shoulders, trailing down my spine across my hips and back up the sides of my waist. I surrender myself to the sensations of his touch.

"I'm going to work you in such a way when you come you will scream" Clayton whispers, his words tickling my ear. I'm on fire.

Clayton removes his finger and hand. I bite down on shouting out for him to continue. I hear him lick and suck his finger and I can feel the heat of his body, he's still close to me.

"Mmmm you taste fucking delicious"

I feel his hands on my hips and he tugs my jeans down my legs removing them along with my socks and shoes in one go. He's left my panties on. I feel his hands travel from my ankles up my body to my back where he unhooks my bra.

"Let go of the chains baby" goose bumps break out across my skin at the husky soft command.

Christ even his voice is playing havoc with my libido. I let go of the chains and Clayton removes my t-shirt and bra dropping them to the floor he kicks them out of the way.

"You can hold the chains again"

Face your fear my mind whispers you have just been blindfolded and self-imposed the restraint and it was erotic as hell. I make a decision.

"Fasten me in" I whisper.

Clayton stills, I've shocked him again. After a moment he nods and buckles me in "Safe word" he says softly, I nod.

He gives me a chaste kiss then steps back. His eyes heat my blood when I see the want and need in them.

"You look so fucking adorable and fuckable like that" Clayton cups himself and adjusts his cock "I really want to be buried balls deep inside you right now baby"

My breathing hitches and my heart pounds making me take shallow breaths through my mouth. Heaven help me I'm panting already and he hasn't done anything to me yet. I'm going to combust when he does.

"Before I use the flogger I am going to use some other things to sensitise your skin. You are not to come until I tell you" bloody hell and holy crap! "Do you understand?" I nod.

Clayton walks over to the cabinet, opening and closing several drawers searching. He makes an "ah ha" sound when he finds what he's looking for. I admire his flexing back and ass muscles as he moves around. He places a few items on the top of the cabinet, closes the draw and turns back to me. As he walks he pulls something onto his hand it looks like a fur mitten.

Standing in front of me he holds up his hand. "This is exactly as it looks. I am going to run this all over your body"

He places his fur covered hand on my stomach and starts moving in slow small circular movements. The soft fur tickles and I resist the urge to pull away. The circular movements get bigger and soon his hand is travelling over every inch of my body, my breasts, arms, shoulders, back, buttocks, legs front and back. I close my eyes and absorb the sensations the fur creates on the various parts of my body, some more intense than others. I enjoy them all.

"Open your eyes baby"

Clayton stood before me, he's removed the fur mitt and in his hand is something I would swear is a pizza cutter but the circular edge is jagged. What the…

"I'm going to run this over your body now, it doesn't hurt or leave a mark" Clayton demonstrates by running it over his hand "let me show you if you don't like it just say and I'll stop" I nod my acquiesce.

Clayton places it on my breast bone and runs it down my stomach; the sensation has my nerves jumping to attention in a good way.

"Carry on?" Clayton murmurs. I nod.

It isn't long before I close my eyes again and I surrender to the sensations this new pizza cutter thing creates. I gasp when Clayton runs it over my breasts and nipples, the sensations head south in a flash. I'm proud I resist the urge to open my eyes.

"I'm going to get the flogger now baby"

I keep my eyes closed and listen to his bare feet padding across the wooden floor, a draw being opened and closed, feet padding back to me. I jerk when I feel something brush across my butt, as tempted as I am to open my eyes I don't.

"Good girl, you are doing so well"

Clayton's murmured praise sends a thrill through me. I can do this. I am doing this and I love every hot sexy minute of it.

Clayton trails the fronds of the flogger over my back, shoulders and breasts then he pulls it away. I hear the swish of the leather fronds seconds before I feel the sting as it lands on my buttocks. I gasp then groan at the pleasure feelings it causes. Clayton continues to trail the flogger then flick it against different areas of my body, thighs, stomach, back, breasts never in the same place twice.

"Well done baby, do you want more?"

"Yes" it comes out as a hoarse desire filled whisper.

"I'm going to use the riding crop but first let's dispense of these" his hands land on my hips and he pulls my panties down.

I can feel his hair tickle my thighs as he lifts each of my feet to remove my panties. I feel his fingers on my slit and they part my lips. His tongue swirls around my clit and folds the delicious sensation pulses through me making my back arch and I pull against the restraints.

"Oh god" I moan. I'm close.

Clayton's mouth closes around my clit; his hands have a firm grip of my hips. He sucks hard.

"Argh, Clayton" I cry out at the intense pleasure he creates, I pull harder against the restraints as I fight to stave off my climax. My heart rate is through the roof, sweat breaks out across my skin. Fuck I nearly come. Thank god Clayton stops and rises to his feet. I hear him move away, at least it gives me a chance to come away from the precipice I feel I'm about to leap off.

"Your skin has a lovely rosy glow to it"

Clayton smooth's his hand down my back and over my butt. Then I feel something cold and hard follow the same path, the crop and excitement pools in my lower belly. I feel the crop go between my legs and tap against my inner thighs.

"Widen your stance baby" I move my feet to shoulder width "excellent" the crop continues its journey over my body "remember to safe word if this gets too much and I will stop" Clayton murmurs in my ear.

The crop rubs against my butt then it left me. Anticipation spikes. I hear the swish and immediately feel the sting. I yelp and my eyes fly open, it hurt more than the flogger. No shit Sherlock what did you expect my mind shouts. Clayton's hand rubs my butt turning the stinging pain into one of pleasure. I close my eyes again determined to keep them closed.

Clayton starts a pattern of light tapping then a sharp flick. He works all over my body. Then he hit my clit. Holy shit pleasure sensations explode through me, I bite down on a scream. My back arches and I push up onto my tip toes, pulling on the restraints at the same time, my head thrown back. I tremble with the effort of holding off my orgasm.

I sense Clayton standing in front of me and the tapping starts all over again. When he gets to my breasts and flicks my nipple with the crop immediately I feel his mouth surrounding my nipple and he suckles me so the shooting pain is mixed with intense pleasure. This has me cursing and pulling on the restraints.

Clayton taps the crop over my stomach moving south, he flicks my clit again.

"Holy fuck" I shout out, the sensation is mind blowing and intense. I know if he did it again I will come, this is something Clayton sensed.

"Don't come baby" he murmurs his command as he continues to tap my sex.

"I can't hold on" I manage to pant out.

"Yes you can"

Clayton flicks the crop and hit my clit. I scream as I fight to stave off my climax, I'm catapulted back to the precipice and clinging on for dear life with the tips of my fingers.

I hear the crop clatter to the floor. Clayton's large warm hands are on my waist and I'm being lifted. I wrap my legs around Clayton's waist as his cock slides inside me easily because I'm so wet and ready for him. The feel of his hard as iron thick cock has my muscles clenching and gripping him, sucking him in deeper.

Clayton pulls back and thrusts deep hitting my g-spot. I swan dive off the precipice screaming my release into the crashing waves of my orgasm. It's so intense I space out.

I come back to Clayton shouting my name as he finds his release, feeling his cock pulse and throb inside me sets off another orgasm or is it aftershocks of the first one? I don't care. I'm wiped out.

I'm vaguely aware of Clayton tugging at each of my wrists. My heavy arms flop over Clayton's shoulders. He lowers us both to the floor, I'm straddling him and his cock is still deep inside me. Clayton rubs my shoulders as I lie limp against him.

"You okay baby?"

I nod my head against his chest. I don't have the energy to talk let alone lift my head.

"Talk to me"

I hum instead.

"That good" he chuckles.

"Hmmm" I give a contented sigh.

"Well and truly fucked I take it"

I move my head to the side and smile up at him then kiss under his chin as it's the closest thing I can reach. Clayton's deep throaty laugh fills the room.

"I'll take that as a yes"

After a minute or so, could be longer I have no idea, Clayton murmurs "Come on let's get you dressed and home before you fall asleep"

He's right I've already been dozing sat on his lap. I'm fighting to keep my eyes open. Placing his hands on my waist Clayton lifts me effortlessly to pull out and he rises to his feet taking me with him. He sets me on my feet.

"Wait there a minute"

Clayton went to the cabinet, opening and closing drawers until he finds what he needs. He comes back with a pack of wet wipes and a pot of cream. Clayton gently cleans me up then applies the cream to my butt explaining it contains a soothing balm as I might find my butt a bit tender when I sit down.

Although I don't need it Clayton helps me get dressed and I love the care and consideration he's showing me, he really wants to look after me. I help him dress with just as much care and consideration.

As we get back in the car my stomach growls loudly, my appetite is back with vengeance.

"What would you like to eat" Clayton asks, I grin at him "food" he mouths.

Wow, da ja vu. I suddenly have the urge to cook us a meal and spend some quality alone time.

"I'm going to cook" I tell him "Paul, take us to the nearest supermarket please"

"Yes ma'am"

Clayton pushes the trolley and follows me around the aisles. I notice all the women stop and stare at him a few blatantly give him the come on which he ignores.

"What are you smiling at?" he asks raising an eyebrow.

"You" the eyebrow goes higher "and all these women staring at you, some even coming on to you"

Before I can finish he cuts me off "What women?" he says innocently and pretends to look around.

"Oooh smooth move" I laugh and reach up to kiss him.

"I only have eyes for you" he counters and I mock hurl "too much?"

"Too much" I confirm.

I have the ingredients for the meal and the essentials I decided to get plus some extra bits for during the week.

"What would you like for desert and don't say me" I add hastily when I see the carnivorous smile on his face.

Clayton pouts, he actually pouts. Oh my god it's hilarious. I laugh.

"Spoil sport" he mutters, then he brightens "ice cream and chocolate sauce" bending down he murmurs in my ear "and I'm going to cover you from head to toe in the stuff and eat it off you if I can't have you"

Holy cow that sounds hot as hell.

"Ice cream and chocolate it is" I whisper all breathy and husky.

Clayton's eyes darken promising a night of debauchment. Bring it on!

"Hello Skye"

A male voice has Clayton straightening and scowling when he sees who it is, I spin round wondering who in the hell could cause such a reaction from him.

"Pete, hi"

Before I can say anything else Caroline the Catty Bitch from Hell walks into the aisle. Shit, shit, shit!

"Oh my god Skye, so good to see you back" she calls out causing other shoppers to stop and look "Oh hi Clay how are you?" she went for a low sultry voice which doesn't quite have the effect she is hoping for and what's with calling him Clay. I don't even call him that, in fact no-one does.

"My name is Clayton, do not bastardize it" Clayton's voice is icy cold and he enunciates every word. Ha! That's told her I gleefully hug myself. Caroline flushes and Pete scowls at her, he's not impressed.

"Congratulations on your engagement" Pete says quickly and rearranges his expression.

"Thank you" Clayton and I answer together.

"So I guess you will be hearing the patter of little feet soon" Caroline says smiling although it looks more like a sneer.

"You didn't tell me we were getting a dog" Clayton says to me feigning hurt surprise.

Oh he's fast and getting good at this.

"Actually I was thinking of a cat, they are much quieter" I retort.

Caroline's face is a picture. Pete looks as if he's about to put her six feet under.

"Anyway it was nice seeing you both. Take care" I layer as much false sincerity into my words as I can without it sounding too sarcastic.

As we move away I hear Pete hiss "What the fuck did you say that for you stupid bitch?"

I look at Clayton, he heard it too. Sniggering like little kids we hurry out of the aisle.

Back in my apartment Clayton vents his anger, I knew on the journey back he was stewing over something, now I know Caroline is the cause.

"What the fuck does she think calling me Clay is going to get her?" he doesn't quite shout but he's close.

I know he meant it as a speculative question but I know Caroline and her motivations "In your or her bed"

Clayton looks at me stunned, then as if I have two heads. I continue to put the groceries away.

"That's preposterous" he splutters throwing his hands up in the air.

"Maybe to you but I know Caroline and her motivation. Practically every guy I have dated" I use my fingers to air quote dated "she has made a move on remember I told you this before I left for Russia. Three of which I know she actually achieved her aim and got them into bed" I walk up to

Clayton and place my hand on his chest "you Mr Blake are way hotter, with a body to die for and insanely richer than any of those guys. She will hit on you every time she sees you and will do her damnedest to get you into bed. I would bet my entire fortune on it if I was a gambling man, woman, whatever"

Clayton put his arms around me. "Well Miss Darcy you had better hurry and make an honest man of me" he kisses the tip of my nose.

"As if that would stop her" I snort "just" I let out a sigh "just be careful around her that's all" it comes out as a soft plea.

"You're genuinely worried aren't you?" he sounds surprised and puzzled at the same time "I will never cheat on you. You are my soul mate, my life. I would never ever do anything to jeopardise us. The thought of losing you doesn't even bear thinking about"

I believe him and every word he says and I don't need the reassurance, yes it's nice to hear but all the same I know deep down he would never cheat on me.

"I trust you and I know you wouldn't. I don't trust Caroline and I know she will do everything she can to get you or make out that she has. All I'm saying is, just be on your guard whenever she is around"

"I promise. Now make me a promise" Clayton says softly.

"Go on" I say warily, where's he going with this?

"That whenever she's around you don't leave my side and protect me from her" Clayton pleads making me chuckle.

"A six foot four hunk of a man scared of Catty Bitch from Hell" I tease "okay I promise" I stroke his face "I love you so, so very much and I don't ever want to lose you either"

I lift up on to my tip toes and kiss him. The kiss only stops because my stomach growls, loudly "Time to get dinner started"

CLAYTON

I sit at the breakfast bar and watch Skye make lasagne and garlic bread, everything done from scratch. The kitchen is soon filled with mouth-watering aroma's which has my stomach growling.

"Do you realize this is the first time we have done this?"

"Done what?" Skye asks as she looks up at me from the oven as she puts the lasagne in to cook.

"Having the full day to ourselves, home cooking and a full evening ahead just the two of us"

Skye smiles sweetly "No I hadn't realized. Have you enjoyed it?"

I get off the stool and walk to her; pulling her into my arms "Every single second" I murmur and kiss her soundly "what about you?"

"Ditto" she whispers and kisses me back "thank you for what you did today, arranging to go to your friends and use his room. It really helped me"

I bite back the "in what way" question which is on the tip of my tongue. I have never asked Skye about the attack although I wanted to but I didn't want to be responsible for putting her through any unnecessary pain or anxiety.

This morning I saw first-hand the turmoil she went through just to get to my friends' apartment and the physical reaction she had just at the thought of being blindfolded and restrained. She shocked the shit out of me when she told me her no-goes on rope and electrical cable. As soon as she said it I knew that was what her attacker had used on her.

"Would you like to go again? He's away all week and I know he won't mind"

I say this as softly and gently as I can to show there is no pressure. I know she enjoyed the experience and she continuously amazed me and the level of trust she had shown in me, it humbled me greatly. Skye seriously underestimates herself in the level of strength and bravery she possesses but the mind is a powerful thing. I had to hand it to her she understood this better than anyone. Skye is determined to rid herself of those bad past memories and I think she even surprised herself on many levels of what she is capable of doing.

"No" Skye pauses chewing her bottom lip "I would" another pause then a lovely pink blush comes across her cheeks "I would like to do those things again but" she sighs "I was thinking maybe we could create our own playroom then nobody would know but us"

"We can do whatever you want. You call the shots on this and set the pace. I've told you I'm not really into the scene and lifestyle but I am willing to be more involved if it's what you want" fuck I will walk into hell and back for this woman "today I showed you and you let me do the things I have fantasied about doing to you since I first met you" Skye gave a wide eyed gasp "plus I told you what else I would like to do and showed you the toys which would help us getting there but if you don't want to do any of that then I am okay with it. So if you want a playroom we'll create one alternatively we can do all those things in the bedroom"

"Bedroom sounds good to me" Skye smiles shyly.

"Or the living room, then there's the kitchen, oh and don't forget the bathroom" I grin wickedly.

Skye's sexy throaty laugh fills the kitchen "You know I've always wondered what it would be like to have sex in a public place" my jaw pops open in shock. The oven pings "time to put the bread in" Skye winks at me saucily as she pulls out of my arms.

"Damn woman you can cook" I sit back rubbing my overstuffed stomach "it was delicious. Where did you learn to cook like that?"

Skye smiles ruefully "When I travel and stay at the client's home I always make a point of going to the kitchen and befriending the cook, if they have one. Swapping recipes is a favourite pastime" Skye shrugs "I enjoy cooking and baking so whenever I can I do"

Skye stood and picks up the plates. I help clear up and load the dishwasher. It's so natural and we move around each other easily, domestic bliss. Picking up our glasses of wine I follow Skye into the living room and sit on the sofa. Skye's phone rings, she looks at the screen frowning then answers.

"Hi Shelley everything okay?" concern mars her features, then her expression relaxes "yeah he's here with me, hang on. Shelley wants to speak to both of us. You're on speaker now Shelley"

"Hi Clayton" Shelley's voice echoes out of the phone, she didn't wait for a response "how do you two fancy going to Vegas next weekend on mine and Phil's bachelor and hen parties?"

"I thought you said you weren't bothering" says Skye.

"We weren't but Phil's Dad and brothers have badgered him into it and he won't go because he doesn't want to leave me and bump. So I have succumbed to peer pressure, I thought hell why not have one last fling, get drunk on orange juice, lose a fortune to the house and shag a gorgeous tall blonde blue eyed geeky looking man"

Skye and I laugh, Shelley has just described Phil.

"You know when I was in Vegas the other weekend it dawned on me I have never done the tourist thing nor have I ever gambled, so I'm game. Clayton, want to lose a fortune with me?"

How can I refuse when she looks at me so full of mischief it makes her eyes sparkle? "I'm in. How many people are going Shelley?"

"I'll have definite numbers tomorrow but at the moment ten confirmed. The plan is to leave Friday afternoon and come back Sunday night"

"You can have my plane at your disposal" I say on a whim "so long as the numbers don't exceed twenty"

I really like Shelley and Phil and if it means I can make their weekend even more special then so be it. Skye smiles warmly and mouths "thank you"

"Seriously" Shelley squeaks "Phil, Phil" she calls out, the conversation on the other end is muffled then Phil's voice comes over loud and clear. "Thank you Clayton, it's mighty generous of you. Are you sure?"

"Absolutely as I said to Shelley the plane can take twenty. Any more than that and they'll have to make their own arrangements"

"It won't exceed fifteen" says Phil.

"Is Shelley still there?" asks Skye.

"We're on speaker" Phil answers at the same time Shelley says "yes"

"Have you sorted out the hotel?"

"We're just doing that now, well after this call" Shelley's voice came over faint as if she'd moved to another part of the room.

"Let me know how many rooms you want as I'm sure I can get a good deal from Marco and Vinny. They did say I was welcome at any time, so no reason to see how welcome they want to make me"

"Oh Skye that would be fantastic" Shelley's voice is louder "let's talk tomorrow when I see you"

"Okay I'll put a call in to Marco now to give him the heads up. See you tomorrow" Skye hangs up "I'm really looking forward to next weekend" Skye says scrolling through her contacts, a salacious grin spreads across her face and it has my cock stirring.

"What are you thinking of Miss Darcy?"

Skye shrugs nonchalantly "I was just thinking about something else I didn't get to try that weekend"

I raise an expectant eyebrow "And that was?"

"You fucking me on the piano" Skye chuckles as my jaw drops and my cock stood to attention. Skye licks her lips reaching down she cups my crotch and strokes "I see you like the idea also" she purrs.

Holy fucking shit did I.

"Hey Marco, how the devil are you?"

Skye laughs in response to something Marco says, her deep throaty laugh resonating through me making my spine tingle and my balls ache. I still can't believe the effect she has on me, emotionally and physically and these grew more intense each day.

Whist Skye is talking to Marco I reach for her and pull her on to my lap and wrap my arms around her. I bury my face in her neck and hair, inhaling deeply. Skye's scent floods my nostrils. I can smell the strawberry body wash and the jasmine perfume of her shampoo all mixed with her natural musk floral scent. Christ she is my drug and I'm hopelessly addicted. I can quite happily overdose on her.

"That's fantastic Marco. I'll call tomorrow with the final numbers and email over the list of names" Skye bringing the call to an end has me focusing back in the present "say hello to Vinny and we'll see you next weekend" Skye hangs up, twisting she looks at me "you okay?" she asks softly.

"Never better" I smile and kiss her.

A soft knocking and a throat being cleared have us breaking apart. Skye looks over my shoulder.

"Paul, what's up?" she says unembarrassed.

"Pardon the intrusion ma'am"

Skye got off my knee and went to Paul. I follow. It seems strange to see Paul casually dressed in sweat pants and t-shirt.

"There is a Samuel Hopkirk downstairs asking or rather demanding to see you. He's refusing to leave, says it's urgent he speaks with you and it concerns your grandfather. He's from a firm of lawyers in England. I've checked his credentials and it's all legit"

Skye has gone very still, her face a complete blank and eyes cold hard stone. She speaks in a monotone voice. "Did he give any indication as to what this business is about?"

"No ma'am. He refuses to give any details except to you. Personally I don't think he's going to go away. If you don't see him now he will be back tomorrow"

Paul volunteers his opinion without being asked but I suppose he knows Skye well enough she will probably have asked for it. Skye nods. "Okay, send him up. Paul will you stay just in case"

"Yes ma'am. Would you like me to get Macy also?"

"No I don't think it will be necessary"

Paul headed out the way he had come. Skye takes a deep breath and shudders, as she looks at me I open my arms and with a distracted smile she steps into me. I hug her.

"Do you want me to get Bruce to help Paul with the just in case?" I whisper in to her hair.

Skye chuckles "No it's okay. The just in case is not to have him escorted off the premises it's to stop me from launching myself at the poor man. You saw what happened in London, anything to do with my grandfather makes me positively violent; you know bringing out my sociopathic tendencies. This guy is only the messenger. Paul is for his protection, not mine" she sighs heavily "I need a stiff drink" Skye pulls away and I reluctantly let her go "do you want one?" Skye calls over her shoulder as she walks into the kitchen.

"No thanks I'll need to be alert and keep an eye on my sociopathic fiancée"

"Ha, ha you're funny not" Skye deadpans.

I listen to the sounds Skye makes as she moves around the kitchen. I'm beginning to feel nervous for her.

"What do you think it could be about?" I call out.

"The old bastard has probably popped his clogs and has devised a plot to try and control me from beyond the grave" she says coming out of the kitchen "I wouldn't put it past the fucker" as Skye sits down voices can be heard coming from the hallway "guess we're about to find out" Skye says taking a drink.

"Miss Darcy this is Samuel Hopkirk" Paul announces.

Skye doesn't bother to stand, she just turns in her seat; the look she gives the guy has me quaking in my shoes. "Mr Hopkirk, take a seat" she nods to the chair.

The guy is dressed in an expensive tailored suit. I guess him to be late forties and he has the same demeanour as Joshua which to me screams lawyer.

"Thank you for agreeing to see me Miss Darcy" he sits putting his brief case on the coffee table and opens it "before I commence I need to, purely as a formality you understand but I am required to see some form of identification"

Skye stares at him, she doesn't move a muscle. If it was me I would be shouting "fuck off, you came to me so that should suffice". Skye takes a mouthful of her drink, put the glass down, got up and walked to the bedroom. I take a seat on the sofa, a few minutes later Skye comes back with a large manila envelope, she hands it to Hopkirk. He pulls out the documents looks at them and nods, returns them to the envelope and gives it back to Skye.

"Thank you Miss Darcy"

Skye sits down next to me. I can feel the tension radiating off her. I want to wrap her in my arms and protect her. I feel helpless and I fucking hate it.

"Miss Darcy I work for Smith, Hall and Evans the law firm that represents your grandfather. I regret to inform you your grandfather passed away four days ago. The reason for this visit is because you are the main beneficiary of his will"

Skye went rigid. I put my hand on the small of her back and rub in small slow calming movements some of the tension leaves her. Hopkirk takes a document out of his briefcase and put on spectacles.

"This is the last Will and Testament of Lord Matthew George Belling" he says looking at Skye over his glasses.

Holy fuck Skye is from gentry. I don't know why but it shocks me.

"If you are agreeable I will only read the part that pertains to you" Skye gives a stiff nod. Hopkirk flips through a few pages and reads "to my only granddaughter Skye Darcy formerly Skynard Lillian Belling I leave the sum of five hundred million pounds on the proviso she legally changes her name back to her birth name and returns to live in England"

Hopkirk looks up at Skye. Deathly silence, Skye turns her head slowly and looks at me over her shoulder. Her eyes cold with fury, I really wouldn't like to be in Hopkirk's shoes right now.

"See I told you the mean old bastard would try something like this" Skye turns back to Hopkirk and I see him shrink back "he can fuck right off. I hope the fucking bastard is burning and rotting in hell" anger is clearly evident in Skye's voice and she means every word.

Hopkirk clears his throat "I take that is a refusal to meet these terms"

"Damn straight, that fucking miserable narcissistic control freak can shove it where the sun doesn't shine. The only reason I would return to England at this moment in time is to throw a fucking party on that manipulative bastard's grave. Sorry you had a wasted journey" Skye finishes sardonically.

"Oh I'm not finished" Hopkirk chuckles and he resumes reading "in the event that Skye Darcy refuses to meet these terms and has mentioned any of the following words within her reply" Hopkirk looks up "I won't read from the list considering you have just used ninety five percent of them" he went back to reading "she has therefore demonstrated her honesty, integrity and independence. Skye I am sorry for the pain and hurt I have caused you and I wish you a life of happiness and love in your marriage to Clayton Blake. I therefore bequeath to you one point five billion pounds"

"Fuck me" I bark out in shock making Skye jump "sorry baby"

I rub her back. She's in shock it occurs to me belatedly. I pick up her drink and hand it to her. With badly shaking hands she drains the glass. Paul appears with a bottle of Southern Comfort in his hand and pours her another generous measure. I nod my thanks to him.

"I can see this has come as a great shock to you Miss Darcy. Do you have any questions?"

"Wwwhat" Skye clears her throat and tries again "what about the rest of the family?"

Hopkirk's expression softens. I don't think it's a question he was expecting but it's typical of Skye, thinking of others first.

"They are all well provided for. Your grandfather was a very wealthy man"

"So what happens next?" whispers Skye

Hopkirk pulls out more documents from his brief case "I need you to sign these and give me details of where the funds are to be transferred to"

Half an hour later Paul shows Hopkirk out. Skye sits with the tumbler in her hands rolling it back and forth watching the liquid swirl. I leave her to her thoughts and pace the room. Skye has had one hell of a shock. Hell I'm fucking shocked. She has gone from self-made multimillionaire to multibillionaire in the blink of an eye. It's a lot to take in. A throat being cleared has us both look up to see Paul.

"Ma'am do you need me for anything else?"

Skye seems lost "No and thank you Paul" he smiles, nods and leaves.

I sit back down on the sofa and Skye climbs onto my lap, something she's never done before. "Hold me" she whispers.

I gladly wrap my arms around her. Skye tucks herself into me and I rest my chin on the top of her head. Skye places her hand on my chest her fingers flex and move slowly. We stay like this for a long time.

"Clayton, how much are you worth?" her question is whispered.

It doesn't surprise me she has asked because I know she wouldn't have done a background search on me preferring to learn about me as we went along.

"Just a little over two billion dollars"

"How do you cope being so rich?" she lifts her head to look up at me, her big yellow green eyes pleading for me to be serious.

"Same as you do. I give back to the community and support various charities, I keep working at what I love doing. Skye you are the same person now as you were this morning that hasn't changed. You do realize you are wealthier than me now" sheer confusion on her beautiful face has me chuckling "Hopkirk said one point five billion pounds not dollars, so with the current exchange rate plus your personal fortune by my reckoning you are worth not far off three billion dollars" Skye went positively green. I grimace "not helping?" she nods.

Skye put her head back resting on my shoulder and remains quiet. I enjoy the feel of her fingers drawing lazy patterns on my chest and of holding her in my arms.

"Can I ask you something" I ask tentatively. Skye nods.

"Your grandfather's name, Hopkirk mentioned Lord does that mean you come from gentry?"

Skye shifts and looks at me a slight smile on her face "No, although he probably wished he was. My grandfather was knighted. He was a captain of industry a self-made man. He grew up in the north of England and his family was extremely poor almost destitute as he was very fond of reminding us at every opportunity" Skye let out a heavy sigh "I just don't know how to feel about it all. My grandfather's test, his message, his remorse"

"Want some help thinking this through" I offer. Skye nods.

"Let's say your grandfather left the five hundred million pounds to someone else in the family who had changed their name and settled in another country. In order to get the money they have to change back to their original name and move back to England. Now think of every family member and put them to the test, would they concede?"

Skye looks off into the distance. I could see it in her eyes as she ran through Uncles, Aunts and cousins after a few minutes Skye stiffens, she has her answer.

"Assuming no-one has changed and by that I mean no-one has had a major personality transplant then they would all do it to get their hands on the money"

"Do you want to hear my thoughts on his message and remorse?" Skye nods.

"Starting with his remorse, in London you spelt it out to him loud and clear the effects his actions all those years ago had on you. The consequence was showing him the anger, hate and contempt you had for him. After you walked away he said I deserved that" Skye's eyes widen "his test and message had he been here to witness would have shown to him you are true to yourself and beliefs, that you wouldn't bend to his manipulations just for money. Your grandfather giving you the bulk of his fortune, to me, was his way of showing he respects and admires you, plus in some way probably trying to make up for the past" I shrug "just my thoughts"

Skye kisses my cheek "Thank you for putting it into perspective" she sighs "I just worry about what people's reaction to me will be when they find out"

"Skye out of everyone you know whose opinion do you value and seek the most?"

"Yours, Shelley and Simon's" Skye says without hesitation.

"So you already know to me it makes no difference whatsoever. You are already and always have been mega rich to Shelley and Simon. Do you think they will change their opinion of you and what do you think their reaction is going to be when you tell them?"

Skye puffs out her cheeks as she considers what I've said then blew out on an exhale. "I'm being an idiot. They will be shocked then happy for me and they will treat me the same as they always have and anyone else can go fuck themselves"

"That's my girl" I grin and I kiss the tip of her nose.

"I can't thank you enough. I would have been a quivering wreck now if you hadn't been here"

"You are a survivor Skye. You will have called an emergency get together with Shelley and Simon and talked it through with them"

"You're right but don't underestimate your part. Yes I would have called them but probably not until tomorrow. I would have tormented myself into a near nervous breakdown and had a sleepless night as well" Skye kisses my cheek "I am the luckiest girl alive to have you in my life. I love you and will you marry me?"

Happiness and joy course through me. My stomach did back flips and my heart thuds so hard it feels as if it's going to break through my rib cage. My face muscles ache I'm smiling so much.

"Yes" I start to laugh, I feel even happier now than I did when I proposed to her in Vegas. I stood with Skye in my arms and carry her to the bedroom.

I place Skye gently on the bed and peel her clothes and underwear off slowly.

"Lie in the centre of the bed and close your eyes. I'll be back in a minute" I give the commands as soft as possible as her nerves are still frayed from the stress of the last couple of hours.

I head to the kitchen and get the ice cream, chocolate sauce and a spoon. I want my desert. Entering the bedroom I take a minute to admire and enjoy the sight of Skye naked and spread out on the bed. She has moved her arms above her head and her legs are open. My cock throbs painfully against the confines of my jeans. I place the ice cream, sauce and spoon on the bedside cabinet then quickly remove my clothes. Skye moves her head in my direction, her breathing picks up as she listens to the sounds I make.

"Good girl" I murmur, she has kept her eyes closed "if you can baby at all times keep your eyes closed and your arms above your head, grip the pillow if it helps" I climb onto the bed "I'm going to be eating my desert off you so you will need to keep still"

I move Skye's legs wider apart and sit between them. Her pussy glistens with her juices she is so turned on. I can't resist, I bend and run my tongue flat against her pussy as if lapping ice cream off a wafer cone. Skye lets out a long low moan. I crawl up her body letting my cock slide along the slit, coating me with her juices. I take one of her nipples in my mouth and suckle making it harder.

"Mmmm I can't wait for the delights dessert will bring" I plant a kiss on her mouth.

I sit up and straddle her, positioning my cock between her breasts and cupping them in my hands pushing them together I rock back of forth.

"Fuck! Your tits feel fucking great against my cock" Skye dips her chin and her tongue darts out and licks the crown of my cock as I thrust forward. Pleasure shoots up my cock and straight to my balls "you're going to make me come if you keep that up" I pant.

Skye moves her arms, she keeps her eyes closed, her hands move mine out of the way and she holds her tits in place then she lifts her head slightly and places her lips on the crown of my cock.

Fuck me! The sight has my balls drawing up tight. I want to fuck her tits now and she is encouraging me to fulfil the fantasy. I place my hands on the headboard and start to thrust, it isn't long before my head falls back and I'm lost to the sensations of the soft skin of her tits against the shaft of my cock and the feel of her lips and tongue swirling around the crown. I start to move faster and I feel the pressure of her tits against my cock increasing the friction.

"Oh yes baby that's it, help me fuck your tits" I gasp out and thrust harder.

My balls tighten, the next instant my cock pulses "I'm coming baby" I thrust again and feel Skye's lips lock on the head of my cock and suck hard "argh Skye" my whole body stiffens as I ejaculate my release then shudder as my orgasm rolls through me. I move slowly back and forth rubbing out the rest of my orgasm. I look down at Skye, she still has her eyes closed and a smug smile plays on her lips as she runs her tongue around her mouth, licking up cum. Some of it is on her chest and neck.

"Put your hands back on the pillow baby"

Skye did without a word. I move back slightly then rub the seamen on her neck and breast into her skin.

"You are mine and now you will carry my scent on you so every man will know you belong to me" my words sound as possessive as I feel. Skye lets out a small gasp, I look at her face and my heart swells as she looks pleased and content.

I reach over to the cabinet and pick up the sauce, ice cream and spoon. I trickle chocolate sauce over Skye's luscious full lips, her tongue snakes out and licks it off.

"Naughty girl" I admonish "that is for me not you"

"Sorry sir"

She isn't at all then she puckers her lips, offering them to me. Chuckling I put more sauce on them. Skye has very kissable lips and a fuckable mouth. I'm going to enjoy this. I run my tongue over her sauce covered lips and along the seam, her lips part. I kiss her deeply dipping my tongue inside her mouth, tasting myself, her and chocolate sauce. Skye responds licking me back and sucking on my tongue, she makes a sound of appreciation at the back of her throat. My cock hardens ready for round two. I pull back.

"So you like chocolate" her answer is to smack and lick her lips "now baby you will need to stay as still as you can"

I move off to the side of her and trail chocolate sauce around her nipples, tits and stomach. I open the ice cream and place a dollop in the centre of her stomach, over her belly button. Skye hisses in a sharp breath and lifts her lower back and hips off the bed, the ice cream slides sideways I catch it with the spoon

"Stay still" I admonish softly, Skye drops her lower body back to the bed and I move the ice cream back into place.

The next dollop I keep on the spoon and run it over her tit before placing it over her nipple.

"Argh" Skye cries out then shudders. I repeat the action with her other tit and again she cries out.

Skye keeps her eyes closed and she's gripping the pillow tightly. I put the ice cream, spoon and sauce back on the bedside cabinet and admire my handiwork.

"Oh baby you look so fucking edible"

The ice cream on her stomach is melting and running down the sides of her waist. I bend and set to work lapping it up. Alternating between her tits and stomach, it isn't long before Skye's legs are scissoring and her hips rotating in slow sensuous movements.

"Open your legs for me" she has them open on the first word out of my mouth "eager aren't you baby" I chuckle picking up the sauce.

I put the nozzle against her clit and squeeze. Skye moans as the sauce trickles down her pussy. I put a spoonful of ice cream in my mouth, lay down between her legs, lift her hips and put my mouth over her pussy pushing the ice cream against her.

"Holy fucking hell" Skye shouts and bucks.

I hold her in place and work the ice cream in with the sauce. I dip my cold tongue inside her hot wet entrance. The taste of her juices mixing with the sauce and ice cream is so ambrosial it makes me groan.

I work a pattern with my tongue swirling around her folds, flick her clit then I cover her with my mouth and suck the chocolate and ice cream off, swirl around the folds then penetrate her with my tongue. Skye's hips gyrate against my mouth. Placing my hand on her lower stomach I spread my fingers and place my thumb on her clit, massaging it then I fuck her with my tongue, pushing in and out in fast shallow thrusts pushing her over the edge. I drink her juices as it hits my tongue. I keep going at her. I'm greedy and I want a second helping. I clamp my mouth over her clit and suck.

"Clayton" Skye screams as she comes hard her back arching so only her head and shoulders stay on the bed.

SKYE

I'm gulping air, I feel as if I'm drowning. Christ the orgasms have been intense. I thought the top of my head had blown off. I stretch my arms out and flex my fingers getting rid of the stiffness from gripping and pulling on the pillow so hard. Clayton crawls up my body planting soft kisses. I'm surprised the pillow hadn't torn in half.

"Desert was delightfully delicious" he purrs "thank you"

Clayton kisses me long and hard bruising my lips, when he pulls away his eyes are sparkling and he looks mighty pleased himself, in fact I'd say smug.

"My turn" I put my hands on his chest and push him away "I'm hungry"

Clayton moves to the side so I can get up then repositions himself in the spot I've vacated. God I'm sticky and about to get even stickier. I grin as I reach for the ice cream and sauce, payback time.

Slowly drizzling chocolate sauce over Clayton's chest and abs I follow the contours of his muscles then dribble the melted ice cream along the same path. There's enough frozen ice cream left to do what I want in a little bit.

I start to lick, suck and nip my way across his body, my tongue following the ridges and contours of muscle. Clayton moans and groans keeping his eyes open, watching me, his hands at the side of his head buried into the pillow. I suck and tease his nipples, he grips the pillow so hard the veins in his neck and arms stand out more pronounced and his hips thrust upwards.

Sitting up I reach for the sauce, tub and spoon then settle in between Clayton's legs. His eyes never leave me. I like him watching me. Clayton has his mouth open, his chest moving up and down in quick succession he's trying to bring his breathing under control.

Clayton's cock lies thick and heavy across his lower stomach reaching his navel. It twitches and pulses, silently demanding attention. I trail my fingers over the shaft and trace the ridges and veins running along it. I love the soft silky smooth feel of his skin and yet he feels as hard as iron when I wrap my hand around him. I pull his cock up-right, fisting him I stroke in long slow pulls, his hips surging with my movements.

"Oh yes baby" he moans.

I pour chocolate sauce over the head of his cock and let it run down the sides. I continue to stroke him, moving my hand lower when the sauce got lower. Using my fingers I smear the chocolate sauce all over his cock, hmm my own kind of chocolate bar. I take him in my mouth, relaxing my throat I take him as deep as I can. Pulling back I suck hard tasting him and the chocolate.

"Jesus, fuck" Clayton barks out.

He's panting hard and I've only just gotten started now I'm the smug one. Smiling, I pour sauce around the base of his cock then lick and suck his balls as the sauce trickles over them. Clayton is moaning and cursing.

I pour sauce over the head of his cock and like last time rub it all over with my fingers. Clayton has his eyes closed, he's concentrating on his breathing trying to regain control, as quietly as I can I scoop a spoonful of ice cream into my mouth. Leaning forward I take him in my mouth.

"Fucking hell" Clayton yells and jerks his hips, a ripping sound follows.

I take him further into my mouth and more cursing follows as I swirl my cold tongue around his shaft spreading the ice cream out. Then I lick and suck it away, sucking hard as I withdraw his cock from my mouth. I take another mouthful of ice cream this time I put my mouth on his balls and suck them into my mouth swirling my tongue and the cold ice cream over them.

"Sshhiiiitttt" a long ripping sound accompanies Clayton's shouted curse.

There goes my pillow, the bizarre thought pops into my head as I work my way back up the shaft of his cock.

I pour more sauce on the head of his cock and put another spoonful of ice cream in my mouth then take his cock.

"Fuck, Skye baby" Clayton barks out and arches his back, he's panting heavily.

I concentrate on setting the rhythm I know will have him climaxing hard. Gripping him with one hand I stroke with firm upward movements whilst with my mouth I suck hard occasionally grazing my teeth over his shaft. With my other hand I cup his balls and massage them, scraping my nails lightly over his sack, extending my fingers to run from his ass along the perineum to his sack and back. Clayton clenches and bucks his hips. His breathing is coming in and out in harsh gasps. The veins in his cock pulse and I taste pre cum he's very close. I suck harder and gripe his cock tighter as his hips move faster. His cock pulses and with one long hard suck I make Clayton come.

"Argh Skye" he bellows his hips thrusting upwards as his back arches off the bed.

The tanginess of his cum mixing with the sweetness of the ice cream and chocolate sauce hits the back of my throat and fills my mouth. I swallow so I can take more of him.

I love this and him. I will take everything he is willing to give. When there is nothing left I crawl up his body and lay down on top of him. The stickiness of both our bodies bonds us together like glue. I place my head on his chest and listen to his racing heart gradually slow. Clayton strokes my hair in a long soothing motion. When his heart and breathing are back to normal he kisses the top of my head.

"Come on baby let's take a bath"

Chapter Twenty Three

SKYE

"How much" Shelley and Simon chorus together in high pitched screechy voices.

I've just finished telling them about the visit from Hopkirk yesterday afternoon and my grandfather's Will, test and message, plus I had to explain what happened in London and the subsequent conversation I had with Clayton about what it all meant.

"One point five billion" I confirm.

"Pounds not dollars?" Shelley asks. I nod.

"Well shag me sideways" Simon says in stunned disbelief.

I smile. His saying always did make me smile. Both of them look as shell shocked as I had been. I called Simon first thing this morning and asked him to meet me at Shelley's for an emergency get together even though I'd arranged to be with Shelley this morning anyway.

Macy is with me, although she's currently sitting in the living room whilst I talk with my friends in the kitchen. Macy already knew. Paul told her after he returned to their quarters. I'm not angry that he had, in fairness Macy said she badgered him until he spilt the beans as she put it and she only did it due to the strange mood he had returned in. She also got him to tell Bruce and they then spent the rest of the afternoon and evening discussing security tactics as they are certain press interest will increase once the news broke and I have to agree, this is definitely newsworthy.

"Bloody hell" Shelley exclaims "it means you are richer than Clayton"

She looks up from her laptop and turns it around so I can see the currency converter website. I didn't want to look at the figure but I do anyway, glutton for punishment. I wince.

"Yeah that's what Clayton said last night. It's still not sunk in. I mean I suppose it will hit home once I actually have the money, it all just seems so surreal"

"At this moment in time what's your biggest concern" says Shelley.

I snort "I had this conversation with Clayton" I take a deep breath "I was worried what people's reaction would be towards me when they found out"

"Oh honey you know you will always be the same Skye Darcy to us" Simon indicates to himself and Shelley "you have always been stinking rich to us and now you're mega stinking rich but you are still the same person inside"

It warms my heart to hear it said out loud and to see the sincerity and love in their faces. I feel myself filling up. Shelley gets up and walks around the table putting her arms around me, holding me to her, rubbing my back. The display of love, affection and reassurance has my bottom lip and chin trembling.

Shelley pulls away just enough to look at me "You had your doubts didn't you?" there is no accusation in her soft voice. I nod.

"I'm sorry but I did. Clayton helped me see through my fear. He asked me whose opinion I valued and sought" I look at my two best friends "obviously it's you two and Clayton, then he asked me how you would react and you both have done exactly as I said which made me realize I didn't care about anyone else and they could go fuck themselves"

"That's my girl" Simon laughs and held his hand up for a high five.

"Okay enough about me" I look at Shelley "Vegas weekend, I spoke with Marco and they have plenty of rooms and will do us a good deal. Macy come in here" I call out, she appears in the doorway and I wave her over "Vegas this weekend, hen party for Shelley. You ready for some drunken debauchery and gambling?" I ask her as she sits down next to me.

"Hell yeah! Bring it on sista" she replies with her usual gusto making us all laugh.

Shelley read through the list of confirmed names, I told her to add Paul and Bruce as they will be there although working. Shelley rang Phil and his Dad to get the last few confirmations. We work out the number of rooms needed and I call Marco, who told me he has reserved a suite for me and Clayton. The same one as last time, yes! piano here we come. Plus he has reserved a suite for Shelley and Phil. Whilst I'm on the phone Shelley takes calls from Phil and his Dad so I'm able to confirm final numbers and rooms then took the email address to send over everyone's name.

Macy is just putting the finishing touches to the email when Shelley takes another call from Phil.

"Don't send that just in case there's a change" Shelley says to Macy as she answers "hi sweetie" within thirty seconds Shelley's face hardens and her eyes flick to me "you are shitting me" she barks into the phone, long pause as she listens to Phil "aw crap... okay... bye"

Shelley hangs up, puts her hand to her forehead and rubs as if trying to get rid of a sudden headache, then looks at me again, pain and regret in her eyes.

"I'm really sorry" she sighs "Phil bumped into Pete and Caroline last night when he was out with his Dad. Long story short Phil paid a visit to the rest room on his return his Dad was telling Pete and Caroline about the bachelor and hen weekend boasting about going on Clayton's plane. Caroline wangled an invite out of his Dad. Phil is still not sure how it happened anyway he's just had a call from Pete saying they will both be coming" Shelley grimaces.

Shit. Fucking shit I scream in my head. "Don't worry, I'm fine" I lie and they know it "hey that reminds me. Clayton and I saw them yesterday in the supermarket"

I tell them what happened taking great delight in quoting Clayton and Pete verbatim, my news gets a mixed reaction.

"Oh my god" says Macy shocked.

"You're kidding" says Shelley in disbelief

"I am so looking forward to seeing what she tries this weekend" says Simon gleefully.

"So long as she stays away from me and Clayton I don't care what she does"

"You can always get Paul and Bruce to operate an exclusion zone around you both" Macy says joking.

"It's a sad state of affairs when you have to resort to that kind of thing with people you know" I sigh.

"I noticed you didn't refer to them as friends" Macy says raising a perfectly pencilled eye brow at me.

I've never really spoken about my past and Pete with her. Macy is aware I knew Pete before I met Shelley and Simon. On the odd occasions Macy socialises with us Pete and Caroline are rarely present so she has no reason to think they weren't friends.

"Oh they're not friends, sweet thing" Simon smiles at me then turns back to Macy ready to dish the gossip "Pete is an old ex-boyfriend of Skye's from years back. Skye bumped into him when he had not long moved here. Being the kind soul she is, she invited him to Gino's. Fast forward to present day, he has a catty bitch girlfriend no-one likes and they go to Gino's every Friday night in the sad hope that we" he points to the three of us "turn up and when we do they have the audacity to sit themselves down at our table, uninvited I might add, then attempt to join in conversations they have no part of. So Catty Bitch resorts to deprecation or trying to belittle Skye whether she is there or not. Needless to say nobody" Simon waves his diva hand "puts our girl down" he gives me a one arm hug "my friends and I play a game called Slap Down Catty Bitch, its good fun. Next time you are out with us and she's around I'll let you play" he winks at Macy.

"That'll be Vegas then" I add miserably.

"Enough about them and lets finalise things for the weekend" Shelley says with such finality none of us argue.

Macy finishes off the email and sends it.

"All we need to do now is sort out what time we fly out and where in the airport everyone needs to meet" Shelley says looking at me expectantly, when I don't respond she widens her eyes as a prompt for an answer.

"What" I say. I'm still clueless.

"Did Clayton give you the details by any chance?"

"Doh! err no" god I sound intelligent "I'll ring him and find out" I say taking my phone out of my pocket and speed dial Clayton.

He answers on the first ring "Hi baby, glad you called. What do you need?" his deep rich husky voice sends shivers down my spine. God! Clayton so has a voice for phone sex.

"Hey, can you talk? I'm not interrupting anything important"

"You and your happiness are my priority therefore important. Business can wait" he says smoothly.

I can't hear any noise which means he's in one of two places; his office or the boardroom. "Where are you?"

"Boardroom" shit "and yes it is full of people"

I laugh "You've called a halt to a meeting just to take my call?"

He chuckles "Absolutely, you are important. So tell me what do you need?"

I have to bite my tongue from saying you. "We're just finalising everything for Friday, all I need to know is flight time and where should everyone meet in the airport?"

"How about we fly out at twelve noon and get everyone to be in the VIP area for eleven" I relay this to Shelley and get the thumbs up "how many people are going and did Marco have the rooms?" he asks.

Crap, I'm going to have to tell him about Pete and Catty Bitch, no time like the present.

"Including Paul and Bruce it makes twenty in total. Listen, I have good news and bad news" Clayton remains quiet waiting for me to tell him "bad news Pete and Caroline are going" he curses profusely "good news, helllooo piano" I sing gleefully.

Clayton laughs it's one of those hearty belly laughs and I imagine him throwing his head back doing it. I'm grinning like a lunatic. My friends give me puzzled looks, I ignore them.

"Now that has made my day, email me the list of names and I'll sort out the airport arrival check in. I'll see you later baby"

Whilst I've been on the phone Macy has made a list of other things which need to be organised for the weekend, things that hadn't occurred to the rest of us. As she reads through the list I decide to add to it.

"Shelley I know it's your weekend and all activities are determined by you but I really want to do one of those helicopter flights over the Grand Canyon and get to see a Cirque de Soleil show"

Before I can finish she cuts me off.

"I would too plus pampering in the spa. I checked it out the weekend of the convention it looks awesome I think that should to be added too. Is there anything you fancy doing Macy?"

Macy looks absolutely stunned at Shelley.

"Come on it's your weekend to have fun just as much as anyone else's. So what have you always had the burning desire to do when we've gone to Vegas and you've never had the opportunity to do it" I say. Macy's eyes shine with tears "come on there's got to be something" I persist gently.

Macy nods wiping her eyes and clears her throat. "I've always wanted to learn how to gamble, you know black jack, roulette, poker, craps" she shrugs "every time I see people play it seems like fun or really serious concentration. I would like to understand the rules of play and not feel an idiot when asking a silly question"

"The only silly question is the one that is not asked" says Simon "I think it's a brilliant idea. I'm in for a private tutorial"

"So am I" I say.

"Me too" Shelley chimes in "so I suggest we do the gambling lesson Friday night. Saturday morning the helicopter trip, spa in the afternoon and the Cirque show in the evening and Sunday will be do as you please. What do you all think?"

The order of activities is given unanimous thumbs up. Further discussion is had around whether to circulate the activities to the girls before the weekend or not, then whether or not to open it up to the boys. It isn't until Simon points out he will be doing the girls activities as strip and pole dancing clubs are not his thing plus he adds Clayton will be doing the girls activities as he wouldn't be leaving my side for one minute, he has a point.

Shelley decrees she will get Phil's list of activities and circulate both to everyone before Friday and then people can pick and choose.

"If anyone has a problem with the activities they can sod off and entertain themselves!" Shelley finishes to a round of applause.

An hour later Shelley and I are alone, Simon has a meeting with a new client, since his TV appearance in Vegas he's been picking up a lot of affluent clients and Macy is organising my business life now I'm officially back in New York. We are in the room Shelley uses as a home studio and I have my bridesmaid dress on. Shelley is making sure no final alterations are needed.

The dress is stunning. A very pale mint green floor length raw silk gown with a corseted bodice which is encrusted with diamante's and sequins. The back is laced up and the skirt of the dress is straight with a slight train at the back. I'm going to be wearing my hair up with a head band of white and dark green flowers. My shoes are silk mint green killer heels, of course.

We talk about what is left to organise for the wedding which is the weekend after next. The ceremony is being held at Phil's parent's house or mansion would be a better description with the whole grounds being transformed for the day.

Shelley has no family, at the age of eight she was orphaned when her parents along with her grandparents were killed in a car crash; she was the only survivor. With no living relatives Shelley then spent years bouncing around foster home to foster home until we met at college.

In contrast Phil's family is huge. I know he has four older brothers, most of them married with kids but he has so many aunties, uncles and cousins it made my head spin.

"How much involvement have you had in organising your own wedding?" I'm curious.

Shelley chuckles "The color scheme, clothes, cake and flowers everything else Brenda has done and she has thoroughly enjoyed herself" Shelley pauses chewing her lip she's contemplating about asking me something.

"Whatever it is, if it is within my power and means you can have it" I say hoping I've made whatever it is easier to ask for.

"You know me so well" she snorts "can I stay with you on the Friday before the wedding?" I nod without hesitation "thank you, it's just sometimes I find Phil's family a bit full on. They mean well but I just know Brenda is going to stress the crap out of me and I want a decent night's sleep"

"Of course you can. Tell you what I'll organise a pamper afternoon and night for us, then in the morning we get hair and makeup done so we only have to get dressed at Brenda's"

"Clayton won't mind will he?"

I hadn't given him a thought when I said yes to her. I shrug. "I'll tell him and if he does have a problem with it he can always stay at his place"

Shelley burst out laughing. "Yeah right, as if that's going to happen. Talking of weddings do you want to see and try on your dress?" she asks uncertainly.

I feel a pang of guilt because I haven't spoken to her about the dress since she told me she'd made it in Vegas. I haven't even asked to see it let alone get her describe it to me. I'm a bad friend.

"It would be rude not to" I grin.

I stare at myself in the full length mirror. I can't find my breath.

"Oh Skye" Shelley's voice is a hushed whisper "you look devastatingly stunning"

My dress is made of ivory silk with a very fine lace layered over the top of it. The bodice is moulded to me, my shoulders are bare but the dress has long lace sleeves ending in a point on the back of my hands. At the back the dress starts under my shoulder blades and has a long row of covered buttons. The skirt is straight with a long train. Within the lace throughout the whole dress in random places diamantes are stitched in so when I walk and move it gives the effect of shimmering.

The dress is simple, understated and highly effective. I can visualise how my hair will look. Piled up in a big mess of cork screw curls woven with gypsy grass, I will wear my moonstone lily shaped drop earrings and I will leave my neck bare. My bouquet will be white Calla Lilies. I can even see Clayton in his top hat and tails. I'm ready to marry him I realize.

"I love it Shelley" I choke with emotion as I look at her through a blur of unshed tears "I absolutely love it. All I have to do now is set a date" I wipe my face "have you got your dress made?"

"It's designed and the pattern is ready but it's not made"

"Why not" I'm puzzled it isn't like her, Miss Super-Efficient. Shelley chuckles at my reaction.

"Skye I need to know your color scheme before I can make it"

"Crap" I mutter which makes Shelley laugh more. How in the hell do I decide on a color scheme "well considering you are my only bridesmaid what color would you like to wear"

Shelley has dark almost black short pixie cut hair, large pale blue eyes and cream colored skin. She is taller than me by a couple of inches but she is petite, she wouldn't look out of place on the cat walk.

"Are you likely to have any other bridesmaids?"

"No. I was thinking of Nessa but she's six months pregnant and not going to be able to travel in another four weeks"

"Does that mean you are thinking of tying the knot before Christmas?" Shelley raises her eyebrows at me, I laugh.

"If Clayton has his way we'd probably get married in Vegas at the weekend. He wanted to do that when I said yes at the convention on the Friday night"

"Oh my god" Shelley shrieks and claps her hands "what stopped you?"

"Too quick for me then I pointed out he would have to tell his mother and face her when he got back on Monday, that sobered him up pretty quick"

"I bet it did" Shelley chuckles "his mother is a force to be reckoned with. She scared me a bit at the charity gala. I can see her heart is in the right place but I get the impression she can be a bit OTT. One of those 'give her an inch and she'll grab a mile'"

"You are absolutely spot-on in your assessment. Clayton is quite strict with her; you know he has actually forbidden Stephanie from asking me anything about the wedding or setting a date"

"No way" Shelley says in wide eyed amazement. I nod.

"It's probably killing her mind you but she knows she will seriously piss off Clayton if she did and that is something she doesn't want to do. He told me when I was in Russia the first two weeks were hell for him as she kept arranging dates for him with various daughters of her friends. He ended up being a real shit to her because she wouldn't back off or stop. When I saw him in London he hadn't spoken to her properly for two weeks, at one point he refused to see her and take her calls. Joshua and Andrew ended up acting as mediators"

"Blimey sounds like your Stephanie is my Brenda" she breathed in wonder "oh I forgot to tell you" she suddenly jolts herself in surprise "Simon is going to give me away"

"That's fantastic!" I shriek, hugging her with joy and enthusiasm.

"Yeah it is. Nicked the idea from you" she beams shoulder bumping me "I thought it was such a thoughtful and lovely gesture at the time when you asked Simon, but the more I thought about it I realized I didn't want to walk down the aisle on my own and since neither of us have a father figure in our lives and Simon is like a brother, he's the only family we've got so who better to give me away. I totally get why you asked him. Hope you don't mind"

"Don't be silly" I admonish "of course I don't mind. It's your day and it's up to you who you ask, so tell me when did you ask him and what was his reaction?"

I grin because I already have a mental image in my head. Simon is such a drama queen.

"Yesterday, he called round whilst we were ringing everyone about the Vegas weekend and of course he cried. Did his diva hands trying to stop himself which made him worse"

Shelley helps me out of the dress, as I put my own clothes back on I realize we haven't discussed color scheme. I'm about to yell to Shelley, as she'd taken the dress into the closet, when she comes back carrying a swatch of fabric samples.

"Great minds think alike" I say pointing at her hands.

"But fools seldom do differ" she deadpans finishing off the quote.

We go through the samples and I fall in love with a sky blue silk. "This would look really good on you Shelley" I say pointing at the sample "plus Clayton has dark blue eyes and it'll work for him as well"

"How about the cravat in this and the vest in this color for Clayton and have it reversed for the best man and ushers" she holds up a darker blue, the two colors work well together "and I'll incorporate the two colors into my dress" she looks at me for confirmation.

"Yes and I can have little flowers made in those two colors and woven into my hair"

"Sounds like we have a plan, all you need to do now is set the date"

I have an idea but I want to check with Clayton first. "I'll let you know tomorrow but make a start on your dress sooner rather than later" I wink at her.

My phone rings. It's Billy telling me he has lined up three properties and when did I want to view them. I tell him I'll get straight back to him after I've spoken to Clayton then I call Clayton and Helena answers his phone.

"Hi Helena it's Skye. If you're answering I take it Clayton is busy"

"Hello Miss Darcy. Mr Blake is in a meeting however I will get him for you"

I can hear her moving around. "No don't disturb him, just let him know I called and ask him to ring me when he's free" I say in a rush, last thing I want is to be perceived as the annoying demanding and needy girlfriend. Helena surprises me by chuckling.

"Oh believe me I would sooner be scowled at for interrupting a meeting than to be berated by him later when he hears you called and I didn't disturb him"

I heard a knock then a muffled conversation followed by Clayton's rich raspy voice. "Skye baby, what do you need?"

"You" the word is out of my mouth before I realize, brain to mouth malfunction. Clayton's chuckle is full of promised sin making me wet and needy. Put your brain back on business girl, I admonish myself. "Billy has rung he's found three properties, so I need to know when you are free to view them"

"Hang on a minute baby" I hear him tapping on his keyboard and he speaks to someone "I can be finished by three how's that?"

"Excellent I'll pick you up outside your office at three" we say good bye and hang up.

I ring Billy and arrange to view all three properties one after the other, then I ring Macy letting her know and ask her to let Paul and Bruce know as they'll all be viewing with us as well.

I end up staying with Shelley and having lunch with her. I really enjoy our girly time together it's been too long since we'd last done this. We talk about anything and everything. Shelley shows me her latest designs, her order book is full and she is taking on extra staff and a lot of it is down to me apparently. When I look at her blank she laughs and reaches for her laptop.

"You really have no clue about the media circus around you do you?" she says as she types my name into the search bar and an explosion of pictures of me appears on screen "you my dear friend are being billed as a style icon"

My jaw hits the table. Holy fucking hell, pictures from various charity and business galas including ones from May, the one in London in July, me with Nessa, me and Clayton, me on my own and pictures from Vegas. The majority of the pictures show me wearing Shelley's creations.

"Are you okay?" the concern in her voice has me looking at her "you've gone awfully pale"

"I had no idea" I whisper, my throat and mouth have gone terribly dry and my stomach somersaults. A cold glass is pressed into my hand, water slops over my fingers. I look down to see my hand shaking.

"Take a drink and breathe" I do as Shelley instructs and on the third breath I feel calmer "I'm sorry I didn't mean to freak you out. Now I know why Simon and Macy don't mention any of this to you, well they do but only the really important things" she clarifies.

I can see Shelley is kicking herself and anxiety has her twisting her hands. I put mine over hers to stop her; mine feel cold on her warm ones. I try for a smile but I don't think it quite works.

"It's okay, in my naivety I thought once the news got fed up of reporting on the engagement it would all disappear, numpty here" I point at myself "forgot about the internet" I pull a face at myself "well Miss Mason I hope you've got some fabulous outfits, sorry creations for me to wear this weekend" my smile is warm and genuine this time. I'm glad Shelley is getting recognition for her work.

Shelley grins back wickedly. "Absolutely and you are not seeing them until the weekend"

"It's a bloody good job I trust you madam" I joke "and on that note I am going to love you and leave you"

Back in my apartment I pull out my art portfolio's and art note books. I want to find the drawings and designs I've done that clients had asked about being made into jewellery in preparation for the meeting with Matthew and Gerrard tomorrow. I remember who the clients are and an idea strikes to do some market research and check to see if demand is still there, two birds one stone and all that.

At two thirty Macy and Paul find me sitting on the floor surrounded by piles of open work books and drawings in plastic sleeves. I also have a list of names and twenty items on order. I feel quite pleased with myself.

"Time to go Skye" Macy calls out and holds out my jacket.

"Yes Mom" I reply grinning, she rolls her eyes at me.

"Paul, when was the last time you saw Jack?"

We are sat in the car waiting for Clayton. It's occurred to me Paul hasn't asked for time off since we've been back. Paul opens his mouth to speak but I cut him off.

"And I don't mean by video link either" Paul grins ruefully and shakes his head. I've rumbled him and he knew I knew "right Wednesday and Thursday I want you spending as much time as possible with him, that's an order. I'm not going anywhere so there's no excuse"

"Yes ma'am but it isn't really necessary" says Paul.

"No argument and it is necessary, he needs his Dad in the flesh not on a screen. In the event I do have to venture out I'm sure Bruce won't mind accompanying me"

"It'll be a pleasure ma'am" Bruce says to me but he's grinning at Paul.

The two of them really do get on and work well together, which reminds me. "Macy tells me you both discussed security strategy and tactics yesterday afternoon. I would like to hear your thoughts and plans"

Bruce's reaction makes me smile. Like Paul he rarely shows emotion but his face is a picture of shocked surprise, I can tell he's still coming to terms with and getting used to how open and honest I am with Paul and Macy and they return the favor. Paul starts to speak when Bruce jumps out of the car and comes round to my side. I look out and see Clayton walking through the foyer. People literally scuttle out of his way. I release my seat belt as the door opens and move to the centre as Clayton climbs in, before the door closes Clayton has me back in his lap and the seat belt fastened whilst kissing me hello.

"Paul and Bruce are going to share their thoughts and ideas on new security measures in light of yesterday's news about my inheritance" I inform Clayton.

"Excellent, let's hear it"

By the time we reach the first viewing Paul has briefed us, the main changes being an additional body guard possibly two and having a safe room. It all makes perfect sense.

"Do you know of anyone for the position?" I ask.

"Yes ma'am I do" Bruce says "actually I know a couple of people"

"Okay get in touch with them and let Macy know when they can come for an interview"

I suddenly remember Clayton has a vested interest in this, crap I bet he's mad at me, I twist to look at him only to see sparkling eyes and a broad smile so not the look I was expecting, which is an angry scowl.

"Sorry" I mouth his grin gets wider he knows why I'm apologising.

I hate the first two properties, too much glass and too clinical and not enough character for me. Although the views are fantastic it isn't enough to win me over. The last property I fall in love with just standing on the side walk and looking up at it. Like my apartment building it's more brick work than glass. It has a modern frontage which blends well with the character of the building. The street is quiet and lined with trees. There is a doorman along with reception come security staff on the front desk all of whom are courteous and polite and they all know Billy.

As soon as I set foot in the apartment it feels like home. The whole place ticks all of the boxes and then some. Macy loves it too, she is animated about the space which will become her and Paul's living quarters. Trying to get a reaction out of Bruce and Paul is like getting blood out of a stone, I tell them that too and much to my chagrin I make them chuckle.

The whole place is empty of furniture so my imagination is having a field day. I'm stood in a room I've mentally ear marked as my studio come office space when Clayton's raspy voice came close to my ear. "You like it don't you?"

I turn to face him "No" I say straight faced, his smile falters "I love it" I grin impishly, I'm rewarded with a big beaming smile coming back full force "come on lets speak to Billy"

I grab his hand and set off out of the room. I stop suddenly when I realize I haven't even asked Clayton what he thinks of the place. Clayton collides into me and manages to catch me before I fall flat on my face.

"Sorry" we say together.

"I've done it again, barrelling ahead and not checking with you for your opinion. I'm sorry"

Clayton puts his arms around me pulling me closer to him. "All I want is your happiness. I would live in a cardboard box with you if that's where you wanted to live" he says softly. He kisses me with so much tenderness it makes my toes curl.

"Guess what I tried on today" a puzzled look crosses Clayton's face and he shrugs in a silent I give up gesture "my wedding dress" his eyes widen and mouth pops open in surprise "how does thirty first of October sound to you as a wedding date?"

The double whammy has made Clayton dumbstruck. I watch his face so I see when he starts to get over the shock I've given him; a beautiful shy smile spreads across his lips and reaches his eyes.

"My birthday, you want us to get married on my birthday?" his whispers in awe. I nod.

Clayton let out a huge bellow of joy, picks me up and swings me around making me squeal. Paul and Bruce come skidding into the room— at least their response time is quick—to see me being spun and Clayton laughing like a lunatic and shouting whoops of joy. In unison they roll their eyes at us and turn to walk out shooing Macy out as they go. Clayton kisses me so passionately it takes my breath away.

"Let's celebrate" his eyes sparkling like sapphires "let's go to Gino's tonight, just the two of us" I nod my agreement smiling like a loon, our favourite restaurant, perfect "come on let's go and speak to Billy and buy this place" he says putting me back on my feet.

We find Billy in the vast room which will become the living room. "Billy we'll take it" I say still smiling broadly "by the way how come this is for sale?" It's a question I always ask when buying property, I like to get the background history.

"The guy selling is going through a nasty divorce and needs to get his hands on cash fast. Actually the whole building is up for sale it only went on the market today"

I look at Clayton grinning, he rolls his eyes knowing what is about to come out of my mouth.

"We'll buy the building as well" I feel giddy.

"Cash buy" is all Billy says I nod "give me a few minutes"

While Billy does his thing I take my phone out and send a text message to Shelley and Simon telling them the wedding date. "Macy" I call out, my voice echoes around the room and I flinch then laugh at myself.

"You bellowed" Macy says chuckling.

"It did come out louder than I expected, even made me jump, just so you know Clayton and I have set a date for the wedding. Thirty first of October"

"So that's what all the commotion was about earlier, she's finally put you out of your misery" she says to Clayton and winks at him. Clayton just smiles and nods, he hasn't stopped smiling come to think of it "congratulations, so I take it we're all systems go?"

"Yeah, we'll make a start tomorrow afternoon"

Venue, the thought suddenly pops into my head. Crap that's going to be a ball ache; delegate, let Clayton decide that one. "Any idea on where you would like to get married?"

Clayton's smile gets even wider "Yes, but I need to make a call first" he pulls out his phone from his inside jacket pocket and walks to the other end of the room.

CLAYTON

I am euphoric. I want to stand on the roof top and bellow my happiness for all to hear. I feel intoxicated, delirious with joy and nothing is going to bring me down from this high. I hadn't felt this happy when Skye accepted my proposal and then I'd been ecstatic.

"Clayton darling how are you and Skye?" my mother's soft and loving voice greets me.

"Hi Mom, we're both good. I'm ringing to ask a favor. Skye and I have set a date for the wedding, thirty first October and I'd like us to get married in the grounds if it's okay with you?"

An ear splitting scream cuts me off and has me pulling my phone away from my ear. It's so loud Skye and Macy heard it from the other side of the room, Skye raises her eyebrows.

"I've just told Mom and asked if we could get married in the grounds"

"I take it that response means yes" Skye laughs and walks towards me.

"Yes, oh yes of course darling" mother has calmed down enough to talk semi coherently and she starts wittering on about things I have absolutely no interest in.

"Mom stop" I feel a slight twinge at being a shit to curb her enthusiasm.

"Sorry darling, please forgive me" she is immediately contrite "there is so much to do"

"Here's Skye, speak to her about it"

I hold the phone out to her, Skye mouths "coward" at me as she takes it off me. I wrap my arms around her and rest my chin on her shoulder. "Hello Stephanie"

I can hear what my mother is saying and her enthusiasm goes stratospheric. Skye lets her ramble on until she runs out of steam.

"I would really appreciate your help Stephanie, can you come to my apartment tomorrow afternoon around three as I'll be sitting down with Macy to start organising everything and it would also help if you and Clayton could have a discussion on who you'll be inviting so we'll have a rough idea on numbers" Skye tilts her head sideways so she can look at me when she says this, I pull a face like a petulant teenager which Skye rolls her eyes at. I hear mother readily agree "that's great I'll see you tomorrow, here's Clayton"

Skye hands the phone back and gives me a quick kiss then heads back to Billy.

"I'll speak to you in the morning to go through the list with you and Mom please bear in mind Skye doesn't have family so don't go inviting every man and his dog of a relative"

"Goodness yes of course" thank god she got the message "can I tell your brothers and grandparents? Gracious!" she suddenly exclaims "it's your birthday, oh how romantic you're getting married on your birthday" she gushes.

"It was Skye's idea and yes you can tell whoever you want, just don't go inviting anyone" I add sternly. Skye is gesturing at me and I start walking back to her "look I've got to go. I'll speak to you tomorrow morning" We say goodbye and I love you then I hang up.

"They are willing to accept a cash offer of one hundred million dollars for this and the building" Skye says gleefully.

"Fuck me, the guy must be desperate to sell" I'm shocked "the whole thing is worth at least double that if not more"

"Like I said nasty divorce and needs cash fast" Billy says "can you complete tomorrow?"

I look at Skye and she nods. "Sure not a problem, I'm curious how did you find out about the seller's situation?"

Skye said Billy was good but to find out this kind of information is pure genius. Billy looks at me uncertain then to Skye for direction.

"It's okay your secrets will be safe, curiosity is his middle name" Skye says joking and nodding her head at me. Billy seems to relax at the reassurance.

"I sold an apartment on one of the lower floors about two months ago. It had quite a lot of interest so I spent a fair bit of time here. As is my practice I befriended the doorman and reception staff, one day the staff were, let's just say agitated. By speaking to them individually I managed to piece together they had been told they might be out of a job as there was a strong possibility the owner might be forced to sell due to personal reasons. I did a bit of digging, found out who the owner was and researched him, discreetly I asked around and that's when I heard about the divorce. When Skye rang on Saturday I came by here yesterday because I knew she would like it and asked if any of the apartments were becoming available as I had a cash buyer. The doorman told me about this" he sweeps an arm out indicating the apartment "I came this morning to speak to the building manager to arrange a viewing and he told me he had literally just been told the building was being put up for sale as of today" Billy flushes and his eyes flick to Skye "I told the building manager there was a strong possibility my cash buyer would buy the building once they saw it and asked if the owner would be willing to hold off going public until tomorrow" he shrugs "they agreed"

"I'm impressed. Skye this guy is fucking good" Billy blushes at the praise, I clap my hands together "so let's get this place bought"

Whilst Billy made his calls Skye and I make ours to the bank and the lawyers, in my case Joshua.

"Christ baby bro you don't hang around" Joshua says when I tell him I'm buying an apartment and building with Skye "I've just had Mom on telling me you've set the date. Congratulations by the way. Do you want me to draw up the paperwork for the pre-nup?"

"Not happening bro"

"What!" Joshua explodes "you've got to protect yourself and all your hard work"

"I appreciate your concern but it still isn't happening" Skye looks at me and mouths "tell him" she's sussed the gist of our conversation "Joshua listen to me, Skye is worth more than me. Yesterday she learnt she has inherited over two point six billion dollars, add her own personal fortune to that she is worth a billion dollars more than me. Even without the inheritance a pre-nup still wasn't on the cards"

"Holy fucking hell" Joshua says in wonder and whistles bringing an end to the pre-nup discussion.

In the car heading back to Skye's apartment she gives a list of names to Macy to email letting them know of the wedding date and to ask for their availability. When she mentions Mr C I know all of them are friends and close associates.

Watching and listening to Skye since I'd first gotten in the car I saw the super-efficient, tenacious and seemingly spontaneous if not impulsive side to her, I've worked out the "seemingly" is in fact calculated. Skye instinctively knew a good business opportunity when it presented itself and she's quick to act on it. I'm touched and amused by how she apologised when she made a decision and acted on it when it should have been discussed and a joint decision made. She'd done it twice in the last couple of hours, I'm not bothered I'm glad she's taken the initiative normally I would have been pissed at someone making decisions for me or on my behalf. Skye is my equal in all things business and personal. I truly am one lucky son of a bitch to have found my soul mate and to be marrying her. Skye touching my face brings me out of my reverie.

"Are you mad at me?" her voice is soft and husky but marred with wariness so are her eyes. I never want to see that look in her eyes ever again, before answering I look around Macy, Paul and Bruce are gone "we're in the underground garage" Skye says in answer to my unspoken question.

"No baby I'm not mad at you" I kiss her tenderly "I love you so very, very much and I can't wait to marry you"

"I love you too husband to be"

Those words send a thrill through me. "Let's get married this weekend in Vegas" I say impulsively.

"Down boy and no" Skye's throaty chuckle fills the car, she laughs even more when I pout sulkily, I even try the pleading puppy dog eyes "still not working" she chuckles and gets out of the car.

"I seriously need to work on that" I mutter as I follow her to the elevator.

"I'm getting immune" Skye retorts.

"Fuck! What the hell has happened?" Skye's living room looks as if a tornado has hit it.

"I was digging out the designs for the jewellery in readiness for tomorrow's meeting with Matthew and Gerrard. I was in the middle of it when we had to leave to pick you up" Skye keeps walking towards her bedroom to get her overnight bag, she's going to be staying at my place tonight "plus I did some market research at the same time. I've got twenty orders already, how good is that?"

Skye positively glows and she has every right to look pleased with herself. I stop at the mess then I see it's actually organised into specific piles.

"Wow I'm impressed, that's excellent and what a fantastic start to a new venture which hasn't even begun yet" I call out so Skye can hear me.

I sit down and pick up the nearest pile and study the drawings. The majority are rough preliminary sketches, the same idea worked multiple times from differing angles or a common theme running through a completely new layout. I linger over the almost complete and detailed pictures. I work my way through each of the piles.

All of this work and no one will ever see it. It's like stepping into the private and creative part of Skye's mind, seeing her thought process as ideas evolve. I'm fascinated by the series of drawings where it's obvious which one is the initial idea and how Skye has experimented with it using tracing paper until she found the one that worked. I also notice the dates and realize I'm looking at her life's work.

There are stacks of art note books. I pick one up and start looking through it, then another and another. I have no idea how long I've been doing this but my stomach grumbles. I look up to shout Skye when I see her sitting in the arm chair watching me.

"How long have you been sat there?" I say in startled surprised, I hadn't heard her.

"Just over an hour" Skye says looking at her watch.

"Why didn't you say something?"

Skye shrugs "You looked so wrapped up in your thoughts, relaxed and contented working your way through all this. It seemed criminal to disturb you" her smile is sweet "but like your stomach I'm ready to get something to eat. If you want to change your clothes from this weekend are clean and in the closet"

"I'll be two minutes" I say getting up and head for the bedroom.

Gino's is surprisingly busy for a Monday night with quite a few families in and other large groups. Gino welcomes us with his usual enthusiasm and he converses with Skye in Italian as he shows us to our table, I notice how all the men and boys gazes follow Skye as she passes and she doesn't pay one bit of notice. There's one young lad in particular who looks as if he is about to faint, must be a fan.

Skye told me about her morning with Shelley and Simon and how they reacted to her news. Then she gives me a rundown of the activities being planned for the girls in Vegas and how Simon would be joining them, she laughs when I say I would be too as I'm not being separated from her, she informs me that's exactly what Simon had said about me.

"So tell me when I first rang this morning how many people were with you in the boardroom?" Skye says taking a sip of wine.

I chuckle, thinking back to this morning "There were twelve, all department heads. It was the monthly business review and yes they all looked at me as if I had finally lost it" Skye giggles "although that is nothing compared the second time you called" Skye's eyes widen and raises her eyebrows "I was in the final stages of negotiating a fifty million dollar acquisition" Skye chokes on her drink. I pat and rub her back.

"Oh my god" she finally splutters out "I did tell Helena not to disturb you, she said she'd sooner be scowled at than berated by you. So did you scowl at her for interrupting?"

I laugh and shake my head. I also realize that Helena likes Skye enough to tell her something like that. I suppose having Skye in my life has mellowed me. I'm more tolerant of things which would normally have me ripping someone a new asshole. On impulse I pick up her hand and kiss the back of it.

"I want to know more about this jewellery collaboration, how do you see it working?"

Skye's eyes sparkle with enthusiasm and her smile lights up her whole face making her even more stunningly beautiful. I can almost hear her mind racing with ideas.

"Well I'm going to propose a seventy thirty split on the profits. The seventy going to Matthew" fucking hell she's giving it away "Matthew is going to be doing all of the hard work so he deserves the lions share" her voice is soft with admonishment at my reaction "my bit is already done. He's the one that has to work out how to get my drawings into the finished product then he has to make them. The poor guy is going to be working flat out"

Skye is right, I just thought about the money. I nod to show I understand.

"Anyway I'm thinking high end expensive range made from platinum, twenty four carat gold and precious stones that my clients will buy without batting an eyelid or balking at the price. Then a cheaper version made from silver, nine carat gold, semi-precious stones and in a price range which will be affordable for the majority of the fans and I've been toying with the idea of a middle range, you know a combination of the high and low end. Obviously all ranges will be available to the fans but there will be a cheaper option available for the majority of the pieces. We will have links from my website and Gerrard's to the new range, orders can be placed online. We'll use my name as the brand and to promote the range to pull the orders in, obviously Matthew and the shop will have credit placement and joint copyright for the designs. I'm willing to put up the bulk of the money to fund the project if it's needed" Skye looks at me and biting her lower lip "that's all I've come up with, can you think of anything I've missed?"

A jolt of surprise goes through me. I hadn't expected Skye to ask for my input and I feel honored. "I have nothing to add, it's obvious you have given this a lot of thought"

Skye shifts uncomfortably in her chair then looks at me sheepishly. "Not really" now that does surprise me and my eyebrows rise, a blush spreads across Skye's cheeks "I only thought about it in between making calls to my clients and sorting through all my artwork this afternoon" she admits.

Fuck me, that's funny; I laugh out loud causing other diners to turn and look in our direction. "You put me to shame baby. It would have taken me days to get to that point. I think Gerrard will snap your hand off when you put the proposal to them"

Our food arrives and we tuck in. We eat in companionable silence, enjoying the food, wine and each other's presence, neither of us feeling the need to fill the quietness. I start to think about tomorrow and the wedding planning Skye will be starting.

The thought of my mother and her likely behaviour makes me uneasy mainly for Skye. This is Skye's day and I'm damned fucking well determined my mother will not railroad Skye into things she doesn't want.

"Skye" she looks up with a mouthful of spaghetti hanging out of her mouth, fuck she looks sexy even like that. Skye bit into the pasta and it drops to her plate "don't let my mother railroad you and takeover when you meet with her tomorrow. I know she will and I can tell her not to say a word about anything and she is to do exactly as you say"

Skye smiles ruefully "And spoil all her fun" what in the hell does she mean by that? The thought races through my mind but I refrain from airing it "don't worry I know exactly how to keep your mother busy. I'm taking a leaf out of Shelley's book" now I'm really confused and my face obviously shows it.

"Think about it, we're getting married in the grounds right" I nod "so who better to give the odious task of sorting all that out. Marquee, tables, chairs, table decorations, catering, invitations and replies, music and evening entertainment want me to carry on" Skye smiles wickedly, oh she's sneaky, I smile and shake my head "the important things are already taken care of, dress, rings and color scheme your mother can do the rest"

I gape at her in wonder "When did you think of all that?"

"Today at Shelley's, she was telling me about Phil's mother. Brenda sounds a lot like yours, you know give her an inch and she'll grab a mile" I chuckle at the over exaggerated analogy, but it's very apt "I asked Shelley how she handled Brenda and that's what she did. By the way Shelley is going to be staying the night before the wedding we're going to have a girlie pamper afternoon and night. She doesn't want to stay at Phil's parents as Brenda is likely to stress the crap out of her. Then we'll get hair and makeup done in the morning so we arrive just in time to get dressed before the ceremony. Oh yes and Simon is giving Shelley away, how cool is that" Skye finishes in a flurry, her smile slips to a frown as she worries her bottom lip with her teeth.

"What's the matter?" I ask softly

"I've done it again barrelled ahead and arranged something without checking you're okay with it first" Skye snorts "Shelley pointed it out to me this morning and I've just remembered I said if you didn't like it you could always stay at your place"

"Fuck no, hell will freeze over before that happens" I bark out.

"Funny Shelley said the same thing but not phrased that way" Skye sighs "I'm sorry I don't mean to be insensitive I just" she sighs again "I just forget sometimes"

I pick up her hand and kiss it "Skye you have been alone for a long time and you are an independent woman. Don't be so hard on yourself, we will both screw up from time to time and we'll learn to deal with it. We will only have a problem if I'd arranged something as well and hadn't consulted you either. As it happens I haven't so" I put on an effeminate voice "invite Simon over and all us girls can get pampered together"

Skye relaxes and laughs hard it's her turn to draw attention to us.

"Excuse me Miss Darcy"

We both look up to see a pimply teenager standing just off from our table. It's the young lad I noticed on the way to our table, the one that looked as if he was about to faint having seen Skye. He has geek written all over him, thin, horn rimmed glasses, pale skin although his face is bright red making his pimples stand out more.

"Sorry to bother you" the kid looks at me warily. Turning back to Skye he holds out a pen and piece of paper, they shake terribly in his hands "could I have your autograph. I'm a huge fan of your work. I even went to Vegas to see you" he blushes even more, Skye takes the offered pen and paper "but I didn't due to the amount of people that turned up"

"What's your name?" Skye gives him her brain frying megawatt smile if it's at all possible his cheeks turn even redder.

"John" he stutters out "wow my friends are not going to believe I've met you here of all places"

"Well let's give them some more proof have you got your phone?"

Nodding and without a word John hands over his phone, Skye stands and gives the phone to me. "Take some pictures" she says wrapping her arms around John's shoulders.

The kid is about to combust. I take a couple of photos then Skye plants a kiss on his cheek I capture it as well. When I hand him his phone back he looks as if he's died and gone to heaven, he holds his cheek where Skye has kissed him. I doubt he'll be having a wash any time soon.

"Thank you Mr Blake sir" he holds up his phone, he shocks the shit out of me but he is a fan so of course he'll know who I am. Holding both the phone and autographed paper as if they are priceless treasures, which I suppose they are to him, he looks at Skye "thanks Miss Darcy you've made my night. Congratulations on your engagement" he nods his head in my direction and practically runs back to his table where his parents and siblings sit gawping at us.

"Time to go I think" I say pulling out my wallet and signal for the bill.

As we climb in the car a thought strikes me. Skye automatically sits in my lap and I fasten us in. "Listen, how about from tomorrow I move into yours. It makes sense because you kind of work from home and you would have more stuff to move if you came to mine. What do you think?"

Skye nods and turns to look at Bruce. "Are you okay with that Bruce?"

A ghost of a smile appears on his lips then he schools his expression as his eyes flick to mine then back at Skye. "Yes ma'am"

"Sure okay why not" huh well that was easy. "what you thought I would want to check with Macy and Paul?" I nod, Skye grins "beat you to it. I asked them this morning on the way to Shelley's"

Skye riddles around on my lap getting her hand in her jeans pocket. The movement of her grinding has me hard in seconds.

"Careful baby" I murmur in her ear she stills instantly and looks puzzled at me. I flex my hips and a salacious smile spreads across her face, she pulls her hand out of her pocket.

"Here you go" she holds up a key.

"What a perfect way to end a perfect day" I say as I take the offered key.

"Oh I can think of an even better one" Skye murmurs as she grinds her ass into me.

Chapter Twenty Four

SKYE

"Everyone is aboard sir" Bruce says as we enter the private section of the runway and the car slows.

"I can't believe we're late" I grumble.

Clayton had a last minute business call to take just as we were about to leave the apartment and he needed to log in to deal with it.

"We are not late, we fly out at noon" he looks at his watch "it is now fifteen minutes to, besides it's my plane and I have every right to play the pretentious owner who doesn't slum it with the lower classes" Clayton puts on a fake posh accent making me laugh and lifting the grumpy mood I've been in.

Clayton is in a playful mood and he has been all morning in fact he has since he moved in with me. On Tuesday night he turned up with a huge bouquet of Calla Lilies along with a number of suitcases. As I helped him unpack he told me his mother had rung him and by the sound of it she called him as soon as she'd left me.

Stephanie is over the moon to be doing the bulk of the work and given free reign. I'd given her samples of the blue swatches so she can match everything.

The ceremony is going to be family and close friends, that still tally's one hundred guests and as expected practically three quarters of them are Clayton's side. Clayton let slip he halved Stephanie's original list and that half will be coming to the reception.

I told Matthew at the end of our meeting on Tuesday about the wedding date just to give him a timeframe to work to for our rings but he said the wedding bands and my earrings would be ready by Thursday of next week. All I have to do now is make the cake. I did the girlie thing on Wednesday and Thursday and searched the internet looking at wedding cakes getting ideas. I asked Clayton if he had any preference on the style of cake to which he snorted "Don't be silly."

I also spoke with Nessa and as I thought she isn't allowed to fly, on doctors' orders she has cancelled coming over for Shelley's wedding next week. I really want her and Chuck to be part of the ceremony so we talked about a live video feed. Clayton loves the idea and is getting his IT man on the case.

The car stopped, Paul and Bruce get out. Macy is already on the plane, she suggested co-ordinating the arrivals to the VIP area and liaise with the crew, Paul and Bruce about status and our ETA when Clayton had to take his call it's a plan that worked well. I know Macy impresses the socks off Clayton. Although we haven't discussed it nor had we said anything to the three of them but already they are answering to both of us.

Clayton and I are also following the new security protocol measures Paul and Bruce advised. We are following one right now which is we don't get out of a vehicle until they open the door, giving them chance to scan the surrounding areas. Bruce opens the door and we climb out, both Paul and Bruce flank us on the short walk to the plane steps then return to collect our luggage as we head up the steps.

The pilot meets us at the top and Clayton greets him warmly. Clive, I remember his name and use it he seems pleased and taken aback. When we enter Phil gets up and comes to greet us, again thanking Clayton for the use of the plane. We're introduced to his parents and the rest of his family, although I've known Phil for years this is the first time I've met them, all express their gratitude. Clayton waves them off and we take our seats, buckling in ready for take-off.

Once in the air the cabin crew come round with drinks and people start to move around. Don, Phil's dad comes and sits next to us. "I really can't thank you enough Mr Blake for doing this for Phil and Shelley"

"Please call me Clayton and it's my pleasure, they are Skye's best friends it's the least I can do"

Clayton brings my hand to his lips and kisses it. From where I'm sitting I can see Pete and Caroline. It appears they are having an argument. Caroline is speaking low and whatever she is saying I know it has something to do with Clayton and me because of the way she is gesturing in our direction with her head and hands. Pete has a hard set look on his face and keeps shaking his head no. Taking a guess she wants to come over and Pete doesn't.

"Whatever Skye chooses to do"

Clayton saying my name brings my attention back to him and Don. "Sorry what was that?"

"Don was asking which of the activities I'll be doing this weekend"

When Shelley and Phil circulated the boys and girls activity lists earlier in the week Clayton didn't bother looking at it saying "Baby there is no point in me looking at them because I'll be doing whatever it is you're doing"

I look at Don "That includes the girlie pampering in the spa so he'll be buffed, polished and having his bikini wax done along with Simon" I deadpan.

Don roars laughing and slaps his thigh. "Well with such a beautiful fiancée I don't blame you. I understand Vegas is where you proposed"

I leave it to Clayton to fill Don in on the details. I excuse myself and go to sit with Shelley, who is with Brenda and a couple of other women who turn out to be Brenda's daughter-in-laws. I listen to them gush about the luxury of the plane and the VIP treatment at the airport. It's the first time for all of them being on a private plane, it suddenly dawns on me I can afford to buy my own plane now that I have my inheritance money. You could before you numpty, well yeah but I don't have to worry about the cost of keeping it and the flight crew now besides I don't need to buy a plane this one will be mine anyway when I get married to Clayton. Holy crap we are mega, mega rich. It finally hits home just how rich we are. I feel queasy.

To distract myself I focus on the women around me. I answer their questions about how I met Clayton, what I did for a living, how Shelley and I met and any personal intrusive questions either I deflect them or Shelley does.

"So what activities are you ladies doing?" I ask and the diversionary tactic works. Shelley gives me a knowing smile and I wink at her.

When the focus of attention isn't on me Shelley leans over and murmurs "They've been arguing the whole time" I look at her trying to fathom who she's on about. Shelley subtly inclines her head in Pete and Caroline's direction. "As soon as they got in the VIP lounge it started. Simon tried to get close enough to find out what they were saying but they moved away if anyone got too close"

"I noticed. My money is on it has something to do with me and Clayton. Caroline was gesturing towards us before"

Abruptly Caroline stands up then bends down pointing a finger in Pete's face. I can only see his face and it's full of anger, his response is spoken through gritted teeth. Caroline straightens. Shelley and I watch as she walks down the aisle and sits next to Clayton, putting her hand on his arm she leans forward making sure her tits brush against him.

"And so it begins" I murmur through a long sigh.

Shelley looks at me sympathetically. I feel sick as I watch Caroline fawn all over Clayton. I try to read his body language but he gives nothing away because he is holding himself so still. Suddenly a scowl mars Clayton's features and I know instantly he doesn't like what Caroline is saying. I look at Don; he has the same expression, interesting. Clayton stands and speaks to Caroline whatever he's saying it shocks her. He might as well have slapped her, such is her startled surprise. Don stands as well and both men leave Caroline where she is without a second glance. Clayton comes straight to me. I stand so he can sit in my seat. Without sitting down properly he is already pulling me to him.

"Fucking cheeky bitch" Clayton mutters loud enough for Shelley and me to hear.

"What did she say?" Shelley whispers.

"Later" I say in a low voice because Brenda and everyone else is watching and listening, plus none of them have gotten over their surprise Clayton has me sat on his lap.

"Ladies" Clayton turns his panty combusting megawatt smile on them and they have no chance of escape "what are you looking forward to most this weekend?"

I sit back and watch as Clayton works his magic and charms the lot of them.

An hour or so later when everyone's attention is elsewhere Shelley comes over and sits next to Simon; as soon as our conversation is finished she looks at Clayton and murmurs "The suspense is killing me Clayton. Details, spill, now" making Clayton chuckle "don't make me use the pregnant lady card on you" she scowls to show she means business.

"Baby girl you use it all the time why should he be any different" Simon says giving his best diva arm wave.

"My plane, mega rich, my plane, best friends fiancée, my plane, good looking, did I mention my plane" Clayton deadpans making us all laugh "First of all she thanked me for the use of the plane but said in such a way it implied I had done it all for her and not you and Phil"

"Cheeky bitch" Simon and Shelley say indignantly together.

"Oh it gets better. She then asked me which of the lame activities was I going to be doing and before I could answer she ridiculed each one, boys and girls. Then she insinuated she could show me a far better time if I stuck with her"

"Fucking bitch" Simon hisses.

Shelley looks as sick as I feel at the revelation. I knew Caroline at some point during the weekend would make a play for Clayton but I never dreamed she would start so early and to make such a bold move in front of Don. I barely contain the shudder at the cold dread I feel seeping into my bones.

"What did you say to her? I hope you put the bitch down" Simon says vehemently.

"I told her if she thought the whole weekend was so fucking lame then why the fuck did she not bother to un-invite herself and if she was intent on showing someone a good time it should be her fucking boyfriend and not me"

All my worries disappear and warmth floods through me chasing away all traces of coldness. Clayton has shown the contempt he has for her to her face and if Caroline continues to persist in pursuing him Clayton will slap her down harder. I suddenly realize this is what Pete and Caroline have been arguing about. Pete knew what kind of man Clayton is and he was trying to stop Caroline making a fool out of herself only she couldn't see it and if she did she's refusing to acknowledge it.

"You do realize she is not going to stop" I say to Clayton "she will get worse"

"How do you know?" Simon asks softly.

"She's desperate and desperate people do things they wouldn't normally do, crazy things, bunny boiler almost. I bet that's what Caroline and Pete have been arguing about. She's probably been coming up with all sorts of plots to get close to you and Pete wants no part of it" I can see my friends concern in their eyes "look I'm not worried" I take hold of Clayton's hand "you have just put paid to any I had. I don't think you realize how determined and relentless Caroline is, she's on par with Maxine maybe worse" I can see from Clayton's expression he doesn't remember Maxine.

"Who the hell is Maxine?" hisses Simon.

"The fucking bunny boiler on the yacht" I use Clayton's words, the one's he used when I first arrived on the yacht in Italy. Clayton's eyes widen and his mouth pops open when he remembers who I'm referring to.

"Aw fuck no" Clayton barks out causing most conversations to stop and people look our way.

I remind Shelley and Simon of Maxine's antics until her husband turned up. "So you see Caroline is doing these things in front of Pete that's what makes me think she will be worse than Maxine" I finish.

"You're worried about me based on past experience aren't you?" It makes my heart ache the look Clayton gives me. I nod.

"She will drive you bat shit crazy and I don't want her spoiling the weekend for you"

"You won't let her" Clayton says kissing the back of my hand. He says it with such conviction and confidence it makes me feel ten feet tall. He believes in me and my ability to pull him out of any dark place she sends him to. I can get creative. I hug myself as salacious thoughts fire up my imagination.

"No I won't" I purr and Clayton's eyes heat in response.

"Oh my it's getting hot in here" Simon says fanning himself, he then touches my arm and makes a sizzling sound "damn baby girl get any hotter you'll be smoking" we all laugh breaking the mood and tension.

"I propose a game for this weekend" Shelley says clapping her hands "Slap Down Catty Bitch, winner for the best slap down gets a prize" she frowns "I'll think of something"

Phil comes over to join us. Shelley fills him in on what has happened with Caroline. He has the same response as the rest of us. "That also explains Dad's pissed off mood. I thought you had upset him Clayton so I apologise. I should have known better"

We talk about the coming weekend. The boys are indeed visiting some strip clubs and Phil tries to talk Clayton into going along. Clayton flatly refuses.

"I've been spoilt because of Skye, why would I pay to see something fake and second rate when I have the premier class real deal here" Clayton pats my knee and I flush with pride and embarrassment. When Phil shouts Clayton's reply to the rest of the men and the responding laughter along with "can't argue with that" comments I wish for the floor to open up.

"Catty Bitch looks as if she's swallowed a wasp" Simon says with gleeful delight.

I notice Pete is sat with the rest of the men and joins in the banter and laughter. Interesting, he seems to be distancing himself.

The captain's voice comes over the speakers informing us of our decent and instructs everyone back to their seats and buckle in. When I'm settled in my seat Clayton takes my hand and squeezes.

"I promise not to let her get to me" Clayton says in a low voice, his face is set with determination. Somehow I know he will find it difficult to keep his promise but I don't say anything. I squeeze his hand and smile.

As we disembark there are squeals of delight from some of the women when they spot the fleet of limousines waiting for us. Macy helps Shelley organise everyone and their luggage into the vehicles.

Clayton and I have our own SUV. Paul and Bruce look impressive and imposing standing next to it in their dark suits and sunglass as they constantly scan the surroundings. It's also the first time the party notice them. I hear Shelley explain who they are which earns them a few furtive glances.

When we arrive at the hotel Marco and Vinny are waiting for us along with a fleet of bell boys.

"Skye, Clayton so lovely to see you again and so soon" Marco and Vinny greet us warmly.

Simon, Shelley and Phil come over and they are greeted in the same vain. Vinny fusses over Shelley telling her to call on him personally if there is anything she needs over the weekend.

"We would like to invite your party to have dinner with us" Marco says to Shelley and Phil "I know you have the tutorials starting at eight so we thought meet at six thirty to sit down to eat at seven"

Thrilled with the dinner invite Shelley and Phil went off to tell the others and when they find out it is with the hotel owners everyone says yes, no surprise there.

"Skye" Vinny touches my arm to get my attention as I'm fascinated watching the bell boys unload the luggage with military precision "I know it's not going to be as manic like the last time you were here but I would like you to know should you need it the hotel security staff are at your disposal"

"Thank you that's very thoughtful and kind of you" I'm genuinely touched.

I signal to Paul and Bruce to come over, I introduce them to Vinny who remembered them from last time. I explain the offer Vinny has made. Paul takes the lead.

"Thank you sir, I would like to meet with your head of security and brief him. Just in case speculation ignites the media frenzy like last time" Paul looks at me then Clayton.

"Good call" Clayton says and I nod my agreement.

"Is there something we should be aware of?" Marco asks speculative curiosity written all over his and Vinny's faces.

"We've set a date for the wedding" both men beam at us "you'll be getting your invite by the end of next week. It's at the end of October, we only decided a few days ago so the news hasn't hit the mainstream yet" I say smiling.

"So naturally if it becomes known you are both in Vegas two add two becomes five" Vinny says and snaps his fingers. A young man in a very expensive silk suit and slicked back hair steps forward "please take Mr Boyd to see Charles Spence" Paul murmurs ma'am, sir and left "now let's get you both settled into your suite" Vinny gives a dramatic sweep of his arm towards the hotels entrance.

Clayton wolf whistles as I walk into the living room. I'm wearing one of Shelley's creations. The cocktail dress is royal blue raw silk, strapless with a corseted bodice. The skirt comes to mid-thigh but it's covered in varying lengths of tiny bead strings which reach just above my knees so when I walk the whole skirt swishes and twinkles. My hair is up in a messy bun, I have that much hair it doesn't look like a bun but I don't care I have the look I want. I do a twirl when Clayton signals.

"You look dazzling baby"

He kisses my cheek so as not to smudge my lipstick.

"Thank you. You don't look bad yourself"

In fact he looks scrumptious in the black suit jacket and trousers, white dress shirt open at the throat. His dark brown shoulder length wavy hair is still damp from the shower. He holds out his arm.

"Shall we my lady?" he gives a slight bow of his head.

"Certainly kind sir" I take his arm and we head out.

Paul and Bruce shadow us to the restaurant. We get stopped, well I get stopped a couple of times en-route and asked for autographs and I pose for photos whilst Clayton waits patiently. It dawns on me he's never once complained about complete strangers talking to me as if they are lifelong friends. It freaked me out when it first happened nearly six years ago. I hadn't realized the size of the following I had but again that's my naivety kicking in. If I look at it logically the companies I did work for sold out of the products the minute they are released even today demand is still high for them and I receive hefty royalty payments, so that in itself should give me a big fat clue.

As we walk through the restaurant to meet our party a huge excited shout went up, a group of guys recognise me and call my name, six of them descend on us. In an instant Paul, Bruce and hotel security surround me and Clayton. The guys apologise for startling me and they're so polite and sweet it's hard to say no to them when they ask for photos and autographs. I pose for individual and group photos they even get Clayton to pose for a few, turns out most of them attended the Fantasy and Sci Fi convention and were gutted when they couldn't get to see me at the meet and greets or the Q&A. They had returned this weekend for a bachelor party, meeting me is the icing on the cake for them, so they tell me. Needless to say we are the last to arrive at our table.

Phil's family are in awe of me as I sit next to Shelley, she leans over and murmurs "They didn't realize just how famous you are as an artist"

"They think I hit the news because I got engaged to a billionaire" I chuckle.

Shelley giggles and nods "Also Catty Bitch tried to make everyone believe you'd been stopped purely because they had mistaken you for someone else. Ged" Shelley nods in the direction of Phil's brother "looked at her as if she was from another planet and said "funny how they knew Skye's name and called out to her, that doesn't sound like mistaken identity to me, does it to anyone else?" then Marco and Vinny told everyone of the chaos you caused that wasn't reported on the news. Me, Phil, Macy and Simon helped as well"

We both snigger like pre-teens when she describes the various reactions the family had to the stories. The waiter came to take everyone's order, when he got to me I recognised him as one of the helpers from the meet and greets.

"Hey Bradley good to see again" I smile at him.

Bradley blushes and beams at me pleased that I remembered him. "Hello Miss Darcy, good to see you and you Mr Blake" he says to Clayton respectfully.

Clayton smiles and nods at him. After Bradley has taken our order and moved further down the table Clayton murmurs in my ear "You really made his day by remembering him"

"At least I know he's not going to spit in my food" Clayton screws his face up in a yuk expression making me laugh "I watch those behind the scenes and caught on camera TV shows" I wink at him making him laugh.

"You're wicked" Clayton leans in and kisses me, his hand stroking my knee and thigh.

"Behave" I murmur against his lips but feeling a thrill at the same time.

"Do I have to?" Clayton's low voice rumbles.

I break the kiss conscious of the others watching us, I mouth "no". Clayton's salacious smile and roaming hand has me shivering with anticipation.

Marco and Vinny are the genial hosts, they sit opposite me and I get them to regale stories of some of the unbelievable things that take place in the hotel and what guests get up to. I love hearing these kinds of tales, as coffee is being served Caroline who's sat further down the table calls out to Marco and Vinny to get their attention.

"Who is the richest person you've had here at the hotel?" Caroline asks with a smarmy smile.

Where the hell is she going with this? I glance around the table to see I'm not the only one with a WTF expression.

"Well it's difficult to answer" Marco says looking taken aback "we have guests from the film and music industries, business mogul's" his eyes flick to Clayton "along with foreign dignitaries"

"Who's the richest person you know Clayton?" Caroline says the smarmy smile is wider or is she hoping for alluring either way she's just shown her real reason for asking her question to Marco.

"Skye" five voices chorus loud and clear, shocking the crap out of me and Caroline's jaw hits the table.

Clayton, Macy, Simon, Shelley and Phil all look and smile smugly at each other then turn and smile ruefully at me, daring me to say differently or deny it. Aww crap everyone else is staring open mouthed, what the hell, it's going to get out sooner rather than later.

I pick up my wine glass raise it and salute Caroline, her eyes narrow. Ha! The bitch didn't like that. I look at Clayton. "So darling how does it feel not to be the richest person you know?" I say in a clear calm voice and smile sweetly.

Clayton bursts out laughing throwing his head back and slaps the table; my friends all join him much to the confused amusement of everyone else except Caroline. She's frowning and talking fast in Pete's ear, he appears to be completely ignoring her either that or he's suddenly become deaf.

"Ladies and gentlemen" Vinny calls out to get everyone's attention "it is time for those of you who are going to have the tutorials. This is Amanda and she will be taking care of you, please follow her and she'll take you to the VIP area"

With the exception of four people, Pete and Caroline being two of the four, everyone else stands up. I think those remaining seated realize it will be boring on their own so they stand to join the party. I notice Caroline is the last to stand and she only does that because Pete has left her sat on her own and doesn't give her a second glance or thought.

There are other people in the VIP area after a few minutes I realize these are the high rollers. Amanda explains which tables have been set up for the tutorials and for the novices whilst we are learning the house will give us chips to play with; when we feel ready to play properly then we will move to the other tables and use our own money.

Earlier I had Marco bring me bundles of high value chips to the suite which I have in my purse and I'm going to give them to my friends.

"Shelley, Simon and Macy can I have a word before we start" the three of them nod and follow me to an area of the room where no-one is likely to overhear me. I open my purse "hold out your hands" they each comply with a puzzled look. I drop a rolled bungle of chips in each open hand "this is my gift to each of you, have fun this weekend"

Open mouthed and speechless, I enjoy their reaction to my gift. It isn't often I can do this to them. Shelley steps forward and hugs me followed by Macy and Simon. In the group hug I savor the silent thanks and gratitude. None of them say I shouldn't have or they couldn't accept it as they knew me well enough to know it would hurt and offend me.

"Come on let's go and learn how to lose it all" I say making them chuckle as we break apart.

I head back to Clayton and he wraps me in his arms and kisses me tenderly. "That was beautiful to watch" he murmurs.

Not once has he asked me about the money after Marco left and I didn't volunteer any information for some reason I didn't feel like justifying my actions. Maybe I was testing him to see if he would try and dictate what I should or couldn't do. Maybe I was unconsciously trying to make a statement like it's my money I can do as I please.

Was I trying to prove to myself I still had my independence? I mentally slap myself I'm being childish and petty. If I continue to think like this I might as well shove a pre-nup under Clayton's nose right now. I would be the one destroying our relationship if I carry on behaving like this.

"Skye baby are you okay?" Clayton's low smooth raspy voice breaks through my mental tirade.

Shit, I'm such an idiot. This fabulous Adonis before me only wants my love and happiness. He would never impose his will, command or demand anything of me. He respects me too much and I will go as far to say he sees me as his equal. The realization hits me like a bolt of lightning, everything he did and said showed me time and time again we are equal on every level of our relationship. He already knew this and here I am playing catch up again. God! I love this man.

"Skye, talk to me baby" concern roils off Clayton.

Reaching up I touch his face and smile hoping the love I have for him shows in my eyes and face. "I had another epiphany" I whisper "thank you for being you. I love you so much" I kiss him.

His arms tighten and pull me closer. I relax and melt into him. "Do you want to share?"

"Later, now I want to learn how to lose money" Clayton chuckles "go have fun Mr High Roller and win a fortune to make up for my losses" I push him in the direction of the tables, not that I can move him it's like pushing at a brick wall. I walk over to the black jack table and join Simon and Macy.

Over the next hour I also have tutorials in roulette and craps. I can feel Clayton watching me and frequently when I look up he is staring, we would smile or wink in Clayton's case he does both. I also notice Caroline circling and trying to get close to Clayton at every opportunity. I also know Clayton is aware of this because he moves at the first chance he gets or he would out maneuver her.

I'm playing black jack with Shelley and Macy. Simon has not long left the table as he'd been losing and decided to try his luck on another table. I really enjoy this game probably because I'm on a winning streak. Someone takes the available seat next to me, I don't look I'm too busy concentrating on the cards being dealt. I yelp at a sudden sharp pain in my ankle and glare at Shelley. She ignores my glare and widens her eyes subtly nodding her head in the direction of the person at the other side of me. Dread pools in the pit of my stomach as I know it's going to be someone I won't be pleased to see. Turning back to my cards and using my peripheral vision I see its Pete. Fucking great and crap on a cracker!

The hand finishes and I'm debating whether to get up and leave or stay. Why should I leave, I'm enjoying myself. Looking for Clayton I see him at the craps table and he's throwing the dice. Caroline is working her way to get next to him. The look on her face is pure predatory. Ignore her I tell myself, Clayton will slap her down. Shelley and Macy stand up.

"We're going to play craps, want to join us?" says Macy.

I know they are giving me an out to get away with dignity "No thanks I'm going to play a little longer here" their eyes flick to Pete then back at me "you go ahead" then I mouth "I'm okay, go" they leave reluctantly.

"Having a good night" Pete asks indicating to the stack of chips in front of me.

"Beginners luck" I say nonchalantly as I add more chips to the stacks which the dealer pushes towards me, then selecting the chips to place my bet. Be civil I tell myself "how about you?"

"Just about breaking even"

He went quiet and I don't feel like small talk or making polite conversation. We play a couple of games—I won, he lost—before he next spoke.

"I hear Lord Belling passed away recently" he states matter of fact and looks sideways at me watching my reaction.

I find it interesting he hasn't made the sentence personal and refrained from saying grandfather. If he's disappointed that he got no reaction at all from me he doesn't show it. However I startle him, he visibly jolts at my reply.

"I know" my voice monotone.

Glancing in Clayton's direction at the craps table I see Caroline has achieved her goal and is standing next to him. Pete clears his throat, I look at him. I can see he is curious as to how I know about my grandfather's death, it's written all over his face. I'm not going to volunteer the information. We play another game in silence, we both win.

"I also heard the family tried to contest the Will but were warned they would forfeit what the old goat had left them" again he's watching me closely.

I already know this because Mr Hopkirk gave me a copy of the Will and I'd read through it, plus I went through it with my lawyer just to make sure I understood the implications correctly of the conditions my grandfather set for the other beneficiaries. I didn't know they attempted to contest it but that doesn't surprise me, however I also know the Will, court and probate records had been sealed by the probate judge.

"I bet they did" I say with no emotion or infliction in my voice. He's fishing, whoever his source of information is knew enough about the family but not all the details.

"Yeah apparently Lord Belling left three quarters of his fortune to someone else but the identity of the beneficiary is being kept secret"

Okay now curiosity is getting the better of me. I want to know who his source is. Time to show some interest and emotion, twisting so I face him I raise my eyebrows and feigned surprise.

"Really, and you know all this, how?"

Pete grins, he had me or so he thinks. "My uncle he knows someone who works for the law firm that handled all of Lord Belling's affairs, plus he's friends with some of the family"

"And they have no idea who the beneficiary is" I want to make sure I heard him right.

"No idea" he nods.

I turn back to the croupier and indicate to them to deal. It's clear to me the family are keeping my identity a secret. They obviously don't want the publicity. I'm famous, well news worthy and the last thing they would want is to admit they had done nothing to help me when I got kicked out and disowned by my grandfather, if the story ever got out.

I doubt Pete's uncle got all the information from his law firm contact it's possible they had just confirmed details but didn't that contravene client confidentiality? I make a mental note to check with my lawyer. I rack my brain trying to remember Pete's uncle and who in the family he would be friends with, I draw a blank and decide not to waste any more energy on it.

I look over at Clayton again. He's scowling at Caroline who is trying her damnedest to flirt. Back off bitch my inner goddess snarls. I place my bet not really concentrating on the cards.

"I thought Clayton was a billionaire" says Pete changing the subject.

"He is" I emphasise the word is.

Pete looks puzzled "It's just at dinner Clayton and the others said you were the richest person he knew"

"I am" I state matter of fact.

Pete looks even more confused. I lost, time to leave. Standing up I toss a chip to the croupier and put the rest in my purse then turn to Pete. "My grandfather died two weeks ago. I'm now richer than Clayton, do the math"

Not waiting for his reaction I walk away and head for the craps table Clayton is playing at. As I approach Clayton is getting ready to roll the dice. Caroline sees me and gives me an evil smile. She leans forward into Clayton and grabs his forearm pulling his fisted hand with the dice toward her, Clayton taken by complete surprise doesn't resist. Caroline's smile turns lecherous as she raises his hand to her mouth and runs her tongue over his closed fingers then kisses them.

"For luck" I see her mouth.

Clayton shudders and looking mortified he puts the dice down on the table, his head snaps up to look straight at me. With panic and horror on his face he pushes his way out of the gathered crowd, who all witnessed Caroline's piss poor attempt at seduction, and walks away from me. I feel a knife slice through my heart. I follow him.

Caroline is looking at Clayton's retreating back with embarrassment and humiliation on her face. What did she expect the silly cow. As I pass I keep my expression blank, I seriously want to punch the fucking bitch, hard, not because I'm hurt and angry but for upsetting Clayton, he will be hurting now. A hushed quiet comes over the table, people are doing the back and forth head thing as if watching a tennis match between me and Caroline.

My eyes lock on Caroline and I maintain eye contact, she tries to look smug and defiant but under my scrutiny and glare it doesn't last long she visibly withers and drops her head.

I find Clayton in the corridor leading to the restrooms. Bruce stands quietly watching Clayton as he paces. Clayton's hands clench and unclench a sure sign he is barely containing his anger. He looks up suddenly sensing my presence. I walk up to him. Clayton holds his hand up in the universal stop sign.

"Don't baby, I feel" he pauses looking stricken "I feel" he tries again.

"Contaminated" I offer, he drops his head and nods. I open my purse and pull out a travel sized anti-bacterial hand cleanser "hold out your hands" he complies and I squirt both hands, he rubs them together "it kills ninety nine point nine percent of germs" I say as I put the bottle back in my purse "does that make it feel better?" I watch him closely, he is still agitated.

"A bit" he says running his hands through his hair and starts pacing again.

He's heading for a dark place. I need to do something and fast, an idea comes to me. "Clayton, look at me" I command softly. He stops and lifts his head. His usually beautiful dark blue eyes are haunted. I have to get him back "come with me" I incline my head in the direction I want him to follow.

I don't reach out to touch him it will be too damaging for both of us. Instinctively I know he has to touch me in his own time and he has to need to do it, need not want, that is crucial.

By the time I get to the VIP room Clayton is walking beside me, close but not touching. Simon sees us and heads over. I subtly shake my head stopping him. He nods his understanding and no-one else approaches us. I don't see Caroline or Pete thank god.

We reach our suite, Clayton went in first and I hang back to speak to Paul and Bruce.

"I'm sorry ma'am I should have done something. I could see she was bothering him. I understand if you are angry with me" says Bruce

Bruce looks as if he really wants to make amends for his lack of action and my heart goes out to him. Instead I put my hand on his arm and squeeze gently. "I'm not angry with you Bruce there is nothing you could have done. Clayton obviously thought he could handle the situation himself. If you had intervened it would have drawn unnecessary attention. Now I'm going to sort my man out and bring him back from the dark place he is in no thanks to that bitch. However I intend to go back out and gamble some more in about an hour, hour and a half tops" I look at both men before me. Bruce looks to be back to his normal self "please make sure no-one disturbs us"

"Yes ma'am" both chorus "thank you" Bruce adds softly. I nod acknowledging his sincere thanks.

I enter the suite to see Clayton stood at the bar as he throws back his drink and pours himself another generous one. His whole body is tense; I can see it vibrating with anger and self-loathing. He doesn't look at me. I don't think he can bring himself to look at me. I feel a pang of hurt, it hits like being kicked in the stomach. I want to scream, shout and throw things at Caroline and it takes all I have to control the urge. I shove my feelings aside this is about Clayton not me, time to get changed, time for action.

"I'll be back in a few minutes" I say heading for the bedroom.

CLAYTON

I savor the burn of the brandy as it works its way down my throat to my gut. Fuck! I want to hit something or someone badly. Rip, shred, tear apart with my bare hands. Christ I would peel off my own skin if I could. I feel dirty, contaminated is the word Skye used it's very apt, even now after using the antibacterial hand lotion I still feel… My body shudders in revulsion as it recalls the feel of Caroline's tongue and lips on my hand. I'd chop the fucker off if it got rid of this horrid feeling but I know it wouldn't do any good, the contamination is under my skin and coursing through my blood making me itch inside and out.

I want nothing more than to hold Skye but if I do I will contaminate her. I don't want to defile someone so precious to me or the thing we have that is so pure. Fuck! I feel sick at the bizarre thoughts hammering around in my head. Shit… what must Skye be thinking and feeling? She had seen the whole god damn thing. I still feel the horror at seeing her stood at the end of the table and like a fucking coward I walked away. I should have called the manipulative bitch out in front of everyone.

I knock back my drink, as I pour another one I hear Skye come in. I can't bring myself to look at her beautiful face. Coward.

"I'll be back in a few minutes" her soft sultry voice washes over me, caressing and soothing my itchy skin.

I close my eyes as I listen to her retreating footsteps. You're a fucking coward Blake, that's what you are. You couldn't look at the woman you love and worship in the eye. I admit it; I don't want to look into her loving yellow green eyes to see the pain and hurt I've caused her. It will kill me.

Stop being a fucking shit and man up go and explain yourself, but Skye saw everything she knew I wasn't at fault, I try to reason.

Skye told you, no warned you to be on your guard when Caroline is around and you thought she was exaggerating, a little paranoid even but oh no being the egotistical bastard that you are you thought you knew better, yeah right. The bitch had been following you around all night, prowling, circling and she finally caught her prey my mind sneers at me.

I should have seen it coming but I was too wrapped up watching that fucker Pete talking to Skye. I felt relieved when Skye stood and left the black jack table. Christ what a fucking mess.

"Want some company daddy?"

My head snaps up as Skye's low seductive husky voice slices through my babbling mind. I spin round. Oh fuck me, my eyes feel as if they're out on stalks just like a cartoon character, my jaw unhinges.

Skye walks slowly across the room giving me time to absorb what she is wearing. A short cropped t-shirt barely covers her magnificent tits and it shows parts of her black lacy bra along with her flat toned stomach, a tartan mini skirt, in fact it's more of a belt it's so short. She's wearing fishnet hold up stockings with a frill running around the top and sky high platform stiletto pumps, the soles light up at each step she takes, hooker shoes. Skye is role playing and her words sink in to my brain as I drag my eyes back up her magnificent body.

I lick my lips, I want to devour her. My cock is painfully hard and straining against the fly of my jeans. Skye has her hair down and wearing bright red lipstick she has also put on heavier eye shadow to complete the hooker look.

Standing in front of me Skye places a finger on my chest and runs it down my stomach, down the front of my jeans and follows the outline of my erection then removes her finger. Fuck my skin feels on fire. She leans forward placing her mouth close to my ear.

"Well daddy, do you?" a shiver of anticipation runs through me, I nod "good, do you want to get down and dirty or would you like a lap dance?"

Sweet fucking Jesus my blood is boiling for her. I clear my throat "Lap dance"

Skye smiles her dazzling brain frying smile, her eyes sparkle full of mischief. "Stay there whilst I set up" she winks saucily and blows me a kiss as she steps back.

I watch her every move, she walks over to the dining table and gets one of the chairs. Skye purposely bends at her waist as she picks it up and brings it back placing it in the middle of the room turning her back to me she bends at the waist to put it down. A groan escapes me as the short skirt flashes her ass and black lace panties. Twisting she looks over her shoulder at me.

"Like what you see daddy?" all I can do is nod.

Skye walks over to the music centre, mesmerised I watch her hips sway the skirt giving flashes of her butt checks as she walks. Her curly long hair swishes and bounces with her movements. Whilst Skye plays about with the music centre I walk over and sit on the chair, I jump when rock music blares out. Skye adjusts the volume. AC/DC Highway to Hell is playing. I'm getting good a recognising the bands and songs Skye likes to listen to.

Skye smiles when she sees me sat in the chair waiting. "My, oh my daddy, you are eager" she purrs.

Skye walks back to me slowly and in rhythm to the music, stopping occasionally to gyrate and swing her hair around.

When she reaches me Skye bends forward placing her hands on my knees she leans so her face is inches from mine. "House rules" her sultry voice washes over me igniting my already burning desire for her "no touching"

Fuck she is going to kill me with anticipation. I put my hands behind me and grip the spindles at the back of the chair.

"How much?" might as well make it authentic.

Skye smiles and runs her tongue over her full red lips "You've got me for the hour so it's five grand. If you want to ride bare back then its double. So which is it going to be daddy?"

"Bare back" I whisper. Skye grins impishly and winks as she pulls away.

"Good choice daddy" then she starts to move.

Skye can dance. She is sensual and erotic at the same time. She came close but never touches me, my eyes greedily follow her every move. When the song starts a second time Skye begins to strip, she takes off the barely there t-shirt then went to remove the skirt.

"Keep it on" I command, for some reason I find it a huge turn on. Skye simply moves her hands up to her bra and waits for my confirmation to remove it. I nod. Her full breasts bounce free. Christ they are fantastic, I can spend hours playing with them.

Skye put her hands underneath the belt of a skirt and turns her back to me; she bends as she slowly pulls the black lacy panties down. Fuck, my cock jerks and pulses, I'm going to come soon if she keeps this up. I grip the chair tighter to hold myself in place, it creaks, as Skye moves toward me smiling salaciously and licking her lips. She straddles my legs.

Aw fuck no. I've no chance as she starts to move. It's agony she's so close yet not touching me. My control is slipping fast, I grip the chair harder. I hear a crack. I close eyes and take a deep breath. Skye's scent fills my nostrils and lungs, bad move, my blood is boiling now. I open my eyes and look at her watching me. One of her nipples is close to my mouth. I can't resist. I circle her nipple with my tongue then close my mouth around it and suck. Skye gasps.

"Tut, tut naughty daddy" she admonishes "that's just cost you another two grand for breaking house rules" she reprimands me by lightly tapping my face. I grin at her. I don't care, it's worth it.

Skye steps back and swings her hair round effectively whipping me with it. I have the sudden desire to feel the sensation across my bare skin, all of my bare skin. I move my hands and take off my shirt, Skye watches me as she continues to dance, running her hands all over her body. I want to do that. I stand and remove my shoes and socks, trousers and boxers then sit back on the chair and resume my position.

"Do that thing again with your hair" I command.

I brace myself as Skye steps forward circling her head on her shoulders to swing her hair around. The cool breeze then the feather light feel of her hair dragging across my skin has goose bumps breaking out and sending tingles racing up and down my body. Skye continues to repeat the motion circling her head in time to the music whipping me with her hair. I close my eyes and open myself up to the sensations her hair creates as it repeatedly cross my face, chest, stomach, cock and thighs.

After a few minutes Skye stops, she's breathing hard from the exertion but she continues to dance. When her breathing is under control she straddles me again and continues her close but not touching moves. My cock twitches and jerks skimming her sex, I can feel how wet she is. I want her no I need her. The chair creaks loudly as I fight to restrain myself from grabbing hold of Skye, the muscles in my shoulders and arms burn with the effort. I surrender.

"I need to be in you. I want to fuck you now" my voice is hoarse.

Skye reaches down and grasps my cock, positioning the head at her entrance and pushes down taking me to the root in one swift movement.

"Fuck, shit" I yell as the feel of her tight hot moist cunt surrounds and grips me. My hands fly to her hips holding her in place. I almost climax. I gulp in air to fight off my imminent orgasm.

Christ she feels so good. I need her. I need to feel her inside and out. My hands travel up her waist to her breasts. I cup them in my hands and roll her nipples. I feel the responding clench of her cunt muscles on my cock. I take one of the hard extended nipples in my mouth and suckle, flicking my tongue over it then suckle again, the delicious feel of her muscle spasms and clenching sends pleasure sensations racing through my cock to my balls. Skye's hands and fingers tangle in my hair and her groans make me suck harder. Her hips grind against me, she wants friction. I thrust my hips upwards and suck her nipple hard making her cry out.

I want her underneath me. I need to feel her writhing beneath me. Grasping her ass with both hands I surge up right, still buried deep inside her I carry her to the sofa. Skye wraps her arms and legs around me. I lower us to the sofa. I need to possess her completely. I kiss her blood red lips, claiming her mouth with my lips and tongue, Skye meets my passion as we explore and taste each other. I flex my hips making Skye groan deep at the back of her throat. Christ I love hearing that sound. I repeat the move over and over, harder and harder. I can feel her muscles spasm and grip me greedily, drawing me deeper. She's close.

"Come with me" I growl out and move fast and hard.

I'm barely holding off my orgasm when Skye reaches hers. I let go throwing my head back and shout my release. My spine hips and thighs locking in place as I bury my cock deep inside her and pump everything I have to give into her. My body shudders and jerks as my orgasm continues to roll through me. I move slowly in and out of her rubbing the last of the orgasm out of both of us.

I lower my head and kiss Skye tenderly relaying my love and thanks as I pull out of her. I get up and gather my clothes, pulling on my trousers minus the boxers. Skye pulls her t-shirt on, picks up her bra and panties then holds out her hand.

"You owe me twelve grand and as sorely tempted as I am to give it to you for free, cos I can count on one hand how many guys have brought me to orgasm but a girl's gotta pay her bills" she snaps her fingers and makes a come on pay up gesture with her hand.

I smile and walk towards her, I like the fact she is still role playing. I put my hand in my pocket and pull out two ten grand chips and hand them to her. "Keep the change, you deserve it"

Stepping into me Skye takes the chips and then cups my crotch. "Appreciate it and call me anytime you need me daddy" she squeezes and rubs her hand against my trousers, my cock jumps to attention, and gives me a chaste kiss "ciao"

Skye heads for the bedroom. I pick up my shirt and put it on and fasten it. Christ I feel great. Comprehension hits me. Skye has cured me of my black thoughts and mood she'd known exactly what to do to get rid of the after effects of Caroline's actions. I head to the bedroom I want, no I need to hold her.

Skye has on jeans and is pulling on a t-shirt when I reach her. I fold her into my arms and hold her to me. Skye wraps her arms around my waist.

"I love you so much" I say against her hair. Skye tilts her head back and kisses me tenderly.

"I love you too" she whispers "hey guess what?" Skye says brightly, I shrug and shake my head smiling "I found these' she holds up the ten grand chips I've just given her "I plan to go lose it all at black jack want to come and help me?"

"Of course" I laugh.

Skye went into the bathroom and I change into jeans and t-shirt then sit on the bed to wait for her. A few minutes later she returns, her full lips are still blood red but her eye shadow is lightened to a smoky grey making her eyes appear larger. She picks up the hooker shoes and takes them into the closet.

"I've got to ask; where in the hell did you get those from?" I call out.

"I found them when I was looking at wedding cakes on line. I got the skirt off the same website. They came yesterday afternoon when I was packing and on a whim put them in my case" Skye came back out wearing low heeled boots "so, you like my hooker costume" she wiggles her eye brows at me.

"Yes very much, especially the belt you wore as a skirt" I'm getting hard just thinking about it.

We head out back to the casino. Bruce and Paul shadow us, on the way Skye tells me about her conversation with Pete; it explains the idiot dumbstruck expression I'd seen on his face when she'd walked away.

When we get to the floor and Skye decides she wants to play the slot machines. I laugh heartily as Skye jumps up and down squealing when she won. Skye doesn't care about the amount it's just the fact she's won.

"Let's stay on the main floor" Skye's eyes sparkle "if it gets mad we'll go to the VIP area" her enthusiasm is infectious, she's having fun.

I signal to Paul and Bruce we're staying on the floor, both nod and Paul speaks into his jacket sleeve more than likely notifying the casino security team who are our back up. Earlier I asked Paul and Bruce not to mention the extra security to Skye because I wanted her to have a normal experience as possible this weekend. Paul reluctantly agreed however that got shot to shit in the restaurant earlier. Skye hadn't reacted at all when the security team surrounded us when the group of guys descended on her. I mentally kick myself because I realize now she expected it, she trusts Paul implicitly to keep her safe.

We join a black jack table; all the men instantly perk up when they got a load of Skye. She soon has them all eating out of her hand and she thoroughly enjoys herself bantering and joking with them. Skye also won a lot. When we left the table Skye tipped the croupier generously from there we played roulette. I had to remind her of how the betting worked.

It's fun gambling with Skye. She gets excited for other people when they win even though she lost. After about an hour we bump into Simon and Macy who are playing craps. Skye said she wanted to have a go at throwing the dice, the croupier having overheard her turned to tell her what she had to do his words dry up in his throat when he sees her.

"Miss Darcy" he squeaks. Skye gives him a dazzling smile "would you like a table of your own?"

Without giving her chance to answer he raises his arm and signals, within seconds the pit boss appears.

"Is there a problem?" he looks at Skye and me with disdain. Skye's eyes widen and I feel her tense.

"No sir" the croupier has seen Skye's reaction to the pit boss's look "I was offering Miss Darcy" he enunciates her name "her own craps table"

The pit boss, it's obvious he didn't recognised Skye, does a double take and blushes, his eyes flicker to me. He visibly swallows and I can see he is internally cursing himself for his blunder.

"Certainly, Miss Darcy, Mr Blake if you'll please follow me" he says with a slight bow.

"Only if we can bring him with us" Skye says pointing at the croupier, who blushes and looks hopeful at the pit boss.

"Of course" the pit boss raises his hand and gives a signal; another croupier appears almost instantly and takes over the table "would you like to go to the VIP area?"

"Nope" says Skye "what's your name?" she asks the croupier as we follow the pit boss.

"Miles ma'am"

Skye introduces me, Simon and Macy.

We have an absolute ball playing craps. I notice security surrounds us and keeps other people away from the table, if Skye noticed she doesn't let on. It isn't long before other members of our hen and bachelor party join us. How in the hell Miles remains professional is beyond me, the girls and Simon flirt outrageously with him. Skye is giddy and bouncing all over the place, when she rolled the dice and got the numbers up all I'll say is it's a good job I have quick reflexes as I just about catch her when she launches herself at me without any warning.

When it's my turn to roll the dice Skye put her hand on my arm to stop me, I watch her open mouthed as she takes my hand opens my fingers and kisses the dice, closes my fingers and kisses them. Fuck that is so hot and my cock stands to attention in agreement, that is how it's supposed to be done. I realize with sudden clarity Skye has just buried the last remnants of Caroline's action from earlier in the night. On a high I roll the dice and hit the jackpot.

Quite some time later Skye says she's had enough and wants to go to the bar to chill out and get a drink. After giving Miles a more than generous tip we head for the bar with Macy, Simon, Don and a few others. We grab a booth and a waitress promptly appears to take our order.

The banter, laughter and conversation from the crap table carried on as we relax and enjoy our drinks.

"Skye, Clayton, I'm sorry but I can't hold it in any longer but I've got to tell you what happened after you left" Simon says looking at both of us with a slight apologetic look "but before I do honey what on earth did you say to Pete"

Skye recounts the conversation, it also means she has to explain her inheritance—although she doesn't give the details of the Will nor did she say she is estranged from her family—to those who didn't know, namely Don and his family. When they get over their shock Skye recaps Caroline's question to me at dinner and by the time she finishes everyone is roaring with laughter.

"You do the math, oh Skye only you could come out with a line like that" Simon says wiping his eyes "well after you followed Clayton out of the room, Robert" Simon points to him "shouts at Caroline "what the fuck do you think you're playing at?" she tries to feign innocence by saying "what do you mean?" to which Don says"

"You've been following Clayton around like a bitch on heat all night" supplies Don.

Simon continues "How dare you she shrieks then she shouts Pete over and basically tells him to defend her honor. Pete says "Why? Everything Don and Robert said is true. Do you really think Clayton would go for someone like you when he has Skye?" Then he walked out leaving her behind. Then Robert says to Caroline "Where do you get off hitting on someone else's fiancé like a whore? Some friend you are" needless to say she got herself out of there pronto"

I'm stunned these guys didn't know me or Skye yet they act as if we are best buddies.

"I'm gobsmacked. I don't know what to say" says Skye equally amazed.

"Sorry if we have offended you" Don says looking at both of us "I understand from Shelley and Phil neither of those two are really friends"

"They're not and you haven't offended me" says Skye softly.

"Nor me" I add "we're just touched you feel strongly enough to say something" Skye nods her agreement.

"The bitch pissed me off on the plane over here, I would have said something to her then if I knew the truth" Don pauses "I am sorry though, it's because of me they're here. I invited them, Phil tried to stop me but I wouldn't listen. Caroline made out you were like that" Don crosses his fingers "I put Phil in such a position he could not say they couldn't come. I sincerely apologise"

"Apology accepted" both Skye and I answer together "will they be at the wedding?" Skye adds with a straight face.

"Fuck no" Don, Robert and the other guys all say in unison making me, Skye, Macy and Simon laugh.

Conversation turns to finding out more about each other; jobs, interests and hobbies. Robert seems to take a shine to Macy and he notices her engagement ring.

"So where's your man while you have fun this weekend?" he says nodding at her ring.

"He's working" Macy looks at Skye and me then winks, a mischievous smile on her lips.

"What does he do?" Robert says turning on the charm.

"Body guard and security detail" she says taking a sip of her drink.

"Don't forget chauffeur duties and sometimes general dogs' body" Skye adds.

"Oh yes that as well" Macy agrees.

"So does he enjoy his job?" Robert leans forward on the table and into Macy's personal space smiling warmly at her. Robert is going to be crucified if he keeps this up. Macy is reeling him in.

Macy nods "He loves it. He gets to travel the world for free, lives in a multimillion dollar apartment and gets paid a stupid amount of money to do it. His boss is lovely, she can be a bit of a scatterbrain" Skye chokes on her beer, I pat her back. I'm enjoying this. Macy unabashedly continues "but saying that she is one shrewd cookie and doesn't suffer fools gladly. How am I doing?" Macy asks Skye. Robert's eyes widen.

"Keep going you can big her up a bit more, less of the scatterbrain though" Skye deadpans.

"His boss not only beautiful and extremely rich is very famous in her field so he has to fend off fans from time to time. Oh and she's just got engaged to a total babe magnet who is also insanely rich"

I grin even more at the description Macy gives me. Robert has twigged Macy is talking about Skye and me.

"You're going to tell me he's here and stood right behind me" Macy smiles sweetly and nods "he's one of the two guys who shadows these two" Robert indicates to Skye and me with his beer bottle "and he's likely to put me six feet under if I don't behave myself" Macy grins even more.

"Aww Paul's a real sweetie when you get to know him" says Simon giggling.

"But he'll still put you six feet under if you misbehave" I add with a wink.

"Message received loud and clear" laughs Robert.

Skye yawns. It's almost one in the morning. "Come on baby, let's call it a night. We're up early in the morning for the helicopter trip"

Skye nods her acquiesce, Macy and Simon also agree as they're also on the trip. I signal to the waitress as we stand. Don stood and says he will cover the drinks when the waitress arrives.

"Mr Blake, sir" she addresses Don "your party's drinks are on the house"

"Marco and Vinny" I ask.

"Yes sir" she nods smiling. I drop three hundred dollars on her tray as a tip and Don follows suit, her eyes light up "thank you"

In the elevator Skye snuggles into me and yawns again, she's crashing the excitement and adrenaline of the night is ebbing away fast.

"Tired baby" I murmur she nods in response not lifting her head off my chest. As we reach our floor I scoop Skye up into my arms and carry her to our suite, by the time I get to our bedroom Skye is almost asleep. She wakes up enough to undress and crawl into bed by the time I get into bed and pull her into my arms she is fast asleep.

Chapter Twenty Five

CLAYTON

In the time Skye and I have been together one of the important things I've learnt about her is if she has to be woken up before she is ready to wake up she is grumpy and snappy for a least an hour, for the next hour she is just plain grumpy. I found this out at my own peril, good job I learn from my mistakes.

Standing at the foot of the bed I look at Skye as she lies curled in the foetal position, her breathing deep and even. Her hair partially covers her body and the rest splays over the pillows and bed. I'm going to wake her in the only way I know that will put her in a mellow mood. My cock jerks and throbs at the thought of what I'm about to do.

It feels like I've been permanently hard since Tuesday when I'd moved in with Skye, well I'm always hard for her but harder, even at work I just have to think about going home to her and I'm aching. When I do get home I have to keep myself in check otherwise I'd be tackling her to the floor as soon as I walk in through the door.

I take hold of the bed sheet slowly pulling it off Skye to reveal her naked body. I crawl up the bed and over her, moving her hair out of the way. I plant kisses on the side of her leg, waist and arm working my way up to her cheek. In her ear I speak softly.

"Skye time to wake up baby'" then I kiss her all over repeating softly the wakeup call.

"Come on Skye, wake up baby"

Skye moves out of the foetal position and mumbles what sounds like "leave me alone"

Her breasts are exposed to me now along with her face. I kiss her forehead, nose, cheeks and lips repeating my words, working my way down to her neck, chest and breasts.

"Wake up Skye, come on baby"

I circle her nipple with my tongue, it puckers and hardens.

"Time to wake up baby" I suck on the nipple.

Skye gasps and groans her body responds to the stimulation, she moves lying fully on her back her hips lift and legs spread wider. I settled myself in between her legs taking my weight on my arms as I position myself on top of her. I kiss and suckle the other nipple, her hips grind against me.

"Skye baby, time to wake up" I say low against her ear and kiss her cheek. Skye turns her head, her mouth searching out mine. I know she's gaining consciousness.

"Skye, wake up baby" I say slightly louder but still coaxing her awake gently. I kiss her lips and she responds.

"Come on baby open your eyes" I cajole, she shakes her head.

"Having a nice dream" she says groggily and surges her hips upwards my cock slips inside her "mmm" she makes the satisfying sound and gyrates against me.

Her clenching muscles suck me in deeper, I groan as the warm moist sensations surrounding my cock send tingling pleasure shooting up my spine. I flex my hips withdrawing and re-entering her slowly.

"Wakey, wakey Skye baby" I sing softly as I set a slow rhythm moving in and out of her.

Skye meets my slow thrusts; a smile spreads across her luscious lips. I place soft kisses over her face as her hands glide up and down my back and ass. I lose myself to the feel of her inside and out.

"Faster" Skye commands softly.

I place my lips over hers and kiss her deeply and increase the pace. I can feel Skye is close to coming. I circle my hips and thrust deep.

"Again" she groans arching and her head pushes further back into the pillow.

I slide my arms underneath her crushing her to me. I want to feel every part of her orgasm. Skye digs her finger nails into my ass and drags them up my back; that feels good, I arch into her hands.

"Oh yes baby" I groan my pleasure as she drags them back down to my ass.

"Please, harder, faster, please" Skye moans out each word begging as she clenches her cunt muscles around my cock. That coupled with her fingers and nails dragging over my back and ass has my climax building fast.

Skye wraps her legs around me taking me deeper, we both groan. I bury my head in her neck. I kiss and graze my teeth across her skin, she climaxes.

"Oh god Clayton"

I hold her closer as her body tenses and shakes. I chase my release pounding into her faster and harder. My balls draw up and tighten. The feel of Skye's tight cunt and her muscles gripping me greedily as she climaxes drives me to the edge, the sweet pain of her finger nails in my ass tips me over.

I lift my head and look at Skye she still has her eyes closed but a smug satisfied smile is on her full luscious lips. I kiss her tenderly.

"Come on baby open those gorgeous eyes for me" I whisper. Slowly her eye lids open and I'm rewarded with a loving look. In the dim light of the bedroom her eyes are luminous "good morning beautiful" I smile.

"Morning" she whispers then kisses me.

"Time to get up baby"

Skye flexes her hips and clenches her muscles around my cock "I thought someone was already up" she teases.

"Careful baby or you're going to be explaining why we're late for the helicopter trip" I move in and out of her slowly.

"I'll just tell them you fucked me awake so I wouldn't be grumpy and I wouldn't let you stop" she circles her hips and clenches down on me "now fuck me again"

"Yes ma'am" I growl.

I can't believe how fast today has gone. The majority of our party sit in the bar relaxing, those who didn't go to the Cirque show are listening to those who did wax lyrical about how fantastic and spectacular the show was. I too thoroughly enjoyed it. In fact the whole day has been highly enjoyable.

The helicopter trip over the Grand Canyon—we arrived just in time at the meeting and pick up point—the scenery was breath-taking, seeing Mother Nature in all her harsh glory. The spa had been relaxing and highly entertaining. Simon and I weren't the only men to join the ladies and a couple more of the guys joined us half way through saying strips clubs aren't all they were cracked up to be.

The only negative I have for the day is that fucking bunny boiler catty bitch from hell. Caroline. She has been a constant presence throughout the whole day. I and practically everyone else ignored her. Pete had been on the helicopter trip and I noticed he and Caroline hardly spoke to each other. Caroline had been in the spa, I'm guessing Pete did the strip clubs and gambling. Both attended the Cirque show.

Every time I looked around Caroline was watching me and Skye like a hawk. At every opportunity I got I held Skye in my arms and kissed her so much so Simon took to teasing me. Something I encouraged. Skye found it highly amusing. Now I have her sitting on my lap as I listen to her talk animatedly with Simon and David, the hair stylist came with us to the show as Simon's guest.

Skye is asking David if he will come to New York to do her hair for the wedding, obviously she will pay for his travel and time. Simon says David can stay with him for the weekend.

"We'll send the plane for you, so you could fly out on the Friday morning" I say because I know Skye wouldn't think to offer it "then we'll fly you back on the Sunday night or Monday morning whichever suits you" all three of them look at me with wide eyed surprise "what? It's not being used to fetch and carry anyone to the wedding, might as well put it to good use"

Skye kisses me and squeezes my hand in thanks.

"When I get back home I'll email the details over to you and of course you'll be at the wedding. How does that sound?" Skye asks. David nods in shocked surprise, it's another couple of minutes before he can verbalise anything.

Skye said David is one of the few stylists she has come across who understood her hair. She got David to work his magic on it this afternoon after the spa session. I finger one of the cork screw curls as I remember the first time I saw him work on her hair, Skye sat on the floor so he could cut it. I went with her to the salon this afternoon, Skye washed her hair at the spa so the look on the other stylists faces when they saw her wet hair reaching her hips was one of awe and pity. Awe at the length and pity for David however this soon turned into professional respect and admiration as they gathered to watch as he talked through how to cut long curly hair, even though it's only been three weeks since the last cut Skye decided to have a couple more inches taken off. Skye offered to sit on the floor much to the shocked horror of the salon manager, instead a foot stool was located and she sat on that.

Now her hair is a mass of beautifully styled cork screw curls with the sides pinned up showing off her ears and the multiple diamond decorated piercing, she is also wearing the drop lily amethyst earrings the purple matching the color of the cocktail dress she is wearing. Skye outshines every female in the group, fuck the entire hotel. I'm proud to have her on my arm.

The stares she draws from both sexes never cease to amaze me, yet Skye seems oblivious to it all actually that's not true Skye is acutely aware of her surroundings.

Paul has taught her well plus she trains regularly with Phillipee and Paul, not just to keep in shape but to be able to act effectively in a real life threat situation. I came home on Thursday to find Skye in the home gym sparring with Paul. Neither held back on the kicks and punches, it made me wince just watching. Skye is fast and she put Paul down a couple of times, likewise when Paul put Skye down I had to hold myself back from rushing to her. Skye just popped straight back up and went toe to toe again with him.

"I feel like dancing, let's go to a club" Skye murmurs in my ear.

"I can think of other ways of getting you all hot and sweaty" I say salaciously.

Skye's deep throaty laugh has my body stirring "I bet you can, but I want to dance and not just for you" she kisses me running the tip of her tongue along the seam of my lips, she pulls away before I can claim her "who fancies going to a club" she calls out. As far as I can make out practically everyone says yes "David where do you recommend?"

It turns out we didn't have far to go as Marco and Vinny have recently opened a night club within the hotel called the Basement. We get shown to the VIP area, the place is busy and the music pumps out loudly. Luckily in the VIP area you can hear each other talk without having to yell. Skye is already moving to the beat of the music as we order drinks. Macy stands and grabs Skye's hand dragging her to the dance floor, Shelley and a few other women follow.

I watch as Skye moves sensuously to the rhythm of the dance music, although she's not dancing in the same way as she does for me to rock music, thank the gods. I notice quite a few other guys watching her and not just from our party. I see a few on the dance floor making a bee line for her; I can feel my body getting ready to vault over the railing in order to fight them off. Macy and Shelley see them and move so Skye isn't easily accessible or to grab. Well done girls, I relax, a little.

"Man! I'd forgotten how those girls can dance"

I turn to see Phil standing next to me. I lean against the rail which separates the VIP and public areas putting my back to the dance floor.

"You know when I first started dating Shelley we would all go clubbing on the Saturday night, as soon as her and Skye got on the dance floor that would be it for the next two hours" he chuckles at his memories "now she'll be lucky if she lasts three songs"

"Oh my god" Simon squeals laughing "close your eyes Phil. Macy is teaching your mother how to booty roll"

I turn back to face the dance floor, sure enough Macy and Brenda are in the centre of the group circle booty rolling much to the amusement of the rest. Macy pulls Skye and Shelley into the centre and they all do it together. I feel myself getting hard watching Skye show Brenda what to do, since she is the slimmest it's easy to see how the action and motion went from start to finish.

Simon calls Don over needless say Phil's other brothers all follow out of curiosity. The reaction is mixed from shocked curses to laughter. By the end of the song Brenda has mastered it and the girls clap and cheer. Don and his sons cheer loudly and whistle drawing the girl's attention which all grin and curtsy before carrying on dancing.

I feel a hand brush across my ass and squeeze, making me jerk in surprise since Skye is dancing. Who the fuck did that? I turn to see Caroline walking away from me; she looks back over her shoulder coquettishly. Fucking psycho bitch, I scowl at her. She either can't see my face or she chooses to interpret my reaction differently as she continues to smile.

Caroline has kept her distance all day so why now? Is it because she has a few drinks inside her? No inhibitions. I look back at Skye enjoying herself, no you fucking moron it's because Skye isn't with me. Shit. Caroline the bunny boiler has been biding her time, waiting for an opportunity. This time she is making her move by stealth, she learnt a humiliating lesson last night and including the fact practically everyone is ignoring her she will get away with it. If I make a scene it will be her word against mine.

Where the fuck is Pete? I can't see him in the VIP area and he isn't stood at the rail with the rest of the men. I glance back at the dance floor and see a man dancing with the girls. He is taking each of them in turn by the hand and twirling them around, it's obvious they know him because they are smiling and laughing. It dawns on me who it is. Pete, he's working his way towards Skye. Oh fuck no! That is so not happening; no one is dancing with Skye but me. I put my drink down.

"Excuse me gentlemen but I'm going to dance with my girl"

"Getting withdrawal symptoms" Simon teases.

I wink at him "Absolutely"

I get to the dance floor and Skye just in time to foil Pete. Skye has her back to me; I put my finger to my lips as Shelley and Macy see me approaching. I place my hands on Skye's hips and pull our bodies close. Skye carries on dancing and doesn't look back instead she places her hands over the top of mine then she grips my little fingers getting ready to bend them backwards, a move which will bring me to my knees with excruciating pain.

I put my mouth close to her ear "I can think of another way you can inflict pain and it would be far more enjoyable"

Skye laughs and releases my fingers. I put one hand flat on her stomach pressing her closer still. I enjoy dancing with her this way as our bodies move together in synchronisation to the beat. At the end of the song Macy and Shelley mime going for a drink, Skye and I stay on the dance floor for another two songs before we head back.

Walking up the steps to the VIP area, Skye in front of me, I feel a hand rub against my ass. Turning round I come face to face with Caroline, she winks at me. I see red.

"Keep your fucking hands off me" I growl menacingly and as nastily as I can.

Caroline does no more than smile and lick her lips, she makes it blatantly clear she isn't going to take no for an answer. I toy with the idea of getting Bruce and Paul to set an exclusion zone as far as she is concerned but it will draw too much attention. I don't want a repeat of last night if I can help it.

An ice bucket full of bottled beers has been placed on the table. Skye takes two out and hands one to me. Skye tilts hers back and downs it in one go then lets out an enormous belch, much to the shock and amusement of the others, the guys make "good one" comments and salute her in respect, Skye bows acknowledging them and making them laugh.

"Such a lady" I say dryly as I sit down and pull an impish grinning Skye onto my lap.

As the night progresses the good natured banter and easy flowing conversation continues. Skye dances with the guys when they ask and I dance with the other ladies of our party. Caroline follows me to the dance floor each time and whenever she can she puts herself in my line of sight. She could dance, I'll give her that but it isn't a turn on in fact it's the opposite.

Everything about her smacks of desperation. Her dress if it can be called that makes her look sluttish. I'm sure it's expensive and designer label of some sort but it did nothing for her. The skirt is too short, just covering her ass. There is no back to it and the front has a split to the navel. The whole thing gives a new meaning to the little in little black dress.

As for her dancing all she is missing is the stripper pole. Caroline is attracting a lot of male attention just not the one she wanted, mine. The more I ignore her, the more desperate she becomes it's laughable.

Fuck, tonight is the last chance she's got to make a move on me. I mentally slap my forehead as it dawns on me why she is doing what she is. Once we are back in New York we wouldn't see each other socially and I'm going to make damned fucking sure we never see Caroline or Pete again and I know Skye wouldn't object.

I'm dancing with Shelley when the third song started and she indicates she wants to get a drink, as I lead her off the dance floor Caroline starts to follow only a guy who's been watching her grabs her arm and pulls her to him and starts to dance. Caroline tries to push him away but it has no effect, she looks at me expectantly to come to her rescue. I give her a fuck off look and I feel no pang of guilt as I walk away.

As Shelley and I approach our table I see Pete sat talking with Skye, aggression surges through me. I really don't like the guy aside from the fact he is an ex-boyfriend of Skye's I find his sycophantic ways to be stomach churning and irritating as fuck. Then I notice Skye's body language she is tense and frowning at him, something's wrong without being obvious I rush to her.

"Why do you want to know that?" I hear Skye snap at Pete as I approach.

Abruptly she looks up as if sensing me, relief floods her eyes. Without a word Skye stands and I sit in her place and pull her onto my lap. Pete looks uncomfortable obviously he wanted to talk to Skye without me around. Skye looks at him expectantly.

"I'm curious that's all" he says rather lamely.

"Well you can stay curious I am not sharing anything with you. It's personal and I would never share something like that with you" Pete opens his mouth but Skye raises her hand to stop him "we are not and never have been close friends" Pete looks as if she'd slapped him "you may think you know me Pete but you don't and never have. You still cling to a memory of who you thought I was all those years ago, that person has never existed and who I really was nine years ago doesn't exist either. Whoever it is you are fishing for information for tell them to fuck off because you know nothing about me or my life"

Even in the dim lights of the club I can see Pete visibly pale, he nods and stands up just as Caroline comes over, the glee on her face disappearing when she sees Pete's face and the hard set look on Skye's. Pete walks past Caroline not even acknowledging she is there, confusion crosses Caroline's face and she's briefly unsure what to do, she follows Pete, good call.

"What was that about?" I pull Skye closer to me and she relaxes with a loud exhale.

"He wanted to know if I'd been in touch with my grandfather before his death plus he was trying to get the exact amount of how much he left me" Skye frowns and chews her bottom lip as she thinks "but he was asking other questions about why I changed my name and took myself to college in London. You know he's never once asked me since he's been here, that's how I know someone in the family has put him up to getting information" Skye continues chewing her lip and looking thoughtful.

"I'm sorry but you're going to have to explain that. I don't get the connection"

Skye chuckles "Sorry" then kisses my cheek "I've changed, Pete hasn't. He is still as self-centred and conceited as he was when I first knew him. When I was seventeen we went out for about three months if that. Pete always thought of me as an attention seeking spoilt brat, I know this because I overheard him telling one of his friends. I was affection deprived never attention seeking. When we split up he wouldn't have given me a second thought and I would be his best friend's little annoying attention seeking spoilt brat of a cousin again and someone to be ignored. Pete has spoken to someone since last night because he knows more about what is in the Will even though those documents have been sealed"

Before Skye can say any more Simon rushes up and pulls Skye off my lap.

"Come on madam you've danced with everyone but me, time to shake that beautiful derriere of yours, you can schmooze all you want with him anytime"

Skye let herself be dragged off, laughing she waves bye to me. I make a mental note to resume this conversation when no-one else is around.

Needing the restroom I stand and make my way towards the back of the room. Luckily I don't have to fight my way through the club as the VIP area has its own. Pete passes me on his way back, there is no sign of Caroline thank fuck. I follow the signs down a short corridor. Bruce follows me and checks the room before I enter; protocol. I tell Bruce to wait for me at the top of the corridor as I went in.

I relieve myself and wash my hands, as I start to dry them I hear the door open and close. I don't bother to look round, my thoughts are mulling over what Skye has said. A hand cups me between my legs and squeezes. I react on instinct. Forcefully knocking the hand away I spin and pin the person by the throat against the wall, fist raised ready to knock the fucker out. Shock prevents me from hitting the perpetrator, when my brain registers who it is I release them and step back putting as much distance between us as possible, I feel dirty, contaminated all over again, rage explodes from me.

"What the fuck do you think you are playing at Caroline" I yell, my voice echoes around the room. I barely contain the anger and animosity coursing through me.

"Oh don't act all shocked and innocent, I've seen you watching me all night and giving me the come on" she says coquettishly.

Caroline runs her fingers up and down the navel split neckline of her dress, supposedly to entice me, instead I shudder. I keep my eyes on hers, she licks her lips.

"I know you want me and I don't blame you after all Barbie is plastic"

The dig at Skye ignites my anger further "You are fucking delusional. I don't want you" I spit out "I never have and I never will"

I turn and walk away. I get three paces out the door when she catches up to me.

"Come on Clay, variety is the spice of life. I can show you a good time, much better than that narcissistic, dim witted, attention seeking excuse of a girlfriend ever could" Caroline is doing her best to sound seductive.

"How dare you insult my fiancée" I roar. Bruce appears and starts walking towards us. I hold my hand up to stop him "Skye is the complete opposite. It is you who is narcissistic, dim witted and attention seeking. I wouldn't touch you with a fucking barge pole, you make my skin crawl you sick fuck" I put as much vehemence and contempt into my words as I can to get my message across "you have a boyfriend remember him?" I add sardonically.

Caroline reaches out and grabs my arm. I shake her off causing her to stumble.

"You don't mean that, I know you don't and we can keep it from Pete and Skye. We will be good for each other" she is trying for sultry but instead it sounds whiney.

"I do mean it and every time I think of you it is with abhorrence" I grab hold of her arm tightly, red mist is all I can see "and I'll show you once and for all just how much"

I frog march Caroline down the corridor and back to the VIP area. I quickly scan the room and spot Pete sitting with Don, Robert, Phil and Shelley. Dragging Caroline with me I head toward them. Skye and Simon reach the group at the same time as I do with Caroline.

The almost murderous raging anger I feel obviously shows on my face as everyone stares open mouthed. I shove Caroline unceremoniously at Pete who manages to stand up and catch her just in time. I step forward and get right into their personal space, both shrink back. I point my finger and bare my teeth.

'I don't fucking care what kind of fucked up relationship you two have got going on but keep your psycho fucking bunny boiler bitch of a girlfriend away from me and Skye. In fact I never want to lay eyes on her again'

SKYE

I've seen Clayton lose his temper before, his bark is worse than his bite but in this case he looks ready to rip Caroline limb from limb. Bruce stands behind Clayton, his eyes never leaving his boss. I think Bruce and Pete see it too because Pete does the sensible thing, without a word he tightly grips the top of Caroline's arm and heads for the stairs with Caroline protesting her innocence all the way.

I went to Clayton. He looks down at me and I can see the anger seething in his eyes and the tremor of his body. I run my fingers down his cheek, something I do to calm him only this time he needs something else to get rid of the aggression.

"Dance with me" I say in a soft command, some energetic dancing will do the trick to work off the negative energy he's carrying.

Clayton kisses my palm and nods, ignoring all the WTF just happened stares I lead Clayton to the dance floor, there will be plenty of time later for Clayton to tell me what Caroline has done to get him so mad.

Halfway through the second song Clayton starts to loosen up and gets more in the groove. At the end of the fourth he indicates he wants to get a drink at least now he's subdued. Back at the table Macy, Shelley, Phil and Simon sit huddled together no doubt speculating about what happened between Clayton and Caroline. They shuffle round to make room for us. Clayton grabs two bottles of beer out of the ice bucket and hands one to me which I promptly down, I'm thirsty.

"Where is everyone?" Clayton asks pulling me onto his knee.

"Mum and Dad and the girls are dancing. Robert and the lads have gone gambling" says Phil.

"David had to go as he's up early for work" Simon laughs looking at his watch "scratch that he'll be up in four hours to open the shop"

"So what did psycho bunny boiler bitch do, by the way that's her new nickname, way better don't you think" says Shelley.

They all grin and look at Clayton expectantly. He looks at me for guidance and possibly debating what my reaction will be.

"You might as well tell them because I'll only tell them later on" I assure him.

Before he answers he kisses me and tightens his arms around me, that's either to keep me in place just in case I decide to bolt if I don't like what he says or to stop me from going after Caroline but it also feels like he needs me in his arms for reassurance, I'm his security blanket.

"Caroline made a pass at me in the restroom, she was extremely insulting about Skye and very delusional about my" Clayton pauses searching for the right words "she has it in her head I want her and she convinced herself I've been watching her all night giving her the come on, she was offering herself to me, that's it in a nutshell" he finishes with a sigh.

Clayton uses my trick of giving information but leaving out huge chunks. It's enough to appease my friends curiosity and for them to add their own spin but I know something more serious happened and I will get it out of him in private, plus he's holding me so tightly I feel as if I'm going to break in half.

"I'm not going anywhere" I murmur to him, he looks at me puzzled "loosen your grip you're cutting the circulation off to my legs" I joke.

Clayton relaxes his arms as his expression changes to apologetic. I listen to my friends speculate whether or not Pete and Caroline will show up tomorrow for the plane back or make their own way home. General consensus is they will show up. Clayton remains quiet when Don, Brenda and the girls come back and leaves it to the others to fill them in on what Caroline had done.

Clayton is too quiet, time to get him to talk, he's stewing and I need to get his mind off the incident.

"Well folks I'm calling it a night or morning rather" I make movements to stand but Clayton beats me to it and sets me on my feet "see you all later"

Macy comes with us, makes sense since Paul will be retiring once we are in our suite.

"Listen I've been thinking about giving Paul and Bruce down time before we fly back. I don't intend to go anywhere, do you have any plans?" I speak softly so only Clayton will hear me.

Clayton shakes his head, he's distracted, bet he didn't hear a word or if he did it's not registered in his brain. When we arrive at the suite Clayton goes in first. I tell Paul and Bruce that between now and checking out the time they can do as they please as we'll be staying in the suite.

I walk in to find Clayton standing by the window staring out at the spectacular night time view of Vegas. I wrap my arms around him and look up at him, resting my chin on his chest. His arms automatically wrap around me but he continues to stare out of the window. After a few minutes he looks down his beautiful dark blue eyes full of sadness. It breaks my heart.

"Come on tell me what really happened" I cajole.

Clayton closes his eyes and sighs "I was in the restroom my back to the door as I dried my hands. I heard the door open and close, I didn't bother to turn round because I was thinking about what you said about Pete. The next thing I know a hand is cupping my cock and balls. I reacted on instinct, knocking the hand away and pinning the person to the wall getting ready to knock two rounds of shit out of them only to find it was Caroline. I released her straight away and put as much distance between us as I could" he opens his eyes silently pleading with me to understand she was the instigator "I lost it as you can probably guess"

Clayton went on to tell me verbatim the conversation between them, how he walked out and she followed continuing to ridicule me and offering herself as the better alternative. Clayton's reaction didn't surprise me in the slightest. I'm just surprised he didn't bitch slap her.

"I am so sorry, you warned me what she's like and to be on my guard, even after Friday night I should have paid more attention. Caroline had made two passes earlier in the club" I raise my eyebrows "she grabbed my ass twice. The first time was when I was stood watching you and Macy teach Brenda the booty roll. Then later on as we came off the dance floor you were in front of me as we climbed the stairs she did it again. I told her then to keep her fucking hands off me. I thought that would have been enough, obviously I was wrong" his eyes fill with remorse.

"Don't you dare take the blame for Caroline's actions" I say sternly "she is manipulative and calculating now you know first-hand just how much, I will admit she has been far bolder with you than anyone else but then again as I've said before you are far more handsome and insanely richer than the others"

"I am truly sorry I didn't take your warning more seriously. How can I make it up to you?" his remorse tugs at my heart again.

I'm about to say I'll think of something when I see the piano in my peripheral vision, it gives me an idea making me smile wickedly at him as a sudden thrill and mischief course through me "Wait right there, I'll be back in two minutes"

I give him a quick kiss and I see his eyes darken. Oh good he's on my wavelength. I head for the bedroom and the closet. I strip off and swap my shoes for my buckled boots, my plan is to walk out naked but I spy the tartan micro mini skirt, hmm, he got turned on by this last night, on impulse I put it on. I take out my dangly earrings and let the sides of my hair down bringing my hair forward so it covers my boobs.

I re-enter the living room, dawn is breaking on the horizon and Clayton has gone back to looking out of the window. On seeing my reflection he turns to face me, his gaze heats instantly and rakes me from head to toe and back again. I love it when he looks at me like that. It makes me feel desirable, sexy, his.

I head for the piano, thankfully the lid is down. I climb up making sure to flash Clayton my naked butt; that earns me a hiss. Christ I'm wet just from the sound he makes. I sit down and put my feet on the lid covering the keys.

"You want to make it up to me, come here" I purr and use my index finger in the come here sign.

As Clayton approaches, all lethal predatory grace like a panther, I open my legs and move my hair back to reveal my naked breasts. Clayton growls his appreciation at the vision I present to him.

"Baby I am going to fucking eat you alive"

I shiver with anticipation, I run my tongue over my dry mouth and lips trying to create moisture, it isn't happening.

Clayton pulls off his shirt and drops it to the floor his abs flex with his movements, my dry mouth waters at the sight of him, my heart kicks up beating faster. Clayton's body and face promise all kinds of sin. Oh yes he really means what he said about eating me alive. Bring it on! Clayton put his hands on my knees and pushes my legs wider apart making me more exposed to him.

"Lie down baby and enjoy being devoured" he rasps darkly.

My back hasn't even hit the piano lid when his mouth is on me and he starts his demanding assault. "Oh god yes Clayton" I cry out as his tongue swirls and flicks then his mouth is sucking hard on my clit, sending a multitude of pleasure sensations cascading through my body making every nerve scream in delight. He's not taking any prisoners... well me... in his quest for delivering pure carnal pleasure. I've died and gone to ecstasy heaven.

The shallow fast thrust of his tongue penetrating my entrance has me heading for the precipice of my climax fast. Hell, he really is devouring me and I love it. I cup my breasts and roll my aching nipples at the same time Clayton slides two fingers inside me and starts to slowly move them in and out gradually moving faster whilst his tongue continues to swirl and lick then clamping his mouth down and sucking on my clit, before I know it I'm diving off the cliff and riding the waves of my orgasm. I know I call out Clayton's name before I'm lost to the crash and roar of pleasure that takes over my body.

Clayton keeps going, finger fucking me and working my clit with his tongue and mouth, a second climax hits me as the first ebbs away, I shout louder.

Clayton picks me up off the piano. I manage to wrap my legs around his waist as my body convulses with aftershocks. His strong arms hold me tight against his hard body. "I'm going to fuck you bent over the sofa" his voice rasps in my ear. Oh dear lord.

As he carries me I can feel his erection rubbing against me, the roughness of his pants further stimulating my clit. My eyes roll to the back of my head at the pleasure it creates, sweet heavens above I'm close to coming again. I feel Clayton's lips on mine, I respond to his kiss tasting myself and him. Clayton has stopped moving but continues kissing me his tongue dipping in and out of my mouth. I unhook my legs and straighten to stand. Clayton loosens his grip and lets me slide down him effectively ending the kiss.

Clayton turns me around and places his hand between my shoulder blades applying a slight pressure to get me to bend over the back of the sofa, when I'm in the position he wants he strokes his hand over my butt and down to cup my sex, his fingers massage my swollen over sensitive clit. A groan escapes me. His fingers trail up towards my back passage then move back to rubbing and caressing my butt.

"Stay as you are baby" he commands after a few minutes and moves away.

I raise my head to see Clayton walk back to the piano and pick up his shirt off the floor, wrapping it in both hands he pulls. His biceps bulge impressively as do the veins coursing his arms. The shirt rips in half. Clayton tears a strip of cloth from the ruined shirt. He moves to stand behind me and grinds his erection into my butt.

"Put your hands behind your back"

With a thudding heart I comply. Clayton ties the material around my wrists, binding them together. I can't move. It isn't uncomfortable and normally by now panic would be flowing through me and I would be a hysterical mess begging to be released, safe wording. It's the first time since the play room Clayton has restrained me and it's the first time I'm immobile in the sense that I will have a hard time trying to get away. I surprise myself at how calm I am and so turned on, in fact I'm looking forward to being taken this way. I realize my heart is thudding with eager anticipation and not fear.

I know Clayton won't hurt me. It makes me aware of just how much I actually trust him with my safety and wellbeing but not only that he's banished my fears about being restrained. Would I let anyone else do this to me? Hell no!

Clayton leans over me; I can feel his warm skin under my hands and on my back. I flex my fingers and feel the muscle definition of his abs; he makes a growling noise at my touch so I do it again.

"Remember to safe word if this gets too much" I nod "good girl"

His hands trail over my shoulders, back and arms sending all my nerve endings into a wild excited frenzy. He positions himself between my legs then holds my bound wrists and pulls lifting my torso and arching my back.

"I intend to take you in this position are you okay like this?"

Holy hell this is so erotic I can't wait to feel him inside me, how deep and full he'll make me feel. I'm soaking wet just at the thought. The sharp sting of a slap on my butt has me groaning.

"Answer me baby I need to know you are okay like this?" his voice is dark and seductive.

"Yes" I pant. I push my butt into him a silent hurry up and get on with it.

"Naughty girl" he spanks me again "I'm going to make you beg for my cock"

What no, that's not fair I want his cock now! "I'm sorry, please don't make me wait" I beg "I want your cock in me now, please"

Clayton's hand rubs in circles over my butt as he lowers me back down over the sofa. "No baby I'll decide when you can have it"

His hand left my butt and I brace myself for the slap but it doesn't come. Instead I hear the rasp of his zip being pulled down. I can't see what Clayton is doing so I listen and sense his movements as he removes the rest of his clothes. Anticipation is killing me what is he going to do.

"You look so inviting and fuckable like this baby" Clayton's voice rasps thickly, I can hear how much he wants me.

I wriggle my butt but it's awkward as I'm bent almost double so it ends up as a rocking from side to side motion. "So fuck me" I make my voice low and husky as the last thing I want to sound like is needy and whiney.

A slap lands on my butt, the unexpected sting has me gasping. "Patience baby" he whispers.

I feel his lips press against my lower back and work their way upwards until Clayton covers me like a blanket. His cock pushes against my sex. His hands cup my breasts and start pumping and kneading them, his fingers roll and tug my nipples.

"Oh my god" I moan as desire and pleasure flood my body. Clayton flexes his hips and his cock slides along the length of my slit stroking and heightening the pleasure. I moan loudly, again.

"I love hearing the sounds you make when I do this to you" Clayton whispers in my ear.

His tongue circles the shell of my ear then he nips my lobe at the same time he pulls hard on my nipples and thrusts his hips forward. The pain and pleasure has me groaning louder still.

Oh sweet lord I like that. Never in a million years did I think I would ever enjoy having pain inflicted on me during a sex act but lord it feels so good. Clayton does it again.

"Clayton, please" I beg. I'm close and I want him inside me.

I move my fingers against his ripped abs, relishing in the tautness as he flexes, his skin is hot and slick with perspiration. He's fighting to keep his control.

Clayton rears up taking me with him, his hands still on my breasts as he continues to slide his cock along my sex as he rolls my nipples between his fingers and thumb.

Oh heavens above I want to come. Clayton's teeth graze the juncture of my neck and shoulder then he bites down and sucks.

"Oh yes, please" I cry out as the myriad of sensations drive me crazy.

"What do you want baby" his lips never leave my neck, his tongue licking and circling, his teeth nipping "tell me" his voice rumbles.

"You" I'm panting heavily "your cock please"

Clayton lowers me back over the sofa, pulls my hips back and widens my stance. I'm so ready for him his cock slides smoothly inside me. Heaven, I'm in ecstasy.

"Yes" Clayton hisses. He has been torturing himself as well as me. Clayton moves in and out slowly, my muscles delighting in clenching and gripping his cock further heightening the pleasure sensations building rapidly in my core. Clayton thrusts deep inside me and holds still.

"I'm going to put you into the position I showed you earlier and I'm going to fuck you hard, ready baby?"

Hell yeah! "Yes"

"Remember if it's too much safe word"

I bite my tongue to stop myself saying "Less talk and get fucking" somehow I know it will ruin the moment, so I nod instead.

Clayton's hands grasp my bound wrists and pulls, lifting my torso. He adjusts his grip to hold my forearms. I feel the pull in my shoulders and arm sockets but it's bearable. The luscious fullness I feel from his thick cock more than makes up for any discomfort in my shoulders.

Clayton pulls back slowly then slams back in, pulling me on to him at the same time.

"Argh" I cry out from the intense pleasure shooting through me. Clayton continues the slow withdrawal and the hard fast entering. Oh I'm in seventh heaven if it exists and I want more.

Clayton is breathing heavily. He circles his hips and plunges in deep over and over again. He lowers me back down and grasps my hips; he begins to move fast in and out, in and out the friction has me standing on the precipice within seconds, one more thrust and I dive off. My orgasm crashes through me with the force of a tidal wave.

"Clayton" I scream out at the intensity of it.

Clayton follows me "Skye, fuck, Skye" he bellows.

I feel his cock throbbing and pulsing as he fills me, my muscles squeezing and clenching, milking every last drop out of him. I love this feeling.

Clayton collapses on top of me, his sweaty brow resting between my shoulder blades, his warm breath gusting over my sweat slick skin. After a few minutes he lifts and I feel tugging as he unties my wrists. When my hands are free Clayton rubs my shoulders and arms all the while murmuring how much he loves me and how well I've done.

Clayton eases out of me and I feel the trickle of seamen run down my inner thighs. Wow! He must have had multiple orgasms if not he'd come hard. Clayton scoops me up into his arms and I wrap mine around his neck, he kisses me tenderly.

"Now I'm going to make love to you slow and long. I'm not going to stop until you beg me to" he says against my lips.

Holy shit he's going to kill me by orgasm.

Chapter Twenty Six

CLAYTON

I watch Skye as she sleeps; she's lying on her stomach with her arms under the pillow, her hair covering her naked body like a blanket. She looks so peaceful I resist the urge to wake her just so I can make love to her like I had earlier. We'd been at each other like a pair of junkies on a binge. We couldn't get enough of each other; both of us were insatiable. I lost count of the amount of orgasms I had. Skye didn't beg me to stop in the end we both collapsed exhausted and tangled around each other.

Once again Skye made me completely forget a nocuous incident involving Caroline. This time it was from the moment she came out of the bedroom wearing only that belt of a skirt and my favourite boots. When she climbed up onto the piano I nearly shot my load just watching her.

And once again Skye knew instinctively what to do to give me what I needed and she let me bind her, put her in a position where I completely restrained her, dominated her. It hit me then how much she demonstrated the level of trust she has in me. Christ I love Skye so much it hurts, my heart aches for her. She really does know me on a soul deep level.

I want to get her something nice, no not nice something beautiful and exquisite. I gently kiss her forehead, Skye sighs contentedly and smiles, and I get up carefully so as not to disturb her. I get dressed quietly and write her an 'I love you and back soon' note leaving it on the pillow so she will see it just in case she woke before I returned.

As I step out of the suite and the hotel security guards on duty stand to attention. Where the fuck is Bruce and Paul? Then I vaguely remember Skye saying she'd given them time off as we wouldn't be venturing out. I smile because Bruce or Paul has gone with plan B.

"Good afternoon gentlemen, who fancies coming shopping with me?"

An hour and a half later I'm back in the suite and I'm feeling pretty pleased and smug with myself. I creep into the bedroom only to find the bed empty then the sound of the shower running registers. I put my bag on the bed and pull out the box, the shower shuts off. I sit on the bed and wait.

Five minutes later Skye emerges gloriously naked with her hair piled up on top of her head so I get to see every fantastic inch of her fabulous body. Standing I open my arms, smiling her megawatt brain frying smile Skye saunters to me and I appreciate the sway of her full breasts, her tiny waist, the swing of her hips and long slender legs. Needless to say my cock shows it's appreciation as well.

"I missed you" Skye whispers as she steps into my arms and lifts onto her tip toes, her arms coming around my neck as I bend to meet her kiss. As soon as our lips meet the kiss deepens and I claim her mouth. I put my hands on her ass and lift her up Skye wraps her legs around my hips. Christ I will never tire of kissing her. When we break apart we are both breathing hard.

"So tell me where did you go that was so urgent" Skye says softly, her fingers flexing and pulling on the hair at the nape of my neck; that does things to me... nice things. I stifle a groan.

"I went shopping" I chuckle as she raises an eyebrow in disbelief "I bought you a present"

Her eyes sparkle with joy "Oooh goody. I like presents. What did I get?"

That makes me laugh; I love Skye's reaction to getting gifts from me. I pat her ass, Skye unhooks her legs from my hips and I enjoy the feel of her naked body as she slides down mine.

I twist and pick up the oblong box. I open it and turn it around to show her the gift. Her eyes widen and her mouth pops open.

"It's beautiful" she whispers as her fingers lightly trail over the ruby and diamond necklace.

"I thought it would go with ruby and diamond lily drop earrings when you get them" a smile spreads across her face and she nods in agreement "would you like to try it on?" again she nods and turns her back to me.

The necklace is a choker made up of square rubies surrounded by diamonds. As soon as I saw it I knew it would complement the earrings. I fasten the necklace, it fits perfectly. Skye walks over to the mirror on the dressing table and looks at her reflection running her fingers over the stones again. I stand behind her, it really does suit her.

"Thank you it's absolutely perfect. I love it" she says looking at me in the mirror "and I love you"

A mischievous grin and a wicked glint appear in her eyes. Holy fuck what is she planning. Shit I don't care because I know whatever it is I will like it, a lot.

Skye steps away from me and drops to her knees, my heart stops then begins beating rapidly faster, she sits back on her heels and spread her knees placing her hands on her thighs and lowers her head down. Oh fuck me! I hiss in a deep breath. Skye has assumed the position of a Submissive. My cock throbs and demands to be freed.

"I would like to show you my appreciation for your gift if you would let me. Master" Skye says in low sultry voice.

I'm momentarily stunned my body however got with the game. I step in front of her. "Tell me how you would show your appreciation"

"I want to suck on your cock until you come in my mouth" she pauses before adding "Master"

The word caresses my skin as it washes over me. I shudder as pleasure courses through my blood and straight to my cock.

"That would please me greatly" I say undoing my jeans and release my cock from the confines of my boxers, I stroke myself. Skye still looks down she's waiting for my command "good girl. Go ahead and please me" my voice is deeper and thicker than usual a sure sign of the effect her words have on me.

Skye lifts her head and rises to her knees; her yellow green eyes sparkling like the rubies and diamonds around her neck. I continue to stroke myself. Skye's eyes drop to my cock and a smile plays on her lips. Slowly she leans forward and her tongue slides out and licks the bead of cum gathered on the head of my cock. She makes an appreciative murmur and smacks her lips at the taste of me.

Skye puts her hands behind her back, opens her mouth and surrounds the head my cock. As I stroke myself Skye sucks and swirls her tongue around the tip taking more of me in her mouth on each rotation and sucking harder as she pulls back, making pleasure hurtle around my body.

"Fuck yes baby do it again" I command.

My balls grow tight and heavy as she does it over and over again. I have to stop stroking myself as I don't want to come yet. I want to enjoy more of the feel of her warm wet mouth and wicked tongue on my cock. I give myself over to the pleasure sensations. My head falls back and my eyes roll to the back of my head.

"That feels so good, use your hands on me baby" I command softly.

Skye's delicate hands wrap around cock and gently stroke, one hand moves to cup my balls tickling and teasing me.

"Yes baby" I groan.

She's torturing me and I love it. I can't hold back any longer. I put my hands on Skye's head, my fingers tangling in her hair, my hips moving in time with her rhythm of sucking. I'm close my climax is building fast. Skye senses this as her hands release my cock and balls and grip my hips, her fingers and nails dig into my ass. I take over and fuck her mouth moving faster as I chase my orgasm.

As I pump my heart beats faster, my breathing becoming harsh and ragged, blood pounds in my ears as pleasure builds, my balls tighten and Skye sucks harder each time I withdraw.

"I'm coming" I gasp just before my release explodes from me.

My spine stiffens as my back arches, my fingers grip tighter in Skye's hair. I throw my head back and my hips forward "Skye, fuck, Skye" I call out as pleasure sensations pulse through me. Skye sucks and licks at my cock taking everything I have to give, prolonging my orgasm.

I'm still panting for breath when Skye rises to her feet, my hands still on her head. I massage her scalp before releasing my fingers from her hair and move my hands to cup her face. I bend to kiss her.

"How can I return the favor" I whisper against her lips.

"Not necessary, besides we don't have time, you can return the favor when we're home" Skye says smiling sweetly.

I know I'm grinning like a goofy idiot. A thought comes to me about her necklace. I raise my fingers and touch the rubies at her throat. "You know this is not intended to be a collar" it suddenly occurs to me she might not know what I mean. I'm going to have to explain.

"I know" whispers Skye.

Well that stops me in my tracks "Someone has been doing their homework" I raise an expectant eyebrow. Skye gives me an impish grin "do you want to get involved in the Dom and Sub lifestyle?" no reason not to have this conversation now considering what she's just said and done.

Skye chews her bottom lip and shakes her head. Both my eyebrows to rise in surprise, she is an enigma. What the fuck! My mind shouts. I must have shown my confusion because Skye chuckles.

"We've already established I'm not submissive however I enjoyed what you did to me last night. I like it when you dominate me like that" Skye raises her hands and cups my face, her smile is so tender and loving my heart thuds "you made me realize last night that all the ghosts and fears of my past have been laid to rest. You are right I have done my homework and I have spoken with a Submissive" her admission shocks the crap out of me "I wanted to find out what it entailed and I thought long and hard about it afterwards. I would be crap at it plus I couldn't do it for prolong periods" she chuckles "I'd probably end up black and blue because you'd have to discipline me all the time for insubordination and I wouldn't like that" I'm speechless she has taken it far more seriously than I had ever imagined "you have awakened me sexually and not just my lady parts" Skye smiles ruefully "but my sense of sexual adventure. I like doing the scenes, I love how turned on you get and it turns me on that I can do that to you. You promised to show me ways to explore and enjoy sex whether it is fucking or making love I want to explore it all with you. If it means dressing up and role playing, using toys or food by that I mean chocolate" I snort a laugh "or if it's plain old vanilla sex" Skye shrugs nonchalantly "I'm game, I'm ready and willing to explore" her eyes search my face for a reaction.

"Wow!" is all I can manage.

"So are you up for the challenge Master" her voice dips lower and huskier on Master.

"Fuck yes" it comes out more of a groan as images flicker through my mind. I clear my throat "when we get home I want you to tell me some of your fantasies because so far you've played out mine" Skye opens her mouth, I put my fingers on her lips to stop her speaking "I know you get turned on doing it but I want to return the favor, tell me what you want and need, tell me when we get home okay" Skye nods and puckers her lips effectively kissing my fingers "now get dressed and let's get something to eat and I mean food"

Skye tries to pout but she's smiling too much.

The flight home is pleasant. Pete and Caroline turned up, everyone ignores Caroline even Pete. It makes me wonder if they're still in a relationship. I squash the thought quickly and return my attention to Skye and listen to her as she discusses her schedule for the coming week with Macy.

Skye has a busy week ahead. She's starting the commission for The Gentleman's Club, renovations to the auction house building are starting, the business partnership for the jewellery range is finalised so the designing can begin and to top it all off she has my mother to contend with to go over the updates for the wedding. It makes my head spin the list of meetings and conference calls Macy reels off.

"We also need to plan in the changes for our new home" Skye adds to the list then looks at me "do you have any objections if Macy and I get on with it?"

I pick up her hand and kiss the back of it "No my love" I smile indulgently, I can't help it "by Friday you'll be ready for the pampering session"

Skye's eyes widen "Oh my god I'd forgotten about that, thanks" turning back to Macy she instructs "clear Friday afternoon and evening as Shelley and Simon are coming over for a pampering, do you want to join us?"

"It'll be rude not to" Macy grins "Paul will be with Jack so why not. Oh I almost forgot Bruce has heard back from his friends about coming for an interview. Do you both want to see them?"

"Yes" we answer together "we'll hold the interviews at my office, speak to Helena to arrange the date and times" I add, then to Skye "you okay with that?"

Skye grins and nods; see I can take over and check in just as well as she can.

Macy stood up "I'll speak to Bruce now to get his friends details and I'll speak to Helena first thing in the morning" she moves off down to the front of the plane to where Bruce and Paul are sitting.

I tug Skye's hand "Come here" I pat my knee "I want to hold you"

Skye's smile got wider as she slid across the seat and onto my lap. I wrap my arms around her and hug her to me. Skye let out a small oomph sound as I squeeze the air out of her. Skye snuggles into me and we sit in comfortable silence for a few minutes. My mind wonders back to our earlier conversation about the Dom-Sub lifestyle and how Skye had done her homework curiosity gets the better of me.

"I'm curious" Skye snort's, I tap her thigh in a playful reprimand "humour me. Who did you speak to when doing your research?" Skye looks at me puzzled after a few seconds I raise an eyebrow "don't keep me waiting, you know what happens when you do" I say in my best Dom voice.

Skye's eyes widen then bursts out laughing when she catches on.

"You're not supposed to laugh" I try to say seriously but fail miserably as her laughter is infectious; it even causes others to look over and smile. Skye wipes her eyes.

"Told you I'd be crap at it" she set off giggling again. I love to hear her laugh. After a few minutes she gets herself under control.

"One of the dancers at The Gentleman's Club is into the lifestyle. It came out during one of the study drawing and photo sessions I did for the commission, actually the timing was perfect'" Skye glances round to make sure no-one is listening, it didn't appear there was but she still lowers her voice "after last Sunday it got me thinking so I rang her. She's a Sub, she came over on Wednesday and I spent quite a few hours picking her brain; getting her to explain various things. She showed me the position, how to act and what to say. It was really fascinating but it made me realize that yes I enjoy being a Sub for a short period of time but I haven't got the self-discipline it would require" she pauses "or the inclination" she adds "to be the perfect Sub, it doesn't appeal to me to be punished because I fail to behave in a certain way. She explained it would be part of the training but I know I will have a hard time of letting go because I have fought and worked too hard for my independence. I understand the Sub has all the power, I get that, I just couldn't do it for hours at a time" she snorts "it took all the control I had not to look at you for those few minutes. I was dying to see your face, hearing your reaction wasn't enough for me"

Skye put her mouth next to my ear "I liked playing the hooker and I want you to call me up to your office sometime" my cock throbs "I like playing the stripper and the naughty secretary. I love it when you spank me with your hand, flogger and riding crop and I want more of it. As for fantasies I don't have any but I do want to try sex in a public place someday, remember on the conference weekend how you finger fucked me at the bar in our suite when everyone was focused on the news reports" fuck I need to be inside her, I nod "and I really, really want to see you in a pair of tight leather trousers especially the next time we play pool"

I'm definitely going shopping for leather pants tomorrow, remembering what we did last time my control snaps and I surge to my feet lifting Skye in my arms. I stride quickly to the back of the plane to the bedroom. I don't give a flying fuck, pun intended, that I have guests who at this moment in time all gawp at me as I pass. Skye is laughing.

"Keep the noise down" Simon calls out making everyone chuckle.

I open the door, kicking it shut behind me as I unceremoniously drop Skye on the bed. I pull her boots and socks off together quickly followed by her jeans and panties. I unzip my jeans and shove them down far enough to release my cock. I'm mounted and buried balls deep inside Skye before she can draw her next breath.

Skye groans "I love it when you take me like this, you lose your control" she raises her hips to meet my thrusts and clenches her muscles hard on my cock; bliss. I kiss her deeply.

"Keep talking, tell me what else you like" my mouth is close to her ear, I nip and tug her lobe with my teeth and I start to pound into her.

"I love the feel of you deep inside me" I roll my hips and thrust hard "oh yes, just like that" her breathing is becoming heavier "I love it when you tell me what you are going to do to me. I love the different positions you take me in. I like the feel of your teeth grazing my skin, your bites feel as if you are marking me as yours"

"That's because you are mine" I growl possessively "you… are… mine" I thrust deeply as I say each word.

"Yes, yours" Skye moans "and you are mine" she clenches and grips me hard.

"Fuck yes, I'm yours" I can feel Skye is close and so am I "come with me baby"

I place my mouth over hers and kiss her hard, our tongues dart in and out tasting, licking, fucking. I brace myself on to my forearms and move faster giving us both the friction we need. Skye whimpers as her orgasm starts, I let go and join her. We cling to each other. Our faces buried in each other, Skye's against my chest, mine in the crook of her neck doing our best to stifle our shouts of pleasure.

"You are a very naughty girl" Skye gives me a really how so kind of look "I told you to tell me about your fantasies when we got home"

Skye schools her expression to one of wide eyed innocence "But I didn't. All I told you are the things I like based on what we have already done and I would love to do more of it. It's not my fault you are so god damned horny and a walking hard on"

I laugh as I realize she's right she even said she didn't have any fantasies. My lust fogged brain had temporarily deleted that piece of information. "So you did. I retract what I said, forgive me"

Skye pouts "I like being naughty" she surges her hips and clenches her cunt muscles on my semi flaccid cock, I harden instantly "ooh feel that, how easily he jumps to attention" she teases.

"Only because it's you" I flex my hips sliding in and out of her. I continue with the slow leisurely pace "you know all last week at work every time I thought about coming home to you I got hard"

"So you are a walking hard on all day every day" Skye giggles.

"Absolutely, it took all of my control not to tackle you the minute I walked in through the door and bury myself balls deep in you"

I pick up the pace of moving in and out of her. Skye wraps her legs around mine and surges her hips up taking me deeper with each stroke. Our faces and lips inches apart.

"I like the sound of that, would you fuck me where I was or in the bedroom" her voice comes out in short breathy pants.

"I will fuck you where you are hard and fast" Skye undulates beneath me and groans "then I will take you to the bedroom and do it all again only slower, where I will worship you and your body with my mouth, hands and cock in whatever position I want"

"Oh yes" Skye moans loudly.

"Shhh baby people will hear you"

I keep up the momentum of my thrusts all the while whispering to Skye what I'm going to do to her. Her answering moans and groans tell me all I need to know. Skye lifts her t-shirt and unhooks her front fastening bra.

"Suck my tits" she commands

I oblige, capturing her hard nipple with my teeth then surrounding it with my mouth and suckle, deep drawing pulls which match my thrusts. Her cunt muscles clench hard and greedily on my cock. Skye pushes her head back into the mattress and arches her back the veins in her neck stand out as she bites back on a cry of pleasure as her orgasm crashes over her. I hold her to me continuing to suckle her tits whilst I thrust harder and faster. I come as her second orgasm hits. Skye turns her head into my arm and bites down on my bicep muffling her shout. I bite down on the crook of her neck.

"I hope you haven't given me a hickey" Skye grumbles as she refastens her bra and pulls her t-shirt down.

I zip up my pants and reach over to move her hair, there's a red mark but it won't bruise. "Just a red mark, nothing your hair can't cover" I say then look at my arm, it's very red with perfect teeth indentations "now that is going to bruise" I point.

Skye looks at it then shrugs nonchalantly "I had to do something to gag myself, look at it this way you've got a memento for being in the mile high club"

Laughing I pick up her panties and jeans and hand them to her.

As we make our way back to our seats the pilot announces our decent and puts on the seat belt sign. Simon grins at me and Skye.

"You must have bloody good sound proofing in that bedroom" he says cheekily.

"Nah, I just bit down on Clayton" Skye retorts quick as a flash. I point at the red mark and teeth marks on my bicep.

"Oh Skye honey you are vicious" Simon squeals with laughter.

"It's his fault for being such a randy bugger" Skye says pointing at me keeping her face straight, she winks at Simon.

"You madam are incorrigible" I put my hand over my heart "and I wouldn't have you any other way".

"Oh yes you would. Given half the chance you'd have me any way you can" she scoffs. Skye is on a roll.

"La la la la" Simon puts his fingers in his ears "too much information, not listening" he sings.

"Serves you right, don't start something you can't finish" Skye says leaning over and punches Simon's arm.

Those around us who have been listening all burst out laughing. For the rest of the descent and right up to the doors opening the good natured banter fills the plane, the weekend finishing on a high. All the while out of the corner of my eye I see Caroline watching and listening to Skye and me. I hope she's finally got the message.

In the car on the way home it suddenly dawns on me Skye hasn't mentioned getting Shelley and Phil a wedding gift. Since Bruce is the only person in the car with us, Paul and Macy are in the vehicle behind us, I ask her what she's getting them. Skye shifts in my lap.

"I've already got it" she lets out a sigh "they've lived together for god knows how many years so they don't need anything for the home. The apartment they live in, I own it" somehow it doesn't surprise me "A few years back they wanted to get on the property ladder but what they could afford was in not very nice neighbourhoods. So I offered to buy a place in an area they wanted and they are paying me back. Like a monthly mortgage payment only interest free, some months they pay more than others depending on their finances anyway it all goes into a special account I had set up"

"So let me guess you're going to give them the apartment and the money back" I keep my voice matter of fact, non-judgemental.

Skye chews her bottom lip, I know she's trying to gage my reaction, she nods "As soon as they said they were getting married I had the papers drawn up and the names on the account changed. I tricked Shelley and Phil into signing the papers" I laugh as Skye winces "I pretended I wanted them to be witnesses on some legal documents. I knew I could get away with it because they trust me" Skye cringes at her own admission "I just hope they're not mad at me for being underhanded"

"I think it is a beautiful, thoughtful selfless act and the perfect gift to give someone at the start of their married life together, especially since they have a baby on the way" I put as much sincerity into my words as I can "I think once they have gotten over the initial shock they will be very happy. When do you plan to tell them?"

"The day of the wedding, what do you think?" it surprises and pleases me Skye genuinely wants my opinion.

"I think it's a wonderful idea if you're ready for all the attention it will draw. Something that generous won't stay quiet for long and I have a feeling you'll suddenly find yourself with a lot of new friends all needing property"

Skye frowns as she considers what I've said. "Good point, I hadn't thought of that" Skye went quiet for a few minutes "Phil will be bringing Shelley over on Friday at lunchtime, I'll do a meal and tell them then"

"If it's okay with you I'd like to join you" Skye looks at me surprised "I was thinking of taking Friday off plus I would like to give them my gift" her eyebrows rise higher "I was thinking of adding to the account"

"You would do that for them" Skye says in wonder, I nod "but you hardly know them"

"I know they are two very important people in your life who love you very much. I saw that this weekend. I like Shelley and Phil; they are two talented unassuming hard working people and I would like to help give your friends, who by the way I would like to class as mine, a head start in married life"

"That's wonderful and very generous" Skye whispers and kisses me tenderly "I'm sure they will appreciate it once they get over their shock" she grins as she says the last bit.

"You don't know how much I'm going to give them" I mock hurt.

"Let me guess your next few moves" she pats my chest "first you'll ask me how much is in the account, then you'll think about matching it, you'll worry it might be too generous so you'll consider a third to which you'll round up to the nearest ten thousand"

I throw my head back roaring with laughter. I'm delighted I am that transparent to her. "Skye how well you know me baby, go on how much is in the account?"

"Last time I checked not far off fifty thousand, so following my hypothesis you'll be adding twenty thou to the pot"

"Okay I'll have a think about it and let you know"

The car stops. Skye climbs off my knee and gets out of the car. I follow and walk to the trunk to help unload our bags.

"Oh and just so you know I've also set up a college trust fund thingy for bump. Once Phil and Shelley have a name I can transfer the fund over as soon as baby bump is born"

I notice Bruce giving Skye an indulgent kind of smile as he hands her a bag. Skye smiles back and carries on talking about how the fund works. I listen but watch Bruce. In all the years he has worked for me not once have I seen him smile, certainly not in the way he just has, that's a first!

Skye has really gotten to him she has broken through the hard man exterior so effortlessly and in an extremely short space of time. Seeing Bruce now I instinctively know and trust he will protect the most precious thing to me in my life with his own, he will take a bullet for her if it meant saving her life.

The thought makes me realize we need to sit down and discuss salaries for the body guards and make sure Paul and Bruce are on the same salary. One of us is bound to be paying a higher salary and I have a feeling that will be Skye.

As we unpack I broach the subject and sure enough Skye is paying considerably more and rightly so due to the higher risk of stalker and delusional fans plus the amount of travel Skye did Paul's pay is compensation for being away from his son.

"Actually" Skye says as she crawls into bed "we need to talk about setting up a joint account so all household bills can be paid out of it including any household staff salaries, then that brings up the question do the security staff get paid out of the household account because at the moment I pay Paul through my business and I'm guessing you do the same with Bruce"

"I do but let's talk about it tomorrow, it's late and I want to devour you"

Skye giggles as I pounce.

Chapter Twenty Seven

SKYE

As I gain consciousness I stretch. My joints pop, my spine cracks and all my muscles are tense and tightly strung. Oooh that feels good. I relax and sag, sinking back in to the mattress. What day is it? My brain groggily tries to work it out. Lord it's been a busy week. Friday! My brain shouts in triumph. Thank god today is a lazy day as far as business is concerned. I can't grumble though, a lot has been accomplished this week.

Work on the auction house building is well under way and the contractors are ahead of schedule four days in, although it could all go pear shaped as the heavy duty work starts today.

The jewellery designs have been agreed on. I smile as I recall the look on Matthew's face when he came over to me Tuesday morning and saw all of my work books and sketches. He was like a kid in a candy shop once he got over his shock. He came by yesterday with my earrings and our wedding rings and brought the finished designs for the first pieces which will be made for my final approval and sign off; he's making a start on them today. Gerrard had, as Clayton predicted, snapped my arm off when I put forward my proposal on the partnership. Matthew, I found out is Gerrard's grandson and hasn't long been working for him; both were stunned when I told them that I already have twenty orders for the high end range.

We interviewed for the additional bodyguard. I was late getting to Clayton's office, due to over running with Matthew. I pretended not to notice but the first guy, who Clayton was half way through interviewing, leered at me when I entered the office. He made my skin crawl. He also had a condescending attitude towards me. I chuckle as I remember I'd drawn a cartoon caricature picture of the guy being kicked out of the office on the pad I was supposed to be making notes on, Clayton saw it and burst out laughing quickly turning it into a coughing fit.

The next guy, Alan, I'd taken a liking to straightaway. Turned out he knew both Bruce and Paul. He also had done his homework on me and Clayton. I asked my usual personal questions around family. He's divorced, no children, parents and siblings live in Texas so being away from home wasn't an issue. Since leaving the military he'd been bodyguard for film stars to businessmen.

"So you're used to dealing with overzealous fans and paparazzi" says Clayton.

"Yes sir, I understand that is a prerequisite in Miss Darcy's case" Alan tilts his head slightly in my direction and smiles. I like his guy.

"Fortunately overzealous fans only happen when I attend conventions" I grin back.

"Yes ma'am I know I was in Vegas as part of the back up security detail" he smiles ruefully.

"Paul and Bruce kept that quiet" Clayton says highly amused. I laugh once I got over my surprise.

We offered Alan the position and he is starting Monday.

I met with Stephanie for an update on progress for the wedding. Invites went out yesterday. We sorted out the menu for the sit down meal and evening buffet. Stephanie showed me pictures of the set up for the ceremony, marquee, table settings and chairs. I told her what I liked and squashed her plans on doves and fireworks telling her I thought it too pretentious and OTT.

All the guys had gone to Shelley's studio for the wedding vest fitting and to get measured. Stephanie commented she was amazed that Clayton turned up; I neglected to tell her I threatened to withhold sex for a week if he didn't go. Clayton laughed when I made the threat but he obviously didn't want to test how serious I was.

The marquee, tables and chairs have been hired and we had the place settings based on the current guest list. Stephanie would make alterations as replies came in. I already know from my guests who will be coming so all the changes would be on Clayton's side.

Finally I went to the new apartment with Paul, Macy and Bruce. Clayton and I made the decision to buy new furniture and appliances so Macy and I worked through each room making a list of what was needed and got the guys to take measurements.

When I told Paul and Bruce they have a blank cheque for security, the pair became quite animated in their discussions. I found them fascinating to watch which I did until Paul told me to go away as I made him feel like he was a science test subject. I laughed mainly at the shock on Bruce's face.

"I've not forgotten about the bells" I retort menacingly, Paul barks out a laugh. As I walk off to find Macy I heard Paul telling Bruce about my threat to attach bells to him as he kept scaring the bejesus out of me because he moves around so quietly.

I found Macy in the kitchen, it's one of those cold stainless steel, grey glossy Formica unit masculine set ups. I hate it. The only thing I like is the cooker.

"I've made a note to get the kitchen units ripped out and replaced with solid oak and I'm going to guess you want to keep the cooker"

"Spot on" I say smiling "also get the black marble replaced with white. I also want the island changed" I drew a sketch of what I wanted and gave it to her. I checked out the sink, fridge freezer and dishwasher.

"Keep the sink and taps, replace all the appliances, actually have you seen a laundry room?"

"Yes it's in the corridor connecting your living quarters to ours, there's another small room next to it which at a guess was used as a storage room for supplies; that reminds me have you considered getting a housekeeper?" Macy looks up from tapping on her tablet.

"Funny you should say that I was just thinking the same thing" Clayton's deep voice came from behind me followed by his arms. He plants a kiss on the top of my head "I missed you" he murmurs in my ear which explains his surprise visit.

So we now have a housekeeper. I didn't need much convincing to hire one. Before I never really stayed in one place long enough to need one, however now I'm going to be more permanently based in New York my requirements have changed. Clayton uses one of those cleaning services but we need someone who will be more than a cleaner, by coincidence Macy just so happened to know of a housekeeper who is looking to relocate to New York. It transpired that for the last few years Macy has kept in touch with a woman who is housekeeper for one of my LA clients. Lisa originates from Brooklyn and is coming back to be closer to her family and elderly parents.

On top of all that I've made good progress on The Gentleman's Club commission. I give a contented sigh everything is falling into place. I turn onto my side and open my eyes. Clayton is lying on his back. The sheet is pooled around his hips giving me a lovely unobstructed view of his chest and abs. He has one arm over his head the other down at his side with his hand resting lightly on his chest. His body is sculpted, not one inch of body fat, all muscles clearly defined. My eyes devour his physique. I love his abs and he has that V thing going on from his hips pointing down to his impressively big cock which I can see clearly outlined under the sheet lying on his thigh.

If the last two weeks is any indication of what our life together will be like we most definitely will be fucking ourselves into an early grave. Since we've been back from Vegas Clayton has kept to his word about tackling and fucking me the minute he set foot through the door. On Monday I met him at the door dressed in my hooker outfit and we christened the hallway. Tuesday I was in the living room painting and I only just dropped my brush and palette in time before a wall of muscle hit me. Wednesday I was in the kitchen cooking dinner and yesterday I played hide and seek, that had been fun, he eventually found me in the laundry room and fucked me whilst I sat on the washing machine.

Clayton also went shopping. He bought a pair of leather trousers and we hot footed it to his apartment and played pool, okay we attempted to play pool. I wore my micro mini skirt and buckled boots; needless to say we didn't pot many balls! His pool table is coming to our new apartment with us. Clayton also bought a flogger, riding crop and paddle along with butt plugs and those love ball egg things.

Thinking about what we've been up to is making me horny. I slide under the cover and make a beeline for Clayton's cock. I'm hungry and I want my morning protein. Taking my weight on my hands I lean forward and run my tongue over the shaft of his cock following the veins. His cock twitches and jerks as it starts to lengthen and harden. This time I circle the head before licking down the length, within seconds he is fully erect. Clayton doesn't make a sound his breathing is deep and even, still asleep. Not for long I think gleefully.

Lifting his cock I gently suck and lick from head to root, after a couple of times of doing this Clayton's legs move further apart, his body responding to my ministrations and telling me it wants me to play with his balls. How can I refuse a silent request, I shift my position so I can cup his balls and work his shaft at the same time. As I set a rhythm Clayton's hips begin to move and he groans, I glance up at him, he's still asleep. I continue slowly increasing the speed of stroking his shaft and how hard I suck. I taste pre cum on my tongue and the veins in his cock pulse, he's close. I continue to work him. His breathing comes in harsh short gasps; his hips pump faster; his hands grip the bed sheets; his head pushes back into the pillow. I suck harder, stroke his shaft faster and squeeze his balls.

Clayton climaxes roaring my name, he comes with such force seamen hits the back of my throat; I just about swallow in time before I choke. I lick him clean then crawl up his body placing kisses as I go. He's still breathing heavily when I lie on top of him and kiss his lips; his arms come round me, gently holding me.

"Good morning my love" I croon. A lazy smile spreads across his face as he opens one eye.

"Good morning beautiful" his voice is croaky, he places a kiss on the tip of my nose "and what a wonderful early morning wakeup call that was"

I grin, feeling pleased with myself. "What would you like for breakfast?"

"You" Clayton says as he flips me onto my back.

"God Skye that was delicious I'd forgotten just how good a cook you are" Shelley says rubbing her pregnant belly. At five months pregnant she is showing now, a neat little bump.

"I'm fit to burst. I just hope I can get in my suit tomorrow" Phil says patting his stomach.

"Hey nobody forced you to eat it all, there's a two letter word in the English language which helps if you use it. It's called no, ever heard of it" I retort jokingly.

"Somehow that word has always eluded me when it comes to your cooking" Phil comes back with smiling making me laugh.

"Does that mean then my cooking is crap because you can say no to it?" Shelley says indignantly to Phil but winks at me. Phil's face drops in horror and uncertainty.

"Be careful how you answer buddy, you might find yourself in the divorce court before you've even got down the aisle" Clayton laughs.

"I'm just messing with you baby" Shelley says patting Phil's cheek.

I get up and clear the table, Clayton helps. As we come back into the living room Phil stands.

"Thanks for lunch Skye, I need to be making tracks" picking up Shelley's hand and looking lovingly into her eyes he says "and you my love I will meet tomorrow at the alter" he kisses the back of her hand.

My heart is fit to burst watching the scene it's so touching and lovely. Clayton prods me in the back. I scowl at him. Clayton inclines his head at Phil. Shit, Phil is leaving.

"Hang on five minutes" I blurt out as I run to my bedroom to get the documents from the safe.

I came back to puzzled looks from Shelley and Phil. I indicate to Phil to sit down as Clayton joins me to sit opposite them. I slide the first envelop towards them.

"This is your wedding gift from me" I slide the second one forward "and this one is from Clayton and me. Open them now"

Clayton had decided to match the figure in the account and transferred the money over during the week so the second envelop includes a bank statement along with cheque book and cash cards. Phil reaches for the first envelop and opens it— my heart is in my mouth as I wait for their reaction—and pulls out the document, confusion is on both their faces.

"What is it" asks Shelley impatiently.

I don't answer. I let Phil read and I know instantly when he's worked out what it is he is holding. His head snaps up, shocked he looks at me then at Shelley then back at me.

"Well what is it" Shelley demands.

Taking pity on Phil I answer "It's the deed to your apartment"

"It's ours. Skye has signed it over to us" Phil manages croak out.

Shelley gasps, she starts to get up and say thank you. I stop her. "Open the second envelop first, it's from both of us" I remind them.

Shelley reaches for it and opens it with shaking hands. This time astonished confusion crosses their faces as Shelley pulls out the cheque book and bank cards. Then they both look at the statement. If we were in a cartoon their jaws would have hit the floor and stayed there.

"That is the bank account I opened for you to make your repayments into. I'm giving you all the money back. Clayton's gift was deposited into the account on Wednesday. We wish you both a long and happy married life together"

Shelley burst into tears "Oh Skye, Clayton" she blubbers getting up. I stand and meet her halfway, Shelley collapses on me crying hard. I rub her back "I'm so happy" she wails "I don't know what to say" Shelley let go of me and went to Clayton crying harder still.

Phil has tears in his eyes as he wraps me in a huge hug. "Thank you so, so very much" he whispers in my ear. As he pulls away he wipes his eyes. Clayton went to shake Phil's hand but Phil grabs him in a hug. "This is the best gift ever and so unexpected, thank you"

"You're welcome" Clayton says patting Phil's back.

I can see he is touched by the strong show of emotion and appreciation our gifts have given Shelley and Phil.

"If it is okay with you can we leave these here until Sunday? I don't fancy carrying them around with me this afternoon" says Phil. I nod.

"How did you manage to get the paperwork in our names for these without our signatures?" Shelley says wiping her eyes.

"Busted" Clayton says gleefully and laughs "time to come clean"

He is enjoying this too much. I narrow my eyes at him, he just grins back at me expectantly. Sighing I pull up my big girl pants.

"Remember back in May a few days before I left for Russia I asked you both to witness some legal documents for me" they both nod, I cringe as I say the next bit "well they were legal documents but it was for that" I point at the two envelopes on the table.

"You tricked us" Shelley says shocked. I cringe more as I nod, I know my face must look like a shrivelled prune I'm screwing it up so much.

Phil burst out laughing. "I knew it" he exclaims "I said to Shelley at the time it seemed odd plus you made sure we couldn't see any of the wording. I was this close" he holds up his thumb and forefinger to indicate a small gap "to insisting on reading what I had just signed but Shelley stopped me"

"I'm sorry, please don't be mad at me" I plead.

"How can we be mad at you? I'm just shocked you managed to think of such an underhanded way to get our signatures" Shelley laughs. Relief floods through me "does Simon know about this?" I shake my head "I'm even more amazed and impressed you pulled it off" I didn't know whether to be insulted or not by her comment "you are way too honest and do everything by the book" Shelley hugs me hard, my spine creaks "I love you Skye Darcy. Thank you so much" I feel tears prickle my eyes. Phil's phone rings as we pull apart.

"Hi Dad… I'm just leaving now, I got held up at Skye and Clayton's" Phil looks at us "Dad says hi and is looking forward to seeing you both tomorrow"

We both shout "Hi Don, see you tomorrow"

I pick up the envelopes and put them back in the safe, as I come back Phil finishes up his conversation with Don and is getting ready to leave.

"Skye, Clayton people are going to ask what you got us for a gift what do you want us to say" says Phil. I can see he is genuinely concerned and wants to protect us.

"Whatever you feel comfortable with" I say.

"Just remember to tell us so we can give the same information also how loose does your tongue get when you've had a few drinks, bear that in mind as well when you decide" Clayton adds.

"How about we say you gifted the apartment to us, Phil's family already know you bought it for us and we are paying you back" Shelley says to me "I would prefer we didn't say anything about the bank account" she says to Phil and he nods his agreement.

"It's going to look suspicious if you don't mention a gift from Clayton" I say "just say he gave you a cash gift and decline to say how much. If anyone pushes you to reveal the amount give them a smack in the mouth for being so bloody nosey"

"Okay that's what we'll do, right I really must get going otherwise my Dad will be knocking the door down" as Phil says that the buzzer went and a look of panic flashes across his face.

"That'll be Simon" I chuckle.

Shelley saw Phil out and let Simon in.

"Well that went a lot better than expected" Clayton says softly as he put his arms around me "actually it was quite emotional, even brought a tear to my eye"

"Ahhh ya big softy" I tease and kiss him.

Not long after Simon's arrival the beauty technicians from the spa and Macy arrived. We all get manicures, pedicures and facials. I got a fit of the giggles for some reason seeing Clayton in a face mask, it was hilarious. I even took pictures for prosperity. I also got waxed and a massage. By six o'clock we're all sitting on the sofa in bathrobes eating pizza and drinking wine. Macy had left to go and spend some quality time with Paul; giving a saucy wink when she said quality time.

Simon is his usual gossipy self, all afternoon he's regaled us with stories. Clayton is amused and amazed Simon knows all the juicy gossip about a lot of influential people, most of them Clayton knows; some are even his business associates and rivals.

"How on earth do you find out all this information" Clayton says bewildered.

"People talk to me for some strange reason. They think I have an honest face and think I'm a good listener" he shrugs, suddenly his eyes widen "oh my god!" he exclaims "I've just remember something you'll find interesting"

Simon sits up straight his eyes bright with glee, taking a sip of wine he shifts so he's perched on the end of the sofa positioning himself so he can look at all of us, must be good gossip.

"I was at a party last night and Pete was there on his own" Simon didn't wait for anyone's reaction "Harry asked him where Caroline was and Pete says we've split up, apparently he kicked her out" shit, shit my mind whispers "Harry then says it's about time you kicked the unfaithful bitch to the curb. So Pete says if you are referring to what happened with Clayton, nothing did. To which Harry replies Clayton, I don't know what you're talking about. I'm referring to the three guys I know of she shagged that at the time were dating Skye a few years back" Simon looks at me unapologetically "Yes, I told him it was too juicy to keep to myself, anyway Harry goes on to say I also know she propositioned two others right under your very nose at Gino's. It doesn't surprise me in the least she tried it on with Clayton but he's too into Skye to even look at a tramp like her"

We all look at Simon in open mouthed stunned silence, he grins back wickedly.

"Anyway I did some asking around; apparently the split was over money. Caroline had spent a lot in Vegas and she expected you" Simon points at me, my stomach drops to the floor "would be picking up the tab only she got a nasty shock at checking out time"

We all laugh, the tension within me eases. I would've loved to have been a fly on the wall to have seen that.

"Pete had to pay her bill on his credit card and when he asked her for the money she was refusing to pay him saying Skye shouldn't have led her to believe it was a free weekend"

Mine and Shelley's jaw pop open. I'm too shocked to say anything.

"Cheeky fucking bitch" Clayton exclaims.

"Oh it gets better" Simon bounces on the seat in excitement "Caroline then accuses Pete of always making passes at Skye and trying to rekindle their past relationship and he'd been doing it for years. By this point Pete has had enough so he packs her bags, took the key off her and threw her out. Caroline was screaming like a crazed banshee and the police were called. They escorted her off the premises, she had no choice but to go because her name isn't on the tenancy agreement and Pete told the police she had never paid anything towards the rent and she only lived there because he allowed her to"

"Bloody hell" is all I can manage to say. I sit in a daze staring at Simon. I'm also starting to feel nauseous and uneasy.

"How in the hell did you find all that out?" Shelley asks sounding as dazed as I feel.

"Pete's neighbour just happens to be an ex-lover of Harry's, he told me and the walls in their apartment building are thin as in paper thin. What information he couldn't get through the walls Pete told him himself"

I don't like the idea of an unhinged Caroline loose on the streets, that's what is causing my uneasiness I realize. I've also got a strong inkling as to why Caroline has always been such a bitch towards me. I look at Clayton, he's frowning. Was he thinking the same thing?

"When did this happen, I mean Pete kicking Caroline out?" says Clayton.

"Tuesday early evening, Graham that's the neighbour said Caroline showed up on Wednesday for the rest of her stuff, she even tried to get Pete to take her back but Pete wouldn't even acknowledge her. Graham helped take boxes down to her car so that's how he knew"

I pick up my phone and send a text to Paul and Macy filling them in, alarm bells are ringing and they're deafening me. After I sent it I remember Bruce, he'll need to know as well. I'm in the middle doing a new text to that effect when Paul appears in the living room. He lifts his hand with his phone and wiggles it then inclines his head in a come here gesture. Dread courses through me. Without a word I get up and went to him.

"I need to tell you something" he looks behind me "both of you" Clayton has followed me.

We went into the room Macy and Clayton use as an office. Paul starts talking as soon as the door shut.

"I apologise for not telling you sooner ma'am. I didn't want to cause you any unnecessary concern or worry. Since we got back from Vegas, Bruce and I have been monitoring these two" Paul lifts his phone indicating to my text message "considering what happened I thought it best. Yesterday Bruce spotted Caroline hanging around your office sir. She tried to follow you home but Bruce managed to lose her. We have already put extra security around this building and we have circulated their pictures to all staff. They are not getting in and neither is anyone else if the resident isn't here to vouch for the visitor. Alan has also agreed to start tomorrow he will be here first thing and will come with us to the wedding"

"Thank you Paul" I nod, I'm so pleased Paul is twenty steps ahead of me on this "please let us know immediately of any developments and if we are out and Caroline is spotted we are told straightaway, she's the one I'm worried about"

"Yes ma'am" Paul hesitates for a moment "I know we will only be here for a few more weeks but I could put up security cameras with the monitors in my quarters"

"Would you be happier if I agree to it?" I knew Paul well enough to ask the question, he smiles ruefully.

"Yes ma'am, I'll sleep better at night"

"Okay, go ahead plus I don't want Macy accusing me of robbing you of your beauty sleep" I deadpan.

"Paul would you ask Bruce to circulate the pictures to the security staff at the office" says Clayton. Paul clears his throat "you've already done it haven't you?"

"Yes sir, I notified them on Tuesday when I briefed everyone here" Paul states matter of fact and unapologetic, Clayton laughs.

"Good man" Clayton says with genuine praise "and am I right in assuming all security personnel have been told Caroline has been spotted outside the office?"

"Yes sir, this morning. I had a call at lunchtime from your head of security. They checked the outside security footage; she showed up around three in the afternoon and is seen to walk past repeatedly until you came out at five. I received a call when she turned up today at the same time. I got notification just before Miss Darcy's text saying she finally left at six"

"Fuck" Clayton whispers all color draining from his face.

"Looks like she's stalking you" I feel sick saying it "but her anger and possibly hate is directed at me. God knows what the crazy bitch is going to attempt"

"I promise you no harm will come to you" Paul says earnestly "either of you, we will protect you"

I try to smile "I know you will" my words come out in a hoarse whisper due to the lump in my throat.

In an unprecedented move Paul steps forward and put his hands on my shoulders and looks me in the eyes. "I will give my life to save yours if it came to that" Paul says solemnly but it's heartfelt.

Mine fill with tears and I pull Paul into a hug "Don't say things like that, never tempt fate" I choke out "I know you will do everything in your power to make us safe, you always have" I let go of him "now go and spend quality time with your fiancée"

"Yes ma'am" Paul's voice and smile are soft transforming his usually harsh features. He nods to Clayton and left.

Clayton holds open his arms and I gladly step into them. We hold each other silently giving reassurance and strength. Neither of us say "it's going to be okay" because we know it isn't. I've dealt with stalkers before. Paul had recognised the early signs too that is why he's taken the lead and initiative in this case.

"Paul really does know what he's doing doesn't he" Clayton murmurs, I nod "I thought at first he was over reacting but when he said Caroline had been spotted again today coupled with what Simon has just told us" Clayton pauses and shudders "I'm glad I took today off"

I lift up onto my tip toes and kiss him. I'm glad Clayton is taking this seriously and he needs to, that way he will be vigilant and ready for any eventuality.

"Come on let's get back and tell the other two" I say softly.

I make a detour to the kitchen and get another bottle of wine—I resist the temptation to get something stronger—and a soda for Shelley.

"What's happened? Come on spill" Simon says as soon as I come out of the kitchen. Concern is etched over both my friend's faces.

I tell them everything, including security being stepped up as a precaution. Shelley and Simon look from me to Clayton with stunned expressions.

"Holy shit" Simon whispers "Psycho Bunny Boiler Bitch really is one"

"Okay let's change the subject" Shelley says with determination "tonight is to be a celebration for my last night of freedom. I hope you've booked a stripper for me"

Simon and I look at each other and grinning we chorus together "Clayton you're up for stripper duty"

In the blink of an eye Clayton stands up and drops his bathrobe, he has his boxers on underneath thank god, but he still makes us squeal with shock and laughter as he gyrates in front of Shelley who covers her face and Simon pretends to faint, that simple act instantly lifts the mood and the wink Clayton gives me as he picks up his bathrobe and puts it back on tells me he did it intentionally to shift everyone's focus.

"I love you" I mouth, his returning smile makes my heart flutter.

Lying quietly in bed wrapped in each other's arms Clayton is in a pensive mood. Normally he pounces on me as soon as I crawl into bed but tonight he simply wraps his arms around me and cuddles. His fingers drift lightly over my back drawing lazy patterns. I lift my head and rest my chin on his chest. Clayton has his eyes closed, he doesn't look troubled just thoughtful. A smile spreads across his luscious lips.

"I can feel you staring at me" he says softly. I place a kiss on his chest and carry on enjoying the view "what's going on in that beautiful head of yours" he murmurs opening one eye.

"Right back atcha" I grin.

Clayton chuckles and then sighs "I was replaying what Paul said earlier and marvelling how calm and in control you were, are even about the whole situation"

"Have you ever had a stalker before?"

Clayton shifts and adjusts the pillow so he can better look at me. "No, it's a completely new experience. I've had over enthusiastic women trying to get close so I would notice them or the women who I dated a few times find it hard to let go and pester me for a week or two"

"What did you do in those situations?"

"Told them to fuck off, I wasn't interested and ignored them" he shrugs "in all instances they got the message and left me alone"

Clayton has been lucky none of those women turned into stalkers. He has to realize himself Caroline is obsessive and I would hazard a guess she is already fantasizing about being his girlfriend and wife, basically being in my position, which doesn't bode well for me if she's convinced herself with me out of the way it left the path clear for her to get to Clayton.

"Holy shit" Clayton exclaims sitting bolt upright and dislodging me to sprawl on the bed. Realizing what he's done he gathers me back in his arms "sorry baby, I didn't mean to do that" he whispers in my hair and kisses the top of my head.

"Are you going to share your epiphany?" it came out muffled as my face is mashed against his chest. He relaxes his hold on me so I can look at his face.

"It just dawned on me you've experienced a stalker before, that's why you are taking this in your stride and you saw the signs with Caroline. You knew and warned me. I just saw Caroline behaving like the other women I just described but the difference is" he pauses frowning "is she mentally unstable?"

"It depends on her level of obsession and if she's convinced herself you really do want to be with her" I sigh and sit up so I can look at Clayton properly "yes I'm calm and yes I've had stalkers in the past but that doesn't mean I'm complacent. I'm worried and scared. It's the uncertainty of what a stalker will escalate to if they perceive things not to be going the way they want"

"Nothing is going to happen to you baby. I won't let it" Clayton says earnestly. I feel like screaming he still doesn't get it.

"It's not me I'm worried and scared for. It's you" Clayton starts to say something but I hold up my hand to stop him "hear me out" he nods his acquiesce.

"At the moment Caroline is fixated on you not me. Simon said earlier Caroline accused Pete of making passes at me and trying to rekindle our past relationship and he had been doing this for years. It made sense to me or I should say the penny dropped as to why she has always been such a bitch to me plus why she has always attempted and in some cases successfully seduced the men I dated. It's because she convinced herself Pete wanted to be with me and in some weird obscure reasoning she was possibly proving to herself that she could take what was mine if I ever took Pete from her. Her insecurity probably pushed her to challenge herself and prove she could do it but over the years it became a game to her, who knows" I laugh a humourless laugh "only Caroline can answer that. My point is you are unfinished business, the one that got away. Based on what you've said of the conversation in Vegas on the Saturday night she has already convinced herself you want her. Now she's single, my guess it's likely she wants to talk to you, that'll explain why she's hanging around the office" I shrug "she wants to let you know she's available and tell you to dump me so you can be together. The worst case scenario in this kind of situation if things don't go her way is that one of us will end up dead" Clayton's eyes widen and his mouth opens in shock and disbelief "if it's me then she'll see it as clearing the path for your life together. If it's you then it will be about if I can't have you, no-one will. My money is on the latter"

Clayton is stunned, staring open mouthed at me. I've shocked the shit out of him. I remain quiet giving him space to work through his emotions and thoughts. Clayton gets out of bed and begins to pace. I've learnt this is his way of dealing with and thinking through a particular difficult problem.

I've watched him do this many times but he's always been clothed. Now he is gloriously naked. In the dim light of the room his muscular sculpted body looks lethal and sexy as hell. I'm mesmerised watching the muscles of his long legs, arms and stomach flex and relax as he moves, his heavy thick long cock and sack swing from side to side hypnotising me.

Clayton is one hell of a virile lascivious man. Lust grabs me and I have to restrain myself from launching at him. I grip the bed sheets, fisting my hands into my lap. I make the mistake of squeezing my thighs together; the pressure intensifies the feelings of desire in my core. My breasts become heavy and my nipples harden.

"Skye"

Clayton's voice has me dragging my lust fogged brain back on line.

"What! Sorry I had trouble concentrating. What did you say?"

I don't attempt to hide my salacious thoughts. I even lick my lips as I look at his cock, my tongue slowly running over the top then bottom lip as I imagine taking him in my mouth, tasting him. Clayton's body responds to mine, his cock twitches and bobs getting harder and longer. Hmmm...

"I said" I drag my eyes up to Clayton's face then back down to his lengthening cock "oh fuck it. It can wait till tomorrow"

Clayton stays where he is. Why isn't he pouncing on me? Once again I force my eyes upwards to his face. Oh my! I can almost see the carnal lust pulsing out of him in waves.

"You want me baby?" his voice is tantalisingly smooth and filled with desire. I slowly nod.

Clayton lifts his hands and rubs them over his chest and down his stomach, my eyes follow their descent. My heart races and I open my mouth to breathe, to get more air into my lungs.

Clayton's hands move back up over his chest, his long fingers circling and tweaking his nipples. A deep growling groan comes from the back of his throat. Blood rushes to the surface of my skin as I feel my body heat up, desire pulses outward from my stomach waking all my nerve endings. My sex clenches and I feel myself getting wetter in readiness for accepting his magnificent cock.

My eyes greedily follow Clayton's hands as they head south. In one hand he grasps his shaft with the other his balls.

"Want this baby?" his low silky voice teases as he strokes his cock and massages his balls. I nod "do you want it in your tight greedy cunt?"

My core muscles spasm at his crude words and the anticipation they trigger. Sweet Jesus it turns me on even more when he talks dirty. Again I slowly nod.

"Are you ready for me, all creamy, nice and wet?" his sinful voice is practically a whisper.

In response I shift the covers out of the way and lie down, spreading my legs wide, opening myself up ready to receive him. I cup my heavy breasts and roll my aching nipples between my thumb and fingers easing the tightness and sending pleasure messages straight to my core. I groan and arch my back. I slide one hand down my stomach, over my newly waxed pelvic mound parting my cleft with my fingers and circle my clit.

Clayton hisses a loud breath through his teeth, looking down my body at him I watch him masturbate as he watches me. Christ this is erotic we've done this loads of times and I still find it a huge turn on.

"Oh baby you look so fucking hot doing that, pull your nipple and put your fingers inside yourself" I do as he instructs, letting out a groan of pleasure as I move my fingers in and out.

"I want you badly" Clayton growls.

"Fuck me Clayton, please" I beg.

He's on me then, taking my fingers he puts them in his mouth, sucking and licking the taste of me at the same time he enters me, penetrating me in one swift thrust.

"Oh yes" I cry out. Clayton grunts as my muscles welcome his thick cock by greedily clamping and gripping him tight.

Clayton places his hands on either side of my shoulders and lifts his weight off me. Looking down our bodies to where we are joined I watch as Clayton slowly withdraws. I can see the shaft of his thick cock gradually materialize then watch as his stomach muscles clench as he thrust back into me. I love every minute of this view.

I lift my hands and start to play with my breasts and nipples. Clayton groans. I shift my eyes to his face. He's watching me roll, pull and tease my nipples. My muscles ripple and clench around his cock in response. I groan loudly at the pleasure.

I let go of one of my breasts and place my hand on Clayton's pectoral and play with his nipple, mirroring what I'm doing to my own to him.

"Jesus Christ. Fuck" Clayton roars and he slams into me.

I feel his cock pulsing as his body stiffens and locks, his orgasm has hit him hard and unexpectedly. I begin to move my hips against him to get friction. Clenching and releasing my muscles I milk every last drop out of his cock. I continue to play with my nipples moving faster against him as I chase my release. Clayton resumes thrusting giving me the friction I crave.

"Come for me Skye baby, I love watching you come"

Three deep thrusts and Clayton sends me soaring into pleasure heaven. We fall asleep wrapped around each other.

Chapter Twenty Eight

SKYE

Shelley comes out of her bedroom looking like crap. She's deathly pale with her dark short hair stuck out in all directions. It's like she's been dragged through a hedge backwards. Shelley collapses on the sofa and groans pitifully.

"Sweetie what on earth is the matter" Simon squeaks in panic rushing to her. He crouches down next to her and rubs her hand then feels her forehead.

"Morning sickness, I'll be okay in a bit" mumbles Shelley.

Simon looks at me as if I have the answer to cure her. Supposedly dry food and ginger helps or so Nessa told me. I go into the kitchen and make toast and herbal tea which has ginger in it.

"Nessa said she eats this and ginger nut biscuits says it helps" I put the dry toast down on the coffee table then her drink "sorry I don't have any ginger biscuits but the drink has ginger in it maybe that will work"

Simon breaks a piece of the toast off and feeds it to Shelley. Halfway through she sits up and finishes the rest herself along with the drink. Thankfully color returns to her cheeks.

"Thanks, I feel human now. I never thought to ask Nessa what she used, wish I'd known this about four months ago. I'm one of those unfortunate women, who by the looks of things, is likely to be suffering from morning sickness throughout the whole pregnancy" Shelley grumbles sardonically.

"Well sweetie now is the time to make you look human, I'm going to run your shower" Simon says patting her knee and getting up.

"Despite what I look like I've had the best night's sleep in a long time, that bed is so comfy" Shelley says standing and hugging me "thank you for letting me stay"

"You're welcome and if you want it you can have the bed" Shelley looks at me surprised, I shrug "we're buying new furniture for our new home so it will go to good will if you don't have it"

"I'm having it" Shelley says with such finality it makes me chuckle.

"Shower's ready Shelley" Simon calls from her room.

An hour later the hair stylists are working on our hair and by lunchtime we are in the cars heading for Phil's parents country estate. Paul and Bruce are in the car with me and Clayton whilst Alan is driving Macy,

Shelley and Simon. We are all going to be spending the night at Don and Brenda's.

Before we set off I thank Alan for starting the job early. He has the same polite professional courtesy as Paul and Bruce. I introduce him to my friends at the same time telling Simon to behave himself to which he pouts calling me a spoil sport. I inform Alan to feel free to turf Simon out of the car if he got too outrageous. Alan tries hard to supress a laugh, thank god he has a sense of humour he'll need it for the journey.

Once we are on the road I decide now is a good time as any to tackle the Caroline issue.

"Right boys" I say addressing everyone in the car "we have" I look at my watch "a little over an hour before we get to our destination so I propose we utilize this time to discuss strategy and tactics for Operation Psycho Bunny Boiler Bitch"

I catch the glance Paul and Bruce give each other and the slight knowing smile on their lips. "Yes ma'am" they say in unison.

Clayton who has been quiet and to a certain extent distant all morning lifts the arm rest and unclips my seat belt then his own, he tugs my hand in a silent command to move and sit in his lap. I've purposely left Clayton alone to his own thoughts, he has to work out how he feels about the whole situation and I've no doubt he's been trying to think of ways to handle Caroline and keep me safe. Unfortunately he also has to recognize this is a team effort.

As I settle into Clayton I carry on "I'll start off with my insights and conclusions, feel free to disagree"

I tell Paul and Bruce exactly what I'd said to Clayton last night including the worst case scenario endings.

"So my questions are as follows one: does Clayton talk to Caroline? In which case, in my opinion it accelerates her actions. Two: have the police been notified?" I feel Clayton jerk and stiffen at this "and finally three: are you guys armed?"

"One: we discuss, two: yes and three: to the teeth" Paul answers.

"The police have been informed" Clayton says startled.

"Yes sir" Paul's eyes flick to mine in the rear view mirror I nod to give the go ahead to continue with an explanation "I did it yesterday since both of you are high profile, as a cursory precaution I have registered a potential situation. At this moment in time there is nothing they can do as no crime has been committed. However should the situation escalate and get out of hand quickly and we have to act to protect you then any outcome as a result to a certain extent will be justified and possibly exonerated should it be fatal"

Clayton nods his understanding "What do you advise Paul regarding Caroline and talking to her?"

"It's your decision to make sir but I agree with Miss Darcy, either way it will accelerate her actions. If you tell her to get lost it could tip her over the edge. If you ignore her it could make her become more desperate to talk to you and tip her over the edge. Personally I think we watch and wait. We continue to monitor her movements and behaviour over the next week then discuss our findings, identify the potential threats and next move at that point"

Clayton seems to visibly relax, I feel all the tension leave his body in one go "I agree, what do you think?" he asks me, pulling me closer to him.

"I agree let her make the first move. Paul, talk us through various scenarios and what we need to do when they happen"

I say that for Clayton's benefit, I already know the drill, hell I've been through it enough times before. I settle back and listen as Paul briefs Clayton and answers his questions in a very factual manner by the time we get to Don and Brenda's estate Clayton is back to his normal self.

Paul and Bruce get out of the car as I make my move to get out Clayton holds me in place. I frown and look at him to see what his problem is only be floored by the love I see shining in his eyes.

"I love you" he kisses me gently "thank you"

"For what" I frown puzzled.

"For making me realize I'm not in this alone"

I smile and touch his face "It's a team effort just remember that and talk, don't bottle up your feelings and thoughts. I gave you a pass this morning mister because this is a new experience for you and you needed the time and head space. It won't happen again buddy" I pat his cheek "I'm the one with the stalker experience and trust Paul, do what he says and when, you'll come out of this alive. We both will"

"Yes ma'am" his eyes sparkle in such a way it makes my stomach flip flop. The car door opens breaking the moment.

Don and Brenda meet us on the steps. Brenda looks lovely in her pale yellow dress and it complements her auburn hair. She starts fussing over Shelley and me immediately. Clayton and I are shown to our room and Brenda gives me directions of where I need to go to put my dress on.

I get changed into my underwear whilst Clayton takes a quick shower by the time he comes back in the room I have my bathrobe fastened and I'm slipping my feet into the mint colored silk covered killer heels.

"What have you got on under there?" Clayton's voice is deeply seductive and it sends shivers up and down my spine.

I glance up. Clayton is leaning against the bathroom door frame, his fabulous sculpted torso and arms glistening with drops of water, his wet hair a mass of damp waves. My eyes greedily take in his fine physique. I have to forcefully drag my eyes up to his face. His expression tells me he's highly amused, his sparkling eyes and knowing smile he's fully aware of the reaction I'm having at the sight of him. Straightening, I slowly undo the belt.

"Look and no touching" I warn as I open the robe and let it drop to the floor.

I'm wearing a cream silk and lace Basque with cream fishnet stockings and lacy boy short thong style panties. I slowly twirl then bend down suggestively, thrusting my butt out and generally tormenting the crap out of Clayton and giving myself a thrill at the same time as I pick up my bathrobe and put it back on.

Clayton has a bath towel wrapped around his hips and I can see his erection, he grips the door frame and his arms are braced. I can tell from the prominence of his muscles and veins along with the slight tremor running through his body that he's fighting to keep himself from launching at me.

Mischief surges through me, I feel like grabbing the tail of a tiger and yanking it. I saunter up to Clayton and cup his cock and balls. I squeeze gently and leaning forward whisper in his ear. "Now all you'll be thinking about as I walk down the aisle is what I'm wearing under my dress and how you are going to fuck me later"

I kiss him and run my tongue along the seam of his lips at the same time I stroke him through the bath towel. A low growling sound comes from the back of Clayton's throat it resonates between my legs and has me wanting and wet instantly. I pull back and look into his dark blue eyes I know he wants to mount me. I take his hand and place it between my legs.

"Feel what you do to me"

Clayton's fingers move my panties aside and slip inside me. I groan as his fingers stroke leisurely. I mirror his movements rubbing his cock as his fingers move in and out.

A brisk knocking came at the door followed by Brenda's voice. "Skye dear I need you to come and get your dress on"

"Okay Brenda I'm coming" I smile at the innuendo of my words "I'll be there in two minutes" to Clayton I whisper "looks like we'll have to finish this off later"

Clayton sighs and removes his fingers and hand. I feel bereft and almost demand he finishes me off. I'm going to be suffering until he did. A wicked idea comes to me, keeping eye contact and smiling I undo the towel at Clayton's hips. Bending I kiss the tip of his cock then take him in my mouth and suck hard making Clayton hiss in a breath then I kiss the head again. Standing upright I kiss Clayton against his lips I murmur "No masturbating, save this for me" I lightly trail my fingers over the soft silky skin of his shaft.

"You're torturing me woman" Clayton growls, he's close to losing control "go before I bury myself balls deep in you"

Smiling coquettishly I back away. "Yes please" I say huskily as I open the door and step into the hallway. Clayton moves towards me, laughing I close the door and head in the direction Brenda showed me earlier.

I enter the room and walk into what I can only describe as a bridal war zone. There are bodies everywhere. The noise is enough to give you an instant headache. I'm the only adult bridesmaid the others are Phil's nieces and ages range from three to thirteen.

Shelley sees me and frantically waves me over; she's in her bathrobe as well. A couple of the younger ones are having a tantrum whilst the mother's try getting them into their dresses, the older ones slouch in the chairs doing their best I so don't want to be here expression.

As I reach Shelley she grabs my hand "Quick let's escape through the window" she says in a mock hysterical panic. At my laughter the whole room suddenly quietens. I raise an eyebrow at Shelley "wow! I should have sent for you sooner if I knew you were going to have this sort of an effect"

Shelley introduces me to the women I hadn't met and the ones who had been to Vegas all give me hugs and a warm welcome, even the older kids want to be introduced.

"Come on let's get our dresses on before Brenda comes back and tells us off" Shelley stage whispers.

We help each other into our dresses and add the finishing touches to our hair and makeup. There are collective sighs and gasps as we present ourselves to the rest of the room. Brenda steps forward with tears in her eyes.

"You both look so beautiful, stunning" she dabs at her eyes and takes a deep breath. I can see her mentally pull herself together "Shelley, I know you have something new and blue" Phil's sister-in-laws have given her a blue garter and I have given her the diamond drop earrings she is wearing "I have the old and borrowed" Brenda holds up a necklace, the chain is a very fine silver on it is a gorgeous tear drop diamond pendant "this was my great grandmother's I would love you to wear it for today"

"Oh Brenda it is absolutely beautiful I am honored to wear it" Shelley says hoarsely.

Brenda fixes the necklace around Shelley's neck.

"Perfect" she says dabbing her eyes again, she's right it is the perfect complement to Shelley's dress and jewellery.

"Time to get this show on the road ladies" Simon calls through the door as he knocks "I hope you are all decent because I'm coming in" Simon stops mid stride as he sees Shelley "oh sweetie you are a vision" his eyes sparkle and fill with tears.

"Don't start or you'll set me off" I warn him.

To give us some privacy Brenda clears everyone out of the room. Simon looks fantastic in his black suit, mint green cravat and vest. His dark hair which he usually has in weird and wonderful master pieces of unmoveable styles is soft and floppy making him look much younger than his twenty seven years.

"My two favourite girls" Simon holds out his hands, Shelley and I take one each "even though I am giving you both away I will never let you go"

My bottom lip trembles at the love and affection Simon put into his words. My eyes fill with tears. I look up at the ceiling and blink fast. I'm not going to cry I tell myself and fail miserably. Shelley hands me a tissue. I blot my face and check my makeup in the mirror. I shove the tissue down the front of my dress. I'll need that later no doubt.

"Shall we ladies?" Simon says holding out his elbows for us to link.

The three of us walk out of the door. In my mind this is the beginning of a new chapter in our lives.

CLAYTON

Damn it. Skye got away from me, if we'd been at home I'll have chased and caught her but I don't think Brenda and Don would appreciate me running around naked with an erection after my girlfriend.

My cock and balls ache like mad but I want to keep to Skye's command. I got really turned on when she said "look and no touching." It had taken every inch of my control not to throw her on the bed and fuck the living daylights out of her or pick her up, have her legs wrapped around my waist as I fucked her hard against the wall.

Christ, I need a cold shower. I walk back to the bathroom and step into the shower. Think of something else. As the cold water hits my chest I start to run through the scenario's Paul talked about and the evasive actions to take. I appreciate and understand now why Skye pays the guy so much he really is worth every penny.

When we discussed the body guard's salary Skye refused point blank to drop Paul's and she insisted the other two be paid the same as him. I tried to reason that Bruce is on the top end of the going rate. I also insinuated Skye was too generous almost gullible. By Christ did I back track on that quickly.

I've never seen Skye lose her temper. I've seen her annoyed and pissed off but it never lasted more than a few minutes if it was longer she tended to go and spar with Paul or Philippe. But to really lose her temper it hadn't happened, yet. However the look she gave me, the hardness in her face and eyes I really didn't want to be on the receiving end of that again. With a cold calmness she said "He deserves every penny, you'll see" and that had been the end of the discussion. At first I thought she was being stubborn but once again she proved me wrong.

I switch off the shower when my cock is semi flaccid, I dry myself quickly and get dressed. I'm the one with the stalker experience. Skye's words bounce around loudly in my head. Shit I've been so self-absorbed I hadn't even asked her what had happened. I really need to stop underestimating her and thinking of her as a fragile defenceless woman.

I want to protect her and she's willing to let me but she is by no means defenceless. For fucks sake she spars with a world champion and an ex-marine and neither of them hold back. A knock on the door intrudes on my thoughts.

"Come in" I call out. Phil's head appears "hey it's the man of the hour" I walk over and extend my hand instead Phil pulls me into an embrace.

"Thought I'd come and say welcome, everything okay with your room" he says looking around.

"Perfect, thanks for letting us all stay overnight. How are you, nervous?" I say as I pick up my jacket and return to the mirror as I put it on giving my appearance one final check.

"Yeah, my Dad and brothers aren't helping though"

"So you thought you'd hide out here" I chuckle when Phil nods sheepishly and grins "tell you what, how about you give me a tour of the place, that'll take your mind off things for a while" I pat his shoulder as we head out the door.

The estate is amazing and less than three miles from my mother's. The house is larger than my mother's although the surrounding grounds are smaller. Phil gives me the history of the place, how it had been derelict when his parents bought it twenty five years ago and over time they've lovingly restored it to its former glory with Don doing the majority of the work himself and extending the house to accommodate an ever growing family.

We walk around the manicured lawn and garden as he points out various features and tells me stories of his childhood growing up here. I recognise many similarities between us, we both come from a strong loving and very close family unit and we've fallen in love with women who have a troubled past and no family. We are workaholics and so are our women. As we make our way towards the marquees Phil talks about his plans to set up his own accountancy firm now thanks to mine and Skye's gift it means he can bring his plans forward by five years.

I see Don come out of one of the marquees and look around on spotting us he hurries over. Phil's parents really have pulled out all the stops for the wedding.

"There you are" Don calls out "I thought you'd run off" he heartily claps his son on the shoulder "Clayton good to see you again" he shakes my hand and pulls me into an embrace again even though he's already greeted me when we arrived earlier "Phil you need to get in position I'll show Clayton to his seat" Phil nods and strides off.

"It's a lovely place you've got here. Phil was telling me you restored it yourself"

"Aye that I did" Don says proudly "Listen Clayton, Phil told me about your wedding gift. I just wanted to say thank you. It's mighty generous of you. Nobody else in the family knows just me" he hastens to add.

Somehow this news doesn't surprise me. I saw just how close Phil is to his Dad during our weekend in Vegas.

"I take it he's also told you what Skye has done?"

"Yes he has, god bless her and I will thank her as well" he sounds quite choked with emotion "I tell you Skye really has looked after them two kids over the years"

"Well she does look and treat Shelley as her sister and she's already referring to herself as aunty" I chuckle.

"The baby will want for nothing" Don laughs heartily.

As we enter the marquee Don introduces me to various people, the ones who had been in Vegas come over and greet me warmly with lots of back slapping and hand shaking. Don takes me to the front, under his breath he explains they weren't doing the separate bride and groom sides due to Shelley not having any family and those she did treat as family are taking part in the ceremony.

I see Macy as we approach talking to Brenda. I quickly glance round and spot Bruce a few feet away then see the back of Alan disappearing through the entrance probably on his way to back up Paul escorting Skye.

"Ladies and gentlemen will you all please take your seats" a woman's voice calls out.

I'm on the end of the row so I have the perfect view of the aisle. I'm surrounded by strangers who nod politely and probably wonder who the fuck I am.

The music starts and a hush comes over the congregation as everyone stands and turns looking at the entrance.

The younger bridesmaids enter first to "ahh's" and the clicks of cameras as they sprinkle rose petals along the path. Skye steps through the opening and my heart stops. Paul and Alan flanking her melt to the sides. Skye is stunning in the pale mint green floor length gown. There are gasps and oohs from the women and appreciative murmurs from the men. Two guys in front of me give low wolf whistles showing their admiration

"Get a load of her" one murmurs "I am so getting me some of that ass later"

My fists clench. I really, really want to smack the fucker, hard.

"Dude, do you have any idea who that is?" ass guy shakes his head "that is Shelley's famous and mega rich best friend Skye Darcy. I hear she's engaged"

"She is! Who's the lucky bastard?" ass guy sounds almost disappointed.

"Me, I'm the lucky bastard" I say smugly, both men spin round so fast I'm surprised they didn't give themselves whip lash.

I give both of them my most menacing smile. Their jaws pop open; ass guy blushes and mumbles an apology. I nod my acceptance and return my attention back to Skye.

Halfway down the aisle Skye spots me and gives me her brain frying dazzling smile. Sure enough my semi hard cock springs to attention as I visualise her in the Basque and stockings, as she drew level I give her a salacious smile and wink. Skye's low throaty chuckle told me what is on her mind as well.

Shelley looks radiant as she walks down the aisle on Simon's arm. Her dress did a damn good job of hiding the fact she is pregnant. Simon cut a striking figure in his morning suit. When Simon stood next to Skye a thrill ran through me as it gives me a strong mental image for my wedding day when he will be walking Skye down the aisle and handing her over to me. I can't wait. I'm impatient as I count the days off. I have to fight the urge of getting the registrar to perform another ceremony immediately after Shelley and Phil's.

Over the years I've attended a fair few weddings and I've always found them to be pretentious and boring but I have to admit I thoroughly enjoy

Shelley and Phil's, maybe it's because it involves more people I like and care for and I'm sharing the day with the woman I love.

I'm impressed by the way Phil's family drew little attention to the fact Shelley only has a few guests. They did away with the long top table; instead they have large circular tables and mix everyone up. I'm sitting next to Skye; the two guys who I'd overheard are also on our table much to their embarrassment. I whisper to Skye what they'd said making her laugh, mischief glints in her eyes. "Behave" I mouth, she pouts calling me a spoilsport.

Simon steals the show when it came to giving the speeches. He is a natural comedian and has everyone crying with laughter as he regales stories about Shelley and then Shelley and Skye, both girls squealing "Oh my god I'd forgotten about that" making everyone laugh harder.

"I think I'm going to vet his speech when it comes to our wedding. Christ knows what he's going to drag up" Skye says wiping at her eyes.

"Spoilsport" I say and laugh when she scowls at me.

The music starts and people begin table hopping and moving around in earnest. Skye's in high demand as the majority of the men want to dance with her and the women want to talk to her. A couple of people ask her for an autograph which she obliges and practically everyone wants a picture with her. Skye makes sure attention isn't taken away from Shelley and I think Phil's family fall even more in love with her because of it.

After the evening buffet Shelley and Phil cut the cake then say thanks to various people and give out gifts to Brenda and the younger bridesmaids.

"We would like to say a special thank you to a very special lady in our lives and she has given us the best possible start to our married life" Phil says, I know instantly he's referring to Skye so I'm watching her instead of Shelley and Phil and I see her reaction when it dawns on her who he's talking about "she has always been a stable constant in Shelley's and my life. Giving her support, friendship and above all her love unconditionally no matter where she is in the world. Our lives have been truly blessed. On a personal note I can't thank you enough for deciding to come and study in New York because if you hadn't I wouldn't have met my soul mate and beautiful wife. I am honored to have you in my life and as part of my family. Skye Darcy"

The room erupts with cheers, whistling and clapping, Phil waves for Skye to come up to the stage. Skye's cheeks are purple with embarrassment and she's clearly touched by what Phil has said as her eyes sparkle with unshed tears. Looking around the room I'm not the only one to be affected as we watch the three of them interact. It brings a lump to my throat watching them hug and talk, the love and affection they share and have in their relationship clearly on show for everyone to bear witness to.

One of the bridesmaids brings on a huge bouquet of pale roses. I'm surprised at Skye's reaction she is genuinely shocked then thrilled as she hugs Shelley and Phil for their gift. You would have thought they had given her the crown jewels. Shelley gives her a box which she opens, on seeing the contents Skye burst out laughing. Skye hugs her friends again.

Skye is beaming from ear to ear and it's hard not to mirror her smile. Sitting down Skye places the pale lilac roses which are bluer in color on the table.

I must have a quizzical look on my face because unprompted Skye informs me "They are Blue Moon Roses" she puts her nose to the flowers and breathes in the strong scent deeply "my favourite flower along with Calla Lilies"

I remember Simon telling me that when he called to let me know Skye was okay after I caused her to freak out by restraining her when I first kissed her. I had apologised turning up with huge bouquet of Calla Lilies because I couldn't find anyone selling the Blue Moon Roses.

"Look what else they got me" Skye opens the box, inside are six small hooped earrings studded with rubies, they are identical to the diamond ones I'd bought her "I showed Shelley my ruby lily drop earrings and the necklace you bought me last night and jokingly I said I had to get a ruby version of these to match" she fingers the diamond ones in her ears.

I couldn't help smiling at the joy she is displaying for her presents. "They are very thoughtful gifts"

Skye nods and let out a snort "Shelley said they had been struggling with what to buy me, apparently the flowers are a no brainer and she could have cried with relief when I said about getting matching earrings. She sent Phil out first thing this morning to go and buy them. You know for an awful minute I thought Phil was going to tell everyone what I had given them as a wedding present" Skye says in a low voice looking around furtively to make sure no-one is eavesdropping.

"Only Don knows" Skye's eyes widen "I take it Don hasn't spoken to you yet"

"No, no he hasn't" Skye shakes her head "about what, what did he say to you?" she whispers.

"It's just to say thank you, he told me as he showed me to my seat, he said he would speak to you separately" I spy Don walking toward us "speak of the devil, here he comes"

Skye greets Don warmly but I can see the tension in her body as she braces herself for what he is going to say.

"I wanted to talk to you sooner but there never seemed an appropriate moment" Don makes a shooing motion with his hand. I turn to see one of Phil's brothers stop mid stride with a puzzled look as he turns away "I don't want an audience and I'm sure you don't with what I'm going to say"

A puzzled and slightly concerned look crosses Skye's face, her eyes flick to mine. I reach for her hand and give it a comforting squeeze.

"Phil told me as a wedding gift you have signed over the apartment to him and Shelley and all the money they've repaid has been given back to them" Skye gives a single curt nod, I can sense her wariness, I run my thumb across her knuckles conveying silent reassurance through touch everything is going to be okay. Don sighs "Skye what you have done for Shelley and Phil over the years has been fantastic but the wedding gift, I can't even begin to thank you or express my gratitude enough. It is beyond generous. I know I have only just met you but I feel I have known you for years because Shelley and Phil talk about you constantly. You have enriched their lives and that of the rest of my family by Shelley becoming a beloved addition as a daughter. If there is anything I can ever do for you please, please let me know"

Don is deadly serious and says all of this from his heart. Fuck even I have goose bumps on my arms.

"Shelley is like a sister to me and by extension Phil is now my brother-in-law. They are my family, all I want is their happiness" Skye says simply.

"I would be honored by extension" Don smiles as he uses Skye's words "to have you as part of my family"

Holy fuck! Skye gasps, she was not expecting that either. Her eyes fill with tears at the sincerity Don displays.

"Thank you" it barely comes out as a whisper. Skye takes a deep breath and let it out slowly through her mouth "that means a lot" Don pats her arm to show he understands "hey does this mean I get to call you Dad" Skye says cheekily with a mischievous grin making me and Don laugh.

"Don you have no idea what you are letting yourself in for" I chuckle.

"I guess I'll enjoy finding out. Skye you can call me whatever you like" he pauses, seemingly re-evaluating what he's just said "within reason of course, so long as it's nice"

We chat about the day and over time Macy, Shelley, Phil and Simon join us along with Brenda and a few other family members including the brother Don shooed away. There is a real sense of family camaraderie.

At first I was concerned Don might be trying to pull some elaborate hustle on Skye by offering her the very thing she has never known growing up, a loving and caring family unit, by giving her that he could try and wrangle money out of her but I needn't have worried. Skye is very astute and she demonstrated to me just how much.

When we were in Vegas I learnt a lot from Don about his business, what he did and his contracts with the city but Skye also gets out of him his financial situation. Turns out Don and Brenda are very comfortable, not millionaires but very happy with their lot and wanted for nothing. Don firmly believes in working hard for your living an ethic he drummed into all his sons and he is also a great admirer of Skye and me and what we have achieved "for ones so young" as he put it.

The DJ starts to play slow music, Phil stands and taking Shelley's hand pulls her to her feet and leads her to the dance floor. I have a sudden desire to dance with Skye.

"Dance with me" I stand tugging her hand to show I wasn't taking no for an answer.

On the dance floor I wrap my arms around Skye and hold her close. "I've been dying to do this for hours" I murmur close to her ear. Skye lifts her head off my shoulder and gently kisses me, my heart flutters at the tenderness "I can't wait for our wedding and I dance with you as Mrs Blake"

Skye raises her hand to my face and gently trails her fingers down my cheek "I love you and I can't wait to be Mrs Blake"

No matter how many times she tells me this, my heart feels as if it stutters then kicks up racing and pounding against my breastbone making me feel giddy and light headed. I am one lucky bastard.

The reception ends and those staying the night make their way inside the house to carry on the party. Skye wants to take the flowers and her earrings back to our room for safe keeping. I go with her.

Skye places the earrings and flowers on the dresser and went into the bathroom. I pick up my phone to check my messages. I'd purposely left my phone behind. Amongst the messages I have several missed calls from my mother and a voice mail. I listen to the message, mother's inviting us to a function the following Saturday. I'm in the middle of sending her a text message when I hear Skye come out of the bathroom. I continue texting.

"Mom has invited us to a function next weekend would you like to go?"

I look up, my heart lurches and my cock jumps to attention, my jaw unhinges and I drop my phone. Skye has taken off her dress and she's stood at the dresser in her Basque, lace panties, stockings and killer heels taking the flowers and hair pins out of her hair. Skye looks at me in the mirror an alluring smile on her lips. Slowly sections of her hair tumble down. My brain has short circuited, I just stand there gormless and watch her.

Taking the last of the pins out of her hair Skye puts her head back and rubs her fingers on her scalp massaging it then she walks towards me very slowly, she is so fucking beautiful, her swaying hips hypnotise me. My eyes greedily rake her body from head to toe and back again. My cock throbs and strains against the fly of my trousers. I feel my body heat from the blood I can hear pounding in my ears, sweat mists over my skin and my shirt sticks to my back. Fuck the effect she has on me, my body. I want her badly but I hold still.

Looking me in the eyes Skye puts her hand over my pounding heart her luscious full lips curve on a sly knowing smile as she runs her hand down my stomach and cups me between my legs. Skye's appreciative hum, low in her throat, sends tingles down my spine straight to my cock and balls. Skye leans forward her mouth an inch from mine.

"Tell me did you masturbate after I left you this afternoon?" Skye strokes my cock and gently squeezes my balls. I bite down on a groan but my hips thrust forward into her hand.

"No" comes out low and husky "Mistress" I whisper.

Skye's eyes widen briefly, this is the first time I've said it to her, recently all our play has been me dominating her, now I want to reverse the roles and see what she will do.

"Good boy" Skye purrs and smiles salaciously.

Skye walks behind me and takes off my jacket I hear it land on the chair with a soft thump. Her hands run over my back dragging her nails over my silk shirt, it feels wonderful, the pull and drag against my skin. As she comes back round to stand in front of me she drags her nails over my chest, a shiver ripples through me, and starts to undo the buttons, I removed my tie earlier in the night. Automatically my hands move and I pull my shirt out of my trousers, I'm eager to get naked.

Skye shakes her head "Keep still" she instructs softly.

"Forgive me Mistress"

A smile plays on her lips as she gives a nod in acknowledgement of my request. Fuck, I want nothing more than to throw her on the bed and launch myself at her but curiosity and anticipation has rooted me to the spot, what is she going to do to me.

Once more Skye stands behind me and pulls my shirt off my shoulders. I realize she hasn't taken my cuff links out. I open my mouth to point this out when she pulls my arms behind my back and uses my shirt to tie my hands and wrists.

Holy fuck! She is giving me a taste of my own medicine it turns me on even more. Skye walks over to the dresser and picks up the stool and positions it in the centre of the room.

"Come here" she commands.

I walk over and stand where she points. Skye undoes my trousers and pulls them down along with my boxers. My cock springs free, hard and proud.

"Sit" a thrill shoots through me and I do as I'm told.

Skye kneels before me taking off my shoes and socks followed by my trousers and boxers.

"I'm going to suck your cock but you are not allowed to come until I tell you" Skye grins wickedly at me.

Holy fucking hell! Now I know why she restrained me. It's so I won't take over she is seriously going to test my control. She's going to torture me with pleasure. I take a deep breath. Skye put her hands on my knees and pushes parting my legs wider. Fuck, that act alone nearly has me ejaculating. My balls hang heavy between my legs as my cock sticking straight out bobs and twitches with eager anticipation and impatient to be touched, I yearn for her hands to caress and stroke me. Sweat is already breaking out across my brow and chest. I flex and pull on my shirt to test how secure she has made the restraint. Secure enough I'm not getting free in a hurry.

Skye runs her hands from my ankles up to my knees and down the inside of my thighs, my breath hitches as she cups my balls in one delicate hand and massages. Oh fuck that feels good, her fingers of her other hand lightly run up and down the length of my cock. A moan deep from the back of my throat escapes me as pleasure races around my body, my head falls back as I absorb the sensations her soft feather light touch generates. I feel her tongue swirl across the head of my cock then her lips cover the tip giving gentle suction, teasing me of what is to come. My hips naturally rock upwards wanting to push deeper into her hot wet mouth but Skye pulls back, and so the pleasure torture begins.

Five times Skye takes me to the brink of climax and pulls me back, on the sixth I beg.

"Please Mistress, let me come, please"

My muscles are trembling from the exertion of controlling myself. I've fought against my restraints and heard my shirt rip a few times as I desperately hold off my orgasm. I've tried and failed to distract myself by thinking of a variety of boring subjects like reciting all the states in alphabetical order to something slightly more interesting like naming football and baseball teams and their players, through to something more taxing like naming all my employees.

My skin is hot and covered in a film of sweat, rivulets trickle down my face, chest and back. Skye gives my cock one final lick and long slow suck. Fuuuccckkk! The room fills with the sound of my groan and the ripping of my shirt.

Skye trails her tongue up my body; licking and kissing until she gets to my nipples then the minx sucks hard and bites first one then the other. I hiss in a breath as the sweet sharp pain goes straight to my balls. I gulp in air trying to slow my heart rate as waves of pleasure crash through me.

Skye stands, slowly peeling off her lace panties and thrusting her ass out as she bends. Sweet fucking Jesus, I close my eyes but the image is seared onto my retinas instead I try to concentrate on my breathing. Feeling hands grip my cock and balls, my eyes snap open.

"Close your legs" Skye murmurs.

Skye straddles me, holding my shaft she positions my cock at her entrance. "Remember, keep still and don't come until I tell you" Skye instructs as she starts to lower herself on me slowly.

"Holy shit, fuck" I curse through gritted teeth as I feel her hot, moist tight cunt slide over me, her greedy grasping muscles have me fighting and straining for control. The sound of my shirt ripping is mixed with our heavy breaths.

Skye moves and lifts a few times until I'm buried deep inside her to the root.

"Please" I beg. I can't hold on anymore.

Skye puts her hands at the back of my head, her fingers twine in my damp hair, pulling and tugging slightly, her lips close to my ear. "You have done well my love. I am pleased you may come when you want but remember keep still" she whispers and starts to gyrate and grind against me.

Skye kisses me, her tongue darting in and out of my mouth, licking and tasting me. I return the kiss and get lost in her. Skye presses herself closer to me, I pull against my restraint as I want to crush her to me, bury my fingers in her hair, hold her in place whilst I take over and possess her.

I surrender and absorb the feel of her cunt muscles clenching and gripping in rhythm to her gyrating and grinding hips, her hands in my hair and the slight sting the tugging and pulling causes at my scalp, her soft luscious lips against mine, her teeth tugging and nipping at my bottom lip and tasting her as she sweeps light strokes of her tongue in and out of my mouth. Her scent filling my nostrils and lungs with each gasping breath I take.

My orgasm explodes and crashes through me like a wrecking ball. Skye releases my mouth and begins to ride me fast and hard, my orgasm seems to last forever. I think I climax again when Skye has her orgasm, if I didn't then it's fucking strong aftershocks.

My head and face are buried in Skye's chest. I'm breathing hard and she rubs my back in soothing circular movements, gently bringing me down.

"Fuck that was intense" I manage to mumble into her tits, Skye chuckles as she strokes my hair.

When she lifts off me seamen trickles down the inside of her thighs; I look down at myself, my cock glistens and drops fall to the floor.

"Holy shit it looks like I've never come before" my voice is hoarse. I don't remember shouting. Skye chuckles again as she undoes my shirt to release my hands and arms.

"Your shirt is ruined" she says handing it to me to inspect and she starts to massage my shoulders "you don't know your own strength" she teases.

"Well that's what happens when you stop me from touching you. I broke the chair in Vegas remember" I stand and pull her into my arms.

"Oh yes I'd forgotten about that" Skye says softly and smiles, I pick her up and carry her to the bed "I take it we're not going back down stairs"

Grinning at her I shake my head "It's my turn to torture you with pleasure"

Fresh from our shower we lie in each other's arms enjoying the peace and quiet. I draw lazy circles on Skye's back enjoying the soft silky feel of her skin under my fingers. We've talked about the day, what we've enjoyed the most, things that we would have done and are doing differently and our hopes for our own wedding being just as enjoyable.

"Can I ask you something?" I ask hesitantly, I'm not sure if I really want to know about her previous stalker but curiosity is driving me.

"Sure, shoot" Skye lifts her head and rests her chin on my chest, her yellow green eyes shining with love.

"I understand if you don't want to tell me and the last thing I want to do is drag up unpleasant and painful memories" Skye's expression becomes wary and she raises an eyebrow probably wondering what the fuck I'm going to ask "would you mind telling me about your past stalker and how you dealt with him? I'm assuming male" I say tentatively.

Skye smiles and nods "I was wondering how long it would be before you asked" she moves to sit up and face me. I sit up also to see her better "to date I have had three stalkers"

"Fuck me" I bark out as a jolt of shock goes through me. I wasn't expecting that. I had it in my head she'd only dealt with one. Skye smiles at me ruefully, without saying anything I know she knows I've underestimated her, again.

"The first two were over enthusiastic and overzealous fans when their behaviour became, let's say worrisome and it was pointed out to them they were about to be treated as a serious stalker threat they were horrified and backed off. The third and last one was a lot more serious. Paul had been working for me about two months when it began. The guy started off sending messages via my website this quickly escalated to flowers and gifts; these started arriving on a regular basis at least once or twice week. Birthday and Christmas gifts were more expensive. He would turn up at events and functions I attended and took to hanging around outside where I was living at the time. When I worked away on commissions within the States somehow he would find me and turn up. To this day we don't know how he got the information, general consensus is he overheard conversations between friends or people that knew of my work commitments" Skye shrugs "this went on for over a year then I had a commission overseas and I was away for just over six weeks, when I got back things changed. Every time I ventured out he was abusive, shouting nasty things mainly and he started sending threatening letters and bouquets of dead flowers would arrive on a daily basis. I got a restraining order but that didn't stop him. About a month later I was coming back from a meeting one late afternoon, as I got out the car he came at me with a knife. Paul disarmed him and the police were called. They arrested and charged him but he was given bail. Two days later he was back, this time with a gun. I was leaving my apartment for a business lunch meeting, he opened fire. The doorman took a bullet in his shoulder. Paul got the next bullet in the top of his arm; he pushed me to the floor and shot the stalker in the leg"

I'm absolutely speechless. Skye is so matter of fact and completely disassociated it's as if she's telling the story about someone else. I completely understood Paul's words to her now when he first briefed us of Caroline's activities.

Skye sits very still and watches me with haunted eyes. After a few minutes of silence I manage to croak out. "Where is he now?"

"Dead" another jolt of shock runs through me "he got arrested and sent to prison. I didn't need to testify at the trial because we kept the police informed and they had enough to prosecute him. Apparently he got attacked in prison and died from his injuries"

"Holy fuck, how did you feel during all that time?"

"Annoyed, angry, pissed off some days because I felt like a prisoner. Freaked out, scared at other times but I never lost trust or faith in Paul. I had complete confidence he would protect me, keep me safe. I did exactly as he said whenever we went out and I was extra vigilant" she snorts derisively "something I have never stopped doing" Skye studies me and takes hold of my hand "the worst thing you can do at a time like this is to bottle up how you feel about the situation. I was lucky I had Simon and Shelley to bounce off, even though there was nothing physically they could do but by giving me the support I needed by listening to me vent helped me handle what I was going through. So please, please talk, scream and shout with me in private when it gets too much. In fact do it before it gets to that stage, it will help you keep perspective and sane"

"I don't know what I would do without you" I'm in awe of her "you have been through so much in your life, you make it seem so easy"

Skye cut me off "I've learnt from my life experiences" she sighs "at the risk of sounding cliché they have made me a stronger and better person. From my stalker experiences I have learnt not to let them rule my life. I refuse to play the victim and I accepted it is okay to be scared but I won't let fear paralyse me into doing nothing and I have every right to be angry and pissed off but my anger is directed at the person causing the inconvenience in my life and I refuse to feel helpless so I get on living my life. They are the ones whose life has stopped as it revolves around me and I pity them, they need help and can't see it themselves"

"Come here" I open my arms and Skye shuffles to me. I hold her close to my chest "you are so brave. I am humbled at your strength" I flex my arms holding her tighter to me.

"Do you want to talk about how you feel about the situation with Caroline" Skye says softly running her hand up and down my arm in a soothing motion.

"I don't know how I feel at the moment" I sigh "last night and this morning I kept running through and replaying all the instances I had interacted with her, trying to see if I gave any signal that could be construed I was interested in her" Skye opens her mouth to say something then stops herself instead she nods for me to carry on "yes I realize now I was looking to blame myself for her actions but I kept coming up blank. I began to feel angry she wouldn't take no for an answer and the more I pushed her away the more determined she became. I have to agree with you I think she does see me as unfinished business and the break up with Pete has triggered" I stop and think of the right word to use "I don't know, this psychotic episode. I admit I was, no I am" I correct myself "scarred for you. My imagination ran riot on all sorts of scenarios. I feel sick at any thought of losing you"

I pause taking a deep breath it's time to come clean "I even went to speak to Paul and Bruce. I told them to keep information about Caroline away from you" Skye immediately stiffens; I feel her start to pull away and move out of my arms. I hold her in place "Paul refused point blank, he said it was important to keep open lines of communication" Skye starts to relax and I carry on "he also said you would instigate a strategic and tactical discussion" Skye let out a bark of laughter, I chuckle "and you proved him right the minute the four of us were alone. I'm sorry I tried to keep you out of it. In my way I thought it would protect you, keep you safe. I was wrong and I am sorry" I pour as much sincerity as I can into my apology.

Skye touches my face and kisses me "I know you want to protect me and I thank you for your honesty"

We stay a while simply holding each other eventually Skye's breathing begins to change becoming slower and deeper as she drifts off to sleep.

As I listen to her steady breathing I resolve to follow all the advice Skye and Paul have given over the last twenty four hours and I will take a leaf out of Skye's book and refuse to become or play the victim. I sure as fuck don't play the victim in any other situation in fact I'm the persecutor in the majority of instances. I'm a ruthless bastard when I have to be which, is all the time in business.

I will only worry about Caroline when Paul tells me to. I have a life to live and no fucking psycho bunny boiler bitch is going to dictate or stop me.

Chapter Twenty Nine

SKYE

I love it when I can get lost in the zone while I paint. Avenge Sevenfold is blasting out, the rock music bouncing off the walls and making the floor vibrate, love it, love it. I'm on my own so I can have the music as loud as I want.

Clayton never complains or says anything about my taste in music, I know he likes some of the milder rock and he isn't so keen on the really heavier rock. I asked him when we first met what sort of music he was into; he shrugged and said he'd never really been into music, even as a teenager, he'd been more interested in working and building his business empire.

This is something I still struggle to get my head around. I would sooner listen to music than watch TV and I have music playing whenever I can. I even go to sleep with music playing. I can escape from the world with music, loose myself.

I suppose it stems from my childhood. When things got really bad I would take myself off on long walks, my favourite was to climb the very steep hill which backed onto my grandfather's estate, it wasn't big enough to be classed as a mountain but to a young restless teenager it was Mount Everest in my mind. I would sit on the summit and admire the scenery with rock music blasting in my ears and I imagined I could fly and soar on the thermals with the eagles and my frustrations, anxiety, woes would melt away. By the time I came back down I would be refreshed and energised, ready to face being either ignored or dictated to.

Clayton understood on some level that music is important to me. He's never asked why he just accepts it, so I still have music playing when he's around just not as loud. In the evening I will draw or paint and Clayton will sit with his laptop working. When he first moved in he used the office but it lasted all of two days actually it wasn't even that, on the second night he'd been in the office less than two hours when he came out carrying his laptop and sat on the sofa.

I think its sweet he feels the need to be close to me, I've noticed that if I paint he will drag one of the lazy boys over to this side of the room and sit near me, same thing happens if I'm at my drawing desk.

My thoughts drift to Tuesday, a shiver rushes through my body and my core clenches at the memory. Clayton rang me in the morning, before I could say hello his deep velvet voice commanded.

"I want you to send me one of your girls over today at twelve noon"

For a fraction of a second my brain stalled, what the.... oh! He wants to play "Certainly sir, any preference to the type of girl you want" my reply is business like playing along.

"Blonde, big tits, athletic, Caucasian" a thrill shoots through me and feel myself getting turned on at his description of me.

"Where is she to meet you and do you have any specific requirements sir" I drop my voice on the last part of my sentence knowing it will get to him.

"My office, my only requirement is for a good time" he growls, I got to him.

After the phone call I deliberate how to get to his office in my hooker outfit without it being blatantly obvious to every man and his dog what I'm going to be doing. I couldn't wear my platform hooker shoes until I was behind closed doors because of the flashing soles, big giveaway. Then I have a brainwave, I put my boots on and my long fitted coat putting a change of clothes into an oversized bag along with my shoes.

Clayton is on the phone when I walk into his office. I lock the door, the blinds are already closed. Clayton watches my every move as I change out of my boots and put my hooker shoes on. Keeping eye contact I slowly undo the buttons on my coat and drop it on top of my bag.

Clayton's eyes greedily rake my body up and down, I'm wearing my tartan micro mini skirt or belt as Clayton calls it, a tight pale pink jersey crop top with the buttons undone over my breasts revealing all of my ample cleavage and parts of my red lace bra, I also have on the matching red lace thong panties. My legs are bare.

I walk slowly to his desk and parade in front of him trailing my fingers over the top of his desk as I pass. His eyes never leave me, I can feel the burn of his lust on my skin. I love how he makes me feel desirable and wanton with just his look, I feel powerful at the same time knowing the effect I have on him. It's a heady mix. Excitement and desire pools in my stomach and between my legs, sweet Jesus on a cracker I'm slick with anticipation.

Clayton continues his conversation and I decide to walk around the office pretending to explore. At the coffee table I bend over as provocatively as I can to pick up a magazine, purposely bending from my waist and thrusting my butt out. Clayton's sharp intake of breath tells me he got the intended eyeful, I smile pleased with myself.

I listen to Clayton's side of the telephone conversation as I flick through the magazine, drop it back on the table and walk to the window. From what I can make out it's something to do with a business deal happening in China and it's in its final stages. At the sound of his call ending I turn round to face him. Clayton has moved from behind his desk and is now in front leaning against it with his ankles crossed and his arms folded across his chest the sleeves of his shirt straining against his muscular forearms and bulging biceps.

Clayton is sexy as hell in a three piece suit but in this casual pose minus the jacket my lust for him goes through the roof. Clayton raises a hand and makes a lazy come here gesture with his fingers. It takes everything I have not to run and launch myself at him. I walk as nonchalantly as I can, I let him see my carnal lust for him as I rake every inch of his magnificent body from head to toe, my eyes lingering on the impressive bulge in his pants. I lick my lips as I mentally undress him. When I stop in front of him I have to drag my eyes up to meet his dark blue lust and amused filled eyes.

"So tell me daddy what would you like to do for a good time" I purr, god I'm so turned on I actually purr.

Clayton stands and walks around me, inspecting every inch of my body and outfit. His fingers lightly trailing a path on my exposed stomach and around my lower back as he walks around me, I bite my cheek to hold back the moan his touch elicits.

"How much?" he asks instead of answering my question.

"Am I here for the full hour?" I counter, his eyes half close as he nods "two thousand, if you want to do anything kinky and ride bare back then it's double" my voice is husky.

"I want you sucking my cock until I come in your mouth and I'm going to ride you bare back and then I'm going to eat you sat on my desk"

Holy shit that sounds so hot. I'm saturated with wanting him. Playing my role I step into him and cup his cock, stroking and dragging my nails over his length. His breath hitches.

"Three thou for the hour and you can fuck me as many times as you want" I pause "or can" I say throwing in the challenge. Clayton's eyes flare then narrow as he processes what I've said.

"So daddy, how do you want to start?" I give him a gentle squeeze. He closes his eyes and takes a deep controlled and calming breath, oh he's close and his control is slipping "I'm ready for your cock daddy however you want to take me" I say in a low voice next to his ear.

"Bend over and hold onto the edge of the desk"

Clayton moves out of my grasp as he gives the command and I comply. Immediately his hand is on my butt rubbing in circular movements. I wonder if he'll spank me but would that be classed as kinky my mind throws out, who cares my inner goddess retorts. His hand left my butt and I brace myself for the spank, it doesn't come. I'm disappointed.

Clayton covers me with his body, his arms over mine, his front pressing down on my back and his hard cock through the rough material of his pants pushes against my butt. I push back into him, grinding and rotating my hips.

"Behave" he growls in my ear "or I will spank you"

Yes please shouts my inner goddess, I continue to grind into him. Clayton chuckles. "So naughty girl you want to be spanked, very well" Clayton straightens and flips my skirt up, grasping hold of my panties "let's get rid of these" he snaps them off me "widen your stance"

I adjust my position and Clayton's hand begins rubbing my butt, anticipation is in overdrive. His fingers slide down to my sex and massage me. Oh that feels good. I moan.

"Fuck, you are so wet, you want this bad" Clayton groans.

The slap and sharp sting of pain has me gasping but I moan as Clayton thrusts two fingers inside me and pleasure takes over. Clayton spanks me six times, massaging my clit and rubbing my butt then thrusting his fingers inside me each time he spanks me. I'm close to climaxing and about to beg for his cock when he removes his hands and I hear the rasp of his zipper.

My sex clenches in desire making me shiver. I feel the head of his cock push against my butt. I tilt my hips as he guides his cock to my entrance, he pushes partway in then holds still his hands grasp my hips firmly.

"Hold on and keep quiet"

I just have time to brace myself when he slams into me.

"Argh" I call out at the sudden feelings of pleasure, fullness and possession that shoots through my body.

"Shhh" Clayton rolls his hips "keep quiet" he admonishes as he pulls slowly out.

His fingers flex and grip my hips then he slams into me again, his balls slap against my clit. Oh god that feels so good. I moan from the back of my throat. Clayton continues with the slow withdrawal and slamming back into me over and over again, each time his balls connecting and stimulating my clit. I climax silently, hard and seeing stars. Clayton picks up the pace and chases his own release. My legs and arms are trembling from the after effects of my orgasm and the prolonged effort of holding myself in place.

"Are you okay?" Clayton asks softly as he places kisses along my spine. I nod as I can't find my voice "good because I am nowhere near finished with you" Oh sweet fucking hell.

For the rest of the hour Clayton is relentless, it's as if he's starved and hasn't had sex for years. He takes me sat on his desk with his head buried between my legs, I suck him off whilst he sat in his chair. Then he starts by taking me bent over the sofa switching us to the missionary position on the floor, then moving into the bathroom and finishing off against the wall.

We help each other get dressed. Both of us have smug satisfied grins on our faces as we look at each other. Clayton picks up my hooker shoes and clothes from around the office and puts them in my bag as I get dressed and put on my coat. Clayton sliding his hands around my waist pulls me to him, kissing me deeply and I lose myself in him. He makes an appreciative hmm at the back of his throat.

"I love you so, so, very much" he mumbles against my lips in between kisses.

Even now I still feel the warm glow that intimate time together had given me. Clayton insisted on seeing me to the car. I'm glad because I seriously doubted I could walk. He kissed me soundly in the street before letting me get in the car, he didn't care who saw us. Maybe that's the point he's sending a message to Caroline.

Bruce, Paul and Alan surrounded us on high alert, constantly scanning the street. I remember Paul's relief as we drove off and asking him if Caroline was around.

"Yes ma'am in the coffee shop across the street"

Each day Paul gives us an update on Caroline's activities. Her pattern has changed from hanging around outside the office from three in the afternoon until Clayton left, to being outside from seven thirty in the morning until he arrived, showing up at lunchtime and back again at three. Clayton said she calls out to him on each occasion. At first it had been requests to talk progressing to she is now free and they can finally be together. Clayton has pretended not to hear her or made out he's on his phone which is true in the majority of cases.

Clayton has really taken the advice Paul and I have given him to heart. Each evening as we eat dinner we talk about the kind of day we've had and that includes discussing the feelings or I should say frustrations Caroline invoked. Since her focus is Clayton it's his time to vent, usually he starts by describing her appearance, the state of her clothes and hair. From Clayton's descriptions her general overall appearance seems to becoming more dishevelled as each day passes.

Alarm bells rang very loud in my head, my instincts screamed she's unravelling fast. For as long I've known Caroline she has always taken great care and pride in her looks and appearance. I brought this up last night after Paul had given us the days briefing. I don't know why but for some reason I expected both men to be dismissive except they'd taken everything I said very seriously.

Paul started talking about having Caroline tailed at all times purely as a precaution so we agreed to hire a private detective. Paul is engaging the services of someone he knows which he did first thing this morning.

My thoughts wander to the new apartment. Everything is scheduled for us to move in at the end of the following week. I'm excited and looking forward to it at the same time dreading the move actually it's the packing I'm not looking forward to. One of the advantages of being rich is you can pay a team of people to do it for you but we still have to sort out what we are taking with us and what is going to good will.

Clayton decided to sell his apartment, assigning Billy to do the honors. His bed, pool table and clothes are the only things to be moved everything else is going to be sold with the apartment. Since I own the building my apartment is going to be rented, again Billy has been given the task of finding a tenant.

I'm thankful Macy has everything under control so I can concentrate on business. The auction house is still ahead of schedule and Matthew emailed this morning saying the prototypes for the first pieces of jewellery will be ready early next week and would I like to come to the shop and see them, I had to refrain from emailing back saying is the Pope catholic. To say I'm excited is an understatement. Stephanie has everything in hand for the wedding. Mike is flying in from Tennessee on Monday to discuss what he wants to commission and I'm nearly finished on The Gentlemen's Club series of paintings. I step back from the painting I'm working on, another ten hours or so and it'll be finished. All in all life is good. I feel complete and soul deep happy for the first time in my life.

The music volume being turned down pulls me out of my musings, I turn to see Paul and Macy walking towards me. Paul's face is grave; Macy is upset tears running down her cheeks.

"What's the matter?" alarm and fear rip through me "what's happened?" panic has my voice going up to a shriek.

Macy can't talk, she tries but nothing comes out. I feel sick and a block of ice forms in my stomach, the cold radiating outwards.

"Skye" Paul's voice is soft but his expression is full of grim sadness. My mind screams something has happened to Clayton.

"No, no, no, no" each word comes out of me as an agonised moan, my knees give out. Paul shot forward and catches me. Terror adds to the cold I'm already feeling inside, I'm shivering "wwwhat's hhhappened" I stutter weakly.

"There's been a shooting" the room tilts "details are sketchy" my brain shuts down I know I'm looking at Paul as if he's speaking gibberish

"Clayton was leaving the office to come home. Caroline had a gun and opened fire. All I know is the wounded have been taken to hospital"

The room spun, my world is crashing down around me.

The wounded, hospital, wounded, hospital the words ricochet around my head. I grasp at those words the wounded, it means more than one casualty, hospital Clayton is injured and in hospital. I have a slither of hope to cling to, he's alive.

"Take me" I whisper to Paul, he lifts me to my feet.

Getting to the car is a blur. The journey to the hospital seems to take forever. I feel numb. It doesn't even register that I'm crying until Macy presses a tissue into my hand. My mind bounces from one nightmare scenario to another. I wrap my arms tight around my middle. I keep telling myself to hold it together; to hold on; we don't know the full story. Paul and Macy keep trying Clayton, Bruce and Alan's phones all go to voice mail. No news is good news, right.

I haven't brought anything with me. I left the apartment in the clothes I stood up in, my old tattered and paint splattered work dungarees with an old crop t-shirt underneath. I still have my bandanna on, I would be barefoot if Macy hadn't handed me my Timberland boots as I headed out the door.

The not knowing is killing me. My worst case scenario nightmare is playing on repeat in my head. I get to the hospital to be told Clayton has died from his injuries and I'm too late to say goodbye. My stomach roils and I dry heave. My heart aches but my soul tells me Clayton is still alive. I hold on to that, I need to believe he is still with me.

Macy and I head into the emergency unit whilst Paul parks the car. The place is manic, staff rushing everywhere and there are a fair few police officers around. We went straight to the reception desk. It appears they are expecting me because as soon as I give Clayton's name and say who I am the nurse directs me to the family waiting room. The nurse couldn't or wouldn't tell me anything about his condition.

Those inside the waiting room look up as we enter. I didn't register faces just noted the room seems full.

"Skye" I look in the direction of the voice that called out my name.

Stephanie is moving towards me, her face strained and pale. I've only ever known Stephanie to be immaculate in her appearance so a jolt of surprise goes through me at her blotchy tear stained face and slightly dishevelled look. Christ knows what I must look like. Stephanie collapses on me, we hold onto each other.

"Have you heard anything?" Stephanie asks with desperation and unshed tears in her voice, I shake my head.

"We just got here" I indicate to Macy "and the nurse told us to come in here. What do you know?"

"All I know is there are three casualties and two are in surgery" she dabs at her eyes.

The room spins and my legs give out, again. Strong arms catch me before I hit the floor. Paul picks me up and carries me to a chair. Macy sits down next to me and takes my hand she murmurs words I don't hear. Stephanie sits the other side of me taking hold of my other hand. We sit in silence for a few minutes.

"How did you get here so fast?" I ask Stephanie, she lives an hours' drive outside the city and that's with light traffic.

"I was already in town. I had lunch with a friend and then a meeting with the wedding planner I was on my way home when Helena called about the shooting. I was a couple of blocks away from here"

I nod and we sit in silence again. I have no idea how long we sit giving each other silent support, it feels like hours but in reality it's probably only a few minutes when the door opens and in walk Joshua and Andrew. Both have worried concern etched in their faces.

Stephanie stands and they all embrace. I feel like an intruder, the outsider looking in on the family's anxiety over a loved one and listening to their murmured conversation as Stephanie answers their questions. My feelings of isolation are short lived however the brothers descend on me as soon as they've checked Stephanie is okay.

My mind begins to play different scenarios of how injured Clayton is. I have visions of postponing the wedding. Bruce and Alan, oh my god! I've been fixating so much on Clayton I completely forgot about our bodyguards. Stephanie said there were three casualties but nothing about fatalities, what if people have been killed; my stomach roils at the thought.

"Paul" I croak out, I stand on jelly legs and take three shaky steps towards him "Bruce and Alan"

Paul guides me back to the chair "I'll go and see what I can find out" he says softly.

The door crashes open, bouncing off the wall making everyone jump and in walks Clayton with Bruce behind him. The sight of him makes me feel as if someone has punched me in the stomach, all the air leaves my lungs and relief sweeps through me like a tidal wave.

"Clayton" cries Stephanie as she rushes towards him with Joshua and Andrew following.

My legs don't seem to want to work, my vision becomes blurred "See, he's okay Skye" Macy whispers rubbing my back and squeezing my hand tightly. I can only nod, I blink to clear my vision and tears roll down my cheeks.

Clayton disentangles himself from his family and comes to me with his arms wide open. I stand on shaky legs as he engulfs. The tears flow and I sob as I hold onto him for dear life. He's okay, he's alive my mind blabbers.

"Shhh I'm okay baby" he soothes me I squeeze him tighter to make sure he really is with me.

Clayton makes an oomph sound and takes a sharp inhale of pained breath instantly I release him and step away.

"You're hurt" I say alarmed and looking for signs of injury but not seeing any evidence.

Clayton pulls me back to him "I'm okay, just a couple of cracked ribs" he kisses me.

I look at him, his face and eyes trying not to show me how much pain he is in. "Sit down" I command softly "Bruce what injuries do you have and where is Alan?"

"I'm fine ma'am, no injuries" he pauses looking at Clayton.

"Alan is in surgery" Clayton finishes.

"Tell us what happened" Stephanie demands before I can.

Clayton sits down and reaches for me and I sit carefully on his lap. Clayton has to explain about Caroline's stalking to his family first, all three of them have the same shocked horrified disbelief look when he finishes telling them. He doesn't give them chance to ask any questions as he launches into the narrative of what happened.

"I decided to finish work early" his arms tighten around me "I missed you" he whispers in my ear, I smile shyly at him "Alan had brought the car round to the front of the building and was stood by the door waiting for me. Mark Ellison, one of the security staff opened the side door and stepped through I followed and that's when the first shot was fired. Mark caught the bullet in his arm. Bruce pushed me to the floor, that's how I got the cracked ribs. As you can imagine screaming and shouting and panic ensued. Alan threw himself in front of Caroline as the second shot went off and he got the bullet in his shoulder. Fortunately a police cruiser was passing at the time and saw the whole thing going down. The police shot Caroline when she refused to stop and fired at them"

"So Caroline is she in surgery too?" I ask tentatively, however my instincts are telling me otherwise.

"No, she's dead" Clayton says in a quiet matter of fact tone.

My stomach feels as if it dropped to the floor, no-one says anything the room is silent, even the other people waiting for news on their loved ones remain quiet. You can hear the proverbial pin drop.

"Have you given a statement to the police" Joshua says in a tone I associate as his lawyer voice.

"Not yet but they know I was the target and Caroline had been stalking me" Clayton looks at Paul "that was a smart move registering the report last Friday"

Paul nods and I beam at him as I know Clayton originally thought it was an overreaction at the time. Now he realizes Paul doesn't overreact. Paul does things that are a means to an end, every action taken serves a purpose. As if on cue the door opens and the police walk in with one of the doctors. Clayton ignores the police and addresses the doctor.

"Any news"

"Mr Blake you are supposed to be in bed awaiting your examination and x-ray" the doctor says sternly.

I scowl at Clayton, he has the sense to look sheepish "In bed, what the hell are you doing here?" I practically shout.

Clayton shrugs "It's a couple of cracked ribs and as soon as I heard you were here I needed to be with you"

Well that took the angry wind out of my sails and I deflate quickly, he sounds so sweet and I can see he means every word. I stand up and pull on his hand.

"Well mister you're to do as the doctor tells you and get back to bed" I say in my best school teacher voice and point my finger at him.

"Yes ma'am. So long as you come with me" Clayton says standing and smiles salaciously at me.

I blush. Macy, Joshua and Andrew all burst out laughing. Paul and Bruce try hard not to, Stephanie, the doctor and two police officers all look amused.

"There's nothing wrong with you baby bro" Andrew says patting Clayton on the shoulder making him wince in pain.

I roll my eyes at them and tug Clayton towards the door.

"Lead the way doctor" I gesture for the doctor to go first, he smiles at me still highly amused "do you have any news on Alan Parker and Mark Ellison the two security detail that took a bullet?" I ask as we walk down the corridor "they work for us" I add hastily before he can say anything.

"Not as yet ma'am. Mr Blake has asked to be kept informed, as soon as I hear anything I'll let you know" he pulls back the curtain and points to the bed as he looks at Clayton.

"Are you supposed to be wearing a gown?" I say to Clayton with a big grin on my face as he carefully lowers himself on the bed.

I'm trying not to giggle at the mental image I have of Clayton in a hospital gown, then the thought of his firm tight ass flashing through the gap at the back has my lust levels rapidly heading for the roof.

"Yeah but do you really think I'd walk around with my ass flashing" he says sardonically.

It's my turn to grin salaciously making Clayton laugh which he stops suddenly and winces. He pales and closes his eyes and takes a few shallow breaths. The doctor is at his side instantly, he opens Clayton's shirt and begins his examination. I can see shadows of bruising forming around his ribs. The doctor removes his stethoscope and hangs it around his neck.

"I can give you something for the pain" Clayton nods "and I need you to rest, no more wandering around" he adds sternly.

"Don't worry I'll make sure he does as he's told" I say.

"The police would like to talk to you if you're up to it" the doctor says quietly.

Clayton keeps his eyes closed, he really is in pain. I sit down next to him on the bed and take his hand in mine.

"Send them in" Clayton's voice comes out hoarsely. The doctor pulls back the curtain and gestures, a police officer and a plain clothed gentleman come in.

"Mr Blake. ma'am, I'm Detective Sanders. I'd like to ask you a few questions about the incident" he pulls out his notebook and flips through a few pages. His whole demeanour says he isn't taking no for an answer and he fully expects our cooperation.

"Sure" Clayton says his eyes still closed, his hand tightens on mine.

"Mr Blake how well did you know Caroline Tanner" Sanders says watching Clayton closely.

"I don't" Clayton says his eyes opening slowly.

"How did you know to lodge a report on a potential stalking threat by her?" the Detective shot back.

"I didn't"

For a brief second the Detective has a look of confusion. I intervene.

"Detective, I'm Skye Darcy"

"I know ma'am" the Detective cut in with a smile, I raise my eyebrows in surprise "my son is a huge fan and so am I"

Huh, well that threw me for a minute. Clayton chuckles then groans and it snaps me back.

"We will give all the information you need but I need to call a few people in here" the Detective nods, I squeeze Clayton's hand "do you want Joshua?"

"Yeah just in case" he murmurs.

"Paul, Bruce" I call out, both men pull back the curtain "Detective these gentlemen are our bodyguards. Bruce please can you bring Joshua" he nods and left. Looking at the detective I point at Paul "Paul is the one who made the report last Friday" I hold up my hand to stop him speaking "we will give you all the information about the events leading up to Paul registering the stalker threat. Joshua Blake is Clayton's brother and lawyer" Sanders eyes widen in surprise but he recovers quickly "him being present is simply as witness to what is being said"

As I finish Joshua enters with Bruce. I make the introductions and I explain to Joshua what we want him to do. Joshua produces a Dictaphone and offers to record the whole interview which Sanders agrees to. The doctor came back with the pain meds and told Clayton they may make him drowsy. Clayton elects to take them after we have told our story, I admire him for that and my heart swells with love for him. Turning to Sanders I start talking.

"Caroline was the ex-girlfriend of Pete Lancaster"

I explain how I know Pete; Caroline's attitude towards me over the years; the guys she cheated with; how they invited themselves on the trip to Vegas. Clayton told how Caroline had come onto him during the weekend. I repeated Simon's gossip from the party about Pete and Caroline's break up. We told everything it felt like being in a confessional. We finish or rather Paul finishes by telling how he and Bruce had monitored Caroline's activities since our return from Vegas. How her pattern and appearance changed with each passing day which caused concern for her mental state and only this morning he hired a PI to follow her when she wasn't hanging around outside Clayton's office. We had no idea she acquired a gun.

"How did you know to place a report?" says Sanders to Paul.

"Miss Darcy has had stalkers before"

Sanders nods his understanding "Do you mind if I talk to your friends" he says to me "just a matter of course to clarify and collaborate everything you've told me"

"Sure we've nothing to hide" I look at Paul "Did Macy put calls out to Shelley and Simon" Paul nods "my guess Detective is you'll find them in the waiting room"

"They are ma'am" Bruce clarifies.

Sanders looks at me impressed "Do you have contact details for Pete Lancaster?"

"No I don't" Sanders raises an eyebrow "I have no idea where he lives nor do I have his phone number. Detective, Pete and Caroline are not friends, as I said Pete is an ex-boyfriend from when I lived in England, that short lived relationship ended over nine years ago. Pete and Caroline would go to Gino's restaurant every Friday in the hope that I and my friends would show up that is the only time I would see or speak to them. Caroline wangled an invite for the bachelor and hen party Vegas weekend via Don, he's Shelley's father-in-law. I'm sure Shelley will tell you, in fact speak to Don"

I manage to keep calm, Sander's raised eyebrow has irritated and pissed me off more than I realized so I feel justified as to why I don't have Pete's contact details. Oh you numpty! I mentally slap my forehead. I've been played. It dawns on me then Paul would possibly know.

"Paul do you know Pete's contact details?" I know he does as soon as I see his face "stupid question I know, of course you do" I say with sardonic humour.

Paul gestures for Sanders to hand over his pad and pen, he wrote quickly and hands it back as a nurse and orderly pull back the curtain, both are startled by the amount of people standing around Clayton and the bed.

"I'm afraid I'm going to have to ask you all to leave as Mr Blake is going to x-ray" she holds up a gown.

I smirk at Clayton as I give him a quick kiss "See you in a bit"

As we enter the waiting room Shelley, Simon, Macy, Stephanie and Andrew descend on me and Joshua firing questions at us about Clayton.

"He's in pain, the doctor has given him some meds and he's on his way to x-ray" Joshua says as he subtly takes Stephanie by the elbow and leads her back to the seats with Andrew following.

"Shelley, Simon this is Detective Sanders. He has some questions about Caroline. Tell him everything, don't hold back"

Both their eyes widen in shocked surprise. Simon mouths "everything" I nod. He looks at Sanders and gives him a dazzling smile. I groan inwardly.

"So handsome what do you want to know?" Simon almost purrs.

I laugh as Sanders blushes. Looking at the detective more closely I suppose he is good looking if you go for the rumpled rugged look.

"Behave Simon" Shelley admonishes swatting his arm.

"What!" Simon exclaims in all innocence "he's cute"

"Detective, I'm going to sit over there" I point to where the Blake family are sitting "feel free to arrest and throw him in jail" I point at Simon "if he gets too much" Sanders chuckles and Simon huffs. Shelley and I roll our eyes at him.

I sit beside Joshua who is reassuring an unconvinced Stephanie Clayton is okay and being taken to x-ray is standard procedure and to confirm if Clayton actually did have cracked ribs as he seems to think. I position myself so I can watch Shelley and Simon talk with Sanders. I can't hear them but I can read body language. Shelley and Simon will tell me everything later but I want to see if the detective believes what he is being told.

"Miss Darcy" the doctor calls out as he opens the door.

I stand and so do everyone else, the doctor points at me and shakes' his head at the others. I follow the doctor with Bruce and Paul falling in behind me. The doctor looks at them then decides they aren't going to take no for an answer.

"Mr Parker and Mr Ellison are in the recovery room, and yes you can go and see them" he pre-empts the question that's on the tip of my tongue.

As we walk down the corridor he briefs me on their injuries. They hadn't needed major surgery as I first thought. Mark has a nasty flesh wound on his upper arm. For Alan the bullet passed right through his shoulder missing anything vital.

"They may be a little groggy as they have been given medication for the pain and Mark can go home in a few hours, Alan we'll keep overnight" the doctor says as he opens the door to the room.

"Thank you doctor"

Alan and Mark are the only two patients in the room and they try to sit up as I enter. "Don't you dare" I admonish softly "the last thing I want is your wounds opening up"

I sit myself down between the two beds and chat with them. I joke with Alan saying he isn't allowed to resign after only a week in the job just because he got shot and telling Mark he should ask Clayton for a pay rise or at least demand danger pay. We'd been talking for about ten minutes when the door opens and a woman and two teenage boys come in, Mark's family. The worry and fear in their faces dissolves to relief and love when they lay eyes on him.

"Hey, I'm okay" Mark reassures his wife as she wipes at her eyes "I was lucky it's only a flesh wound and the doc says I can come home in a few hours"

The door opens again and in walks Clayton, he isn't wearing the gown, my inner goddess grumbles "what a pity" and pouts. Clayton introduces himself to Mark's family and expresses his gratitude and thanks to Mark for putting himself in the firing line then told him all medical expenses are covered and he is to take the next month off with full pay. I get a dig in about paying Mark a danger bonus as taking a bullet for the boss isn't in his job description like Alan's. Mark and his family gawp at me for my audacity.

"You're right my love" Clayton says taking my hand and kissing the back of it "I'll sort something out" he says to Mark.

"Thank you sir, but it isn't necessary" Mark says stunned.

Before Clayton can reply the doctor walks in and tells him off again for not being where he should be. Tut-ting and rolling my eyes I push Clayton out the door much to everyone's amusement.

Clayton has badly bruised ribs and shoulder, the result of landing awkwardly when Bruce pushed him to the ground and covered him when Caroline opened fire. The doctor said he needed a couple of days rest. Hmm chance for me to play nurse, I'm sure I still have my naughty nurse Halloween costume from a few years ago in the closet somewhere. We call in on Alan and Mark again before going back to everyone in the waiting room. Clayton asks Mark how he is getting home when Bruce tells him everything has been arranged. We say goodbye and head for the waiting room.

"We should call in on Mark tomorrow at home, check he's okay" I shrug when Clayton just looks at me, his expression is hard to fathom "just a suggestion"

Clayton stops and pulls me to him; good job the corridor is quiet. His fingers lightly stroke down my cheek "That's a wonderful suggestion" he whispers and gently kisses me "come on let's go get the others"

"The press are outside in force" Simon says as we enter.

"Shit"

"My sentiments exactly" Clayton murmurs in my ear. Huh guess I said that louder than I thought "do you want us to stay quiet on this Detective?"

"For the time being if you don't mind sir" Sanders says putting his note book in his jacket pocket and standing.

"Simon is our PR guru" I say "do you mind if we put a statement out saying Clayton and the injured are doing fine, as I'm guessing they know Clayton was brought here and are speculating he was Caroline's intended target along with her reasons for shooting at him"

"I can work with the hospitals publicity department and I'll find out if there's certain protocol to follow" Simon says, he's in full business mode.

Detective Sanders looks momentarily speechless at Simon "Sure, keep all reference to Caroline Tanner out of anything you put out. I have your contact details should I have any other questions"

I look at Macy and she nods to confirm she's given him our details. "Thank you detective" I smile at him.

Sanders becomes bashful and hesitant, I raise an eyebrow "I know it's unprofessional of me but my son is never going to forgive me if I don't ask for your autograph"

Clayton starts to laugh then hisses in pain, making me chuckle, I really should have more sympathy for him. I sign Sanders note book and offer to pose for a picture with him, further proof for his son I joke. As Macy takes the last photo Paul walks into the room. I didn't even notice he had disappeared.

"Ma'am, sir" he says addressing Clayton and me "the hospital security has agreed to allow us to leave through the back door so to speak"

"Is it that bad?" asks Clayton.

"Yes sir, I went to look for myself as soon as Mr Hanson mentioned it. Taking into account your injuries you won't get to the car without being jostled. Bruce is bringing the car around to the service entrance as we speak"

Thankfully we get out of the hospital without attracting the attention of the press or the paparazzi. We time our exit with Simon and the hospital's publicity person giving a statement so all attention is at the front of the hospital whilst we sneak out the back.

Once home and I tell Clayton to go straight to bed and rest. He lets me undress him and I know he is indulging me as he has 'that' smile on his face the whole time. His eyes never leave me, he constantly touches me, gentle caresses with his fingers trailing my arms, exposed mid riff, my cheeks and neck. I couldn't hold back on the gasp at the sight of the huge bruise which is forming along the ribs of his right side. I place kisses along the bruise.

"How badly does it hurt?" I can feel myself filling up.

Clayton cups my face and kisses me tenderly "I can bear any pain so long as you are looking after me" I melt in a puddle on the floor at his words.

I turn down the bed sheets and plump the pillows "Okay mister into bed"

Clayton's arms snake around me "Join me" he says whispering and nipping my ear lobe, the sting resonates in my core.

"Behave" it takes every ounce of my control to say that "now get into bed"

"Bossy" Clayton grumbles.

I tuck him in and head for the closet, time to find the nurse outfit.

CLAYTON

I get myself comfortable settling into the pillows and mattress as Skye disappears into the closet then make the mistake of taking a deep breath. Fuck! It hurts; a dull throb starts up in my right side.

I'm just thankful Caroline was such a fucking lousy shot. Talk about my life flashing before my eyes as I heard the first shot and landing on my side, all images and thoughts were of Skye.

Closing my eyes images of Skye in the waiting room flood my mind. I relive the moment. I know she had come straight to the hospital, to me, the minute she got the news. She hadn't changed out of her tattered work dungarees or removed her bandanna. She looked so young, small and fragile and so god damn fucking sexy.

Grief and pain marred her beautiful face changing to relief and love as soon as she saw me it had my heart pounding and my arms aching to hold her. I had to reign myself in as I nearly told my own mother to get the fuck out of my way so I could hold her.

"Would you like something to eat" Skye's husky voice asks softly.

I slowly open my eyes which snap open wide when I get a load of what she is wearing.

"Fuck me!" I sit up too quickly and pain shoots through me making me wince and brings tears to my eyes.

Skye gently pushes me back down "Careful, if I'd known you would have this reaction I wouldn't have put it on. I better go and take it off"

"Hell no" I snap at her "stand back so I can get a better look"

Skye dutifully takes a couple of steps back so I can get the full impact of what she is wearing, not that I need it because my cock is already demanding we get the party started.

Skye is wearing a nurse outfit, a very, very short nurse outfit. It fits her like a glove showing off her fuckable body and the buttons are open to reveal her ample cleavage. She has on white stockings and suspenders. The hem of the outfit finishes about two inches above the tops of her stockings, on her feet are sky high white platform killer heels, as she calls them. To add authenticity a watch is pinned to her chest and a nurse's hat on her head. My cock is pulsing and twitching in appreciation of the view. I lift my hand and signal for her to give me a twirl, smiling Skye obliges.

"Come here" lust makes my voice lower "so nurse, are you here to look after me?"

Skye bends over and puts the covers straight. I can't help myself and run my hand up the back of her leg and cup her ass, Skye wiggles and pushes into my hand.

"Absolutely Mr Blake" I can hear how turned on she is with those few words. Skye smooth's the covers and brushes her hand over my erection "I'm here to look after your every need"

I groan as she caresses and gently squeezes my cock, my hips surge upwards of their own volition. I move my hand between her thighs and run my finger along the seam of her panties. Skye's breathing becomes shallow and her lips part. I push her panties aside and run a finger parting her cleft. I slip it inside her.

"Oh baby you are so wet for me. I want to eat you" I lick my lips as I remember how sweet she tastes.

"I'm desert Mr Blake" purrs Skye as she continues to stroke me.

"I want you as my starter" I pull my finger out and put it in my mouth "hmmm you taste so fucking good, as sweet as honey"

I make a move to grab her but pain shoots through my side halting me in my tracks. Skye takes advantage and moves out of my reach.

"Rest and I'll bring you something to eat" Skye chuckles as she heads out of the room.

I close my eyes and get comfy again. I'm going to really enjoy the next couple of days especially with Skye parading around in that nurse uniform. Fuck she's going to put me in an early grave.

I feel the bed dip and Skye's fingers gently stroke my face, slowly opening my eyes I see her beautiful yellow green eyes full of concern and a sweet smile on her luscious full lips.

"How are you feeling?" her voice is soft and it makes my heart flutter.

"Better now you're here" I smile back "I guess the pain meds are finally kicking in" I'd taken them after the x-ray but I was still pumped with adrenaline from all the events of the afternoon for them to have any effect. "How long have I been out?" I give a huge yawn making my jaw crack.

"Just over an hour; I've made soup do you feel up to it?"

"Feed me" I command making Skye rolls her eyes.

Skye helps me sit up against the headboard and sits beside me reaching for the bowl of soup.

"I want you straddling me"

A smirk crosses Skye's full lips, without a word she put the bowl down, takes her shoes off and climbs across my lap. I put my hands on her thighs effectively halting her descent. Lazily I run my fingers around the tops of her stockings then up to meet the hem of her outfit, slowly I move my hands up under the skirt to her panties and grasp them. Skye's breath hitches, the sound makes my cock pulse.

"You won't need these, nurse" I pull and snap them, throwing the ruined panties to the floor "are you ready for me baby?" I look up into Skye's lust filled eyes as I run my fingers over her slit, parting her I can feel how wet she is but I want her to tell me.

"Yes"

"Good. I need to be inside you. I need to feel you inside and out" my voice rasps with desire. I have this undeniable strong urge to connect with her, to be connected to her.

Skye maneuvers so she can pull the covers back revealing my rock solid cock. I'm aching for her. Fuck the sight of Skye wrapping her dainty hand around my cock nearly has me coming. She strokes me gently making me groan, my head falls back with a thud on the headboard. I feel her warm wet entrance on the head of my cock. Lifting my head I watch as she lowers herself slowly onto me.

"Oh fuck baby you feel so good, just what the doctor ordered"

My head falls back again as I absorb the sensations of her surrounding me. I feel grounded and connected just what I need. Skye rises and lowers herself a few times on the final lower she settles into my hips taking me to the root. I feel her muscles clench and grab me, my cock jerks in response to the pleasure. A small soft groan escapes Skye. I grip her hips and thrust mine up and grind into her making her groan again, her head is thrown back and her hands rest lightly on my shoulders.

"Kiss me" I command.

Skye's hands cup the nape of my neck, her fingers tug on my hair as her lips meet mine. She's being gentle afraid she's going to hurt me. I need to feel alive, I need something life affirming. I wrap my arms around her, pinning her to me and kiss her hard. Skye responds, our tongues dart and circle tasting each other. Teeth nip, pull and suck on lower lips. Skye slowly rocks and circles her hips. I am consumed by need for her and it is so strong I feel my orgasm hurtling forward and I don't stop it, I do nothing to speed it along either, I enjoy the feel of Skye working me. As the orgasm hits I break the kiss throwing my head back.

"Fuck. Skye" I bellow, pain along my side blends with the rush of pleasure coursing through my body.

Skye continues to rock her hips going faster, chasing her own orgasm. I put my hand between our bodies and massage her clit.

"Clayton, yes, Clayton" Skye shouts out. I love hearing her.

Skye collapses against my chest her head rests on my shoulder; her hot panting breath tickles my neck, our hearts pound in unison. I tighten my arms around her and bury my face in her hair inhaling deeply taking in her scent.

"I love you" I whisper in her ear. Skye lifts her head and kisses me.

"I love you" she whispers.

After a few minutes Skye makes a move to get off me, I hold her firmly in place. "Stay where you are, now feed me"

Skye's eyes widen in surprise then she laughs her deep throaty laugh. I'm still inside her and I feel my cock hardening back to full strength, so does Skye.

"I can see you're going to be a demanding pain in the arse patient" Skye mutters under her breath, I smile as sweetly as I can at her as she reaches across and picks up the bowl of soup.

Skye stirs the soup and lifts a spoonful towards my mouth. I rest my hands on her thighs as she feeds me. The soup tastes good.

"Homemade?" I ask.

Skye smirks "If you call opening a can and heating it up in the microwave homemade, then yes it is"

I laugh then wince as pain shoots up my side. Skye is immediately anxious.

"You okay?"

"I'm fine baby it just hurts when I laugh" I rub my hands up and down her thighs to give her reassurance. I can't help myself as I surge my hips upwards making her gasp.

"Behave" Skye mouths at me as she feeds me another mouthful "oh by the way; whilst you were asleep your mother and brothers rang checking up on you, plus a bunch of other people. Macy's fielding the calls now but you should call your Mom" I roll my eyes which earns me a light tap on the shoulder, I feign hurt "nice try but it's your other shoulder that's injured" Skye says pointing at the bruise which forming nicely "ring her and put her mind at rest otherwise you'll probably have her on the door step first thing in the morning"

"Shit you're right" I sigh. I reach for my phone on the bedside cabinet, again Skye moves to get off my lap with one hand I hold her in place "stay where you are" I growl.

Skye places the now empty bowl on the cabinet as I dial my mother's number. It's a short conversation. I have no remorse when I lie to her saying the pain meds are making me drowsy and I want to sleep in order to end the conversation. I want my desert.

"Liar, liar pants on fire" Skye sings as I toss my phone back onto the cabinet.

I push and roll my hips upwards "Good job I'm not wearing any" I thrust again making Skye gasp as I make sure she feels every inch of me.

Clasping Skye to me I roll so she's beneath me. I kiss her gently as I flex my hips moving slowly in and out of her "Christ I can never get enough of you" I say as I trail kisses down her throat.

"Hmmm" Skye responds arching into me, running her hands up and down my back.

"I really like this outfit, when did you get this?" I start to undo more buttons so I can get better access to her tits "fuck there's no bra"

"Disappointed?" chuckles Skye.

"Hell no" I run my tongue over a nipple making it harden. I blow lightly over it and circle my tongue around it. Skye lifts her chest up a silent demand her body wants more. I surround the nipple and suck, drawing it deep into my mouth flicking my tongue over the nub. Skye writhes and grinds her hips into me "answer my question" I gently bite the nipple.

"What question?" Skye gasps, she's lost to the pleasure.

"When did you get the outfit?" I move to the other nipple drawing it deep into my mouth.

"Couple of years ago, Halloween" she pants out.

Jealousy pounds through me. She went out in this for a party and other men ogled her, wanted her. I put my mouth close to her ear "Did you go out in this?" I thrust deep and hard with my hips. Skye's muscles greedily clench down on my cock.

"No" relief sweeps through me. I thrust deep and hard again.

"Why not?" I push. I keep up with the slow deep hard thrusts, Skye's breathing is laboured. I thrust hard again "answer me" I demand, I lift up onto my arms so I can see Skye's face "open your eyes"

Skye struggles to open her eyes, when she does they are hazy and glazed until she focuses on me. I continue thrusting hard and deep, she fights to keep her eyes from closing.

"Party... cancelled"

I have an overwhelming urge to mark my territory, stake my claim.

"Good girl" I increase my thrusts striking as deep and as hard as I can "this is for my eyes only. You... are... mine" I say through gritted teeth and punctuate each word with a deep thrust, Skye meets each one by raising her hips, fuck she likes this "who do you belong to?" Skye groans out incoherent words "answer me" I thrust hard.

"You" the shout rips out of Skye "again" she commands.

"You like it hard baby?" I pound into her.

"Yes" it comes out as a low groan.

"Let me hear how much you like it. I want to hear you scream" I slam into her and I'm rewarded with a shout.

I set a punishing pace, ignoring the pain lancing my side and shoulder. It's worth it seeing Skye beneath me writhing and calling out as I pound pleasure into and from her, feeling her tight hot wet cunt muscles greedily grab my cock wanting more. Sweat trickles down my face, chest and back. I feel Skye's climax building as her muscles spasm and with each thrust she shouts louder.

"Who do you belong to?"

"You Clayton you" Skye screams as her orgasm detonates.

I wrap my arms around her as her body jerks and spasms. I continue to pound faster, deep and hard. I bury my head in her neck. Pleasure explodes through me causing all my muscles to constrict, throwing my head back and holding me still as I come hard filling Skye.

"I love you Skye" I bellow, the strain pulls at my bruised ribs and muscles. There's no separation between the pain and pleasure I'm feeling.

I collapse on top of Skye and her arms wrap around me, one hand runs up and down my sweat drenched back the other through my damp hair, soothing me, bringing me back down.

"You are mine" she whispers in my ear "you belong to me and this" she clenches me inside and out "is for my eyes and me only"

My heart swells she's staking her claim. I lift my head and kiss her for a long time pouring all of my love and need into it, into her.

We've both been quiet, lost in our thoughts, since getting into the tub. Skye is leaning against me, I have one arm wrapped around her shoulders holding her to me with my free hand scooping and pouring water over her body, watching the rivulets trickle and caress the skin over her chest and stomach. Skye's hand rubs my leg in long slow movements whilst her other hand mirrors the same action along my arm that crosses her front.

"When Paul told me there had been a shooting I felt my world collapse" Skye whispers softly, my arm tightens pulling her closer "my legs gave out, he caught me before I hit the floor. Actually it happened twice the second time was when your Mom told me there were three casualties, two were in surgery. I assumed one of them was you"

"Who caught you the second time?" I feel a pang of jealousy and regret it wasn't me.

"Paul" she sighs "the journey to the hospital seemed to take hours and we couldn't reach you, Bruce or Alan on your phones"

Skye twists, I loosen my hold as she turns to face me, lying on my front, her movement causes pain to shoot up my side but I mask it, I think. Skye reaches up with one hand and gently strokes my face. I turn my head and kiss her palm.

"My imagination ran riot, my worst fear" she says softly "was getting to the hospital and being too late to say goodbye" her eyes are overly bright with unshed tears, my heart aches for her "I don't know what I would do without you" her voice cracks and she bites her bottom lip to stop herself from crying. It doesn't work. My heart feels as if it's shattering. I cup her cheek and brush away a tear with my thumb.

"You are a survivor Skye" I can hear the emotion in my own voice. Skye shakes her head.

"I realized today I'll never survive you, if you left me. I'll be a broken empty hollow shell"

My heart shatters into a million pieces. I pull her up my body and hold her tight "Baby you're breaking my heart. I love you so much" my words are filled with raw emotion.

My throat burns and I can't swallow past the lump. Tears sting my eyes, I bury my head into her neck and let go. Big wracking sobs. I cry like a fucking baby. Skye holds me, her hand stroking my wet hair, she doesn't say anything just hums softly, calming and soothing me.

The events of the day have affected me more than I thought. I can't remember the last time when I cried. After a while I manage to find my voice.

"When the gunshots were going off all I could think about was you. At the hospital all I wanted was you with me, when the nurse told me you had arrived nothing was going to stop me getting to you. I needed to hold you. Feel you. Be with you" I lift my head and cup Skye face pulling away so I can see her beautiful eyes and face "you are my world. Everything I do revolves' around you. You make my life worth living; you give me a reason to get up every morning. I was nothing but an empty shell of a man then I met you and you made my heart beat for the first time in my miserable existence. You are the piece I was missing, you complete me. I am never, ever going to leave you and no-one is ever going to take you away from me. You are mine and we belong together" tears are rolling down Skye's cheeks "why are you crying?" my question comes out as a soft whisper.

"I'm so happy. I love you so much. I never let myself dream or hope I would find someone I could love so much that it hurt, let alone find my soul mate" Skye half sobs and laughs the last few words. My heart shatters all over again.

"You are so fucking beautiful, inside and out. I love you" I pull her to me and hold her in a fierce grip. Skye clings to me as desperately as I cling to her. We remain like this until the water is too cold to stay in any longer, reluctantly we let each other go and climb out of the tub. I fight Skye off so I can dry her and wrap her in towels to warm her up, she only relents when I tell her, her lips are turning blue and she's shivering. I dry myself off quickly then scoop Skye up, ignoring the screaming pain of my ribs and muscles, and carry her to bed.

"You're supposed to be taking it easy" Skye complains and sulkily pouts, she actually pouts.

"You look so fucking adorable when you do that" I laugh and plant a chaste kiss on her lips.

I climb into bed and before I can pull Skye into my arms she jumps out of bed and dashes back into the bathroom. I hear the cabinet open and close, then the tap turn on and off. Skye reappears holding a glass of water, her other hand is closed.

"Here take these" she says holding out her closed hand, my hand automatically lifts to accept whatever these are, she drops two pills onto my open palm "pain killers, doctor said to take two before you sleep"

"What makes you think I'm going to sleep" I wiggle my eyebrows as I rake my eyes up and down her naked body. Lust kicks in immediately.

"Behave and take your meds or no sex" Skye says sternly.

The threat of no sex works like a dream, just like it did when she threatened to withhold sex for a week if I didn't go to Shelley's for the wedding vest fitting, there is no way in hell I'm going to test how serious she is, and like a good boy albeit scowling I take the pills. As soon as I finish drinking the water Skye holds out her hand for the empty glass, I grab her hand and yank her to me at the same time I drop the glass to the floor, Skye yelps as I flip her onto her back and I pin her down with my body.

"You're supposed to be taking it easy" Skye scolds me giggling and tries to push me off her "I know you're in pain, you can't hide it from me"

Damn the woman is too observant.

"Pain killers work wonders and I am going to take it very easy" I grin wickedly at her and bend my head to kiss her. I move from her lips to her jaw down to her throat.

"You're a pain in the backside. Do you ever do as you're told?" Skye pushes her head back giving me better access to her throat. I've got her.

"Nope" I grin against her skin.

Skye's attempts to push me off change to pulling me closer to her, she groans as I lick, kiss and nip my way very slowly down her body.

"Now for my desert" I say settling myself in between Skye's thighs, her legs over my shoulders. I run my nose over her pussy inhaling deeply "hmm, this smells delicious I just know you're going to taste divine"

I run my tongue flat against the length of her cleft, just as if I would ice cream off a cone, Skye cries out and her hips buck. I love watching her respond to my touch. I place my hand on her lower abdomen and hold her in place as I get ready to devour her.

"Sweet as honey, I think I'm going to gorge on my desert, what do you say?" I run my tongue over her again, this time I latch onto her clit and suck hard.

"Oh god" Skye cries out, the words are long drawn out, her hips push upwards and her hands find my hair, pulling and tugging.

"Hmm definitely having seconds, possibly thirds" I swirl my tongue around her folds and clit, biting lightly then plunging my tongue deep into her.

"Argh" Skye arches off the bed, her arms fly out to the sides and she grips the bedding.

"I'm definitely going to have thirds you simply taste too fucking good"

I blow over her sensitive bud, she's close and I want to make this last. I kiss the inside of her thighs and across her hips following her scar, when her breathing calms down, I devour her again. Three times I take her to the brink before Skye begs me to let her come. I rear up to my knees and move her into the position I want.

"Put your arms above your head and grasp the head board" I command softly.

Skye does it immediately. I twist her so she's lying partly on her side; I lift one leg and move to straddle the other lying flush to the bed. Her raised leg I place against my uninjured shoulder. Taking hold of my cock I tease her entrance and slowly push in.

Her swollen tissues and muscles greedily grab me "Oh baby, you were so made for me" I groan at the pleasure their touch triggers.

I have to hold still and take deep breaths to regain my control. Skye's muscles spasm and contract around me, she's very close. "Don't come until I tell you"

Skye moans and takes deep breaths, I withdraw slowly and she whimpers.

"Hold on baby" I grasp her leg in one hand placing the other on her hip and thrust forward hard.

"Argh, fuck" Skye calls out.

"Again baby?" I slowly withdraw.

"'Hell yes" Skye shouts.

I slam into her, screaming her pleasure and whimpering as I withdraw, over and over again.

"I can't hold on any longer" Skye's whole body is trembling with effort staving off her climax.

"Not yet" I bark the command through gritted teeth and I drive back into her.

Skye screams as her orgasm rips through her, moving quickly I place her leg down so she's on her back and I thrust in and out hard and fast, a second orgasm hits her before the first ebbs away. Skye bites down on my pectoral as she tries to muffle her scream. The sharp pain coupled with her muscles spasms and clamping down on my cock triggers my orgasm and I release hard.

"Fuck, fuck, Skye" I bellow as my body clenches and I still as my cock twitches and pulses deep inside her. I gasp in short shallow breaths trying not to hurt my abused ribs. I start to move slowly in and out drawing out the pleasure for both of us.

I fall asleep with my arms wrapped around Skye and my face buried in her hair breathing in her heady floral scent. I'm never going to let her go is my last thought.

Chapter Thirty

SKYE

I can't move, panic surges through me and I jolt awake. My heart is pounding in my chest and I can feel a scream bubbling, threatening to break free, my body is shaking. A grumbling noise resonates in my ear and air is squeezed out of my lungs. What would have been a full blown blood curdling scream comes out as high pitch wheeze. The grumbling sound and the tightening of the restraint came again. 'Clayton!' my mind shouts with relief making my whole body sag, I suddenly feel boneless, limp as his arms flex and tighten around me again. Clayton has me in a vice like grip; I've woken up in exactly the same position as I fell asleep, neither of us has moved during the night.

A light knock on the door has me lifting my head—it's the only part of me I can move—as it opens slightly.

"Skye" Macy's voice calls softly.

"Yeah" my voice is thick with sleep. The door opens a bit more and I can see the outline of Macy's head against the light spilling in behind her.

"Sorry to wake you but Mrs Blake is here and she's insisting on seeing Clayton. I've told her you're both sleeping but she won't leave" I can hear the peeved irritation in Macy's voice. I know given half the chance Macy would have told her to fuck off and I know Clayton will give her permission and his blessing to say it but he hasn't so she can't.

"What time is it?" my voice is still croaky, I clear my throat.

"Ten thirty"

Blimey, we've had twelve hours sleep! I think that's a first for both of us. "Okay, give me ten minutes"

Macy closes the door. I try to move but Clayton's arms tighten even more and he grumbles again. He really doesn't want to let me go. Instead of trying to move out of his arms again I wriggle round to face him. Clayton is adorable when he sleeps. I place my lips to his and kiss him; he responds and makes a contended humming sound.

"Clayton baby wake up" I coax "Clayton time to wake up" I kiss him again "come on Clayton you need to wake up" I manage to prize an arm free and gently stroke his face, his morning stubble prickling my fingers.

I stifle a giggle as it's usually Clayton waking me up and I know I can be a real grumpy cow if I'm woken before I'm ready. I kiss him again.

"Come on sleepy head wakey, wakey" I'm rewarded with a sleepy smile "open those lovely blue eyes for me"

They slowly open "Morning beautiful" he whispers and kisses me tenderly.

"We need to get up" I say softly against his lips.

Clayton's hand pushes against my butt so my hips meet his and he grinds his erection into me "I'm already up" he says with a cute sleepy salacious grin.

"As much as I would love to make full use of this right now" I grind against him "you'll have to save it for later. Your mother is here to see you"

Clayton's eyes snap open, he's fully awake and alert now. "Ah fuck what does she want?" he groans "and what's she doing here so early?" he sounds like a petulant teenager and I fail miserably not to laugh.

"It is ten thirty and I'm guessing she wants to see if her beloved son is being properly taken care of. She's worried about you so stop being a grouch"

"Kiss me" Clayton demands grumpily. The kiss I give him is tender and slow, our mouths and tongues lazily move against each other. Clayton soon gives a contented hum and sighs "you sure I have to wait till later?"

"Later" I reiterate "you can fuck me against the wall and I'll even wear the nurse uniform if you want me to"

A deep rumbling growl told me he did as he attacks my lips with a deep hard kiss. "I'm going to fuck you hard and fast now baby"

My core clenches as he flips me onto my front and lifts my hips. I just have time to raise myself onto my elbows as he enters me. We both groan. I love the fullness, the stretching feeling I get from his magnificent cock. Clayton moves slowly in and out a few times letting me get used to the feel of him.

"Ready baby" he grasps my hips.

"Yes"

I'm panting with anticipation, I enjoyed his roughness last night his need for me coming out in pure carnal brute force and this is going to be a repeat. I'm in heaven. Clayton withdrew slowly and I clench my muscles so I can feel every inch of him, he groans his pleasure. Clayton's grip on my hips tightens it's my cue to get ready; he slams back into me pulling my hips onto him at the same time. Oh he's deep. Clayton repeats the slow withdrawal and fast penetration a few more times, we both groan loudly then he starts to move fast in and out, over and over. It's not long before we are both climaxing. Clayton trails kisses up my spine as he pulls out of me. I collapse face down on the bed, my heart is still racing and I take much needed deep breaths. A sharp slap on my butt has me jerking up right.

"Come on baby you're not leaving me to entertain my mother on my own, get dressed"

Clayton laughs when I scowl at him as he walks into the bathroom. I take a minute to enjoy the view of his tight butt, long lean muscular legs and the flex of his broad shoulders as he strolls in his graceful gait. At the door Clayton turns and winks at me, I blush because I've been caught ogling my man and husband to be. Butterflies summersault in my stomach, in four weeks I'll be married.

I'm going to keep my name professionally now I just need to tell Clayton and after last night's possessive declarations I have a feeling it will go down like a tonne of bricks or a cold bucket of sick as Simon is fond of saying. Sighing I drag myself off the bed and into the shower thinking of various ways to bring up the subject. In the end I decide and agree with the coward in me to leave it a few days.

I walk into the living room to see Stephanie fussing over Clayton, who is fast losing patience. I'm not going to rescue him, instead I head straight for the kitchen to make breakfast or should that be brunch considering its nearer lunch time. The smell of food and coffee soon has Clayton coming to me with Stephanie hot on his heels.

"Smells good, what are we having?" Clayton wraps his arms around me and nuzzles my neck.

"Bacon, poached eggs and toasted bagels. Stephanie would you like some"

"No thank you Skye dear, I just stopped by to see how Clayton is"

I lean to one side and grin up at Clayton mouthing "told you". He rolls his eyes and moves away to pour coffee for him and Stephanie.

Whilst I finish cooking and sit down to eat Stephanie gives a rundown of everything to do with the wedding and numbers to date. I only have twenty people attending, all of whom have said yes so I switch off and leave Clayton to converse with his mother about their various relatives and family friends.

"Skye the wedding planner wants to know who is doing the cake so she can liaise with them. Give me their details and I'll pass them on" Stephanie says in her superefficient no nonsense voice.

"I'm doing it" I say around a mouthful of food.

Stephanie is momentarily stunned. "You're making the cake" the disbelief she feels is clearly evident in her voice and face.

Clayton scowls at her "That's what Skye said, she's making it" he snaps, he doesn't hide the fact she's just pissed him off.

"I'm sorry dear" Stephanie's eyes flick nervously to Clayton as she apologises "I know you said you were sorting it out, I just didn't realize you meant you were actually making it" poor Stephanie looks distraught at me.

I reach over and squeeze her hand "Don't worry about it and no offense was made or taken" I smile at her then give Clayton a meaningful look one I hope conveys a go easy on her message. He got it as he rolls his eyes and huffs.

A throat being cleared has the three of us looking up at Paul. "Excuse me ma'am, sir. Detective Sanders is here, he has an update"

"Show him in" Clayton and I say together. I can't help but laugh at Stephanie's surprised wide eyed look.

A few minutes later Paul brings Detective Sanders into the kitchen.

"Good morning detective, would you like a drink" I offer as I get off the stool and head to the sink with the dirty plates.

"Black coffee please and apologies for the intrusion but I was passing and thought I'd give you an update" Clayton pours him a mug of coffee "thanks, how are the ribs?" I hear Sanders ask as I load the dishwasher.

"A lot better and the bruise is coming along nicely" Clayton chuckles "this is my mother Stephanie Blake"

"Ma'am" Sanders nods politely to Stephanie who in turn gives him a dazzling smile.

"Let's go sit in the living room" I pick up my tea and lead the way.

I falter sitting down when Sanders exclaims "Holy cow" in shocked wonder. I turn to see he's spotted the five large canvasses which make up The Gentlemen's Club commission. He whistles and walks over for a better look. I hear another low whistle as he takes in each canvass.

"These are fantastic" he says to the room in general.

Clayton and Stephanie join him scrutinizing the extremely sensual paintings. They are my take on futuristic pole dancers. I realize it's probably Stephanie's first time seeing my work up close and personal. She has a mixed stunned and fascinated look on her face. I sit curling my legs up on the sofa and wait patiently.

Clayton is the first move away which seems to snap Detective Sanders out of his trance, remembering where he is he blushes and looks at me apologetically "I'm sorry ma'am, forgive me they are truly amazing. I have to ask, who are they for?"

"It's a commission for The Gentleman's Club the painting on the far right has about another ten hours work then it's finished"

Clayton scoops me up and sits me on his lap, if Clayton's action surprises the detective he doesn't show it.

"Well I'll get to the point of my call" Sanders says sitting on the arm chair "do either of you know Della Johnson?" in unison we both say "no". Sanders nod indicates he expected that response "I only ask because that's who Miss Tanner stayed with and it was her gun used in the shooting. I've spoken to Pete Lancaster and your friends and all collaborated with your information given yesterday so I'll be making my report as soon as I get back to the station and the case will be closed. From Miss Johnson's account Miss Tanner did indeed display increasing erratic and unstable behaviour"

"How did Caroline get hold of the gun?" says Clayton.

"Miss Johnson kept it in her night stand, she wasn't aware it was missing until I turned up on her door step. It was quite a nasty shock for her"

"I bet it was" Clayton says dryly if not a tad sarcastic.

"Thank you for letting us know Detective" I say smiling at him.

"Well I'll leave you to enjoy the rest of your day" Sanders says getting to his feet "it was nice meeting you both" we shake hands and Paul shows him out.

Clayton stands behind me and surrounds me in his arms, he rests his chin on my shoulder turning his head slightly he kisses the side of my neck. A shiver runs through me. Stephanie is still looking at the paintings, she is unusually quiet. I look at Clayton with raised eyebrows, he shrugs and shakes his head looking at his mother he's clueless as well about her behaviour.

"Ma'am, sir" Paul says coming back into the living room "Alan is being released from hospital within the hour. Bruce is going to collect him and bring him back here; we've rearranged my quarters to accommodate him"

Alan is going to be moving in with us at the new apartment until then he's staying at his own place however yesterday's shooting put paid to that. Macy insisted Alan come and stay with us because he needed someone to keep an eye on him whilst he recovers, nobody argued well Alan tried but gave up when Macy said "I don't care how tough you think you are, you're still going to need help" I on the other hand had forgotten all about it, until now.

"Of course, if you need to use any of the spare rooms here because things are cramped please do" I say feeling a tad guilty, suddenly remembering Clayton has a say I wince and look up at him only to find a loving smile on his face.

"The guy took a bullet that was intended for me I'm not going to begrudge them more room" he tightens his arms around me.

"Thank you ma'am, but it shouldn't be necessary. Macy needs to speak with you on some business matters she asks if you can let her know when would be a good time"

Before I can say anything Clayton says "Send her in now" Paul nods and disappears, I look open mouthed at Clayton in peeved disbelief "I need to speak to Helena and sort some business things myself. If we both do that now it gives us the afternoon free"

Clayton dips his knees and pushes up into my butt telling me exactly what he has in mind. I grind and rotate my hips and push back into him.

"You're forgiven" I whisper, Clayton hardens even more.

"Are you both still going to the function tomorrow night?"

Shit, Stephanie. I'd completely forgotten about her, so had Clayton judging by the way he jerks away from me at the sound of her voice.

"Yes Mom we'll be there"

"Good, well I'll be off then and let you two get on"

We both see Stephanie to the door and say goodbye. For some reason Stephanie cups my face in both her hands, her eyes sparkling with love and wonder then she gives me a huge hug taking me completely by surprise.

"What an earth was that all about?" I ask Clayton as he shuts and locks the door.

Clayton picks me up so I wrap my legs around his waist and my arms around his neck. He carries me back to the living room.

"I've no idea, but hazarding a guess I think it's just dawned on her that you are one seriously talented artist and not just a pretty face" he stops in front of the canvasses "Mom is a huge art fan and she spent the whole time studying these" immediately I understand what he's getting at because Stephanie is also a huge gossip and any juicy titbits to be had she will be first in line only on this occasion she chose to ignore the detectives update "the figures are so life like they look like photographs. It wouldn't surprise me in the least if she goes home and researches more of your work or I should say she'll pay closer attention"

"Oops sorry I didn't mean to intrude" Macy calls apologetically.

"Come back Macy, you're not" I shout after her retreating figure. Clayton takes the hint and puts me down.

Macy and I sit in the living room and go through all the business issues whilst Clayton uses the office. Two hours later we're wrapping up when we hear Clayton cursing and ranting at the top of his voice. Macy startles and looks apprehensive towards the office. It's the first time she's heard Clayton angry at home, there's a loud thump making us both jump. A few seconds later the thumping continues along with a lot more cursing.

"I better go and see what he's got his knickers in a twist over" I say getting up.

"Rather you than me" Macy mutters under her breath.

"I heard that"

"You were meant to" Macy grins at me "good luck"

Standing in the doorway I look into the office to see Clayton with his head down and his hands in his hair, pulling at it. He's seriously frustrated.

"I don't give a fuck" he roars, I flinch "how can you have fucking let it get to this stage and not fucking notice you fucking imbecile"

I really don't want to be the person on the other end of the phone actually they're probably thanking their lucky stars Clayton isn't in the office because he'd more than likely launch the poor sod through a window. As if sensing me Clayton's head snaps up his eyes are blazing with anger, his whole body is trembling.

"Go back through everything with a fine tooth comb and come back with a decent fucking explanation" the menace in his voice makes me want to run for the hills "stop, no more fucking excuses, do it now" he rips the ear piece out and throws it onto the desk as he stands.

I step into him wrapping my arms around his waist. Immediately he wraps his around me dropping his head on top of mine and breaths deeply. After a few minutes I feel all the tension leave him as he calms.

"Tell me about it"

Clayton sighs heavily "There's an acquisition I'm working on with a company in China. Someone in the office has fucked up big time. We're supposed to be finalising the deal by end of play today. I could get answers from the Chinese but they don't speak English and the interpreters have to be given twenty four hours' notice if we want to use their services and that will be too late"

I lift my head and look up at Clayton with expectant raised eyebrows. Clayton looks at me puzzled; he's forgotten I speak Chinese.

"What! You're looking at me as if I should know the fucking solution" he snaps at me, that's a first but I let it slide because he's frustrated and stressed when he should be relaxing.

"How many languages do I speak, no don't answer let me rephrase. Which languages do I speak?" I deliberately say it slowly as if he's mentally challenged.

Clayton's brow furrows in concentration and he chews his bottom lip. A minute later the light bulb pings on.

"Oh you fucking beauty" he roughly clasps my face and kisses me hard then dashes to the desk picking up his phone.

A half hour long conference call later which includes the team from Clayton's office and the team from the Chinese firm disaster is averted and the deal is back on track for completion. Throughout the whole call Clayton has me sat on his lap with his arms firmly gripping me and holding me in place it's almost as if he's afraid I'm going to bolt. Clayton wraps up the call by issuing orders and expected time frames for updates; he really does put the fear of god into people, even when he's not shouting.

"Thank you my love" Clayton murmurs in my ear as soon as the conference call is over "that is the second time you have saved my business a fortune" he pauses "actually it's the fifth time"

"Really" I'm puzzled "I can only think of Mr C and the fraudster's incident"

Clayton's low rumble of a chuckle vibrates against my back. "Remember the week we spent together in May" I nod "you gave me a number of suggestions and you made me re-evaluate a couple of my business practices. I implemented three of them straight away and I saw returns instantly, since then it's more than doubled"

"Huh, go figure. I can't remember for the life of me what it was I suggested, but I do remember you telling me when we were in Italy" I shrug "anyway I'll send you an invoice for my expert knowledge, see I'm not just a talented artist with a pretty face" I tease as I stand up.

Clayton winces as he stands, he tries to hide the pain but I know he's in agony. "Time for your pain meds and don't try to tell me you're okay I can see you're not, come on" I take his hand and tug he follows me out of the office.

"Yes ma'am. Christ you're a bossy little thing" Clayton grumbles then he brightens, a salacious grin slowly turning the corners of his mouth up, his voice drops low and seductive "is nurse going to administer the medication"

I stop and look up into his lust filled dark blue eyes. I put my free hand down the front of his sweat pants and stroke his semi erect cock, he hardens instantly.

"Are you going to be a good boy" I grip him tighter, stroking him with firm slow pulls.

"Fuck no" Clayton's salacious grin gets wider and he thrusts into my hand "I'm going to be naughty as hell and you're going to wear the nurse uniform whilst I do rude and dirty things to you" his tongue runs suggestively over his lips and he thrusts into my hand again to make his point.

I drag him to the bedroom.

Clayton has given me two earth shattering orgasms; we lie side by side panting. I see him wince as he does his best to get air into his lungs. I bite my tongue to refrain from saying something stupid like no more sex until he's better, neither of us will be able to stick to it. My stomach lets out a long and very loud growl, pangs of hunger follow. Clayton lifts his head and looks at me with a raised eyebrow.

"Still hungry baby" he winks.

I reach down and fondle his flaccid cock which quickly becomes semi hard "Up for giving me a protein drink" I grin wickedly.

"Ha, you're a minx and insatiable" he kisses me long and deep, my toes curl "make us something to eat baby" he says against my lips.

Sighing dramatically I get up and straighten the nurse outfit—Clayton really does like this—as I head for the door. "I'm going to call in and see Alan…"

"The fuck you are" Clayton roars, I flinch and turn to look at him only to see six foot four inches of prime muscled naked male with a furious scowl on his face hurtling towards me.

"What the…" is all I have time to say when he's on me, spinning me round and I'm pressed face first against the wall.

Instinctually my hands fly up, palms flat at the side of my shoulders. I push back but get nowhere. Clayton is a solid wall of muscle behind me, caging me in and pressing against me. I could quite easily get out of this and cause some major damage but I don't want to hurt Clayton plus I'm seriously turned on.

"No-one sees you like this but me" he growls in my ear, his hot breath tickling and sending goose bumps all over my skin. Clayton is angry and possessive, his hands move from the wall and roughly grab my hips, he pulls me backwards "keep your hands on the wall" I comply.

Bloody hell this is a huge turn on. I'm not in a rush to enlighten him I have no intention of letting anyone see me dressed in my naughty nurse outfit. However I can't resist poking the hornet's nest.

"Why not?" I challenge.

I feel Clayton's cock slide along the crack of my butt as his hands travel up my back moving round to the front and grasp my breasts, his hands and fingers flex and knead them. My head falls back against his shoulder as pleasure surges through me.

"You are mine" his hot breath gusts against my ear, his teeth nip my ear lobe the sharp sting heads straight between my legs, his mouth moves down to graze my neck. One of his hands travels south, down against my stomach and cups my sex "my eyes only" he whispers darkly as his fingers apply light pressure to my clit.

I hold back on the moan at the back of my throat, my heart is hammering against my rib cage and I'm breathing heavily. Clayton adjusts his stance and I feel the head of his cock brush my entrance; he pushes forward and enters a fraction. The moan escapes me. He pushes further in. Clayton moves his hands to my hips the heat of his chest against my back disappears.

"You belong to me" Clayton bellows and slams all the way in, pulling my hips back on to him at the same time.

"Oh god" I yell at the sudden invasion of feeling so deliciously full.

Clayton holds still, he's breathing hard. He rotates his hips and withdraws slowly. I clench my muscles down hard holding onto the feel of him.

"No fucker is going to see you dressed like this but me" possessiveness drips from his every word.

Clayton's fingers flex on my hips cluing me in he's about to thrust back in. "Do you hear me" he growls, thrust.

"Yes" I shout as he hits deep inside.

I love the feeling of possession and his display of passion, claiming me, owning me. At the back of my mind by rights I should be angry, fighting against his jealous dictatorial declarations but at this moment in time I don't care, no-one has ever shown me how much they love and care about me, with such ferocity it makes them unreasonable.

Clayton's hands move from my hips to my breasts, he pulls me upright altering my position as he flexes his hips in shallow thrusts, his cock continues to massage me inside as he slowly undoes the poppers on the uniform, releasing my breasts. He peels the dress off over my shoulders and pushes it down to my waist.

"Hands back on the wall baby" his voice is softer, no trace of anger in it.

I place my palms back and he circles his hips, stirring his cock inside me as his hands run over my back. His fingers and thumbs lightly massage their way up to my shoulders.

"I love the feel of your skin, so soft silky and smooth" he says trailing kisses along my spine.

My skin tingles at his touch. My whole body is thrumming with pleasure. His hands snake around to my stomach his fingers tips lightly stroke then move upwards and palm my breasts.

"And I fucking love these beauties" he says rolling my nipples and tugging them, pleasure trails rush straight to my core.

"Yes" I moan my head drops forward as I absorb the feelings he's creating in me.

"Every delectable inch of your fucking fantastic body is for my eyes only" he whispers in my ear, his teeth nip and tug my ear lobe "hold on baby because I'm claiming you"

Clayton's voice is dark and sensual, excitement thunders through every molecule of my body. My muscles clamp down hard on his cock in anticipation for the hard fuck I know he's about to give me.

"Fuck baby I can feel you want this, your greedy cunt is telling me so"

Clayton circles his hips and withdraws agonisingly slow. I moan low at the back of my throat in response to the pleasure he elicits. Clayton places his hands back on my hips. I lock my arms, his fingers flex and grip. He thrusts forward as I push back. We both yell our pleasure.

Good lord he's deep. He circles and grinds his hips then slowly withdraws. Clayton sets a delicious rhythm of hard thrust, circle and grind, slow withdrawal.

"Mine" he growls each time he thrusts deep inside me. His movements are controlled "feel me baby" he swirls his hips and withdraws "you feel so fucking amazing"

He picks up the pace, powering into me faster and faster, again and again, in and out, in and out, over and over. Pleasure is spiking, I'm hurtling towards the precipice. His hands grip tighter almost painfully as he plunges into me, pulling me back on to him to meet his thrusts.

"Oh god, yes" I shout, I'm close to the edge.

"Who do you belong to?" Clayton barks out the demand as he powers into me "whose eyes, tell me?"

Clayton moves faster, the friction stokes the inferno in my blood, sweat breaks out across my skin, my heart pounds in my ears, short shallow gasps of breath as I reach the precipice.

"Tell me" Clayton roars slamming into me.

"Yours" I scream as I swan dive off the cliff.

My legs buckle under the force of my orgasm. Wave after wave crashes through me, I'm vaguely aware of Clayton lowering us to the floor. I'm sat straddling his lap, a hand still on one hip holding me in place, the other wraps around my front with his hand at my throat, cradling my head against his shoulder. Clayton continues to push upwards into me as he chases he release and draws out my orgasm.

"I love you Skye" Clayton shouts as he spills into me, filling me. I feel his cock pulsing and pumping deep inside as his body jerks and shudders with the aftershocks of his orgasm.

His head is buried in the crook of my neck, his warm breath gusting over my overheated sensitive skin. I can feel Clayton's racing heart hammering against my back as he places tender kisses along my neck and shoulder. We stay like this for several long minutes as we both come down from the intense orgasmic high.

"Tell me" I clear my throat as my words come out croaky "what on earth makes you think I would go out and see Alan or anyone for that matter in this nurse outfit?"

Clayton's arms tighten around me. I feel him shrug, he doesn't give an answer. I'm not going to scream and shout at him but now I can think clearly I am going to tear him a new arsehole if he continues with this possessive dictatorial crap.

"So are you going to let me finish my sentence" I ask sardonically. I feel his head nod "I'm going to go and see Alan after I have changed and we have eaten" I enunciate and emphasise the words after and changed to make my point "do you want to come with me?"

Clayton lifts his head "I'm sorry baby. I don't know what came over me" he sighs "yes I will come with you"

"I know exactly what came over you, it's called the green eyed monster" I make my statement light "hell you can fuck me like that again anytime you want, just give me some credit on my wardrobe choices for visiting a sick employee" the sardonic reprimand is clear in my voice. I can't help it.

Clayton lifts us off the floor and turns me around to face him; his big hands cup my face. "You're right about the green eyed monster, I'm sorry"

I can see Clayton is doing his best to look contrite and he's failing miserably, he releases my face and wraps his arms around me, I slip mine around his waist and rest my head on his chest savoring his warmth, heady masculine scent and the strong rhythmic beat of his heart.

"I was thinking I am one lucky fucking bastard having a stunningly beautiful woman who is about to become my wife, who dresses up and plays nurse just for me when you said you were going to see Alan and overwhelming feelings of possessiveness hit me. I'm not going to share you with anyone. I make no apologies for that" I hear the challenge in his softly spoken words "you are mine" his arms tighten "and I will see off any fucker who tries to take you away from me. I'm never letting you go"

I lift my head and pull back to look up at him, my breath hitches when I see the fierceness of his burning love for me in his face. I put my hand on his cheek and stroke the day old stubble.

"I love that you own me, claim me and possess me. I do belong to you; body, heart and soul. Remember that, just don't treat or speak to me like I'm an idiot that has to be dictated to" now Clayton does look sorry "and bear in mind mister if you do I'll do the same to you and I guarantee it'll piss you off quicker than it will me, I grew up with that shit"

Clayton gives me a heart breaking and breath taking smile "I consider myself told off, message received loud and clear" he kisses me gently "for what it's worth you own me body, heart and soul too"

"I know" I run my fingertips down the side of his face "I love you"

Clayton gives me the heart breaking and breath taking smile again, my smile, the one only I get to see. Clayton lowers his head and tenderly kisses me again, our lips skimming and moving against each other softly. I lose myself in him until my stomach grumbles loudly. Clayton chuckles as we break apart.

"Sorry for being such a dick" he says as he places a stray piece of hair behind my ear.

"Apology accepted"

I pull out of his arms and go to the closet to get changed.

"I've been thinking" Clayton says walking in behind me "after we see Alan will you come with me to see Mark"

"Of course, that's a great idea" I say pulling on a pair of jeans.

I'm a bit surprised Clayton suggested it actually I'm surprised he even thought of it even though I mentioned it yesterday. I kick myself that's unfair of me. Clayton is generous and kind hearted and he is getting more considerate of others. It's not that he's selfish or self-centred I've learnt he's led a life where he's not had to or been made to consider others needs before his own, it's just not on his radar.

"What would you like to eat" I ask as I pull the hair pins and tie out of my hair.

"Surprise me" Clayton says as he pulls on a pair of jeans. I'm momentarily distracted as I watch his chest and ab muscles flex and contract, there is not one ounce of body fat he is all defined sculpted muscle.

"Like what you see baby?" Clayton whispers like the devil himself.

"You know I do"

I reach out and run my fingers over his stomach, up over and across the expanse of his chest and back down. I lean forward and kiss between his defined pectorals. My lust for him ricochets through the roof. I take a deep breath filling my lungs with his scent. "Not helping" my inner goddess shouts. Mentally and physically I shake myself. Clayton's laugh is low and seductive he knows exactly what is going through my head and the impact he has on me, my body.

"Helloooo, anybody here" Shelley's muffled voice breaks through my lust filled mind.

"Damn" I mutter.

"You can have me all you want later baby" Clayton's seductive voice does little to dampen my lust "go on before we give Shelley an eye full" he spins me round and slaps my butt as he pushes me out of the closet.

"Hello, Skye" Shelley calls through the open crack of the bedroom door.

"Come in Shelley" I open the door wider, the look of relief on her face at seeing me dressed makes me smile.

In her hands she's holding a garment bag "I'm not stopping I just called to drop this off, it's for tomorrow night" huh, I must have a puzzled look on my face "the charity function you've got tomorrow. Stephanie's invited me and Phil, plus she's invited Simon, here" she explains holding out the bag. I take it from her.

"Can I look at it now?"

"Sure, I'm surprised you didn't tell me about the function" Shelley says a tad reproachfully "it's lucky I finished it yesterday"

"I'm sorry Shelley. I forgot, Stephanie only invited us last weekend and so much has been going on this last week it slipped my mind"

Shelley looks mortified and blushes "I'm an idiot, ignore me. Here I am selfishly thinking my best friend doesn't want me to dress her anymore and you've got a tonne of shit to deal with" Shelley's eyes fill with tears.

It's not like her to get upset over something like this. Hormones, the thought flits through my mind. I put my arms around her and give her a hug.

"I'm thankful Skye has such a loving and thoughtful friend who looks after her" Clayton's voice is full of warmth coming from behind us.

Shelley lets out a sob and takes a shaky deep breath, she frantically rummages in her purse and pulls out a tissue, wiping her eyes.

"Stupid hormones are all over the place" Shelley barks out a watery laugh "poor Phil has been getting the brunt of it"

"Where is he" says Clayton.

"In the living room" Shelley waves over her shoulder in the direction of the living room.

"I'll leave you two to it I don't want to spoil my surprise for tomorrow" Clayton kisses my cheek, then kisses Shelley's cheek too "thank you" he says softly to her.

Shelley touches her cheek "Wow I'm never washing my face again"

Chuckling Clayton heads out to the living room.

I open the garment bag and pull out the dress. The dress is made of a deep ruby red silk and is overlaid with swirling patterns of black sequins. The bodice is fitted to the hips with the skirt flaring out and finishing just above the knee. Underneath the skirt are layers of fine black netting, just enough layers to give the full skirt some shape, as I lay the dress on my bed it's then that I notice the skirt actually has a series of slits, as they fall open it reveals the next layer of black silk. The overall effect as I walk and move around will be quite something. The dress is strapless and the back is tied corset style.

"I made it with your ruby and diamond necklace in mind" Shelley says tentatively.

"It's fabulous" I breathe "hang on a minute" I head to my closet and bring out my red killer heels and a black pair "which ones" I hold up a shoe in each hand next to the dress.

"Actually I got you these" Shelley reaches down into a bag I hadn't noticed by her feet and takes out a shoe box "I hope you don't mind" she cringes as she opens it.

Inside are red silk platform killer heels with a delicate black lace covering the enter shoe and heel. I instantly fall in love as I run my fingers over the shoes, I unashamedly drool.

"Oh wow!" I say as I lift them out of the box "oh wow! These are fantastic, thank you" I sit on the bed and pull off my trainers and socks. The shoes fit perfectly. I walk around the room testing them out. They are comfy. I stand in front of the full length mirror to admire them "I love them, thank you so much" I look at Shelley's beaming face in the mirror "you really do look after me"

"Don't" Shelley holds up her hand "you'll set me off again"

I take the shoes off and put the dress back in the bag placing both in the closet.

"When did Stephanie ring you" I ask as we walk into the living room.

"She didn't, she called in at the studio this morning after she'd been here. Stephanie said she thought we could all do with a bit of cheering up after the events of yesterday, she got me to ring Simon so she could speak to him" Shelley shrugs "you don't mind do you"

"Hell no, why would I? At least I know tomorrow night is going to be more bearable and fun with you and Simon there" I put my arm around her and squeeze.

There's no sign of Clayton or Phil in the living room, I head for the kitchen with the obscure hope Clayton might be making something to eat. Nope it's empty.

"I wonder where the boys have got to" Shelley says echoing my own thought.

"God knows, unless they've gone through to Paul's quarters to see Alan" I say as I start pulling bread, cheese, ham and salad out of the fridge to make sandwiches "oh by the way we had a visit from Detective Sanders this morning" Shelley's eyes widen.

As I make sandwiches I fill her in on what Sanders said and the gun belonging to Caroline's friend. In turn Shelley gives me a rundown of what she and Simon told Sanders at the hospital yesterday, it was almost verbatim to what I told him.

"I guess Pete must have said the same thing or very similar to us for the detective to be satisfied and to close the case so quickly" Shelley says thoughtfully.

I nod "Well he did say you all collaborated my story so Pete must have" I snort "the bitch in me wishes to have been a fly on the wall to have seen that interview"

Shelley grins wickedly "Oh to have been a fly on the wall indeed"

I put the plate of sandwiches on the breakfast bar, as I get drinks from the fridge I hear Clayton and Phil coming in through the front door, both of them are laughing at what the other is saying.

Shelley calls out to them "Where have you two been, and what's so funny?"

"I've just taken Clayton downstairs to see the media circus for himself, he didn't believe me" Phil says still chuckling "when the lift doors opened he nearly shit himself, I wish I had taken a picture of his face" Phil mimics Clayton's shocked, horrified and possibly terrified expression making us all laugh including Clayton.

"In my defence" Clayton puts one hand over his heart and holds up the other one palm facing out "there are millions of them out there. I just wasn't expecting that many"

"Yeah right, that means there are probably five pap's out there" I scoff.

"Add a zero on the end and you won't be far off" Phil says as he leans over taking a sandwich "we had to come in through that lot. I'm just thankful your reception and security guys know us"

"Holy shit" I say spraying a mouthful of food over the counter, which earns me a few scowls "I've not even given a single thought to the poor staff on the desk and door"

"Don't worry baby" Clayton says wiping up the remnants of the food I'd sprayed "I spoke with them and they are all fine, plus Paul and Bruce have been checking in with them on a regular basis"

"I guess I should send a letter out to all the residents apologising for the inconvenience, did reception say whether or not they've received any complaints"

"They didn't mention it and I didn't think to ask, tell you what how about we send everyone in the building a bottle of wine and a bouquet of flowers" Clayton leans across and squeezes my hand.

"It's a lovely idea" I say sliding off the bar stool and walk over to the intercom phone "but I'm going to check first if there have been any complaints"

"Don't want to stir up a hornets nest if there's no need to" Phil says grabbing another sandwich.

I wink and give the thumbs up as the front desk picks up. After a quick conversation and reassurance that all staff are okay, not that I didn't believe Clayton, I'm also informed there haven't been any complaints from the residents but its early days and hopefully the media will quickly get bored.

"Well there haven't been any complaints yet" I say hanging up the phone "so we'll send the wine and flowers when we get some"

CLAYTON

"Penny for them" Skye's soft husky voice brings me out of my reverie.

Lying in the bath with Skye's back to my front and one arm wrapped across the top of her shoulders the other drawing lazy patterns on her flat stomach I find I'm trailing my fingers back and forth across her scar running from hip to hip then back to lazy swirling circular patterns on her lower belly and back to the scar.

"I was just reflecting back over this afternoon" I murmur into her hair and place a kiss just under her earlobe.

After Shelley and Phil had left we went to see Alan, who was touched as well as embarrassed by all the fuss from Macy and Skye. As we headed down to the car park Skye joked about lending Macy her nurse uniform, she laughed even harder when she saw my pouting face. On the way over to Mark's house Skye insisted on stopping off at the florists to take a bouquet, then nipped into the off-licence to get a couple bottles of wine to take with us. We were lucky not to have the paparazzi following us since they were camped out at the front of the apartment building en masse, however it didn't stop people from recognising us and asking after my health. When we got to Mark's house it was a different story, the media were camped outside and if it wasn't for Skye's quick thinking it would have been bedlam getting to the front door. Skye got Paul to ring Mark's mobile and told him we were outside and to open the front door as soon as we knocked so luckily we were out of the car and in Mark's house before the press had time to react. Bruce and Paul looking menacing stationed themselves outside the front door.

In the hour we spent with Mark and his family the amount of press tripled thankfully Paul called in reinforcements. It was scary as hell getting back into the car, even being surrounded by a team of body guards it was more frightening than what I experienced in Vegas at the convention, all the shoving and pushing, questions being fired one after another, some reporters shouting out untruthful and obscene things to provoke a reaction.

Skye had the hindsight to call Simon and got him to come down and give a press statement asking them to leave Mark and his family alone so he could recuperate in peace. Thankfully Simon arrived as we left otherwise I think Mark's poor family would be still under siege. Skye also organised a delivery of groceries "Just in case" she said, when we got back. An hour ago Mark's wife rang thanking us profusely and said only a couple of media people lingered outside the house.

As we sat in front of the TV eating dinner the news came on and we made one of the leading stories, there was a brief shot of us entering Mark's house followed by the jostling scrimmage of us getting into the car then Simon giving the press interview in his usual cool calm charismatic charming way.

"Hindsight is a wonderful thing, would you do anything differently?" Skye says lifting her head to get a better look at my face.

"No, I'm glad we went to see Mark and his family. I think it was worth all the hassle afterwards just to see their surprise and appreciation of our visit" their gratitude had really touched me "what about you?"

"Part of me thinks we should have left it a few days and waited for the press to lose interest but then my commercial logic kicks in and from a public image stand point it puts you in a good light, you have this reputation as a ruthless hard ass in business but it shows you care about your employees"

I give a snort of laughter "I don't think the poor bastard I chewed out today would agree with you"

We fall silent, enjoying the relaxing closeness of the moment.

"I never found out who did it" Skye says in a small voice after a few minutes, my whole body stills including my trailing fingers over her scar, all I can hear is my heart thumping loudly in my ears. I let out a shaky breath as my mind races trying to work out what she's referring to. Skye places her hand over mine and trails her fingers along the scar. Fucking hell is she….

"It was my eighteenth birthday and I went out with some friends to celebrate" holy shit, she's telling me "we'd gone on a pub crawl and ended up in a night club. It was a good night, we were all single and none of us were interested in picking up a guy, just a group of girls out for a laugh and a good time. At the end of the night I was tipsy but not drunk, anyway we left the club to get taxis home. I was the only one going in my direction so as we came out of the club my friends got in the only two taxis that waited outside I said I was fine waiting for the next one. Anyway I remember wanting a cigarette, the wind had picked up so I stepped into the side alley to light it and I got hit from behind" Skye took a deep shaky breath "when I came round I couldn't see or move, I was blindfolded and tied down. Later I found out that it was a derelict office and I'd been tied to a desk"

I close my eyes and groan as I remember saying to Skye about keeping her chained to my desk, twice. As if reading my mind Skye let out a humourless chuckle.

"It's okay you weren't to know. All I remember is how sound echoed around the room and I know there were two people in the room but as hard as I tried I couldn't identify their voices. I'm certain only one of them carried out the attack. He kept screaming at me "how did you know" and "what do you know" and "who have you told" over and over. To this day I have absolutely no idea what he was referring to. As you can imagine each time I said I didn't know I got hit, he even gagged me to muffle my screams. He hit me so hard I blacked out, when I came round he was… he was…" Skye's voice faltered "he was raping me. He was saying all sorts of vile things and calling me derogative names and how he was going to beat and cut me up until I told him what he wanted to know. I struggled with all my might, I tried to fight him off but they'd tied me down too securely. I begged him to stop but he kept on and on"

I pull Skye's shaking body closer to me, instinct is telling me to stay quiet as this story isn't over. Fuck I feel sick to my stomach and my blood is now ice. After a few minutes Skye continues "I lost count of the number of times he raped me. All in all I passed out three times either out of pain or he hit me so hard I blacked out, the last time was when he plunged in the knife. I vaguely remember hearing an argument happening beforehand it was something to do with evidence" Skye shakes her head "that's the one word I remember clearly "evidence" when I woke up again I was in hospital with two broken ribs, a dislocated jaw, lots and lots of bruises all over me and part of my womb missing"

"Jesus" I whisper into her hair in horrified disbelief.

"Speaking with the police later they reckoned the word evidence probably related to the fact the attacker, the police believe, didn't use a condom so he attempted to get rid of any DNA. He was successful because the knife wound caused internal bleeding which resulted in the doctors performing an immediate partial hysterectomy and they weren't able to get any DNA traces from me. The police said an anonymous emergency call was made at ten in the morning. I left club with my friends at around one so I'd been held for at least eight or nine hours" Skye sighs heavily "anyway the Police also believed I was attacked by someone I knew due to the questions the attacker kept asking or the attacker believed I was partial to some information I unwittingly stumbled upon and I had passed onto someone else" Skye shrugs "with no leads, the only DNA at the scene and on the rope, electrical cable, blindfold and gag was mine, there was no CCTV footage either so the case went cold very quickly"

I feel numb. My heart is breaking for her. I desperately want to protect her yet I feel so helpless. "Baby I have no idea what to say" I squeeze her to me "I love you" I whisper holding her tighter. Skye lightly squeezes my forearm and continues running her fingers across my arm.

"My grandfather turned up later that night well after visiting hours, because of the bad shape I was in the nurses let him in. I was doped up to the eyeballs yet I remember every word he said to me. The nursing staff were disgusted it had taken him so long to come and see me since they had notified him as soon as I was admitted" Skye's voice is flat, emotionless, detached "they were even more shocked when he left after five minutes. He came to say his piece and went"

"What did he say?" shit I want to bite my tongue off, the question is out of my mouth before I engaged my brain. Skye is quiet for so long I didn't think she was going to answer.

"In a nutshell, I deserved everything I got for being a drunken slut and there was no doubt in his mind I was a junkie, being constantly high on drugs and I was no better than my pathetic, weak, spineless parents. He wasn't prepared to stand by and watch me destroy my life and bring further embarrassment to him with my wayward and capricious behaviour. Oh, he also called me a delinquent. Then he really put the boot in by going onto say, and I quote "I no longer see you as my granddaughter. I wash my hands of you. You are dead to me. You don't exist anymore in my family, I disown you. I don't ever want to see your face again. From this day you have a month to pack your things and get out of my house" then he walked out, that was the last time I saw him. July was the first time I'd seen him in eight years"

"No wonder you reacted the way you did in London when you saw him again" It was like huge pieces of a jigsaw were falling into place for me in understanding Skye better.

"You know that night was the first time that I had allowed myself to get tipsy. I never had before because of what I witnessed as a child seeing my Dad drunk and, high and drunk. It was the thing to do sneaking into pubs underage, being in England it was quite easy to doll yourself up to look eighteen or older, the alternative was to nick bottles of booze from your parents drinks cabinet and go round to your friends for impromptu parties, but I never did any of that. The other thing that hurt, I have never touched drugs it was my cousin Alfie who was the pothead" Skye says quite indignant "out of all the grandchildren Alfie was grandfather's favourite. Just before I left England to come here I heard Alfie got arrested for possession with the intent to supply and the bastard didn't disown him"

"How did you hear about that?" curiosity gets me every time.

"I bumped into an old school friend who happened to be in London for the weekend on a shopping trip. Apparently Alfie was the hot gossip of the town for a couple of months. Grandfather tried and failed to cover it up however he got Alfie into rehab as part of his slap on the wrist. As you can imagine that pissed me off even more"

I felt for her, I really did "If it was me baby I would have kicked up a stink, big time"

"Oh I was tempted, I wanted to but my grandfather was so pig headed it wouldn't have made any difference. Shelley and Simon talked me down and when I realized it wouldn't get me anywhere I put it behind me and focused on my new future"

"Did any of your family make attempts to get in touch with you, even after seeing your old school friend?"

"No" Skye shifts in my arms "I didn't leave a forwarding address when I left my grandfather's estate and lucky for me the school friend was one of those people who loved to talk about themselves so I didn't get to tell her where I was living in London nor did I tell her I was leaving for New York the following week. I've no doubt she would have told as many people as possible that she'd seen me and the only gossip she could give out was the fact I was in London studying Art, she didn't have my new name nor which college I was at, she also didn't ask why I left town so quickly" Skye sounds smug, for some reason I can't help smiling "come on let's get out the waters getting cold" Skye sits up pulling the plug. I wrap her in a warm towel and rub her dry.

"Did you ever worry or hope your grandfather or any of your family would get in contact as you became famous?"

Again Skye took her time answering, from the expression on her face she was seriously working through her thoughts and feelings. Picking up a towel she starts drying my chest.

"There was a time very early on that I hoped someone would get in touch, namely my cousin Alfie he was the one I was closest to, especially when Pete came to work in New York as he is or had been Alfie's best friend" Skye shrugs her shoulder "I thought maybe Alfie would make contact through Pete after a couple of months I gave up expecting to hear news and I assumed Pete was no longer in touch with him. I don't know why but I never asked Pete about my relations and he never volunteered information until Vegas that is, he gave himself away"

"Ah, now I understand what you meant that night, you never did finish off telling me"

"Did I not" Skye looks up at me puzzled, I place a kiss on her frown line between her eyebrows.

"No, Simon dragged you off to dance then the Caroline incident happened" I remind her. Skye's mouth forms a little O shape and the frown line disappears "after that I completely forgot about it"

Bending down I scoop Skye up into my arms and carry her to the bed. Pulling her onto my chest I wrap my arms around her.

"Thank you for telling me" I murmur and kiss the top of her head.

Skye lifts her head to look at me. I see a mix of apprehension and love in her beautiful yellow green eyes. Her fingers gently stroke my cheek.

"I've never told anyone the complete story of what happened to me before. Not even Shelley and Simon know everything, you're the only one" Skye's voice is low almost a whisper.

A surge of love for her so strong cripples me. I can't breathe and my heart stops. Moving slowly I roll her onto her back and kiss her with reverence. Skye matches the softness and tenderness.

"I love you so, so very much" I whisper "let me love you"

"Yes" Skye whispers softly arching her back exposing her throat for me to kiss. I worship every inch of her for a long, long time.

Chapter Thirty One

CLAYTON

We make a start sorting through Skye's stuff and packing to take to the new apartment. All day Skye has been quiet, too quiet for my liking. I'm getting worried. She hasn't been withdrawn she's just has this contemplating thoughtful kind of air about her. I have to refrain from asking her every five minutes if she's okay, on the occasions I succumbed she's given me such a beautiful smile, reached up and stroked my cheek and kissed me. Sometimes she says yes other times she squeezed my hand. A couple of times I had to stop myself from shaking her and demand she talk to me. I really, really, want to climb inside her head to know what she is thinking. Christ this is fucking frustrating.

Out of sheer desperation when Skye and Shelley left late afternoon to go to the beauty salon I ring Simon for advice on how to handle Skye's mood.

"I've never seen her like this" I finish saying to Simon after I explained Skye told me everything about her attack and her grandfather "I'm at a loss I don't know what to do"

"Wow, she's told you everything" Simon's amazement is evident in his voice "even Shelley and I don't know the full story"

"Yeah Skye did mention that"

"I'm sorry my man but there's nothing you can do" Simon says sympathetically "when Skye is in a quiet contemplating mood she obviously has something on her mind, you've just got to give her space to work it out, she'll talk when she's ready"

Sighing heavily I try not to vent my frustration "I feel so helpless and I don't want to piss her off by asking if she's okay every five minutes and I just know that her mood is a direct result of what she told me yesterday"

"You're worried and you want to shoulder her burden I get that but from experience if you continue to push, Skye will shut down even harder" Simon's exasperated sigh rattles the ear piece "I feel for you Clayton, I really do. Skye will talk when she's ready"

Hanging up and feeling even more wound up I hit the gym to work off the pent up helpless aggression surging through me.

Now I'm pacing the living room weaving in and out of packing boxes like a caged tiger as I wait for Skye. The living room is organised chaos as Macy would say; the overstuffed book case is now empty. Some of the books are in boxes but the majority are stacked in piles awaiting their fate.

The canvasses for The Gentlemen's Club commission have been wrapped and packed ready for delivery, the contrast of the sparseness at the top end of the room to the cramped living area is staggering.

"I'm ready"

Spinning round I see Skye weaving her way towards me. She looks stunning and as always my heart misses a beat then kicks in beating harder. Shelley really knows how to dress Skye, the red and black dress is moulded to her, the skirt flaring out and showing flashes of the under skirts through the slits as she walks, the effect is amazing. Skye is wearing her ruby earrings along with the ruby and diamond choker even her shoes match. With her curly white blonde hair piled up on her head and honey tone skin the effect is dramatic and sexy as hell. I feel myself getting hard. Skye stops and gives me a twirl.

"You like"

Taking her hand I place it over my groin and kiss on her temple "Oh I like" I murmur and being the randy fucker I am I thrust my hips into her caressing hand.

"Guess what" Skye purrs, I shake my head I don't want to guess. Skye takes my hand and parting the slits of the layered skirt puts my hand on her stocking thigh "you don't have to push up the skirt, easy access through the slits"

A growl rumbles deep in my chest, Skye's eyes glitter with mischief. Her earlier melancholy state seems to have lifted. Before I can raise my hand any higher up her thigh a cough interrupts us. Looking up I see Bruce, he can't see what I'm doing but I remove my hand anyway.

"Sir, ma'am the limo is outside however so is the press. Do you wish to go in the limo or the SUV that's in the car park?"

"SUV" we say together, we all grin at each other it's a no brainer really.

"Thought as much" Bruce chuckles "we're ready when you are"

As Bruce leaves Skye moves to follow him I hold her back, she looks at me with wary questioning yellow green eyes before I can ask Skye pre-empts me.

"I'm okay"

"I was going to ask that but I want to rephrase my question" it has suddenly dawned on me I've been asking the wrong question all day "what's on your mind?"

Skye gives me sad smile "I don't know. I can't put my finger on it. I've just got this niggling feeling that something is eluding me and I have no idea what that something is. Does that make sense?"

"No but promise me you'll talk to me once you figure it out"

Skye gives me her megawatt brain frying heart stopping smile "I will"

The press go into frenzy when Skye and I arrive at the venue, as I help Skye out the car I'm momentarily blinded by all the flashes going off. As we pose for the photographers questions about Thursdays events are hurled my way but I ignore them, after a few minutes I guide Skye into the building. Entering the ballroom people converge on us, well me. All are asking the same thing. How was I feeling? Was I scared? What actually happened? I feel Skye move behind and away from me making room for the sycophants to surround me. I stop answering the questions, turn my back on the people surrounding me and grab hold of Skye's hand I raise a "where the fuck do you think you're going" questioning eyebrow at her. Skye throws her head back and laughs, I grin like an idiot I've got my girl back.

As I answer the questions I scan the room, being tall has its advantages. I spot Andrew then the rest of our group, I make my excuses and pull Skye along with me and head over to them. On the way over I see an unwelcome face "Fuck"

"What's the matter?" Skye asks looking around, concern marring her features.

"Nothing" I try for light hearted innocence, last thing I want is her to be upset or her evening spoilt by that fucking prat. Skye stops walking and tugs my arm making me face her, guess it didn't work.

"Tell me" her voice brokers no argument.

"Pete is here" Skye's eyes widen with surprise then dart around the room searching for him "he's over by the bar talking to a group of men"

"Shit" Skye vehemently hisses as she spots him.

"Come on. I doubt he'll make a scene and as long as the fucker stays away from us I won't either" I tug her forward.

As we reach our group Andrew hands us our drinks. My family greet Skye with enthusiasm even Mandy seems to have gotten over her aversion of Skye or she's a fucking good actress. Mandy doesn't attempt to give me a hug and her voice quavers as she says hello to me. I nod at her, I still haven't forgiven the fucking bitch and I know my face is showing it.

"Be nice" Elizabeth murmurs besides me.

"I am" I say curtly, Elizabeth rises an eyebrow at me "I acknowledged her, what more do you want?"

"Can't you forgive and forget?"

"Fuck no, I'll never forget and I am most definitely never going to forgive that fucking bitch and if you push the matter we'll be falling out as well"

Elizabeth laughs and kisses my cheek "No we won't because I won't let you"

"What are you two whispering about?" Joshua says suspiciously.

"I'm attempting to get your dear brother to bury the hatchet and to be more civil to Mandy" Elizabeth brazenly informs her husband.

"Why the fuck would he want to do that? Even I haven't said two words to her"

"At least you don't look at her like she's something on the bottom of your shoe" Elizabeth sighs.

I've had enough of this conversation so I leave them to it and move to Skye's side as she's talking with Shelley and mother, hearing wedding talk I plant a kiss on Skye's cheek and move over to Simon and Phil.

"We've decided to go away for a long weekend next week, and once the baby is born we'll have a proper honeymoon then" Phil's face is glowing as he looks over at Shelley, who is looking radiant in a flowing dark blue gown that shows off her baby bump.

Simon is looking around the room no doubt eyeing up the male talent "Oh my god, oh my god" shocked surprise is all over his face "you'll never guess who's here"

"Yeah I can, Pete" Simon's eyes widen even further as he stares at me "I saw him earlier stood by the bar as we came in and yes Skye knows he's here"

"Jesus" Phil whistles "where is he and has he seen us?" Phil searches the room.

"He's over by the dance floor" Simon nods his head in the direction trying to be subtle "he's definitely seen us all now. Do you think he'll come over and talk to you or Skye?"

"He's got some balls if does" Phil says with a humourless laugh.

"I agree, let's just say I hope for his sake he doesn't" I say with a hint of menace in my voice.

"Ladies and gentlemen, please take your seats, dinner is served" the toast master calls out.

The banter and conversation during dinner is easy and free flowing, no one mentions Thursday. I come to the conclusion that my family and Skye's friends must have made some sort of pact between themselves before we arrived and I'm thankful. After dinner the band starts playing and people start to table hop and get up to dance.

"Come on Clayton you can dance with me" my mother says standing up. I'm torn, I don't want to leave Skye yet I don't want to upset my mother.

"Go on" Skye chides "there's someone over there that I want to talk to" I stand as Skye does "go, dance with your Mom. I'll be alright" Skye pushes me in the direction of my mother and the dance floor, reluctantly

I go but I watch Skye as she walks towards her target, hips swaying. Every man's eyes follow her as she passes.

"She'll definitely keep you on your toes" my mother chuckles as I lead her onto the dance floor.

"She does already" I grumble.

Whenever I can I watch Skye as she talks to a bald fat guy, he smiles like Alice in Wonderland's Cheshire cat and puffs his chest out. The women at the table all look at Skye with sour jealous distaste whilst the men sit straighter holding in their stomachs and smooth back their thinning hair. Thankfully Skye doesn't stay long enough to be introduced to the table and she makes her way back to ours which is now empty. The band finishes playing and I start to lead mother off the floor, another song starts up.

"Oh! One more dance" mother pleads, begrudgingly I agree. As I glance at our table I nearly trip over my own feet as I see Pete making a bee line for Skye. Rage surges through me.

"Ouch, loosen your grip Clayton" mother winces as she reprimands me, immediately I relax my hand as I become aware I'm crushing hers "what's the matter?"

"Sorry" I mumble and choose not to answer her question "tell me is all well with the wedding preparations?" I switch off as mother drones on and I observe Skye as she talks to Pete.

SKYE

I see our table is empty as I head back from talking to the owner of The Gentlemen's Club, looking at the dance floor most of our party are on it then I spot a couple others table hopping. Hopefully I'll have a few minutes peace, all day I've been reflecting back on what I told Clayton the night before. The attacker's questions keep bouncing around my head and I've been racking my brain to find a possible meaning, it's frustrating as hell, a constant unsettling feeling has been with me all day. It's telling me I should know, do know even yet it eludes me. It's like having a question that you know the answer to and it's on the tip of your tongue yet you can't grasp it enough to verbalise.

Clayton, bless him, is worried about me. He's been so attentive almost to the point of smothering. In myself I feel fine it's just this damn frustrating connection I'm not seeing.

"How did you know?" a low almost threatening voice jolts me out of my musings, my stomach churns as the question resonates, it's what my attacker asked. A flash of fear has me breaking out in a cold sweat. The person asking the question sits down next to me. My feeling of unease amplifies as I look into the drawn pasty face of Pete.

"About what" I manage to keep my voice calm.

"In Vegas you knew I'd spoken to someone in the family, how did you know?" Pete doesn't meet my eyes instead he hutches over the table and watches the dark amber liquid swirl in his glass as he turns it with his fingertips. I glance around the room Clayton is still on the dance floor with Stephanie although his cold hard murderous stare is on Pete. Paul and Bruce are on the other side of the room by the doors we came in through.

"I'm not discussing anything with you" I say standing and walk away. I'm surprised my legs aren't quivering.

In front of me is a set of double doors. I head through them. The corridor is empty; down at the bottom is a sign showing ladies and gents washrooms I walk in that direction. Suddenly I'm hit from behind and pushed against the wall, winded. Instinctively my hands come up to stop my face being smashed against the wall, dropping my purse it lands at my feet. I'm pinned in place by a man's arm across my shoulders pushing up into the back of my neck, his hips pushing into my lower back and buttocks. The stench of stale alcohol and cigarette breath assaults my nose and wafts close to my ear. I can't move my head to get away from the revolting stomach churning smell. After the initial surge of panic a soothing calm comes over me, I know I can get out of this situation.

"This time when you're asked a question you'll fucking answer it" the mean threatening voice is Pete's.

"And what if I don't" I mentally pat myself on the back with how calm and defiant I sound as I ready myself to throw Pete off.

"Oh you'll fucking answer and not play dumb like you did all those years ago" I freeze, sick with fear as realization hits me that elusive connection suddenly clicks into place "I'd hate to resort to Alfie's methods" Pete taunts, his free hand caresses my thigh and starts to hitch up my skirt.

"You were there" I whisper fighting down the bile at the back of my throat so I can speak "you were there and did nothing to stop him" my voice is getting stronger as anger floods through me replacing the fear, my heart is pounding against my breast bone and I feel the surge of adrenalin building.

Pete pushes his weight against me "Yeah I was there. Alfie was convinced you rumbled him and his little enterprise. He was shit scared you spilled your guts to that dearly departed fucking shit of a grandfather. So how did you know?" Pete's voice is full of barely contained menace.

Pete's hand is now on my thigh, flesh touching flesh. I shiver with revulsion. Oh hell no, he's not going to intimidate me. Gathering all my strength I push back from the wall and throw my head back hitting Pete square in the face.

"Fucking bitch" Pete screams, releasing me.

Moving quickly I kick my shoes off and take up a fighting stance. Pete's bent holding his bloody nose.

"You fucking bitch, you'll pay for that"

Pete rushes forward with his arm pulled back to hit me, I dodge the swing and channelling all my anger I punch him in the gut. I take a step back as he clutches his stomach and drops to his knees.

"You want to know how I knew" I spit at him as he gasps for breath "the Will is a sealed document and for someone who's not family you knew too much you fucking stupid imbecile"

From his kneeling position Pete launches himself at me, I side step and use his momentum to send him crashing into the wall. Pete howls in rage and spins to face me. Hate and anger twist his no longer handsome face. For the first time I see how much he really hates me.

"After all these years you've never been interested nor asked why I changed my name and went to London. Why did you want to know?"

I'm breathing heavily. I can feel another surge of adrenalin pumping through me. I resume my fighting stance all the while watching Pete's body language to tip me off for his next move.

Laughing manically Pete swipes his hand across his mouth "Money, why else"

That doesn't make any sense "I don't understand" I can hear the confusion in my voice.

"You dumb fucking bitch, I was paid to come to New York. It took us that long to find you. We had to be certain you really didn't know"

I don't need to ask who he is referring to, Alfie put him up to this, of that I'm certain "Know about what?" I shout at him in frustration "what the hell are you going on about?"

"Drugs" Pete says in a low growl, a sinister sneer on his face.

An incredulous humourless laugh escapes me "Drugs! All I knew was Alfie liked dope. Christ anyone could tell that. He reeked of the stuff and it wouldn't surprise me if he was doing coke as well. So what are you saying? That his little enterprise was dealing?"

"Oh, it is more than that" Pete says with a delighted sneer, his lips pulled back over his teeth.

"What… trafficking, as in importing and distributing?" Pete nods his head. I know my shocked surprise is showing on my face.

"You really didn't know" Pete's own surprise momentarily showing in his face.

"'Why would Alfie think I did?"

Pete moves forward. I hold myself still determined to stand my ground even though instinct is screaming at me to run. Pete's face is inches from mine, his horrid stale breath blasting in my face.

"Because you walked in on a telephone conversation he was having. He was in the middle of finalising the details and closing a deal on a big shipment"

"When was this?" I'm racking my brains trying to remember.

"Two days before he attacked you. He was in the library"

My brain coughs up the memory, flooding my vision. I remember seeing Alfie sat in the dark green wing backed leather chair by the window, me browsing the books taking my time selecting one to read as I listened to music.

"I didn't hear anything" Pete's look is sceptical, his face twists in a mean sneer "I was listening to music, I had my iPod on" I add quickly.

Surprise flits across Pete's face then resumes its hateful twisted sneer "Oh dear that's a shame"

Pete lunges, slamming me against the wall, banging my head. I see stars. His weight is pinning me again. His mouth is inches from mine.

"Now I'm really going to have to make sure you keep quiet" I really don't like the tone of his voice or the implications of his words.

His mouth crushes hard against mine. One hand is at my throat keeping my head still, the other gripping my wrist hard against the wall. A fresh surge of adrenalin roars through my veins. I open my mouth and take hold of Pete's bottom lips between my teeth. Pete misreads my intentions and releases my arm, snaking his behind my back cupping my butt, he grinds his erection against me. I cup both my hands and bring my arms up. I smack each hand over his ears and bite down hard on his lip. Pete howls in pain and releases me, staggering a few steps away. I move away from the wall.

"Fucking bitch" he yells and lunges, raising his fists.

I spin and roundhouse kick him square in his chest, Pete staggers back, bending over clutching his chest. I step into him and hit him with an upper cut punch. A punch that has me pouring into it all of my anger and hate I feel towards him and Alfie for what they did to me all those years ago.

Pete drops to the floor like a sack of potatoes. I ready myself for him to get up and attack. He doesn't move. Tentatively I step forward and push him with my foot. His body is a dead weight. Shit, have I killed him? The thought spurns me into action.

Dropping to my knees I put my hand on his neck feeling for a pulse. Relief floods through me when I feel it beating strong. Shifting Pete's body I put him into the recovery position. I pick up my purse and shoes. I should head back to the ballroom and get help but I really need to be alone right now and sort through my memories and feelings. Up ahead is an exit to the stairwell, on shaky legs I head for that.

CLAYTON

Mother is still prattling on about the wedding. I can't take anything in because that fucking creep is talking to Skye. My mind is racing trying to come up with an excuse to get back to the table.

"Swap partners" Joshua's words don't register until it's too late, the bastard whisks mother away leaving me with Mandy who I can feel trembling under my hands.

"Will you ever find it in your heart to forgive me and start a fresh?" Mandy asks meekly. She quakes even more as I glare down at her.

At this moment in time I'm more likely to rip her limb from limb. Christ I'm such a shit, of all the times Joshua can pull a stunt like this. Take a deep breath and count to ten I tell myself. Mandy doesn't push the matter and remains quiet as we move around the dance floor. Looking into her sad pleading eyes I relent, a little.

"Honestly, I don't know" I say simply "I'll tell you one thing, I'll never forget and at this moment in time the animosity I felt towards you on that night is still as strong today so if you want your answer now, it's no. As for starting a fresh, you burnt that bridge because I'm not going to forget"

"I understand" Mandy's eyes fill with tears "I really, really wish I could turn back time and restart that day again. Andrew and I are on the brink of splitting up because of it" now that shocks me "he can't forgive me either"

"I have absolutely no idea what to say apart from I'm sorry to hear that Mandy" a tear trickles down her cheek "have you tried counselling?" fuck I'm clutching at straws here, I really don't give a shit about their relationship.

Mandy swipes the tear away "He won't go with me" she says miserably.

"Do you want me to speak to him?" why the hell did I just say that I mentally admonish myself, I haven't got a fucking clue what to say to Andrew.

Hope lights up in her eyes "Would you?" she whispers.

"I'm not making any promises but I will talk with him"

Glancing around the room I see Paul moving quickly across it talking into his sleeve. Suddenly alert I scan for Bruce. I spot him at the top end moving just as quickly in the same direction as Paul, both are heading for the double doors that are closest to our table, which is minus Skye. Something's wrong.

"Excuse me" I say hastily to Mandy and leave her on the dance floor as I rush after Paul and Bruce.

Andrew, Simon and Shelley are sat at our table laughing and joking. Andrew stops when he sees me. "What's wrong?" he says standing as I pass, the others follow suit.

"I don't know"

I sprint to the double doors—I know they'll be following I don't have to look round to check—and practically take them off their hinges as I burst through into the corridor. First thing I see is Paul crouching down over a body.

"What's happened?" I shout as I drop down next to him, I recognise the prone body as Pete.

"Not quite sure sir" Paul says checking Pete's pulse "I saw Miss Darcy leave through these doors about five minutes ago, thought she was visiting the ladies bathroom. Bruce saw him" Paul points down at Pete "go through but not Miss Darcy. I'm sorry sir but we just put two and two together during our check in"

"Shit, where's Skye?" panic settles over me.

"She's not in the ladies room sir" Bruce says striding back up the corridor.

"There's security footage" Paul nods looking up behind me "there's a camera"

"I'll go the security office" Bruce says as Simon comes through the doors with Shelley, Phil and the rest of my family.

"Oh my god, what's happened?" numerous shocked and startled voices chorus.

"We don't really know" I say bewildered.

"This is definitely Miss Darcy's doing" Paul states matter of fact "she didn't come back into the ballroom. Anyone have any ideas where she will have gone?"

"If we were in the country I'd say find the nearest hill or mountain" Simon says with a shaky laugh.

"The roof" I shout out in overjoyed relief getting to my feet.

As I sprint to the exit and crash through the door I hear gasps and my mother saying "Oh my goodness please tell me she's not going to jump"

As the door swings shut I glimpse Shelley reassuring her, no doubt explaining the significance of Skye's need to be high up. By the time I've cleared two flights of stairs Simon, Phil and my brothers are following me. Simon is the only one who keeps up with me as we race up the stairs. My lungs and bruised ribs are burning along with the muscles in my legs as I burst through the roof door. It registers the door has been propped open, at least Skye had the sense of mind to do that, the thought eases some of the desperate panic I'm feeling. Unable to speak I indicate to Simon through hand and arm gestures we split up to search the roof.

When I have enough breath in my lungs I shout "Skye" but the wind is so strong it rips the words from my mouth. I search frantically moving around air conditioning pipes, telephone masts and skylights. Simon appears in front of me pointing and gesturing me to follow. I sprint over to him.

"She's there" I follow his pointing arm "go get her my man" Simon pats my shoulder, my bad shoulder. I wince and ignore the burst of pain.

Skye is sat on the ledge looking out over the city. The wind has loosened parts of her hair from its pins and it's whipping around her as the gusts circle and move on. It is bitterly cold yet Skye is sat so still and serene, only her hair is moving doing its frenzied undulating hypnotic dance.

I approach slowly and quietly. I don't want to startle her, the last thing I want is for her to jump back in surprise and go over. As I kneel down next to her I hear the roof door bang open, Phil and my brothers have finally arrived, automatically I glance over my shoulder to see the three of them bent double, hands on knees wheezing badly.

I don't say anything to Skye. I know she knows I'm here, although I'm dying to know what went down with Pete. I trust and know she'll tell me when she's ready.

After what seems like an eternity Skye takes a shuddering breath and turns to face me. Skye tries to smile but the hurt and sadness in her face makes it impossible. I desperately want to take her in my arms but instinct is telling me to keep still. The blustering wind drops and the only sound we can hear is the rumble of traffic in the streets below.

"It was Alfie, he did it and Pete was there and did nothing to stop him" Skye's agony is palpable in her whispered words.

It takes me a few seconds to work out the meaning of her words. I feel the sledge hammer blow to my stomach as comprehension hits. Her own fucking cousin raped her, the one person in her family who she felt anything for had betrayed her. She knew there had been two people in the room that day the other person being Pete, bastard. It leaves me reeling then anger takes over. I fight the urge to race back down stairs and tear that creepy mother fucker apart with my bare hands. Only Skye's desolate and sad look stops me. My baby girl needs me. I stand and open my arms. Her sad smile yet filled with so much love shatters my heart. Skye stands and steps into me, welcoming her I wrap my arms protectively around her as she slips hers around my waist. I feel her trembling against me yet neither of us makes to move, we stand for a while simply holding each other.

"Come on let's go home" I say pressing kisses to the top of her head. Skye nods meekly in agreement. I look over to at the door to see the others have already left.

At the top of the stairwell Skye stops to take off her shoes, noticing that her lips are blue I start to take off my jacket.

"No I'm okay" Skye says softly "I'll soon warm up going down" her sad smile suddenly becomes mischievous "race ya" she shouts as she turns and quickly descends. I laugh, my girl is back.

Breathless and extremely warmed up by the time we reach the bottom of the stairs Skye's eyes have their sparkle back.

"Will you tell me what happened?" I ask tentatively as I run the back of my fingers down her cheek.

"Yes" Skye whispers and kisses me.

"I love you" I murmur and kiss her back.

Opening the door I'm taken back at how packed the corridor is with people. Medics are attending to Pete who is now conscious and sat propped up against the wall. Police are milling around talking to my family and our friends. Plain clothed detectives are talking to Paul and Bruce.

"There she is. Arrest that fucking bitch for assault" Pete screeches angrily pointing at Skye.

Pete's outburst has everyone turning towards us. My desire to rip the bastard sleazy mother fucker apart resurfaces in a flash. It doesn't register I'm moving forward snarling at him until the detective talking to Paul blocks my path.

"Mr Lancaster it is you who is under arrest for assault. Miss Darcy's actions were in self-defence. I've seen the security footage" the detective speaking looks familiar "read him his rights"

"Oh thank god for that" I hear Skye mutter under her breath. That alone disperses the red mist.

"Don't do anything you may regret Mr Blake" it's Sanders "I'd hate to be making another arrest tonight. Miss Darcy, are you up for giving a statement?" Sanders smiles kindly down at her.

"Sure" Skye nods "do you mind if I give it to you at home, there's a lot to tell"

Sanders ponders her request "Tell you what, how about I find a quiet room here and get drinks and snacks sent in"

"Deal" Skye says smiling "although I want Clayton's family and my friends present as well" looking up at me she says "it's time they knew everything and I really don't want to have to repeat the story"

If Sanders was going to object he buried it, he seemed to be the kind of guy who followed his gut and I can tell he understood Skye.

Ten minutes later all of my family, Skye's friends, Paul and Bruce along with Detective Sanders and another detective he introduced as Monaghan are sitting in a meeting room. Skye sits at an angle, facing the detective but also able to see everyone else in the room. I sit next to her, as close as I possibly can. I'm fighting the temptation to sit her on my lap somehow I don't think the gesture will be appreciated by Skye or the Detectives.

"Detective Sanders in order to better understand what happened tonight between myself and Pete Lancaster I need to tell you about something that happened to me eight years ago on my eighteenth birthday" Skye's husky voice is calm and confident.

There is a knock on the door making everyone jump such is the tension in the room. The waiters bring in tea, coffee, water and sandwiches. Once they've left and everyone has helped themselves and settled back down Sanders with pen and note pad poised looks at Skye.

"So tell me what happened on your eighteenth birthday?"

"I was raped"

A collective gasp goes around the room. I look over at my family. My mother, Elizabeth and Mandy all hold a hand over their mouth with unshed tears in their eyes. My brothers are grinding their jaws. All have looks of shock, sadness and pity.

As Skye's story unfolds those looks turn to horror and anger. Skye tells Sanders everything about the attack, the words her attacker used and about two people being present. She told him of her grandfather's hospital visit, being disowned and kicked out. Changing her name and moving to London and eventually to New York. How two years later she bumped into Pete. She told him about seeing her grandfather again in London in July and her inheritance, then the subsequent conversations she had with Pete in Vegas on the bachelor and hen party weekend.

"Then last night" Skye pauses and turns to look at me, picking up my hand and looking me in the eye "I told Clayton all of this" I raise her hand to my lips and kiss it, she turns back to Sanders "all day I've been going over and over all of this, something has been niggling at me, something that I should know but not being quiet able to put my finger on it" Skye shakes her head "anyway tonight when everyone was on the dance floor Pete sat down next to me. He wanted to know when we were in Vegas how did I know he had spoken to someone in the family. I told him I wasn't going to discuss it with him and got up and walked away. My quickest exit was through the double doors, I walked down the corridor heading to the ladies next thing I knew I was hit from behind and pressed up against the wall. Pete said" Skye closes her eyes and takes a shuddering breath before opening them again, I rub the back of her hand "he said "This time when you're asked a question you'll answer it" I replied "And what if I don't" Pete said "Oh you'll answer and not play dumb like you did all those years ago. I'd hate to resort to Alfie's methods". I knew and said to him "You were there and did nothing to stop him"

A ripple of gasps and cursing goes up around the room as the meaning of her words dawns. Skye hisses and imploring looks at me. I immediately relax my grip and kiss her hand again mouthing "sorry".

"Pete admitted he was there, he went on to say Alfie was convinced I had rumbled his little enterprise and he was scared shitless I had squealed in particular to our grandfather. At this point I felt Pete's hand on my thigh pushing up my skirt he asked again "How did I know". Anger surged through me. I pushed back against the wall and threw my head back hitting him in the face. As he fell away from me calling me a fucking bitch I kicked off my shoes, he called me a fucking bitch again and I'd pay for that he lunged towards me with his fist raised. I ducked his swing and hit him in the gut. As he went to his knees I shouted the Will was a sealed document and for someone who wasn't family he knew too much and I called him a stupid imbecile. He launched himself at me again I just helped him along to smash into the wall. I asked him why after all these years he was so interested to find out why I changed my name and moved to London, his reply was money. I said I didn't understand to which he called me a dumb fucking bitch then went on to say that he had been paid to come to New York, "It took us that long to find you. We had to be certain you didn't know" I knew instantly he was referring to Alfie. Know about what I shouted at him. Drugs Pete replies" Skye took a mouthful of water.

"Detective, all I knew was my cousin at that time anyway was a pothead and it wouldn't have surprised me if he did coke. I told Pete this. I asked him if Alfie's enterprise was dealing drugs. Turns out it was more than that, he was trafficking and distributing. From the shock on my face Pete could tell I really had no idea. I asked him why Alfie would think this. Apparently two days before he attacked me I had walked into my grandfathers' library and Alfie was on the phone finalising a large shipment. I remember seeing Alfie sat in the chair but I was listening to music, I had my iPod on whilst I chose a book so I didn't hear anything of Alfie's conversation. I could tell I surprised Pete when I told him this. Then he said "that's a shame, now I'm going to make sure you keep quiet" and he slammed me against the wall. He had his hand against my throat and he kissed me. I sucked in his bottom lip, he released my arm so I cupped my hands" Skye releases my hand so she can demonstrate to the detective "I bit down on his lip and smacked my hands over his ears. It's a simple and highly effective way to get someone off you. He came at me again, I did a roundhouse kick to his chest and as he bent gasping for breath I hit him with an upper cut punch. When he didn't get up I checked for a pulse then put him into the recovery position" Skye sighs "Detective I know I should have gone for help but I needed to be alone to think through everything Pete had said and to jog my memory"

The room is deathly quiet. I was going through a myriad of emotions and I'd heard three quarters of the story already, fuck knows what my family were going through. A chair being scrapped back startles everyone. My mother visibly trembling walks towards Skye on shaky legs.

"You brave, brave girl" she whispers softly and envelopes Skye in a hug "so very, very brave"

The room is so quiet everyone heard each word as if it had been shouted. The room erupts then. I hear Simon, Shelley and Phil discussing the parts they did and didn't know. My family expressing shock, anger and outrage at the injustice Skye has suffered and praise for her bravery, finally the detectives discussing certain points.

I tug Skye's hand to get her attention "I'm immensely proud of you, it was an extremely brave thing to do. I love you"

I kiss the back of her hand. What I really want to do is wrap my arms around her and kiss the life out of her. A loud knocking on the table quietens the room and looking towards the source, Sanders.

"Miss Darcy I have a few questions. From my previous conversations with you and your friends" he nods in Simon and Shelley's direction "you mentioned that you only saw Pete on Friday's if you went into Gino's" Skye nods "during that time did he ever bring up the topic of your past and family?"

"There were rare occasions when we'd all share a story from our childhood but I don't remember him trying to steer the conversation specifically about me or my move to London and changing my name"

"I do" Shelley says looking at Skye apologetically then at the detective "Skye was away working on a commission. It was about six months after we had first met him and he hadn't yet met Caroline. There was me, Phil, Simon and a couple of Simon's friends. We had got to Gino's earlier than normal that night so we were half way through eating when Pete came in. He joined our table. I remember him asking where Skye was and being put out he hadn't been told she was working away. Simon told him to get used to it as only those in the inner circle were privy to her movements. Simon meant it as a joke but Pete got quite shirty. He said something like "Oh so you all think you know Skye, well you don't. I know things about her none of you know"

"Oh my god, I remember that night now" Simon says in surprised wonder.

"I do too" Phil adds "Simon asked him like what and Pete wouldn't say at first. Simon goaded him until Pete said Skye Darcy isn't her real name. I must say Pete was quite malicious when he said it"

"We all know that, Marty my friend says. She changed it when she moved to London" Simon says gleefully "anyway she changed it legally so it is her real name. Pete didn't like that one bit"

"We then proceeded to tell Pete everything Skye had told us about him" Shelley says smiling at Skye.

"I bet that shocked the shit out of him" Skye says laughing.

"It did" Shelley, Phil and Simon say together.

"Come to think of it" Simon went on "when Pete started seeing Caroline it was her that would ask those questions, you know, why move to London and New York but never why Skye changed her name. And she'd ask the three of us individually bringing up the question every couple of months until one day I asked her if she had a sieve for a brain because she asked the same bloody question so many times. I think Pete put her up to it"

"So what did you tell her Miss Darcy" asks Sanders.

"To study art for both moves" Skye shrugs.

"You mention that you knew Alfie was a" Sanders pauses and consults his pad "pothead, how did you know that?"

"My father died of a drugs overdose when I was ten, he smoked it all the time so I'm very familiar with the smell and Alfie reeked of it whenever I saw him, actually a better way of phrasing it would be you could smell him before you saw him"

"Were drugs a regular occurrence in the family home?" Detective Monaghan asks nastily.

The look Skye gives him chills my blood even Sanders shifts uneasily in his seat.

"My mother committed suicide by booze and pills when I was three. By the time I was ten I had witnessed my father trying to take his life three times by OD'ing. So yes detective if you're asking if drugs were a regular occurrence, but if you want to know did I see them and use them the answer is no. What relevance does this have to what is being discussed?" Skye's words are cutting.

"My sentiments exactly" Joshua says angrily. There's a collective agreement from the rest of the room the atmosphere instantly becomes hostile towards Monaghan.

"I apologise Miss Darcy for my colleague's inappropriate question" Sanders says glaring at Monaghan who has the audacity to look nonplus "whilst you were on the roof did you remember anything else about Alfie, his habits, routines maybe?"

"Yeah I did" Skye sighs "Alfie is two years older than me. I remember when I was sixteen Alfie was going to Ibiza with a group of friends, he wanted me to go as well but grandfather wouldn't allow it. Anyway on his return he and his friends all got pulled in and arrested at customs. Nobody would tell me what it was about. I just remember grandfather being terribly angry and pulling strings to get Alfie out. Grandfather made Alfie's father stop his allowance and ground him. Even though Alfie had no allowance for six months he always seemed to be flushed with cash. He bought a brand new Porsche, designer cloths, going out to the best restaurants and clubs. Alfie didn't care if he got caught sneaking out and he told Grandfather he'd been saving up his allowance to buy those things"

"And your grandfather believed him" Sanders asks incredulously.

"I don't know" Skye shrugs "Alfie was his favourite. Not long after that Alfie told grandfather he had set up a business in the entertainment industry and demand was very high. I guess grandfather turned a blind eye or Alfie well and truly hoodwinked him. And before you ask I have no idea if Alfie is still in business that's a question for Pete. Apart from seeing my grandfather in London back in July I haven't seen any of my relations since the day of my eighteenth birthday"

"Thank you Miss Darcy. I have one last question" Sanders smiles ruefully "where in god's name did you learn to fight like that?"

Skye bursts out laughing, the sound easing the tension in the room "Phillipee Belgarde"

Sanders gives her a puzzled look, I take pity on him.

"What she's not telling you" I say grinning at Sanders "is that Phillipee Belgarde is a three times mixed martial arts world champion and that she spars with him at least once a week. Hell she spars with these two" I point to Paul and Bruce "on a daily basis and they're ex-marines"

Paul and Bruce both smirking shrug and nod. All of my family and the two detectives are open mouthed.

"Seriously Skye you take on these two" Andrew asks in amazement, he whistles when Skye nods "wow that guy really did pick on the wrong girl" he chuckles.

"Thank you for your time" Sanders says standing, Monaghan follows suit "I'll be in touch if I have any other questions"

"What happens now? Will you be charging him?" Skye asks shaking Sanders hand.

"Do you want to press charges?" Skye shakes her head "thought as much. I'm going to have a chat with a couple of contacts in the DEA first just to check if he and possibly your cousin are on their radar. I'll keep you posted. Good night ma'am"

SKYE

I snuggle into Clayton trying to bury myself deeper into his arms. He moves to accommodate me, flexing and tightening his arms around me, pulling me closer still. We've been like this since getting into the car.

"You okay?" he whispers in my ear, his warm breath tickles my skin.

"Hmm very, if I was a cat I'd be purring extremely loudly" I whisper back.

I move my head and put my lips to the underside of his chin then drag my teeth lightly across the skin. Clayton shudders and chuckles darkly.

"Behave" his voice rich, dark and promising. He drops a kiss on the tip of my nose.

"Spoilsport" I grumble and nip his chin again with my teeth before snuggling back in his arms.

I feel safe and strangely energised. After everything that's happened over the last couple of hours, the emotional roller coaster I've been on by rights I should be exhausted, physically as well as emotionally drained.

My mind starts filtering through the reactions of those around me in the meeting room to the things I revealed. My friends had known about three quarters of what I revealed from my past and their loving hugs and murmured we'll speak tomorrow told me nothing's changed, if anything our bond has become stronger.

Clayton's family are shell shocked to say the least at my egregious revelations. They all hugged me and said how brave I was as we said our goodbyes but I couldn't get a read on how they felt. Suddenly I have an overwhelming desire to find out what Clayton thinks about his family's reaction to my background, will they still want me as part of the family? Would they put pressure on Clayton to call off the wedding, our relationship even because they would class me as damaged goods, too damaged?

"You know you impressed the shit out of my family tonight" Clayton murmurs thoughtfully.

"You are psychic" I bark out laughing "I was just thinking about asking you what you thought their reactions would be once they have chance to digest all of my sordid past"

Clayton looks down at me smirking "Not only is Joshua more in love and awe with you. Andrew is as well. When we were collecting our coats all they could talk about was how much damage you did to Pete in such a short space of time, how incredibly brave and well-adjusted you are considering the shitty start in life you had"

"So they don't think I'm damaged goods and won't try to talk you into dumping me" I cringe as the words of my inner most fears and insecurities are out of my mouth before my brain kicks into gear. I cringe even more when I see the anger in Clayton's face.

"Why the fuck would you think that?" he explodes. I shrink under the force of his glare. I can't meet his eyes. I drop my head. I feel ashamed of myself for thinking it but I can't help it, tears fill my eyes. Clayton lifts my chin with a finger, I keep my eyes cast down "look at me" he says more softly. He takes in a sharp breath as he sees the unshed tears "is that what you think?"

I shrug "I don't know, I just…" I take a shaky breath "I don't really know them, someone like me with my background there are people out there that will run as fast as they can in the opposite direction in order to distance themselves"

"Oh Skye baby" Clayton wraps his arms tight around me, squeezing me "if any of my family thought that I would disown them. You mean everything to me and if they can't see what a beautiful person you are now then they don't deserve to be in our lives. However I can categorically say that they think the sun shines out of your very beautiful ass and you can do no wrong"

I'm filled with an unbelievable amount of happiness it makes me light headed. I settle in and breathing deep Clayton's heavenly manly and earthy musk scent fills my lungs.

"Mandy told me tonight that she and Andrew are on the verge of splitting up" Clayton murmurs, that jolts me off my happy cloud.

"Whatever over"

"She asked me if I would ever find it in my heart to forgive her, you know for what she said to you when you first met" I look up at Clayton, he's gazing out of the window "she said Andrew can't forgive her either" I don't say anything, hell I've no idea how to respond to that. Clayton sighs heavily "I said I'd talk to him, but after your revelations tonight" he looks down at me and gives a helpless shrug "I think that might be the final nail in the coffin"

"How long have they been together?"

"Fuck knows, years" Claytons brow crinkles as he thinks "must be at least seven could be as many as ten"

The car comes to a stop. Paul and Bruce get out. The door opens and Bruce helps me out, he lightly squeezes my hand before he releases me, surprised I look up at him. His eyes are soft and kind he gives me a slight bow. It dawns on me that Clayton's family are not the only ones where my revelations are the first time to be heard. I look across to Paul who nods and bows also. The reverence of their actions coupled with admiration in both their faces for some reason makes me blush and all I can manage is a shy smile. Clayton gives the three of us a puzzled inquisitive look as he takes my hand and we walk over to the elevator.

"Are you still going to speak with Andrew?" I ask as a way to divert his attention.

"Yeah, I said I would" Clayton puffs out a loud breath "fuck knows what I'm going to say to him. I mean I tore into her before I knew all of your past. I told her my animosity towards her was as strong today as it was then and I'd never forget and at this moment in time I honestly don't think I can forgive her. What the hell am I supposed to say to Andrew?"

"How about we both speak with him? Send him a text invite him for breakfast tomorrow say ten o'clock"

"God I love you" Clayton exclaims and kisses me soundly.

I watch as he taps out a text message to Andrew. I have an ulterior motive to being involved in this conversation and it's primarily selfish. I want to find out exactly what it is Andrew can't forgive and if he's using it as an excuse as a way out of his relationship. Clayton's phone pings at the same time as the elevator door.

"Andrew says he'll see us at ten and do you want him to bring anything?"

"No just himself" I say opening the door and flick the lights on "do you want a night cap?"

Suddenly my feet disappear from the floor and I let out a startled squeal. Clayton hoists me up in his arms "No I'm going to eat and devour you instead" he growls in my ear as he strides towards our bedroom. My heart clatters in my chest, heat and desire flares in my stomach and between my legs in anticipation.

Chapter Thirty Two

SKYE

Hands and fingers are running over my back and buttocks, massaging, kneading. Oh that feels good my sleep filled brain whispers as I start to surface towards consciousness. Feather light kisses and damp swirling patterns of a tongue follow my spine downwards. My legs are pushed further apart. Hands on either buttock knead and push upwards, opening and separating me. Warm breath blows along my seam followed by the swirl and lick of a tongue, penetrating, probing. A moan escapes from deep within me at the pleasure it creates, my hips rise of their own volition wanting more.

A low throaty chuckle brings me to consciousness, large warm hands grip my hips gently lifting. A thick long hard steel cock slowly slides in.

"Oooh god" I groan out loud as my muscles clench down welcoming the invasion.

"Morning baby" Clayton whispers as he starts to move slowly in and out.

"Hmmm" I love being woken up like this, I shift up onto my elbows and push back as Clayton thrusts forward taking him deeper.

"Want it harder baby?" Clayton's dark velvet voice is temptation itself.

"Hmm please" my voice sounds gravely.

Clayton adjusts his grip on my hips and pounds into me. My body and nerve endings suddenly awaken and light up as he plunges over and over again. Oh this is heaven and a stark contrast to the slow gentleness of last night. This time my orgasm is building fast, my core is tightening, the pressure of pleasure waiting to detonate. Clayton releases one hip and I feel him wrapping my hair around his arm, his hand clasps at the nape of my neck. Tugging he lifts me and plunges deeper again and again.

"Yes" I call out throwing my head back into his shoulder. His hand releases my hair and his arm snakes up around my front, holding my throat and chin he tilts my head to the side, exposing my neck. I feel his mouth and teeth nipping and sucking, his tongue trailing along my pulse.

"Come baby" Clayton growls the command in my ear then he bites down and sucks hard at the juncture of my neck and shoulder as he thrusts hard and deep inside me.

Pleasure detonates. I'm helpless as my body spasms and judders riding out the waves of my orgasm.

"Fuck, Skye" Clayton bellows as he joins me. I feel his cock twitching and pulsing as he empties into me.

We both fall forward. Clayton's weight is welcome as he crushes me into the mattress, his hips move languidly making the pleasure last for both of us. Our heaving breathes and beating hearts are in sync. Clayton nuzzles my neck where he bit me.

"Am I going to have a hickey there?" I say muffled into the pillow.

"Sorry baby I couldn't help myself" there's not one iota of remorse in his voice.

"So that's a yes then" I try to sound sardonic but it doesn't work because of my post coital orgasmic haze.

"I love you" he whispers as he pulls out of me.

"Humph" I snort doing my best to show my displeasure at being marked.

Clayton's phone beeps with an incoming text message, I watch and admire his abdominal muscles stretch and flex as he reaches across to pick it up off the bedside cabinet.

"Andrew's on his way" he reads out "time to get up" he slaps my butt making me yelp then drags me out of bed grumbling.

The warm morning autumn sunlight spills in through the window into the kitchen. I'm going to miss my kitchen, I think with a pang of sadness as I prepare breakfast. At least the bleak monstrosity in the new apartment is being replaced with wood, for me wood gives a kitchen that homely feel. The kitchen was the only room in my grandfathers' huge house that felt welcoming. Where in the hell did that thought come from. Huh go figure!

Memories start to flit through my mind of the times I spent in the farmhouse style kitchen with the cook and servants. All the wooden cabinets and welsh dressers holding china plates and serving platters, the scrubbed worn wooden table in the centre of the room, the stone tiled floor. It dawns on me my passion for cooking stems from old Mrs Benson, I spent hours with her as she let me watch and as I got older teaching me to cook. As I stand stirring the sauce for the eggs benedict I look around the room and realize unconsciously I've modelled it around that very farmhouse style kitchen which holds the few happy childhood memories I have.

Clayton's arms coming around my waist brings me back to the present, he steps into me getting as close as he can, he bends his head and kisses the juncture of my neck and shoulder.

"I'm sorry" he murmurs contritely.

I tilt my head sideways so I can look at him "What for?"

"This" he kisses the spot where he's bitten me, exposed by my oversized sloppy t-shirt slipping off my shoulder "I know you don't like hickeys. I didn't mean to mark you. I got carried away in the throes of passion. Forgive me?" Clayton gives me his puppy dog eyes and pouts, making me roll mine.

"You're forgiven, I would say don't do it again but it'll be a waste of breath" I laden as much sarcasm into my voice as I possibly can. Clayton's face lights up and grins like a naughty school boy.

"You're the best" Clayton plants a kiss on my cheek, there's a knock at the door "that's Andrew"

As he bounds away to answer the door my mobile rings without looking at the call ID I answer.

"Miss Darcy, it's Detective Sanders" internally I groan I'm not going to like this.

CLAYTON

I open the door to be met by a huge bouquet of flowers, Calla Lilies to be precise.

"Ah bro you shouldn't have" I grin at Andrew as I step aside to let him in.

"I know and I didn't" Andrew grins back "these are for your lovely lady"

I'm hit with a pang of jealousy "Don't tell me you've fallen in love with her as well"

Andrew laughs and slaps me on my shoulder "Baby bro you knew that already" he pauses and stops walking "look Clayton I know why you've invited me for breakfast" apprehension hits me square in the gut and wipes the smile off my face "Mandy told me what she said to you" all humour has left his face "I called it quits on our relationship last night"

"Fuck me" I'm amazed, I never in a million years thought he'd act so quickly or rashly. Out of the three of us Andrew is the one that takes forever in making life altering decisions.

"Come on I'm starving and something smells delicious" Andrew's back to being jovial, he doesn't appear to be cut up at all "wow, this place is fantastic. Is Skye selling?"

I watch Andrew as he walks slowly around the boxes taking a good look around getting a feel for the room; I mentally slap myself as I realize this is his first time being here, he looks at me expectantly.

"No, she owns the building so she's going to rent it out, the whole floor will be, as the staff quarters take up the rest of the floor" I point in the direction of Paul and Bruce's living quarters. I can hear Skye talking to someone in the kitchen, my curiosity is roused "this way" I indicate.

Skye is serving up breakfast onto the plates her shoulder hunched up to her ear with her phone sandwiched in between as she ladles sauce onto poached eggs.

"No I told you everything I know last night…….. eight years….. really" Skye sucks in a sharp breath "I have absolutely no idea" there's a long pause as Skye listens to the other person, she smiles at Andrew and mouths "thank you" as she takes the flowers off him and he kisses her cheek, that is so unlike Andrew, I feel my eyes narrowing at him. Skye moves to the sink and puts the flowers in it. Skye carries on moving around the kitchen, getting knives and forks, glasses and drinks, she motions for Andrew and me to sit down and start eating "Oh my god" Skye sits suddenly on her stool, shock written all over her face "I knew he'd been left out of the Will but I had no idea that was the reason… no I don't want to press charges" Skye lets out a bark of laughter "thank you detective, bye"

"Detective Sanders" I ask. Skye nods as she tucks into her breakfast.

"Yes, good morning Andrew and thank for the flowers, they're lovely" Skye gives Andrew her brain frying megawatt smile which temporarily stupefies him "he was giving an update, apparently when Sanders told Pete everything I'd told him last night Pete got a case of verbal diarrhoea" Skye resumes eating.

"Come on" I cajole after a few minutes when she isn't forthcoming with more information "you can't say that and not carry on, I'm dying here" Andrew laughs at Skye's impish grin "see what I have to put up with" I appeal to my brother for support which just makes him laugh harder "Christ give a man a break will you"

"She knows your Achilles' heel baby bro" Andrew chuckles, Skye winks at him.

"Damn right I do" Skye leans over and kisses my cheek to pacify me "Pete told Sanders he's been in touch with Alfie the whole time he's been living in New York and Alfie is still in the drug business. According to Sanders Alfie and Pete are persons of interest" Skye air quotes "to various drug agencies in different countries. I knew Alfie had been left out of the Will but not why. Apparently grandfather disowned Alfie just over four years ago for one too many drug related offences. Alfie wanted Pete to find out exactly why I legally changed my name and moved to London so he paid for Pete to come to New York when they eventually tracked me down, I guess my grandfather never did tell anyone in the family he disowned me. Anyway Alfie managed find out what was in the Will however my two Uncles, one obviously being Alfie's father, refused to name the majority beneficiary as the crafty old bastard made it they would forfeit their inheritance if they revealed my identity. So thanks to Caroline's who is the richest person you know Clayton question in Vegas Pete started putting two and two together. Hence his questions to me and when I told him to do the math he got straight onto the phone to Alfie. What they didn't know was how much I had inherited. Between the two of them they came up with a blackmail plot that included threatening to leak my true identity and the rape to the media"

"Fucking hell" Andrew and I say together.

"Before they could do that they needed to know how much I knew about Alfie's drug operations, just in case I had leverage to come back at them with. Pete had been waiting for an opportunity to speak to me or I should say threaten me on my own. Unfortunately for him Caroline's stalking happened and threw a spanner in the works. Alfie was putting pressure on Pete to set the blackmail plan into action so when Pete saw us at the gala last night he jumped in with both feet and you both know how that turned out for him"

Andrew looks how I feel, stunned. Skye finishes eating her breakfast. Sanders' information certainly hasn't diminished her appetite.

Andrew clears his throat "So what's happening now?"

"Well as you heard I'm not pressing charges" Skye looks at me imploringly "I can do without the extra publicity, I'm sure you can"

Fuck, I love this woman so much. I pick up her hand and kiss the back of it "I agree"

"All Sanders said is that he's handing Pete over to the relevant government agency since he's singing like the proverbial canary, so your guess is as good as mine" Skye shrugs.

"You don't really care do you" I chide jokingly and shoulder bump her, Skye play acts falling off her stool and comes and stands by me putting her arms around my neck automatically my arm snakes around her waist my hand resting on her hip.

"No I don't, does that make me a bad person?"

"Hell no" Andrew barks out before I can answer "after all the shit you've been through you have every right to be indifferent" Skye's eyes widen in surprise at Andrew's outburst "sorry, I didn't mean… I just…" Andrew flushes.

"It's okay, thank you" Skye says softly "sometimes I just need to hear someone else's perspective"

"I agree with Andrew" I kiss her temple "personally I hope they throw the book at him and your cousin" that makes Skye laugh.

"I'm going to get going and let you two get on" Andrew says standing "thank you for a lovely breakfast"

"Oh, no you don't, sit down" Skye commands Andrew.

"Skye it's okay. Andrew has already told me he's broken up with Mandy" I say standing.

"No, no, no it's not okay. Both of you sit" Skye glares at both of us, we do as were told "I want to know your reasons for breaking up with Mandy because I'll be damned if you're using me and Clayton as an excuse. I have no problem with Mandy and just because Clayton can't forgive and forget it doesn't mean you can hide behind his animosity towards her"

Andrew looks momentarily taken aback by Skye's outburst then a huge smile breaks out across his face giving her a look that I can only describe as adoration.

"Wow, you are tough and bossy for such a little thing" Andrew looks at me "bro you seriously need to get this woman down the aisle, fast"

"Humph" Skye scowls "you've been talking to Joshua" both of us laugh at her reaction.

"Yes I have" Andrew smiles warmly at her "and now I see first-hand what he's been going on about. Honestly, the reason I broke it off with Mandy is because I realized we don't have what you two have, we never did. You two" Andrew pauses struggling to find the right words "you sizzle together, even when you're not stood next to each other, I can practically see the electricity jumping across the room. Mandy and I have never had that kind of attraction, connection or passion. That night when Mandy first met you Skye she revealed a side of her personality that I'll admit I didn't like but I got to thinking, questioning and comparing myself to you Clayton along with my relationship"

Holy shit, I raise an eyebrow and Andrew grins at me sheepishly "You were, no you are, so protective of Skye, ready to rip apart anyone who questions her motivation and character. Hell you even dropped everything to be with her not once but multiple times, my workaholic billionaire baby brother who puts no-one before work travelled halfway around the world and across the country to spend time with the woman he loves. Christ you even gave up your penthouse and moved in here. Don't get me wrong this place is fantastic" he adds quickly "but Clayton even you've got to admit that before meeting Skye there was a time you expected everyone to bend to your will" I shrug and nod, yeah he's right

"Skye my brother has changed so much since he's met you, it's a pleasure and a joy to see him so happy and when I compared myself to him, the things he's done since being with you, I asked myself if that was me and Mandy would I have done the same thing. The answer that kept coming back was no. In the eight and a half years we were together not once have I felt that passionate about her" Andrew chuckles "not once have I experienced withdrawal symptoms that I have to ring her up just to hear her voice or rearrange my day so I can have lunch with her or finish work earlier just to be with her because I missed her" Skye laughs, I smile Andrew really has been talking to Joshua.

"Then last night when you sat there in front of everyone and revealed all the horrors of your past I watched the two of you, how silently you gave each other strength and support. I saw how strong your love for each other is" Andrew's eyes become overly bright as his voice cracks, he takes a deep shaky breath "and I want that" he whispers.

Skye stands and walks over to Andrew, she wraps her arms around him and holds him. Andrew's shoulders shudder, poor guy is fighting not to break down. Skye rubs his back. After a few minutes she steps back.

"Promise me one thing" Skye says, Andrew nods "that you tell Mandy all of this"

"I already have" Andrew gives her a small resigned smile.

Skye doesn't say anything instead she reaches up and kisses his cheek. Fuck I feel emotional at the tenderness she shows my brother. I get up and join them. I give him a hug.

"Have you told Mom and Joshua?"

Andrew shakes his head "That's the next port of call and somehow I don't think Mom's going to be overly upset and on that note I best get going"

We both walk Andrew to the door.

"Let us know if you need anything" Skye says as she hugs him good bye.

"You've got a good woman there baby bro, make sure you hang on to her" Andrew whispers to me as we hug goodbye.

"I intend to" I murmur back.

SKYE

I step back and give Clayton and Andrew some privacy in their whispered goodbye conversation. I'm still reeling from Andrew's candid confession. Never in a million years would I have guessed he had scrutinized our relationship so closely. Hell, even I've seen subtle changes in Clayton from when I first met him but for Clayton to have made such profound changes that it impacts on his own family's relationships I'm flabbergasted, gobsmacked, dumbfound because I'm the reason for his radical change. I'm not quite sure how to feel about that.

"Tell me what's going on inside that beautiful head of yours" Clayton wraps his arms around me and picks me up, my legs and arms automatically wrapping around him as he walks us back to the living room.

"I was just thinking about what Andrew said about how much you've changed since meeting me and how much it has affected him in his relationship"

"All because of you baby and it's all good" he murmurs darkly in my ear sending a shiver down my spine.

"Is it?" Clayton's eyes smoulder as he nods "it's made me realize just how much I've changed as well. There was a time when I would have literally crucified myself with angst and worry over everything that has happened in the last twenty four hours, hell I should be ranting and raving over Alfie's and Pete's betrayal but I feel strangely calm"

"You've had closure" Clayton kisses me gently "you have the answers you needed about your past, revealing everything last night helped you draw a line underneath it. Time to start afresh"

The jolt of realization Clayton is right hits me like bolt of lightning. For the first time in my life I feel utterly complete, content and happy, whole. I'm no longer going to be influenced and tainted by my fears and the ghosts of my past. I have a new life and a bright future with the man I love. My soul mate and I can't wait.

"I love you" I whisper "take me to bed and make love to me"

Clayton growls his approval and stalks into the bedroom. He kicks the door shut. "Let's go to Vegas and get married now, today" Clayton murmurs as he places kisses along my throat.

I laugh because I know he's deadly serious, my heart bursts with overwhelming happiness and love. "Okay, let's do it"

THE END

About the Author

K L Stockton lives in south Manchester, North West of England, UK, with her husband and daughter. She is an avid reader, loves to paint, watch movies, listening to rock music and going to gigs, and spending time with her family and friends.